By Richard S. Wheeler
from Tom Doherty Associates

The Far Tribes

Yellowstone

Richard S. Wheeler

A Tom Doherty Associates Book / New York

THE FAR TRIBES AND YELLOWSTONE

The Far Tribes copyright © 1990 by Richard S. Wheeler

Yellowstone copyright © 1990 by Richard S. Wheeler

All rights reserved.

A Forge Book
Published by Tom Doherty Associates, LLC
175 Fifth Avenue
New York, NY 10010

www.tor-forge.com

Forge® is a registered trademark of Tom Doherty Associates, LLC.

ISBN 978-0-7653-8214-6

Forge books may be purchased for educational, business, or promotional use. For information on bulk purchases, please contact the Macmillan Corporate and Premium Sales Department at 1-800-221-7945, extension 5442, or write to specialmarkets@macmillan.com.

First Edition: August 2015

Printed in the United States of America

0 9 8 7 6 5 4 3 2 1

Contents

The
Far Tribes

For Sara Ann Freed

Prologue

The old Virginian, Colonel Augustus Bullock, USA Ret., eyed his visitor shrewdly.

"You want information about Skye," he said cautiously, surveying the man. "Lots do. You've come to the right place, suh. I know more about Barnaby Skye than any man alive."

The colonel motioned for his guest to have a seat in the wooden chair opposite his desk. "If you're planning on hiring him, I'll send word along. I do that for him. It's part of my business. I'm his agent."

Bullock settled himself into his swivel chair. He liked nothing better than to talk about Skye. "I also do some weeding," he said, and waited for the response. There was none. "Folks clamor for him since he's the best there is. Even back in the States, they know of him. But he's choosy. He's told me a hundred times he wants clients with courage and common sense. Out in those wild lands, the other kinds could get him killed—and themselves."

Bullock smiled at that. It always put them on their guard, he thought. They wandered into his Fort Laramie sutler's store about this time of year, maybe a dozen every May or June, and he sent some of them along to Skye. He stroked his white Vandyke beard, studying the man.

"You ask how he treats folks out there—women, children, cultivated folks. Out there in that wild land, full of hostiles, roaring rivers, hailstorms, starvation, white and red renegades—and heaven knows what. Oh, he'd surprise you, Barnaby Skye. He's read more than you have, I'll wager. He takes people of all sorts—scholars, women, clerks, children—even missionaries. He did that in fifty-five, and no one thought he could. Just as long as they have sand, suh. Courage and common sense."

His visitor perked up at that. Bullock's eyes went soft with memories, with visions of a giant among men.

"Recently he escorted a party composed largely of women—some of them the sort to make a man blush, I say—from here clear to the diggings at Bannack. He pulled them through. Maybe I should say, suh, he showed them how to pull themselves through. Through hell, I'd say. Pure hell on earth. Oh, that was a trip! That was eighteen and sixty-three, I believe. Not long ago.

"But from what you've told me about you and your party, you'd be more interested in one he guided back in fifty-two. Yes, eighteen and fifty-two. He met his party up at Fort Benton, to the north. He hadn't been guiding long. Since the midforties, anyway. He had a new wife then, Mary, and their little boy, Dirk. The lad's back in the States now, getting a schooling. Yes, Mary of the Shoshones, as well as his other wife, Victoria of the Crows . . ."

Bullock saw his visitor startle. "Oh, suh, the mountain men do that a-plenty. Those wives of his are an army—an army. Those and that horse of his, Jawbone. A young animal in fifty-one, but a beast, a *beast*!"

Bullock watched the man, weighing him. "Want to hear that story, do you? Oh, that's a story. It tested Mister Skye clear beyond the limits of his powers—the powers of the best of the mountain men! And he brought them through trouble I lack words to describe, my friend. Believe it or not, life or death hinged on a large cradle his wife Mary used to tote that boy. Life or death! But I won't get into that now, my friend. Just remember this: whenever men of the frontier talk about the best of them all, they all whisper the name Barnaby Skye—*Mister* Skye to you, suh. . . . And it sounds like a prayer."

Chapter 1

The setting sun caught Fort Benton like a torch. They rounded the last bend of the Missouri and beheld a gold-flamed building of dried earth, stout and precarious in an empty land. Elkanah Morse watched, fascinated, as engagés in red calico shirts and greasy buckskins boiled out of its single narrow entrance facing the river and hordes of savages poured from brightly painted skin lodges to crowd the levee. These would be the Blackfeet, the most warlike and hostile of all northern tribes. They made an awful racket, fusils exploding in the air, throaty cries, the cacophony of rattles and beads and jingles. But they camped here to trade, not to make war, and that was what brought Elkanah Morse from far off Lowell, Massachusetts, to this desperate place.

Still, the sheer savagery of these tribesmen sent a shudder through him, and he momentarily regretted bringing his dear wife Betsy, and his spinster daughter Arabella. Two months late. Would his guide, Barnaby Skye, still be there with all the horses they would need? Morse scanned the distant levee anxiously, looking for a white man with two squaws and a baby boy. If Skye hadn't waited, the whole trip would be doomed.

He rested on his pole, letting the cordeliers propel the keelboat. These last weeks had changed him. He couldn't bear to watch the brutal labor of the cordeliers while he and his family lounged on the foredeck, so he found a pole and joined them as they made their circling promenade around the cabin, along the narrow passageways on either side of the boat, by turns thrusting their poles into the river bottom to propel the boat ahead. When the current ran swift or it grew windy or they struck rapids, they could not pole the boat at all, and then the long ropes were pulled up from the hatches, and sweating men dragged the keel-boats upstream by stumbling along the banks, through brush and swamp and rock, often in water, surrounded by maddening mosquitoes and horseflies. So Elkanah Morse had joined them, and in turn grew hard, sloughing off the soft body of a middle-aged manufacturer and becoming firm-muscled and young. The Frenchmen had laughed at first, then admired the doughty industrialist, and shared the *tabac* with him. All the while they toiled up the swift river, his restless mind sought better ways, ways to meet this need. A small steamboat, he thought. He would offer to build American Fur a small boat just a bit larger than these keelboats, to churn up the shallow western reaches of the great river.

In the second keelboat rode the rest of his party, portly Percy Connaught, a shrewd scholar and Utopian and owner of a successful book bindery in Hartford. With him was Captain Jarvis Cobb, West Point, on detached duty to reconnoiter the unknown lands of the West. And finally, Elkanah's old and dear friend Rudolpho Danzig, Swiss-born geologist and naturalist now teaching at Harvard. Elkanah liked to tease him, call him "the world's greatest expert," which was not a bad description of a man who seemed to be on intimate terms with everything in the universe. Danzig and Cobb had helped the cordeliers pole and haul the laden keelboat, but Percy Connaught, soft and bookish, made excuses and probably, Elkanah surmised, thought the brutal labor was beneath him. He didn't know Connaught well. The man lived down in Connecticut and bought bindery leathers and cloth from him. Cobb he knew even less: a desk-bound instructor at West Point who had found out about Elkanah's journey and asked to join it.

This last stretch had been uncomfortable because there was no room in the keelboats for living space. They had camped on the banks of the great Missouri each night, beneath incredible bluffs, crenellated white towers of rock cut into fantastic forms, that had his wife Betsy exclaiming and painting furiously with her watercolors. Danzig exclaimed, too, but for other reasons, and could be found in twilight studying strata and chipping out fossils and making prodigious notes.

Almost two months late. If the river had been higher, the American Fur steamer *Chouteau* would have continued up the river, offloading part of its burden at Fort Union and then pushing on, with higher draft, perhaps even as far as old Fort McKenzie. Almost August, and Elkanah Morse had the whole business ahead of him. He would personally visit the far tribes and see what he might manufacture for them. He would expand the Indian trade. He would apply Yankee genius to the labors of neolithic tribesmen, for mutual profit. But 1852 had been a low-water year and the fur company's steamboat had snagged on every sandbar on the endless river. They'd skirmished with wild Indians while cutting firewood, been delayed by vast herds of black buffalo swimming the great river, hung on snags. Once they anchored for a week in Dakotah to cobble up a patch where the hull had been pierced by a piece of driftwood that the captain called a sawyer. For over two thousand miles the little steamer had fought the mighty river, from St. Louis clear up to Fort Union at the confluence of the Missouri and Yellowstone. Beyond that, the water flowed too low, and the trade goods going on the additional three hundred some miles to Fort Benton had to be cordelled upstream by fierce profane sweating French engagés of the fur company.

Two months late. Elkanah scanned the boiling crowd anxiously, hoping that his guide had waited. Barnaby Skye was his name. Mister Skye, they called him with obvious respect. Pierre Chouteau himself, master of the fur empire, had written Elkanah that no man in all the northwest would be more capable of taking him out to the far tribes in comfort and safety than Skye. The tribesmen knew him and respected him. He and his two squaws—the idea of two squaws fascinated Elkanah—were a small army. The guide even owned a strange fierce horse, Jawbone, that had become a legend in the far country for its warlike ways. Skye, it seemed, had once been a pressed British sailor but had jumped ship with nothing but a belaying pin and the clothes on his back at Fort Vancouver on the Columbia, and had become a top man in American Fur before turning to guiding.

No man better . . . Elkanah peered anxiously into the savage mob, looking for such a person, hoping the man hadn't given up the long wait.

"Well, Betsy, this is where it starts!" he said, finding the hand of his dear buoyant wife and squeezing.

"I want to paint this place! See the colors, Elkanah! See how the sun brightens the adobes where they're building the blockhouse. These yellow cliffs! All the red calico of these people. Even the river's turned yellow in this light. . . ." She paused. "Do you suppose we'll be safe?" she asked, suddenly cautious.

"As safe as Mister Skye can make us in such a place.

And of course Alec Culbertson must think of safety all the time. Look at that fort. Just one small entrance there. I wonder how it feels to live here, one of a handful of whites surrounded by the most savage and warlike tribe of all, and thousands of miles from the frontier."

He glanced at the awesome river, swift and golden in the low sun. Somewhere far to the south and west rose its headwaters, and from those mountain fastnesses known only to a few white men, flowed the snowmelt water past here at Benton, past Fort Union, down through a continental prairie, ever south and east, until it poured muddy and thick into the Mississippi. The sheer distances awed him. Back in Massachusetts he'd scarcely grasped the length of the journey.

What if Skye hadn't waited? Two months the man had been compelled to idle at Fort Benton. Elkanah's letter, sent last winter to the guide, care of the sutler at Fort Laramie, requested that he be at Benton the first of June . for a lengthy business trip among the far tribes. The guide apparently was an educated man. In due course a response arrived in Lowell, in a fine hand, saying he'd be at Benton, and the seven-hundred-dollar fee would be acceptable. He would have the necessary riding horses for the Morse party and packhorses and mules for the goods Morse wished to take to the Indian villages. The rest of Skye's brief letter contained advice about what to bring and what to wear. But now it was a day shy of August.

Could the trip still succeed? Could this man Skye get him and his party to the villages he wished to visit so that he could study the Indian life, devise helpful goods that might civilize their life and open new markets for his products? He manufactured a variety of goods for the trade, eagerly bought by the American Fur Company. His

Lowell mills spun calico and gingham tradecloth in bright colors. He loomed blankets of various weights, modeled on the Hudson Bay ones, with points, or bars, signifying the thickness. His four-point blankets were prized here in the North. His foundries turned out cooking kettles and skillets, iron arrow points, lance points, ladles, spoons, and knives.

Nor was that the end of it. His busy companies turned out satinets, cambrics, canvas, muslin, laces, silks, carpeting, bed quilts. He produced wallpaper and oilcloth. His tannery produced binder's leathers, saddler's leathers, harness leathers, trunks, and valises. He made steel pen nibs, bar iron, hoop iron, brass and steel wire, coffee mills, church bells, saws and augurs, as well as plows, scythes, spades, shovels, bullet molds, and locks. He had with him a sheet-metal camp stove of his own manufacture, designed to fit into a canvas tent of his own manufacture.

Among the carefully chosen goods he brought here was a complete canvas lodgecover that could replace the buffalo cowhide skins now in use. In his kit were lathed hardwood arrowshafts, more true and perfect than anything manufactured by the tribes. Iron arrow points, large and small, long, barbed, wide, short. He had ready-made arrows, a whole panoply of kitchen goods, knives galore, bolts of fabrics these tribes had never seen, needles and threads, awls, ready-made rubber moccasin soles in various sizes. He would try these out, bring the benefits and blessings of modern civilization to these people, learn how they manufactured their possessions. Hide scraping, for instance. He had several scraper designs in mind that would ease the work. He had the ash and iron fittings for a wheeled travois. He would attach lodgepoles to it and see what these people thought. He would transform their lives!

This man, Skye, who came so highly recommended by top people at American Fur, would take him and his party from place to place and deliver them at last to Fort Laramie before cold set in. If it wasn't too late . . .

At last the weathered gray keelboats were poled to the levee and made fast. Elkanah slipped an arm around Betsy and held tight as the boat bumped land and crowds of wild Indians swarmed close, pointing at them, gesticulating wildly.

"I believe they're seeing their first white woman," Elkanah said. The stares of these half-dressed people were upon Betsy and Arabella, and squaws pointed and babbled in a strange tongue. Arabella's face pursed with fear, but Elkanah laughed, and Betsy smiled.

Working through the buckskin-clad throng was a ruddy, stout, bulbous-nosed man Elkanah took to be the bourgeois here, Alexander Culbertson, a legendary veteran of the fur trade.

"Morse?" cried the bourgeois. "That you? We'll get a plank up in a minute." He paused, staring at the women. "I'll be—didn't expect . . . now ain't this a treat," he blustered.

A peculiar burly man stood apart, walled by ten feet of space that none of these tribesmen penetrated. He was a barrel of a man, medium height, whose small blue eyes, almost buried in the crevasses of a weathered face, studied Morse intently. The man had a nose such as Elkanah Morse had never seen, a vast bulging prow, ballooned and battered by brawling, that dwarfed the rest of his clean-shaven features. Beside him stood two squaws and a boy, all of them somehow separated from the rest of the throng.

Elkanah Morse had never seen such a man, though he was well aware of the peculiarities of mountain men. He had a hunch this one would be Skye, and studied him closely as engagés swirled around him, preparing to unload cargo. The man had dressed Indian, in red-beaded breechclout and fringed leggins. His long tan shirt hung to his hips, and had fringes also. He'd cinched it at the waist with a heavy belt that supported a sheathed knife and a holstered revolver. He wore square-toed whitemen's boots. But it was the grave alert face that drew Elkanah's attention. The man wore his black hair shoulder length, common enough in the mountains, but crowning all this was a black silk stovepipe hat, set rakishly to the man's left.

It was not so much what he wore, but the way he stood, and the way space opened around him, that told Elkanah Morse something about this man. Something about him spoke of calm power, utter competence in the wilds, and faint menace. They locked eyes briefly, and the man smiled, but then his glance turned to the keelboats, appraising them, peering at plank hulls, wide-flared bows, and the low wooden cabin amidships with plank thick enough to stop a rifle ball.

Beside the man the squaws hung close. The older one, rail thin and weathered and seamed, glared angrily at this surging mob. The younger one, full-figured and golden-fleshed, her jet hair in braids, looked more amiable. She clutched the little boy who was plainly a breed, child of the mountain man and herself.

Skye, he thought. Had to be Skye, from all the descriptions. The man had waited! Elkanah was putting his life and safety and the lives of all his party in that man's hands. There surged through him something beyond words, some animal instinct that the man down there would shepherd them safely through a land as dangerous and wild as any left on earth.

"Morse," yelled Culbertson. "The plank's up. Bring your lovely ladies down. Just in time for supper. Here now, the plank wobbles like a drunken Frenchman."

In Culbertson's arm nestled a small, shy, dusky, and altogether beautiful woman, dressed in brown taffeta with an ivory cameo at her throat.

"Mister Morse, I'm Alec Culbertson, and this is my dear wife Natawista," he said. "She's of the Bloods, and the light of my life!"

"I'm so pleased to meet you," said Natawista in flawless English. Her small brown hands caught Betsy's and pressed them, then Arabella's, and finally slipped into Elkanah's.

Everywhere around them now life whirled. Connaught, Cobb, and Danzig waited for a plank that would let them off the second boat. Elkanah caught Skye studying them, even as Skye had studied himself.

Blood and Piegan squaws swarmed around Betsy and Arabella, pinching fabric, touching flesh, muttering and pointing. Arabella looked ashen, but Betsy smiled bravely and touched back, admiring bone necklaces, beadwork, soft-tanned skirts.

"Come on in now," Culbertson yelled. "Your truck is safe. My engagés will haul it all in." He tugged his guests after him, weaving away from the levee, straight toward the burly man in the black silk hat.

"Elkanah, this is Mister Skye. This is your guide. And these are his wives, Victoria of the Crows, and Mary of the Snakes. And this tyke down here is Dirk."

"Delighted, Skye," said Morse, gripping the rough hand of the guide. "Saw you from the boat and thought it was you."

"You'll do, Mister Morse. You'll do indeed. We're set

to go in the morning," rumbled this man, with a voice that echoed like thunder. "And call me Mister Skye, if you would, mate."

Engagés had run a plank up to the gunwales of the second keelboat, and soon the rest of Morse's party threaded through the boiling bronze crowd. Elkanah waved them over.

Rudolpho Danzig, a short, compact, dark-haired man, studied the Blackfeet and French-Canadian engagés with amiable curiosity as he came. Young Captain Cobb, with full muttonchops of yellow-brown hair and a receding hairline, studied things about him as if making notes. But white, soft Percy Connaught looked jumpy, if not terrified.

"Gentlemen," said Elkanah, "come meet our hosts, Alec and Natawista Culbertson, and our guide, Mister Skye, and his wives Victoria and Mary. And the little lad is Dirk. . . . Now, sirs, let me introduce Professor Rudolpho Danzig, a geologist from Harvard College with a lively interest in natural sciences and everything else on earth. Professor Danzig is Swiss, from Berne, and an old friend who badgers me to make scientific instruments for him.

"Now here is Percy Connaught, of Hartford, who owns a book bindery there and is an old business acquaintance. Mister Connaught has come here to write a book about the West."

"Two books," corrected Connaught. "One for the vulgar—it'll cause a few sensations, I hope—and one serious one, to influence public policy concerning the Far West."

"And finally, Captain Cobb, who instructs cadets at West Point about something or other, and is here to gather information for the army, and reconnoiter the West."

"My field's intelligence," explained Cobb. "Knowledge wins wars. It's a pleasure, sir," he said, offering a hand to Culbertson. "And you, sir," he said to Mister Skye. He offered no hand to the Indian wives. Elkanah realized that Connaught hadn't either, but Professor Danzig had cordially clasped hands with each person present.

Mister Skye was visibly sizing up the party, his obscure blue eyes darting from Danzig to Cobb and finally gazing a long moment at Connaught, absorbing the man's pasty corpulence and apparent nervousness.

Then Culbertson steered them toward the fort, which lay thirty or forty yards back from the levee.

"Is our property safe? I should think these savages would snatch it the moment we turn out back," said Percy Connaught in a nasal New England twang. "They're all famous thieves."

"My engagés will have it inside directly," said Culbertson. "They'll be busy all through the night. All these tribesmen—Blackfeet mostly, Piegans and Bloods, and a few Sarsi, Crees, and others—about three hundred lodges, have been camping here waiting for this moment. We'll shelve the trade goods tonight and open the window in the morning.

"The window?" asked Elkanah.

"Right here," said Culbertson as they wove into a long low corridor with a stout gate at each end. "This is the trading window. It opens onto our trading room. They'll bring in the buffalo robes and pelts in the morning and trade for the goods. They'll clean us out of everything—two keelboat loads—in a few days, but the keelboats will bring more from Fort Union. All the trading takes place right here at this window. Only a few at a time, you see, with the inner gate, here, shut."

"Is it that dangerous—that you must deal with these people through a small window?" asked Elkanah.

"Not at all," Culbertson said. "But there are times— when they've sampled the jug, especially—we prefer to be careful." He smiled faintly. "I can't imagine where the spirits come from," he added.

"They're barbaric!" said Connaught, oblivious of Natawista Culbertson, Victoria and Mary Skye. "Animals. I have always opposed white settlement of these western lands. This is like the Sahara, like Australia's Outback, a huge burden the Republic must now maintain for no good purpose."

Mister Skye glanced sharply at the man, and Elkanah wondered whether there'd be trouble on the trail. He thought to say something to Connaught, who seemed utterly unaware that the company he addressed included Blackfeet, Crow, and Snake women. Those he called the vulgar were always invisible to him.

But the moment passed. The inner yard of Fort Benton was redolent with cooking odors and the faint smell of other things—leathers, hides, horses, urine, and human sweat. From a small pen across the yard, an ugly blue roan horse with yellow eyes and narrow head flattened its ears and shrieked, its stare on Mister Skye.

"The engagés live over there," said Culbertson, pointing to a barracks building. "The kitchen's there. Hide storerooms here. My quarters, offices, and spare rooms over there. A few married engagés live nearby in adobe cabins. We've started that northwest blockhouse—my men make about twelve hundred adobe bricks a day—and then we'll build another one on the southeast corner, the river side."

"Not much wood to build with," observed Rudolpho Danzig.

"Not much," Culbertson agreed. "We cut firewood over in the Highwoods, twenty miles south. Adobe's the only building material here."

"Why here? Why this site?" asked Professor Danzig.

Culbertson shrugged. "These river flats are rare. And up above are the great falls of the Missouri. Also, there's a ford here, and we're close to the tribes we trade with, the heart of the Blackfeet country."

"Ah, so," said Danzig. "Always a reason."

"My friends," said the bourgeois, "Natawista has magically prepared us a great feast of buffalo hump. We'll see you to your quarters now, and expect you in a few minutes."

Elkanah Morse looked forward to it, and the good talk, keenly. He would plumb Mister Skye at table.

Chapter 2

So long had Mister Skye hunkered at campfires that a proper chair felt uncomfortable and strange. He had not sat in one for about twenty years. He tried to remember his manners, dredged up from his forgotten boyhood, and it made him clumsy. Natawista Culbertson had managed a great feast, with succulent buffalo hump, rib, tongue, spiced sausage made of boudins, and potatoes and turnips fresh off the keelboats. Alec uncorked a flagon of good port wine for the occasion, but Mister Skye managed to avoid it. Not now, he thought, not now. In his possibles rested a three-gallon cask of bourbon from the sutler at Fort Laramie. It warmed him to think of it.

The hour was late and he felt sleepy, but across the massive plank table sat one of the most astonishing men Mister Skye had ever encountered. Even now, in the torpid wake of the feast, Elkanah Morse peppered questions at his hosts and guide, his blocky tanned face animated and young in the amber light of the oil lamps. Here lay Yankee genius of a sort entirely new to the guide.

"What are the most successful trade items, Mister Culbertson?" Morse asked.

"Why, blankets, I suppose. Calico. Anything metal, cooking pots . . ."

"I have them all. I have copper kettles that weigh half as much. What about arrows? I have ready-made arrows, with shafts that are truer than anything they can make."

The bourgeois frowned. "I don't think ye'll git far with those, Mister Morse."

"Why not? It's progress! A better arrow. Each shaft milled to a thousandth of an inch. Exactly identical iron tips. Good turkey-feather fletching, scientifically cut and measured."

"Medicine," rumbled Mister Skye. "An arrow must have medicine. So must a bow. Each tribe makes bows and arrows their own way. Each warrior or hunter has his own marks dyed or notched on an arrow."

"Tradition. You're really talking about tradition. That's the barrier to all progress, Mister Skye. I'll show them a better thing, and they'll see it eventually."

"Ah, no, mate. I'm talking about Indian religion. Medicine is how Indians understand power and success and failure and the forces of nature. I'm afraid your ready-made arrows—"

Elkanah Morse laughed easily. "Hope I can prove you wrong," he said. "But that's why I'm here, to get answers. I'll pester you with questions the whole trip!"

Mister Skye enjoyed that. A man who asked questions proved better on the trail than one who had all the answers.

"Now let me try another on you, gents. I've brought a sickle. We make them, too, good hard steel edge. Sickles and scythes, shovels, pickaxes, hatchets, we make them all. Now I thought a sickle might be right handy among these tribesmen. Cut hay. Pile up a winter's supply of prairie hay. Now take a hunting party, out camping somewhere and afraid their ponies will be stolen. They could cut hay, bring in grass, keep their ponies picketed right in camp."

Alec Culbertson laughed. "Woman's work. No self-respecting warrior would cut hay. It's beneath them. That's for beasts of burden, not warriors or hunters, who lounge away their lives like any proper prairie Indian."

"How you talk!" cried Natawista. "But it is true. Maybe you trade sickles to women."

"Son of a bitch!" cried Victoria, Mister Skye's old woman. "Maybe them damn warriors will learn to use this sickle."

Conversation froze. Betsy and Arabella gaped. Rudolpho Danzig grinned. Jarvis Cobb looked uncomfortable. Percy Connaught pursed his lips, drew himself up in his chair, and peered disdainfully.

Only Elkanah Morse chuckled. "You are a lady after my heart, Mrs. Skye! When I ask hard questions and want straight answers, I know where to come."

"I forget," muttered Victoria. "I learn this talk from the trappers that came to Absaroka. I forget you got some damn good words, and damn bad words. In Absaroka, all words are good words. Son of a bitch!"

"There are occasions, Mrs. Skye, when I envy you your freedom," said Betsy Grover Morse. "A New England woman has a want of words."

Arabella Morse looked bored. "I'm tired, Papa. I think I shall retire."

"By all means," said Elkanah, watching her sweep away and into the shadowed yard. "I dragooned her into coming," he said. "She's bent upon making life as dreary as possible for herself."

Mister Skye watched Elkanah's daughter thoughtfully as she fled the table.

For half an hour more, Elkanah Morse peppered questions at his hosts and his guides, and Mister Skye marveled that a man who had cordelled and poled a keelboat all day, beneath a blazing sun, could be so awake deep into the summer night. The guide studied Morse, studied the others, trying to fathom the character of these people. He had to. His safety, the safety of his family, the safety of these people themselves would be at stake. Arabella seemed pouty and rebellious. A problem.

Covertly Mister Skye eyed the others. Danzig had said little, but seemed as alive and vital and curious as Elkanah Morse. Captain Cobb seemed an enigma, poker-faced and polite. West Point and competent, he thought. Connaught reeked of trouble, his pasty soft face reflecting disdain and contempt the whole evening. But Betsy, vibrant Betsy the watercolorist, there was a good match for Elkanah, a woman of innate happiness and strength.

Suddenly Elkanah called it off, just as Alec Culbertson showed signs of dozing, and gentle Natawista drooped. "Time for bed. Off in the morning. Try to make up time. One thing, Mister Skye. Before we leave, I'd like to drop in on the opposition, find out what they trade, get the measure of their needs. I see it's just upstream a piece."

Culbertson came suddenly awake. "Wouldn't advise it," he muttered.

"Sounds like there's some animosity," Morse said.

"More to it than that," rumbled Mister Skye. "It's not just competition. There's bad blood. Harvey is, shall we say, hostile to us. To Alec here, and to me. Fort Campbell has not yet been resupplied this year, so he hasn't a thing on his shelves. Mister Morse, I'll put it plain. Alexander Harvey is a killer of the most brutal sort, unforgiving, cruel, vicious. He's murdered Indians and his own engagés without cause. Twice when I was employed by this company, I stopped him from shedding blood. Alec, here, had him thrown out. He will take you for an agent and provocateur of American Fur."

"Sounds formidable indeed, Mister Skye. Nonetheless, I shall visit Fort Campbell in the morning. I'm a businessman and manufacturer, looking for opportunities in the Indian trade. I'll tell him that, and tell him what I have to offer. He may order from my companies on just as competitive terms as American Fur."

There was a bit of steel in the reply, Mister Skye thought. Well then, he'd accompany Elkanah Morse in the morning. Just to keep the unpredictable Harvey from murdering the entrepreneur on the spot.

"I will take you there then," Mister Skye said.

"Why, that's not necessary. I'd prefer that you'd see to the packing. You have the horses, I trust?"

"I do, but I'm going with you to Harvey, Primeau and Company."

"If there's bad blood, why, I'd prefer to go alone, and you may organize our caravan."

"Mary and Victoria will organize it."

"I see you're determined. All right then. I've put myself and my loved ones and friends in your hands because they told me you're the best in this wilderness. I'll defer to your judgment, Mister Skye. If you feel the need to go with me when I visit this man Harvey, why, you must have cause. Come with me, then. Is this man mad?"

It was a question Mister Skye couldn't answer for sure. "No, I don't suppose so. Suspicious. Obsessed. Surrounded by imaginary enemies. And ready to murder."

"Then I am glad you'll be with me, Mister Skye."

In the quietness of a rose and burgundy dawn, Elkanah Morse stared at the ponies. The sun lay so low that a long umber shadow from the engagés' barracks along the east stockade fell across the yard, almost to the horse pens.

"These are Indian ponies, Mister Morse. Small, tough, with hoof horn so hard they don't need shoes. They prosper where grain-fed horses die. High-bred horses from the States can outrun them—for a while. But for sheer endurance, these mustang ponies will outlast them. I have your dozen, and I've picked them for this country."

"They seem small and thin—"

"They're that, mate. Trust them. They'll all take saddle or pack. I dickered half the spring for the best. Now, how do you want this done?"

Beside Morse and Mister Skye lay a mound of gear, all of it so new and clean and well built that it astonished the guide.

"I'll need two to carry my sample goods. Need two ponies to carry the goods up to Fort Campbell. Each of my party will have a riding horse. Those two sidesaddles are for my ladies. The remaining ponies will carry foodstuffs and camp supplies. Of course, sir, you'll be providing us with meat. . . ."

Mister Skye nodded. He caught a tough hammerheaded pony with spots over his rump.

"Let me show you how I want them," said Morse. "I've gone to some lengths so's not to gall the animals." He dropped a fine brown wool saddle blanket over the pony, and then a pack saddle with a fleece lining that astonished Mister Skye. He'd never seen a pack saddle like this, fleece-lined, with cinches of the finest harness leather. After he'd tightened down the saddle, Morse hung the panniers to it. These fine canvas bags astounded Mister Skye as much as the saddles themselves. They were light, durable, riveted along the seams, with fitted buckle-down covers, and probably waterproof.

"Like them? I designed them myself. Had them custom-made in my tannery." Some delight animated Elkanah's square, craggy face.

The river was a live thing, throbbing without pause. It rippled orange and salmon in the dawn light as Mister Skye and Elkanah Morse walked past somnolent Blackfeet lodges toward Fort Campbell, leading two packhorses.

The opposition post was a smaller version of Fort Benton, also on the north bank of the Missouri. Mister Skye banged on the massive plank door with the butt of his Hawken and waited. Fur posts rarely stirred until midmorning, and this one was no exception. He banged again. At last they heard a bar being lifted within, and the heavy cottonwood door creaked open a bit. In the rose light they could see an eye, a hand, and a heavy blue revolver.

"You," said Alexander Harvey.

"We have business, Harvey."

"Not likely. American Fur Company monkey business."

Mister Skye sighed. "I'd like you to meet Elkanah Morse, Lowell, Massachusetts. He manufactures goods for the Indian trade. Harvey, Primeau probably buys them in quantity. He has two pack loads of samples. New goods. Things he thinks the tribes might cotton to. He came all this way to find out."

The door creaked open a bit further, but the heavy revolver never wavered. Harvey had straight coarse black hair, disheveled now, burning brown eyes in a hollowed rough face, and the build of a bear. Now those burning eyes settled on the panniers, noting the fine cut of the canvas, double buckles, and pack saddles that pampered horses.

"Mr. Harvey? I'd like to ask a few questions. Mostly, I'd like to know what the tribesmen want. What to manufacture. It seems to me if I get a sense of—"

"No," said Harvey.

Mister Skye glanced at Elkanah Morse, and at Harvey's unwavering revolver that had somehow lifted slightly until it bored into Morse's breast.

"Well, let me show you the goods I've brought along."

"I don't need to see them. Tell me what they're worth and I'll trade in robes. My resupply isn't in and my shelves are bare."

"Don't you want to see . . . ?"

Harvey shrugged. "They trade for anything I've got. It doesn't matter."

"Well, at least you could tell me what is most—most sought for. I can then make sure your St. Louis people know . . . and I can usually improve the product. Lighter, stronger, more efficient . . ."

Harvey stared at him, then at Mister Skye. "I'm not telling my trade secrets. This is just another damned American Fur snooping party. And you're just another damned American Fur lackey come sniffing around here to find ways to steal my business. Skye, there, is American Fur and always has been."

"It's Mister Skye, Harvey."

The man half-hidden behind the massive door leered.

"I'll show you," said Elkanah Morse firmly. He walked to the nearest packhorse, ignoring the revolver that swung along with him. "I have here six types of iron arrow points; lance points; lathed hardwood arrowshafts. Skillets and kettles, light and heavy, cast iron and copper. Scythes, knives, hatchets, ax heads, double- and single-bitted. Copper rivets, long and short—"

"Rivets?" asked Harvey.

"Why, sir, I thought the Indians might use them in leatherwork. Punch a hole with an awl—I have awls—and run the rivet through leather along a seam, and flatten down the opposite side."

Harvey said nothing.

"And here I have canvas, oilcloth, calico, cambric, and an entire presewn canvas lodgecover. Do you suppose they'd go for a canvas lodgecover? I had a hide lodge shipped to me a year ago, at great expense, for the pattern."

"Oilcloth. Waterproof?" asked Harvey.

"Of course. Red checks, yellow, white. Also a bolt of canvas impregnated with India rubber. Great covering for a canoe. How about wire? I have brass wire, steel wire, fine gauge. Do you think they'd want it?"

"American Fur must be trying to pawn off crazy stuff on me."

"I'm an independent manufacturer, Mister Harvey.

American Fur is a customer. So is Harvey, Primeau. You use my blankets. Now tell me, what colors do the tribesmen prefer? Striped, like the Hudson Bay ones? How many points? Four-pound sell best?"

"I told you I don't share trade information. Tell Culbertson it's a good joke. And you can leave that truck right here. It'll give me a little something to peddle while we wait for the pack train."

Elkanah Morse drew himself up, eyeing the revolver at last. "Those are my private samples, Mister Harvey. I'm on my way to the far tribes with them."

Harvey grinned. "American Fur samples, you mean. Gonna go out and lure the redskins into AFC. Uncinch those loads and drop them."

"I think not, Harvey," said Mister Skye.

"He obeys or he's a dead man, and so are you."

Harvey's threat was real, thought Mister Skye. With that revolver the man could put bullets into Elkanah Morse and into himself before he could bring his Hawken to bear. And he was half-hidden behind that door, too. Time ticked by. Morse stood paralyzed. Mister Skye thought the man would be dead before he even started here. Harvey might well murder him after the packs were off the horses.

"I said move," snapped Harvey.

"Murder will put you in a federal prison," said Elkanah quietly.

Alexander Harvey laughed cynically.

"Mister Harvey. I'm going to turn my back and lead these packhorses with my goods away from here. If it's murder, you'll do it whether I'm armed or unarmed, whether I face you or have my back turned."

Deliberately, Elkanah Morse turned and walked to the packhorses and took hold of the halter stales. Mister

Skye stood rooted, watching Harvey's black revolver follow.

"I will live long enough to kill you," muttered Mister Skye.

Harvey's burning glance caught him then, and the revolver swung toward Mister Skye. A laugh. The heavy door creaked shut, and the bourgeois of Fort Campbell had vanished from sight. Mister Skye stood stock still, his small blue eyes searching out loopholes and finding none. Heart pattering, he trotted up to Elkanah Morse.

"You were frightened?" asked Mister Skye.

"Never so frightened. My legs tremble under me."

"But you did it. Stood him down, mate."

Elkanah Morse shuddered. "I did what I had to. I should have taken your advice, Mister Skye. You and Mister Culbertson warned me. This is a wild land with wild men in it."

"Aye, mate, it is that. There's something a bit wrong, mad I'd say, about Harvey, but you stood him down. Don't think it's over. Harvey never forgets. When he makes an enemy, there's but one thing in his head, and that's the finishing of what's begun."

"Does he really think I'm some sort of American Fur man?"

"No telling. The opposition comes and goes. AFC beat out Bridger, Sublette, Fitzpatrick, Ashley. Beat out Campbell, Fox, and all the rest. They get murderous, thinking about AFC, thinking about the rich Chouteaus back in St. Louis. They get to hating AFC the way a Bible thumper hates the devil. If AFC did half the things they say it does, the government would have lifted its license long ago."

The entrepreneur pondered that as they walked along the riverbank back to Fort Benton. Life stirred in the

Blackfeet lodges now; dusky women bathing at the river silently watched their progress.

"How about these? Piegans and Bloods, are they? We could show my goods to these. Can you talk their tongue?"

"Sign language," said Mister Skye. "I'd say no to this. These Blackfeet are waiting to trade later today, as fast as the keelboat goods are shelved. You won't get an answer out of them. Not the kind of information you want. Mostly they'd be confused, and Culbertson might not be entirely happy. Maybe, if you'd like to stick around a day or two, you could sit at the trading window, see what they want most, watch the whole thing."

"I don't think that'll show me much. What they want shows up in the purchase orders. So many four-point red blankets. So many of such and such an iron pot. No, Mister Skye." He beamed at the guide beside him. "I'm itchy. Let's be off. I've some fancy camping goods of my own design I'm rarin' to try!"

"And you'd like to put a few leagues between yourself and Alexander Harvey, eh?"

Elkanah Morse sighed. "I'm glad to be free of him. We'll leave directly, right after breakfast, and then we'll be free."

"Don't count on it, Mister Morse."

Chapter 3

Percy Connaught kept two journals. One would be turned into a book about far west policy. The other would become a book full of Wild West episodes, strange encounters, and amazing sights—for the vulgar, of course.

The first book would make him influential among the best minds in the Republic; the second would be a sensation among the masses, and make him rich.

Not that he was poor. He had inherited a bindery in Hartford, and it provided a comfortable return and largely took care of itself, giving him time for more important things, such as advancing civilization. Every Whig instinct in him had fought Manifest Destiny, but in 1846 the avalanche had come, and now the Republic stretched clear to the Pacific, and we owned the Spanish possessions as well as Oregon. But what had we gained? A vast wasteland! A Sahara that could not support civilization and might well bleed the Republic to death. The western armies numbered a few thousand, and should number a few hundred thousand to control and defend this vast waste. Everything on this journey so far had confirmed him in his view, and he intended to write a book so compelling that it would affect the nation's destiny for decades. And here was Captain Cobb, reconnoitering for the army. An opportunity! Percy intended to convert Cobb to his view, and between Cobb's reports and his own, they'd overcome the inflammatory Senator Thomas Hart Benton and his mad son-in-law Fremont and establish a rational Western policy.

But now, in the yard of Fort Benton, he labored on his other journal, the one for the vulgar. Each of his journals—five hundred blank pages bound in fine red morocco—was filling rapidly with his penciled fine script. Not ink, of course. Not nib and ink in a wilderness. Here before him labored Skye's two squaws organizing this caravan. The barbarous guide himself had vanished at dawn with Morse—off to the opposition mud pile—but these squaws looked downright industrious. Two squaws, one an old hag and the other comely and voluptuous, wives of a barrel-shaped Briton without a nation, who arrayed himself in scandalous fringed leggins and breechclout like the children of the wilds. Now there was a thing to describe to the vulgar!

Grudgingly, he admired them. In the same way he admired Skye, too. Morse found out Skye was the best to be had in the Far West; half-savage himself, fierce, wild, and uncanny. A party could feel as safe as the wilds permitted when Skye was running it. A comfort. He knew there'd be few comforts in the coming months, but having a trained lion along would be one. He chuckled. Trained lion. He'd remember that, use it upon the vulgar. A lion and two catamounts. How they'd laugh, back in the States, to read of a man with black hair to his shoulders and a black silk stovepipe set rakishly on his caveman skull!

"You!"

Percy removed his gold-rimmed spectacles and peered up. Why, it was the old hag herself, the one called Victoria.

"You. Stop making the words, and git your pack on. We're going to go soon. Son of a bitch, we don't go nowhere with a mess of lazy."

"Right with you, old woman!"

"Me old? Maybe tougher. You soft as sheep wool, and you gonna feel it until you get toughed up."

"You have me there, Victoria," he admitted. He paused a moment to scribble it in his journal. He'd record her language as best as he could—using a dash, of course, to form some expressions. Like G———m. It would be inconsiderate to teach the vulgar unfortunate expletives. Then he snapped his red morocco journal books shut and tucked them in his pack.

"That's some hell of a pack. I never seen any so light and strong," said Victoria, fingering the riveted canvas.

The packs were, in fact, one of Morse's uncanny marvels. The frames had been cut from thin hickory, tough as steel, and swathed in fleece-lined harness leather pads. The panniers were compartmented with canvas dividers to keep things in place. The canvas itself was lightly impregnated with rubber, making them watertight.

Victoria flipped one of Morse's thick saddle blankets over a scrawny pony and dropped the loaded pack saddle over it, muttering and exclaiming in her strange tongue all the while, as Percy Connaught watched, amused.

Culbertson and half the engagés here hovered around, too, fingering equipment such as they'd never seen, exclaiming, hefting Morse's weapons, bantering with Betsy and Arabella, the first white women they'd ever seen here. Amid the hubbub Mister Skye and Elkanah Morse returned, leading packhorses and looking peculiarly grim on a crisp morning. Connaught wondered at it, but neither of them said anything. They wolfed a breakfast of buffalo steaks and oat gruel that Natawista had ready for them.

Everything seemed ready. The women, in matched gray cotton dresses with pleated skirts, sat their sidesaddles, looking enchanting. Rudolpho Danzig sat a restless spotted pony, eyeing this horde with intense interest. He wore a tweed suitcoat with leather patches, and a flat-crowned gray felt hat that shadowed his pale face and black spade beard. Jarvis Cobb sat easily aboard one of Morse's light cavalry saddles, with a roll tied behind him. They had rehearsed all this over and over in the East, with Elkanah Morse's driving genius organizing everything, inventing and manufacturing devices for every need. They had even gathered in Lowell before embarking and tried it all out, tents and saddles, hatchets, and revolvers supplied them by

Connaught's Hartford neighbor Sam Colt. There was nothing more that Yankee genius could do. If the hand of science, progress, and civilization could not conquer the wilderness with such as this, then it couldn't be done.

Mister Skye—how Connaught enjoyed the name!—rolled with a sailor's gait to the pen where that peculiar horse paced. Percy had never seen such a beast. Skye's animal stood tall, ugly, rawboned, with evil yellow eyes and a blue roan hide marred by a hundred scars and cuts. The thing shrieked wickedly as Skye approached, and butted the guide with his head.

"I'll help saddle, Mister Skye," said Elkanah, closing behind the guide. Even as he stepped ahead, Skye's burly arm caught the industrialist and spun him back ruthlessly. Morse gaped, barely holding his temper.

"Sorry, mate." Skye addressed them all. "I don't want any of you getting close to this horse. Never closer than ten or fifteen feet. For your safety."

"He kicks, I suppose," said Elkanah, rubbing his bruised arm.

"No, Mister Morse, he kills."

Even as they stared the strange horse with the narrow-set vicious eyes bared his teeth and snapped at the air, murdering flies and men. He squealed eerily as the guide threw a light pad saddle of Indian manufacture over him and slid his sheathed Hawken over that.

Percy Connaught shuddered. A murderous blue horse would be something for his journal, the one for the vulgar, of course. The guide paused, as if looking for something, studying the high mud-brick walls, testing the cerulean skies with knowing eyes. He rolled over to Alec Culbertson and Natawista and roared like a sore-toothed grizzly, hugging the bourgeois while they slapped each other on the back. And then a gentler hug for Natawista. All much too demonstrative, embarrassing actually, to Percy Connaught's taste. But they'd educated themselves back East about the mountains, and had got that veteran of several rendezvous, Nathaniel Wyeth himself, to tell them what to expect. That taciturn ice dealer had mentioned the mountain hug and a lot of other strange customs, and told them to respect the ways of the mountains and their men because such things were natural and good for the place and the circumstance. They had listened with care.

Outside of the fort, a milling crowd of savages watched silently. Percy studied them a bit fearfully, wondering at their feathers, calicos, half-naked brown bodies, vermilioned cheeks and heads, and calf-high black-dyed moccasins that gave these people their name. *Pieds Noirs*, the French trappers had called them. Stone Age people, without the wheel, without metal, without writing. But no doubt murderous.

Skye's old hag glared at them, and Connaught remembered that the Crows were mortal enemies of these Piegan and Blood savages. Her weathered old body grew rigid, as if she expected an arrow to bury itself in her breast. Even the guide, Skye, peered sharply at the throng. But at the gate of Fort Benton, Culbertson yelled something in their tongue, and the savage mob thronged toward the trading window. Resupplied, Fort Benton was in business.

The ford of the Missouri turned out to be right in front of Fort Benton.

"Follow my path, mates. Water's low. It won't even reach the bellies this time."

He steered his ugly blue horse down the levee and into

the swift current, angling upstream. The guide's pack-mules and ponies followed, each carrying its burden in dyed parfleches. Their skin lodge went over on two horses. One carried the hide cover on its back; the other carried two bundles of lodgepoles that floated behind. The guide's word was good. At no place in the hundred-and-fifty-yard river did water blacken a pony's belly.

Elkanah, Betsy, and Arabella ventured out next, the women laughing and watching the cold water tug at their mounts. And lastly, Connaught, Cobb, and Danzig crossed, each leading two packhorses. They gathered on the south shore beneath a pitched yellow bluff, and the ponies shook off water, violently rattling the packs. But nothing came loose.

It was easier than he had supposed, Percy thought. Maybe all the tales of hardship he'd heard about the Wild West suffered a bit from exaggeration.

But over here, away from the dun-colored fort, things seemed somehow different. Mister Skye sat quietly on Jawbone, letting them all feel it. Feel how it was to be alone in a vast and menacing wild.

"All right, mates," he rumbled. "From now on, your safety depends on heeding what I say. If anything happens to me, trust my good women, Victoria and Mary. They're better at this than I am. Alec Culbertson told me most of the Piegans are in the Judith basin, two or three days south. They were enemies of you Yanks for years; many still are. Trade and smallpox tamed them—a little. They are great thieves, and thieving is an honor on these plains. Mister Morse, they'll want to trade for the sample goods you'll be showing them, and if not trade, then steal them. I'll be thinking of ways to deal with it. I don't speak their tongue, and sign language won't explain it. Be thinking on it."

For several hours they toiled quietly up long yellow draws, down into an old bed of the Missouri, and finally up again and out upon a plain so vast it stretched to infinity, with only a few amethyst buttes and lavender mountains roughing the surface. Percy Connaught found the vast silent emptiness frightening. The old hag rode off obliquely left, or southeast. Mary and her infant boy trotted off obliquely right, until each of them turned into black dots, often mysteriously invisible. Scouts, Percy Connaught thought. Scouts, like cat's whiskers, like the antennae of a bug, out to search the bunch-grassed silvery prairie for enemies. Sam Colt's .31-caliber baby dragoon revolver belted to his waist was a comfort.

Aeons ago, this had been the bed of a great sea. That was plain enough from the stratified sedimentary rock they'd passed as they wound upward from the Missouri River valley. The rock lay angled, broken, and faulted here, no doubt tumbled by the upheavals of the nearby mountain cordillera. They rode through a second channel of the Missouri, dry now except for a small creek, probably in use as recently as the last ice age. Somehow this land had been lifted up from the sea, and then the erosion began, thousands of feet of it, leaving those distant blue flattopped buttes where a cap of more resistant rock had prevented the erosion. Limestone, probably. Here in an arid climate, limestone would endure.

Before retiring at Fort Benton, Rudolpho Danzig had pulled out his sextant and measured the height of the North Star. The higher in the sky it appeared, the farther north they must be. Fort Benton was, he determined, approximately forty-seven degrees and fifty minutes north. Not far from the forty-ninth parallel, where the British possessions began. Longitude was a tougher matter, and he wasn't particularly worried about it. Someday the world's nations would have to decide where to start, where to run the arbitrary zero meridian. This republic wanted it to run through Washington City, in the District of Columbia. France insisted that the prime meridian run through Paris. Spain was holding out for Madrid. But he guessed that someday the world's nations would settle on London, the Royal Observatory in Greenwich in particular. There were ways to measure just how far west they had come. An accurate clock and a sextant measure of the noonday sun, for one. But he had only a pocket watch. Time was meaningless in these vast and entertaining wastes. He had with him the brand-new book published by the U.S. Naval Observatory, *American Ephemeris and Nautical Almanac*, listing the position of various celestial bodies each day of the year, based on a prime meridian at Washington, D.C. He had also a copy of *Bowditch's Practical Navigator*, for additional help. And, of course, a magnetic compass, which turned out to be several degrees off true here.

None of which concerned him a great deal. He had come for fun, and found every minute, every breath he breathed in this endless land, a joyous experience. He'd grown up in Berne, Switzerland, and won his doctorate in natural sciences from the new University of Berne, and then hastened to the New World and broader horizons than Switzerland could provide, using his doctorate as a handy passport. Harvard had embraced him. He was nominally a geologist, but his mind refused to be straitjacketed and his real study was the whole world and its people, geography. His students got geology enough—plus biology, cartography, topology, botany, paleontology, history, anthropology, and more. Academia couldn't contain a mind like his. Nor his compact body, either, for here he rode, on Morse's expedition, observing everything and setting it down cryptically in his journals. Except for the impressions of a few mountain men, this country remained unmapped and unknown.

From the moment he met Elkanah Morse, he knew they were kindred spirits. The manufacturing genius and the professor had restless tinkering minds, boundless curiosity, and an itch to see what lay beyond the horizon. Rudolpho Danzig had said yes, yes, yes, before Elkanah Morse was half through explaining his westward journey. In Morse's kit lay a mountain of gadgets. Not to be outdone, Rudolpho Danzig had a few of his own, including the whole paraphernalia of Louis Jacques Mandé Daguerre, inventor of the daguerreotype, a photographic image made on a silver-coated copper plate treated with iodine vapor. Elkanah's cousin, Samuel F.B. Morse, had introduced it to the United States, and Rudolpho had hastened to purchase one of the things, seeing at last the tool geologists and naturalists needed to record their finds and help cartographers. He lacked plates—weight was a crucial factor—but he hoped to make a few images of some of the aborigines, perhaps chiefs or headmen.

Ahead of him rode Elkanah and Betsy, side by side, enjoying the wilderness and each other. She perched in her sidesaddle as if she'd been born to it, though in fact she learned to ride only recently. She refused to be left behind. Where Elkanah went, she would go! He'd discouraged her at first, with tales of hardship and danger, but that had only whetted her appetite. She began riding lessons at once and became an equestrienne as swiftly as she'd become a noted watercolorist. Between them, they'd dragooned their daughter Arabella—whose feelings about this expedition were displayed in a fossilized pout—and thus the whole Morse family rode along behind the rude mountain guide.

For a moment Rudolpho felt a pang. His own Sarah declined to come, and he missed her sorely, along with their three boys. But ah, that Betsy! What made these women of the New World so much bolder and more vital than their sisters of the Old World? Scarcely a woman of Europe would have ventured into a wild like this, but here rode Betsy Morse, braving it all, enjoying herself, tasting life, risking everything, drawing air into her lungs as clean and dry and transparent as any air on earth. How could there be diseases in a place like this? The sunbaked plains bred health and life and strength!

That evening they camped in a peculiar gulch on the northeast edge of a looming flattopped butte, black with ponderosa on its precipitous slopes. Square Butte, Mister Skye labeled it. To the west lay the Highwood Mountains, black-forested and mysterious. Danzig eyed the terrain carefully, noting the white cap of resistant rock that formed the butte when softer dark rock below it eroded away over aeons of time. This place alone, with its tumbled land, could occupy a geologist for months, he thought. He had observed a giant dry riverbed here, and wondered what vast stream had cut it not too long ago, probably in glacial times. Maybe the Missouri itself, he thought.

Camping was a familiar drill for all of them now. They'd camped along the Missouri from Fort Union, on the banks beside the keelboats, as the burly French beasts of burden roped and poled them west. But now Mister Skye's choices of campsites would be based on different considerations:

good water, good grass for the stock, shelter, wood for fires, and defense. Danzig paused to admire the choice. All those things seemed abundant here.

Except perhaps defense. They had stopped in a broad riverbed gulch and could be observed from dun bluffs, not to mention the vast butte that loomed over them. At least, Danzig thought, their guide had chosen a place where a campfire could not be seen far in the night.

Mister Skye addressed them all. "Let the ponies graze and water freely until dusk, but under guard. Perhaps you will oblige us by staying out among them, and armed, Mister Connaught. Later, we'll picket them close to camp. My horse, Jawbone, does excellent sentry duty all night."

"Why—why—I had thought to do my journals, Skye."

"It's Mister Skye."

"Oh, dear, yes, it's Mister Skye!"

"The camp seems to be equipped with fine lanterns, carbide lanterns, Mister Connaught. Light for your journals later. I will climb Square Butte yonder with an eye to our safety."

He did not wait for a reply from the Hartford man of letters, but trotted off into the russet twilight. A bit later Danzig caught glimpses of the burly guide clambering easily up slopes fit for only a mountain goat. Connaught had ignored Mister Skye, settled before the fine canvas tent with collapsible light ash poles Morse designed, and had taken to whittling his pencil and scribbling in his red book. Rudolpho Danzig sighed, plucked out the carbine Morse had lent him, and strolled out among the loose ponies and mules, keeping a sharp eye upon the nearby tree lines and the rim of bluffs. The ponies rolled in dust, slaked a fine thirst at the cold spring, and ripped the tops off of bunch grass greedily.

Danzig watched the animals, watched Jawbone herd them all, king of this equine tribe. He watched the squaws, Victoria and Mary, erect Mister Skye's skin lodge into its conical form. Back in Massachusetts, Wyeth had told them about these lodges, calling them marvels, perfect adaptations to the nomadic life of these plains people. The squaws adjusted the wind flaps to the direction of the breeze, thus drawing fresh air from the bottom of the lodge to its top and sucking off smoke if there were a lodgefire within. But this amiable summer night they'd cook outdoors after butchering the antelope old Victoria had somehow slain with a silent arrow during the day. Danzig intended to learn about these lodges. Indeed, maybe they'd try out the canvas lodgecover Morse had fashioned.

Mister Skye slid silently into camp a half hour later, just before blackness snuffed the gray northern twilight. He stared hard at Percy Connaught, saying nothing.

"Picket the horses now," he said shortly. "And hobble one or two close to your tents. I'm going for a little ride. We've been followed, and I'm going to find out why."

Chapter 4

Mister Skye rode down the backtrail quietly, through an indigo night, with only a fat amber moon hanging in the east to light the way. Jawbone glided over the undulating prairie, making no noise. Near the hollow, Mister Skye circled west. Not a whisper carried through the silent night. Along the northwest horizon, a faint gray afterlight lingered, the detritus of a spent day.

When he reckoned he was near, he steered Jawbone into

a slight crease and left him there. On foot, he stalked the remaining hundred yards up a gentle grade dotted with ghostly sage, and finally to a crest where he could peer down. Nothing. The dished land before him lay empty in the salmon glow of the moon. No fire, but he hadn't expected one. Stalkers rarely lit a fire. He eased silently to earth and studied the inky hollow, seeking the rock or log or thicket of sage that might be something else. His instinct, honed from a life in this wilderness, told him someone lurked there, though he could see or smell or hear nothing.

He set his silk stovepipe hat aside now, and flattened himself, his dragoon Colt in hand.

"If you're Harvey's man," he said conversationally, "forget it. These people are exactly what I told Harvey they were."

Nothing. And yet Mister Skye sensed that his words had reached human ears.

"If you're Pikuni," he said, using the Piegan band's name for itself, "know that I am Mister Skye. I am Mister Skye."

His name was big medicine and well known in every village on the northern plains. All warriors thought twice before tangling with the man named for the heavens and the horse that made war all by itself.

"I am Mister Skye!" he said sharply.

Only profound silence greeted him. He waited, dissatisfied, for a long time, his senses alert. Then he crabbed back from the breast of the earth, and retraced his steps to Jawbone, and rode through a dim night back to camp, the massive black hulk of Square Butte always before and to the right of him.

At his own camp he found them all gathered around a blazing fire, except for Mary and Victoria, who hung back in shadow. His own buffalo-skin lodge loomed off a bit from Elkanah Morse's camp, where the fire flared and spat sparks into the night breeze. From the darkness, he admired Morse's camp, with its lightweight ingenious tents and handy gear. Just beyond the rim of firelight, he spotted the picketed horses, shifting bulks close at hand. But it would not do.

He appeared suddenly in their midst, startling them as he knew he would.

"I'd suggest you douse the fire, mates. It's a comfort on a chill night, but it silhouettes you all."

"You found someone behind us?" asked Morse.

"Someone is behind us," Mister Skye said. "I didn't see him nor do I know his purposes. Probably a man Harvey sent."

"The fire's a pleasure, Skye. I'm finishing my journals by the light. Surely you don't mean some sort of danger lurks out there? Wolves, I suppose, but the rest, why, it's hoodoos and hobgoblins," said Percy Connaught.

"A lobo wolf, in human form, Mister Connaught."

"You make it sound like the nights are full of menace," said Betsy Morse.

"They are that, Mrs. Morse. I have been in the mountains for about a quarter of a century now. About two-thirds of the men I've known here have gone under. Sometimes from sheer accident or disease, and sometimes from carelessness."

"Well, Skye, we'll certainly have to be careful, what with assassins prowling the night," said Connaught.

"It's Mister Skye. Come with me, sir. We'll walk out to the crest of that rise yonder and let you look down into this camp."

Reluctantly, Connaught followed Mister Skye into the blackness.

"I can't see the way," he muttered.

"Of course you can't. Your eyes are fire-blinded. If something lurked out here, you wouldn't know where to shoot."

Connaught laughed.

From the slope a hundred yards out, they stared down into the camp. Each figure around the fire shone brightly against the black canvas of the night. Metal glinted in flickering yellow light. Skye's lodge, off a bit, was a ghostly cone.

Behind Skye, off in the blackness, something scurried through brush. Instinctively, the guide grappled Percy Connaught to earth and flattened both of them on the crest of the hill. Breath exploded from Connaught.

"Now see here, Skye! Are you mad! You demented fool, do you always tussle your employers to the ground?"

Mister Skye said nothing. Some shadowy form in the blur of the moon slid off through dense sagebrush, whisper of cloth or leather scraping brush.

Connaught laughed. "All very dramatic, Skye. And now a hare or a coyote has slithered into the sinister night!"

Mister Skye said nothing. He had dealt with obtuse men before and had come to the conclusion that nothing could change their opinions except bitter experience.

They trudged silently back to camp as Connaught dusted grime off his britches.

"Why, we scared off a rabbit," Connaught announced airily.

But Elkanah Morse read something in Mister Skye's face and hastened to shovel the loose dry soil of the plains over the fire, until they all sat in blackness and only a lingering of smoke remained.

Slowly the night came alive around them. Orion, Big Dipper, North Star. The horses and mules grew visible now, silvery moonlight glistening from their haunches and manes. Sharp night air curled about them. They grew aware of Jawbone hovering protectively in the murk, nipping bunch grass and then examining dark horizons, all senses alert.

From a far hill, coyotes laughed and chattered, but the answer came from wolves, barking sharply into night, or howling like souls caught in perdition.

"Where the buffalo gather, so do the wolves," said Mister Skye as he settled himself cross-legged in the circle of these people. "Tomorrow we'll reach the Judith basin, a bowl of knee-high golden grass, cold creeks full of trout, surrounded by low mountains. Full of buffler, usually. Piegans likely will be on the south side, living fat, making a little jerky and pemmican with these August berries. Until a few winters ago, they killed any white man they saw. Terrorized every tribe south and west and east. My wives hate them. I hated and feared them, too—lost many a friend to them. But times change. . . ."

"It was smallpox, wasn't it?" asked Captain Cobb.

"That and the trade for buffalo robes and white man's goods. Captain Cobb, do you approve of sitting here in the cold dark, without a fire?"

Jarvis Cobb laughed easily. "You want a military opinion, and I'm on detached duty. Well—to answer your question—yes, I suppose. Safety before comfort. Always assuming, of course, that there really is someone out there. I notice you haven't posted night guards."

"My night guard is that ugly evil horse. Captain Cobb, why might someone be following us?"

"You have me there. I'm a textbook soldier with no field experience. I've hoped to organize an intelligence service. The army has none, you know. I'm hoping to prove the value of it with this jaunt. Cartography, topology, detailed information about each tribe, weather . . . all of it. Now— to answer you with a textbook reply—I'd say a stalker is after one of two things—intelligence, what are we up to? Or—damage. Striking us down at a vulnerable moment."

"If a lone stalker wanted to do maximum damage to us, what might he do, Captain?"

The young officer sat quietly in the darkness. "Why," he said at last, "kill you, I suppose."

It was a good answer, Mister Skye thought.

"Who do you suppose he's working for—or is he on his own?"

"I'll answer that," interrupted Elkanah Morse. "Harvey sent him to keep an eye on us. I never met a man so suspicious. He thinks I'm an American Fur man, instead of a manufacturer out to deal with the far tribes."

"How would you deal with a stalker, Captain?" asked Mister Skye.

"Snare him and find out what he wants."

"If he's Indian, Captain, he'd consider torture an honorable death. If he's white or breed, you might get something out of him if you are ruthless enough."

"I confess, Mister Skye, I hadn't even thought of such means—"

"This is a hard land, Captain. Put that at the top of your notes."

Mister Skye sat contentedly, feeling fingers of cold air

pluck under his elkskin shirt. It always took him a few days on the trail to take the measure of his clients. Now, at the end of their first day, he had some inklings. Connaught had shirked when asked to do something vital. But the thin professor, the spade-bearded Swiss geologist Danzig, had quietly filled in without being asked. Cobb remained an enigma—intelligent, bookish, distant. Elkanah and Betsy Morse delighted him with their natural strength, curiosity, joy, and grace. Pouting Arabella could cause acute problems. He sat amiably in the dark. This would be a better party than some.

They found Weasel Tail's band of Piegan Blackfeet on the south edge of the Judith basin, where the Judith River emerged from the humped foothills of the Belt Mountains. Through the hot cloudless day they passed innumerable buffalo, most of them shaded up or lying indolent in the August sun. They fascinated Betsy with their dark stupid power, and she resolved to paint them when she could.

Mister Skye's squaws hung closer to the pack train now, Betsy noticed, not wanting to be too far away from their husband in this land of their enemies. Inexorably he led them southward toward the upper Judith, as if he somehow knew where the band would be. Midafternoon, half a dozen horsemen boiled down from the bluffs to the south, dusky men on dark ponies, and Betsy's heart hastened. Fierce almost-naked men surrounded them, pointing and gesticulating. She found herself under their inspection. They stared at her, at Arabella, at their way of sitting sideways upon their horses.

"Easy, mates," said the guide. "They mean us no harm. Curious about the white women, first they've ever seen.

These are the police. Every plains village has them. They protect the village and keep order."

Still, their savage power, bows, quivers, and befeathered fusils, alarmed her. They stared flat-eyed at her, revealing not the faintest warmth, and she thought surely she'd be murdered or worse. Beside her, Arabella had gone pale, and she stared back at them with all the arrogance she could muster. Connaught wasn't doing well either. He rode rigid with terror. Cobb seemed self-possessed enough, and that peculiar Swiss, Danzig, positively enjoyed the experience, just as her own Elkanah was delighting in every second of it. She blushed to think how nearly naked the Piegans were, and how attractive their tall, lean, muscled bronze bodies looked to her. She thought to paint them, too. Every one of them an Adonis, she thought wryly, remembering her grand tour through Italy. She smiled. They did not smile back.

Ahead, Mister Skye reined Jawbone and waited. One of the warriors approached, and the flash of hands and arms began. She'd heard of this and now she was witnessing the hand talk of the plains. At last they traveled again, these village police flanking the caravan.

"It's Weasel Tail's village," Mister Skye explained. "These are Brave Dog Society soldiers, doing camp duty. Every one a seasoned warrior. I talked with Blue Heron Running, a headman of the village. Told him we wished to pay our respects to the chief. They're plenty curious about the women. He wanted to know whether you ladies are to be gifts for Weasel Tail."

Betsy blanched. The thought of it suddenly alarmed her—that she might be considered property, traded off to some savage at the whim of some male.

Elkanah laughed and reached across the withers of his

horse to clasp Betsy's hand. His eyes danced with mischief. "Maybe they'll trade some dusky beauty to me," he said. She didn't think it was funny.

Mister Skye saw the tension lacing the faces behind him. "Peaceful visit," he rumbled. "Enjoy their hospitality. Have your little gifts ready, Mister Morse. Twists of tobacco will do. They're not painted up, not fighting us— not currently, anyway. Likely just whiling away a sunny August here, making a little meat for winter. You'll be perfectly safe. Even your possessions will be safe."

"About as safe as chickens surrounded by foxes!" Betsy blurted.

"You have medicine, Mrs. Morse," replied the guide. "You ride a trotting horse sideways, and these great cavalrymen of the prairies have never seen such a thing. Wave your wand, and they'll do your bidding."

Betsy laughed nervously, feeling a froth of emotion that was not far from hysteria.

They followed the glinting clear river now—a creek, really, this time of year—and rounding a bend, beheld a forest of conical lodges on a crescent flat.

Bedlam. Her watercolorist's eye picked out yellow and gray curs, all howling. Naked brown babies with jet hair. Girls in leather skirts; boys wearing nothing. Squaws gaudy in red and purple tradecloth, primary colors, yellow calicos, loose billowy skirts, soft dove-gray doeskin shirts. Blue-black hair in glossy braids, hanging loose, tied into a long ponytail. Shrieking ponies. Thick bullhide medicine shields, daubed with white clays, red and black and white—or rather, she thought, carmine, burnt sienna, cream, russet.

All about her rose golden lodges of sewn hide, their tops blackened by smoke, their sides flaunting symbolic suns and eagles and stick figures, and buffalo, and fox, in gaudy color. The lodges seemed to stand in some order, each opening facing east, and she thought some religion must be in it. At the top of each rose a forest of sticks, lodge-poles actually, making the horizon furry with limbs, as if the village were a forest.

They stared at her, pressed, fingered her cotton skirts, boldly peeked at her black high-top shoes, touched her saddle, an excited buzz and murmur, currents of surprise and astonishment running through them. Arabella looked ashen. Betsy followed the lead of the squaws around her. She reached down, touched bone necklaces, claw orna-ments, and laughed. In spite of a moil of fear, she enjoyed herself. Everything she and Elkanah had talked about for months suddenly became real.

Before her, Mister Skye rode easily, his silk hat raffishly tilted. These dusky villagers seemed to know all about him, and his blue roan, and they gave the horse wide berth, seeing Jawbone's laid-back ears and wicked glar-ing eyes, clacking teeth, and lips twisted into a perpetual snarl. Strung out, the visitors made a considerable pro-cession with their packmules and ponies, and the Skye family travois and parfleches bobbing ahead of her. But at last Mister Skye drew up before a larger lodge, this one painted the cerulean of the skies about its lower circum-ference, with yellow sunbursts above it. Before it stood a tripod, decked with black and white eagle feathers, weasel and ermine tails, and—thirteen black scalps. Betsy watched old Victoria eye the dangling scalps ferociously.

She beheld the chief and he beheld her the same mo-ment. His dark intelligent eyes surveyed her sandy brown hair and oval face, the swell of her bosom within her gray cambric dress. And finally her sidesaddle perch on her pony and slim ankles encased in black shoes. She in turn found herself peering at a young man with none of the seams and weathering of age she'd expected in a chief. This one stood tall, inches over six feet, she imagined, taller even than Elkanah. Lean, the color of waxed cherrywood, scarcely thirty, she supposed, peculiar scars upon his hard-muscled chest, and straight as any captain of industry. He wore a necklace of giant gray claws from some animal she could scarcely imagine, but that was all, save for a skin breech-clout so small she jerked her gaze away. Upon his loose jet hair perched a bonnet, but not the kind she had imagined. This one was a crown of vertical eagle feathers, with no elaborate tail. Only the upthrust feathers and two small ermine tails at either temple. His fierce animal magnetism fascinated her, and only reluctantly did she focus upon his three wives, each a stunning young beauty wreathed in smiles for these white visitors.

She would paint them! Her anxieties eased.

Mister Skye could not speak the tongue of these fierce people, and now his hands and arms flicked this way and that, and the chief's fingers replied. At last the chief commanded something, and a warrior scurried off into the crowd of onlookers. Mister Skye dismounted easily in that circle of quiet space around Jawbone.

"We'll be having a smoke," he said to Elkanah. "When the pipe comes, puff it and pass it along. It's the ritual of peace and welcome. Bring your gifts. Explaining your purposes here is beyond the sign language, but we're in luck. They've a Crow woman, married now to one of their warriors who captured her years ago. They're fetching her now. My Victoria will translate for us into Crow; this woman will translate the Crow into Blackfeet. We'll go slow, but we'll get it across. You're big medicine,

Elkanah—the man who makes the white men's magic. They already know that—I was able to sign that much, anyway."

The Crow woman who now lived among these people hustled forward, and Victoria eyed her sharply.

"River Crow—Absaroka of the prairies," she muttered. "Ain't any friend of mine."

Weasel Tail motioned his guests into the lodge—Mister Skye, Elkanah Morse, the Crow woman, and Victoria. The flap fell closed behind them. Betsy gazed at poor Arabella and sighed. The girl hated every moment of this, and didn't need to. It all lay in her head.

"Arabella, dear, enjoy yourself!"

"I hate these savages! I despise them!" her daughter cried.

"They'll sense that. People sense things unspoken, dear. Try to learn about them. Interesting, don't you think?"

"They'll slit our throats while we sleep!" Arabella retorted.

Professor Danzig spoke up kindly. "Not inside a village. Not to guests, Arabella. If I've learned anything about such people, it's that they are most hospitable."

The calm professor calmed her daughter, Betsy thought. And herself.

Chapter 5

Elkanah Morse's fertile imagination ran riot as he stalked through the Piegan village on a shimmering cool August morning. He watched people doing everything the hard way! He paused before lodges, running a hand over his balding brow, smiling at squaws and children, observing the daily work of the village. That's what he had traveled across a continent to see! Already he was concocting new products in his mind, devices expressly for the Indian trade. He paused before a rack of poles burdened with thin slices of buffalo meat being jerked. Every one of those hundreds of thin slabs of meat had been sliced from a carcass with a knife. He'd make it easier! His mind churned with the image of a device that would have multiple blades parallel to each other, all hooked to a powerful lever. One tug of the lever and there'd be a dozen perfect slices of meat ready for jerking in the hot sun. Saving labor! That was the key to progress! He eyed the rack itself and decided to design a lightweight, folding, portable one these people could take anywhere. Then they could jerk meat far out on any prairie, far away from trees and wood needed for poles. He scribbled furiously in a small notebook, smiled at a busy kneeling woman, who smiled back, and meandered onward.

He spotted a woman making pemmican, battering berries and fat and meat. Why, the woman could use a food grinder! He chastised himself for not bringing his Morse Foundries food grinder, which clamped to any kitchen table and augered any sort of meat or vegetable through a perforated head. A perfect device to help a patient squaw, but one no trader in the fur business stocked. He'd talk to Culbertson about that! Better yet, the Chouteaus themselves, and all the rest of the St. Louis entrepreneurs. That seemed to be the trouble with most businesses. They did things the way they always did, under some rule of inertia, never seeing new opportunities, never experimenting. Well, he'd change that! He'd ease the lives of these far tribes forever. For a few buffalo hides, they'd soon have labor-saving devices that would ease the brutal toil of these women.

If Elkanah Morse seemed curious about the life of the village, the villagers were no less curious about these strange visitors. By the scores, they flocked around the campsite of their guests, touching everything. Trim watertight canvas tents with collapsible hardwood poles intrigued them. Betsy's folding cookstove of hinged sheet metal fascinated them. Who had ever seen such wonders! Betsy laughed, opened the door of the oven to show them the tiny fire of twigs that heated whole pots of food on the oven, and Piegans clapped hands with joy and fascination. Such medicine! Would the wonders of the longknives ever cease?

Elkanah watched amiably, knowing that soon, when Betsy erected her easel and began portraits with her fine English watercolors, she'd be the belle of this ball. And that would be only the beginning. In the afternoon, these Piegans would attend their first trade fair. It had taken some talk, but eventually the Piegan headmen were given to understand that Elkanah Morse hadn't come to trade, but to show his wares, find out what the villagers desired, and discover what they needed. All that, from English to Crow to Blackfeet, had been a difficult exchange, but not impossible. Elkanah inclined to the belief that very little was truly impossible.

All seemed well in camp. Their tents and Mister Skye's lodge had been erected just upstream from the Piegan village. Old Victoria hovered close to her lodge with a face etched in granite, and Elkanah remembered how bitterly these two peoples regarded each other. Even lush young Mary stayed close, playing with the infant boy.

The old crone glared at him as she fleshed an antelope

hide. "Damn! How come you want to sell fancy whiteman stuff to these dogs, eh? These people all killers, murderers, bad. . . ."

She seemed not to understand what he was doing any more than the villagers. "Why, Mrs. Skye, I'm not here to sell. I'm here to find out what they want, what I can manufacture, what I can invent that might be useful to them. I'll be doing the same for your own Crow people."

"They take all these things you make and kill us with them," she muttered.

"Wait until I get to your village," he said.

He wandered back into the village, drawn toward Jarvis Cobb, who had hunkered down near a group of old weathered men and several solemn warriors, who glared at Cobb fiercely. Elkanah wondered if perhaps the army captain wasn't welcome there, even in his civilian clothes. The older men, he discovered, were arrow makers, which meant that the young men with them surely were warriors and hunters. No one forbade Elkanah, so he hunkered down close to Cobb to watch. No Piegan said a word.

There seemed to be no division of labor here. Each of the artisans made an entire arrow. On an ancient fleshed hide lay piles of chokecherry shoots that obviously had dried a long time, some of them bumped and bent, irregular in various ways. Several of the artisans had small heaps of iron arrowheads made from hoop iron. Using an old ax head buried in the ground for an anvil, one old man patiently chiseled a piece of metal from a barrel hoop and began hammering it into a pointed arrowhead. Another old man, with black hair braided far down his naked back, shaped a nock in an arrowshaft with a knife and a thin piece of sandstone. Deftly he sanded the chokecherry shaft until a smooth notch for the bowstring had been cut in it.

Other bits of sandstone turned out to be files that he used to shape the hafts of iron arrow points.

Satisfied at last, he placed the chokecherry shaft next to an iron arrow point and chanted quietly for a minute. The nasal chanting mystified Elkanah. What had it to do with making an arrow? The ribby old man had yet another sandstone block, this one with a long groove cut into it. The groove, it turned out, had been perfectly fashioned to sand down the chokecherry shoot into a straight smooth arrow. With practiced but gnarled hands, the old arrow maker ran the shaft back and forth in the sandstone notch, slowly scraping off bark and smoothing nobs until, in a few swift moments, he had a fairly straight shaft of dried wood. Still, it bowed slightly. Where the wood bowed, the old man wetted it with saliva, biting and licking the reluctant wood until the shaft straightened and lay true to the eye.

Swiftly now the arrow maker slitted the thinner end to take the point. With a small tool made from a white man's nail, Elkanah supposed, the arrow maker grooved his shaft, running a wavy little groove—lightning-bolt-shaped it seemed—down each side of the shaft. Why did he do that? Elkanah wondered. Was it to release blood and thus kill an animal—or enemy—faster?

Mister Skye joined them there, observed the surly silence, and began to flash his fingers. For some minutes he finger-talked with one of the arrow makers.

"Not sure you should be here, mates. Making arrows is big medicine and war. It means good hunts. These young braves buy arrows from the old ones, pay for them in ponies or meat or sometimes tobacco. They don't think much of having white men watch something pretty close to religion for them."

"Didn't know I was that obvious," said Cobb.

"I'd like to watch," said Elkanah. "Think I can help them make better arrows, Mister Skye. Could you explain my purpose to them?"

The guide sighed, made signs with flying hands, and waited. An old man nodded at last, but two of the muscular young men stared sourly at the intruders.

"You can watch. Be careful and diplomatic, mates."

"That old gent there is making arrows with obsidian points," Elkanah said. "Where do they find a glassy black rock that chips like that? I've never seen such fine points."

"That rock's famous among all tribes, Elkanah. It used to be traded in every direction, clear back to your States. It comes from a whole cliff of it up in the geyser country where the Yellowstone rises. Whole mountain wall of black glass. They don't use obsidian much anymore. Just a few old men clinging to the old ways. They like iron points and make them from hoop iron they get at the trading posts."

"Probably my own hoop iron. I sell a lot to American Fur."

Cobb scribbled a note on a small pad. The army intelligence man at work, Elkanah thought.

"What about bone? Don't they use bone points?"

"They don't go for bone much. Too light, and not very effective in an animal. If they have to, they can make bone points from buffler ribs, but it's not common."

"What about those wiggling grooves down the shaft? To let blood?"

Mister Skye paused a moment. "That, and medicine—they think of arrows as man-made lightning. But mostly, those grooves keep the arrowshafts from warping. Takes some kind of pressure off the wood."

The old arrow maker dyed the shafts, using mineral and vegetable tints he had concocted, and set them to dry.

"Every warrior or hunter has his own marks, his own colors. And each tribe has its own signature, I suppose you'd call it. That way there's no arguments about who counted coup or who killed the buffler."

Elkanah watched the old man fletch the arrows, anchoring the trimmed and dyed feathers with a glue made from boiled hoof, while another set an arrowhead on its shaft and wrapped it with wet sinew so smoothly that scarcely a bulge rose around the base of the arrowhead. A wizened man examined his finished arrow, peered down its straight shaft, and suddenly smiled at his white visitors. He handed the finished arrow to Elkanah, who admired the craft that had created it.

"Tell him it's a fine thing that will slay the buffalo, Mister Skye. Would he like to see metal points, and my hardwood shafts, and ready-mades? I suppose this is as good a test as any."

"Don't see any harm to it," Mister Skye replied thoughtfully. "But I think you'll be surprised by what happens."

"I hope your iron points don't ever pierce the flesh of United States soldiers," said Cobb shortly.

The trial of the arrows drew the whole village. Here would be something to see! Elkanah had brought six of his ready-mades, each as anonymous as the others, differing only in their points. His lathes had milled each shaft true and even; the three turkey feathers on each had been trimmed to the exact same size and glued down. No shaft or feather had been dyed in any way, and beside the Piegan arrows they looked pale and featureless.

Warriors, children, squaws, headmen, Weasel Tail himself examined Elkanah's ready-mades without comment. The arrows passed from one tribesman to another, and Elkanah hadn't the foggiest notion what these people thought of them. Neither did they ask questions about them, although Victoria and the Crow woman were on hand to translate.

Elkanah wondered what they'd use for a target in this grassy flat along the Judith River. A giant headman whose bronze muscles rippled in the high sun snapped some guttural order, and soon a youth led an ancient horse, swayback and mangy, before them. It stank from suppurating wounds that succored armies of flies.

"There's your target, mate," said Mister Skye.

Elkanah was horrified. "But not a live target—" he said. Betsy looked stricken.

"Dog food," said Mister Skye.

A boy led the scruffy brown stallion about forty yards downstream and turned it broadside. No one bothered to tether it.

"I didn't quite expect living targets," said Elkanah tartly.

"This isn't Lowell, Elkanah."

"Why are they so silent? They've passed my ready-mades around without comment. Without a smile, frown, exclamation. Without pleasure or distaste."

"Medicine, mate. No spirit helper guides your arrows. No dye gives it a home or owner among these people."

"If I make them, will they buy my arrows?"

"We'll see," said Mister Skye. "But I doubt it. Medicine is everything, and nothing is done without it."

The honors went to the headmen. Three powerful men, each a leader of a warrior society, selected two arrows impassively. A squat thick graying man with thick cheekbones, naked but for a breechclout, nocked an arrow.

"He's the leader of the Bulls, the oldest and highest Piegan warrior society," Mister Skye muttered.

Jarvis Cobb scribbled notes.

The headman's richly painted, sinew-wrapped bow seemed short to Elkanah's eye. A sudden silence settled on the crescent of villagers here. Elkanah saw Betsy firmly shut her eyes; Arabella had vanished.

In a single smooth motion, the warrior drew the bow-string while the arrow pointed skyward, arced the bow downward, and loosed the arrow, which flashed white across space, and buried itself in the brown hide just back of the forelegs. The horse shuddered. Its neck lowered. It convulsed. It drew its lips back even as a froth of pink blood slobbered from its mouth. It swayed.

Elkanah scarcely realized the warrior had nocked his second arrow until he saw the white blur. The second one buried itself six inches from the first; a little above. Blood trickled from both wounds. The second arrow pene trated clear to its fletching. The horse shuddered and collapsed, landing with a soft thud. Its lungs still labored.

A gray cur skulked toward the carcass, but a sharp shout from someone stopped it.

The villagers remained silent, raptly watching death creep over the ancient pony. Elkanah had the sensation that death was something these savage people enjoyed and studied. Solemnly, a younger man, tall and lean, with a peculiar reflexively curved bow of wide flat material wrapped in sinew, stepped forward and sent one of Elkanah's ready-mades into the pony's dun-colored underbelly. The creature spasmed once again and sighed into quietness. A sudden whip of air announced the next shot, also into the prone belly but a few inches back. Both arrows had pierced up to their fletching.

The third headman, a cruel scar jagging his face, and peculiar scars on his chest, drew a heavy but short bow back and loosed an arrow. It pierced into belly just an inch from the previous warrior's first shot. The final arrow also went true, entering an inch or so from the previous man's second shot.

Ah! There was fine shooting! The villagers whispered and explained and chanted things. They all surged ahead to the carcass to watch the warriors tug Elkanah's arrows out of it. The shafts came hard, but finally slid out, slippery with gore, and the warriors solemnly handed them to Elkanah, who washed them.

To Victoria he said, "I wish to know whether they like these arrows. Would they buy them?"

She glared at him and caustically repeated the question to the Crow woman, who raised the question among the Piegans.

Warriors muttered to each other. A man Elkanah took to be a shaman cried nasally, picked up dust, and threw it to the wind. For what seemed hours the Piegans debated, and when the answer came back, the words had been formed by Weasel Tail himself.

"Tell the man his arrows are very fine and true. But we would not trade robes and ponies for them."

That was all. Elkanah wanted more answer.

"Medicine," said Mister Skye. "About what I thought."

Elkanah Morse laughed easily. He'd come to find out things. He'd offered them a better arrow than their own, but they'd have no part of it. "Well, perhaps I can manufacture bows for them. Are bows medicine, too?"

"You bet, mate. And their bows are better than any you'll ever make."

"Surely you're not serious."

"I am. That third bow is made from osage orange, brought here clear from the Mississippi Valley, and highly prized as the best of all bow woods by most of the tribes. French call it *bois d'arc*. The first headman's bow is local, either willow or chokecherry. Middle man's bow is bone wrapped in sinew and reflexed. Every one is shorter, more powerful, and handier than an English longbow. Try shooting one of your European longbows from horseback and you'll see."

"The bowstrings are twisted sinew?"

"That they are. A good enough string if handled carefully and kept from water. Indians don't make war or hunt in the rain, Elkanah. Your scalp's safe enough when the clouds are emptying."

Jarvis Cobb scribbled that, too, and looked almighty pleased.

"Each of my ladies, Mary and Victoria, have light osage orange bows, and each have taken a lot of meat with them. Kept my belly full. But I did insist on one thing: I got some good linen cord from the sutler at Laramie, and made tough linen bowstrings for them. They hunt in rain. In my business we need all the edge we can get."

"I'll sell linen bowstring!" cried Elkanah, scribbling his own notes furiously.

Jarvis Cobb frowned. "If you sell them linen bowstring, the savages can strike the army in rain," he muttered.

"If the tribes buy it. Lots of medicine wisdom about wet hunts and wet war, mate."

Yellow and gray curs, half-wolf, mobbed the pony carcass, gashing bloody holes in it, snarling and growling and howling wild songs upon a blue-domed afternoon.

Percy Connaught eyed the carcass disdainfully. He'd disappeared just before the first arrows sailed.

"A fine tale to tell in my journal for the vulgar," he said.

"Utterly savage and heartless. Oh, it will cause a sensation in the States."

With all these chattering villagers about, Elkanah thought it would be the ideal moment to display his goods. He corraled Victoria, who stood stonily beside the creek. "I'm going to set out my things near our camp," he said to her. "Please invite them all. And explain once again my things are not for trade; I wish to learn what they think of them."

Dourly, Victoria wheeled off to find the other Crow woman.

At his tents he found Betsy setting up her easel, and before her, perched daintily on a log, sat a silent solemn slip of a girl with loose blue-black hair, small brown eyes, and an unhappy look. But she was adorned in a tiny festival dress of soft doeskin, decorated with dyed bone and rimmed with red tradecloth.

"I'm going to paint her!" Betsy said. "It cost me one trinket mirror."

Even as Elkanah unloaded goods from his panniers and spread them on blue-and-yellow-striped thick blankets he manufactured, Piegan villagers drifted in to finger pots and skillets, sample the textures of cloth, cerise and umber and gray, tug at tan canvas, puzzle over copper rivets, delicately feel the hone of shining hardened steel knives, finger rubber moccasin soles, giggle at a galosh, examine bridles of fine russet harness leather, study awls and drills and axes, red-painted hatchets, black lance points, iron arrowheads, long and short, wide and narrow, barbed and hooked. Solemnly they poked and fingered them all, exclaiming and yet telling him nothing. But all of Elkanah's goods together were no attraction at all compared with the image of a little girl swiftly and surely taking shape beneath Betsy's wondrous brush.

Chapter 6

Arabella Morse wandered through the afternoon up the Judith River, between bald grassy bluffs, feeling petulant. The Piegans were so alarming it had taken all her nerve even to go for a walk along the mountain stream. She scarcely noticed the shimmering beauty around her, the sweet-scented air, silvery-green sage, or the way the cottonwood leaves trembled with each zephyr.

The summer had turned out exactly as she had feared. Unbearable! Her father had dragooned her into this; wouldn't let her stay in Lowell and enjoy lemonades, croquet, picnics, poetry reciting, mental improvements, the pianoforte, calling at teatime, and above all, her serious pursuit of marriage. Unless she married soon, she'd be an old maid, and her life a ruin. Twenty-one was almost old. She had no serious beaux, but many came calling, and she delighted in sorting them out: some wanted to marry money; some were too bold; most were uneducated oafs, like her father, who could think only of business and inventions and sales and new processes, and never of art, or sculpture, or novels, or moral enlightenment, or the world's destitute. Too many males were like that, unrefined, unaesthetic, insensitive.

But he'd insisted and she was here, and another sweet summer under the green canopies of Lowell had been lost. How could she ever make up the time? Time is lost forever, if it's lost! He'd plunged her into a wilderness unfit for refined people. Thrown her in with savages, brutes who shot arrows into horses for sport, murderous, smelly, cruel, spontaneous human children! Everything had disgusted her, not least the reek of the village when the winds eddied the smell of offal and dung into her nostrils. For what purpose was civilization other than to escape all this, and refine mankind? Maybe they'd even slaughter them all! She felt pity for herself, seeing in her mind's eye a solemn gray granite obelisk over her lonely grave. "Arabella Morse, Born November 28, 1831, Died August 12, 1852. She Lacked Only Life."

So absorbed was she in visions of tombstones that she scarcely realized for a moment that Jarvis Cobb had caught up with her, and walked beside.

"Want company?" he asked.

"I'd love company," she replied. Good company, even if he had left his wife and two children in New York. He was a young man, anyway, and an officer, and that was all she could ask. But of course too old—thirty, he told her.

"Escaping the village?"

"Let's not talk of the village. I don't want to hear a word about it."

"I've filled two pages of my notebook with intelligence about them. Things the army should know. They don't fight in rain, for instance. Sinew bowstrings go soft, their flintlocks get wet. A good time for us to strike. Their buffalo bull-neck shields turn arrows. Even deflect a half-spent ball. But they use no horse armor. I even saw a shield stop an iron-pointed arrow. I know where they get their iron, and how to interdict their supply. If we kill off their buffalo, they won't have much good bone to work into points—or food for that matter. You see . . . some intelligence, some knowledge, and we have the means to win wars. . . ."

She sighed. "Must you?" she asked, putting an aggrieved inflection on it.

He laughed quietly. She liked his laugh. Actually, she

knew, Jarvis was bookish, a man of mind rather than action, and she liked that, even if his thoughts ran along military lines.

"This is a valuable trip. I'll revolutionize the army's way of going into battle. 'Know Your Enemy' will become its standard when I publish. And I will rise to the top ranks. But that's not what interests beautiful young ladies."

She felt pleased. Her beauty was borderline, she felt whenever she peered into her looking glass, and she ardently welcomed reassurances. Her nose seemed a bit thick; she preferred the narrow patrician variety. Eyes too wide set, and a mousy hazel color. Oh, to have big azure ones, blue as cornflowers! And a creamy-tinted flesh instead of her fishbelly white! Still, she was molded well, tall and slim, swelling at just the right points. And what she lacked, she made up for with dashing dress that kept dressmakers and milliners gossiping and ecstatic about her tastes.

And now she read frank appreciation of all that in Jarvis Cobb's gaze that so casually floated from her lustrous brown hair to the swells of her bodice and hips. She laughed easily, finding a moment of flirt even here, thousands of miles from home.

"Do you miss your family?" she asked softly.

Cobb remained silent as they strolled through bunch grass, alarming big black and white magpies. "I must confess, privately, Arabella—that I'm glad to be away. My . . . domestic life, my family—has turned sour. Not my children, of course. Delights of my heart. Little Peter's five; the infant—Elise—barely a year. But oh . . . there are difficulties."

She waited, saying nothing. How males revealed themselves to her! She had wormed every secret from every beau, just by listening and clucking and nodding her head!

"We quarrel, my Susannah and I. Her tongue's sharp. Her words cut deep. She tells me she regrets marrying me. It was a great comedown for her, for one of her caste. A captain's pay is unbearable. Officers are all oafs. I'm a slave of the army, at its beck and call. I pay her no regard. I love my books and charts more than I love her. I spend my time by the midnight lamp rather than, ah . . . rather than attending to her needs. I confess, Arabella, I've wearied of it. And am glad to escape."

"But you're a man of honor, of course, and will endure it rather than pitch her out."

"Oh, of course. Divorce—that's unthinkable. But how good it is to have a kindred spirit, one whose mind touches upon my concerns. We've shared our deepest feelings for months now. Across a continent. At the bow of the steamer, just you and I, talking. Is there anything about me you don't know? I'll tell you! Tell all my secrets to you! How good you're here a million leagues from anywhere, touching my soul, Arabella."

She peered solemnly at him and found him returning the gaze, his eyes windows of soft pain. She liked his thick muttonchops and high-domed brow and his wavy yellow-brown hair.

They'd reached a boulder-strewn bend of the river, a mile or so above the Piegan village. The sun had settled into the purple west, and the breezes had died.

"I think I will cool my feet," she said. "If I walk like this, I surely will have bunions."

"I'll cool mine, too," he said. "I see just the rock."

He led her to a large rosy boulder that diverted clear water around its base. She settled herself on it, arranging her tan Bedford cord skirts carefully. Then she unhooked her shining patent pumps and wiggled white toes. He settled himself beside her, unlaced heavy grimed boots, and rolled off gray and faintly odorous hose.

"Oh!" she exclaimed, dipping feet into mountain water. "I fear I shall wet my skirts."

She tugged the Bedford cord skirts upward, and the embroidered cotton petticoat up, too, letting a little show, along with shapely ankles and too much calf.

"This is better," she said. "Therapeutic. I do dread misshapen feet. Bunions are terrible."

"Yes, terrible," he agreed. "We are so far from everything. I'd count it a loss to be so far from sweet feminine companionship but for your tender presence here. Indeed, we share so many things of the soul. To sit here is to enjoy some ethereal union of spirits in a vast wilderness."

Her heart tripped a little at all this—she'd never flirted with a married man before, much less one unhappily married.

"I'm enjoying it, Jarvis. Oh, my!"

Thus they sat, wiggling feet in cool water, neither venturing further, until the sinking sun reminded them that they dallied far from safety and food.

"It's getting chilly," she said, "but my heart is warm."

"Mine is, too! I suppose we should be getting back. The savages set guards at night and would put an arrow through us if we were to surprise them."

"I didn't bring a button hook! I don't know how I'll keep my shoes on."

"I'll carry you if I must, but I imagine you could walk with your shoes loose, Arabella."

"You could carry me easily," she said. "You're so strong."

He sighed. "You flatter me. It's a mile, and I'm a desk soldier."

She smiled and touched his arm. "I'll manage," she said. "I've enjoyed the afternoon. This has been just the nicest day this summer. You're a dear friend, and we have things to seal, two good refined minds uniting, clear out here."

"May I seal our kindred spirits with a kiss?"

"Why, yes, Jarvis. I can't think of a nicer way to seal a friendship than with a chaste kiss of platonic love."

He kissed her lips softly, tentatively, awaiting response. She kissed him back firmly. She felt his strong young arms slip around her and tug her to him, and the hardness of his chest against her breast.

Then he released her.

"Our union of the spirit is sealed," he said, breathing rapidly. "Let's fly back to camp before they come looking."

The small blue pebble in Rudolpho Danzig's hand piqued his curiosity. It looked like blue glass, except that the abrading of the Judith River had ground and dulled its surface. But in the warm sun the blue within flared a saucy azure. He'd found only the one, poking around at a place where the creek ran shallowly over a rock ledge. Corundum, he thought. Back at the Piegan village he'd see how it scratched, and what would scratch it. Corundum was among the hardest minerals, and if that's what it proved to be, he had found a sapphire. That amused him. He'd already found a few flakes of free gold caught in a small crevice in another creek bottom.

It didn't surprise him, though. Here lay a great mountain cordillera, with vast hidden treasure waiting for the world to find it. He squinted up into the Belt Mountains, a dark featureless range set at right angles to the great north and south chains of the Rockies. Perhaps untold wealth here for someone, someday. He laughed. It didn't set his

heart pounding or fire the furnaces of ambition in him.
Long ago he'd wrestled with all that. From boyhood onward
he'd been seized by ambition. He knew he had intelligence;
the other boys in the province had seemed dull-witted to
him. He would conquer the world! He raced through the
natural sciences at the new University of Berne, intent
upon becoming the world's greatest geologist and naturalist. He would write great papers, make breathtaking
discoveries, change the way science viewed the earth, and
his name, Rudolpho Danzig, would be revered through
Europe.

All of which, he thought wryly, had made young Danzig
desperately unhappy and discontent. He'd been too busy
to enjoy the days he lived, too consumed with the fevers
of success to enjoy the moment, treasure company. Worse,
when he burrowed into the Alps to win a geologic picture
of them, he'd seen nothing, missed everything. Feverish
with ambition, he'd wrested his doctorate from Berne and
skipped across the Atlantic to begin his teaching career at
the great old American university called Harvard. And
there, in quiet amiable Cambridge, in his thirty-second
year, he'd descended into the bowels of hell, living in
anxious fear that greatness would pass him by. Some instinct told him he had done poorly. Around him, those
Americans were doing better fieldwork, drawing brighter
conclusions. He'd failed, and he'd kill himself.

One January night he sat in darkness holding an Allen
and Thurber pistol. He'd neglected to keep his stove fed
with channel coal, and now the ice in his digs matched the
ice of his soul. But something stayed his hand. An image
formed of his native Alps, sidelit just before sundown,
one of the few precious images he had permitted himself.
His discontents roiled within him. Why had he always

been so miserable, so unhappy, so dissatisfied, so alive to the future and numb to the present? He'd rejected everything. He set the old-fashioned pistol down on top of a pile of foolscap and traced the thread of a shadowy idea. If he'd rejected everything in his daily life, then perhaps the thing to do would be to accept everything.

From that night, he'd accepted his life and circumstances. Was he poor? He accepted that. Was he obscure? He accepted that, too. Was he single in a foreign land, and unlikely to find a woman who'd tolerate his accented English? Well, he'd accept that, too. He huddled under cold blankets, and the next morning began to practice his new approach. He'd had no revelations. No blinding light or heavenly voice had felled him on the road to Damascus. No emotion had flooded him. No release, no tears, no joy, no epiphany. But if he could accept what he was, accept his circumstances, he would do it. He began by accepting the grim quarters that his scholar's pittance afforded. Comfortable, really. He accepted the clothes he wore, the breakfast of oat gruel he downed, the dreary winter classes he would teach that day. In fact his callow students found him less snappish that day, and willing to answer their questions instead of merely ridiculing them.

Gradually his life changed. Merely by accepting each day, accepting his circumstances, accepting the people around him, accepting students and faculty, accepting his new republic and its tumultuous politics, and accepting himself, he emerged into a new life. Ambition deteriorated even as he grew more absorbed in his field and began to see pattern and purpose in the workings of the earth. Once geology existed to fuel his vanity. Now he came to his work humbly, fascinated with everything around him, poking and probing, questioning, playing with hypotheses, unaware of self because he was lost, childlike, in a garden of wonders. Rudolpho Danzig gradually disappeared, and in the place of the taut, dark, desperate man with a thick accent came a new creature who enjoyed life around him, and studied it casually, coming to not-so-casual conclusions. That's when he married his Yankee bride Sarah Percival, who adored him and basked in the warmth of his love.

Now in this wild of the American West, he held his dazzling blue pebble in hand and laughed. Wealth meant nothing. Here was a whole world to explore, and that was wealth for his soul beyond imagining. He dropped the pebble into a glassine bag and labeled it. He'd tell them nothing. He understood his contentment, and the discontents of others who didn't practice his daily acceptance of his life. He paused to sketch the terrain in his notebook, and drew a crude map of the whole country, carefully dating it and locating its latitude, which he had determined last night by sextant: forty-six degrees north, fifty-eight minutes.

He wished he had time to probe upstream toward the clay dike that probably held the sapphires, but tomorrow they would leave Weasel Tail's village. August marched ahead, and time grew short even before they got well into the adventure.

Back in the village, Rudolpho found Elkanah displaying his last and greatest innovation. There among the smoke-blackened, paint-daubed lodgecovers made of laced cowhide, stood a virginal white cone of immaculate canvas, triple seams connecting each of the gores to make a perfect cone that rose like a white New England church in the village. Around it stood most of the village, gazing silently at the wonder. A few young squaws ventured inside, past the canvas flap, exclaiming at the amount of light within, fingering the hard cloth, giggling. But old women glared at this thing and wouldn't step inside.

"Danzig! There you are! I borrowed fourteen lodgepoles from Chief Weasel Tail himself and set it up. That drew them in a hurry. Now I'm going to show them something."

Elkanah hastened to the Judith River and filled a canvas camp bucket brimful and carried the sloshing burden back. He motioned the curious women inside. They saw the bucket and fathomed his purpose and giggled through the hemmed hole. Then Elkanah dumped the bucket, and water rivered down the steep slope.

"Now we'll see!" he cried. From within came chatter and giggles. Elkanah ducked in. "Not a drop!" he cried. "Dry as bone! See here!"

Standing outside, Rudolpho didn't doubt it. Whatever Elkanah Morse manufactured, he made well. This lodge-cover had been cut out of his tightest, heaviest canvas and sewn on Elias Howe's new automatic sewing machines, which Elkanah had seized upon for his own manufacturing purposes.

Morse squeezed out of the door hole and into the afternoon sun. "It weighs maybe a quarter of what the buffalo cowhide covers weigh. Why, they have to kill and skin anywhere from eleven to twenty or so hides, and lace them all together with watertight seams, to make a lodge the old way. Imagine, Rudolpho. Imagine what a boon this'll be to them!"

But Rudolpho could sense no great enthusiasm for this wonder. His keen black eye caught these villagers staring impassively, rather than feeling liberated from inferior old ways.

"They'll get used to it. I've learned that wild Indians

have to think about new things for a while. I suppose their medicine religion is all tied up with it."

Old Victoria squinted up at him. "Damn right," she said. "This ain't got any medicine. It ain't a lodge. Probably cold as hell in winter. Thin cloth instead of good thick hide with an inner lining to keep out the Cold Maker."

Elkanah laughed. "You always tell me true, Mrs. Skye. Will they buy it? I can make it for about twenty dollars, and I suppose traders here might sell it for seventy or eighty. It wouldn't take many buffalo hides to buy a house."

"Maybe goddamn whitemen kill all the buffalo off, then they buy it."

Danzig thought that was an acutely perceptive reply.

"That's what I'm here to find out," said Elkanah. He unlaced the lodgecover as one last demonstration of the genius of his device. His whole cover could be dismantled by pulling linen cord out of the eyelets of a single waterproof seam. In only a moment the cover shrugged free and sagged to the ground, leaving naked poles poking heaven. He folded the canvas bundle and dropped the entire cover in one pannier of a packsaddle, while Piegans stared thoughtfully.

"Let them think on it for a year. I won't put any on the market until next year," Elkanah said. "They're steeped in their traditions. All my stuff must seem pretty radical, strange, to people who lacked the wheel and iron. But they'll come to it. They'll see it. And maybe add their own medicine to it."

That was the thing about Morse, thought Danzig. Realism and optimism, and a strange kind of certitude that fueled his genius.

That cool evening, the Morses gave a feast for the chief

and headmen, cooking one of the plentiful fat buffalo of the Judith basin. It went well, and even the old Absaroka woman, Victoria, seemed to relax among her tribal enemies, Danzig thought. At its conclusion, while the fire flickered low and the seated headmen smoked contently, Elkanah gave each a twist of tobacco, and then Betsy unrolled her surprise—a fine portrait of Weasel Tail in his full ceremonial regalia. She'd caught him well. He gazed at this image of himself, of the eagle-feather headdress with its ermine trim, at the very face he'd seen mirrored in quiet waters, at his ceremonial shield and lance. And his face kindled into delight.

"It is a good likeness," he said through his translators. "Come again to my village and show us such things."

Beyond the corona of the fire, Rudolpho Danzig thought, the night seemed uncommonly cold.

Chapter 7

Victoria's heart sang. They'd left the Siksika dogs behind and now rode south, toward the lands of her people, the Absarokas. All the while they'd languished in the village of Weasel Tail, she'd made medicine in their lodge and kept her Green River knife close at hand, so she might scalp one first, before they scalped her. That was one thing she didn't like about being Mister Skye's sits-beside-him wife: sometimes she had to visit the enemies of her people. These Piegans were worst of all; more terrible even than the Lakotah people to the east.

She rode ahead and to the west of the caravan, along the Belt Mountains and into Judith Gap, the place where the prairie grasses lay between the mountains. To the east, the black-timbered slopes of the Snowy Mountains vaulted upward. To the west, the black slopes of the Belts. But in the gap lay emerald grasses and buffalo trails, as well as the trails of the People. And that made it dangerous. Great battles had been fought here, mostly between Absarokas and Piegans, but also others, such as Assiniboin and Gros Ventre.

She eyed the somnolent prairie sharply, seeing nothing. She had good eyes, Absaroka eyes, better even than Mister Skye's. She saw the floating eagles and the way the ravens flew. That's what caught her eye now, ravens flapping hard, eastward, in flight. Something had disturbed them upon the western slopes. Some whites thought her people took their name from the crows, but Absaroka really meant the giant bird. Even so, she saw the crows flapping and knew her spirit helpers were signaling. In her mind, the vision of trouble formed. She had the medicine gift, seeing what was not seen.

The verdant prairie that crested between the mountains seemed smooth enough that nothing could hide upon the breast of it, but she knew otherwise. Coulees and creeks, invisible to the eye unless one had almost come upon them, snaked north or south, into the drainage of the Musselshell, or the Missouri. She paused, resting lightly in the pad saddle of her old bay pony. He sensed her alert calm. Far off to the northeast, she saw the pack train trotting southward. Mister Skye directed it into the Musselshell valley, looking for a village of Gros Ventre that Weasel Tail said would be there.

She spat. Gros Ventres killed Absarokas. More enemies. They called themselves Atsina, but the French trappers called them Gros Ventres, Big Bellies. Victoria snorted.

The French trappers also called her cousins the Hidatsa, the Absaroka people who lived on the great river to the east, Gros Ventres, too. Couldn't those thickheaded French keep the Peoples sorted out?

Perhaps hunters to the west set the black birds flapping. She scanned the shimmering prairies, seeing nothing. Only the quiet of a warm sunny morning and the snuffle of her pony reached her senses. But something would be there. Not deer or elk or buffalo or antelope, for those four-foots didn't make the ravens croak across the dome of heaven. She glanced behind her. The pack train looked to be a short pony run, maybe five hundred beats of the heart. In the transparent air she made out her husband leading, with that whiteman things-maker beside him. Victoria liked him. He had merry eyes and so did his woman Betsy. She didn't like their daughter, or the one called Connaught, who stared arrogantly—and blindly—upon Creation. The rock collector she liked. Peace shone in his eyes, and acceptance of the Peoples. The other, the young man Cobb, she wasn't sure about, but didn't trust.

She turned west, away from her people, riding crosswise of the grain of the land. Just as she knew, in this direction the land lay corrugated, and at times she slid her pony into long swales where she would be invisible even to someone nearby. She continued westward until she struck a longer coulee, close to where the raven messengers had taken flight. There she slid off her pony and set him to grazing. She found nothing there. No hoofprints of passage, no green horse dung. Nothing to make the blackbirds fly.

Still, she knew something had passed and left its presence behind, where she sensed it, sensed the ephemeral shadow of man passing. Maybe some Piegan warrior dog, going to murder them all, she thought angrily. She stalked up the west slope of this long shallow draw until her black head rose just above the breast of land, so that anyone looking her way would see only a stray dark rock there. Nothing. Softly she padded back to the bottom and slid down upon her knees, sniffing the grass. She slowly drew in the scents of the land, savoring them, and smelled moccasin. So! Now she spotted a bit of bent grass, silver in the sun. Sharp-eyed, she stalked on foot to the south, her senses aware, her Norwester fusil primed and ready. The faint trail revealed itself now, the passage of a single man sneaking south out of sight of her pack train, shadowing it, ahead of it.

She slid up the east slope until she could see Mister Skye and the rest due east. Soon they'd be south of her. Swiftly, she trod along the vague trail, at one point finding the faintest impression of a moccasin in dun dust. A large light man, she guessed, one who stalked with the feet of the mountain cat. Ahead the soft coulee wheeled southeast, and she grew wary. She could not see what lay around the bend. She squatted low, calculating. Whoever stalked them would be gazing east, watching the passage of the pack train. Alertly, she slid around the soft curve, a few inches at a time, and froze. Ahead the distance of a good shot, a whiteman peered cautiously through the tall grasses toward Mister Skye's party a mile east.

Son of a bitch! she thought. A whiteman, a killer man. She knew that from the voices within her. Killer, as elusive as a mountain lion. This one had no horse. He padded across this empty land on his moccasins and carried only a small leather bag, which rested beside him. She pulled back a little. If she stared long, he would feel it, the way an animal felt it when stared at. In brief glances she took the measure of him. Black-bearded and thin, so

thin the flesh clung to bone and pressed tight to skull.
Old, dark-seamed face, black hair almost gone, no good
scalp to take! She felt she knew this man. Mister Skye had
pointed him out once. Yes, a dangerous man, an enemy. A
fur man. She studied his weapon—a fine percussion lock
with a black octagonal barrel that did not glint in the sun.
A stalker's rifle, she thought, carefully dulled. French. She
sensed that. In grease-blackened skins with the fringes
half-gone, all so dark that it made him only a shadow even
in bright sun.

Tortu. Philipe Tortu. It sent a chill through her to know.
Philipe Tortu was a lone lion, killing in the darkness, invisible by day, slaughtering one by one any man his masters
bid him to slaughter. Some of her Absaroka people had
died at his hand, she knew. He always left his sign, a
small cross of Christ, the whitemen's medicine chief,
carved upon the back or chest of the dead. Her own heart
clutched within her. He had strong medicine. Her own
ball would not harm him, but his ball would kill her, his
thrown dagger would bury itself in her. Tortu, the wolf of
Alex Harvey, come to see what the white toolmakers were
doing among the tribes, and stop it.

He seemed restless, peering for something. Looking for
her, she realized. He should be seeing her scouting, but he
wasn't seeing her. She crabbed back around the bend of
coulee, sensing his eyes would soon study his own backtrail. Afraid to turn her back and glide back to her pony,
she crouched, her knife out and in hand. Not that it would
do much. She possessed no medicine against such a demon as this. Still, Tortu did not come. And she dared not
peer around the bend, into his flat brown eyes.

She needed to get back to her pony. For a long way ahead
the coulee lay straight. She edged up it, fearful she'd cause

birds to explode from her, giving her away. But nothing happened. The somnolent sun arced over a quiet grassland that seemed empty of life in the noonday heat. Everything had shaded up, even birds, until the Heat Maker slid low. She reached her pony and climbed on noiselessly, riding north before cutting east in a wide arc. She cut the pack-train trail and urged her hot sweat-whitened animal into an easy lope. Her man and his party had ridden so far ahead she couldn't see them. But twenty minutes of easy loping brought them in sight. In fact, they were nooning. Mister Skye stood on a knoll, looking for her. Mary, the only one still mounted, sat her pony a little east, the infant slung on her back. Around the sun-pierced camp hip-shot horses stood half-asleep, tails whacking at flies, necks lowered and eyes closed. Only Jawbone stood erect, and at peace, with his ears perked up and his evil yellow eyes calm.

A quiet, pacific place. The whitemen, Cobb, Connaught, and Danzig, each had their pencils out and were making the talk signs in their books of white pages. What did they say in their pages? Did they say this land held no danger, lay sweet and quiet in the August sun? Did the rock-picking man talk of his rocks? They made pictures, too, sketches in their journals. The rock man made drawings of the hills and mountains. As she slid off her pony, she saw him set his journal aside and pick up his curious instrument he called a sextant. What it did she couldn't fathom, except that he made it level with a little ball of liquid metal inside glass—what a wonder, liquid metal—and then peered somehow at the sun without burning his eyes, when the sun was highest, or at the star of the north at night. And then he made more of the talking signs in his book.

But that scarcely concerned her now. Her man stood expectantly on the knoll, watching her, waiting. She loved him. He stood there, thick and powerful, breezes playing with the fringes of the elkskin shirt she'd made for him, strong with great medicine, his blackened Hawken in hand and the many-shooter holstered at his side.

He gazed at her expectantly, knowing somehow she had news. His faded blue eyes were so small and so buried in the crevasses of his flesh she could never see into him, scarcely knew when he peered at her. But she felt them on her now.

"Tortu," she said, and saw his eyes go cold.

By Percy Connaught's standards, the Musselshell wasn't much of a river. It ran eastward where they struck it, in a shallow dish of prairie that had turned dun as the grass cured. The small flow of murky water confirmed him in his belief that the Far West would always be too arid to be of much value to the Republic. It'd cost more to police and soldier these wastes than it was worth. To the south rose remarkably jagged gray mountains Skye called the Crazies, their north slopes still holding snow in their crevasses. Anonymous unnamed ranges dotted the west.

The creek—for that was all it was, really—rolled lazily between thick emerald bands of cottonwoods and brush. The guide, Skye, had splashed across it to the south shore, woven through giant shimmering cottonwoods until he emerged at the low dissected bluffs beyond, and made camp there well back from the creek. He'd become angry, Connaught thought, and barked at the whole party, telling them dangers lurked here, there, everywhere. It amused Connaught. Dangers indeed. The Indians seemed peaceable enough if approached peaceably. What else could there be? An occasional prairie rattler. Grizzly bears in these cottonwoods, according to Skye. Well, fine, they'd avoid the perils of nature, especially with Morse's remarkable equipment. Really, the guide seemed afflicted with ghosts and goblins.

They cooked a meal from provisions on Betsy's portable stove, because the guide wanted no campfire illumining them. Really, it all seemed overdone, and Connaught wondered whether this theater was spun out to impress Morse, and maybe win more money from him, or at least gratuities later. This campsite, he noticed, had an open field of fire in all directions, and was a little beyond effective range from either the south bluffs or the dense riverbank cottonwoods and brush. Well, fine, he thought. Safety, even if it meant dragging firewood some distance. Skye picketed the horses close that evening—how short the days were becoming!—except for that ugly thing he rode, which wasn't picketed at all and hung about Skye's tipi.

No sign of Gros Ventres had shown up in the afternoon, nor of buffalo either. The guide debated it with his squaws, in English, Crow, and what Connaught thought must be Snake. It didn't matter: he had impressions to put down in his journal before the lavender twilight settled into indigo. This would be for his serious journal, the one that would affect public policy.

This arid land, he scribbled, might support light grazing, but everywhere the want of water would prevent serious settlement. True community—homes and mercantiles, schools and churches, industry and husbandmen—could scarcely root in a land without water. Thus would this desolate country be a burden on the public treasury, for no vacuum of power existed long: it would have to be soldiered or lost to rapacious Europeans. Maybe not the British, who seemed complacent with the Oregon settlement, but others: Russians, French, even Chinese. This might well be sold to them and the westward boundary of the Republic drawn at a waterline, east of which enough rain fell to farm the soil.

Satisfied, he slipped his journal and pencil back into its waterproof oilcloth bag Morse designed for him. Cobb and Danzig had finished theirs and sat uncomfortably about the stove, warmed in front but feeling cold-bitten in back, as Connaught felt. He'd beaten the darkness by moments. It seemed an unpleasant camp, with no light save for pricks of orange around the hinged sheet metal of the stove. Skye had not asked again that Connaught do any camp duties, and now that pleased him. They'd paid Skye and the squaws to do all that, and the guide had gotten the message earlier.

Neither Skye nor his squaws joined them that evening. The old squaw vanished into blackness. The young one hovered close to their lodge. They seemed to expect trouble. Then, out of darkness, the guide materialized and squatted beside them.

"We'll be turning east tomorrow, mates. Down the Musselshell valley. My wives don't think the Gros Ventre village is above us—no buffler that way, far as we can judge. You can bloody well hear them, you know. Bawling, restless sometimes. Especially at night, when sound carries. Hope to find the village tomorrow."

Elkanah Morse nodded. "Long day," he said to his women, and they silently rose and headed for Morse's taut rectangular tent. Connaught headed for the bedroll himself. A camp without firelight seemed empty and dull, and no one made conversation by the snap of a tiny tin stove. He saw Cobb catching up with Arabella in the darkness, and caught some whispering. The two of them had been visiting with each other constantly for days. The bookbindery executive slid into the darkness to water a dry land, and into his bedroll.

The howl rose eerie in the night and made his flesh crawl under his thick blankets. A wolf? Lion? Bobcat? No. It sounded almost human. In the murk beside him he heard Cobb mutter something and knew Danzig lay wide-awake, too. Cobb scratched a sulfur match on something, and for a blinding moment the three stared at one another until the match blued and the inside of the tent caught wavery shadows.

The howl filtered through night air again, distant and indistinct, and Connaught swore he heard sobs, too, human sobs. He poked his head through the tent flaps. A star-flecked dome of indigo sky gave faint light. Enough to see their guide, Skye, wearing only a breechclout, heft his glinting revolver.

The howl rose again, muted and broken. Out in the open air, Connaught realized it rose in the east, down some-where in the thick brush beside the Musselshell. It be-came a broken sobbing, ragged and vagrant in the eddying air of night.

Skye disappeared into his lodge and emerged moments later dressed in skins, and much less visible than his white flesh had been.

"Mary," he whispered softly, "stay and guard here."

Jawbone snorted restlessly and tromped sideways, but Mister Skye ignored him.

"You—Connaught. You stay and guard the camp. Guard the women. The rest of you come," he said in a rumble that carried only a few yards.

Danzig and Cobb materialized, dressed and armed. From his tent Elkanah Morse emerged, also ready. A moan rose through the night, ending in a blood-chilling shriek.

"I'm coming, too," said Connaught tartly. He'd make his own choices and not let a hired man direct him so.

"Need someone to guard Mrs. Morse and Arabella, mate," said the guide softly.

"Do it yourself," Percy retorted. If you gave these hired men an inch, they'd be directing your whole life.

In the starlit shadows he saw the young squaw settle herself in shadow, a flintlock in hand, and also her small bow and a quiver. She could deliver death enough, he decided, and followed the other men and Skye eastward.

The guide turned to them. "Spread out, walk softly, keep out of the brush and trees, where you'll snap sticks. Stay in deep shadow. Stay behind me. When we get close, let me go ahead. Don't talk, don't whisper, don't sneeze. Keep your arms ready but don't shoot, don't fire at shadows, don't kill one of us. If you're not sure what to do, do nothing. If we come to Indians, start no wars, kill no one. We're few and any village can mount enough warriors to hunt us down. Do you hear me, Mister Connaught?"

An insult. Plainly, an insult. Percy bristled. "Yes," he said, obviously pained, "I hear you."

"All right then, mates."

They slid silently through bunch grass. The sobbing swelled on the night zephyrs, terrible to hear. Some ghastly thing was happening to some human being. They hurried on, galvanized by the screaming. The sound rose from within the cottonwood belt beside the river, and there, curtained by brush, they glimpsed a fire. A half mile from their own camp, Connaught estimated.

"You stay. Stalking in woods is tricky, mates."

But no one could obey. The sobs impelled them forward, and only the shrieking masked the sound of their passage over snapping sticks and around grasping brush. At last they pulled up in darkness, fifty tree-dotted yards or so from the red tableau.

Indians. All males, their bodies copper in firelight, muscular, sinister, laughing softly. All males except for one. The Indian woman's brown flesh glistened sweat in the amber firelight. She wore nothing. She'd been tied to a slender tree, her arms bound around the trunk behind her, and her legs bound as well. She writhed violently, groaning. From scores of places all over her young body, slivers of pitch-laden pine projected. They'd been jabbed into her, and hung from small bleeding wounds across her chest, her breasts, her arms and shoulders, her cheeks, her nose, her thighs and calves and feet. Slowly, a few at a time, these pitch-laden ponderosa slivers had been ignited and burned hotly toward her flesh until flame consumed her, and the smell of burnt skin suffused the air. A flaming sliver flared upon a taut brown breast, and she shrieked.

Never had Percy Connaught witnessed a thing so terrible, slow torture and inevitable death.

"Ritual torture, mates. She's an enemy of theirs, and they count it good to kill her as slowly as they can," the guide whispered. "She looks Flathead. They're probably Gros Ventres. Stay back and let me handle it!"

Chapter 8

Ritual torture. Killing an enemy of the People. Common enough, thought Mister Skye. Not much time left. The warriors looked to be Gros Ventre, but in the flickering amber light he could scarcely tell. The very people they would soon visit. If he saved the woman, he'd enrage them, break medicine.

A flaring splinter burned into her belly and she screamed, then moaned, writhing against her taut bonds. The warriors gazed approvingly. This enemy dog screamed and wept, and that was good.

He turned to the taut transfixed faces dimly white behind him. "I'm going in. Let me handle this. Don't shoot. If I call out, Elkanah, put a shot in the fire, scatter some sparks to let them know I'm not alone. I'll save her if I can. But remember, I'll break their medicine. We'll be visiting these very people."

He peered at the appalled men shadowed in the cotton-woods.

"Mister Connaught, please hand your weapon to Elkanah."

"But—they might kill me!" Connaught refused, clinging desperately to his revolver.

Mister Skye didn't have time to argue. The woman shrieked again in mortal pain and fell into a wild sobbing, slumped against her rawhide bonds.

"Spread into a half circle. Two of you on that flank," he whispered, and glided softly toward the glow. The seven ponies had sensed him, and stared into the night straight at him. But torture has its own fascination, and the war-riors didn't notice—for the moment.

A stick cracked under him, masked by a shriek.

When their backs were to him, he slid into the open, his Hawken cocked, his big Colt revolver ready.

"I am Mister Skye," he roared.

They wheeled violently, recognizing a name and man who had become a legend among all the northern tribes. Some carried glinting knives, awaiting the next step when they would slice living flesh from the woman bit by bit, keeping her alive as long as possible to prolong her agony.

Some circled, so they could rush him from all sides.

"Stop!" he roared. He didn't know their tongue, but his command had its momentary effect, backed by the swinging bore of the Hawken.

A burning splinter flared against the woman's nose and she shrieked, too lost in pain to notice her salvation.

One of the Gros Ventre, a tall, muscled warrior the color of mahogany in the wild waving flamelight, snarled something to the others.

The leader, then. But they were about to rush him.

"Elkanah, let them know," he commanded.

From the darkness a heavy shot boomed, and the fire blew apart, careening glowing brands in various directions.

"That's enough," yelled Mister Skye.

"Sit," he commanded, pointing a finger at the grass before each of them. These were fine experienced warriors, not young ones. As dangerous and murderous a band of Gros Ventre fighting men as the village possessed. A scar laced across the cheek of one, cocking an eye. Amber light shadowed the scar furrows across another's chest, a place where battle-ax or lance had gouged a vicious trough. Not one of them, he realized, studying each one by one, had the unmarked body he started life with. Medicine bundles hung from their necks, but beyond that they wore little. Some had painted, great greasy slashes of white clay mixed with fat, black ash, yellow and ocher.

War it was, and war they celebrated; he thought.

As fast as they settled sullenly, peering sharply into the blackness beyond the aura of the tiny fire, Mister Skye raced to the woman, who slumped nearly senseless and out of her head. He yanked the remaining slivers of pine from her tormented body, each tug another burst of pain. Blood oozed from the small wounds. Where the burning brands had reached flesh, there were ugly festering cauterized holes.

With his free hand he cut her rawhide bonds. She fell sobbing, curled up at the foot of the tree, still lost in her torment.

"Mister Cobb," he said quietly. "Please attend to this woman. Find her clothes, and carry her, if you must, back to Victoria and Mary."

Cobb materialized out of darkness, his revolver glowing orangely in the light.

"Holster it, mate. The next part of this is peaceable, and they know me anyway. I've already broken their medicine."

Reluctantly Jarvis Cobb sheathed his weapon, staring sharply at the sitting warriors. He found the woman's torn red calico blouse and skirts, but when he attempted to slide them over her, she wailed. She couldn't bear the touch of anything upon her brutalized flesh.

"Let her stay, mate. Let her weep. I'm going to have a little talk with the headman here, and I'd take it kindly if you'd keep an eye upon the others, watching for the throw of a knife."

The captain stood beside the huddled woman, ready for trouble. Mister Skye settled himself on the grass before the headman. He would do the rest of this with sign talk.

The warrior watched him impassively, with eyes as flat and feral as a rattler's.

"I am Skye," he said, making the arched sign for the heavens. "I come at peace. We come to your village with gifts. We wish to buy the woman to be our slave. What will you sell her for?"

For a long time the headman said and did nothing, until Mister Skye thought he didn't understand.

"Who is with Skye?" he finally signaled.

"Whitemen who make pots and iron arrowheads and blankets. Friends of the Atsina, come to see what Atsina people like."

"They will give us many things for the slave. She is a Flathead and a dog and deserves to die. She has no bravery in her."

"One bolt of blue cloth for the woman. A fair price," signaled Mister Skye.

"Cloth, ten twists of tobacco, and one pony."

"No horse. The tobacco, yes. She is a Flathead dog and that is all we will give."

"One iron arrow point for each of us." The headman's hand included the six others.

Mister Skye lifted his voice to the darkness. "Elkanah, can you spare seven iron arrowheads?"

From the blackness the entrepreneur called back, "Anything at all, Mister Skye. Anything to spare that wretched woman."

The guide nodded, and his fingers flew again. "Ten twists, seven iron arrow points, and a bolt of blue cloth."

The headman pondered. "One thing more," his hands said. "You have broken our medicine. Our hearts are on the ground. The night is bad. We will take those things for the dog, and we will all count coup on Mister Skye. That will make our hearts good."

"No. No warrior counts coup on Mister Skye. It is death." The guide's hands jabbed angrily. "The great blue medicine horse would kill each of you."

"We are Atsina warriors. We must have our medicine back. You have taken it. You cannot enter our village until we count coup."

From the thickening dark, the other Gros Ventres watched intently, following the fingers.

"You have counted coup upon the Flathead woman."

The headman retreated into stony quiet.

Mister Skye pondered. To let them count coup on him would end his medicine. The news would race like wildfire from tribe to tribe, wiping away the respect and wariness he'd fostered. No. He'd have to offer them some other atonement, some other christ.

"Mister Danzig," he said into the black shadows. "These Gros Ventres wish to count coup. It restores their medicine. Would you volunteer?"

"They wish to touch me, right?"

"Right, mate. They will each touch you. Maybe hard."

"I will be the Gadarene swine, and maybe even rush into the Musselshell afterward," said the geologist amiably.

He sauntered easily into the light, his dark eyes filled with concern for the weeping woman curled near Jarvis Cobb.

They watched him, seeing a compact graying man with wise eyes, walking fearlessly to them.

"You are a brave man, Mister Danzig," said the guide. "Walk to each warrior and let him strike you. Some may wish to hurt you."

The geologist ambled easily to the first and waited. The warrior gravely tapped him. The second warrior shoved hard, staggering him. The third touched him lightly. The others tapped firmly, and then he stood quietly before the headman.

"What is your name?" signaled Mister Skye.

"I am called Snow Hunter."

"Snow Hunter. This is Rudolpho Danzig." The guide spoke the name aloud. "He is a wise man, a medicine man of the whites. A teacher. He studies the earth. He knows about the rocks upon the breast of Mother Earth."

That was as much as Mister Skye could convey with his sign talk.

"Now you have counted coup upon a great man of the whites," he signed gently.

The Atsina leader stared hard at the quiet professor, sensing some fine thing about Rudolpho Danzig. Then he offered a handclasp. Surprised, the geologist found himself shaking hands.

Mister Skye felt pleased. "Now we will smoke," he said. "Mister Morse, we'll need a bolt of blue cloth, ten twists of tobacco, a pipe, and seven arrowheads. And please bring Victoria to tend to this woman. We have acquired a slave."

"I'm here," came a familiar hard high voice from the dark. Victoria padded into the glow of the coals, her bow strung and an arrow nocked in it. "I'll fix her good. Flatheads, they friends of the Absaroka people."

Her presence astonished Mister Skye's clients. They peered distrustfully into the dark, wondering what other surprises it might harbor.

The episode shook Percy Connaught to the depths of his Whig soul. Civilized people, he wrote in his public policy journal, can scarcely imagine the savagery of these inhabitants of the plains. They must either be civilized and enlightened, or meet the fate that nature reserves for inferior species.

Then he turned to his journal for the vulgar and described the same episode in lurid terms, alluding delicately to the burning brands that blistered the woman's limbs and face but avoiding the brands that burned pits in other flesh. It would make a sensation in the East, he knew.

The whole business set his mind churning. No longer did he feel comfortable in these distant wilds. Not even Mister Skye offered much protection against barbaric tribesmen such as these. He saw himself tied naked to a tree, convulsing as each pitch-laden brand blistered into his flesh, slowly dying in an agony beyond the comprehension of civilized men.

In such desperate pain had the short broad Flathead woman been that they could not clothe her. The softest touch of calico set her to gasping in the night. Victoria muttered and cursed and finally asked Skye to carry her back to their camp, after he had smoked with the barbarous Gros Ventres.

That took an hour. Percy had crouched suspiciously in the outer darkness the whole time, unwilling to let those murderous Indians know of his presence. But at last the warriors left for their village to the east, and Mister Skye solemnly carried the groaning Flathead woman to his lodge.

There the woman's moans lifted through the night, and he saw Victoria scurry in and out, digging in parfleches, stirring balms and salves of root and powder of her own barbarous manufacture, muttering and cursing while the others sat silently, unwilling to return to sleep.

When finally he slipped into his tent and bedroll, he slept not at all. He lay rigid, and not one muscle relaxed.

The morning found him crabbed, tired, and full of nameless terrors. He sipped coffee dourly and turned silent. He tended to be honest about himself, and discovered a truth in the middle of the night he didn't much like: he had no particular sympathy for the Flathead woman. Indeed, where he ought to feel pity, he felt wild fear that a similar thing might happen to him in this terrible desert. That was not the only distasteful discovery he'd made about himself this trip. He knew he was a slacker, sloughing off camp duties on the pretense that he had more important things to do. He did: the journals were priceless records. But he knew that he alone wasn't carrying his weight, and he felt half-annoyed with himself, and slightly ashamed, and he couldn't rationalize away his conduct.

When Mister Skye emerged at last from his lodge, yawning, Elkanah Morse cornered him, bursting, as usual, with questions.

"How is the poor woman, Mister Skye?"

"She'll be all right, mate. Nothing internal got hurt—just her skin. She'll be scarred the rest of her life. She's in such pain we can't dress her, and not the lightest cover either."

"Who is she—do you know?"

"Just found it out this morning, Elkanah. She's Flathead, all right. Kills Dog Woman. She and a few other women, and a party of Flathead hunters came over here to make meat. Flatheads think the Musselshell country is their buffler ground. The Gros Ventres jumped them, got her."

"Barbarous!" exclaimed Percy.

Mister Skye fixed him with a stern gaze. "Don't know that some slaves in your South get treated much better."

"That's barbarous, too, and I'm ashamed of the white South!" he replied.

The guide nodded. "Those Atsina aren't exactly appreciated by the people around here."

"I suppose Mrs. Skye has a few simple unguents for those wounds," said Elkanah.

"Lot more than that. She has medicines made from roots and leaves. Powders she blows or dabs into terrible wounds and they don't ever mortify. She put Kills Dog Woman to sleep with a leaf tea last night in spite of the woman's pain."

"You're saying they have effective medicines, better than our scientific ones?" Elkanah asked.

"I don't know what your medicine back in the States is about, mate. But yes, Victoria and most any tribal practitioner here can do amazing things."

"Would she share her secrets? Get me leaves and roots and tell me what they do and how to use them?"

"Ask her, mate."

"I may have a new business," Elkanah said. "One that'd bring healing to the world. That's what business is all about—bringing good things to everyone. I'm not a chemist and know little about pharmacopoeia, but Danzig knows chemistry and I'll set him on this."

"What of the woman? You said you'd bought a slave last night. Is that what you intend?" asked Connaught indignantly.

Mister Skye laughed heartily. "No, that's what I bloody well told the Atsina. We'd buy the slave. Why else would a whiteman buy a Flathead woman? That was for their understanding, Mister Connaught. She's welcome to stay with us; welcome to return to her husband. But for a while she'll be with us."

Elkanah asked, "Won't she be terrified when we visit the Gros Ventre village?"

"More like hate. She'll know she's safe with us. Gros Ventre won't harm a hair on the head of my slave."

"Will we be welcome?"

"I imagine." He paused, hesitant. "But the Atsina—Gros Ventre—are known for treachery. One of the reasons they're hated. They're even quarreling with their old allies the Blackfeet just now." He sighed. "We smoked. We gave them their medicine back. We bought rather than captured the woman. I think we'll be out of harm's way. But let's put it this way, Elkanah. That tribe, above all tribes, needs watching. Stay alert, pick no fights, never use your arms or you'll be tortured to death before every man, woman, and child in the village."

"Let's just go elsewhere!" Percy Connaught exclaimed.

The guide's flinty gaze rested on the man of letters. "Can't. I told them we're coming. They said we'd be welcome. If we turn tail now, they'd say our medicine left us. Do you know what that means?"

Percy Connaught felt annoyed. This barbarous man lectured him, presumed him to be utterly ignorant, even though Percy had taken pains to read every journal of wilderness travel he could lay hands on. He supposed, secretly, that he actually knew more of Indian medicine than the guide.

"Why, we must save face," he replied.

The guide's gaze rested on the distant yellow bluffs, dotted with cedar and jackpine, missing nothing. "I suppose you could put it that way," he muttered.

The rest of the camp stirred. Betsy had a fire kindled in her portable stove and the aromatic smoke of juniper sticks perfumed the camp. Arabella vanished into brush. Mary and Victoria busied themselves around Skye's lodge.

"We'll go to the village as soon as our guide wishes," said Elkanah briskly.

"Tomorrow," said Mister Skye. "Today we'll let our guest heal."

"I have a theory," said Elkanah. "And this is the place to prove it out. I hold that trade brings peace. Traders are the emissaries of one civilization to another. They bring goods and goodwill and buy what the others have to offer, making valuable exchanges that bless both parties. Let's go to the Gros Ventre. I'll wager my products will excite them, kindle the desire for trade—"

"Or theft and murder," broke in Percy.

"Yes, that's possible, Percy. But I'll wager on trade. Wait until they see what civilized men can offer them. Every modern convenience. Freedom from famines, as soon as they learn to till the earth and plan ahead. I have for sale every implement that will help them transform themselves into modern men with all the blessings of true civilization. Trade, gentlemen, is the unifying and civilizing force of modern times!"

Jawbone screeched, and plunged away wildly.

Mister Skye responded by diving to the grasses.

A distant shot racketed and a ball plowed earth where the guide had stood, barely missing his flattened body.

A faint bloom of blue powder smoke spread along the top of the bluff a hundred fifty yards distant.

"Son of a bitch!" snarled Victoria. She dove into the old lodge and sprang out with her flintlock, hard fierce gaze upon the rim of distant dun rock. She fired, and the bark of a gnarled pine flew into the sky.

"Tortu!" she muttered, a word that baffled Percy Connaught.

Mister Skye scrambled to his feet, running to fetch his Hawken. His evil horse kept on screeching and whirling.

"Mister Morse, your theories aren't worth a bloody damn," the guide muttered.

Chapter 9

Hunting down Tortu would be as futile as snatching smoke. Harvey's assassin had a way of vanishing into wilderness. Even so, Mister Skye trotted up the south slope to search for the faint tread of moccasin he expected to find, and follow it. Probably that human phantom had crossed the river by now and had holed up far to the north. But it had to be done: if Mister Skye hoped to live to ripe old age, he had, to stalk the stalker.

It all puzzled him. Why now? Years ago, Mister Skye had booted Alex Harvey out of American Fur for brutally murdering two Blackfeet who had come to Fort McKenzie to trade. That, actually, was the culminating incident in a long string of brutalities Harvey had inflicted upon his engagés, tribesmen, and those above him in the fur company's chain of command. Plainly Harvey wanted him dead and had set the most vicious and elusive killer in the Northwest after him. Tortu meant twisted, and that described him perfectly. No man possessed more cunning and cruelty, less warmth and human kindness than Tortu.

All of it had something to do with Elkanah Morse, too. Mister Skye puzzled that one, because Harvey, Primeau could as easily stock Morse's products as American Fur, though perhaps at higher prices. The opposition couldn't afford to buy in the quantities that were routine for American Fur. Surely Harvey didn't believe that the Morse party engaged in actual trade. Morse had only two packhorses laden with goods. A trading venture out among the tribes would have required scores of packhorses or mules. No, it had to be that Harvey, Primeau couldn't afford to risk loading its shelves with Morse's new trade items. Harvey'd always hated anything new. And Morse brought the new and untried to the far tribes, threatening to weaken the opposition even more.

He stared hard as he approached the bluff, his eyes alert for the glint of a rifle in the dawn sun. But he found nothing, not even the faintest moccasin track. Any good assassin avoided horses that might betray him with noise, droppings, and a trail easily followed. About him lay a vast and silent wilderness where a man without a horse could hole up silently in any crag of rock and wait. Mister Skye sat quietly, watching for the explosion of birds or the flight of antelope on a distant slope. Nothing.

He had little time. Tortu meant death. Not only to himself, but also Mary and Victoria and the child; to Elkanah and Betsy and Arabella Morse; to the rest. The only safety lay in a village. Almost any village. Tortu would be unlikely to assassinate guests in a village and face a hundred or so howling vengeful warriors, as skilled at rooting out elusive quarry and as knowing of the wild as Tortu himself.

Mister Skye would get them to the Gros Ventre village, then. Not that the treacherous Atsina would offer much more shelter than the wilderness. Below him, he spotted Victoria stalking angrily, checking out every scrub pine and juniper bush within rifle shot of the camp. Nothing.

He eased down the slope, his flesh flinching, awaiting the explosion that would be the last thing he ever heard. Nothing happened.

"Victoria," he muttered. "We'll head for the village. Rig a travois for Kills Dog Woman. We can't stay here."

"We go among dogs to hide from rabid wolf," she snapped.

Nonetheless, she began at once to break camp and ready

a travois to carry the tormented woman, who'd face screaming pain with every jolt of the poles over a rock or into a gulch.

"Captain Cobb, I could use your counsel," said Mister Skye.

"What was that all about?"

"Killer named Tortu. Sent by the opposition. Harvey's nursed grudges for years, and probably thinks Elkanah's venture here works against him in every way he can imagine. That's how his mind works. I know it well enough . . . Tortu. Shadowy French-Canadian fur man who's turned lobo. Always on foot and shadowy as a panther at night. We get him, or he gets me—and you. I'm heading for the Gros Ventre village at once. How would you suggest we defend ourselves en route?"

Captain Cobb scanned the mounded hills and their copses of pine and juniper nervously. "In pairs," he said at last. "If you set single flankers and scouts, he'd murder them. Pairs are harder to deal with."

"I was thinking the same bloody thing." Mister Skye lifted his black stovepipe hat, tugged at his long hair, and screwed the hat down again.

"You and my Mary on one flank—and don't underestimate her, Mister Cobb."

"I certainly don't."

"Victoria and I on the other. The Morses and Mister Danzig can handle the packhorses, travois, and the rest."

"What about Connaught?"

"He can do what he wants."

Jarvis Cobb stared, smiled faintly, and turned to break camp.

They splashed across a ford and up the north slope, onto level open bench land that offered few possibilities of ambush. Kills Dog Woman lay on the travois stoic and silent now, in acute pain but drained of the terror of death. Mister Skye watched her pass, repelled by her swollen gashed face, angry and scorched, the nose so bloated she could barely breathe. Their eyes caught a moment and then hers closed. No one had told the burned woman where they would go today.

The morning remained cold, a haze robbing the sun. Not long, he thought. He had to hurry these people to Fort Laramie and army transport down the Platte. He and Victoria rode the south flank, keeping an eye on the breaks tumbling down to the river, where Tortu would likely lurk. Far off to the north, Captain Cobb, erect and military in his saddle, guarded alertly, along with Mary, who rode twenty or thirty yards back of him. In the pack train itself, Elkanah Morse rode with his revolver in hand, as did the doughty professor, and Connaught.

Beneath him, Jawbone sensed the wariness and minced with ears pricked up and his nose testing the chill air. At the faintest scent or sound of trouble, the ferocious horse would alert him in various ways. But the morning slid by quietly, broken only by a burst of antelope bounding white-rumped to the northeast.

They ventured at last into buffalo grounds. They lay, for the most part, in the lush dun cured grasses, having filled themselves early in the morning. A few black hulks stood on distant swells of prairie, sentinels. One group caught the scent of the intruders and indolently trotted over the horizon. Others didn't bother to stand and seemed oblivious to their passage through the haze-chilled morning.

They nooned on a dry swell that offered no chance of surprise in any direction. Even so, Victoria hovered angrily, her old flintlock in hand, while Betsy and Arabella doled out slices of cold antelope that had kept well in the cold night.

The wiry dark professor took the opportunity to shoot the noon sun with his sextant.

"Where are we, Mister Danzig?" asked the guide.

"Why, sir, I believe—given my lack of adequate equipment—we're at forty-six degrees and thirty minutes north. I get that by deducting the sun's altitude from zenith, or ninety degrees, and then adding the zenithal latitude of the sun on this date from a table I have. In fall and winter one deducts the zenithal latitude."

Mister Skye laughed. "I'd say we're on the north bank of the Musselshell, with the Snowy Mountains off to the north, the Crazy Mountains over there in the southwest, and some of the best grazing land in the world beneath our feet."

Connaught bridled at that. "More a desert waste," he muttered, scribbling something in his endless journal. "Can't imagine human beings surviving here in any but the most barbarous circumstances."

Elkanah approached him. "I've been pondering this whole business of Harvey's assassin," he began. "It appalls me. Have I misunderstood something? Is my trade expedition at fault here? Is my family endangered? Should we turn back to Fort Benton to put a stop to it?"

The more Mister Skye saw of the entrepreneur, the better he liked the man. Elkanah asked questions, got to the heart of things, and had a mind open to possibility. Mister Skye tackled the history first, describing Alex Harvey's troubled, brutal, unstable years working as an officer of the American Fur Company until Skye booted him out. Now he had a powerful opposition company, backed by the amiable Robert Campbell himself in St. Louis, as wily a master of the fur trade as the Chouteaus.

"Yes, to answer your question. Harvey sees a threat. They don't have the cash to risk on new shelf goods—all these items like ready-made arrows you've toted along."

"But surely that's not an excuse for bloodshed—for murder—for taking the lives of, of you and yours, and me and mine!"

"This isn't the East, and what you're seeing is not competition among trading companies, Elkanah. Out here beyond law and civilization, the struggles of the fur companies are something else, more primitive, brutal, vicious. The walls and that bastion being built at Fort Benton protect not just against Indians, Elkanah. They bloody well protect against pirates. Consider this an ocean, and consider it full of privateers and freebooters."

Elkanah Morse grinned wryly. "I can see that free trade and certain civilized rules and order complement each other. Mister Skye, are my wife and daughter in grave danger?"

"Yes."

"What do you propose?"

"Get to the safety of the Gros Ventre village. And then I'll have to deal with Tortu somehow—stalk the stalker."

"Let's go then," said Elkanah sharply.

These Gros Ventre looked terribly poor, Elkanah thought, with few of the ornaments of the proud Blackfeet. They fashioned their lodges from ragged mended hides, rarely daubed with the medicine decor that leaped to the eye when one viewed a Blackfeet village. Few of the haggard tribesmen they passed wore decorated clothing. Most of it was simply crudely tanned hides or rough-sewn tradecloth in various subdued earthy colors, carelessly cut and laced, all of it ill-fitting.

"These are the homeless wanderers of the prairies, Elkanah," Mister Skye said. "They rarely stop long enough to manufacture what they need, and spend a lot of time mooching on other villages until they wear out their welcome."

"Maybe I can help them. For a few buffalo robes, they can have my ready-made lodges, arrows, and all the rest."

The guide sighed. "Not that simple. They steal and war and sponge for a living, and that's the way of it with them."

These people seemed less eager to have visitors than the Blackfeet. Perhaps hospitality wasn't a part of their way, thought Elkanah. The camp crier had announced them, and the village police escorted them as they rode into the concentric circles of lodges on a cottonwood-dotted flat along the Musselshell River. Few dogs met them, no doubt because the rest had vanished into the stew pots. No one seemed surprised. News of their coming had preceded them. But many a brown eye gazed boldly at the delirious Flathead enemy bound tightly to Victoria's travois, now a slave of Mister Skye.

"The Blackfeet camp was like a rainbow," observed Betsy, "but this is all brown and dreary. I didn't know villages and tribes could be so different! It'll be a challenge for my paints."

The whole trip Betsy had fussed and worried about Kills Dog Woman, begging to help any way she could. But Victoria had shooed her off, and the woman herself remained barely conscious. The torture had unsettled Betsy and turned Arabella silent and distant. But his dear bright wife hadn't thought of herself; her heart had gone out to the suffering woman, and Betsy's innate love for the creatures around her had worked into a rage against torture, against these Gros Ventres, and a determination to preach Christian love to them all. That was his Betsy! Elkanah thought. Never content just to observe, and always eager to make herself a part of things, and change things for the better.

"They're an evil people!" she had said. "I shall rebuke them and teach them!"

"I'm afraid most of the tribes engage in ritual torture, Mrs. Morse," the guide had replied. "It's medicine, part of the way they dominate their worlds."

Elkanah realized as they threaded through the quiet village that few people watched them. The young men had vanished, and only the ancient ones, with furrowed brown faces, observed their passage, along with scampering children. It puzzled him.

"Out fetching buffler. There's a pishkun near here, about a mile east."

"A what?" asked Elkanah.

"Buffler jump. Natural place where they can stampede a herd over these cliffs and make meat."

"How can they possibly make use of hundreds of carcasses at once?"

"They can't. They take what they want, and feed the wolves and coyotes with the rest."

"Can't they do it some more efficient way?"

"They're horse-poor. Don't know much about training a buffler runner, either. They bloody well steal what few buffler runners they've got, so why learn to train them?"

"Are there no other ways?"

"In snow, they can sometimes drive buffler into a drift so deep they can't escape the arrow. Or they can kill an old bull or cow before the wolves do."

"Can they do anything well?"

"Steal, war, and kill. They're as fierce as any around here, and their women are fiercer than the men. Some years ago, some trappers tangled with them near a rendezvous and took a licking no fur trapper's ever forgotten."

"Mister Skye," said Betsy, "will we be safe here?"

"Your persons, probably. But not a single item you own. We'll have to set guard over the supplies and ponies, even though we're guests."

"Mercy!" exclaimed Betsy. "I shall give them a piece of my mind!"

They drew up before the lodge of the chief, who stood with his befeathered staff of office in hand, awaiting them. This dreary lodge stood no taller or wider than the others, and its only decor was a collection of black scalps laced around the entrance flap.

He'd lost his front teeth and muttered amiably to Mister Skye, ancient hands lazily making sign as he mumbled. But his cataract-fogged old black eyes shown merrily, and his ancient body, withered down now about his bent frame, jerked and bobbed spastically as he talked. A merry old rogue, Elkanah thought. An ancient crone, as withered and toothless as the chief, sidled out of the lodge and grinned her gummy pleasure.

"He's called Horse Medicine, mates," explained the guide. "He says the whole village is up on the prairie north of here driving buffler. There's some squaws east of here, waiting to slice up the bloody herd. The village is mostly run by the war chief, White Beaver. Younger man. We'll smoke now. Have some tobacco and a few things ready, Elkanah."

An hour later, after a lot of finger talk, smoke, an old man's babbling, and a long hard effort by Mister Skye to explain their purposes here in the village, the guide and

Elkanah emerged into a cold sun. The village dog soldiers had led a sullen Victoria and the wary visitors to a campsite just east of the village, hard by the banks of the Musselshell. There'd be wood and water, but no graze for their ponies for a mile or so.

"We're invited to watch the jump, mates. But you'd better have the stomach for it. A whole herd of terrified buffalo going over a cliff and dying in a heap, bones and blood, isn't a pretty sight."

"It's not a sight for women, Betsy!" said Elkanah. "You and Arabella had better—"

"Oh, pooh! If squaws can manage it, so can I! I'm going to paint it later anyway."

"I think I'll stay here," said Arabella dryly.

Elkanah himself wondered whether he could stomach a sight like that. But he'd go. He'd find ways to make the labor easier. He'd study what they did, how they dealt with a pile of black limp carcasses, and what they salvaged and abandoned.

Victoria came with them, muttering, intending to make meat herself, and maybe snatching a hide or two after the Gros Ventre squaws had abandoned the pile.

"I suppose they'll leave this village site soon. The smell of decaying flesh will be awful here," said Jarvis Cobb.

"Few days. It doesn't rot all that fast in this colder weather, Mister Cobb."

"Interesting erosion," said Danzig. "Lot of it from wind over countless years. Wind-whipped sand hollowed that yellow sandstone. Frost cracked those slabs loose, and there they perch until something tumbles them."

Percy Connaught came along, pinch-faced and white, looking so grim that Elkanah wondered how long he'd last when the horror of it slammed into them. They'd all come except for Mary, Arabella, and Skye's little boy. Elkanah hoped Mary would guard the camp from these thieves, and relaxed only when he realized that Mister Skye didn't seem concerned about it.

The jump itself loomed above them, its lip about a hundred feet up, and the fragmented face nearly vertical. At its foot lay a pile of yellow detritus that had weathered off the rim. The cliff rose only forty yards or so from the lazy river and was naked at its crest here at the jump, but to either side thick stands of jackpine and juniper sprang almost miraculously from native rock, their roots jammed between loosened sandstone strata. In the detritus lay ghastly heaps of white bones, hollow-eyed skulls, grown dry and porous in the relentless prairie sun. In fact bone was spread over a wide area, an acre or so, Elkanah supposed.

A dozen or so squaws waited solemnly, some of them kneeling and making medicine of some sort with guttural chanting. They eyed the whites curiously. Several wore only filthy old skin skirts, nothing covering their sagging brown breasts. Elkanah glanced tautly at Betsy, who seemed to be perfectly at ease with the nakedness.

"They won't be wearing their Sunday best while slaughtering the sacred buffler," Mister Skye explained softly. "If the hunt is good, you'll see them all fixed up tonight in finery for a happy dance and a lot of medicine making. They'll thank the One Above. Most of these tribes know what gratitude is, and reverence of nature is born in them. And likely they'll apologize to the buffler spirits they've taken."

It seemed a strange, mysterious place, Elkanah thought. On a tripod hung some sort of medicine, a weasel tail and feathers and other things. But there was something else:

some palpable power he felt here as they all stood quietly, anticipating thunder and death, some brutal climax that would sunder the sun and earth.

Then a strange excitement shivered through the squaws, and their keening crescendoed into whispers and new alertness. Elkanah heard nothing and wondered. Some of the women lifted naked arms toward the bluff, in some kind of supplication. A strange fear settled on them all. Percy sweated, drops of wetness blooming suddenly on his forehead as he licked his lips. Death lurked and prowled here, setting teeth on edge. Victoria glared contemptuously at the whites about her, daring them with her sharp black eyes to weaken and flee this place of carnage. From above now the wind carried faint hoarse cries, and Elkanah spotted a boy on the edge of the tawny cliff, far to the west, waving a red trade blanket frantically.

The earth trembled. They heard nothing, but felt a strange vibration in the soles of their feet, a tremor that rustled grass and turned the cottonwood leaves silver-sided. Then came a faint mutter, a throaty boom of distant thunder, fearsome. Elkanah involuntarily stepped back, stepped away from this tawny lip of death looming above. The others did, too.

"Oh, God!" cried Betsy. "I shouldn't have come!"

The squaws wailed now, mouths open, dancing small circles, even as thunder rolled toward them and the sound battered ears with the howl of death.

The first buffalo, a great bull, sailed over, legs flailing, grunting and whistling, defecating as it somersaulted down, and smacked the earth shoulder-first with a sickening thud, twitching. Even as he fell a dozen more sailed into space, grunting, thundering, spinning and tumbling, smacking earth on their backs, splintering legs, breaking necks, spewing blood, geysering guts and urine, dying fast and slowly, shuddering and spasming, landing on the ones underneath, ten, a hundred, two hundred, thunder, and awful silence.

From above, the chanting of the hunters.

Next to Elkanah, Percy Connaught vomited and huddled into a ball, sick. Betsy stood pale, her lips drawn down. Elkanah settled his own stomach and turned to watch the squaws attack.

Chapter 10

From the top of the heap a calf bawled piteously, its forelegs shattered. The terrible black pile did not lie quiet, but pulsed with fading life. Limbs rose and settled and shuddered. Bright blood gouted from compound fractures. Yellow bone pierced through woolly brown hide. Mouths yawned open and black lips drew back into eerie grins. Dun dust twisted upward in a column and drifted east. Above, on the lip of doom, bold gray wolves surveyed the feast below.

Elkanah had never seen death wholesale, and it sickened him. Betsy couldn't bear it, turned her back upon it, and clutched him.

"Oh, God," she wept. "I didn't expect—I hadn't thought—"

On all fours, Percy Connaught heaved up everything in his stomach. Even Rudolpho Danzig, who took life as it came, looked unusually solemn, if not shaken. Mister Skye didn't like it either, Elkanah realized. His face had a drawn look in the presence of so much death.

He estimated a hundred seventy or eighty, old and young bulls, cows, calves, yearlings. Dead or dying in two or three minutes of cataclysm. Even as he watched, Gros Ventre squaws in ancient tattered skirts swarmed into the heap, often carving upon the still living. A hundred, maybe a hundred and fifty women materialized, each with glinting silvery knives, and began sawing. Tongues first. Easy to butcher, and a delicacy. The women crawled over the pulsing pile, slicing out tongues and tossing them into a bloody heap on the grass.

"I ought to make a daguerreotype," said Rudolpho, "but they're so black I'd have only a black mound on my plate. Too bad. No one has made an image of a buffalo jump."

"I had thought to paint it, but I can't. I never will," muttered Betsy, still in Elkanah's arms. "I think I'd better go back to our camp," she said softly. "It will be a long time before all this fades from my mind."

Elkanah watched her go. Even his buoyant Betsy, who rode storms and troubles like a cork, had suffered some sort of shock. He wished he had discouraged her, but then he smiled. No one ever discouraged Betsy when she set her will upon something.

Mister Skye's gaze had shifted to the rimrock and the cottonwoods along the riverbank and studied the far shore, and Elkanah realized that even here, surrounded by Gros Ventre, he watched for the slightest sign of that madman who dogged him—and maybe the others. It filled Elkanah with rare anger: he'd had enough of slaughter.

"Where are the men? Where are the hunters?" he asked the guide. "There's work to do here, more work than I can imagine!"

"They've ridden back to the village. They'll celebrate and smoke now, and laugh. Their work's done."

"But if they helped—these creatures must weigh a thousand pounds or more—if they helped turn the carcasses, pull them out of the heap—"

"Woman's work."

"But that's madness. They could butcher so many more—start meat to drying—collect hides—"

"Woman's work. No self-respecting warrior would think of it. If you tried it yourself, these squaws would chase you away, or just laugh at you."

Instead of slicing down the stomach cavity and pulling off the hides, these women sawed down the neck and back, cutting a good hide in two.

"Why do they do that? What a waste of a hide!"

"They can get a split hide out of it, mate. Sew the two pieces back together with sinew. The buffler are too heavy to turn over—too heavy for women to drag at all. So they're slaughtered about the way they fall. See, they're going after the hump meat, best of all meat, and that thick white backfat there—great delicacy. From the stomach they'll take some boudins—intestines—and liver. Raw buffler liver, now there's something to taste. Kept many a fur man alive and happy."

"I'll make block and tackle! I'll show them how to set up a simple tripod and pull these carcasses up with good rope and some hardwood pulleys. Then they can slaughter the whole animal, take the whole hide off—"

Mister Skye laughed. "Don't think you'd get far, mate. Look at those hides. Few of them worth anything. They've been torn to shreds by horn and hoof landing on them."

"You mean most of this is waste?"

"That's the way of it."

"What'll they get out of this?"

"Why, more meat and trim than they know what to do

with: hump roasts, boudins, liver. Plenty to jerk before it gets too cold, and plenty for pemmican. Backfat, that adds flavor to stews. Sinew. Hides. Dorsal bone, off the hump, for kitchen things. Brain for tanning. Maybe twenty, thirty hides to trade. Mostly splits—worth less, but still something they can give for whitemen's truck."

"What percentage of all this carnage'll get used?"

"Oh . . . ten, twenty. Rest feeds the carrion eaters for a week or two. See the wolves, mate? They're waiting. You'll hear them all night. Coyotes, wolves, badgers, crows, hawks, magpies—you'll hear them at dusk, soon as the squaws clear out."

Rudolpho said, "It seems a waste, at least to a European, to whom meat is always precious."

"Millions of buffler," said Mister Skye. "Sometimes the land is black with them, far as the eye can see. But if the robe trade builds, they'll thin down."

Jarvis Cobb said, "It's their whole economy, isn't it? Kill off the buffalo, and the warriors of the plains are tamed. I'll discuss that in my reports."

"Hate to see them go, Mister Cobb," said the guide.

"These buffalo prevent forward progress of civilization," Cobb replied. "These tribesmen won't stop roaming and warring until we destroy the buffalo. Then it'll be easy to start them farming and ranching."

"I suppose you're right," said Mister Skye crisply. Elkanah was not surprised at the bitterness in the guide's voice. Abruptly Mister Skye left them, stalking toward the Gros Ventre village and his own lodge.

"He hates to see his own way of life fade," said Rudolpho gently. "I can understand it. They get to love this life, out beyond the known world. The freedom. Even these tribesmen who are traditional enemies of his wives seem to command his respect."

"We've witnessed something few whites have ever seen, or will see," Elkanah said softly. "Write it up, Percy—" He peered around, discovering that Connaught had vanished, too. "Something for Percy's journals."

Before them, blood-soaked squaws sliced and tore red flesh from black carcasses. Greasy gray guts covered the grass. Flies swarmed in great green masses. The Gros Ventre women chattered among themselves in a hoarse sharp tongue, and sometimes slipped morsels into their mouths to chew as they worked—chocolatey liver especially. The silent heap of buffalo turned redder and browner, and yet scarcely diminished. On a far side of it, Elkanah spotted Victoria, fiercely hacking back hide with a honed hatchet to get at hump roast. Elkanah scarcely felt like eating, and wondered if he'd manage even the succulent rib roast coming that evening, a roast more tender and tasty than anything beef cattle could offer.

Most of that chill afternoon Elkanah watched, while squaws chipped away at the dead, not even touching a hundred or so animals trapped at the bottom. If they wouldn't hang the animals for slaughter, there seemed little he could offer to save labor or make this gargantuan task easier. It boiled down to humble whetstones. These squaws butchered with dull knives, making hard work brutal work. The other possibility that came to him was smocks of some sort, some sort of cotton shifts they might use for this filthy work and then wash easily. The whole thing might go easier with some division of labor. Teams of strong men to hang the beasts from a stout rafter. A group of hide specialists who did nothing but peel back the valuable brown skins. Gut specialists, who gathered the boudins and liver. Head specialists, who scooped out brain for their tanning process. Backstrap specialists, who cut out the fine hump meat, took sinew and backfat, and the succulent tenderloin. Then it'd all work.

But even as Elkanah thought it, he knew it'd never happen. This monstrous mound would feed wolves rather than people, for the most part. While he watched, shamans snatched bits of buffalo—eyes and noses, ears and tails, magic and power for them. This entire labor seemed infused with tribal medicine and religion, as warriors raised arms to the One Above, as squaws followed ancient rituals and would do things no other way. How, Elkanah wondered, could you offer a people a better way if it invaded something sacred in their life? He had no answer for it.

In the village he found old women, crippled women, and girls engaged in the same relentless labor. Patiently they sliced each thin strip of red meat to be jerked, while children hung loads of the slices over cottonwood racks for the blessing of the sun. Warriors and hunters loafed, smoked, gambled, joked, snatched bits of meat to chew, and enjoyed the late afternoon. Whetstones, thought Elkanah. He'd make whetstones and ease this labor.

Tomorrow and maybe the next two or three days, these people would be much too busy to examine his wares, study his ready-made lodgecover, finger his remaining arrow points, axes, kettles, saws, hatchets, bolts of cloth, thick blankets, and the rest. Percy would scribble. Cobb could study the warriors and their fierce ways of war. Betsy could paint. Danzig had whole cliffs of weathering sandstone to probe for fossils. Working with his pocket watch, which he'd set to the riverboat's chronometer at Fort Union, he found that noon at this location came two hours and twelve minutes later than noon at Washington, D.C. In each hour, the earth turns fifteen degrees of longitude, and in each four minutes of time the earth spins an additional degree. Thus they were thirty-three degrees west of Washington City; one hundred-ten degrees west of a prime meridian running through the Royal Observatory at Greenwich, England. Elkanah grinned. He measured it as twelve or thirteen hundred miles from the farthest edge of civilization.

Barnaby Skye came all awake at once in the blackness of the lodge. The preternatural quietness had jolted him awake. His mind cleared swiftly, and he listened for Jawbone's warning mutter or shriek, but heard nothing. Through the smoke hole above, a few stars winked in a clear moonless night. He sat up in his robes, senses tingling. Victoria sat up with him, listening, but Mary and the child slept peacefully. Kills Dog Woman didn't stir. He could see none of them.

The silence itself had awakened him. The whole night had been alive with the eerie howl of carnivores feasting on the heap of buffalo a little to the east. They'd heard the throaty howl of wolves inviting their brothers to feast; yapping of coyotes, the scream of foxes—now all gone silent. One thing—no, two—might do that. A grizzly at the carrion, lord of the wilds, whose very presence chilled every living creature around. Several times, Mister Skye had experienced a sudden silence, when bird songs caught in their throats and the shimmer and rustle of forests ceased, and even wind seemed stilled. That meant Old Ephriam lumbered near with small weak eyes, vicious temper, and claws that could shred any creature in moments. Maybe a grizzly had found carrion. Or maybe Tortu. Fresh, still-warm liver for the stalker, boudins, hump meat to take somewhere else and roast over a tiny smokeless fire.

In the blackness Mister Skye found moccasins and pulled them on, and buckled his heavy belt with its holstered and sheathed burdens.

"Son of a bitch, Tortu," muttered Victoria. "You go kill him now. He is rabid, like a bad wolf." She paused. "You kill him first. I want you to come back. You be careful, Mister Skye."

Her fear reached him. Rarely did she admonish or caution, but now her terror spilled from every taut word. "I don't know why that Harvey sent him. If he hurt you, if he send you to spirit land, I'm gonna kill him back. He don't see an old squaw with a knife."

Her crabby love reached him, and he drew the taut old woman into his arms and hugged her. She hugged back ferociously. "You be careful, Mister Skye. He got bad medicine, lots of it. Baddest man there ever was. You come back to hug your old Victoria. I'll fix you good hump ribs and make a new elkskin shirt. . . ."

"I don't know what's in Harvey's craw either," he muttered. "It's been nine years since I booted him out of the fur company. And if I hadn't done it, Alec Culbertson would have."

"Maybe these people. Maybe this maker of things, Morse."

"Maybe," Mister Skye agreed, thinking of Alex Harvey's suspicious mind, seeing threats where there were none.

"I'll come with you now."

"Stalking has to be done alone, Victoria. You'd best watch over our lodge and the two tents."

"I got a bad feeling. Tortu's bad medicine. Has the medicine power of hydrophobia and wolf. Never so bad."

The old woman's nervous outpouring troubled him. He'd never heard her worry so much. He pulled open the door flap and peered cautiously into an inky night with not even a sliver of moon. And yet, some sort of light shimmered, an eerie green that undulated and wobbled and made shadows writhe on the black ground. The eerie light triggered alarm in him. He'd never known such a thing, as if heaven had released every soul trapped between heaven and hell, and now they all danced. He spotted Jawbone, ears laid back in the weird light, head up but not sounding alarms. Good. Victoria knew Jawbone's language.

His senses screamed. He peered hard at shadows, at the quiet prim tents of Morse's party. He padded softly past wavering cottonwoods, alive with the greenish light, padded lightly through quivering bunch grass toward the great black pile of carrion. Things passed him, soft as a feather. Creatures with sharp teeth slinked his way, giving him wide berth. Quietness clamped down on the night like plague. Had he been wrong to leave Victoria and Mary and the child? Would a cruel killer strike swiftly, killing all that he loved in a few silent slashes? Would the killer murder a great entrepreneur, a genius, in his bed, and exterminate a brilliant scholar, a captain, and Connaught as well? Plunge a cold knife into bright, bold Betsy's breast?

He felt the silence thicken as he approached the black mound. He smelled no bear. Abruptly, fear crawling in him, he retreated and padded almost back to the Gros Ventre village. There he cut north to the dark bluff and scaled a steep watercourse until, puffing hard, he stood on the rim of sandstone and beheld a night alive above the prairies.

Across the whole northern quarter of the heavens, curtains of wavering green light plunged and erupted, fountains of weird light, mostly green, but sometimes phosphorescently yellow or pink, the color of long-bruised flesh. Northern lights. He'd never seen such a frightful display of them, a heaven gone mad and devouring stars, devil's light turning the earth to dancing jelly.

Swiftly he padded east across open prairie, up a small cuesta that angled northwest, down its rock-strewn far side—it formed a natural wall to funnel buffalo toward the rim—and then, warily, toward the lip of the buffalo jump. He crept on to its other side, where scrub pine grew and their shadows quivered in the phosphorescent light. There, in the rock and pine, he peered down over the edge, into the shadowed mass of dead buffalo below, where the northern lights didn't reach. Slowly he studied every night form. Nothing. But something stalked there.

"Tortu!" he said in a silky, carrying voice. "Go back to Harvey. Tell Harvey to forget it. A long time has passed. The people I'm guiding mean him no harm. Go now, or meet your fate."

He slid sideways to new shadow, not wanting to be where his voice had risen. Nothing. He peered sharply about him. The wavering light made it tricky. Every shadow undulated, multiplying Tortu by a thousand.

Some violent thing hissed by and shattered on sandstone a few feet ahead. Arrow! From up here! He rolled violently, finding cover behind jagged sandstone rimrock. Another thing slapped rock, this time inches from his face. Now he sweated. Tortu stalked, but the wavering green light hid the stalker. Mister Skye felt his heart trip, the pulse so loud in his ears that it surely reached Tortu's. Arrows in the green night. Bad medicine, bad as Victoria had feared. He lay still. To crawl would be to die. His elkskins blended with the sandstone, and his head pressed deep into the grasses. But he inched his arm down to his dragoon revolver until he gripped it. In that position he waited, his nerves screaming. Time ticked, and the weird light faded back into blackness until he could scarcely see a few feet ahead of him.

The voice lifted from somewhere in the blackness of the jackpine. "Ah, Monsieur Skye! So it is a standoff tonight, eh? Too black now. The lights of the north died before you did!"

"Tortu! What does Harvey want?"

A weird chuckle drifted back, from a different locale. "Why should I say, eh? You want to know why you die, *oui*?"

Mister Skye remained silent. Tortu seemed inclined to talk.

"Harvey, he don' care about old times. He's making much more as the opposition. American Fur pay him a little. But now, he's—how you say?—a principal. Naw . . . he wants dead the man Morse—*mort*! Morse *mort*!"

Mister Skye waited in the blackness, alert for the slightest shadow against the stars. The metal of his revolver wouldn't shine now, with the liverish light gone. He slid it out and pointed where last Tortu's voice had floated over the cold air to him.

Nothing. Tortu said nothing. Mister Skye wondered what Harvey, Primeau and Company had against Elkanah Morse. Why they'd sent an assassin to kill the businessman. He had no answer, and he wasn't about to speak up again. An endless time slid by, and Mister Skye felt bone-cold in the freezing night. But still he lay rooted to the spot, relatively safe in the sandstone cleft, every sense alert. Vision came with gray dawnlight, and still Mister Skye lay quietly, feeling his life at stake. Gray gave way to color, gray sky and grass and trees turning pastel blue and dun and jade. He lifted an arm and waved it. Nothing. At last, with a blinding sun creeping over the east horizon, he sat up. Still nothing. He stood, stretched, pumped life into locked muscle, and padded back to camp.

Victoria stared at him sharply, more angry than relieved.

"You scare me bad," she muttered, turning her head aside. "How come you stay away all night?"

He saw wetness rimming her crabbed old eyes. Mary, who was feeding his boy, Dirk, looked up at him solemnly, anguish in her eyes, too. They'd been sharing their fears, he knew.

"He had me pinned. Better eyes than mine," Mister Skye said quietly. "I never got a shot. Never even saw him. But he talked a little. He's after Morse, and I haven't the faintest inkling why."

Chapter 11

The terrible death of so many buffalo darkened Betsy Morse's spirit. She had witnessed something too brutal to fathom, and the memory seared her mind. Of course animals were slaughtered for meat. But in the East she'd been insulated from it, and in any case the throat-cutting of a single cow or ox seemed different in its very nature from this violence she'd observed.

This wild land frightened her now, though she hadn't started the trip with Elkanah harboring fear. In the space of hours she'd seen a woman rescued from ritual torture and death; seen a mad assassin shoot at their guide, Mister Skye. The importance of order and a policing hand and punishment of crime dawned on her. She had taken them all for granted in civilized Lowell. If someone stole or murdered, why, punish him! But here . . .

She hastened back to their tents, glad that Arabella hadn't witnessed the buffalo hurtling to their doom. She wanted only to rest quietly until the searing images left her. Perhaps then she'd set up her easel and paint. How the tribesmen—especially the children—loved to watch! But there at their camp at the edge of the Gros Ventre village, the tortured Flathead squaw, Kills Dog Woman, sat quietly before Mister Skye's lodge, beside Mary and the child, Dirk. The woman's face remained a ghastly ruin, her nose blistered and swollen, arms pitted with vicious suppurating pockets of burnt flesh, feet swollen and blistered so badly the woman couldn't stand on them.

And yet, she noticed, the Gros Ventre paid the woman no attention. Hours before, their warriors had started to torture her to death. Now the woman belonged to Mister Skye, and she had ceased to exist, even as a curiosity, to the Gros Ventre. Betsy's heart tugged, and she sat down beside the Flathead woman and smiled, unwilling to touch her tormented flesh.

Mary sat quietly, sewing a new sole on a worn moccasin, using an awl and sinew.

"Perhaps you could tell me, Mrs. Skye—is the Flathead woman comfortable?"

"You bet. Soon she'll be fine."

"But isn't she—afraid? These are the very people who tortured her!"

Mary shrugged. "No. They be enemies of Flatheads—Crow and Shoshone, too. She gets caught, she expects it.

If the Flatheads catch the Atsina, the Gros Ventre, maybe they torture the Atsina squaw. This one, she wasn't very brave. She wept and cried and screamed, so they did it slow. After burning, they'd slice off little bits of skin, make as much hurt as they could but not kill her. If she didn't say nothing, just stood quiet, they'd kill her quick, honor her medicine."

Betsy tried to digest all that, but the very ideas repelled her. She gazed gently at the impassive woman, who was dressed in a loose orange calico shift that lay lightly on tortured flesh, and felt pity.

"Mrs. Skye, would you ask her if I can help—I could whip up a new dress in no time, very light cloth. . . ."

"Hard to make Flathead words." But Mary muttered at the woman, her fingers gesticulating.

The woman replied through lips too swollen to speak.

"Maybe later. You make a dress and maybe she becomes your slave. She thinks that's a good idea. Take her with you back to your home in the East. Maybe good medicine."

Betsy sighed. Some instinct warned her not to say no to this or express her dismay. "She'd be a fine helper, I'm sure," Betsy said. Mary seemed satisfied with that and translated it. Kills Dog Woman managed a smile through puffed lips.

On a nearby gray cottonwood log, Percy Connaught scribbled furiously in his two journals. He had the red-bound one open now—the one he would publish for ordinary people. No doubt he was describing the killing of the buffalo in language as florid as he could muster, Betsy thought. And no doubt he would not mention that through it all, he was on hands and knees vomiting! She laughed suddenly, some of the horror of the day sliding away.

Rudolpho Danzig rummaged through one of the panniers near his tent and pulled out his daguerreotyping apparatus. A strange device, Betsy thought. He set up a wooden tripod with telescoping legs that he anchored in place. On this he attached a curious box with black bellows and a spyglass lens in front. Well, she thought, what on earth would he make an image of?

He approached the women diffidently, his warm eyes resting gently on Kills Dog Woman. To Mary he said, "I'd like to make an image of the Flathead woman."

"But why on earth now!" Betsy exclaimed. "Wait until she's healed. I imagine she'll be rather pretty."

"Ah, Betsy, that's the point. I wish to record the life of the tribesmen as it is, for my colleagues who are ethnologists. The picture of the tortured flesh would be most impressive. . . . But of course, if this is an affront—"

Mary eyed the apparatus suspiciously. Rudolpho turned to her. "This makes an image, like a painting. Like Betsy's watercolors, but faster. In just an instant. I'd like to make an image of Kills Dog Woman. No harm will come of it."

Mary tried to convey all that to the injured woman, who finally shrugged and muttered something.

"She says she is a slave and awaits her fate."

Betsy's spirits sagged. What strange people! But Danzig nodded and pointed his contraption at Kills Dog Woman, and then vanished under a black velvet hood.

"Ah!" exclaimed the Flathead at the peculiar sight. A white man wiggling around under a black hood in bright sunlight. "Ah!"

Something clicked. The eye blinked. Danzig emerged, beaming, with a rectangular thing in hand, and vanished into his tent. Betsy waited, wondering what these squaws would say. Her whole family had been daguerreotyped, and now the lovely images in oval frames rested on Elkanah's polished walnut desk at home. Betsy had been astonished that hers had come out so well. But not so well as a good color portrait, she thought. Those black and silver images lacked life compared to her clear, transparent watercolors splashed gaily on good absorbent paper.

Danzig's image making had caught Percy's attention too, and he scribbled that into his red-bound journal while Danzig fussed inside his tent. Betsy thought to have Danzig make images of Arabella and Elkanah, too, mementos of this astonishing adventure, but Arabella had vanished. Oh, yes, she was strolling with Captain Cobb. A good thing, Betsy thought. At last Arabella had found someone to talk to. Ever since she'd befriended Cobb, Arabella had become almost amiable. Or at least less sulky.

At last the slim professor emerged from his tent, carrying a thin copper plate. He knelt before Kills Dog Woman and showed her the silver and black image on it, an image of herself, blistered and wounded.

"Aiee!" wailed the woman, startled. She peered at the image and lifted a swollen, blistered hand to touch her puffed cheeks. Her tormented eyes darted to the daguerreotype and then to the dress she wore, and she wailed.

"Bad medicine," said Mary solemnly. "You have stolen her spirit and made it evil."

Betsy peered at the image. The likeness was perfect, but shocking. The wounds had become black blotches, and the grotesque swelling of her face had become monstrous on the plate. "Oh, dear, Rudolpho. I think this was a mistake!"

"I fear so," he said contritely. "I was most callous, and now I've done some black magic. So much for science and knowledge! How can I make it up?"

Betsy turned to Mary, but Mister Skye's squaw wasn't following the drift of it.

"Mary," he said gently. "I have injured her, and wish to express my apologies but don't know how. May I give her something according to the traditions of her people?"

Betsy watched Mister Skye's beautiful dusky wife frown silently. What a golden beauty! she thought, a bit enviously.

Mary tried again to convey something of Danzig's feelings to the Flathead woman, but ended up shaking her head.

"She says the bad medicine is because she is now a slave."

"Ah—Mrs. Skye. Tell her I will make her a good-medicine image of her. When she is healed, I'll make an image that will show her beauty, her virtue, her—strength!"

When that was conveyed, Kills Dog Woman smiled.

"Professor, would you make an image of Mrs. Danzig in such condition?" asked Betsy.

"Why—I don't believe so."

"Well," Betsy said triumphantly, "Kills Dog Woman feels just the same way!"

"I am duly chastened," said Professor Danzig. "Do you suppose old Chief Horse Medicine might sit for a portrait?"

"Let's find out!" said Betsy. "You'll either be a sensation or they'll torture you to death!"

Jarvis Cobb helped Arabella up the last steep grade to the top of the amber stone cliff, northwest of the Gros Ventre village. Twice as they puffed their way up, rattlers slithered off, while the city-bred young woman yelped her fear. Below, dog soldiers—the village police—watched them impassively. At the top, on a rough plain dotted with somber green jackpine, they got their wind. But what struck them at once was the view. To the north lay a blue belt of featureless mountains their guide had called the Snowies. Far off to the south, maybe even fifty miles in that crystal air, rose jagged gray peaks with snow still trapped in the north crevasses, a range called the Crazies. Still others lay blurred on distant dun horizons.

"It's beautiful, Jarvis . . . but I cherish smaller vistas, green canopies, tea and tarts in our side yard in Lowell."

"It's a lovely place," he replied. "Bereft of people we know and cherish. We must make our own companionship here."

"Yes! The wilderness is so stern. I've been writing poetry. Everyone is keeping notes and journals, so I thought I would write, too. My poems keep me from going mad here!"

"I hope you'll share them sometime."

"Oh, would you read them? But I must see whether they'll embarrass me first."

The slim maiden before him looked, if not beautiful, uncommonly pleasant, and everything about her had been enhanced by costly clothing that fit her lovely form to perfection, tantalizing the male eye. With her cheeks flushed from the hard climb and a faint glisten of moisture on her temples, she seemed vibrant to him. Stray locks of glossy brown hair—all the Morses had rich brown hair—fell over her forehead in enchanting disarray.

He sighed. Honor raised its firm barrier. To violate it would stain his career, offend his host, lead to endless difficulties. She flirted and more; she teased and toyed and aroused. They waded one day at a creek, and she had lifted her skirts high, flashing visions of trim ankles and calves, knees and thighs. She'd had every advantage of education, grooming, training in the women's virtues, and all these dazzled him, and no doubt a long procession of beaux. Each day they'd wandered off to some private bower and hugged, and the hugs had ceased to be merely affectionate. Each day they'd come closer to a brink, but hadn't fallen over it. So far. But just being here away from prying eyes would tempt fate again.

"You're ravishing, Arabella," he said, almost involuntarily.

She smiled gently. "It's so grand to have a dear friend. I would die here in this awful place without someone to cling to," she replied.

He wanted to cling and dreaded it. Something about this wilderness over two thousand miles from his home and family had loosened bonds, commitments, ties. He could scarcely conjure up a vision of his Susannah, or his boy Peter. Some savage force severed the threads, one by one, crumbling promises. He cringed at it and yet welcomed it, heart pounding, drawn ever closer, each day, to the time of no turning back. Even now she stood before him smiling brightly, soft lips parted, eyes shining instead of pouty.

"I'm rested; let's walk," she said, waltzing toward the somber copse of gnarled ponderosa and juniper piercing out of the crannies of broken dun sandstone. He trotted after her, scarcely keeping up with her rushing strides toward a new bower deep within the pines.

They plunged into dappled shade, surrounded by yellow-barked pines with long needles. They treaded down a long gentle slope covered with brown needles, into a bowl that emptied over the bluffs they'd scaled. She pushed ahead, aiming toward a ledge of lichen-covered stone that formed a natural seat in a sunny place. She'd done it again, he thought restlessly—found a very private bower for them to dally in, surrounded by curtains of needles as opaque as bedroom doors.

"What a place to rest!" she exclaimed. "See how secret it is! This is where friends can share the things in their hearts and souls. Tell me what's in your soul right now."

She sat down, leaning back on her arms until the polished tan cotton of her dress strained over her bosom. She waited quietly, her large shining eyes intent on him, wanting confessions and intimacies.

"Why"—he said hoarsely—"I am missing my Susannah. It's been so many months now. My family. My little cottage. My fine staff position . . ."

"You must miss her embrace."

"Oh, I do. A great sweetness. A great tenderness."

Arabella sighed. "I sometimes can't bear being a maiden and unembraced. But of course I must be patient."

"Yes, be patient. Be patient, Arabella. You'll find just the right gentleman for you."

"I don't know that I want a gentleman. This wild land does strange things to me. Naked Indians. Blood. Life and death in the raw. I fear it's making me half-savage myself."

"There's honor, Arabella. One of the things a good officer tries always to live up to—at the Point we encourage duty, honor, country."

She laughed wildly. "Honor," she said, and giggled.

It seemed time to turn conversation away from these dangerous things. Why was it, every time they strolled, they ended up at the very brink? How weak he was! He let her lead him toward forbidden things each time, as fascinated and hungry as she, as probing and eager as she. He glanced into her face, and found her wide eyes intent upon him.

"Arabella, let's talk of other things," he said quietly. "We may be alone and unchaperoned and free and two thousand miles from our friends, but what could happen here might lead to our ruin, your shame, and my disgrace, divorce, the end of my happy posting as a teacher and scholar at the academy, ostracism for us both. . . ."

"I know." She sighed softly. "I don't mean to violate honor and I'm sure you don't. I only am curious about things I—haven't experienced, and the wilderness drives me."

"Then let us be friends, comrades of the soul and mind," he said, relieved.

"Yes, let's."

They sat quietly side by side, sunning.

"It's so private here," she said. "There's not a view anywhere, only the trees. Tell me what it's like to be a soldier. To be someone called upon to shoot human beings if necessary."

"I'm not really that kind—the army has all sorts of people, and my work is scholarly, really."

"You research better ways to shoot people," she said saucily.

He winced. "If the army didn't exist, would you feel safe?"

"No, of course not. Lots of people want Daddy's money and factories. I suppose lots of countries would like to possess ours."

"But that's only one view of it," he rejoined. "What if the army exists to help take land and possessions away from other people—these Gros Ventres, for example."

"You sound like you're speaking against your own army."

He shrugged. "I'm a realist. Manifest Destiny is making

this whole continent—its central area at least—the property of the Republic. My army will soon be corralling these tribes, one by one. My task in the field of intelligence is to learn how to do it efficiently and without bloodshed."

"I suppose it's going to happen. But I hope not for a long time. This land is just right for these savages, and I can scarcely imagine whites living here. They'd turn savage because the land would make them savage."

"The key is buffalo," he said quietly. "The army doesn't need to wage war at all."

She seemed bored, and they lapsed into silence again. Mountain bluebirds flitted boldly from branch to branch around them, splashes of color.

"Would you hold me again?" she asked shyly.

"I'm afraid to, Arabella."

"I know. I'm afraid, too. But we can still be friends of the soul and mind if you hold me. I just—this wild land stirs up some need, is all."

"Honor," he said quietly.

"I know. But hold me gently anyway."

He knew he would. His heart tripped with the mounting hunger that galvanized him. "All right. Just for a moment, Arabella. Then we must let go."

She stood and faced him, her gaze intense, her wavy fine hair tumbling loose about her face. She smiled and still he hesitated, feeling out of control, not wanting to stand, not wanting her to experience his desire. But slowly he stood, drawn up by some relentless force larger than his will. She glanced briefly at him, with quick intake of breath, and they slid arms about each other softly, not pressing, a last crumbling barrier still between them.

Then they pulled each other desperately close and he felt

her melting into him, felt her loins molding to his own thickening desire, felt her breast upon his.

"Oh! Jarvis!" she whispered, and kissed his lips with her own parted ones. He returned the kiss furiously, finding her lips sweet, touching her tongue with his. He kissed her lips and eyes, kissed her nose and throat, drew the fine hair away from her ears and kissed them, kissed the cotton fabric over her breasts, felt her hands slide down to his buttocks and draw him tighter to her, felt her arching her own inviting loins against his throbbing.

"Stop! We must stop, Arabella!" he cried.

"*Non!* Eet is ver' entertaining. Don' stop."

Jarvis felt the shock of terror pierce his lust. He whirled. Arabella gasped, withdrew, pulled down high-hiked skirts.

"What a pity. Ver' pleasant to watch," said a cadaverous man with coarse black hair and sallow skin stretched over a skeletal face. One hand held a bow with a nocked arrow; the other rested lightly on the haft of a sheathed bowie knife.

"Tortu," said Jarvis tightly, his own mind a turmoil of fading lust and sudden terror.

"I'm going to take this lady, daughter of Morse. You go back and tell Monsieur Skye, tell Skye and Morse, and then they come out of the village after me to save the mademoiselle."

"I won't go," snapped Arabella.

Tortu laughed wickedly.

She sat down. "Drag me," she said, fear and defiance blazing in her.

"You have no horse, Tortu. I think it's a standoff," said Jarvis. Something of his long training, his own life work and passion, intelligence, began to assert itself even in the midst of his terror. "Tell me, Tortu. Why do you want her?"

"It make my task easy." He glared at Arabella. "Up. Up or taste the blade."

She shook her head, weeping now.

"Who, Tortu? Who do you want? Morse? Skye? And why?"

Tortu gazed at him with hooded black eyes as flat and opaque as a rattler's. "You are full of queries. But it make no good. I am paid to send Monsieur Morse to paradise." He laughed softly. "Ah, paradise, where the spirits float. Who has employed me? Ah, *mon ami*, that is amusing."

"Where'll you take her? What will you do with her?"

Tortu smiled. "Not far. Far enough to choose my . . . ah . . . terrain. Maybe I keel her, *oui*?"

"You've stolen a guest from the village. All the Gros Ventre will swarm after you."

"And the belle Arabella die, *oui*? *Non*."

"And what if Skye doesn't come?"

"The mademoiselle, she is good sport."

"She can't go far on foot."

"Ah, the prick of the knife—what miracles it can perform!"

"What if only Skye comes?"

"Then I kill but one, and the way is open to Morse."

"Morse is wealthy. He could make you rich the rest of your days if you forget this."

"Ah, bribe! Ver' entertaining. But I like to keel. Tortu—the name, a legend of the north. But enough talk. Now you go back to the village. I will leave clear tracks to follow, *oui*?"

"No!" screamed Arabella. She began howling at the top of her voice, a piercing scream that would carry beyond this grove, maybe to the ears of a village dog soldier.

Catlike, he jabbed the glinting blade lightly into her

side, his gaze never leaving Jarvis. She gasped. Red blotted her cotton dress. *"Allons, mademoiselle."*

The pain subdued her. She rose shakily and followed Tortu, her last desperate glance on Jarvis.

He watched until they disappeared into the northwest.

Chapter 12

Jarvis Cobb stopped before them, wild-eyed, running his hand over his high forehead and receding hair.

"Tortu! He took Arabella!"

Mister Skye felt cold dread run through his blood. Elkanah Morse heard it and dashed to the guide's lodge. From her cookstove, Betsy gaped.

"We—were—strolling up the rimrock. He—just— materialized out of nowhere, where the pines are thick."

"Oh, God," breathed Elkanah. Betsy sagged, holding tight to the entrepreneur.

Mister Skye waited, already knowing.

The captain got his breath and gradually composed himself into a military officer. "He had a bow and arrow, and a knife at hand. He made Arabella go with him. He told me to go back and tell you. . . ."

"Wants us to follow."

"Yes. Said he'd leave tracks. He wants to suck you out of the village and kill you."

"What else, Mister Cobb? Why did you stray so far from the village when you knew—"

"The view!" he cried. "We climbed up to see—to see the Crazy Mountains and the Snowies. . . ."

Cobb seemed peculiarly flustered. "I was able to ask—to gather some intelligence. He's—threatening to kill her if you don't come. He's—really after Elkanah, not you, but sees you as a barrier. He . . . wouldn't say who employs him or why. He's on foot, can't go far; can't haul Arabella far. When she—she refused to follow, he pricked her—pricked her with a big knife."

"Oh!" cried Betsy. Elkanah looked ashen. "Oh, dear Arabella," she wept.

"I offered a reward—a bribe—for him to lay off, but he just laughed."

"What did he say to the offer?" Mister Skye asked thoughtfully.

"He said he likes to kill. Likes to be a legend, a terror, in the northwest."

"You're not telling us everything, Cobb," said Mister Skye.

"I swear that's it. I wasn't expecting—wasn't even armed with a revolver."

"Your mind was upon other things, perhaps," said Mister Skye. "As an army officer, surely you know better. Unarmed. Taking a young woman beyond—"

"I know, I know!" he cried. "I am in torment!"

"We have no choice but to go after her and try to trick or overwhelm him, Mister Skye," said Elkanah quietly.

Mister Skye shook his head. "No, mate. This isn't something for you. I'd be pulling an arrow out of your chest in minutes. I want you and Betsy to stay here." He stared at the others, who had gathered around. "Mister Danzig, Mister Connaught. Please guard the camp. Captain Cobb will stay here as well, guarding the Morses. For the moment, say nothing to our hosts. In fact, Elkanah, if you can summon the courage, I'd be pleased to see you begin your presentation to them—your trade show. Their buffler cutting and hide fleshing's slowing down now."

"I couldn't possibly do that, sir."

"Very well, mate."

He nodded to Victoria and Mary and began to saddle Jawbone. Behind him Betsy wept, and the others gaped silently. Danzig finally galvanized himself into action and found rifles for them all.

Mister Skye slid his sheathed Hawken over the saddle, checked the loads on his dragoon Colt—the caps were all seated—and clambered on Jawbone, waiting. It took Victoria longer to fetch her pony, which had been grazing in the Musselshell River brush. She anchored a small pad saddle over her bay pony and the sheath containing her old fusil. Over her shoulder hung her quiver and unstrung bow. She glanced at him solemnly, a small taut aging Crow woman perched lightly. Mister Skye loved her in that moment.

"What are the chances we'll—see Arabella alive?" asked Elkanah hoarsely.

"Pray," said Mister Skye.

"I'd like to go. I think I could offer money—enough—"

"Tortu doesn't care about money." He turned to Cobb. "Where do we pick up the trail, Mister Cobb?"

"Climb the bluff west of the village—there's only one way. Walk west. Continue into a ponderosa pine grove— a thick one sloping down into a hollow. . . ."

"Some view, Mister Cobb. All right then."

They walked leisurely through the village. The squaws paused in their labor to stare, and to summon children away from the terrible medicine horse, Jawbone. They walked through quiet space, the village opening silently and closing behind them. They passed the lodge of the war chief, White Beaver, who sat smoking before his tipi, watching them intently.

"Hunting," Mister Skye said with his fingers.

An odd thing to do with a village groaning under buffler meat, he knew. But all Indians honored whim. The chief nodded amiably.

"How you do this?" asked Victoria irritably. "Maybe we both die for those people. Tortu stalks and they go for a walk."

In truth, he didn't know how. He was going by invitation, with ambush in Tortu's mind. Going because he had to. Cobb had gathered some useful information, at least. No horse. On foot—well, maybe. It'd be easy enough for Tortu to snatch a couple of Gros Ventre ponies. He could do it even under the watchful eye of the youths herding the ponies. No one could stalk so invisibly as Tortu. . . .

Why? How? Where? He might never catch Tortu. He might find Arabella with a slit throat, a simple pawn to draw him away from the village. Or he might find her— violated, demented . . . Cobb should have had more sense. He'd acted as if he didn't understand about these wilds, as if the quiet sunbaked plains were as safe as the streets around West Point. . . .

Put him out of mind. What Cobb did or failed to do didn't matter. Tortu mattered. . . . And a plan to outwit the craftiest and most dangerous killer he knew of.

He found a steep watercourse breaking the dun cliff and rode cautiously up, feeling Jawbone gather muscle under him to spring up the crumbling rock and over clinging juniper. Behind him Victoria followed. Three of them— Skye, Victoria, Jawbone—against one. That'd help. But Tortu had a hostage, a living shield to prevent shooting, to prevent even aiming. Mister Skye sighed. He probably would disappoint Elkanah and Betsy. This trip among the far tribes would probably come to a bitter end today.

The view above was stunning. Cobb had that right at least. To the west lay the wooded hollow, densely covered, a place with no view at all, neither in nor out. A place to hide, Mister Skye thought, and with the thought came some inkling of how it might be between Cobb and Arabella.

He reined Jawbone lightly. The forested slope loomed darkly ahead, and a rifle poking from any shadowed pine within it would be invisible to him. Jawbone minced, feeling the guide's tension. Jawbone knew; he always knew, and his ears pricked forward and his nose sniffed high, bobbed, sniffed, and pointed. He'd picked up man scent in the woods island on this vast prairie.

The woods covered a dished depression that emptied over the bluff and into the Musselshell. Open prairie lay around it. He turned Jawbone north, steering around the woods. He'd try to pick up a trail on the far side. Northwest, Cobb had said. Intelligence. Observant officer. Give him credit for that. Victoria followed quietly. She rarely spoke in tight moments, but always knew what to do, often better than he knew. They circled the dark woods, always out of rifle shot, and studied the open prairie as well. Tortu was famous for rising up out of nothing, a place of no cover, a place that might seem as safe as the slope of a field outside of London.

Mister Skye grew desperate for want of a plan, but he couldn't think of a thing. He'd simply been invited to his own death, and he had to go or lose Miss Arabella. North of the copse he'd realized the sun had sunk low, and the late August chill had already pierced into his buckskins. Arabella would be spending a bitterly cold night—if she lived. Tortu might just slit her throat and wait, free of any encumbrance.

Twilight was always the most dangerous—a time when stalkers stalked invisibly, hidden by tricky light. This twilight would be no different. It might also obscure the trail, but Tortu didn't want that. He wanted to lead his prey to the slaughtering place. Off to the west, the plunging sun sank behind a purple cloud bank turning the heavens amethyst, jade, and pink. A band of ocean green lay along the horizon, reminding Mister Skye of the high seas he knew so well. The western flanks of the mountains flamed yellow, while the eastern slopes turned indigo. Beneath his feet, the grass glowed burgundy and rose. He'd rarely seen such a sunset.

They found the light tracks of two unshod horses in a dusty patch on the far west side of the grove, two or three miles west of the Gros Ventre village. Tortu had deliberately steered the horses into the dry dusty area. And for good measure, Tortu had dropped a strip of tan cotton cloth—a mocking signal. The tracks headed straight into the sunset, west by northwest, across an utterly empty land, with scarcely a slope or ridge to distinguish it. So it would be like that, he thought. The thing Tortu did best.

He reined Jawbone, feeling a prickle of fear, even though Jawbone sent him no signals. Victoria reined beside him.

"Son of a bitch!" she said crossly.

In minutes the path ahead would thicken into a purple murk. He studied it, seeing nothing but sensing murder. Beneath him Jawbone stood rigid, not even swishing his tail, turning the horse and man into sunset-splashed statues.

No, he thought. Why do what Tortu wanted? He dreaded

what they'd say in camp when he returned without Miss Arabella.

"We'll go back," he said. "If he kills her, he's lost his chance to draw Morse—and me—out of the village."

They rode quietly back, around the forested area, and finally down the cliff to the Musselshell valley. The fragrance of buffalo ribs broiling struck them. In the village an idea struck him.

"Victoria," he said quietly, "let the Morses know I've returned temporarily, and that we followed a clear trail of two unshod ponies."

She glared at him. "Dogs fight dogs," she snapped.

He grinned. She rode toward the Skye camp in the east edge of the village. He turned Jawbone toward White Beaver's lodge, dismounted, and scratched softly on the door flap. Light shone translucently through the amber lodge-cover. A massive square-faced squaw invited him in.

He settled in the guest's place proffered him. The war chief, who wore only breechclout and leggins, seated himself in his proper place, his powerful torso and shoulders glinting in the tiny fire. He offered no pipe. Mister Skye and his entourage were scarcely friends of the Gros Ventre.

Mister Skye regretted that he had only his hands and arms to convey meaning. The sign language of the plains was crude and failed to convey detail. Still, he would try. It took a long time, hands whirling, an occasional word, Tortu. Arabella. White Beaver knew Tortu. What northern Indian didn't? Knew Harvey, too. At the news of the abduction, White Beaver frowned. Stealing a guest from the protection of his people? Ah, there was war. And where were this Tortu and the woman?

Hovering close, northwest, mocking. The guide said nothing, letting the whole story run through White Beaver's mind.

Why does Tortu do this to your people? he asked, fingers flashing.

We don't know. Could be many reasons. Morse makes the trade goods stocked by the trading posts, both American Fur and the opposition.

White Beaver reached above him and lifted a sheathed medicine pipe from a hook on a lodgepole. They smoked quietly. The evening raced by. Darkness settled on the village. The war chief seemed lost in thought. At last he signaled. This is a great wrong done to the village of Horse Medicine. I, the war chief, will lead our warriors this very night. Tortu might hide from white eyes, but not from the eyes of the People. We will kill him and bring the girl. You will not come—my medicine says we must do it, avenge the wrong done this village. I will gather every warrior, young and old, ten times the fingers of my hands, and we will kill Tortu. Go to your camp and wait.

I'd like to question Tortu—find out reasons, the guide replied with his fingers.

White Beaver frowned. We will try to bring Tortu here alive, he replied. And shrugged. The gesture dismissed Mister Skye. He stood, nodded, and slipped into the icy night. Even as Mister Skye rode back to camp, he heard the town criers quietly summoning warriors from their lodges. Within a few minutes, something like a hundred of them would be mounted and begin a vast infiltration of the prairie where Tortu lurked. This one would be beyond his ability to solve himself, he thought, glad he'd recognized it. He'd bloody well learned to be humble in this wilderness—be humble or die. What would he prove, riding out to rescue a maiden in man-to-man combat, like some Arthurian knight? He was no knight, and here no rules, no fairness, governed the way men warred. Why did he always take battle so personally? Was it some male pride in him? They'd think ill of him in camp, turning the task over to the village. Coward, they'd think—Connaught especially. Well, they bloody well could think what they would. He smelled frost in the eddying air, and would be glad of the fire in his small lodge.

They heard him coming and waited quietly in the night. He dismounted, slid the saddle and bridle off Jawbone, and turned the ugly blue loose to graze.

"It's a tribal matter, Elkanah. Every warrior in the village is mounting up right now. Abducting a guest of the village is a mortal insult to them. Think what you will—it's the one way to fetch Miss Arabella back. She's safe enough, I think. Wouldn't be if Tortu killed me. We'll have to sit and wait."

"You're not even going?" asked Connaught disdainfully.

Mister Skye fixed his gaze on the man. "Say it, Mister Connaught. Say what you think—that I'm too cowardly to go at this alone."

"Why, I—well, yes. You're the vaunted guide, a white man, too. This conduct is, well—"

"I think Mister Skye is doing the right thing," broke in Elkanah firmly. "We must wait. This wilderness and its tribes do things in ways we would be wise to understand. Don't you agree, Jarvis? Rudolpho?"

"Of course," said Jarvis. "What better safety for Miss Arabella than a hundred dusky warriors swarming through the dark?"

"Keep your guard up, mates. With every warrior out of the village, nothing keeps Tortu from coming here. I'd suggest lights out in your tents and patience. We may not know anything until morning."

"Oh, Mister Skye, thank you for doing what you could," said Betsy. "We trust your judgment. You've lived here and we haven't. If our dear child can be made safe and this strange threat to us, to you, ended this way, why . . ."

"We'll give this village gifts," cried Elkanah.

Mister Skye nodded. "Tell me again, Elkanah. Has the opposition company any reason to hold a grudge? Have you treated them differently from American Fur?"

"No . . . Well, maybe. We offer volume discounts. American Fur's orders of trade goods are larger, and qualify for larger discounts. But that's scarcely reason to send an assassin . . . or kidnap my innocent daughter."

"Doesn't make sense," Mister Skye agreed. "But someone wants you dead for some reason. And this wild land is a perfect place for it to happen."

With that they adjourned sadly into their tents and lodges to wait while the desolate night slowly passed. The village lay quiet in the frosty night, with only the dog soldiers present to protect it from wolves of all descriptions. Mister Skye sat in his dark, warm lodge, playing with his little tyke, Dirk. An odd name to these Yankees, but a British one he'd always liked. Scarcely a Dirk in this American republic. His women sat quietly through the somber night. None of them could sleep. He feared for the lively, bright, spoiled young woman. His reputation as a guide who could get his clients past any peril of the West hung in the balance here, and it lay in the hands of tribesmen who had been enemies of the fur trappers, enemies of his wives' tribes. He didn't like it. But his every instinct told him that Tortu would be more than a match for him.

He peered out of his lodgeflap into the blackness and

eventually made out Cobb, who sat with his back to a cottonwood, holding a fowling piece. A soldier faithfully at guard. Good enough. Cobb and Jawbone made a formidable force against an intruder.

Midnight passed according to Mister Skye's reckoning, and a bit later the heavy thud of hooves reached him, the sound of returning warriors. Muffled cries. Harsh commands. By the time the horses and warriors had arrayed themselves before Mister Skye's camp, every person there had bounded out of a tent or lodge and stood waiting, dreading.

Mister Skye made out White Beaver on a white medicine stallion, and sitting behind him, skirts hiked high, rode Arabella.

"Oh, dear!" exclaimed Betsy. "Oh, thank God! Oh, Arabella!"

The warrior lifted the young woman easily and set her on earth before her parents, who hugged her.

"It was awful, Daddy. What a pig! He stabbed me a bit to make me docile. And then he put me on a horse and we rode to a place where he waited—he called it a buffalo wallow. Just mud and smell."

"Where is he? Is he dead?" cried Elkanah.

But Arabella was sobbing, pent-up terror flooding out of her. "Pig, pig, pig, pig," she sobbed.

At last, Elkanah turned to Mister Skye. "Please tell them we are grateful. Please tell them I have gifts—much of what I brought—for them in the morning."

"Hard to make finger sign in the night, mate. You get her story. I'll walk back to White Beaver's lodge and get his story by the firelight, where we can see each other."

Mister Skye trudged wearily toward the war chief's lodge, more tired than he thought he'd ever been. There before the lodge lay a dark hulk, a human being on his side. In the soft light radiating from the skin covering, he saw Tortu—and an arrow protruding clear through his belly. It had entered from the rear, and its metal trade point projected through his buckskin britches in front, dark with blood.

The assassin breathed raggedly, wheezing. "Ah . . . Skye . . ." he said, coughing. "You are coward. Afraid of Tortu . . ."

Mister Skye knelt down to hear the whispered words. "Yes," he said simply. "Afraid is right, mate."

Tortu grinned, wheezing. "So I am more man. Tortu, you send the whole village against Tortu."

"Tortu!" said Mister Skye sharply. "Why did Harvey send you? What started this?"

The dying Frenchman laughed, a rattle in his throat. "Not Harvey! He don' know about it. I get employed by St. Louis men, and they say they get money from . . ." The last words mumbled and blurred into a spasm of choking. Tortu's mouth leaked blood. And Tortu died.

Mister Skye stood up slowly. White Beaver and other warriors stood, seeing death slip into their midst. Then the war chief barked something, and warriors hauled the dead man away. He beckoned to Mister Skye to enter the lodge where they could finger-talk in wavering firelight.

Chapter 13

Elkanah stood before the opened panniers, puzzled. "What would be appropriate?" he asked.

"Tobacco. Powder, galena. One of those bolts of cloth if you can spare it. But they don't value material things the way we do. Have Betsy paint his portrait—he'd be truly honored. That or one of Mister Danzig's daguerreotypes."

"Gold?"

Mister Skye hesitated. "Yes, if White Beaver understands it."

Moments later they stood in chill pale sun before White Beaver's lodge and waited. Perhaps they'd come too early, Elkanah thought. He'd noticed that male Indians arose at a late hour and lounged through most days having fun and accomplishing little.

The flap parted, an eye peered out and they waited some more. At last White Beaver's squaw, Hide Scraping Woman, ushered them into the warm, softly lit lodge. A boy slid outside. White Beaver yawned. They had awakened him. He seated them, and slipped outside to the bushes a moment, and returned wider awake.

The guide's fingers flew once again, and Elkanah wondered whether he might invent some way—maybe pictographs—by which these plains tribes could communicate faster. Little cards, the size of playing cards, with lots of pictures—ah, there'd be something to sell them. . . .

Questions and gift giving. They wanted to find out from White Beaver what had happened. Arabella's account of the night was semicoherent. The assassin had prodded her along, leering and laughing, making obscene jokes and threatening to violate her. That much Elkanah had found out. And now he wished to give generous gifts to the war chief. Mister Skye had assured Elkanah that the chief would share them with the others who rescued Arabella.

He watched White Beaver reply, doubting that much real information could be transmitted in such fashion. At last Mister Skye turned to him with the story.

"White Beaver says their best scouts sniffed out Tortu—he stank, it seems—and worked around him. He'd left the buffler wallow and had dragged Arabella back into a gulch. It was White Beaver's arrow that got him. Some of them diverted Tortu in front, and the war chief slid in from the rear. Turned out to be easy."

"You've thanked him?"

"Not exactly a concept like that. But honored him, yes. Gave him your praise. And debt. Told him you're owing him, and had gifts. You can fetch 'em now."

Elkanah ducked out into sunlight and dug into the pannier. He found the bolt of royal blue velveteen, shimmery in the sun. On it he piled the other things, a pound of powder, bar of lead, a spare skillet, ten twists of tobacco. These he carted in and laid before the chief, who grunted, fingered the cloth, and then smiled, saying something unintelligible.

"He's well pleased," said Mister Skye. "Now I'll tell him about Betsy if I can."

In a moment it was arranged. White Beaver would put on his ceremonial dress, bonnet, bearclaw necklace, and sit for Betsy. She'd paint others if she had time. Elkanah would at last show his trade goods and the guide would try to get some reaction to them.

White Beaver dismissed them—he was obviously hungry for breakfast—and Elkanah and the guide led the pack pony back to their camp.

"Mister Morse, before Tortu died he told me Alex Harvey had nothing to do with all this. Tortu was working for someone else."

Elkanah felt puzzled. "This whole thing makes no sense at all," he muttered. "But I'm so glad it's over. I've been sick with worry—for me, for you, for dear Betsy and Arabella—"

Mister Skye waited. Then, "Tortu said he'd been hired out of St. Louis. I don't have more than that."

"St. Louis? Why—you mean, someone back in the States?"

"You have enemies back in the States?"

Elkanah puzzled that. "No . . . business rivals . . ." A thought came to him. "One firm grew very bitter, or at least a principal in it did. I'd undersold them on many things—kettles, arrow points, cloth . . . American Fur finally quit buying from them because I simply had better and cheaper goods."

"Mister Morse, for as long as I can remember, this wilderness, out here beyond the frontier, has been a place of revenge, murder, plots spun out back in the civilized East but executed here. Back in the trapper days, the rendezvous days, there were often some hunters showed up at the frolics—only they hunted heads, not pelts. That's what a frontier does, mate. The things they can't do back there, they hired done out here. If you think life's savage here, maybe you might see just how savage business competition is back there, on your manicured lawns, in your safe cities."

"You really think a business rival . . ."

"You have any other ideas, mate?"

In fact, Elkanah didn't. Always, like the dark drone of bees, men had resented his successes, his inventions, his bright new marketing ideas, his sheer interest in improving the way people lived, and the fact that he'd earned a fortune doing it. Why did the world hate progress?

"You think it's over, Mister Skye?" he asked, shaken.

"We'll keep our guard up and look for a confederate. But Tortu was a loner if there ever was one. He'd have gone into a rage at the idea he couldn't handle it alone."

"It never occurred to me that others might resent my successes so much," Elkanah muttered.

The kidnapping shocked him. Arabella's terror had turned into smoldering hatred of everything in these wild lands, and especially of its people. "I want to go back to civilization!" she'd told him at dawn. "Take us back! Wild-men and savages! I didn't want to come and be exposed to madmen! It's all your fault, making me come. This is the most awful place!" Elkanah couldn't think of a thing to say. He wished devoutly he'd left her back in Lowell, well chaperoned and safe.

Within an hour, Betsy had her easel and watercolors set up at White Beaver's lodge. The war chief refused to sit, and stood patiently while Betsy brushed fine transparent color on the white sheet until a stern proud war chief began to emerge. Around her stood a horde of children and squaws, watching in astonished silence. Some of the young warriors feigned not to notice, but ended up staring at this amazing spectacle anyway. At last even old Chief Horse Medicine watched enviously.

Betsy saw him. "I'll do you next!" she said.

A while later she rose and carried her swiftly done portrait to the war chief.

"Ahiee!" he said, and Elkanah wondered what that meant. But White Beaver held it up solemnly so that all the onlookers might see. Then he paraded it back and forth, holding it in a way that suggested pride and magic. Then he motioned abruptly to his squaw, who ducked into the lodge and emerged with a handsome bone necklace. The hollow white bones had been strung like two small washboards, forming a V at the center. Solemnly Hide Scraping Woman tied the necklace thongs around Betsy's neck.

Betsy smiled. "I'm so pleased," she said. "Thank you. It's beautiful!"

They understood the tone but not the words.

That day Betsy painted old Chief Horse Medicine, his wife, Makes the Moccasin, and an old cross-eyed medicine woman, revered because she could see in two directions and into herself. She sketched three of the warriors in their finest regalia, holding their bows and quivers and trade fusils studded with brass tacks, and feathered lances. All of these she gave away, though Elkanah wished she'd keep them to take East.

"Don't worry, dear. I've made pencil sketches, too, and I'll fill them in with the colors later. I remember just the colors," she said happily. "I'll have a fine portfolio to display in Lowell."

Elkanah's own trade show turned out to be disappointing. The enigmatic Gros Ventre stared at his goods, exclaimed in guttural tones at his canvas lodgecover, fingered his fabrics, studied his russet leather bridles—and kept him in the dark. No one in the village could communicate with him. He held up his milled-perfect arrowshafts and ready-mades, and warriors stared politely at them. No medicine in them. No medicine. He'd never sell goods that lacked medicine. Disappointed, he packed things back into the fine panniers and gave up.

Rudolpho Danzig was having a better time, he noticed. The professor had his daguerreotyping apparatus out and was making portraits. He had too few plates to make images of one at a time, so he was lining up Gros Ventre into rows, like some chorus back East, and then squirming around under his black hood, adjusting focus. Whole crowds of villagers waited patiently while he finished the process by treating the silver-coated copper plates with iodine vapor in a box inside his tent. Each time he emerged with a new plate in hand, villagers mobbed him, exclaiming, pointing. They passed the plate from hand to hand, chattering and laughing and fingering themselves.

This visit to the Gros Ventres had been a failure, Elkanah thought. He'd learned nothing helpful to his business. No one could even talk to him. At least he was coming to understand the daily life and labor of the villages, although their religion continued to mystify him. And the whole alarming business of Tortu had ended— in death—and he and his loved ones could hope for safe passage through this wilderness now. If anything, he felt even more confident about Mister Skye.

Back in camp he found Arabella sitting sullenly, saying nothing to Captain Cobb, who had attended her faithfully during and after the ordeal. Good man, Cobb. But a bit careless to wander so far from the safety of the village. Percy Connaught attacked two journals at once, whittling his pencil furiously and scratching in one and the other leather-bound journal in a fine hand to save space.

Connaught looked up at Elkanah. "These are becoming priceless!" he exclaimed. "So valuable. I'm pouring out all my impressions. Forming policy about these people. Recording every nuance. Describing every chief. Examining every event. Can you imagine how the tale of that Flathead squaw's torture and rescue will be received back in the States? So valuable!"

"Wrap them in oilcloth," cautioned Elkanah.

"Oh, I do that! And in your bag, too. The safety bag you designed for me!"

Elkanah smiled, glad to see one of his little things in good use. He glanced over at Mister Skye's lodge and saw the injured Flathead, Kills Dog Woman, sitting solemnly beside Mary, talking in some fashion with uttered phrases and finger signs. She had healed somewhat, and had the affection of Mary and Victoria to help her along. That pleased him.

From the Musselshell valley their guide took them south over rugged humped prairie and down the east flank of the Crazy Mountains. Outside of the Alps, Professor Danzig had never seen mountains so glacier-sculpted. They were crested by knife-edged ridges of extruded igneous rock, volcanic in origin, with flanks as steep as sixty or seventy degrees. A little like the Alps, he thought. Cirques lay between the ridges, with traces of snow still in some of them. The range seemed to extend forty or so miles north and south and looked to be narrow across, maybe fifteen or twenty miles. Sometime in recent geologic history, molten rock had pushed up through a crack in the crust of the earth to form these stunning razor-edged purple peaks.

The caravan rode easily now, with the danger from that madman gone. Betsy and Arabella perched comfortably in their familiar sidesaddles. Danzig thought that Arabella had weathered her abduction well enough. The girl was too ill tempered to brood about it, and all they'd heard from her for days had been sulfurous comments about natives, red and white. A good spoiled-rotten rich girl would be too busy living to let a mere abduction get her down. Still, he thought, for all her nastiness, Arabella could be witty and warm when she chose to be. He liked her, somehow, against all odds. She'd be slow maturing, but would finally blossom into a lovely woman.

Back a way, Cobb handled the packhorses easily. Far ahead and to either flank rode Mister Skye's squaws, like the antennae of a caterpillar, looking for trouble and finding none in this somnolent country. How the old woman's eyes shone! he thought. They were riding into her country, the home of her people, the Absarokas. She seemed to know this land, steering them to water and safety and sheltered campsites each evening. Her people were Kicked-in-the-Bellies—what a name! He had written it in his journal, and no doubt so had Connaught and Cobb. She would find them without difficulty, Mister Skye had said. She always knew mysteriously where they would be, any time of the year, including this bright beginning of September.

They crossed Sweet Grass Creek, which angled southeast, but Mister Skye hewed to the eastern flanks of the mountains. When they reached Big Timber Creek, the vast valley of the Yellowstone lay ahead. Mister Skye followed the creek, along cottonwood-dappled banks and still-green meadows that drew moisture from the high water tables. Frost had yellowed some of the foliage, Danzig observed, and it faintly worried him.

He touched his heels to his pony and trotted up to Percy Connaught.

"I've never seen such a land, Percy. What noble mountains—a little like my Alps. And how rich these lands. We ride in perfect comfort day after day, dry sweet air, lush cured grasses for our horses. . . ."

"It soothes the eye," agreed Connaught. "It lends a nobility to these savage people. These mountains and vast prairies have shaped them, I suppose. A harsh people fitted to a harsh land. In the space of hours we've seen torture and death as well as cheer and festivity and feasting."

"I suppose you're recording all that in your journals."

"I am. Few whites have been here, and those who came didn't record it properly. Not even Frémont in his explorations south of here. But I am. I am not only catching every detail—especially about these savages, who fascinate me—but recording my observations about them. Oh, Danzig—when this is published, I'll—I'll—"

"You'll make your name," said Danzig, who knew Connaught's churning ambitions very well.

"I'm forming a theory," said Percy, almost ecstatically. "Maybe someday it'll bear my name. The land forms the people. We whites live in moderate climates without extremes, you see. Flatter land, fertile, well watered, temperate. It affects our character, you see. With natural industry we make our soils yield, our mines produce. Our own nature is temperate, measured, thoughtful. Now you take these savages out here—everything is extremes because the land is extreme. Little water, so they must hunt instead of farm. Vast prairies, scarcely a tree on them. How radically they must affect the soul. Vast barbaric mountains like these on our right. Barbaric! Violent walls of rock, not at all like the gentle slopes of New England or Appalachia. It must provoke these savages to war, to violence, you see. There's not a stitch of temperance in them. Give them spiritous drink and they'll instantly stupefy themselves. Give them weapons and it's an excuse for bloody battle. Give them buffalo and they slaughter whole herds! Why, the more we wander here, the more my journals fill up with the true picture of savages!"

"I come from a country whose landscape is even more violent than this," said Danzig quietly.

"Well, yes," admitted Connaught. "But Switzerland is an exception. A mountain island in a settled temperate continent. It doesn't really challenge the truth of my theory.

Look at Skye's squaws. Wild and savage, even after living for years with a white man. Of course this savage land has turned Skye savage. He's a deserter from the Royal Navy, I hear. No wonder he lingers out here, afraid to go home. He wouldn't even dare to step into the Canadian possessions."

"He was impressed," corrected Danzig. "A man who's dragooned onto a ship against his will has a right to free himself, don't you suppose?"

Connaught didn't reply. Then: "It's a mystery why he stayed here. He could have gone East to the States safely enough, made a good life for himself. He obviously has nothing put by. A ragged tipi and two squaws and a half-breed brat. Oh, I tell you, Danzig. This land is dangerous! It tears away every virtue and civilized restraint in a man! I fear for the Republic if it's ever settled! And I am going to publish on it—these journals, this trip, why, what I have packed away in oilcloth here will be the most important book of the decade!"

Rudolpho Danzig grew silent. He could scarcely imagine a more enchanting place to settle, a place that would invite warm Swiss villages, healthy living with mountains and meadows stretching from one's very yard, game, crystal water and air. . . .

The water-worn cobbles in Big Timber Creek were igneous and metamorphic, he noted, granite, diorite, down from the mountains, but the country they rode through was sedimentary, an ocean bottom once. Rising to the south were the snow-tipped Absarokas, as formidable as any range he'd seen. They rode, he mused, along the farthest western edge of the Great Plains, a corner of the plains that he increasingly described within himself as paradise.

At the shimmering Yellowstone they paused, admiring

the wide clear river with its gravelly islands and easy banks. The river ran slow this late in the year, and it didn't seem formidable to cross. Across the river a large stream debouched, and Danzig knew at once where they were: Lewis and Clark had called it Rivers Across and had camped here. Danzig had their journal in his bags and had studied it closely.

"That's the Boulder flowing in across there, mates," said Mister Skye. "We'll cross here, a little above, and camp on the Boulder. Victoria says her people will be up the Boulder valley a way. We'll find them and have a good visit. Some speak English. They've been friends-—give or take a little horse stealing—of the whites from the fur days. Many trappers stayed with them. That's how I met my Victoria. Their customs are, ah, a little unusual. . . ."

Mister Skye looked pained, at a loss for words. But Danzig laughed. He knew what the guide was trying to say. The Crows were notoriously bawdy. The journals of the mountain men brimmed with it. He glanced covertly at those prim New Englanders, Elkanah and Betsy and Arabella, but their faces didn't register understanding, and the guide couldn't bring himself to say more.

"Son of a bitch!" muttered Victoria. "Let's cross!" She slipped off her pony and began unloading a travois. In minutes she and Mary had strapped Mister Skye's lodge and parfleches on the backs of their ponies and mules and were ready. Confidently she led them west a bit and struck into the water at a southwest angle. Danzig watched her progress as the swift current tugged her pony's legs. But the ripples scarcely reached its belly and it bounded up the far side, shaking and spraying violently, while Victoria laughed and chattered like the darting black and white magpies along the great river.

Rudolpho Danzig was pierced with understanding. Victoria had come home. For a moment he felt a pang for his own Switzerland, for his Berne, for the sweet people who lived there. Homesick, suddenly. Homesick out upon a North American wilderness half a globe away from Berne. But Victoria danced and laughed on the far shore, transformed, the heartland of the Crow people beneath her feet. These people Connaught called savages—these people loved their homes and families and villages as much as any on earth. Was Connaught, beside him, seeing love? Seeing Victoria's joy and anticipation? Tomorrow, the Kicked-in-the-Bellies! Parents, brothers, sisters, cousins, nieces, nephews, chiefs, headmen, clans, news, births and deaths, the old squaw's people! He doubted it. Theories could imprison the mind, he thought. And Connaught's mind lay trapped deep in a prison of his own making.

They crossed the gentle Yellowstone easily and made camp on the south shore, with breathtaking views in most directions as the setting sun painted the mountains.

"Tomorrow, mates, we'll head into one of the most beautiful intimate valleys in the West and find Victoria's people," said Mister Skye. "Enjoy yourselves. With Tortu behind us, this looks to be the happiest journey we've had."

Chapter 14

Victoria dashed ahead of the caravan, looking for her people. The Kicked-in-the-Bellies usually camped here in the valley at the beginning of the coolness. She touched moccasins to her pony and it spurted ahead, galvanized by her excitement. She ran beside the boulder-strewn river, following it upstream, through mounded plains at first, and then foothills, and finally into the great mountains, where forested slopes shot upward from the intimate verdant bottoms.

And then before her sat two Kit Fox Society warriors, camp police, on restless ponies. Her people! She knew them by their society shields. She knew all the warrior societies: Lumpwoods, Big Dogs, Hammers . . . They sat easily, almost naked even in the icy morning air, watching her. Close, then! These were the guardians of her village, ever alert for surprises from the Piegan or Lakotah—she spat the names of the enemies of the People from her mouth.

"Ah!" she cried, reining before them. She couldn't think of their names; they'd been boys when Mister Skye had taken her away from the People. But they knew her. Every person in that village of almost two hundred lodges knew her.

"Many Quill Woman!" cried one, a powerful bronzed youth with massive cheekbones and a single braid of jet hair. Victoria loved to hear her Absaroka name spill over his tongue.

"Ah, Kit Fox Society man! I'm so happy to come to my people! The others come, my man, Mister Skye, and whitemen we are taking from place to place."

"It is a good day to visit," said the other, a thin hawkish young man. "Tonight we have a dance. The Kit Fox Society is done with the village policing, and we will dance. Then the Lumpwoods will dance, and they will become the village police. But we do better. We guarded well and kept the village safe."

"A dance! We will be happy to see you dance!" exclaimed Victoria. "And how is our chief Many Coups?"

"He has blessed the village. We are rich with buffalo meat and new hides, and the women are busy making pemmican and gathering roots for the time of the cold," replied the heavier youth.

"I will not wait. I'll go ahead to the People!" she cried. She kicked the pony forward, and one of the Kit Fox warriors rode beside her. The other would escort Mister Skye.

Ahead a mile lay a thin layer of blue smoke from the village fires, trapped in the narrow mountain valley. Close now! Here and there along the river, Absaroka women plucked berries, pulled up good roots. Others busied themselves on the steep slopes, gathering pine nuts. Her people! How she ached for news, ached to hug them all, gather her own Otter Clan loved ones about her and chatter with them into this night! She loved Mister Skye and knew it was a great honor to be the woman of the great white warrior, but this visit would be pure joy. Always, unless her village was grieving, these visits marked the high points of her life. And the Kit Fox warriors had no bad news to give her!

The camp crier, old Coyote Tongue of her own clan, met her and wheeled about to announce her, crying among the lodges, galvanizing women and children. Many of the young men had gone off to hunt, but would ride in soon for the great dance.

She rode her pony into a great forest of bright-daubed lodges, whose doors opened to the east to greet and revere Sun when he came to make the new day. She collected a crowd, scampering, shouting children, boys who drew mock bows and sent mock arrows at her, and laughed. Women who rose up from their hide fleshing and moccasin making to welcome her. The Kit Fox escort pushed through them all importantly, guiding her to the great lodge of Many Coups.

The chief was not there to greet her when she and the crowd halted before his fine lodge with its black-painted suns and new moons. Beside the lodge a brush arbor had been erected, and in its soft dappled shade his sits-beside-him woman, Black Deer Nose, scraped a new hide. Many Coups was off counseling with the medicine men this afternoon, she explained. Soon he would come.

By the time Many Coups appeared, Mister Skye and the whole entourage had also, wending through the shouting villagers who kept a respectful distance from the terrible blue roan, Jawbone.

"Big feast and Kit Fox dance tonight," she said to Mister Skye. "Son of a bitch, we gonna have fun."

The powerful chief threaded his way, unhurried, among his people, stared at the visitors, his eyes long upon Elkanah and Betsy and Arabella—he'd never seen white women except once at Fort Laramie—and vanished into his lodge. Welcoming required ceremony. A welcome formed a sacred bond between the village and its guests. In a moment he emerged, wearing his ceremonial regalia. His chief's bonnet of black and white eagle feathers above a blue-beaded headband was without a tail. He held a staff of office, befeathered at the top, with totems hanging from it.

Victoria barely heard the welcoming as Many Coups droned on. She had spotted her father and his new woman, one she'd never met. And her brother and two sisters. And others of her Otter Clan, the clan of her dead mother, to which she belonged by birth. Mister Skye, Elkanah, and the other whitemen vanished into the lodge for the ritual smoke and gift giving. Then at last they emerged from the chief's lodge, and Mister Skye led his party to a place on the outskirts of the village and made camp there.

Crossly—she wanted to be free—she erected Mister Skye's lodge with Mary and Kills Dog Woman and looked to the comforts of the Morse party.

"Big doings tonight, mates. Kit Fox Society dance. And a feast of buffler. Boudins and tongue, hump meat and ribs. They'll honor the spirits. Honor their guests. Thank the One Above. There'll be a solemn ceremony transferring the police duty to the Lumpwoods—that's another warrior society. This is the season of dances and feasts and medicine. Last fling before it gets too cold and winter closes in. Tomorrow night, a Lumpwood Society dance and another feast. We're among friends—Victoria's people—and you'll enjoy meeting them all," Mister Skye explained. He turned to Victoria, who stood muttering. "I figure there's some folks you want to see, old woman." He grinned and pulled her to him with his massive paws, and she felt happy in the tight circle of his arms.

"No one here I care about. All dogs," she retorted. He laughed, more at ease than she'd seen him in many moons. In a way, this village was his home, too, the place he'd always returned to in the winters of his trapping days, so that he was almost Absaroka himself, and had counted coup and fought beside many of the graying men of the village. Crow enemies were Mister Skye's enemies.

"If you find a beautiful Absaroka girl and pay fat gifts for her, I could use another slave. Got too goddamn much work. Got Mary, and maybe this Flathead, Kills Dog Woman, unless she goes back. But they're goddamn lazy and I got to do everything! Damn. You find a pretty Absaroka girl and go into the bushes with her!" She laughed raucously. Mary grinned impishly. The healing Flathead women, who didn't know English, smiled politely. Victoria glanced covertly at the whites and saw the strange one, Percy Connaught, gaping. She cackled and winked at him.

With that, Victoria fled into the large village to find her old father and meet her stepmother, who came from a band of river Crows. Her heart felt as light as her feet as she dodged shouting children and barking yellow dogs and passed smiling women who had returned to their endless labors. Many of them, she noted, were making winter moccasins from the smoke-blackened tops of lodges. The smoke-and-grease-cured leather turned water and made a fine outer moccasin against the Cold Maker's fiercest weather. And that would come all too soon, she thought, feeling the late-afternoon chill as the sun slid toward the towering western slope, plunging the valley into a lavender cool.

Her people! How rich they all were. Fat times, plenty of buffalo. Parfleches full! Fresh red quarters hanging from alder branches and heavy tripods! And here in this green valley, she knew, roamed more deer and elk than could be counted, and sometimes the great brown bear, too. Bear spirit claimed this valley and would hunt fall berries and eat pine nuts and catch trout and maybe roar at them here before going off to his den for the long winter's sleep. But now as she threaded through the lodges looking for her father's, everything delighted her approving eyes. How fat they looked! She saw few women with hair cut off—not many warriors had died this year. Fat women beaded and quilled together, or strung thin white bones into handsome heavy necklaces. They knew Victoria and smiled, but did not detain her, for she would first visit with her clan, and then the People.

She passed young bronzed men sitting with graying elders and scraping and sanding bows of six-month seasoned chokecherry and willow, good medicine bows to kill the Piegan dogs. The Blackfeet were as numberless as the stars on a moonless night, and the Absaroka were few, and her people survived only by sheer force of will, and much good medicine, and a determination to hold on to this Elk River land, what whites called Yellowstone, that gave them food and skins and health and cool summers and protected winters. Where else could life be better?

She passed the lodges of great warriors, lodges daubed with red or yellow figures showing them counting coup, killing the sacred buffalo. Before them on tripods hung the medicine of the lodge and the trophies of war—Piegan and Lakotah scalps, dry and black. She knew instinctively where to go, what quarter of this giant village her father's lodge would be in. And at last she found it, and found him, ancient, rheumy-eyed, toothless, and grinning as she swept him up in her arms, an old woman greeting an ancient man.

"Come tell us the news, Many Quill Woman. And meet my new woman, Digs the Roots, who was two times widowed by the Piegan and Assiniboin dogs."

She slipped inside and found brother and sisters, nieces and nephews she barely knew, her father's medicine bundle hanging from a lodgepole, and her father's new woman, much younger, with two fingers cut off in mourning, smiling at her joyously.

"It's good to be home!" she exclaimed. "I will stay here for a few days and let Mary and Kills Dog Woman, the Flathead, take care of my man."

Oh, he had a thirst. It felt worse than the rendezvous the day before Broken Hand Fitzpatrick's pack train arrived.

He thought lovingly of the juices corked into the soldered tin cask in his panniers, juices he had saved just for this.

Absaroka was home, and the Kicked-in-the-Bellies his people. Tonight at the feast and the dance he'd gather old gray Buffalo Tail and others of his friends around, and roar like the grizzly. He could jabber passably in Crow, and they could hump along in English some, and what more did they need, except plenty of the amber juice to light the way? Ah, what a thirst! Oh, what a night! He would disappear, go over to the Other Side, as Victoria angrily called it. She'd be too busy with her kin to notice, he thought smugly.

But he had business to attend to first. He hoped to conclude it before evening, before the great feast and dance, before he corralled his warrior friends and slapped backs and hoorawed and bellowed. What a surprise he had for Buffalo Tail, the widower! But it would take some doing, he thought.

It took only an hour or so. First he corralled the headman, Buffalo Tail, and had a smoke. Then they invited in the shaman, Bull's Eye, and smoked again. Then they trotted among the conical lodges until they found the squaw of Raven Wings, who was one of several Flathead women in the village. Mister Skye still needed to round up Elkanah Morse, but the businessman had disappeared someplace. Probably somewhere where something was being manufactured, he thought. He steered them all toward a gathering of middle-aged men patiently sandstoning wood into trim bows, and there sat Elkanah, studying it all.

"Come along, Mister Morse. You have business to attend," rumbled the guide.

Puzzled, Elkanah followed Mister Skye's party back to

the guide's own shabby lodge, where Mary and Kills Dog Woman sat happily, minding Dirk and resoling Mister Skye's moccasins.

At once the Flathead squaw cried out and ran to Kills Dog Woman, babbling in the tongue none of the rest understood. They hugged, and the squaw tenderly examined the healing wounds, turning Kills Dog Woman's face from side to side, running a finger over the new pink flesh on her arms, all the while muttering and wailing. The Flathead woman had nearly healed now, and as the swelling receded her beauty had blossomed. Her eyes shone to discover her friend here among the Crows.

More translating now, thought Mister Skye, but the Flathead squaw of Raven Wings would do.

"Would Kills Dog Woman like to go back to her Flathead village now? She's free to do so."

The answer came in a flood as Kills Dog Woman poured out her story, which finally was repeated in Crow, which Mister Skye could understand.

"What's this all about?" asked Elkanah impatiently.

"Why, mate, she's saying that the Gros Ventre killed her husband when they jumped the Flathead buffler hunters. That was before they caught her and started to torture her to death. She's saying that it'd be fine to go back to her people, but the Absaroka have always been good allies of the Flatheads, and she likes it here, she's happy here. But she says the decision is not hers—she's been bought and is a slave of the whitemen."

"Well, what has that to do with me?" asked Elkanah impatiently.

"You bought her, mate. She's your slave."

"What!"

"You own Kills Dog Woman. That was your bolt of

stuff that bought her. Your goods and arrow points. She's all yours, Mister Morse."

Elkanah gaped helplessly. "But that's ridiculous! I was merely trying to keep the poor woman from being brutally tortured to death!"

"Well, you got yourself a slave." Mister Skye could not quite keep the grin off his face.

"But I'm an abolitionist! I give her her freedom right now!"

"Not that simple, Mister Morse."

"What would Betsy say? How did I get into this?"

Mister Skye enjoyed this hugely. All the more because an audience had collected. Professor Danzig watched with a cocked eyebrow. Captain Cobb stood quietly, enjoying himself. Even Percy Connaught observed the affair with stuffy interest. And then, to make it all perfect, he spied Betsy coming, her paper and colors in hand, and waited a moment until she joined them.

The headman, Buffalo Tail, eyed Kills Dog Woman closely. A comely woman, Mister Skye thought. Slim, with liquid brown eyes and heavy cheekbones and a full chunky figure. Tall and strong. Buffalo Tail stared and nodded. Kills Dog Woman, sensing what lay ahead, smiled shyly.

"Ah, Elkanah, and Betsy. Meet my old friend and war companion Buffalo Tail. He's a headman here, leader of the Kit Fox Society, maybe the next chief of the village. Buffalo Tail is a widower. The pox took off his woman a year or so ago. He thinks maybe this Flathead lady of yours would make a fine fat bride for him, warm his nights, make his moccasins."

"Woman of ours?" asked Betsy, puzzled.

"Good God," muttered Elkanah. "Is it that simple?"

"No, quite complex. We've consulted the shaman, had

a smoke. And we've come to see the woman. They admire her, of course. Anyone who's been tortured by those dogs the Gros Ventre is a friend of these people. Especially a Flathead."

"Well, fine," said Elkanah, relieved. "I'm pleased. I'll just give her to Buffalo Tail here." He sounded hopeful.

"Well, that'd be an insult, Elkanah. You're putting no value on her. Break her heart. You're saying she's worthless."

"Oh."

"Tell you what, mate. Buffalo Tail here is offering two fine ponies and a rare cream-colored buffler robe for her. Those cream robes are mighty precious, and this one is tanned so soft it's like velvet. A whole robe, too, not a split."

"But what would I do with two more—Mister Skye, I am in your hands. Let me be putty in your hands."

"Now don't be hasty, Elkanah. You must think over the proposition. Shortly, two good ponies and the robe will be placed before your tent. You think on it. If the ponies are a suitable bride price for Kills Dog Woman, then put them out in our bunch and take the good robe into your tent. Buffalo Tail will observe that you have accepted his gifts and come fetch his bride."

"What is this about?" cried Betsy.

"Sounds like a right good proposition, Elkanah," said Rudolpho Danzig. "If two ponies aren't enough, maybe I'll trade my sextant for her."

Elkanah Morse sighed. "I came to find out how to trade," he muttered. "Will I be invited to the wedding?"

"Not exactly, mate. Buffalo Tail will just come and claim her, move her into his lodge."

"That's it? No blessings, no ceremony?"

"Oh, you might hold a feast to celebrate it if you and Betsy are inclined. But that would be more correct if Kills Dog Woman was your daughter rather than your slave."

"She's no slave of mine! You bought her!"

Mister Skye howled gleefully and slapped Morse on the back. "Well, mate, you don't have to trade her off to Buffalo Tail. Maybe you'd like another wife, eh? Why, Betsy just might be delighted to have all her burdens shared."

"Another wife!" Betsy gasped. "Elkanah, how could you?"

"Mister Skye, you are a rascal."

"I think two wives would be a good proposition, Elkanah," said Rudolpho. "It might take a little explaining in Lowell, though."

"I think Betsy would be pleased to share," said Cobb.

"Like those Mormons," added Danzig.

"Why! What? How dare you!" Betsy howled.

The guide's laughter boomed across the happy village. He addressed the Flathead squaw. "Tell your friend Kills Dog Woman that the headman here, Buffalo Tail, is mighty pleased to take her for a wife."

Kills Dog Woman listened, smiled broadly, ran a finger tenderly over her pink wounds, and then suddenly wept softly. She clung to the other Flathead woman, weeping. Then at last she pulled herself free and walked to her new man and solemnly took his hands in her own and pressed them gently to her lips, saying something in her own tongue.

"She says she's proud and pleased to be chosen by the headman, and grateful that the whiteman has given her, and she'll do her best to bring good medicine and good work and love to the lodge of Buffalo Tail."

Love suddenly hung on the air. Elkanah muttered to

himself. Connaught raced off to find his journals and pulled out the one intended for the vulgar.

"I must explain all this to Betsy," muttered Elkanah.

"You don't have to explain anything. I don't want to know!" she snapped. "Don't you ever tell me! Sometimes I don't understand men!"

Buffalo Tail wandered off to fetch two fat ponies and a robe. And Mister Skye dug into his panniers for a tin cask. A happy journey, he thought. Almost idyllic, in spite of the bad moments with Tortu. Fine people he was guiding. Yes, a good trip, nothing wrong with any of them, even Connaught. A fine little adventure among the tribes. He found his soldered cask and tipped some gurgling amber juice into a crockery jug.

"Ah!" he exclaimed. "A happy trip."

Chapter 15

To Jarvis Cobb, the Kit Fox Society dance seemed less a dance than a military parade passing in review. It had begun about twilight after a vast feast on a grassy area rather like a village square or plaza near Chief Many Coups' great lodge. The society apparently numbered about fifty warriors, plus those who still stood guard vigilantly out on the periphery.

Captain Cobb's business was intelligence, and he'd spent the afternoon counting lodges. One hundred and sixty, he numbered them, times an average of eight persons to a lodge. The Kicked-in-the-Bellies numbered twelve or thirteen hundred people. A huge village, he thought. Feeding a community so large must be a pressing, constant prob-

lem. This feast, this single meal, had consumed ten buffalo, six elk, and uncounted deer, plus a vast array of roots
and berries patiently gathered from the abundant Boulder
valley. One meal! Cobb grew suddenly aware of the burden on Chief Many Coups, the importance of buffalo to
the Crows and all the plains people, the power of the shamans and village site selectors to name each place where
the village would stay and to set the times of travel. How
long could it last? he wondered. Only as long as the buffalo lasted. Food was everything: cut off food, and the
plains tribes would be brought to heel without war.

Carefully he recorded his intelligence in his journal for
future military use. On its pages he numbered the lodges
and people, named the warrior societies, and wrote in the
names of every headman and war chief and shaman he'd
learned of so far. Knowledge wins wars, he thought.

Before him, to the quiet throb of drums, the Kit Fox
warriors paraded in endless naked array. No intricate
dance step here, but every lance, shield, scalp, bow and
quiver, and rifle, paraded over and over before the people,
as if to tell them something of the power and prowess of
this society, of these protecting warriors. Chief Many
Coups stood solemnly the whole while, rather like a
president or general reviewing troops. Each of these seasoned senior warriors paraded his personal medicine,
his shaman-blessed war shields made from the thick hide
of a buffalo-bull neck and so strong they could sometimes
stop a rifle ball as well as an arrow. They carried befeathered coup sticks proudly, many strung with withered black
scalps. Enemy dead, big medicine.

The village watched respectfully: the Kit Fox Society's
fame and honor were known to every adult and child. Cobb
wondered when it would all end. The warriors had circled

fifteen or twenty times now, in continuous parade, and showed no sign of stopping. It seemed a little boring actually. Then at last a change came: one at a time, the warriors began to address the chief, probably telling him of their personal feats at war, Blackfeet and Sioux killed, coups counted, praising their personal medicine, the personal help of badgers and buffalo horns, mountain sheep and pack rats. . . . So religion took a part in it, if medicine could be called that, he thought. The things that whites separated from one another seemed blended together here, war, power, personal prowess, spirit help, God, magic. Captain Cobb wondered how he could describe all that in his journals; how it might help future officers in future Indian wars deal with savage peoples.

Indigo night settled, and still the drums throbbed in the darkness, at the rate of heartbeat, mesmerizing in their intensity. Several small bright fires lit the parade route, casting amber light upon brown faces. Squaws and children sat quietly in their ceremonial best clothing. Affairs of state seemed to be dress occasions, he noted. The women wore softly tanned and fringed doeskin dresses, almost white in the night, with bone and bead necklaces and exquisite calf-high moccasins on firm comely legs.

Close by, the Morses sat quietly enjoying the pageantry, Betsy making small pencil sketches in the dim gold light. Arabella looked pained, and kept glancing at Jarvis. But across the way, near Many Coups, Mister Skye sat cross-legged, methodically lifting a brown jug to his lips, smiling stupidly. That savage oaf of a guide was imbibing spiritous drink, Cobb thought distastefully. Connaught had noticed Skye, too, and was whispering to Danzig about it.

"He's drunk!" whispered Percy Connaught. "Skye's drunk as a lord! What an insult to our hosts. I've never seen anything so disgusting! It'll go into my journals along with a description of this barbaric parade."

"I hope he stays quiet and doesn't insult these people," replied Captain Cobb. "These are his wife's people and there he is, making a spectacle of himself."

"He looks quiet enough to me," rejoined Rudolpho Danzig. "Just a quiet little drunk, eh?"

"Why, he's passing the jug to his Mary, the young one!" exclaimed Percy. "A swine of a man. I knew it all along!"

"These drums are giving me a headache, Captain Cobb," whispered Arabella. "Would you walk with me? I don't think I can stand another minute of them."

"The beat's so steady it's like the human pulse. Have you noticed that when these savages pound those drums faster, our pulses speed up? Fascinating!" said Cobb. That, too, would go into his valuable journal.

He rose and escorted Arabella beyond the vibrant arena and into a vast blackness in which countless lodges loomed conically in the night, each with a forest of sticks thrust into the starlit sky. Something like a thousand villagers had gathered there at the dance, Cobb thought. And now these silent tipis seemed deserted, though many others, infants, the very old, slumbered in them. Slowly the drumming faded as they wound among lodges, and the other sounds, crickets, the ripple of water in the river, the soft flurry of breeze on the ear, restored peace in him.

"Thank you, Jarvis," she said, taking his arm. "I was going mad there. I never want to hear another drum."

He paused, not quite sure where they walked. In a village so vast, on a black night, getting lost seemed all too easy. Still, there was the river, and he knew they followed it generally south, away from Mister Skye's camp at the north end of the village.

He felt Arabella's presence beside him, and found himself struggling again. Not since the moment they'd been surprised by Tortu had they been together like this. Arabella had been so shaken that she had avoided him. He, in turn, cursed himself for his carelessness, for letting temptation overcome his own scruples. But here they were, and he found himself keenly aware of her lush form in the black night, the lithe young figure tightly wrapped in beige gingham, the softness of her lips. . . .

At the south edge of the village they could scarcely hear the drums.

"Oh, Jarvis," she whispered, taking his hand and pressing it in hers. "I had to get away. I'm so lonely. So alone here. You've been such a comfort. Would you hold me gently? I draw such peace from your quiet embrace. . . ."

"I'm married, Arabella," he replied hoarsely. "I can't let what almost happened—"

"Of course not," she said. "But we're friends, and we share something in our souls. We both hate this barbarous life and yearn for the comforts of civilization. Oh, Jarvis, hold me gently or my heart will break!"

She faced him eagerly. He hesitated, feeling the stir of his loins and the race of his pulse. Perhaps for a minute, he thought. They still walked among the lodges, though open meadow lay just ahead. Not a private place at all. A village street, though a midnight-black one. It'd be safe . . . and wouldn't lead to anything. He'd return to his dear family at West Point in honor. . . .

He drew her to him, slid his arms around her crisp dress and under her shawl, drew her tight until her breasts crushed against him and their thighs pressed tightly through layers of cloth and restraint. Her lips lingered on his. His lips found her eyes and cheeks and then pressed hard. He felt her arms and hands tugging him tighter, racing greedily up and down his back. . . .

"Oh!" she cried, and pulled back a moment, uncertain.

A woman's nasal voice erupted softly close by, and they leaped apart, discovered, hearts racing. Their eyes, long free of the mesmerizing fires at the dance, could see clearly now in the starlight. An old crone, bent, wizened, toothless, grinning. One of the ancient ones, probably very poor by the looks of her. She grinned, gummed strange words, hissed in sibilants, and beckoned.

"She wants us to follow," Arabella said tightly, her voice quivering. The toothless grinning woman clawed at Jarvis's sleeve, tugging. They followed her reluctantly between black cones. The old one tittered and giggled, like a girl, and pointed at the door flap of a small sagging lodge.

"She's inviting us to come in," said Arabella. "I guess she wants to entertain us."

They clambered through the low door hole. Within, a tiny twig fire flickered, supplying more light than heat. Black buffalo robes lay thickly, making a bed along the far side. Three dyed parfleches contained the woman's whole possessions, except for a bow and a quilled quiver with a few arrows in it, hanging from a lodgepole. The lodge smelled pleasantly of leather and smoke and sagebrush. A poor lodge, a poor woman, Captain Cobb thought.

"It's so quiet, so . . . private!" exclaimed Arabella. "Why, I can't even hear the drums. I didn't know a skin lodge could keep out the world so well."

"Yes," said Cobb.

The old woman grinned, tittered, pointed cheerily at the mounded robes, and waited. Cobb understood. The Crows loved lovers, loved dalliances, loved assignations. That drunk, Skye, had told him that. Told him that Crow squaws had become famous among the mountain men, famous for their boldness, for their incredibly bawdy jokes . . . and here stood an old toothless crone grinning and waiting.

"What does she want?" asked Arabella.

"I think she wants to leave us here, so we can . . . talk . . ." said Cobb. "I think she's given us a little bower. I suppose she's expecting a gift."

Gifts he had, a pocketful—a hank of crimson ribbon, a polished tin looking glass or two, some twists of tobacco. He dug in his pockets, found a ribbon and a twist of tobacco, and presented them to the old woman.

"Ah!" she exclaimed, sniffing the tobacco happily. Then, suddenly, she darted out.

Utter silence embraced them. Cobb stared across to Arabella, his pulse hastening. Her lips opened, her eyes shone brightly. She pulled a ribbon out of her glossy brown hair, and it cascaded loose about her shoulders. Artlessly she undid the top button of her gingham, and then the next. He struggled one last time with duty and honor. "I think we should just talk, Arabella. Just share the things of the soul as friends must. We have the future to think of. My . . . family. My career. Your reputation . . . I mean, your future marriage . . . If we just sit down now, it'd be best."

"I don't care about the future!" she cried. "We'll probably be killed or scalped anyway. I don't want to—to die without knowing about—about . . ."

She rushed to him, pressed her hungry body against his, knowing his thick desire. He pulled her to the mounded robes and began undoing buttons while she kissed and tugged him furiously.

Elkanah Morse spent a ragged night. The throbbing of the drums had a residual effect on him, like some savage narcotic. It had heightened all his senses, made his hearing, vision, smell sharper. But most of all, the lingering throb of them prevented sleep, like black coffee.

Arabella had come in late, just when he had become alarmed about her and was considering going out into the darkened village for help. But he'd been daunted by that prospect. With Mister Skye apparently stupefied by strong spirits, he didn't know where to turn. But she'd arrived at last and slipped into her bedroll.

"Where were you, Arabella?" he asked softly.

"Talking," she replied crossly. "We had lots to talk about."

"We were growing worried."

She didn't reply.

Had the night been still, he might have drifted off then among the chirping crickets. But it wasn't. Periodically, from the vicinity of Mister Skye's lodge, roaring and bellowing shattered the peace. It sounded like a sore-toothed grizzly, but he knew the voice rose from a human throat. Between the roars, he heard cackles and giggles, not to mention the splash of someone making water very close, and other grunting he hoped Betsy didn't recognize.

But she did. "Dear me," she said. It struck her funny. "Dear me!" she said, lacking words. "Oh, my!"

Elkanah Morse laughed, feeling irked at the same time. Back in Boston, that former mountain man Nathaniel Wyeth had warned him that nature held sway in the wilds of the West, that one could only be tolerant of voluptuary excess. That was how he'd gently phrased it: voluptuary excess. One New Englander to another.

Jawbone shrieked and snarled, an unearthly snapping scream Elkanah could scarcely believe erupted from a horse. The creature obviously hated Mister Skye's excesses.

Mister Skye had roared back, shivering the night.

Once, when Mister Skye had bellowed louder than usual, a night-shattering honk that vibrated the earth and stilled the coyotes in the hills, Elkanah sat up with a jerk. He'd step out and still the monster. He clawed open his tent flap and peered out into the starlit tableau. There indeed sat Skye, cross-legged, before his lodge, jug in hand, muttering softly, baying at the North Star. Leaning on him and in worse condition, slumped his younger wife, Mary, who snatched the jug and guzzled and barked like a coyote while he pawed her with his big hands. Nor were they alone. Sitting to the other side of Skye, an Indian Elkanah made out to be Buffalo Tail, teetered like a slowing top. And flat on the ground lay Kills Dog Woman, her skirts scandalously high.

"Oh dear," muttered Betsy beside him. She peered out, too.

"I must do something," whispered Elkanah. "You mustn't look."

But Betsy had fallen into a fit of giggles.

"Be quiet!" snapped Arabella from her black corner.

"Look!" cried Betsy as she peered out the flap. She pointed at two ponies picketed beside their tent. And a mounded something in the grass.

"It's the bride price," muttered Elkanah. "But I think Buffalo Tail has jumped the gun."

Buffalo Tail wobbled to his feet and began to make water.

"Oh dear," muttered Betsy, and ducked back in.

Elkanah peered around sharply, thought he saw Connaught's distraught face peering from the other tent, and then closed the flap. It'd be a night to endure.

But Betsy had other ideas. Silently, in the total blackness, she snuggled tight against him and hugged.

In the haggard dawn he crawled crabbily into the gray light, finding frost on the grass. Mister Skye had vanished along with Mary. In their lodge, he supposed. Buffalo Tail had vanished, too, with or without Kills Dog Woman. The ponies stood patiently. One looked to be a dun, the other a chestnut, both fattened by fall grasses and clean of limb. Before him lay the dew-soaked buffalo robe, amber, almost yellow in color, lighter than any of the buffalo he'd seen. He spread it out, admiring its rare beauty.

He'd had no sleep at all, and felt it. He'd speak to Mister Skye, of course. Tolerance indeed; he could understand the ways of these mountain people. But they might at least have reveled somewhere else, away from camp, away from the eyes of his women. Yes, he'd say that to the guide when he sobered up. It would have scandalized most white women, and maybe did scandalize Betsy, though she'd made light of it. And of course he would prefer that Arabella not see or hear such things. The girl had lived a protected proper life, and while this trip and the sight of naked Indians had surely informed her about certain things, he hoped it wouldn't affect her grace and innocence and the lovely purity he enjoyed in his daughter.

Wearily he tugged on his boots and laced them, and wandered into the misty river bottoms for his ablutions. The others slept, or pretended to. He slapped cold river water on his stubbled face and enjoyed the icy shock of it.

"Wakes a man up, eh?" said Rudolpho Danzig.

The professor had kneeled nearby to wash.

"Can't say as I needed awakening this morning. Up all night," replied Elkanah sourly.

Professor Danzig laughed. "At least we're in a friendly village," he said. "Do you suppose our guide might remain in this condition for some while?"

"Maybe until he runs out of spirits," Elkanah replied. "He can't possibly have a bottomless reservoir of them."

"We could spill them," Danzig replied.

Elkanah sighed. "Let's wait and see. Today I'm going to show my wares, pitch the canvas lodge. These people know English! I can talk with them, Rudolpho. I'm not going to worry about Mister Skye today. But tomorrow, if he's not with us, we'll have to find our way down to Fort Laramie without him. Or find some other guides to escort us. I have no idea just where we are."

"Why, to be exact, we are at forty-five degrees and forty minutes north, provided that I was holding the sextant exactly level when I shot the North Star. At sea, there's always true horizons, but here on land, surrounded by mountains, we have none, so land sextants have a spirit level or some similar device. If I didn't get the bubble right last night in the dark, I could be off a few degrees."

"You're a big help, Professor!"

Danzig grinned. "I always know where we are," he said. "All we need is a sober guide to get us to the next place."

They laughed, and the day seemed better.

The valley lay deep in cold blue haze, but far above, the rising sun blazoned the eastern slopes of the mountains, fired the ridges yellow and white and orange.

"The warmth'll be welcome, Professor," said Elkanah softly. "Frost last night."

"So I've noticed. Elkanah, we should hasten on, I think. In these latitudes, the weather can turn on us—turn into brutal icy rain, mud, snow. . . . This summer's over. Indeed, my fall term has started; I'm missing classes. Hoped to be back about now . . ."

"You're right. I'll talk to Victoria if I can find her. These lodges all look alike. I'll show my wares today, and tomorrow we'll be off for Fort Laramie and the military caravan home. I'd hoped to visit half a dozen tribes this summer, but we've gotten to three at least, and I'm getting some idea of what can be done and what won't sell. It's less easy than I thought to change the lives of traditional people, Rudolpho. But that's what I came out here to find out about."

Percy Connaught joined them at the misty riverbank.

"Discharge that lout," he said. "Worthless."

"You'll guide us safely home, Percy?"

"Hire these Crows. Or find some other white renegade who's at least sober."

"No . . ." said Elkanah. "Mister Skye pulled me aside at the beginning to offer some words of advice. As I look back on it, it almost seems as if he knew he'd stumble along the way. Trust old Victoria, and young Mary, he said to me. Those women would be better guides than he could ever be. That's what I'm going to do, Percy."

"Put our lives, our safety, into the hands of two savage squaws?"

"That's it, Percy. Two squaws."

Chapter 16

Mister Skye lay stupefied in the shadowed lodge. The bad-medicine smell repelled Victoria as she peered in. Gone to the Other Side again, she thought crossly. He often did that in the village of the Kicked-in-the-Bellies.

The People didn't mind. Mister Skye had married into the village, had fought beside its warriors, and had helped them all many times. And when Mister Skye guzzled the spirit waters, they smiled and helped him to his lodge. Actually the spirit juices gentled him. He always roared like a wounded grizzly, but it was only roaring. Still, Victoria hated it when he uncorked his jug. Hated it when Mary joined him. That left her to take care of little Dirk, because Mary slept as stupidly as Mister Skye.

She had to feed Jawbone. The horse hated it, too, and laid his ears back and snarled whenever Mister Skye went to the Other Side. Jawbone turned even more menacing in these periods, and eyed the world murderously from narrow-set yellow eyes. Still, she had to feed him.

"Damn, you gotta eat grass, Jawbone," she muttered, approaching him cautiously, wondering if this would be the time he chose to slaughter her with his vicious hooves or teeth. But he stood evilly while she tied a halter on him and led him to fresh pasture. It would be a long walk because the pasture close to the large village had all been chewed down to dirt. The evil blue roan followed her reluctantly, unhappy about giving up his sentry duties. When Mister Skye drank, Jawbone stood like a soldier over him, letting no one close except Victoria and Mary.

She thought she'd try the hills rather than the Boulder River bottoms and steered Jawbone up a long western slope and into a pine-park area where grass flourished thickly. She'd leave him there unguarded. No one could capture that fierce animal. A rope landing over him was signal enough to him to attempt to butcher any human in sight. Big medicine, she thought fearfully. Bigger medicine in Jawbone than in any horse of any tribe. She left him there, chewing and glaring yellow-eyed down upon the long village below. He'd return soon and resume his duties.

Winded from the long steep climb, she paused. Below, her people's village spread along the river flats, and she could see the women working on robes, sewing, making clothing to ward off the cold. Far to the south and north she made out the horse herds, two of them for a village so large, each guarded by youths as well as the Lumpwood Society warriors now policing. In the northern band, picketed close together, grazed Mister Skye's and Elkanah Morse's horses and mules, including the two fine ponies given to the white-man by Buffalo Tail, for Kills Dog Woman. A fitting price for the Flathead squaw, she thought. Two fat ponies for the fat woman.

Down below, she spotted Elkanah Morse setting up his displays. He'd borrowed some lodgepoles, and even as she watched, he erected his ready-made canvas lodge. When he got it up and laced, it gleamed whitely, and drew hundreds of villagers to it.

She hurried on down the slope because she'd promised the things-maker she would translate for him, tell him what her people thought of all his big-medicine wares. She liked him. Elkanah Morse seemed to be a good man, not contemptuous of brown-skinned people. He spoke truly, asked questions, respected the sacred ways of her people, and had a good laughing heart, just like his squaw Betsy, who enjoyed people and accepted the differences among them.

"There you are, Victoria! Now we'll begin," he said. She wove through the silent villagers, who stared impassively at pots and skillets, bolts of cloth, blankets, ready-made blanket capotes, assorted awls, saws, knives, axes and hatchets, arrow points, ready-made arrows, and above all, at the canvas lodge. Not a soul among her people said anything or gave the slightest indication of how they felt. That would be impolite. But she sensed something more than politeness here. She sensed fear and worry about all these new ways. She'd have to press them for answers, she knew, because they'd say not the slightest thing critical about the things of these guests.

"I'd like to get some sense of how they feel about these goods—whether they'd trade robes for them at the posts. And so on. Your people are so polite!"

Victoria smiled at him and began questioning her people one by one. Ah, Many Quill Woman, how can we tell? We do not know the medicine of these things! The more she queried, the more evasive they became. Maybe these things are not the Absaroka way. Maybe the medicine men, like Buffalo Bull's Eye, would find evil in them. Maybe they'd be good to have. Maybe they shouldn't tell the whiteman anything, so that he has no power over them. Maybe this man Morse is a bad-medicine man, a witch, and these things are witch things? Who can say? Maybe we'd trade robes for these. Maybe we won't. Witch things are bad medicine. Do his arrows know our bows? Have our bows met his arrows? Who can say, Many Quill Woman! How can one talk about such a lodgecover as that? We see not a medicine picture on it, just cloth. Who would live in cloth, unprotected from witches? Who is this man that Mister Skye brings here? Have you brought us a witch or a demon, Many Quill Woman?

At last, she returned to Elkanah. "Son of a bitch!" she muttered. "I don't get the answers you want. They say maybe yes, maybe no. Maybe good, maybe bad. Maybe they'd trade robes, maybe not. Maybe it's the Way of the People, maybe it ain't."

"Could you tell me more? Am I violating your religion, Victoria? Do these ready-made arrows violate—is something spiritually wrong?"

She shrugged. "Goddamn. They say their bows don't know these arrows. Ain't never met these arrows. These here arrows ain't met the bows. Bows and arrows got to meet. Feathers and arrowshafts got to meet. Arrow points got to get to know their brothers."

Elkanah looked baffled. "But these arrows will shoot true—go truer."

"Naw. Each warrior knows his arrows and arrows know him. He can make his arrows go where he wants. But not yours."

"Well, what about the canvas lodgecover? Isn't it a convenience, something new and better—especially in the summer? Won't it save them labor? Isn't it lighter, easier to carry, easier to set up?"

"Damn," she muttered. "I can't say it right in English. It's no place to live, they say. No spirit helper, not the One Above, to protect it. They think maybe you're a witch."

"A what?"

"Bad-medicine person, making bad things. They'll go visit the medicine men, find out about you."

"Good God! I mean them no harm! I wish them no evil!"

"I'll go visit the shaman, tell him whitemen son of a bitches ain't bad medicine. Unless he says so. If he says so, we got to get out of here. No one will want us to stay in the village."

"I'd like to go with you—would you translate for me? Let me make my case? He'd listen, wouldn't he?"

She squinted at him angrily, unable to make up her mind. Maybe this man she liked was a goddamn witch.

That's what the People thought. "Go get a good pony. Get lots of twists of tobacco. I'll take you to Buffalo Bull's Eye. Maybe he accepts your gifts, maybe not. Maybe he tells you to stay, and you're not a witch. Maybe he says you're a witch and you gotta go. It ain't just you. The professor man, he gets inside his black cloth and steals the images of people, bad magic, takes the image of a good Absaroka person. And last night they see him out with a thing, stealing the North Star. He looks in, and aims at the star to take it from us. And your squaw, she makes the images, and the people see she's captured their medicine. Maybe she's a witch, too. Goddamn, if you're witches, I'm staying with my people and you and Mister Skye can get out!"

Elkanah stared at her, speechless. "Are we in danger?" he asked quietly.

"Naw. They maybe make you go, and burn all the witch things you got."

"I'd like to talk with Buffalo Bull's Eye. And also the village headmen. Would you translate?"

"Goddamn," she muttered.

He hurried off, pausing long enough to warn Rudolpho Danzig and Betsy of possible trouble. The silent crowd of villagers drifted off, leaving Elkanah's displays naked and forlorn. In a few minutes Elkanah returned, leading one of the ponies he'd received and carrying a handful of tobacco twists. He followed her silently as she threaded through the village, heading not for the small lodge of Buffalo Bull's Eye, but toward the emergency council of village elders and shamans gathering in the grass before Chief Many Coups' great lodge.

She squinted at Elkanah, who looked drawn. Mister Skye gone to the Other Side, too. Maybe Mister Skye could explain to his Absaroka friends about this white witch.

Maybe he could make things right. But he got drunk, and he was no damn good now.

Seated in a semicircle in the grass, the elders and sub-chiefs waited, along with two shamans. Victoria stopped at the edge, awaiting an invitation.

"You have business with us, Many Quill Woman?" asked Many Coups.

"Yes. Elkanah Morse here has brought a gift to Buffalo Bull's Eye, and a twist of tobacco for each of you. He wishes to talk with you and tell us what he is here for, and that he is not a bad-medicine man. Not a witch. That is what he will say."

The elders sat quietly, not responding, waiting. Then old Bull's Eye rose slowly, lifted his medicine staff with a rattlesnake head at its crest, shook it in each cardinal direction, and slowly walked to the pony, circled it, and led it to a nearby shaded place. They would listen, let Elkanah Morse address them.

One by one the other whites arrived, looking solemn, and settled themselves in the grass opposite the headmen. Danzig's arrival seemed to evoke some sort of tension among the Crows.

Elkanah stood, eyeing the assemblage amiably. "We are pleased and honored to be guests in your village, gentlemen," he began graciously. He praised the headmen, Victoria, and the Crow people, and admired their way of life and their arts.

Victoria translated easily, except when ideas didn't translate well. Oh, if only Mister Skye hadn't gone to the Other Side! Elkanah began to explain his reasons for making the arduous journey among the far tribes.

"I employ many workers to make things that people find useful," he continued. "We make new things to make life easier, too. Things to make less work. Just as a steel knife makes cutting meat easier than one chipped of stone or shaped from bone, so does a canvas lodge make life easier for your women."

The shaman interrupted, and Victoria translated now for Elkanah. "Why should we want to make life easier for the women? Then they would have nothing to do and feel worthless."

"They would have more time for fun, more time to enjoy their children," replied Elkanah.

"But you steal their worth from them, things-maker. If they have much to do, they are proud and happy and know they are good wives. That is our way. If they have nothing to do, they will get into trouble. It is for women to labor, and men to hunt and war. A woman is valuable and revered among us if she works. Would you have our women become like men?"

Betsy smiled amiably. Arabella looked cross.

Buffalo Bull's Eye stood, raising his arms. "The First Maker, Ah-Badt-dadt-deah, has made our ways!" he cried. "Where is the First Maker's hand in these cloth lodge-covers? The lodges must be made of the sacred buffalo, our protector and our food. Why do we worship buffalo and dance around the skull of a bull? So that we may have his blessing upon our lodges. Who blesses the cloth lodges of this whiteman—except ghosts from under the earth and demons from the dark waters? Evil spirits profane the cloth lodge!"

The shaman sat down suddenly amid silence. The enunciation of the sacred name of the First Maker required silence and reverence. The lesser spirits, even Sun and Earth Mother and Moon, the Absaroka might joke about, for they were like magic people. But not the One Who

Made All Things. Victoria translated quietly, using the whitemen's word, *God*, for the more fearsome one she barely dared pronounce.

Elkanah paused, finding words. "I do not wish to violate the beliefs of the Absaroka people," he began. "No evil spirits from under the earth live in my canvas lodgecover. I made it so that the life of the Absaroka people might be easier, and I might be paid something for the making of it."

A powerful headman, No Scalp, stood in his ceremonial robe of wolfskin. Over his brow rested a desiccated wolf head, the medicine of his spirit helper. "I despise the arrows of the white things-maker," he began in a nasal harangue. "They are not made in the proper way, and the bad spirits in them would turn them around in war so they come back at us. What Absaroka made incantation to the spirits? Who prayed that the arrows would fly true, into our enemies, or into the buffalo, or into other meat? Who set the arrow points next to the shafts so they might get to know each other in harmony? Who told these whiteman arrows what bow would shoot them, what Absaroka warrior or hunter would possess them? These are arrows made by the underwater spirits to weaken and deceive us and make us think we will be safe."

Elkanah nodded. "I suppose these things are not for your people, then. That is what I came to find out. I will pack the things and put them away."

Many Coups himself rose, holding his hooked staff of office. His word, Victoria knew, would decide their fate. He addressed the whites in English. "The man Danzig, with the black hair flowing from his face. Some among us say he is a bad-medicine man, a white witch. At night he goes about with a strange weapon and steals the star of the north from the Absaroka. And when Sun comes to visit, he makes images of the People with another strange thing, secretly under a black robe where we cannot know what medicine he practices. He steals images from us and takes them to the demons under the earth. So it is said among us. No man can make images as perfect as these, so they must be made by demons. The evil ones then can possess my people and bring evil upon them, and upon the village."

Rudolpho arose thoughtfully. "Chief Many Coups, no harm is intended, and if you could see inside me where my spirit is, you would know I am a friend. The thing you refer to is called by whites a sextant, and it is a little like a spyglass. With it I can tell how far south or north we are. The farther north we are, the higher in the night sky is the North Star."

"We know where we are! Why should it be a mystery to whites?" asked Many Coups impatiently. "We are at the center of the world. To the south it is very hot. To the north it is very cold. But First Maker brought the People here because here it is perfect."

"Ah but—my good chief—you see, we whites believe the world is round like a globe, like a perfect ball, and right here we live very far to the north—"

"A ball? We would all fall off of a ball, and the sides would be too steep!" cried the chief.

Professor Danzig retreated. "The other device that makes images was invented across the sea by a Frenchman, the kin of the French trappers who often visit your people. It does not steal images, and no demon or bad medicine is in it. It works with metals and chemicals—elements of nature, not evil spirits."

"We believe no man, white or of the People, could make

images so perfect," Many Coups retorted. "You are hiding from us the demon people under the black robe who do these things."

"No demon people are . . ." Professor Danzig paused, helplessly. "I tell you what. I will give the images to you, so each of your people will get his image back and no evil spirit can take it away. Would you and your people like that?"

Many Coups consulted with his elders and headmen for a while. "We will take the images the bad-medicine people have made," he said.

Danzig had the plates with him and handed them to the chief, who gave them to the shaman.

"Now my council will talk about these things among ourselves. You will go to your camp and wait, and do not leave it or wander in our village." He turned to Victoria. "Many Quill Woman, we will let you know, too. You have translated well."

She followed the whites back to the camp, her heart heavy; her own people shunned her because she might be in the company of a witch. She ached inside, and felt ripped apart. At camp, the whites vanished silently into their tents. She peered into her own lodge, where Mister Skye lay muttering, and the sour smell of his spirit juices smacked her. She elected to sit outside with Mary and Dirk and to tell Mary about all the terrible things that were happening.

Her people deliberated slowly, and she knew it would be a long time before a message came. But at dusk one did come, and it was delivered by Many Coups himself, flanked by two shamans. She knew by the set of his face that things were bad.

"We find that this man with the black beard, Danzig, is

a bad-medicine person. We are divided about this man Morse, the things-maker. Some say he is not a bad-medicine person. Others say he is. I cannot make up my mind."

Witches, Victoria thought. Mister Skye is guiding bad-medicine men of the whites.

"The council says that the whites must leave the village at once. We cannot permit witches to stay in our village and harm the People. Evil would come to us in the night. The spirits would rise out of the earth and sicken us with pox or make us starve. We must honor our way and cleanse ourselves. After you leave we will burn everything of the whites, and purify ourselves in the way, and make offerings to the First Maker and the others who protect us."

"At once?" asked Victoria.

"At once. Before the darkness. If you do not go, the Lumpwood soldiers will kill them. We have spoken now. Be careful, Many Quill Woman; you are among witches. Come back with Mister Skye when you are not among witches."

The chief wheeled off into the quiet village. Not a soul stirred in it; each villager knew that bad-medicine whites would send demons upon them unless they stayed within the safe circles of their lodges.

"We must go," Victoria said sharply. "If we stay, you will be killed. When the dark comes, we must be away or you die!"

Elkanah stared at her. "We are not bad-medicine people, Victoria," he said firmly.

"The medicine men say one here is," she spat. "They have all-knowing. They know!"

Elkanah chose not to argue. "Let's get packed and off," he said quietly. The whites had already loaded their panniers, and the Lumpwood Society police had already brought their horses and mules. In a few moments they could leave. Jawbone snarled, ears back, as she lowered her lodgecover and loaded the travois.

I will have to lift Mister Skye upon him, Victoria thought, despairing. She wanted to weep.

"Son of a bitch!" she cried. "Hurry up! We go now!"

Chapter 17

Mister Skye defied the laws of gravity. Rudolpho Danzig had never seen the laws of gravity suspended before, and observed the matter with scientific curiosity. From his vantage point on the back of a pony a few yards behind Mister Skye, the professor maintained a constant vigil, awaiting the moment when gravity, king of all natural forces, would reassert its dominion. Danzig had heard of only one previous case, in which the Subject had walked on water. But there the similarity ended. Mister Skye belonged at the opposite end of the spectrum from the Other One, and seemed inclined to sink like a stone to nether regions rather than float or defy nature's law.

But the professor's own eyes recorded the fact that Mister Skye tilted considerably further than the Leaning Tower of Pisa, first to port, and then with a shudder and desperate convulsion, to starboard. His degree of declination fell clearly into the impossible.

"I will bet you two bits, payable in Lowell, that the silk hat falls to earth in the next five minutes," said Elkanah, riding beside Rudolpho.

Indeed, it seemed likely. Mister Skye rode heavily starboard, and the black stovepipe jammed rakishly over his cranium leaned even further starboard, virtually horizontal, and seemed to cling to the guide's skull only by force of habit.

"Done!" said Professor Danzig. He was witnessing one miracle; why not two?

"I believe Jawbone is unhappy," observed Elkanah Morse. It had to be the understatement of the day. Jawbone loathed every moment of the journey, and minced with his ears flattened back and a snarl frozen on his lips, staring viciously at the topsy-turvy world through yellow eyes.

Mister Skye reached the apogee of his starboard journey and convulsed himself back to equilibrium, muttering and clutching his brown jug. A moment later he began sliding to port side, and Jawbone clacked his teeth.

"I think you lost, Elkanah," said Professor Danzig.

"Five minutes aren't up yet," the entrepreneur replied, consulting his silver-cased turnip watch, a gift from Betsy.

They rode quietly through an icy morning. Victoria had led them out of her village the previous twilight and pushed on into the dark, seeming to know where they would go. North of the village, she suddenly cut east, riding out of the Boulder River valley and into rough foothills for several miles until her mysterious trail led down into another drainage, a cottonwood-lined creek. There they camped, eating a late supper from their few stores in the panniers.

Victoria had turned sullen and wouldn't even speak to Professor Danzig, whom she firmly believed was a bad-medicine man, a witch. When they awoke this frosty morning, she continued to ignore him and wouldn't even come close to him. Apparently she thought he was the author of all their troubles. Her village medicine man had told her so.

She rode a hundred yards ahead, as if to dissociate herself from these evil whites, a lithe angry ancient woman resting lightly on her rawboned bay pony. She steered them due east, too, by Danzig's magnetic compass, taking them across drainages, up and down vast swales and ridges, rather than following the easier route of the level Yellowstone valley. It puzzled Danzig a little. To the south loomed vaulting mountains that looked to be the roof of the world. From the ridges he could see the Yellowstone valley way to the north and angling northeast. And between them, the country had convulsed into giant shoulders of the mountains, half-forested, half-prairie, rocky and cut by rushing clear creeks. Not a good place to take a caravan, he thought, but she seemed to follow a fairly easy Indian and game—probably buffalo—trail. Ahead, Mister Skye's travois-laden ponies and mules negotiated the rugged country with no difficulty beyond an occasional jarring bounce of the travois. But Mary rode ahead, keeping an eye on all that, and on little Dirk, sitting on a travois as well. Unlike Victoria, Mary revealed not the slightest hostility.

"How does it feel to be a witch?" asked Elkanah, whose mind must have run in the same direction as Rudolpho's.

"About the same as feeling Swiss," he replied. "About the same as feeling married."

"It's not a good thing. Is there any way you can reach her? Change her mind? Stop this superstition? I dread to see our little party divided."

"I will ask to speak with her at this evening's camp. I'd like her to look through the sextant and see what I'm doing."

Mister Skye slid almost horizontal and then righted himself heavily, like a half-flooded ship wallowing in heavy seas.

"You owe me two bits," said Rudolpho triumphantly. "Once a man defies natural law, there's no stopping him."

The horses straggled up a long grade. Sandstone, Danzig thought. So convulsed by the upthrust mountains that the strata stood on end. Wind-eroded, too, hollowed and curved into fantastic shapes by the abrasion of sand upon sand. Indeed, a violent cold gust whipped at his back, lifting dust and debris from the slope.

"Cold, isn't it?" said Elkanah. "I asked Mrs. Skye to take us to Fort Laramie directly. I fear time's run out. I'd hoped to get to two or three more villages—Sioux, Arapaho, Northern Cheyenne—but that's out. We'll be lucky to scrape by in pleasant fall weather."

"Those army ambulances from Fort Laramie to Leavenworth may not exactly be comfortable either in October and November," Danzig observed.

He felt the pony bunch its muscles under him and plunge over a sandstone step in the trail. He'd come to an understanding with this line-backed coyote dun—that's what Mister Skye had called the beast—long before, soon after they'd left Fort Benton. His diplomatic protocol with the beast required that he sit quietly and let the horse make all the decisions in true monarchial fashion. It had been hard for the republican Mister Danzig to swallow, but in time the dun showed the wisdom of it. The little malformed low-rumped mustang picked gentle grades, carried him uncomplainingly, and seemed to survive on snatched mouthfuls of bunch grass and weeds. Its unshod hooves were remarkably hard, and never wore out, even in such rock as they now traversed.

Professor Danzig's head had found the protocol with his mustang agreeable, but his tailbone didn't. The Harvard geologist had rarely been on a saddle horse for more than an hour or two in all his life. But here he lived atop this animated conveyance, and he'd discovered new ways to experience pain. He believed his hammered behind would no longer rest comfortably upon cushioned Harvard chairs or even outhouse seats and he would have to install saddlelike chairs in his home for future comfort. Still, he rode easier now than when he started the voyage. The mustang had become affectionate, too.

Behind him rode Betsy and Arabella in their sidesaddles, their pleated long riding skirts tucked neatly about their legs. Professor Danzig had always marveled at Betsy, but never more so than here in a vast empty wilderness. Her natural buoyancy turned all hardship and discomfort into adventure, and her ready laugh and affection turned each camp into a happy picnic. Even dour Arabella had relaxed her tart hostility, and seemed softer and more a woman, he thought.

Behind the lovely ladies rode Percy Connaught, always complaining of discomforts or exclaiming about the entries in his priceless journals, and last, Captain Cobb, who tended the pack animals and seemed competent in his phlegmatic and deliberate way. Elkanah had asked the pair of them to handle the pack animals and supplies, but only Cobb did, patiently saddling and unsaddling each animal each day, making sure the loads in the panniers were even, taking the horses to water and pasture, and all the while being useful. Connaught had not helped. He alone was the slacker among them, forever finding his morocco-bound journals more important than the camp chores. So they'd all waited on him because there was no help for it. Saddling his horse mornings, unsaddling and picketing it at night. Danzig had done much of that. Good training for a geologist in North America, he thought privately.

That evening Victoria sullenly halted them beside a twisting creek, barely running in this dry season, that had cut a deep narrow canyon in its rush to the Yellowstone.

"Has this creek a name?" Danzig asked politely. Victoria glared, and turned away silently. Through the whole journey he'd sketched maps, inserted creeks, given peaks and rivers whatever white trapper and Indian names he could commandeer from Mister Skye or his wives. But now his principal source had become unavailable. Indeed, incoherent. Danzig watched Victoria and Mary ease the inert muttering guide off a twitching and biting Jawbone. They couldn't quite support him, and he landed in a heap, trembling the earth, gazing stupidly from his obscure blue eyes at his new universe before vanishing into his own world again.

"Goddamn," Victoria muttered fiercely.

She avoided Danzig through all the camp chores, but at last he cornered her before their shabby lodge.

"Victoria," he said softly. "May I say something?"

She wheeled, glaring, frozen, waiting.

"For me to be a bad-medicine man, a witch, I'd have the wish in my heart to do evil to you and your people and others. I have no such wish. You call God the First Maker. I hope the First Maker blesses you and brings you goodness."

She glared, muttering, and returned to her butchering. Sometime during the day she'd put an arrow through a doe, though no white in camp knew just when, and now she and Mary peeled the hide off of it.

He tried again. "Tonight come look at the North Star with me through my sextant. I will show you that I only look. I am not stealing your star or making bad medicine. I can use it to look at the sun, too, when it is highest at noon, and tell you how far north or south we are."

She glared, muttering. "Maybe I'll think about it," she snarled. "Maybe you a witch and make Mister Skye stay on the Other Side. He never stay over there this long before."

"We could take away his whiskey," he said.

"No. I don't take away nothing. He got to make up his own mind. You take away his whiskey and I get mad."

He left it at that, detecting some softening in her that might turn into something better soon. He wanted to poke around the stratified sandstone here before dusk anyway.

Two things happened at the equinox. It rained, and Mister Skye sobered. Jarvis Cobb surmised that the former caused the latter. They awoke to leaden gray overcast the first day of fall, and a temperature barely above freezing. Indeed, the water in the camp buckets had iced over, a clear solid skim reminding them to hurry to safety.

For days, old Victoria had steered them east by southeast, following the humped prairie foothills of the Absaroka mountains. Grand country, Jarvis thought, but hard to travel compared with the flat belly of the Yellowstone angling to the north. They'd pierced through a vast silence, made all the more profound by Victoria's dour hostility to them all. They'd seen not a soul, not even another Crow band. It seemed almost as if the whole Crow nation knew a bad-medicine party pierced through its lands and had steered far away.

They'd splashed across a laughing clear river horse-belly deep, beneath towering blue peaks, that Danzig identified as the Stillwater. Then another, less formidable one he called Clark's Fork of the Yellowstone, boulder-strewn and murkier than the first. Lewis and Clark's careful journals had become Danzig's basic source because Mister Skye remained lost in his own world. Elkanah bet Danzig that

Mister Skye would fall off Jawbone and into Clark's Fork. It looked as if it might happen. The angry blue roan splashed viciously across the slippery rock-strewn bottom, as if weary of the leaning stupefied load he carried. At one point Mister Skye defied gravity again, righting himself at the last moment, but not before Jawbone splashed him thoroughly by pawing icy river water. Danzig won another two bits. Percy recorded the bet in his fattening journal for the vulgar.

The Crow woman swung through a wide dry gap in the mountains. Pryor's Gap, Danzig called it, after consulting Lewis and Clark again. At once Captain Cobb could see its strategic importance. They'd come to the eastern end of a vast range of mountains that blocked southward passage. But off to the east rose the featureless Pryors, and beyond, the Big Horns. A strategic gap, he thought; a gap that funneled villages, armies, and horse-stealing expeditions. The country grew sandy and arid, with thick bursts of silvery sagebrush and sharply eroded dry watercourses. All the beauty and grandeur of the Yellowstone country vanished, and a new dark mood lay upon this lunar land: loneliness. This huge empty basin seemed somehow inexpressibly lonely. The Big Horn basin, Danzig called it. A natural home of wild horses. The explorers' journals recorded that the Pryor Mountains—which they named after a sergeant on that expedition—were full of them.

They'd dined the last evening of summer on an antelope Victoria had shot. The white-rumped pronghorns seemed abundant here, and were gathering now into vast winter bands. Prairie-goat meat seemed tough and gamy, and didn't please him. But it filled his belly. In these frosty days it kept well, so they tied unused haunches on their packs against the time when Victoria might not be able to down

an animal. Rudolpho pulled out his sextant as night thickened, and shot the North Star again in a sky growing
cloudy.

"Just south of forty-five degrees north," he said. "Let's
call it forty-four degrees, fifty minutes."

Jarvis Cobb recorded that in his tersely written journal,
along with other military considerations. White haze
ringed the full moon, and Captain Cobb recorded that, too.
Also that their lout of a guide, Mister Skye, had now completed his eleventh day of inebriation. Victoria no longer
eased him off Jawbone; she yanked him hard and let him
crash to earth. Always his first act upon smacking into dirt
was to stumble to his feet and make water, which invari-
ably caused Betsy and Arabella to hasten elsewhere.

"Have you no decency!" Connaught bellowed.

Bitter wind flapped at their tents that night and eddied
into them. This expedition had not outfitted itself for winter, and their shelters and bedrolls seemed barely adequate
as the days shortened and the night frosts clung to the
bunch grass far into the days.

Icy horizontal rain whipped them just as Betsy got her
portable tin stove fired with sagebrush stalks for breakfast.
Each drop hissed as it hit the hot stove. Eventually the rain
drummed so violently that it cooled the metal surfaces in
clouds of steam, and she could cook nothing. In any case,
she got soaked in icy water while the rest huddled in their
tents. Cold breakfast, then. Or no breakfast. They crawled
inside their chattering tents to wait.

Captain Cobb, the army man, knew it would only be a
matter of time before water oozed into their dank, gloomy,
crowded quarters. Neither of Elkanah's tents had been
set up on high ground or ditched to carry off water. The
prairie clays under them would turn to grease and soak

bedding. And everywhere a hand or finger touched canvas above them, it perspired, coating the inner walls and ceiling with collected water.

From out in that icy drizzle, Victoria bellowed at them. "Pack up now! We got to git!"

Captain Cobb stuck his head out the flap, into the stinging wind-borne spray. She stood before him, small, soaked, and glaring. Astonishingly, Mister Skye's lodge had been neatly folded and anchored to its travois, and its poles hung in two bunches from the second horse. Mister Skye sat upon Jawbone, rain dripping from the brim of his silk hat, the shoulders of his buckskins black with water. He looked almost sober. Mary sat her pony impassively, cuddling little Dirk before her, bundled tightly in some sort of capote.

"Surely you're not traveling on a day like this!"

"It gets cold soon. And you ain't got anything for cold. We got to get you to Fort Laramie fast."

"Well, we're not going," replied Cobb. "We'd take pneumonia in this."

"You got those slickers. You each got the slickers."

True enough, he thought. Elkanah had provided each of them with a bad-weather coat of canvas impregnated with India rubber. That was another of his strokes of genius. Ever since his friend over in New Haven, Charles Goodyear, had learned to vulcanize rubber by adding sulfur and heating it, Elkanah had experimented with rubberized fabrics. When Howe invented the sewing machine, Elkanah had plunged into ready-made storm gear.

From the other tent, Elkanah peered around, observing Mister Skye sitting silently and possibly soberly on Jawbone. The guide said nothing—not yet ready to speak—but stared back with knowing in his eyes at last.

"I think we'd better be off, gentlemen," Elkanah said quietly.

"But that's madness!" cried Percy. "We'll all be soaked and take the fever. My journals will be ruined!"

Mister Skye said, "Have you looked around the walls of your tent, Mister Connaught? Do you wish to sleep in muck tonight? Perhaps we'll find a better place down the trail a bit. Do you see any firewood here to dry out with? Only sagebrush, sir."

They stared, astonished, at the guide.

In fifteen minutes they packed and broke camp, settling themselves gingerly on cold wet saddles. The whites, in fact, had more protection from the driving rain than Mister Skye's family, who sat stolidly absorbing the drizzle in their water-black skin clothing.

They struck southeast under a leaden sky, through a day without light, across a landscape without feature. Arabella turned sullen and vicious, snapping at her mother. Percy muttered complaints and imprecations. But off they went into a gray gloom, as hungry as when they rose.

By noon the clay beneath them turned to gumbo, treacherous and slick. Horses skidded, and not even the utility of four legs kept them from sliding and careening. Water trickled down Captain Cobb's neck, slicing vicious streaks of cold down his back and chest. Travois poles skidded silkily behind the guide's horses, cutting clean furrows in the liquid clay. And still they rode across a land that seemed almost desert. The only happy creature in the whole caravan was Jawbone, whose ears perked forward and whose step had become bold again, now that he carried a man on his back rather than a drunk.

Connaught's complaints turned into hate.

"If you hadn't gotten drunk, we wouldn't be in this mess your squaw got us into, Skye!" he cried.

"Mister Skye, mate."

"Drunks don't deserve to be called mister. Why don't you and your stupid women find us shelter and warmth? Where are caves? Overhangs? You'll kill us with the ague, the chills. Have you no thought for the Morse women?"

"Hard to find those things in this basin."

"Well, find them! And we'll wait for sunshine there."

"Might not be sunshine for days. And we're a long way from Fort Laramie." Mister Skye spoke with a peculiar gentleness that seemed to rise from some remorse and sorrow. Cobb noted it, and found himself oddly sympathetic even to a man who had been falling-down drunk for eleven days.

"Percy," said Elkanah, "let's endure. Let's get along. Let's see what the day brings. We're not suffering terribly in these slickers. Not as much as Mister Skye and his brave women."

But the rain kept driving, mixed with sleet, and they found no place to hide. They crossed a swollen muddy river Mister Skye called the Greybull, and made a miserable wet cold camp in a grove on its south bank. That night they were all sullen and quiet.

Chapter 18

All the next grim day he led them southeast under a sullen sky that blotted all landmarks and emptied icy water in gusts and bursts the whole hard trip. He knew where he was going by instinct. Four times horses skidded to their knees, usually when clawing up the slick gumbo of a grassless draw. In places hock-deep muck mired the horses, clotting on hooves and pasterns and exhausting them. They splashed so much muck on their legs and bellies, and on their riders and packs, that not even drenching rain washed it off. It caked heavy on the beasts, adding to their burdens.

Late in the day, when the dull light imperceptibly melded with twilight, he struck the valley of the Big Horn. Just then orange sunlight pried at the world from under the belly of the storm, turning it purple and gold, and blazoning a vivid emerald smear of valley set between ocher bluffs. The light lasted all of thirty seconds, and then vanished like a vision, or a visitation of angels, spurring strange yearnings in him for the sight of England.

A bruised dark cloud spat ice at them as they skidded downward, horses mincing and going rigid under them, into the bottoms.

"We'll camp down here tonight," he said to the sullen people beside him.

"I hope there's dry firewood," snapped Percy.

"We'll show you how to find it," Mister Skye replied. He had started to hunt for the right sort of place, preferably sandy and a bit up from the bottoms; protected from the gusty winds, and with a thick cottonwood forest nearby, plenty of brush. He would have preferred a good overhang, but little rock lay exposed in these gentle water-cut bluffs.

He swung south, up the Big Horn, riding under the west bluff through a bottom partitioned into parks and dense thickets. They scared up mule deer. Partridge exploded from brush, spraying rain. They crashed through thickets of fall-yellowed foliage that drenched them as they passed.

He chose a place on a gravelly delta beneath the bluff, a place that had shed the water. Thickset majestic cottonwoods loomed darkly in every direction save for the bluff on the west, and masses of brush burgeoned up in the gloom. He preferred camps with sweeping vistas, but this cloistered one would do on a drizzling and bitter night.

He'd gone numb long ago. The ice water had purged the last of the alcohol from his body and forced his mind out of its long haze. He felt subdued, stung by nature and guilt, quiet and humbled, in need of forgiveness.

They all dismounted, mud-caked and hard-eyed, surveying this brush-walled place in obscure light. Victoria and Mary erected the lodge. The two wall tents rose. He'd chosen well. They'd sleep dry and warm tonight and wouldn't even need to trench around the tents because the rain vanished into the gravel. Wordlessly, Victoria slipped into the gloom of the forest with her hatchet and reappeared later with semidry wood. A lot of the small sticks looked entirely dry, ripped from some obscure corners. Other wood seemed moist-black on top, but gray-bottomed. Elkanah and Rudolpho examined her load with interest and plunged into the gloom to duplicate it.

Percy dove into the erected wall tent and refused to budge, leaving the camp and horse chores to Captain Cobb once again. Elkanah rigged a fly sheet he'd rarely used this trip in front of his tent, giving protection from the drizzle. It chattered in the wet gusts. Betsy could cook comfortably under it, using her little folding camp stove. But this night none of them would be as comfortable as the Skye family in its skin lodge with the smoke vent and wind flaps above, to draw off the smoke from a small hot fire in the very center of the lodge, a fire to cook on and radiate heat into a cone of comfort.

Well, thought Mister Skye, they had slickers all day; my Victoria and my Mary and my Dirk have a warm dry night ahead. The smoke-cured lodgeskins turned even a driving rain and captured warmth within. The smoke of Victoria's fire lifted lazily into the rain and then sank to earth, oddly perfuming the little park. Betsy's stove pumped smoke up its tiny chimney, too, and Elkanah's party crowded close to it, heat-starved, under the canvas fly.

The guide sighed. They'd not collected wood enough for a night like this, and gloom lowered into gray now. He braved the stinging rain some more, and checked the horses, too. He found them in a neighboring park, greedily chewing grass at the end of their pickets. All except Jawbone, who ranged freely and would return to the lodge shortly. They seemed safe enough here, though invisible from the camp. It wouldn't be a night for horse thievery. He snapped squaw wood from trees and carted it to the Morse camp. Three armloads. Then another for his lodge.

"Is that enough?" asked Rudolpho. "I'll help you. And watch how you select dry wood."

"Glad for your help, mate," the guide rumbled, and together they examined wood, finding it dry on sheltered sides, finding sticks caught in brush that seemed barely moist.

"This is the Big Horn. And upstream a way it becomes the Wind River on my charts. How do you explain that?"

"Cuts through a red and purple granite mountain, Mister Danzig."

"But it's still the same river!"

"No . . . not really. On the other side of the mountain it's another river, headwaters in the Wind Rivers, pulsing out onto the Great Plains, or anyway an arm of the plains. When it hits the canyon, it starts running uphill."

Danzig laughed. "You mountain men," he said.

"Tremendous hot springs this side of the canyon. We'll go there for a little holiday. You might even feel warm again. We could make it in less than two days."

"Connaught claims his writing fingers are frozen stiff." Mister Skye didn't laugh.

In his lodge he pulled off his clammy soaked fringed shirt of elkskin and let the tiny hot blaze warm his naked flesh. His wives had anchored down the lodgeskirts with rock to keep chill gusts from sliding into this haven. Soon, when it became colder, they'd tie up the inner lining and anchor it with rock, giving them double-walled comfort that made lodges livable even in bitter cold. Victoria looked up at him from her cooking pot and the sliced antelope and bread root she was dropping into it, and suddenly crawled over and hugged him.

"Goddamn!" she exclaimed angrily, squeezing him. It was her signal that she'd forgiven him, and more. Her way of telling him she loved him. Mary smiled, too, loving without words.

He sat peacefully in his small home, cleaning caked wet powder out of the cylinder of his dragoon Colt and setting the soaked powder to drying safely back from the spitting fire. On occasion a gust of cold wind rattled the lodge and sent a few drops whirling down the smoke vent, but it didn't matter. This rain seemed relentless but not vicious. He half expected to see a sheen of snow in the morning, though. He poured fresh Du Pont into six bores of his cylinder and rammed balls home, and pressed fresh caps over the cleaned-out nipples. The old caps had vanished during its long neglect. That done, he set to work on the soaked Hawken, gouging gummy wet powder out of it, cleaning the chamber and nipple, and replacing powder, wad, ball, and cap.

He'd order some of Elkanah's slickers for his women, he thought. Maybe even buy Elkanah's if he'd sell them to him at Fort Laramie. Mostly, Indian ways worked better here—he glanced at his comfortable lodge and thought about the cold wall tents of Elkanah's—but those slickers had value and might save his family from a death of a cold or ague or lung congestion.

Almost over, he thought. Maybe two weeks of autumnal travel to Laramie if they could make thirty or so miles a day. He'd give these half-frozen mud-caked pilgrims a little comfort where the hot mineral waters boiled over white-limed rock and into the Big Horn. That'd lift their spirits. All in all, it had been an easy trip, without calamity, and Morse had found out what he came for. Morse's party still faced seven hundred miles of prairie travel with an army supply and mail train east, but they'd have excellent covered wagons to ride in.

Even stripped to his breechclout, he felt perfectly comfortable in the warm lodge. His leggins and shirt steamed in the radiant heat. Little Dirk was in a jolly mood, freed of the cradlebasket that trapped him on Mary's pony, and Mister Skye horsed with the tyke in the glow of the lodge. Everything inside seemed golden and tan and brown tonight: the dark inviting buffalo robes, the tawny lodgeskins, the rosy brown faces of his women, the amber smoke of the fire coiling out upon a lowering blackness. He felt happy to have the rot out of his blood and to be here, now, at peace. His soaked silk hat lay to one side, and he'd tied a red bandanna around his head to keep his long graying hair out of his face.

The Skyes entertained visitors that night after supper. All except Percy Connaught, who scribbled in his tent by the light of Elkanah's lantern.

"Back in Boston, Nat Wyeth told me these skin lodges are marvels," said Elkanah. "I was slow to believe him . . . but I'm learning."

The entrepreneur's grin, along with his endless capacity to adjust his thinking to new insights, delighted Mister Skye. Betsy and Arabella sat to either side of Elkanah, at first a bit put off by Mister Skye's furry near-nakedness, but warming to him and to the fire and the radiant cheer of this little home.

"Well, mate, what have you learned this trip? What'll ye be manufacturing for us?" asked the guide amiably.

"I've learned to trust the trading companies—for the most part," Elkanah said. "They seem to know what the tribes will buy and what cuts against the grain of their lives. Like those ready-made arrows of mine."

"I think you'd find a market for your slickers," Mister Skye said. "Handy things. I don't fathom any medicine problems with them."

"I'll remember that," Elkanah said.

Beside Betsy sat Rudolpho Danzig, quietly avoiding talk and glancing from time to time at Victoria.

"You, Danzig. Dammit. How does your star shooter work?" she asked suddenly, in a stutter of the conversation.

"Why, I'll show it—"

"Nah, I seen it. Don't go out. You couldn't look at the star tonight. We know where we are, but you don't know where you are!" she said triumphantly. "Inside my head is better than them charts you draw."

He laughed easily. Victoria had forgiven him, too. Or declared him a nonwitch just by talking with him.

They didn't stay long. The visit had been a reconciliation more than anything. Shared comforts, shared anecdotes about a brutal day, and a renewal. Drowsily Mister

Skye saw them off, his gaze following them to their dark chill canvas tents. For all of white men's genius and innovation, they didn't know how to live out here, he thought. Didn't know how to live Injun.

That blustery night two wives snuggled up tight beside him, and he enjoyed them both, slipping at last into an amiable dreamless sleep.

Jawbone's screeching awakened him. He knew that wild screech, and his heart labored from rest to violent banging, not catching up with his need for blood. He yanked his robes aside and clutched his Hawken, easing out the door flap. A dull streak of light shone through black cottonwoods to the east. That was the last he saw. Something cracked his head from above, and he sagged into the wetness.

Mary bolted up in the robes. Victoria slid up in the blackness. Outside, a shot, a thud, a male yell, a woman's scream. Another shot. Naked, Mary crept toward the lodge door, stumbling over her man's prone form, half in, half out, blocking the way.

"Son of a bitch," muttered Victoria, her old fusil in hand. She peered out, into murk. Mary did, too, seeing the shadowy forms of warriors. One leaned over Mister Skye, just a few feet away, a scalping knife catching the gray of dawn. Victoria fired, flint on frizzen. Spark and sizzle. She'd failed to clean out the soaked powder.

Mary grabbed Mister Skye's legs and tugged violently, yanking her man's entire body back into the lodge just as the warrior grabbed a handful of Mister Skye's long graying hair. She yanked so violently the warrior tumbled in with Skye, muttering Shoshone words Mary understood.

Victoria clubbed the warrior with her fusil.

Dirk squalled in his robes. Mary lifted the big chunky boy, slid him into the lined cradlebasket she used now.

Then the entire lodge ripped away from earth, yanked by some giant force, leaving them naked in dawnlight. The old lodge crumpled in a heap. Around them crouched more warriors—nearly naked even in this bitter air—than Mary could count, ready to kill, lances and war clubs poised, trade iron tomahawks in hand. No bows. Rain had softened the sinew bowstrings.

Wildly she peered out. Both the wall tents had vanished, ripped from their pegs and thrown aside. One dark form—Cobb's, she thought—lay inert. Danzig sat quietly. Percy Connaught in white linens whimpered, choked, pleading for mercy in a strange whine. Where the other tent had been, Arabella cowered in her bedroll. Betsy sat up in her petticoats, a blanket drawn tight about her. And Elkanah in a nightshirt struggled to his feet, his face wild, his receding hair prickling in all directions.

All this Mary absorbed in a glance. Jawbone screeched, wheeled through camp, tumbling these raiders, kicking murderously at one and another, biting viciously. They turned to lance him, missing because of his demonic speed and violence. A flaying hoof caught a warrior, crushing his thigh into bloody pulp. He fell, writhing, screaming words Mary understood: "demon horse . . . medicine horse . . . I am gone. . . ."

She crabbed around her possessions, found her own fusil, probably wet, too, and brought it up, but a cold hand clamped her, ripping away the rifle. "I'll take that, squaw," said a voice in a tongue she understood. Shoshone? Would her people, ancient friends of the longknives, friends of Mister Skye, do this?

"Stop!" she cried in her Snake tongue. "This is Mister

Skye! I am Mister Skye's woman! This is the medicine horse Jawbone! Do this and you die!"

Jawbone screeched and plunged, berserk and murderous. A lance caught his flank, drawing a thin sheet of blood, and he bulled into its thrower, toppling him. Mary screamed. Victoria crawled to Mister Skye, who stirred woozily.

Elkanah Morse managed to stand, but a warrior smashed him to earth with one brutal blow. Betsy screamed.

"Don't hurt me, I'm a friend," Connaught whined. "I'm a friend, a friend. I'll give you anything, anything."

The light had intensified a little. Cobb, flat on his belly, stirred. Mary could make out a bleeding gory lump on his head where he'd been knocked unconscious.

Mary stood up, naked, and yelled, "If you hurt Mister Skye or us, you will die! The spirits will kill you. The spirits will torture you and take away your children." Some of the milling warriors glanced at her, understanding her words. Her Shoshone. She felt shamed beyond description. The warrior who had ripped the rifle from her tossed her to the ground again, and she sprawled over Victoria and Mister Skye.

"Goddamn," Victoria muttered, drawing her dagger. "They kill us all, but I will kill one."

Jawbone went insane, screaming an eerie sound that could not possibly rise from a horse throat, plowing viciously into one after another of these night raiders, scattering them. From the little park where they'd picketed their horses, she heard screaming and hooves and finally a thunder of fleeing animals.

Mary wheeled upon the warrior beside her whose hand gripped her hair. "You! You've disgraced my people!" she snarled. "You've attacked friends!"

"Not Snakes," muttered the powerful stocky warrior. "Bannock. No friends of these longknives."

Bannocks! Not her people. Not exactly her tongue, either, but one she'd understood. They lived in the mountains to the west, like her own people.

"We come for the sacred buffalo," he said with a strange accent. "We see no buffalo for our winter meat and hides, but this is almost as good." He laughed, and deliberately slapped his lance across Mister Skye's naked back, raking flesh and drawing blood with its iron point, counting coup again. "We will all count coup on the big-medicine white-man who lies at my feet."

Mary stared at the hard-muscled warrior. He hadn't painted for war. This had been sport, at least until Jawbone went berserk. Now two of them lay injured or dying, one with a crushed hip, the other with a caved-in skull. So many! A few had taken off after the captured herd. Jaw-bone bolted after the herd, too, intending to turn it back, as he always did. So many! Bannocks slid out from behind cottonwoods where they'd fled from the terrible medicine horse. Mary counted swiftly. Maybe twenty more.

"This is Mister Skye. We have captured the greatest of all longknives," cried the warrior. "Come count coup before we torture him to death!"

"You will die! His ghost will haunt you forever and soil your villages forever," cried Mary fiercely. Her words were different but somehow the same as theirs.

They laughed easily. One by one they filed past, each slapping a lance or a war club across Mister Skye's back. One snapped a hatchet down, and Victoria deflected it ferociously. The warrior snarled, shoved old Victoria aside, and swung the ax viciously. Mary sprang into him, sent him sprawling. "You will die!" she hissed. He grabbed her hair, lifting her bodily, intending to bash her skull with his hatchet. That's when Mister Skye bit him. The guide gripped a calf and sank in his teeth and spat out a mouthful of flesh and blood. He'd ripped a mouthful of calf from the leg. The Bannock screamed. Betsy screamed. Victoria snarled and snatched the hatchet from the staggering warrior and clobbered him with the flat back of it.

Victoria stood wildly, a vicious old naked squaw daring any of them to come closer, to count more coup on Mister Skye. The Bannocks laughed. Over twenty of them had counted coup on the greatest of all whites. That made the Bannock people the greatest of all tribes!

Mister Skye sat up dizzily, staring about him in the dawn-light. He felt the lump on his skull where he'd been clubbed. His back bled from a score of wounds where the coup counters had jabbed lances and knives into him.

Elkanah stood again, and they let him. "Who are they, Mary?" he asked weakly.

"Bannock!" she hissed. "I know their words. They live far to the west. They came for buffalo."

Elkanah peered around him. "We are all alive," he said.

"Not for long. They will torture us! They will kill us slow, just like Kills Dog Woman."

She stood ferociously, utterly unconscious of her young voluptuousness until she grew aware of staring. She knew the One Above had given her a perfect body. Imperiously, she picked up her dried doeskin dress and slid it on. Then she picked up Dirk's cradlebasket and anchored him into it, pulling its well-greased elkhide cover over Dirk's head to keep the rain off of him.

Mister Skye stood nakedly, a hairy barrel of white flesh, and as he did, a dozen warriors lifted their deadly lances and pointed them at him.

He made signs with his hands. Signs for medicine, for killing, for bad medicine. What he was saying to the one who seemed to be the Bannock headman was, leave at once or die of bad medicine.

The stocky scarred gap-toothed headman, who wore waist-long hair in a single braid plaited around German silver medallions, grinned back. "I don't hold with medicine," he said, letting Mary translate. "It is foolishness. White trappers taught me it is foolishness. I know of only three things: The power of warriors. The power of hunters. The power of squaws. Right now we have the power of warriors over you, and we will do what we please. Slow-Death Man has said it."

Chapter 19

A Bannock freethinker, Mister Skye thought to himself. His head ached. Cold penetrated his naked body. He turned his back to the whites and tied his elk-skin belt—a gift from Victoria—around his middle and picked up his breechclout. This he slipped between his legs and stuffed the red-beaded ends under his belt fore and aft and let them drop.

"Get dressed," he said to the rest sharply. If they didn't get dressed, and fast, they'd likely not have any clothes.

Victoria slid her fringed doeskin dress over her and tied on her high moccasins. Mister Skye slid his elkskin shirt on and immediately felt warmer. He pulled up his heavy leggins and tied them with thong to his wide soft belt. He started for his square-toed whiteman's boots.

The pocked headman growled something at Mary.

"He says no shoes. Whitemen have tender feet and can't go anywhere without shoes," she said.

The guide stared toward his clients. Elkanah was tugging trousers up under his nightshirt. Arabella cowered in her blankets. Betsy pulled a woolen emerald dress over her night shift. Cobb had been dressed when he plunged from his tent and got clobbered. He sat up now, rubbing his head. Danzig dressed quietly, his back turned to the women, buttoning the fly of his black britches. But Connaught seemed paralyzed, cowering in white linen smallclothes that stretched down to his knees.

Mister Skye's mind whirled with possibilities. Their herd had bolted, and several Bannocks had ridden off to corral it. Jawbone's occasional shrieks drifted through the morning fog. He would be gathering the horses, too, or maybe conducting his one-horse war on the mounted Bannocks. They might put arrows into the horse—if they had dry bowstrings.

He turned to the smirking headman. "If your friends were trappers, you know English," he said flatly.

The headman said nothing, his eyes mocking.

Deliberately, he reached for his big boots and slid his feet into them. The lance stabbed earth viciously, half an inch from his fingers. Mister Skye stood again.

"So you don't believe in medicine," he said calmly. "But you counted coup twice—big medicine—and invited all your warriors to count coup. You believe in medicine, my friend."

"Medicine is nonsense," replied Slow-Death Man in slurred English. "Counting coup is like the ribbons your soldiers wear. Bravery ribbons."

He spoke something sharply to the warrior nearest

Rudolpho, who threw the geologist into the gravel and yanked his shoes off.

"Oh dear," cried Betsy faintly.

Danzig rubbed a sore arm and sat quietly.

"They have been told," said the headman.

"Slow-Death Man. How did you get that fine brave name?" asked Mister Skye, meeting mock with mock.

"In the New Grass Moon, after the trappers had wintered with us, I killed them slowly. Three days it took because I am expert. They told me medicine is not real—just cloudy thinking. There is only power. Power to kill, that warriors and hunters have. Power to grow life, that squaws have. Spirits. Ghosts. Witches. Vision quests. All nothing. Animal helpers, spirit helpers, whitemen's God, all the same. I asked them about the blackrobe, DeSmet, who came to us with the cross, and black book. They laughed. Medicine, they said. No good. Only rifles and axes and bows and arrows make power. So I killed them slowly to see if they were lying. They lied. They screamed and prayed to their medicine, the one called God. So I took my new name."

Mister Skye nodded. A headman without the constraints of medicine. Bad business. He'd known whites like that, trappers in particular, turned murderous and brutal by the very mountains.

"These people with me have come peacefully—even their women are along—to show new things, good things, to the people like yourselves. That gentleman there makes these good things, arrow points, metal pots—and he came to find out what you like, and make them for you. We wish to smoke the pipe with you, and then be on our way."

The headman laughed sarcastically. "One of my men

lies dead, kicked in the skull by your horse. Another lies badly injured, his hip smashed by your horse. And another, there, you have bitten in the leg, and he hurts."

"That's the price of war and horsestealing," replied Mister Skye. "Your power was not enough."

"Bad medicine," snapped Victoria. "You got bad medicine."

The headman turned serious for a moment. "Some of my warriors think it. They keep to the Ways of the People. I am different. I think of luck and power. I think we will do what we please. You are helpless. We have power. We will torture Mister Skye to death, and kill your horse. I don't know about the others. I will think about it."

The remaining Bannocks returned, driving the stolen herd before them. Five more, Mister Skye thought. Jawbone hovered beside the herd, bunching it, doing Bannock work, squealing and dancing like a spirit animal, making the Bannocks restless.

"See how your great medicine horse does our work for us, Mister Skye. It has killed one of us, and we will kill it soon."

"Unless it kills you first," Mister Skye retorted. The blue roan looked confused, he thought. Never had it seen him captured. It didn't know friend from enemy just now. It paced restlessly, ignoring the Bannocks. One warrior tried to touch it with a coup stick, but Jawbone whirled, arcing murderous sharp hooves inches from the warrior's chest. After that they let it alone.

The headman barked some nasal command, and the newcomers slid off their ponies one by one, paraded before Mister Skye, slapping him with lances and coup sticks, counting coup. Jawbone paced nearby, half-frantic.

Mr. Skye felt the club and scrape of their lances bruising

him. They had not counted coup gently. Twenty-five Bannock hunters, sporting. He wished Jawbone hadn't killed one. But it was what he'd trained the ugly blue roan to do. Crazy horse. Jawbone walked along an edge. Mister Skye stood obdurately, never flinching as the coups rained over him, staring each bloody warrior in the eye.

"Now we have all counted coup on the great—and helpless—Mister Skye," said the headman, mocking. "Now we will see what these whitemen have in their bags for us."

The breath of their ponies fogged the cold air. The whites looked miserably cold, standing half-dressed beside their torn-down tents. Warriors trotted gleefully toward the plunder. One reared back on his heels and burst into coyote song, barking and yapping in coyote joy—the sound of a fresh kill.

"Be patient, mates," said Mister Skye softly. "We have our lives so far. Remember that."

"So far. So far!" The headman snickered. "Maybe I will drain it away slowly to pay for our losses."

"Sir, I will help your injured men!" Betsy said. She walked resolutely toward the two who lay groaning, one with a lacerated and smashed hip, the other with a gouged calf.

The headman beamed. "See, it is as I say. Squaws have power to heal and grow. That is woman's power. Man's power is to kill and be a lord over the world. That is all there is—power."

Betsy ignored him. The warrior whose calf had been bitten sat on the gravel, clutching his calf, trying to slow the sheeting bright blood. He'd lost a great deal and sat sternly, gray-faced, ignoring pain but weakening.

"Oh, dear," she said. "I can't stop this."

"Let the dog die," snarled Victoria.

The headman snapped a command, and two warriors shoved Betsy aside and wrapped soft leather that had been a saddle seat around the bright-blooded wound and tied it tightly with thong. The other warrior's problem was different: his hip was broken. The lacerations on his thigh had crusted over and barely bled at all. Bouncing brutal travois all the way back to bitterroot country, Mister Skye thought.

He considered turning Jawbone loose. A sharp command would do it. But not against twenty-five able-bodied Bannocks. They'd kill Jawbone with their lances, and then slaughter the whole party. Maybe drive arrows into the roan if they had any dry bowstrings.

"Easy, mate," he rumbled at the horse. Jawbone shrieked.

"You're wise, Mister Skye. We'll count coup on the famous horse, too, the terror of the plains." He laughed again.

"Not before he kills half of you," muttered Mister Skye. "And you first. If power's all you know, then taste Jawbone's when you're ready. Your widow will wail and cut off her finger. And because you don't believe in anything, your spirit will wander without a home forever."

Slow-Death Man nodded solemnly. He understood the language of power, even if he laughed at the language of medicine. He stared triumphantly at the huddled fear-stained whites, the captured herd steaming in the cold fog, and then at the bags and parfleches, the debris of Mister Skye's lodge, the canvas and ropes and metal pots of Elkanah's, the thick blankets that still covered Arabella, and all the rest, wet in the mist.

"We will see what the whiteman makes!" he said, muttering something to his warriors. At once they prodded the whites toward Mister Skye, yanking Arabella out of her blankets. She wore a loose white nightdress that hid little of her. Terrified, she tenderfooted her way across gravel, too frightened to object. All the whites minced on bare feet over coarse rock until they gathered close to Mister Skye. Connaught, dressed only in his white smallclothes, had gone blue with cold, and sat down shivering beside the others.

"Easy, mates," said Mister Skye. "We're going to be all right if we stay patient."

Slow-Death Man heard it and laughed nasally. Betsy and Arabella huddled close to Elkanah, drawing and giving warmth. Mary, clutching Dirk in her cradlebasket, and Victoria settled down, glaring hot and defiant, beside Mister Skye. The others—Danzig, Connaught, Cobb—sat huddled and cold in the bitter wet fog of dawn. The sun had vanished behind a new cloud bank, and Mister Skye thought it might rain hard again, or sleet. If a wind came up, these people could die of exposure, even partly dressed as they were.

"Mister Headman, my name's Elkanah Morse. I'd be delighted to show you my goods and demonstrate their uses to you. I've brought fine things to show your people. . . ."

"Quiet!" snapped the headman. He pricked his lance into Elkanah's back, making the industrialist wince.

Squat muscular warriors spread gleefully through the camp, wrestling goods from panniers and parfleches. Bolts of cloth, blue and red, flower-patterned and gold, velveteens, canvas, rubber moccasin soles, ginghams, cottons, wools . . . shiny tin pots, gleaming copper kettles, iron arrowheads, steel awls with wooden handles, red hatchets, blue axes, the black slickers, silvery knives, readymade arrows, black iron lance points, Betsy's folding tin cook stove, thick four-point blankets with Hudson Bay–

type stripes at either end, rubber ground sheets, the tan lodge-cover, ghostly in the fog, copper rivets, rolls of wire, cord and string, scraping tools, files, augers . . . collapsible tent poles with brass fittings . . .

"No!" cried Percy Connaught. "No!" He bolted up and ran, stumbling barefoot, toward the one who lifted his journals. "No!" he shrieked as the warrior solemnly unwrapped the oilcloth bag and slid the blue leather and red leather volumes out into naked day and leafed through them. "No!" screamed Percy, ripping them from the warrior. The Bannock whirled, smashed Percy into the gravel, and kicked the sobbing man. The thump of it jolted them.

"Oh dear," said Betsy. "Oh dear!"

"Those are everything. Those are my life! My work of months! My reputation and fortune! Every insight my mind possesses!" Percy babbled. The warrior stared, flicked through the pages of fine writing. He ripped a page and set it floating to earth.

Behind him, Mister Skye heard the headman chortling. "What is in the sign books, Mister Skye? Big whiteman medicine!" he mocked, drawling out medicine. "White power!"

"His journals of the trip, Slow-Death Man. You might leave him that. Means a lot to him."

"So does our dead warrior—Falling Buck—mean a lot to me! What is writing compared to a Bannock life? All one winter trappers showed me the letters and words. They said those were power, too, power like guns and arrows. I can read. I will take the books with me and cipher the words. See what this weeping man thinks is so important."

"Oh God, no," wailed Connaught. "I'll read them to you. I'll pay anything. I'll send it, send gold, give you whatever—"

"Quiet, weeping man. Your words are all foolishness. See how you wail like a dozen mourning squaws."

The headman muttered something, and a warrior handed him the two journals, along with Cobb's and Professor Danzig's.

"I will see what's in them!" cried the headman.

Both looked stricken, Cobb sat tight-lipped, saying nothing, but his dreams and hopes rested on his journal, Mister Skye knew. Cobb's might be damaging. If the headman really could read, he'd find coldly gathered military information, cold assessments made for armies bent upon defeating Indians. Professor Danzig's would be a compendium of geological notes, sketches, maps, weather notes, anthropological observations about the tribesmen, flora and fauna notes . . . But Cobb's journal—it could get them all killed, Mister Skye thought. He'd never thought of that, that a military intelligence journal could pose such menace.

He peered up at the headman behind him, who stood thumbing through pages, frowning. Mister Skye felt sudden relief, discerning that Slow-Death Man could pick out very few words. "Want me to read it for you, Slow-Death Man?"

The headman glared at him and slid the heavy journals into a soft leather sack dangling from his pad saddle. He strutted out among the goods strewn about by warriors. Everywhere, gleeful muscular young men—were there no old ones in this party?—dug through goods, shouting. These Bannocks were a squat broad wide-cheeked people, with lidded Oriental eyes. They seemed impervious to cold, stripped down for the buffalo hunt to breechclouts and calf-high moccasins. Most wore their coarse hair shoulder length and loose. A few guarded the herd, their own poor ponies—the Bannocks had never been a horse tribe—and the stolen animals. The rest dug industriously through the loot, howling at women's chemises and pantalets, yapping at Elkanah's folding razor, brush, and strop, wiggling Arabella's black lisle stockings in the fog and then making a neckerchief of one.

One found Betsy's portfolio, jerked out her watercolors, forty-three of them now, and bugled like a rutting elk. "Ah!" he cried, waving them. Warriors gathered around, exclaiming, admiring. He waved a watercolor, bugling and howling, making his elk medicine.

"Atsina!" cried one, staring at a portrait of a Gros Ventre warrior. "Ah!" he bellowed, and tore it to shreds. An enemy. Then they found portraits of the Blackfeet, squaws, little girls, warriors. . . .

"Ah!" they cried, spreading Betsy's deftly done works on the gravel and grinding their moccasins into the soft absorbent paper. "Piegans!" they howled.

"Oh, Lord, no, oh dear . . ." breathed Betsy, and sobbed into Elkanah's arms. Elkanah Morse held her tightly, his face resolute and wary.

"I'm so sorry, Betsy. Who would suppose that these tribesmen would—hate portraits of others? How little about them I understood . . ." His voice trailed off.

"Mrs. Morse," rumbled Mister Skye softly. "We have life."

That set her to sobbing more, and Arabella, too, and Mister Skye supposed it was the wrong thing to say. And yet it made a point among them. Some of them. Percy Connaught had sunk into some desperate blubbering despair.

"Mister Connaught. Go get dressed," Mister Skye snapped. "Miss Morse. You too! Now or never. Before they take—do you understand?"

Arabella clung tighter to Elkanah and wouldn't budge. Percy huddled in a heap on the gravel, his white knees lacerated.

Mister Skye watched the warriors shake and flip clothing item by item and toss it into the growing pile. They'd take it all, this loot for Bannock squaws, whitemen's clothing. Connaught and Arabella would go almost naked in the wilderness in late September.

Mister Skye stood. He'd try it himself. With his rising a half-dozen warriors surrounded him with lances. He walked anyway, ignoring them until the iron points pressed viciously into his guts and thighs.

The headman leered. "Power, Mister Skye. That's all there is. See what we have got! Two hundred fine robes could not get us this at the posts. Warrior power got this!"

"I am going to get a dress for the young woman and some britches and a shirt for that man whose books you've stolen."

"Whitemen need clothes. See us, with only our breechclouts. We don't feel cold. Whites are clever but weak. They die without all their clever things, food, weapons, clothing, tents. Let them see if they can live—like us."

A pocked warrior handed the headman two of Danzig's devices.

"What is this?" asked the headman, holding up the sextant.

Professor Danzig himself answered quietly. "It tells me how far south or north we are," he said. "I will show you how to use it." The lithe dark Swiss seemed calmer than the rest.

Slow-Death Man laughed and set it on the ground. The other device before him was the daguerreotyping machine, varnished box, glass eye, black velvet. Plus a handful of exposed tintypes.

The headman examined each, passing them along to exclaiming warriors. Miraculous images. Like Betsy's only all in brown and white and exact, just as the eye sees. One warrior burst into wild talk, gesticulating, pointing. The headman grabbed the tintype.

"He knows this Atsina. He counted coup on this Atsina. He wants this image so he can make medicine and kill the Atsina in the future!"

"Medicine," muttered Mister Skye, feeling the lances pressed into him.

Slow-Death Man said, "Yes, medicine. I do not follow the way of my people. But all the rest follow the way. I think White Weasel is foolish, wanting this image to make medicine. If he wants to kill this Atsina, he should go kill him. No medicine!"

"I will give him the image," said Professor Danzig.

The headman looked amused. "You talk like making gifts!" he exclaimed.

Danzig said, "I am making him a gift."

"Make me a gift. Make an image of me."

"I can do that. I will need this, and these"—he pointed to a box of unexposed plates—"and other things. I have nine plates left."

"Make nine images of me. Ah! Make nine images of me counting coup against Mister Skye."

He would show the world, thought Mister Skye. Very well. It might win them something.

Professor Danzig set up his wooden tripod, screwed the daguerreotyping machine to it.

"You will have to be very still. There's little light, and

this needs lots of sunlight. But if you stand still, perhaps I can make an image."

He vanished under his black cloth. The warriors halted their plundering to gape. The headman grabbed his coup stick, rammed it roughly into Mister Skye's ribs, and held it there, proudly. Danzig fussed. They heard a whirring click and the eye blinked.

"Now I must pull my tent over me and do some things," Danzig said calmly.

"Son of a bitch!" exclaimed Victoria in a rage. Counting coup meant a lot to her. Sacred business to a Crow, Mister Skye thought. And Slow-Death Man would count it eight more times before the whirring lens. He didn't much like it himself, but he'd gotten the message of the lance points. The message wasn't medicine; it was power.

Chapter 20

Betsy wept as these whooping naked savages destroyed the work of months, work she could never replace. Every rip of matted paper ripped her heart. She remembered each of her subjects, sitting before her in high summer sunlight. Little girls, proud warriors in all their regalia of fur and bone and feather, work-worn women, some dressed in softly tanned finery, others in shabby bags of skin worn for messy and grueling tasks, such as fleshing a buffalo hide. All gone, each delicate stroke that had caught shadow under cheekbone, sheen on a bearclaw necklace, pride in a chief, mystery in a squinting sour shaman.

"I have lost everything," she whispered to Elkanah, sitting beside her. He squeezed her hand.

"Not everything. Not life. They'll take my display goods and we'll be on our way," he said. "Memory will help you redo them."

She shook her head. Memory wouldn't help at all. Memory wouldn't sort out quillwork, beads, the slant of a feather, the scars on a warrior's arm, the sag of lodges. No, it was gone.

"I'd hoped to have an exhibit. I'm the only woman. . . . Hardly anyone's been here. Catlin. Bodmer. Miller . . . I thought—I could almost read the Boston papers . . . 'Splendid Exhibit of Wild Indian Scenes at the Athaeneum . . . Fine Transparent Colors Boldly Put to Paper by the Lowell Artist . . .'"

She sighed shakily.

"We'll pick up the pieces! We'll gather every scrap, and when we get back, we'll puzzle them together. Then you can copy, Betsy."

But even as he whispered, gusts of chill air scattered fragments of color into wet grass and off into thickets of brush.

Beside them sat Jarvis Cobb, pale and drawn. She glanced covertly at him, wondering if he'd suffered a concussion. And poor Percy in his muddied smallclothes, huddled on gravel into a ball of anguish. Everything he'd scribbled gone, too, unless they could get it back from that strutting smirking chief. She didn't particularly like Percy, but she pitied him now and felt a kindred loss. He was a fusty bachelor, too, and lacked the ties she had, so he probably had wrapped his whole life, his future, his dreams, in those vanished journals.

They were dividing the weapons now. That dreadful

smirking headman had buckled on Mister Skye's belt and holster with his old revolver and had claimed Mister Skye's heavy dark Hawken. Except for that, they hadn't plundered Mister Skye's belongings. Too many things of Elkanah's and Rudolpho's fascinated them. They'd gotten Elkanah's weapons, too—everything. The custom fowling piece, and English rifle, and Sam Colt's revolver. Some subchiefs of some sort fondled them, along with every other weapon they could find, plus powder horns, paper cartridges, and all the rest of it. She felt a chill. The more these Bannocks plundered, the more helpless they all became.

"I don't think they're going to take just your trade goods, Elkanah," she whispered. "I think they'll take everything. Everything!"

"We're alive," he replied, echoing Mister Skye. "Surely they'll leave us a few things to get along with."

"But . . . !" she exclaimed, and then couldn't say what dread thoughts crowded her mind. Would they . . . kill? Would they torture? The image of poor Kills Dog Woman of the Flatheads filled her mind, and she shuddered. What if they killed Elkanah? Tortured him before her eyes? What if—what if— She tried to chase a terrible thought away, but it wouldn't go away. What if they used her, crawled on her and used her, and used Arabella, right before Elkanah's eyes? She'd die; she couldn't bear the thought; she couldn't imagine this profane thing happening to mock what had been sacred and sweet and private between them alone. Elkanah might go crazy and they'd kill him. Arabella—she might go mad, poor thing, those things unknown to her. . . .

Betsy shuddered and stared around. What-if's could drive a person mad, she thought. Just thinking about what-if's. It hadn't happened. They all sat here unharmed. She clutched her arms tight around her in the vicious cold and stared helplessly at the whirl of her small wet world.

Professor Danzig emerged from under a huddle of canvas, toting a tintype. Slow-Death Man had grown impatient and had gone back to plundering, but at the sight of Danzig he leaped to the professor and snatched the daguerreotype.

"Ah! I am here, counting coup on Mister Skye!" he cried. "I will show this to everyone, to the world! I will have another now!"

Mister Skye hadn't moved, indeed couldn't move with three lances jabbed into his belly and back. Danzig quietly ducked under his black hood, the headman brought his coup stick down viciously on Mister Skye's skull, staggering the guide, and the next click trapped an image of humiliation.

"That is all," the headman said to Danzig. "This image making takes too long." He barked something in the Bannock tongue at some of his cavorting band, and they began at once to load Elkanah's fine panniers with their loot. And exactly as Betsy feared, they weren't stopping with Elkanah's trade goods, either. She watched in horror as every scrap of equipment—things that could mean life itself—vanished into the bulging panniers of the pack saddles. Their whole kitchen. Her shoes and dresses. Everything of Arabella's. Their sleeping blankets. The rubberized ground cloths that Elkanah had invented for cold damp earth. Everything of his—razor, strop, shoes. The lanterns and lastly the tent itself with its shining fittings. Everything. Everything! A sudden sense of utter nakedness and helplessness swept through her, and a vision of death from exposure.

Instinctively she clutched Elkanah. "We must be brave!"

she whispered. "We will be brave!" She reached across Elkanah's lap and patted Arabella tenderly. The girl looked stricken. "If worse comes to worse," Betsy said softly, "I wish to be worthy before our Maker. I want to find the courage to bless them, whatever they do to me—to us."

Elkanah stared at her, some anguish boiling bleakly in his eyes, some guilt.

She read it. "Do you think for an instant I'd have let you come here alone—without me? Keep your Wild West adventure from me?" She smiled. "If you had, you'd have found me curled up in the bottom of a pannier!"

She felt his hands responding, his fingers intimately tugging her closer, pressing her rib cage. Maybe, she thought with renewed dread, they were saying good-bye to each other. She stared at his familiar face, seeing it in profile now, his high forehead and receding brown hair and the clean strong line of his determined jaw. She would remember it while there was breath in her.

Danzig crawled out from under his sprawled canvas, stood quietly, and handed the second tin-backed image to the headman.

"I suppose I could show you how all this is done," Danzig said. But Slow-Death Man didn't hear. He studied the new image gleefully. "See! See how I have power over Mister Skye, greatest of all the whitemen! See this! I am the greatest."

"Don't know about that," rumbled the guide. "Let's you and me find out."

"You are my captive," the headman retorted.

"You take a knife. I'll fetch me a wooden club I've got in my things. I've busted a lot of sailor skulls with it; might as well bust yours. Belaying pin."

"Goddamn," muttered Victoria.

The headman glared. "I have heard of how you fight with this club. I will think about it. Maybe this is not the day."

"Any day's the day to smash the skull of a Bannock coward."

"I will think about medicine."

"Ahhh!" mocked Mister Skye. "Maybe those images showing you counting coup are lies. Three of your warriors have lances against me, and you count coup. Great warrior you are, my friend."

Mary heard all this and instantly translated it into the Shoshonean tongue Bannocks understood. The headman's boasts; Mister Skye's challenge.

"What is Mary doing?" Betsy whispered.

"I think she's telling the Bannock warriors that Slow-Death Man is refusing to fight Mister Skye—even when Mister Skye would have only a belaying pin against his knife."

"Mercy!"

"They're about the same height—medium. I think the Bannock has longer arms, but Mister Skye is heavier. But a belaying pin . . . I've never heard of such a thing. . . ."

The young warriors had stopped their plundering and stared at their headman. Slow-Death Man rose and paraded before them, showing them the images—counting coup against the big-medicine whiteman. Swiftly his nasal voice rose and raged.

Mary translated. "He is saying they should torture us all to death. That Mister Skye's challenge is nothing, a bluff."

Betsy felt a sickening fear flood through her. Torture . . .

Mister Skye tried to stand, but the lancers thrust at him and kept him sitting.

"Slow-Death Man," muttered Mister Skye. "If I kill you, we will take all our things and leave. You will not kill me. I always have medicine."

The warriors waited for the headman to translate. Just to make sure his message reached them all, Mister Skye repeated himself with the hand language of the plains. His three guards permitted it warily.

"No such thing as medicine. Only power," the headman retorted. But his warriors stared. At last one of them began his own oration, snapping strange-sounding words to the others. Betsy listened, mystified by the man's powerful oratory and fierce gestures. He pointed at the piles of booty, at Mister Skye.

"He says they should take everything and go," translated Mary. "He says Mister Skye got big medicine, and the Bannock chief don't got medicine because he says he don't follow the Way of the People. So Bannock chief get killed and Mister Skye takes everything back. He says they'll take everything, and he's chief now, and Slow-Death Man ain't anything anymore."

"I don't understand," whispered Betsy.

Victoria heard her. "They want all this stuff and think maybe that son of a bitch gonna lose it because he ain't got any medicine or spirit helper. So they say he ain't the headman anymore and maybe they all go away."

"I'll fight the new headman," rumbled Mister Skye. "Tell him that, Mary. Give him a knife. I'll have my belaying pin. He's got Bannock medicine. Let him try it."

Mary translated that back to the new headman, a young stout one with protruding eyeballs. At that moment Jawbone screeched eerily, feeling the tension in camp.

Theft or glory? Loot or prowess? They argued briefly among themselves and settled for loot.

"They're afraid," snarled old Victoria. "Goddamn!"

"Of Jawbone," whispered Elkanah. The warriors eyed the terrible blue horse warily, afraid of a murderous shrieking assault that not even lances would stop, at least before the horse would slaughter several of them.

The new headman-by-consent snapped commands, and warriors loaded Mister Skye's possessions, the parfleches of pemmican and jerky, the fine robes, the women's old fusils, and their osage orange bows. One of them discovered the linen bowstrings and exclaimed. They nocked the strings of both bows and drew them, howling. One of them dipped the bowstring into a puddle until it was soaked and drew it. The string didn't fly apart. The bows passed from warrior to warrior, and each pulled the string to its limits but it didn't break. Magic! It dawned on them what those bowstrings meant. Horse raids in rain! Hunting in rain! Defeat of enemies in rain when sinew bowstrings went soft and flew apart!

"Ah! More whitemen's medicine," said Slow-Death Man, ignoring his recent humiliation. "Bows that shoot in rain."

They folded Mister Skye's lodge and bound the cover to a travois. They abandoned the lodgepoles, which would only hinder them on the long trail west. When they were done, everything from Elkanah's party, and every possession from the lodge of Mister Skye, had been stuffed into panniers or bundles and tied down on horses and mules. Victoria muttered angrily. Betsy watched with fascination and terror, knowing her fate in these autumnal wilds. Even as she clung to Elkanah, the numbing cold—just above freezing—relentlessly chilled her. She couldn't get warm. Poor Arabella—even worse off in her gauzy white nightdress!

"Slow-Death Man! Tell them I want my belaying pin back. If I don't get it, I'll come after you," growled Mister Skye.

The deposed headman had recovered something of his mockery. "Maybe not," he said. "We maybe still torture you to death. That is to be decided. You and the others."

The bleak news chilled Betsy. She felt an overpowering urge to go to the bushes. None of them had done it. They'd been dragged from their tents an eternity ago, though now she realized it had scarcely reached midmorning. In the back of her mind lay another purpose: she hoped to find a piece of sharp-edged stone, sharp enough to sever the artery at her wrist, sharp enough to spare her and Arabella days of utter torment, hours of debasement too evil to imagine. Fast death would be a mercy.

"I must do chores," she whispered, freeing herself from Elkanah's comforting grip. "Come along, Arabella."

No one stopped them. In fact, Victoria and Mary joined them. They wobbled tender-footed over stone, cringed over grass and sticks, and finally turned around a drenched thicket that sprayed ice water over them, intensifying the cold. She found no sharp stones there; only river-rounded cobbles. But along the bluffs lay fragmented sandstone. . . .

Victoria stared at her. "What are you looking for?" she asked sharply.

"Nothing."

Victoria, all-knowing, discerned Betsy's mood. "You got to die proud," she said. "Kill them if you can. If they torture, you say nothing. Don't cry. Don't scream, no matter what. Laugh and make them see you got a big spirit. You show them a big spirit and maybe they kill you quick, honor your spirit."

Arabella wept. Betsy tried to comfort her, drew an arm

around the girl's soaked cold nightdress and gasped at the coldness under her hand. Her daughter could not be far from danger from cold.

"Run, Arabella! Dance! Wave your arms! You're much too cold!" she cried. "We all will. I will, too!"

Betsy began running in place, swinging arms. Arabella stared.

"It's no use," mumbled Arabella. "We'll all be dead."

"What are you talking about? They go away, we get fixed up quick," growled Victoria.

"We have nothing," mumbled Arabella.

"I don't understand goddamn white people," muttered Victoria. "We got a whole world here. We can walk two days and sit in hot springs, so warm you can hardly stand it. We got a whole river valley here full of stuff."

"Two days without shoes! Two weeks to walk there barefoot!" cried Arabella, actually saying what Betsy was thinking privately. "Without clothes! Without food! Without fire! Without shelter! And if it rains again—it looks like it—the cold will kill us. I don't want to die!"

"Who's gonna die? I ain't," muttered Victoria crossly. "You do like your mother now, make your heart pound. Only don't make sweat or do too much. Just enough to make your blood go fast."

It began to mist, fine cold drops that wet Betsy's face and hinted of death. It occurred to her that this day had scarcely begun. It would stretch into the longest of her life, or mercifully the shortest. She'd come to an age when she'd thought about her own death. One does that upon turning forty. And yet it had always seemed so distant, and she felt so young and full of life that she'd put off coping with it. But here it was, sitting right here like a wolf on its haunches, waiting. For her. For Elkanah. For Arabella. And the others . . . Now that she peered about, she saw death lurking everywhere, but no more than in the lowering dreary clouds that blanketed heaven with bulging black bellies and hid horizons as surely as they hid the future.

They limped back in the thickening icy mist and found the Bannocks loading the last of the stolen pack animals. Not a scrap of the comfortable camp remained, except for the shreds of Betsy's paintings, scattered forlornly. The mist settled on the scraps, blurring the watercolors, streaking the remains of hundreds of hours of loving labor.

The Bannocks seemed excited, and she realized they clustered around those bows that had been Victoria and Mary's, endlessly pulling back the linen strings. Others of them fondled the percussion lock rifles they'd commandeered.

Mary listened to their excited talk. "They're thinking they can hunt the buffalo now, even in the rain. They can shoot them bows. They can shoot them rifles with the caps. They got one or two flintlocks that ain't no good in the rain. But now they got these new ones they can shoot. They're saying they can shoot buffalo now."

"Maybe the rain will rescue us, mates," muttered Mister Skye.

But Betsy couldn't see how. It'd kill them in this desolate cold place in hours.

Their minds made up, the Bannocks herded the pack animals west, and up the bluffs. Betsy felt so cold in the thickening mist that she scarcely cared what the Bannocks did. Everything she possessed went in that caravan. At the last moment, the three grinning Bannocks who had guarded Mister Skye with lowered lances released him and swung up on their waiting ponies.

Only the deposed headman, Slow-Death Man, remained,

sitting on his coyote dun. Mister Skye stood, stretching after his long immobilization on the gravel. The rain had soaked his heavy graying hair, and now it matted blackly about his skull and neck. He, too, seemed as cold and defeated as the rest, Betsy thought.

"Mister Skye. We talked about whether to kill you all. But we don't need to. The rain will do it. Whites have magic things—and are helpless. We'll go kill buffalo now. Maybe it'll rain for many days, but we'll kill buffalo anyway, and go back across the mountains. They will welcome us in our village! We will sing many songs about this day."

From under the black slicker he'd commandeered, he pulled out Mister Skye's old hickory belaying pin, flared thickly at one end, but lathed narrower at the other. He tossed it to earth.

"Here! Take your wooden club, the club that Mister Skye always has. Maybe you can kill buffalo with it!"

Some faint light seemed to flare in the guide's eyes.

They watched the Bannock trot off and catch up to the others. They watched the pack animals top the slippery bluff and vanish into gray mist. They stared at each other, seeing ashen, cold, gray-fleshed, half-dressed, blue-lipped barefoot mortals with utterly nothing, and only a few hours from doom.

Chapter 21

Mister Skye faced them. "You are alive," he said. Numbing rain stung him. "I want you to listen. But before you listen, I want you to huddle together."

No one moved. Jarvis Cobb stared up at him. "No use,"

he muttered. "Don't rally us with nonsense. I'm an officer. I know about this."

"Huddle anyway. Press together. Mister Connaught, get up."

The man lay curled in a ball on the gravel, his white underclothes mud-smeared and soaked. He peered up and said nothing.

Mister Skye walked to him, feeling harsh gravel under his soles. He lifted Connaught to his feet, but the man didn't help and would have sunk to earth but for Mister Skye's support.

"All gone. Let me die. I know perfectly well what our true condition is."

Mister Skye dragged him to the others. Listlessly, Betsy helped Connaught down and drew him close, her face a mask. Professor Danzig stood, flapped arms to make blood move, and walked over, squeezing close to Arabella and slipping an avuncular arm about her shoulders.

"Cobb?" The officer sat apart, head sunk into his chest.

"Goddamn," snarled Victoria. She and Mary slid over to Cobb and embraced him from two sides, making a tight ball of human flesh.

The icy rain fell heavily now; not a deluge but a cruel drizzle.

"We don't have much time. I won't take time to explain everything now. We have important things to do. First, forget about your hunger. We can live for days without food. Second, fire and shelter will keep us going. Fire is the first priority. If not fire, then shelter."

"Have you flint and striker? Sulfur matches? Dry wood?" asked Elkanah wearily.

"No. But with luck, we'll have a fire. And if we can't

start one in this, we'll have a shelter. But tonight and the next days will be the worst."

"I suppose you have a convenient cave, with dry wood stashed in the back and a pouch of lucifers hanging on the wall," muttered Cobb.

Mister Skye gazed at this country. The Big Horn cut through gently sculpted hills here, occasionally baring outcrops of gray sandstone. No caves or even overhangs in this country. But maybe, just maybe, an upright cliff of rock that'd form a warm wall they could prop brush against for a shelter . . . He'd set them looking.

"No, we're not so fortunate. But I intend to get us through. Get you safely and comfortably to Fort Laramie."

Connaught laughed crazily.

"It's midmorning sometime. We have enough daylight. If all this had happened late in the day, we'd be in trouble."

"We're not in trouble?" asked Cobb, mocking.

"Captain Cobb, I'll argue later. Just now there's no time. I'm going to set each of you to a task. Do it. Your lives depend on it."

Arabella started laughing crazily too. Her body convulsed and shivered, a bad sign.

"Elkanah and Betsy, press yourselves over her. Pin her down and warm her with your own bodies."

Betsy stood. "I'll give her my dress—"

"No, your body heat's more important."

Reluctantly—this intimacy ran against their grain—the Morses clambered over chattering and shivering Arabella and pressed her. Professor Danzig helped, too.

"Damn," muttered Victoria. She stood, slid off her soaked doeskin dress, and handed it to the Morses. Her old

withered naked body seemed to defy the elements, and
Mister Skye knew that she could go awhile with nothing.
Indians seemed to have a gift of endurance. Elkanah and
Betsy wrestled the trembling young woman into the dress,
and then pressed over her again.

"Thank you, Victoria," said Betsy.

"Cattails," Mister Skye said gently to Victoria and Mary.
Instantly they trotted off on hardened feet toward the river,
hoping to find a slough.

The tall flat leaves of the cattail could swiftly be woven
into good mats. Weak ones but usable tonight. The bulbs
of the cattail were edible, and could be dried and pounded
into a good flour.

"Mister Danzig. Your training as a geologist might save
the day for us. We need flint or obsidian—both actually.
And any rock with a sharp edge."

"These hills—there'd be little flint in them. Obsidian—
not likely here. That's volcanic glass. Flint's a type of
quartz. . . . But the river. It's low and there's gravel beds
exposed, and I'll probably find it. . . ."

"Flint for weapons, knife edges. But mainly flint for fire,
if we can find something to strike against," said Mister
Skye. "Let me see your belt buckles, gentlemen."

Cobb's was brass. Elkanah had no belt on. Neither did
Professor Danzig. No steel.

Disappointed, he turned to other things. "Mister Cobb,
work your way north, downstream, as far as your feet can
stand it. Look for a cave, an overhang, a vertical rock wall
or cliff. Look also for deadfall limbs or thick grasses. If
you see any chunk of rock—from these bluffs—that has a
sharp edge, get it. If you find an antler, bring it. If you find
vines, wild grape or anything like it, mark the place. If you
spot animal burrows or dens, remember them. Look for

dry-bottomed thickets. Carry a stick to club any small animal—sometimes in bad weather they sit stupidly. But food is secondary. Our first business is shelter and warmth."

Captain Cobb sighed, ran a hand tenderly over the bloodied lump on his head. "This is utter futility, you know. I'm not feeling well," he muttered.

"Give up and die then," Mister Skye retorted sharply. He didn't have time to argue. With a cliff, some deadfall limbs for rafters and beams, and grass for thatching, he could make a serviceable and almost waterproof shelter.

The rain bit at them all. He felt icy water sting down his back and belly. So little time. He saw Danzig walking off, each step tentative, bare feet testing. Slow going.

"Mister Connaught. Stand up. Run in place. Make your heart pound at once, until you're warm."

The miserable man curled tighter into a ball and didn't reply. "Break off brush as thick as you can manage, Mister Connaught. I want to find you under a large pile of it when I get back."

The man laughed weirdly. Mister Skye didn't have time to argue.

"Elkanah, we're going south, upstream, together, looking for shelter and gathering some things. We have things to talk about."

Even buoyant Elkanah seemed rudderless, shocked, and shivering cold.

"Up! Up, man! I need your manufacturing wisdom!"

Actually, he needed his squaws' Indian ways more, but Elkanah's inventive and flexible mind would help. The entrepreneur stood, hollow-eyed, and wobbled over harsh gravel, grimacing whenever a sharp pebble bit his white wet feet.

Good. He'd come.

"Mrs. Morse. When my wives return with cattails, they'll show you and Arabella how to weave simple mats from the leaves. If you weave the leaves tightly, they'll turn into a mat that will hold heat and turn the wind, and even shed some water."

Betsy, who lay over her daughter, peered up, wet hair falling over her white face, and nodded.

"Come along, Elkanah," he said. They walked slowly and silently south, the misery of the icy drizzle subduing them.

"Lots of ways to make shelter and fire, Mister Morse. Lots of ways Indians survive in these circumstances. We're going to turn Indian for a while. Don't give up! Don't let any of the others give up! I'm regretting I spoke sharply to Mister Cobb, though he and Connaught are the ones most likely to collapse and die. You and the professor and Betsy—I have to rely on you. Captain Cobb seems—I think he's got a concussion."

Elkanah sighed. "Tell me honestly, Mister Skye. Our chances are about zero, aren't they?"

"Fifty-fifty, Elkanah. And better than that if we can get through tonight alive and well. Our enemy's despair—that more than nature or weather."

They struggled painfully southward at the base of the gentle western bluff of the river, past cottonwood parks and thickets closer to the stream.

"I don't see it," Elkanah said.

"The Indians managed very well before they had a single trade item from whites, Elkanah."

"But the things they had took time to manufacture. It took time to shape a bow with bone or flint knives, sand it with a block of sandstone, sand arrows, chip arrow-heads. . . ."

"You're going to find ways of doing it, Elkanah."

The industrialist winced along silently. "I'm already starved. I'm sure the others will soon be dizzy with want of food. I don't know where we'll get the strength—"

"My women are gathering cattails right now. There's other edible roots and nuts and berries. Fall's a good time, in a way. We can rob squirrels, snare ducks—lot of things. Tools. You'll be in charge of tools, Elkanah. Knives. Flint's only one way. If we find a new buffler skeleton, we'll have good knives. Those dorsal bones that make the hump, they're flat and wide and can be sanded down with a chunk of sandstone into useful knives. We'll need knives and clubs, stone hammers and flint-edged hatchets. Lances whittled to a point, the point hardened in fire. Arrows, bows . . . Put your mind to it, Elkanah. The Indians call you things-maker."

Elkanah laughed shortly. "Maybe we can scrape and sand green wood into some kind of bow, but how would you string it? Surely not with these whangs on your buckskin shirt."

"No, they won't work. Jawbone, Elkanah, will supply us with a temporary bowstring. Plaited from his long tail hair. Poor doings, but maybe we can make a weak bow."

"Horsehair!"

"I'm looking for a sharp-edged stone right now to cut tail hair. Need it for a fire bow."

"Fire bow?"

"With a wrap of bowstring around some bone-dry hardwood, a bow can get that wood spinning into a hollow of another piece of hardwood until it smokes from friction. We've got to get a bit of dry tinder in there to ignite."

"But this rain! This water!"

"Squirrel's nest in a knot, in a tree hollow, should have

plenty of tinder. Dry wood'll be harder. And we'll see what Danzig comes up with by way of flints."

"But we have no steel."

"I've seen spark from smacking rocks, Elkanah."

"Ow!" cried Elkanah. He'd stepped on a vicious stick. He lifted his cold white foot and found blood.

"My feet aren't much better," said the guide. "I never cottoned much to moccasins except around camp—always wore big square-toed boots."

His own feet had been lacerated by this walk, he knew.

Elkanah stopped. "Mister Skye, I've never been this cold. I'm cold down in my center. I'm wet and numb, and— I'm losing heart. We don't have much time. Poor Arabella! Poor—"

"Look here," muttered the guide. He stood before a small corner of stratified stone with roughly vertical walls about five feet high, with sloping prairie above it. It needed only deadfall limbs propped against it and thatching. Not much, but something.

"This might do," he muttered. "But I want to check thickets first. Animals hunker down in hollows under thick brush and stay warm and relatively dry. But getting to them in the river brush is going to be bad, Elkanah."

Step-by-step they threaded into the dense brush closer to the river, placing tender feet with care and even then wincing. Slow, wet, miserable going. Nothing. Just water-laden willow and serviceberry and chokecherry brush, open at their bases and cold as January.

They heard a crashing behind them and discovered Jawbone, following and curious. The horse! He'd barely thought of the horse. He'd grown as cold as Elkanah but wouldn't admit it. He'd never been as cold as this in all his years in the mountains.

"Elkanah, I'm going to help you up on Jawbone and take you back. I want you to huddle together with the others—make each other warm."

"But Jawbone—he'd kill me."

"No, not now."

He hoisted the exhausted man up, while Jawbone twisted his head back, wary and ready for trouble. Wearily Mister Skye stumbled back, step by painful step, the horse following unbidden. The three hundred yards seemed more like three miles to him because his muscles weren't working right and his feet bled from scores of small lacerations. But he trudged ahead.

"The horse feels warm under me," muttered Elkanah. His feet dripped blood.

Back at camp, or what remained of it, things had gotten worse. Betsy still lay upon Arabella, but both of them convulsed with shaking. Victoria, still naked, pressed close beside them.

"I am sorry, Mister Skye," she muttered. "I got goddamn cold."

The guide's heart sank at the sight. But Mary sat stoically, weaving cattail fronds into a mat as fast as numb fingers could manage it. She'd found a sharp piece of sandstone to cut off the bulbs, and these she piled beside her. Her dress had blackened with cold water, and the icy rain ran down her goosefleshed arms, off her braids and face. And yet she endured. His heart went out to her, too. A cattail mat would be a pathetic barrier in such a cold as this—but a start.

Time. He needed much more time. An hour more and these people would be beyond help. He helped Elkanah down and bade him lie close to the others. A vicious gust of wind sliced through, chilling their numb bodies further.

"Mister Cobb!" he roared. "Get over here! Get tight against the others."

Jarvis Cobb had curled into a small ball, shaking spastically inside of his drenched tan shirt and britches. He peered grayly up at Mister Skye and laughed through clenched lips.

Mister Skye grabbed him by his shirt, lifted him bodily, and slapped him. The wet smack echoed weirdly.

"Oh!" muttered Betsy.

Cobb laughed harder, maniacally. Mister Skye slapped him again.

"Very good of you, Skye. Hit me again," muttered Cobb, teeth chattering beyond control.

Mister Skye didn't know whether he had the strength left to drag the man to the others, but he tried. He hauled Jarvis Cobb across abrading wet gravel and dumped him next to Victoria. Then he hauled a whimpering Percy Connaught to the same pile and jammed him hard against Cobb. His heart thudded painfully. A small task, but the coldness had sapped him.

Mary finished a cattail mat, and Mister Skye laid it over the pile of them, a pathetic green thing. She didn't have enough cattails for another.

"Let me borrow that stone," he muttered. The sandstone had a rough jagged edge, not bad as a cutting tool. He found Jawbone's tail and grabbed it.

"Easy, boy," he muttered. The horse peered evilly at him, through yellow murderous eyes. "Easy . . ."

He sawed at the tail hair. It didn't cut readily. The horse shifted restlessly, barely tolerating it. He sawed more and cut some of the long hair loose until he had a fistful.

No time, he thought. No time. They'd be dead of exposure before he got enough done. . . .

He took the hair to Mary, who stared at him soberly.

"Mary, you're beautiful. Did I ever tell you how beautiful you look in the rain?"

A flash of smile rewarded him, and he hugged her, feeling the sopping cold of her doeskin dress, and the warmth of her faintly. "We have to hurry," he whispered.

She nodded, pressing tight to him. It felt good.

"Lots of cane grass in these bottoms. This knife of yours—cut it fast. We'll gather it into bunches and I'll tie a horsehair around one end . . . thatch."

"What is thatch?" she asked.

"Grass'll shed water," he muttered. "Hurry!"

He had to find Danzig. Probably half-dead somewhere. He tried to crawl over Jawbone and couldn't. The strength had gone out of him and the horse's back was slippery wet. He led the horse toward a cottonwood log and managed to clamber on. He could steer Jawbone with his knees. He trotted north, weaving through majestic cottonwoods with yellowing brown-specked leaves, glistening with water. A long silvery log caught his eye, and he steered Jawbone toward it. Hollow end, rotten reddish wood reduced by weather and insects to pulp along the bottom. Maybe, he thought. He slid off the horse and peered in, on his hands and knees. Hollow and dry, the gloomy light showing distantly from the other end. Big enough for women, two women. His naked Victoria, and Arabella, the farthest gone.

He climbed up on Jawbone, knowing he himself had reached his limits, and trotted back to the inert shivering people. Mary had cut and tied three grass bundles and laid them on the others.

"I've found a safe warm place for two women," he said. "Victoria, come with me. Arabella, I'll carry you."

Nothing. They peered at him dumbly. He slid down from Jawbone once again and gently pried them apart, lifting the mute Betsy off her daughter. Arabella shook violently. He lifted her, dragged her, to Jawbone, who sidled warily from him.

"Steady, boy," he muttered. He lacked the strength to seat her properly, and slid her over the horse on her stomach, hanging on the animal like dead game. He turned around and found Victoria standing grimly behind him, her eyes desperate and ice water trickling down her naked flesh.

They followed him, Jawbone with his half-dead cargo, and Victoria, silently. The log lay two hundred yards distant, close to the Big Horn. It took a long time, and then they stood before it.

"Help me," he muttered. Together they slid Arabella off Jawbone and twisted her wet skirts tight and wrestled her feetfirst into the hollow log. It got harder and harder to do as the friction increased, but with a last vicious push against her shoulders, he got her head under cover. They stood panting.

He stared at her, then wrapped his tired arms around his old naked woman. "Forgot to tell you how I love you, Victoria. Forgot to say thanks. Maybe we won't get out of this. It's getting worse by the minute. If we don't, I want you to know—to know—you've given me a good life. Most lucky man in the world to have you. I love you now . . . love you in the spirit land to come. . . ."

She hugged him mutely, too tired to talk. Then she slid herself into the other end of the log.

"Goddamn, it's warm in here," she said.

Chapter 22

Life-and-death crisis galvanized something in Professor Danzig's mind. As he limped through cottonwood forest and brush toward the sprawling Big Horn River, his keen, analytical mind surveyed possibilities. He'd never felt such cold as this, with icy rain slicing into him and sluicing heat out of his compact body. But he ignored it. Rather, his fertile mind furiously examined one material after another in these bottoms.

Not much time. Perhaps an hour for the weakest; two or three hours for the strongest. He reached the river at last, after wincing his way through a barrier of thick rushes and sedges, dense stalks as high as three feet. They could be cut and thatched, he thought. They had insulating qualities. But cutting them would be a problem. He tried tugging some, breaking some, and found they resisted, as he expected. Oh, for a knife! In an hour they could have a shelter of bulrushes.

He stumbled at last out upon a gravelly streamed area. In spite of these first autumnal rains, the Big Horn ran very low, exposing long beaches of mud and gravel and cobbled stones, rounded by aeons of river passage. The variety of them surprised him. Red granites and gray gneisses, pale rhyolite, gabbro and basalt, most of these igneous rocks probably from the great Yellowstone batholith to the west. But also sandstone from the surrounding area, gray limestone, mudstone, shale, chunks of quartz, good news because it might mean flint. Other rocks he couldn't identify. Some of them looked burnt.

But finding flint on a dark gray day in a sheeting rain presented problems. Flint had a luster and could range from translucent to opaque. But in this relentless rain, all the rocks had luster. He stumbled slowly over gravel, hunting the telltale gray or brown, seeing nothing. Then, before him, an arrowhead, finely chipped of tan flint, with two knife edges and the haft intact so it could be anchored to a handle. He fondled it, rejoicing, and slipped it in his pocket. He debated. Head back with this or search further. He decided to search. This would give them a knife, but they needed flint for a fire striker and many more tools. He wobbled on, feet numb on wet icy rock. In ten minutes he had one additional piece of flint he felt sure of, and two rocks he classified as doubtful. Only then did he notice that his limbs were refusing to function and he was shuddering spasmodically, as his body fought against the murderous cold. Time to get back, hug someone for dear life.

In the thick bankside rushes he paused and began cutting. Slower than he thought, a few stalks at a time. Too long. He began slashing savagely, forcing work from his numb body, feeling his heart begin to pump. When he had an armful of the wet rushes and sedges, he unbuttoned his shirt and stuffed them in, working them around to the back until he could jam no more into available space. The rushes dripped cold water but then, slowly, caught a bit of body heat and began to feel warmer than his drenched cotton shirt. He rejoiced and slashed at the rushes around him until he had another armful, and began carrying them back. They might be the salvation of someone back at camp.

He worked his way through dense cottonwood bottoms, noting that the huge rough-barked trees seemed relatively dry on their eastern sides. People could lean against their trunks on that side, somewhat protected from the northwest winds and the driving rain. As he walked, his restless mind hunted for burial scaffolds—he'd like nothing better than to rob the dead of robes and blankets and weapons, so the living might live. But he saw nothing. Only wild things in an empty land.

That's when he came upon Mister Skye, riding Jawbone.

"Worried about you, mate," the guide said, his gaze taking in the bulky deformed shirt and Rudolpho's armload of rushes.

"I'm a stuffed shirt," said Rudolpho gleefully. "It helps. It keeps bunching up but if it's spread evenly in my shirt, it insulates."

"How'd you cut it?"

Danzig grinned, dug in his wet pocket, and pulled out the flint arrowhead.

Mister Skye took it, admired its sharp edges, and handed it back. "A treasure. It could bloody well save our lives." He slid down. "Hop up here now. Your feet are leaking blood."

"That horse'll kill me. No reins either."

"No. Not now. First week or so he might have. He'll allow it now." Mister Skye relieved the professor of his armload and helped him up.

"Warmth between my legs," said Danzig. "Feels almost royal."

Oh, for horses, Danzig thought. They could all ride, barefoot or not, to any sheltering point. Or even down to those hot springs Mister Skye had talked of, a day or two south. And just wait out the storm immersed in hot water. His convulsing stopped, thanks to Jawbone's warmth and the rushes in his shirt.

"Professor, I think we have less than an hour, at least for some. I found a hollow log for Victoria and Arabella."

"Any chance of a fire?"

"A chance," Mister Skye muttered. "If only things would be a bit easier. I need to make a bow. Need to find a bone-dry stick, and a bone-dry log with a small pit in it—with your arrowhead we can hollow a pit. And bone-dry tinder—maybe from a squirrel nest, or a bird nest in a knothole or decayed hollow trunk. Bone-dry, Professor. I'll get some horsehair to Victoria and hope she can find room enough in her hollow log to plait hair into a bow-string of some sort. With your arrowhead I might be able to cut a long thong from my leggins, but the wet leather won't be strong enough. That arrowhead, Professor—that'll make some moccasins for two of us."

"From what?"

"My leggins."

"That'd leave you too naked in this weather."

"I got this long elkskin shirt and breechclout."

No one remained in the gravel bench where they'd camped. But Elkanah called from within the cottonwood forest, and they turned that way. They'd all removed to the trees, even Cobb and Connaught. The gusting wind cut at them less, and they'd discovered the dry east sides of the massive trees. At one, Elkanah sat with his back to the tree, holding Betsy tightly, warming her as well as he could. And she held Dirk's cradlebasket. The baby fussed, hungry, but was better off than the rest inside his warm cocoon with a hood of leather over it. The cradlebasket itself, in Betsy's arms, gave her some additional protection.

Mary sat in the lee of a tree, stoically making grass bundles, using horsehair to tie the tops of each. She looked numb.

In the dry lee of other trees sat Cobb and Percy Connaught. Cobb sat ashen-faced, in only his wet shirt and pants. Connaught had commandeered all of Mary's grass bundles and had packed them around him. Both trembled convulsively. Their gaze followed Mister Skye and Professor Danzig and the horse, but they said nothing.

"Up with you both now," said Mister Skye gently. "I want you to run in place, wave your arms, make your body work hard. Then we'll stuff these rushes around you."

Cobb laughed sarcastically, between chattering teeth. "Make us die comfortable," he muttered, shivering.

But Percy Connaught obeyed, casting aside all the grass bundles and standing in his muddy underclothes. He flailed clumsily, shivering. In the lee of the cottonwood little rain hit him. In moments he puffed and quit.

"We're done for," he muttered.

"No, mate. The professor here has found an arrowhead that may save us all."

Cobb laughed wildly, but the laugh died away into a shudder and spastic rattle of the throat.

"Mister Cobb," said Mister Skye, "you've lost faith. If you won't save yourself, we will."

Danzig slid off Jawbone to help. Together, he and Mister Skye stuffed the rushes into Cobb's shirt, working them around into an insulating barrier. The rest they stuffed up his pants legs, while Cobb watched inertly, chattering.

"I'd rather die fast than slow," Cobb muttered.

"You'd be better off sitting there with Percy, your back against his chest."

Cobb grinned grayly. "Too intimate for males," he said, convulsing again.

"Professor," said Mister Skye, "perhaps you could sit here with one or the other. I'll take Jawbone and the arrowhead and cut another load."

"I'll go with you," said Danzig. "The rushes in my shirt have warmed me some."

Mister Skye peered at him sharply. They stopped at the tree that sheltered the Morses.

The baby gnawed at a cattail bulb, but fussed.

"If you find some moss," said Mary, "I'll clean him. He's soiled. He's warm, though."

"We'll look," said Mister Skye. Then he addressed the Morses. "Elkanah, Betsy, we'll make it, thanks to the arrowhead that Rudolpho found. It's flint, too, and later we can strike a fire with it. We'll bring back more rushes now, and you'll find them helpful when spread evenly inside your clothing."

Elkanah sighed. "I'm sorry I'm so helpless, Mister Skye. I've become so numb . . . this tree offered a little relief . . . do you really believe that we—can—get out of this? Or are you just buoying us up in hopeless circumstances?"

"It's very bad, mate. Especially without a fire. But there's a chance. When there's a chance, fight for it. Eat on those cattail bulbs. They're nourishing. Full of sand or grit and not pleasant, but they sustain life. All of you, down as many of them as you can. Later we can pound them into an excellent flour."

Cobb laughed weirdly. "With what?" he yelled from his tree. "Our handy kitchen?"

"I'm coming with you," said Elkanah quietly. "Betsy, will you be warm enough?"

"I'm coming with you, too," she said firmly.

"We've only one tiny arrowhead to cut with, mates."

"I'm coming anyway. I can be looking for things."

The Morses came. They all stopped at the hollow log and found that Arabella and Victoria were almost comfortable.

The girl nodded mutely, too miserable to talk. But they

could see she wasn't shivering. At the other end of the great log, Victoria shivered nakedly.

"I'm damn cold," she muttered. "Dry, anyway."

"You gave your dress to save my daughter. I've got my wool nightdress under my dress, and I'm going to give it to you now!" Betsy cried. "Go ahead, gentlemen. I'll catch up."

"Goddamn, that'd feel good," said Victoria.

As they stumbled ahead Elkanah seemed to gather strength. "I'll hunt bone while you cut rushes. Give me a rib bone and some sandstone to sand with and I'll make a knife and speed this up."

"Don't look for skeletons in these cottonwood bottoms. Look on open ground," said Mister Skye. "That's where you'll find sandstone anyway, along the bluffs. Keep moving. Start calling if you go numb. Make your blood work. Better yet, Elkanah, I'll go on Jawbone while you and Rudolpho cut rushes here. I'll return directly. I can cover a lot of ground on a horse, far more than a barefoot man. You keep warm cutting hard. Here, I'll cut some more of Jawbone's tail hair and you can tie the rushes into bundles. We'll take the big load back on Jawbone."

They watched Mister Skye wheel Jawbone west, through cottonwood forests and brush. Rudolpho cut first, slashing a small handful of rushes with the arrowhead, finding some warmth in the work. Elkanah stuffed the first batch into his shirt, and then began tying them into bundles.

"Let me cut awhile, Rudolpho. I'm cold again. I never knew what cold was until now. I never even knew I could live, make my body work, feeling as heatless as I do now."

Danzig handed him the tiny brown arrowhead, and Elkanah began slashing at rushes furiously.

"I'll be back in a bit. I'm going to walk the river flats again. There's got to be some sharp rock I can use to cut with," Rudolpho said.

Elkanah stood a moment, looking haggard. "It's up to us and the Skyes, isn't it, Rudolpho? We've got to try. Use the last bit of our strength if we must. Figure things out. I've never needed to think to save my life, but now I'm trying to think and act to save my life—and Betsy and Arabella's. It's all impossible, I know. But I don't want to die from a lack of trying. Who knows? Some tribe or village might show up. We might find a warm cave. Sometimes these Indians leave ceremonial lodges or shelters. Never give up, Rudolpho. We must never, never give up!"

Danzig smiled. He'd gotten numb standing, and hobbled off toward the riverbank. He kept his back to the driving rain. It seemed warmer somehow than when rain lashed his face and trickled icily down his chest and belly. Behind him he heard Betsy arrive and take over the cutting while Elkanah bundled the rushes.

So many problems, he thought. Shelter and fire first. But food, too. They couldn't put that off. Tools and weapons to make. Bows and arrows, lances, clubs. Clothing . . . he wondered if the rushes could be woven into something much more durable than cattail mats. Surely they'd make carrying baskets. Ancient people and modern all wove baskets from rushes.

He spotted an antler and picked it up. Mister Skye said he wanted one, but the reason for it eluded the geologist. Along the gravelly flats he hunted, his eye alert for something, anything of value. He found the remains of a dead mallard, long since devoured by predators. But the heap contained feathers, and feathers made arrows. He grabbed a handful and stuffed feathers in his pocket. He thought about down, but this duck carcass yielded none. A tough vine tripped him. Vines! he thought. Vines to tie shelters together! He ripped it loose and followed its long snaking stem, finally gathering ten feet of it. He couldn't break it, but with a rock he smashed it off from its roots. Feather, antler, and vine, he thought unhappily. And they were all freezing to death.

A covey of ducks burst from rushes ahead of him, whirring into the air and honking loudly. Meat, he thought ruefully, at last feeling pangs of hunger. The exploding ducks startled something else, and he glimpsed a brown form—deer probably—bounding off. The thought of hot, steaming, tender meat, of hides, filled him with a vast yearning. His eye caught some dun chert among the gravels. Maybe it'd make sparks. He pocketed it. He probed around the gravel with his antler, and then it came to him—he held a knife in his hand.

Excited, he stared at the antler. Not one knife—ten knives! But he needed sandstone in hand-sized smooth chunks to start shaping it. Easy enough. The bluffs to either side of the river were made of it. He hobbled over a carpet of sticks, oblivious to the jabs and slices, and struck through grassy parks, past dense brush, and finally to a sandstone outcrop. Plenty of it, stratified and weathered. Feverishly he began grinding on an antler prong. It'd probably be hollow or spongy in the center, but he could still fashion an excellent knife from one side of it. He set the prong on rock so he could apply pressure, and delighted to see the sandstone in his hand begin to cut into the antler, flattening one side. He turned it over and flattened the other, sanding violently, barely aware of the rain. Gradually he shaped a knife, two flat sides about four inches long, plus a comfortable handle. But he didn't know how to cut the prong loose from the antler. Then it occurred to him to notch it and snap it off.

So intense was his labor that he scarcely realized people called for him. Then Mister Skye rode up on Jawbone and sat, observing the professor's progress.

"That's the most valuable thing so far," said the guide. "We'll cut rushes fast with that. I didn't find any buffler bones, but I found a shelter place. Little overhang, couple hundred yards downstream. Only three, four feet of overhang, but it's dry and we can block off the rest with a wall of brush or thatch. Professor, don't go back to the old place. Just head upstream along this bluff. Do it now. You can sand it in a dry place, get out of the wet."

"Mister Skye, I'd be more than delighted to get out of the wet," he said. He gathered up his antler and sandstone blocks, plus a sharp-edged piece he thought might help snap the prong off, and trudged north. Some of the others had already arrived, carried there on Jawbone. Cobb and Connaught sat under the low overhang in a completely dry place. Rudolpho even noted dust and dead leaves and twigs untouched by rain here. Maybe the sort of debris that'd kindle into a fire.

"I don't see that this rock is any better than the tree," muttered Connaught. "It'll just prolong the agony. I've never been so cold. No heat left in me. I can't imagine why I ever consented to this journey."

"Here, Percy, come here and work this sandstone over the antler. Keep you warmer," said Rudolpho kindly.

"You really suppose that your little toolmaking exploits will rescue us from exposure and starvation, thousands of miles from civilization," Percy said.

But the dry protected hollow had awakened the possibility of survival in Cobb. "Percy," he said sharply, "we're probably within fifty miles of comfortable lodges with warm fires in them. Bridger runs a trading post somewhere southwest of here. Victoria's people, the Crows, claim this basin as their own. We can't be far from a warm Crow village. Mary's people, the Shoshones, often hunt and camp in this Big Horn River basin. I don't know how far we are from Fort Laramie itself—our goal—but I suppose it's not far."

"Without moccasins," muttered Percy.

Rudolpho said, "Jawbone will carry two of us. Mister Skye says his leggins will make a couple pair. And as we make weapons and fire-starting things, we'll get clothing and warmth. In Europe, many people wear wood-soled clogs. And don't forget sandals. Even an old desiccated buffalo hide might yield sandal soles. Come help me, Jarvis. My arms are so tired with this grinding I can't make them work anymore."

Jarvis Cobb came at once, a different human being from the one who sat listlessly in the rain, mocking the gods. "I don't see how we'll make it—unless we're rescued by friendly Indians—but trying is better than not trying," he said. He took over the knife making, bearing down with the sandstone in long smooth sweeps across the prong.

"I'm starving to death," said Percy. "Not that there's any reason to live. I've lost everything. I won't even be leaving my insights behind when I go."

But Rudolpho didn't listen. He'd spotted Mister Skye, Elkanah, and Betsy on Jawbone, all of them carrying bundles of rushes. And struggling barefoot behind them came Mary, with Dirk in his cradlebasket on her back. All gathering here, hauling their few possessions, cattail mats, bits of rock, the clothing on their backs. The rain, if anything, lashed down harder.

The newcomers huddled gratefully in the dry air, all three of them spontaneously hugging each other tightly. Mary set her heavy cradlebasket down. Dirk howled lustily now—he needed food and attention at once. From outside, Mister Skye turned Jawbone around for one last wet trip, to bring Victoria and Arabella from their log. To Rudolpho, this shallow hollow, this dry place, seemed more marvelous than all the palaces of the Hapsburgs and Bourbons in the Europe he left behind.

Chapter 23

Mister Skye had no idea how long it might be until nightfall. The gloomy overcast hid the sun. A lot of time had elapsed since the Bannocks had ridden off in the morning, but perhaps that had been more recent than it seemed. Ordeals did that: time went haywire through trouble. Hunkering under the shelter of the low overhang, he studied a sky that held its secrets perfectly, neither hinting of the end of this icy rain, nor revealing the hour.

Beside him, the others huddled miserably, trying to draw heat from each other. The overhang might keep fresh rain off them, but it achieved little else. Freezing wind gusted and eddied through it, turning wet cloth and leather to ice. Every scrap of material they'd gathered—rushes, grasses, cattail mat—they'd put to use in and over their clothing, with little effect. They eyed him, waited for him, the gaunt despair in their faces telling him that he alone could save them, that they had run out of ideas. The expectant and defeated looks told him something else, too. None of them wished to venture out into that stinging rain again. Here in the lee of the cliff, when they clung tightly enough to each other, the soaked rags they wore grew slightly warm, or at least didn't suck the last heat out of their bodies. So they cowered there, a bit warmer than out in the weather—but in mortal peril.

Up to him. Their stares said it'd be up to him. He felt as cold as the others, a deadly numbness that seemed to go deep. He shivered violently on occasion, unable to stop the convulsing and shaking of his limbs.

Fire, he thought. They had shelter of sorts, and the only additional thing they could do would be to pile up brush around the overhang to cut wind. Maybe thatch a wall if they had energy enough—and the daylight to do it, which he doubted. He guessed it had reached late afternoon, and an hour of the gloomy light remained before a pitch-black, starless, moonless overcast night descended.

Fire, or some, maybe all, would die this night. He probed around in the debris. Their drenched clothing had wet much of it, but he found a few small dry twigs, some dry leaf, weed seeds, a bit of fluff. One good-sized ancient cottonwood stick, maybe four inches in diameter. Half-wet where someone had sat or dripped on it. Enough to try, he thought.

The baby squalled. Mary had pulled him from the warmth of the cradlebasket and wiped him with wet grasses. The shock of the cold set the tyke to howling and sent pain through Mister Skye's heart. Mary had found a flat rock and a river cobble and began pounding a cattail bulb into an edible mush for the baby. She'd stopped nursing him only a few months ago, and now Mister Skye wished she still might have milk. He watched her slide some of the cattail pulp into the child's mouth. The boy spat it out and bellowed. She tried again and this time the child munched on it, whimpering. He'd be warm again soon, back in the cradlebasket with its seasoned leather outer shell and blanket lining inside.

Fire. He began gathering the dry debris, twigs, fluff, dust and the half-wet stick. Fire. Make a fire with this.

"Victoria," he said, "if your fingers still work, would you make a horsehair bowstring for a fire bow?"

"That hair ain't long enough, Mister Skye."

"I know," he said. "Try it anyway."

Muttering, she pulled herself away from the warmth of the other women and sorted out three small bundles of Jawbone's tail hair, twisted each, and adding new filaments of the twelve- or fifteen-inch hair, began plaiting them into a cord that would run not much more than three feet long, less when she wove the ends into loops for the bow.

The others watched intently, hope and discouragement showing in their gazes.

"Mister Danzig," Mister Skye said. "I need to have a small smooth conical pit chipped out of the dry side of this stick here, maybe half an inch in diameter. A single drop of water will ruin it. I will need a similar little pit dug into a hand-sized piece of wood. That doesn't have to be bone-dry, but it mustn't be wet or spray water."

"I'm so cold that any work will help," Professor Danzig muttered. He dug the wet flint arrow point from his pockets, wiped it on the inside of the cradleboard—the only thing approaching a dry place—and began gouging tiny bits of wood, trying to keep water out of his work.

"I'm going to go out on Jawbone and hunt down a dry stick. Need a bone-dry stick, maybe a foot high, inch in diameter, to spin in that hole. While I'm gone, gents, I'd like you to brave that rain one more time—gather the driest firewood you can find—from the lee side of trees, underside of deadfall. Once it gets dark, it'll be too dark to gather anything beyond firelight—and there's no wood to speak of in here."

Elkanah nodded. "I'll do it," he said, rising wearily. "Will you join me, gentlemen?"

Cobb stood, trembling, and hobbled out.

Connaught said, "I'd not be any good, I'm afraid." He drew grass bundles about him and settled back. "I don't believe in fighting fate or defying destiny," he added.

No one replied.

"I'm trying to reconcile myself to what must come," he muttered.

Elkanah and Jarvis plunged into the sweeping rain.

Mister Skye dragged himself out, felt the terrible icy lash again, and caught Jawbone by the mane. He led the slippery horse to a log and mounted painfully. Then he rode numbly into the cottonwood forest, hunting for the single dry stick he had to have. The rain assaulted him in sheets deep in the forested flat of the river, missing him one moment, deluging him icily the next. He couldn't stand it long, he knew. Perhaps he imagined it, but the light seemed to grow murky and fade. He studied each tree, looking for a knothole containing squirrel debris, scrutinizing each deadfall log that might be hollow or rotten and hold the stick he wanted. At last he found a giant trunk that had lodged against another tree when it fell, so it remained high enough for him to crawl under if he wished.

There in the dull light stood the sticks he wanted, spikes from the old log, projecting straight down, ancient and dry apart from whatever minor windborne spray had touched them. He slid off the horse and hunkered before them, staring. Yes, he could break them off. But then he realized he had no way to carry the precious sticks back to the overhang without soaking them. Bark, perhaps. A piece of hollow log he could put them in? Nothing.

He boarded Jawbone again from a stump, feeling his legs slide over the slick wet hair, and went hunting for a stick carrier in the dimming light. Running out of time. Nothing. He stopped, wondered if there might be something, anything, up at the overhang.

An idea came to him, and he rode back to the others, after sharply peering around to memorize this place in the dying light.

"Need the cradlebasket for a few minutes, Mary," he said. "To keep a stick or two dry."

Her dark glance seemed despairing, he thought, but she wordlessly pulled little Dirk out and clutched him to her cold wet breast. Mister Skye took the cradlebasket gratefully, folded its hood over to keep rain out, and rode Jawbone down into the gray forest again. He felt the slap of yellow cottonwood leaves plastering him with every gust. At the fallen log, he dismounted.

How could he keep his hands dry? He wiped them futilely, first on leggins, then on Jawbone's underbelly. Nothing. He'd have to snap the spikes from the log wet-handed and hope not to touch the ends. As a last measure he rubbed his hands along the underside of the log and then gripped the first stick. It cracked off and he darted it into the cradlebasket. The second snapped harder, but he slid it in also and nestled the dressed leather over his precious cargo. And rode back.

"Keep those sticks bone-dry," he muttered to the others. "We need only one, but keep them both dry. Professor, whittle the ends into points if you can with the antler blade."

Then he turned Jawbone back into the gloom. He still needed bow wood and began searching for a box-elder stalk, maybe an inch or two in diameter. Or anything like it that he could break off. It had grown almost too dark to see. Close to the river, he found chokecherry brush and snapped off the cold wet sapling, having trouble with the clinging bark. He finally mashed off the bark with a rock, hammering viciously until the last of the fibrous material parted. The light had died, and he'd have to make his bow in virtual blackness. He wished he'd done this earlier, but when you're trying to stay alive and keep others alive, time grows peculiar and irrelevant.

He slid off Jawbone at the overhang and plunged under it, bone-cold again, feeing water trickle down his chest and belly, catch in his loincloth, drip from his plastered-down hair. Elkanah and Jarvis had returned with some pathetic, mostly soaked sticks. And they'd managed to pile some brush at the north end of the overhang to slow the gusts a bit. Both of them walked back and forth in the confined space, willing their bodies to move.

"Don't know how we'll see to do this," he muttered.

"I have these," said Danzig, holding up a couple of pieces of wood with small hollows pitted in them, blurred shadows in this light.

"I don't see this hair no more," muttered Victoria. She eyed his crude chunk of chokecherry disdainfully. "That's too fat. Gotta be thinner to make a bow. I'll go get one," she said.

Before he could stop her, she plunged out, a wraith in her white nightdress.

"Don't!" he cried. "Too dark! You'll get lost!"

But she ignored him. Some lingering eerie light gave her passage. He waited, dripping, desperately cold again, and finally peeled off his sopping skin shirt and wrung water from it. His flesh had become icy. He sat down, easing back into the cold rock wall. Mary slipped down in front of him and pressed her warmer back into his chest. That felt good.

Like a ghost, Victoria reappeared in the blue dark, dripping water. She held a proper wand of wood.

"Goddamn," she muttered. She peeled off the borrowed nightdress and wrung it out carefully, her wizened body all but invisible in the murk anyway. Then she put it on, tugging the resisting wet wool.

"Where's that arrowhead, Danzig? I gotta scrape this into a bow and put nocks on the end," she said.

They could hear her in the dismal darkness. Her teeth chattered. The others huddled silently, night upon them, finding only each other for warmth.

For an endless while, they heard only her steady scraping, her profane muttering, and the soft movement of arms and fingers in the night. Mouse scratching, rat gnawing. It grew colder. Mister Skye could no longer control his shaking. He couldn't see the others, but supposed they might be better off welded together as they were.

Night settled into utter emptiness. They could not see each other, even a few feet away. Vicious winds gusted down the slope from above, chilling them. In pitch black, Victoria sandstoned the little piece of bow wood, tapering and notching ends for the bowstring, muttering in her strange Absaroka tongue. Mary crooned softly, quieting the restless child. Somewhere in that inkiness, Harvard Professor Danzig whittled tiny chips of wood from a dry stick, feeling his way as he chipped a broad point at either end.

Mister Skye stood and paced. He feared his body would

quit if he didn't. But he bumped into someone else, two others, also pacing. He didn't inquire who.

"Goddamn!" exclaimed Victoria. "Where's that horse string?"

Silence, and anguish.

"Ah!" she said. She muttered and mumbled. "We make it go now, Mister Skye," she said. "You kneel down here."

Danzig sat there, too, holding things. Victoria handed him the little bow, first. He felt its tension, felt the taut horsehair string looped and tied at each end. Good, he thought, but so short he'd hardly get up any speed. Danzig found Mister Skye's hand, led it to the wood on the ground, and showed where the tiny pit in it was. Mister Skye assembled it all, the fire stick, with a twist of the horsehair around it, a small hand-held block on top to serve as a bearing, and the bow.

"Now, Mister Danzig. A pinch of that dry stuff off the floor here into the hole, please. And then hold the bottom piece firmly."

"It's done," said Danzig.

He sawed at the bow slowly, feeling and hearing the stick whirl in its sockets, beginning the friction that he hoped would set the tiny bits of debris smoldering. From above, he pressed down gently, taking it easy on the hair bowstring. Blackness multiplied the difficulties. He scarcely knew whether his fire stick stood upright. He sawed at the bow, the stick whirled and squeaked—good, squeaking might mean it's dry, he thought. He couldn't see a damned thing. Gently, gently, he sawed, back and forth, spinning one stick in the socket gouged into another.

Nothing. "Victoria, I'm going to lift the point out of the hole. If your finger is dry, see if there's heat. And add a pinch of tinder. . . ."

"Goddamn, it's warm," she said. "Ain't hot, though."

He set to work again, this time whirling harder and faster, less careful of the bowstring. He sawed madly, feeling the stick spin under his palmed pressure, and finally smelling—he thought—a bit of smoke.

"Close!" he muttered.

"I think I smell smoke!" cried Elkanah.

In the blackness Victoria pinched more of the tinder into the little charred hole, and Mister Skye sawed the bow back and forth. The exercise and tension heated him, at least momentarily, driving back the circling wolves of cold. Smoke again, close, so close.

"Oh, God," cried Betsy, "let it happen, have mercy on us!"

"Oh, please," added Arabella, lifted from her long silence by hope.

"Have mercy on us, Lord!" exclaimed Percy Connaught. "Have mercy on your poor servants!"

"We'll do it, man!" exclaimed Elkanah. "If the Indians did it before flint and steel, we can do it!"

Mister Skye spun the stick, jerking the little bow back and forth viciously. Too short. The bow didn't let him spin the stick for long before he had to go the other direction. He grew tired, but sawed anyway—

—until the horsehair string broke.

"What happened?" cried Jacob Cobb.

Something sagged lower and lower inside of Mister Skye. He felt his muscles weigh down, his body sink, icy air eddy over his bare feet.

"String broke," he muttered.

"Don't give up!" cried Elkanah. "We can make another. Try thong. Can we cut thong with Rudolpho's knife—from leggins?"

"Wet thong's weak, mate. And this bow's too short."

Mister Skye's words sounded like the rattle of a falling guillotine blade.

"It's in the hands of God," breathed Betsy. "If we had moonlight, we could cut a new longer bow and start over. Oh, I'm so cold. . . ."

"Hands of God," murmured Rudolpho, sounding puzzled.

Mister Skye sat in the blackness, seeing nothing of past and future, not even seeing in his mind's eye. Cold and despair snuffed his inner vision, turned this moment into an eternal midnight. Hell, he thought. Hell must simply be a place without light and heat.

"I'll give you my shoestring. Tie two shoestrings," muttered Captain Cobb. "I'll give you my West Point belt."

"We can fix it!" Elkanah exclaimed firmly. "Never give up! Never give up! I'll find something. Who's got something for a string?"

No one answered.

"Some spin the stick by rolling it hard between hands, mates," Mister Skye said. "Hold the bottom one, Professor. Victoria, pinch in some more tinder."

He tried again. Between his palms he whirled the stick in its socket, harder and harder until crouching exhaustion sprang upon him. He stopped.

"How hot is the hole, Victoria?"

She muttered, didn't reply.

"Anyone else want to try?"

Elkanah tried and wouldn't quit until he fumbled, exhausted, sobbing wildly.

"Hold me," whispered Betsy. "We must be together now."

Mister Skye heard shuffling, and Elkanah's soft sobs, buried upon the breast of his wife.

He peered into the night and saw exactly nothing.

Little Dirk squalled violently, and ratcheted sobs. Mary exclaimed, "What?" The child's sobs muffled.

"Who took the cradlebasket?" she cried.

It took Mister Skye a moment to understand. And when he understood, he still felt too tired and cold to care. His son whimpered and coughed, while Mary soothed.

"Whoever took Dirk's cradlebasket, return it now," he said. "Return it now and I won't be coming for you."

"Oh, God!" Betsy cried. "God have mercy!"

No one stirred.

"I'll be hunting you down," said Mister Skye.

Silence met him. Betsy sobbed. Victoria cursed. Mary soothed the cold infant.

"I'll be hunting right now. And you'll feel my hands," Mister Skye rumbled, in a voice as black as the night.

A miserable thing, he thought. He found someone and patted ruthlessly. And another. And another. His sixth sense told him someone moved silkily, always knowing where the guide was. He jabbed out toward the rain with both hands, touched a bare wet foot, he thought, and met silence again. Nothing.

Not that a cradlebasket would help much . . . he thought. Still, the outer lining and hood would run maybe three feet square. . . . Warm someone a lot.

"Cradle robber!" he roared. "I don't know who you are, but I'll find out!"

From the darkness, Elkanah's voice. "I intend to find out, too. We'll survive this. And someone will return East in shame."

His voice quivered with cold.

"Let's all huddle close now," he added softly.

"No, mates. If you do that, you'll die before this night's

over. We'll walk. Every last one of us—get up and walk, all night, right to dawn. We'll walk until we drop, round and round this little place, stooped under here. Up and walk! You—the one with my Dirk's cradlebasket, and his little robe—you won't make it under that. You've got to walk all this long night!"

Chapter 24

The baby whimpered at her breast. She felt its icy limbs and wondered why the little thing wasn't bawling. A placid child, she thought. Her people withstood cold much better than these whites, and the blood of her Shoshones ran in Dirk. She clutched the naked boy, trying to protect him with her hands and with the wet elk-skin of her dress. But it seemed hopeless.

She felt the cold and hungry baby's needs as keenly as she felt her own: food, warmth, dryness, relief from the murderous cold that pressed so relentlessly. It had not reached freezing. Winter Man had not come, making Earth white. But he hovered not far away, and could kill wet and unclad people even before water turned to ice. She hugged Dirk tighter, trying somehow to cover the child.

What manner of man would do such a thing? Had these white people no honor? Did they not love children? Her people loved children. Not only her people, but the other Indian people, too. Only rarely did they harm a child. Not even enemy children. Sometimes they captured the little ones of enemies, not to kill or harm them, but to raise them as their own. She knew of enemy Blackfeet children in the village of her people. Arapaho, Cheyenne, Lakotah, too.

But someone among these white people stole from her child, stole selfishly so he might live and the child might die. It seemed so terrible to Mary she couldn't grasp it. Unspeakable, this deed. Were all of Mister Skye's people like that, evil in their spirits, empty, without good medicine? The question brought its own answer in her mind. No, they were not all like that. She thought of each of them here and decided that three would never do such a thing, but the other three might.

The child stirred restlessly in her hands and sobbed softly. Everywhere her hands touched its smooth young flesh, she found numb cold. Its back had grown numb, its legs stiff. Surely that child of her womb and Mister Skye's love, surely it would cease to breathe before Sun came. A terrible bitterness sang through her, and she thought she would find out who did this thing, and kill. Yes, kill. The bad-medicine person who had evil must be driven out, sent to the spirit land, sent where his spirit would wander forever without a home.

Medicine. Her own medicine helper and friend had always been the magpie, bold saucy bird, black and white, daring and smart. Well, Magpie, what would you say to me now? she thought. How would you save my child from the Winter Man?

Dirk sobbed steadily now, choking on his sobs.

"Blanket stealer," muttered Victoria, who trembled next to Mary. "I'm gonna go look," she whispered.

Mary's own coldness consumed her mind when Victoria vanished. How dark! She'd never known a night so black, so black that even the people next to her seemed a long way away, and she seemed all alone. Only the sound of their breath, or a subtle sense of their presence, told her that she wasn't utterly alone with her freezing child under a naked overhang. Just beyond, the subtle whisper of splashing told her the rain still sheeted down.

No one complained about Dirk's soft sobbing. Some shame pervaded them all, the utter evil of the theft of the cradlebasket grinding heavily upon other souls and hearts.

"Let me hold him, Mrs. Skye," said Betsy. "I have skirts that might warm him."

Mary didn't answer.

Mister Skye paced angrily, staying warm, she knew, but also driven by boiling rage.

A clatter. "Here!" hissed Victoria. A moment later Mary felt the old Crow woman touching her, handing her the cradle frame.

"Found the damn thing almost in the rain," she whispered. "Here—feel this!"

Mary felt, and touched wool! The inner liner she'd fashioned from an old Hudson Bay blanket remained inside the basket, a little bag of wool she'd carefully sewn for Dirk. She used it in cold weather. In warm, the outer leather lining sufficed to keep the child comfortable and protect it from rain and sun. That laced-down leather skin had been stolen. No doubt at the crack of dawn, she'd find it on the rock somewhere, carefully abandoned before telltale light came. Wool!

"Thank you, Magpie," she whispered. "We have stolen it back. You have sent Victoria!"

She felt, rather than saw, Mister Skye suddenly crouch before her.

"What?" he muttered.

For an answer, she found his hand and guided it to the cradlebasket and the wool, letting him hold it while she pulled Dirk off her soft breast and slipped the little boy into the dry woolen sack, and felt the child slowly relax in the sudden warmth.

"Goddamn," muttered Victoria.

From afar, Elkanah's sad voice came to them. "I am afraid to ask this, but is the baby—he's stopped crying. . . ."

"Dear God," wept Betsy.

Mister Skye addressed them all, his voice a low thunder in the bitter night.

"Victoria found the cradle," he rumbled. "Outer elkhide's missing. Someone's snatched a robe for himself. But inside, Mary had a wool lining, sewn from a blanket. Dry wool, a bag. She's put my boy in it and he'll weather the night. . . ."

"Thank God!" Betsy cried again, weeping.

Mary heard others cough and sigh.

Mister Skye continued quietly, soft words floating out into the inkiness. "I'm talking now to the one that stole the liner," he said. "All you had to do was ask. We'd have given you that hide liner. We'd simply forgotten about the wool inside. Whoever you are, you stole life from my boy. I'll not forget this. We're all cold, but we'll survive, I think. And one of you'll go back East with a shame in you, a stain you can't erase, a deed you'll never undo."

Cobb laughed sarcastically. "Come on, Skye. I'm so cold right now I know I'm dead before dawn. What time is it, do you suppose? Nine in the evening? Ten? And who's to say tomorrow will be warmer? The sun will rise on corpses."

"Don't give up! Never give up!" exclaimed Elkanah. "Mister Skye's right. Walk. If we sleep, we'll die! Make our muscles work and we'll live! I've walked this whole time, and I'm still living!"

Mary listened for more. Neither Arabella nor Percy

Connaught spoke. And neither did Professor Danzig, now
that she thought about it. Maybe Professor Danzig was a
witch, just as Victoria thought. Bad-medicine man, bringing evil upon them all. She clutched the woolen bundle to
her breast, warming the baby within it with her caress,
warming herself, too. Beside her she felt Victoria trembling in her wet nightdress. Mary handed the woolen
bundle to the older woman, who clutched it to her own
chest. She felt Mister Skye gathering them into his arms,
sharing what small heat remained in him. And then, when
he discovered Victoria's trembling, he pulled off his elkskin shirt and pulled it over her, and Mary heard Victoria
weep.

It surprised Elkanah Morse that life remained in him.
He didn't see how his body could possibly function, his
heart beat, his lungs pump air, when his flesh and bone had
lost their warmth. He wondered what his body temperature might be. Whenever he felt the fatal drowsiness seep
into him, he bolted up, sometimes hitting his head on the
low rock above, and paced a tiny circle furiously, flapping
arms as he went. Tiredness had long since consumed him,
but he scarcely cared about that. Cold remained the enemy,
the stalking killer.

   Betsy prayed. He knew that, heard her soft whispers and
entreaties. He dragged her up from her seat where she
slumped against the rear rock wall, forced her to walk beside him, and all the while she whispered and sobbed and
trembled. He'd found Arabella, too, tight beside someone—
Cobb probably—and pulled her up and forced her to
march, she protesting bitterly all the while. Some of the
dampness had left Arabella's borrowed doeskin dress as
well as Betsy's linen one; he could feel that with his hands.

They'd been under the cliff for hours and body heat slowly dried clothing.

Still it poured. He jabbed a hand out and felt the icy sting. Heard its soft murderous song, too. He sensed Danzig paced also, but not Connaught, who huddled inert somewhere. The shame and rage of the cradleboard affair boiled through him. He could understand the desperation. He felt the same cold, the same frantic need to wrap himself in anything at all. Not Danzig, surely not Danzig, his fine dear friend, and a man of honor. Not Betsy, not Arabella . . . his mind stumbled uneasily upon his daughter. Had she done something so dishonorable? The others, surely—the two he didn't know well, who'd tied on to his plans. He hadn't known Cobb at all; knew Connaught only through business. One of them! He would deal with one of them! The world would know about one of them!

He returned to his pacing, his mind mad with ideas. That's how his mind worked, thinking, trying, planning, studying. No problem he'd ever faced in a long life had ever been so desperate as this. No telling what dawn would bring. Could it only be nine or ten, with a whole night ahead? Surely they'd die. What heat remained? What shelter? He thought of weaving rushes into tight blankets and discarded it. No one could see a thing. In any case, most of the rushes had been consumed, shoved under clothing into thick layers of prickly grasses that did insulate them a bit.

He peered out. Not the slightest sign of a star or moon. What would they do tomorrow? Try a fire again, he supposed. If anyone was yet alive. Make a new bowstring from Jawbone's tail hair. Or Mary's . . . the woman's jet hair hung to her waist when she hadn't braided it.

"Mister Skye?" he whispered. "Let's try the fire bow with Mary's hair. It's longer!"

He waited for a reply. At last the guide responded. "Bow itself's too short, mate. I couldn't get it to spin the stick long enough. Also, hair's slippery. Victoria's loop and knots slid apart. And how will we see to braid it?"

Elkanah heard Cobb laughing sardonically again. "You'll invent something, I'm sure, Elkanah. In Lowell, you'd sit at your warm desk and invent something, sipping tea and eating tarts while you do."

Elkanah didn't reply. Hunger worked on him as it did the others. He'd tried a cattail bulb and found it gritty and bland, smelling of swamp, but he'd managed to get it down, sand and all.

Jawbone. Jawbone! "Mister Skye," he began. "What about Jawbone? Could you get him to lie down here? He's a thousand pounds of warmth. We could all draw warmth from it if the horse would lie still."

"Afraid not, Elkanah. I couldn't get that horse to lie still for that."

"But —a half a ton of warm flesh! Try, Mister Skye!"

Jarvis Cobb said, "Kill him. That heat would last all night. In the morning we'd have meat and a hide for shoes. You've got that belaying pin, Skye, and you can approach him, lead him here, and drop him right here. One horse for nine lives. How about it?"

Mister Skye didn't respond, and when he did at last, the answer surprised Elkanah.

"Ten lives, not nine, Captain Cobb. If you try to touch that horse, he'll kill you, if I don't kill you first."

Mister Skye's tone seemed so terrible that Elkanah couldn't imagine a reply from Cobb, but the captain laughed wildly.

Elkanah said, "That horse is our transportation, our ambulance if one of us becomes ill, Jarvis."

"Too late," muttered Cobb. "Dawn—if there is a dawn—must still be ten hours away, and I'm going right now. Half hour left for me . . ."

The man's desperation pierced the night. Probably true, Elkanah thought. Maybe none of them would live. If only they could have Jawbone . . .

Elkanah himself couldn't get Jawbone off his mind. He could almost feel the warmth of the animal radiating from its wet hair; he found himself conjuring up tasty steaks of horseflesh, cutting crude moccasins from the scarred blue hide of Skye's animal. Using its thong and sinew to make weapons, clothing, stone-head clubs and hatchets, horsehair from tail and mane woven into shirts . . .

He knew his own mind raced. Tiredness caught him again and he slumped beside Betsy, found her numb and inert. "Get up!" he cried, dragging her to her feet. She slumped down, unable to support herself. He lowered her to the cold rock and massaged her limbs, pumping arms and legs, hugging her.

"Mister Skye!" he cried. "Betsy's going."

"I'm coming," muttered the guide. "Keep talking so I can find you."

Together they lifted Betsy and dragged her, but her legs no longer worked and she wasn't responding.

"Elkanah," said the guide. "We'll have to press her between us. Hope you don't, ah . . . Let's ease her down, mate. I'll lie behind, you face her, and we'll press her."

Between them they sandwiched Betsy. Elkanah felt Mister Skye's massive hands reach past Betsy and onto his own back, pressing the three of them together. For a bit, Elkanah felt almost warm. He felt Betsy's heart and lungs work—she lived, sandwiched in a fragile warmth.

Cobb laughed relentlessly. "Should have killed Jawbone,

Skye. We'd all make it to daylight with a warm carcass like that. Funny, Skye. You've railed and raged about a missing bit of skin covering for a baby, talking shame and honor and dishonor. But there you are, refusing to save ten human lives by killing a horse."

That accusation had justice in it. A deadly silence sifted through the desperate camp. Jawbone's body would indeed help them to dawn, Elkanah thought quietly. They might also manage to eat some raw hot meat, or hot blood, too. . . .

Mister Skye sighed. At last he said, "When Mrs. Morse is warm enough, I'll fetch Jawbone."

"Goddamn!" cried Victoria.

Mary wept. Elkanah fathomed that killing Jawbone would be akin to killing a brother or a child or a husband.

He felt Betsy's body slowly relax in the cocoon that he and Mister Skye had given her. Perhaps they could make such cocoons, taking turns at being the one in the middle. He lay quietly, his mind more and more on Jawbone, almost feeling the beast's hot warmth, Hair, hide, blood, hooves for glue perhaps, horseshoes to hammer into knives and . . .

"Mister Skye," he whispered. "Is Jawbone shod?"

"Of course, mate. Had him shod at Benton."

Elkanah felt a pulse of wild excitement. "We have fire!" he cried.

Cobb laughed nastily.

"Rudolpho! You found flint?"

"I think so," the geologist muttered. "Maybe some chert, but the arrowhead is definitely flint."

"Where is it?"

"Against the back wall of the overhang, drying out. Couldn't sleep with rock in my wet britches."

Elkanah bolted up crazily. "Mister Skye, get Jawbone fast. Iron! We have iron! Not as good as steel for sparking, but many a horseshoe has struck a spark! Will he hold for it?"

Mister Skye thought. "He stands for shoeing well enough, mate, as long as he knows the shoer. I haven't a halter, but I've got whangs enough on my leggins and shirt sleeves to cobble something."

"Can we get the shoe off?" cried Elkanah.

"Not in pitch black. Those nails, clinched over. I don't see that we have the tools—"

"We can sharpen an antler prong—" Elkanah shouted.

Betsy stirred in his arms. "I'm all right," she whispered. "Go make the fire!"

Mister Skye said, "I don't think we need to take the shoe off, Elkanah. Victoria can hold him with a halter I'll lash up; I'll hold his foot steady. You and the professor can strike flint and get that tinder under it." He sighed softly. "I don't know that we can ignite the tinder, especially in total darkness. I'd give my arm for my charcloth."

Charred cloth, or charred cotton, heated until little but carbon remained, but not allowed to ignite, made perfect tinder, Elkanah knew. A spark settled on it, glowed into life, and a gentle breath often flared it into flame. But they had none of it.

"Betsy, we'll carry you to Arabella. Never stop hugging her. . . ."

Moments later, Mister Skye stood at the edge of shelter, whistling up Jawbone. They heard a rustling, a soft snort, and then felt the presence of the horse they couldn't see. "Easy," muttered Mister Skye. The very presence of the animal seemed a good thing. Not that they could feel its heat, but they sensed its presence. Mister Skye worked at something, and Elkanah realized the guide pulled whangs from his skin clothing and was tying them into something. In a bit, he heard Jawbone being turned around, the horse's deadly hind legs facing into the shelter, its shod hooves clicking on rock.

"Easy," muttered Mister Skye.

Then the guide's voice, very close. "Professor? Elkanah? Have you your things?"

Elkanah felt around for the tinder while Danzig fetched his rocks.

"Easy," said Mister Skye. "I'm holding his off rear hoof, gents. Hunker down here. Who's doing the honors?"

"I suppose I am," said Professor Danzig. "If I can hold the rock. My hands are numb."

"Easy," said the guide. The horse stirred restlessly. Both Rudolpho and Elkanah reached out, felt the hoof, traced the iron shoe, memorized it. Mister Skye held the foot toe-down, making the shoe vertical.

"The shoe's wet," said Danzig.

Mary materialized from somewhere and handed them a scrap of wool from the cradle—the only dry cloth among them.

"If he kicks, it's as good a way to die as any," Rudolpho joked, "and faster than some. Elkanah, is the tinder down?"

"Piled right below the shoe, Rudolpho."

"Well, let's be about it," the professor said.

He snapped a rock across the hoof. The horse stirred but held, with Mister Skye soothing him.

"That wasn't promising. Felt wrong," said Danzig. "Let's try this one."

Another harsh scrape, and a spray of sparks like fireworks.

"Ah!" cried Elkanah.

"Oh, God!" cried Betsy.

Behind him, Elkanah heard them all babbling.

Danzig struck again, and this time one tiny orange spark caught and glowed in something below.

"More, Rudolpho!" Elkanah cried.

Danzig struck flint again, and a spray of tiny shooting stars dropped through the darkness. Three sparks struck tinder and continued to glow. Elkanah blew gently, cursing the damp air, the humidity.

Then, grudgingly, a bitter blue flame wavered.

Chapter 25

Too late, too late.

Jarvis Cobb stared at the dazzling little flame flickering heatlessly as Mister Skye fed it twigs and sticks. It guttered dangerously in the cold gusts, but grew, crackling and wavering, casting a yellow wash over the dun rock of the overhang. Light out of darkness. Fire out of promises and hopes. They all gazed, bewitched, at this miracle of life snatching at least some of them from the lip of doom. Mister Skye, Professor Danzig, and Elkanah Morse huddled around it, nursing it protectively with their very bodies.

In it lay the possibility of life. Betsy wept. She'd come closest to doom, but others weren't far behind, minutes from the very end.

Light blossomed, glinted yellow off of wet rock just beyond, probed into corners previously black as pitch, struck the planes of flesh on faces, shadowed other planes.

Jarvis rejoiced along with the rest—until he realized that they stared at him silently.

Too late, too late. The soft, well-oiled elkskin robe he'd unlaced from the cradlebasket remained tucked up under his armpits, wrapped tightly about his torso, offering steady life-giving warmth.

Too late, he remembered it. He stared at it, this insignia of dishonor, feeling the heat and scorn of their gazes. His mind leaped to find excuses, explanations, mitigating words, but he could think of none. His brain went soft, addled, rattled, and he couldn't string an idea together.

None of them said a thing. What was there to say? He stared wildly about, unable to meet their eyes, and then pitched the robe off with a small strangled laugh. Victoria picked it up and wrapped her small cold frame in it and returned Mister Skye's shirt to him. With the fire and his blanket bag, Dirk wouldn't need the outer lining.

"See? It wasn't needed," Jarvis babbled. "See, she took it."

No one spoke. Mary slipped to the fire with the restless child in her arms and let the rudimentary warmth begin its work.

Jarvis chuckled amiably. "Nothing ventured, nothing gained," he said. "What counts is the life of a man in his prime, fine-honed and educated, and not the life of a little-breed."

No one spoke.

Their obdurate stares told him he had become a pariah, an outlaw here in this community.

He ceased to make light of it. "We do what we have to to survive," he muttered. "You'd do the same if you were dying."

Still no one replied.

"This is nothing. I've done us a favor. The child doesn't even need it—he's got a wool bag. Now we've got moccasin leather from it."

The words drifted out into the strange silence, marked only by the snap of twigs in the tiny wavering fire. Its heat barely reached him where he sat with his back to the wall of rock, and he shivered, not daring to move closer to the life-giving flame.

He trembled, hugged himself. He'd do it again, he told himself. We all do what we must to save ourselves. He had that right—save himself or perish—and he took it. No harm done, either. They'd found the woolen inner lining. . . . He'd been scarcely aware of that lining when he unlaced the cover in the pitch black. It snugged into the other side of the willow hoops of the cradle frame.

Jarvis Cobb had a sense that his life had changed in a moment, that some great dread crushing force had forever damaged his progress through his days and years. He sensed that he would live with this thing forever, that it might sneak up upon him in his nights, catch up with him as he taught at West Point, follow him about in whispers, ostracism, isolation, pointed fingers, lack of promotion. His wife, if she didn't know of reasons, would wonder why he seemed so isolated, why they never advanced. . . .

Sitting there against the cold rock, he sensed all that, less thought out than intuited in a flash. What rotten luck, having to deal with this, for surely it would follow him. Not a lifetime of valiant service in combat on the frontiers would wipe it away. And yet it had been nothing: a civilized scholarly life for a minor threat to a breed child of the wilderness, half-blooded of a Stone Age people.

He laughed. He'd made a perfectly logical choice; save

what was valuable, a lifetime of study, of intelligence, and its applications. Save what was valuable if one had to make hard choices. Save himself, as he had every right—indeed, a firm duty—to do. Still, he thought, it'd go badly, badly. . . . A melancholy settled over him and he tried to turn his thoughts to other things.

A fire didn't mean much anyway. They were all half-naked and shoeless, without food or weapons or shelter, and autumn thundering in—what did it all mean, this shaming?

Mister Skye set aside his damp elkskin shirt and then stood under the low overhang, stripping off his leggins until he wore only his breechclout. Jarvis wondered at this public disrobing.

"Throw a bit of the dry kindling on, Elkanah—give me light. I'm going out for squaw wood. Don't have near enough here, and what we've got is half-wet. While I'm out, pile it close to the fire and start it drying."

"I'll come with you!" cried Percy Connaught. It startled Cobb. Connaught volunteering to do a nasty job in icy rain. But the big ungainly scholar with ghost-white flesh peeled off his undershirt and winced out into the rain, teeth clenched, behind Mister Skye. Cobb caught the glance that Elkanah gave to Rudolpho, the faint smile. A man redeemed, it seemed to say. No one glanced at Cobb. He'd ceased to exist, he thought.

From out in the darkness he heard snaps and the slap of wetness, and then Percy Connaught minced in carrying an armload of sticks snapped from trunks, dry wood but wetted black.

"Mister Skye says we'll need a lot more. We'll need enough for two fires, and enough to be drying and feeding fires at the same time," Connaught said. He slipped tender-footed back into the gloom, ice water trickling down his cold-pinked body.

Between them, Mister Skye and the Hartford bookbinder brought in ten armloads of broken sticks and set it all to drying around one side of the fire. Connaught looked determined and proud, even when he'd gotten so chilled he could no longer keep his arms and legs from spasming.

"Come sit here, Mister Connaught," said Betsy softly. She made a place for the dripping man close to the fire.

Mister Skye returned almost empty-handed. "That's as far as we can see for wood," he said. "Mostly I'm just feeling trunks for sticks that far. We need much more."

He shook himself like a hairy bear and found a place close to the flames.

Jarvis Cobb found no place at the circle around the fire, but sat with his back to the stone wall. Still, a faint heat reached him, radiation from flame, warm air whirling and eddying through the overhang. He felt colder than he had without the fire, but he knew the whole place would warm gradually.

An outcast, he thought. For doing what anyone would do. Even Arabella, who'd sat beside him through the night, who loved him and shared hardship with him, had deserted him now, gone to sit beside her parents, refusing even to glance his way.

Well, he thought, too bad. A sudden hardness filled him. They had no right to judge. Fools, all of them, or canny rustics like Skye and his squaws. They'd go back East and babble and tell dark stories . . . if they got back at all. Skye and his women and brat might survive out here, living their savage lives, but he doubted they'd say anything, or that the army would take a squaw man seriously anyway. Such drunken louts lived off the scraps from army forts all along the frontier. But Morse might talk, his women might gossip. Connaught might whisper. Danzig might tell a tale or two. If they all got back, of course.

Jarvis Cobb wondered idly whether they'd all make it. Betsy looked haggard; Arabella half-sick. Connaught, soft and scholarly, seemed half-dead in his underdrawers. Oh, they'd try. The squaws knew how to turn rock and wood and bone and hide into useful implements, bows and arrows, knives, snares, hooks, traps, deadfalls. Given time, they'd make shoes and clothing of sorts, lay in wild foods, and hobble their way back to Fort Laramie. Morse had a kind of genius at it—he'd come up with the means to make a fire, something that had eluded even Skye and his savages.

Cobb wondered where he stood in this cozy little society. Would they feed him? Make shoes and clothing for him? Offer fire and shelter? Bid him to come along East? The more he pondered it, the more he doubted it. He'd be there, a presence, but outside of them. Some wall had lowered between them and him. All the sensible argument in the world wouldn't breach that wall, he knew. Well, he thought, if they cared so little about him, for some minor transgression—if it was a transgression—he needn't care about them. In fact, it'd be most inconvenient for them ever to reach the East and whisper their nonsense about him. He had a whole life ahead, glory and honor, and he didn't want it stained by something as absurd as this. Perhaps, if he used his brains, he could contrive to arrive at Laramie alone.

They awoke ravenous. The cloud bank cleared off about the time the smoky sun probed over the tops of the distant Big Horns walling the east. A warm dry day, a day to achieve important things, thought Elkanah. In a curious way, he found himself enjoying the challenge of all this. He had to solve problems—manufacture urgently needed things—or he and his dear ones would perish.

It had been a strange night. With the building heat came relaxation, and drowsing. Yet no one had slept much. Each wished to guard the wavering fire, feed it, nourish it as one nourished a child at breast. The strange brooding presence of Jarvis Cobb troubled them all. No one knew what to do about him, and each bottled his private thoughts about Cobb within. Not a word had been spoken. In the breaking dawn-light, the captain sat a little distant, walled off from the others.

By common consent, the remaining cattail bulbs had been left to Mary, who washed the grit from them and then mashed them gently, using a river cobble and a flat slab of wet deadfall she had found. It made a poor meal for the infant, but a meal at any rate, and in the end hunger won over his distaste for the whitish pulp.

Their clothes had dried. The fire along with body heat had done that for them. But if the others felt the way Elkanah did, their stomachs howled and the beginnings of faintness from starvation pressed upon them. The last full meal had been two evenings earlier, cooked under the canvas tent fly Elkanah had rigged for Betsy.

Elkanah sat quietly, his mind chewing furiously on the looming problems. He could scarcely even list them, much less arrange them in some order of priority: food, footgear, clothing, firewood, tools, weapons, carrying bags, bedding, means of building a fire more easily, dry tinder for future use. . . .

Mister Skye's women handed the infant to Arabella, who accepted it a bit sourly—the child had soiled its blanket bag—and then walked out into the wet woods and the icy dew-laden grasses. Each found a digging stick, and then the pair of them separated, one working upstream, one down, their gaze steadily upon the autumnal yellow weeds and grass. Root gathering, he supposed. They'd had bread root the squaws dug up several times during the trip. The white meat within the black and repellent skin seemed edible enough. They'd boiled the roots then. He wondered whether they could come up with something to boil them in now—short of fashioning and firing clay pots, a process that intrigued him. He knew nothing about doing that.

Mister Skye, too, had busied himself right from dawn, roaming widely through the cottonwood bottoms, hauling sticks and logs in great profusion back to the overhang, where he carefully set them close to the fire to dry. He gimped along on bare feet, wincing and wobbling while he labored. Only his squaws seemed able to go barefoot without much difficulty.

Footgear. Surely one of the first things, Elkanah thought. A knife to cut moccasin leather from Mister Skye's leggins. The flint arrowhead would do it, but slowly. Rudolpho's antler knife would be too weak and dull too fast. He needed metal . . . such as Jawbone's shoes. Then an idea came to him: horseshoe nails. If Mister Skye would permit it, he'd take a single nail out of each rear hoof—one to beat into a tiny but effective knife; the other to turn into an awl. Elkanah worked the idea around, growing excited. With a stone hammer, he'd flatten out one nail into a tiny thin blade, and bang the nail head into a haft and anchor the haft into wood, or antler. Then they'd have a real knife—something to cut leather, gut animals, whittle wood. . . .

And the other nail would make an awl to punch holes,

drill, manufacture. . . . Excited, he wobbled out over gravel and sticks until he cornered Mister Skye.

"If you'd let me remove a nail from each of Jawbone's rear hooves, Mister Skye, I'd turn them into valuable things—a real knife, a good awl. . . ."

The guide paused in his wood gathering and grinned. "You're the man to do it if it can be done," he said. "I suppose the shoes would stay on minus a nail. Usually do. But we're still a long way from Laramie—well nigh four hundred miles. Maybe a little less. A lot of wear on an unshod hoof." Then he frowned. "How do you propose to get the nails out, Elkanah? Those nails are clinched tight over the hoof."

"Rudolpho's antler spikes . . . and patience."

"You'd better make a mallet first, mate."

"I have that in your belaying pin, Mister Skye."

"What if the nail gets stuck halfway?"

"Pry the whole shoe," replied Elkanah.

"Jawbone's trained to kill people who fool with him," Mister Skye muttered. "But I can usually keep him calm enough for shoeing. It seems like a way to start. Make tools to fashion what we need."

Elkanah felt mounting excitement. "With a little knife, sir, I can whittle wooden soles, clogs. We can attach sandal straps to them and walk, even if there's not enough leather for moccasins."

"Go to it, things-maker. I'll join you soon as I get this load of wood in. If we stay warm, we'll survive the rest."

Elkanah fumbled his way back, his cold wet feet discovering every stick and rock and cactus on the way to the cliffside. Tools and weapons, he thought. Bows and arrows for the hunters. He paused before a chokecherry bush, seeing wands of wood two or three inches in diameter. Bow wood, he thought. Not the best, not dried hard, but useable. Better than the other choices in these bottoms, coarse splintery box elder and cottonwood. He tried to break some off but couldn't. Well, too early to think of bows anyway, he thought. Hunger hung in him maddeningly, souring a bright day that would turn warm and golden by afternoon.

"Daddy, I can't bear this hunger. I'm half-mad with it!" Arabella cried crossly when he returned.

He squatted before her as she rocked little Dirk in her arms. "We're alive, Arabella," he repeated softly. "Before we can get much to eat, we must be able to go out to find game and roots. That means shoes, moccasins, at least sandals. And that means tools to make them."

Tears welled in her eyes. "I'm so hungry. I didn't want to come. I wanted to stay home. I've slept on hard ground. I've gone unwashed for weeks. And now this . . ."

The baby squalled suddenly, and she began crooning, rocking it with unaccustomed arms, half-desperate.

Professor Danzig joined them. "I've been scouting the riverbanks as much as my feet permit," he muttered. "I have more flint. Scared up mallards and mud hens and some Canada geese going south. Things splashed ahead of me—otters, I suppose, or muskrats. And deer. I startled a deer. And fish—I'd even eat fish."

Danzig looked so forlorn and famished that Elkanah laughed. They both laughed sharply, feeling the hollow of their bellies. For a moment Elkanah allowed himself a vision of dripping venison, roasted dark, of tender duck cooked in its own fat, of juicy buffalo hump meat or rib roast half-pink and juicy within and browned hot and fire-bathed on the outside. . . .

"Food is my nemesis," muttered Danzig. "I'd sell my soul—I'd do most anything for a juicy platter of buffalo just now. . . ."

The selling of soul reminded them all of Cobb, and they glanced covertly toward the edge of the overhang, where the captain had isolated himself. He had disappeared somewhere.

We all have Cobb's temptations and weaknesses in us, thought Elkanah. No need to be too hard on the captain. Who among us might not do the same thing, if a bit more desperate? Maybe hunger would drive another to do it, to stealing food rather than warmth. . . .

Ten mouths to feed, he thought. Actually a staggering task without the means. No gardens here or dairies or swine or cattle or orchards—other than what Mister Skye's remarkable women might discover in nature.

"Betsy," he said softly, "if you can manage it without shoes, go with Victoria and Mary next time, and learn, learn everything, and ask questions about every leaf and stem you see."

"Oh, Elkanah, I'll do all I can. But I'm so weak for want of food . . ." she murmured. "And my feet are bleeding."

"Percy," he said amiably. "I'm appointing you our fire tender. Keep it going all day, at least a bit. Bring in wood, and hunt down dry tinder and twigs—rob squirrels!"

Connaught seemed pleased. "Trust me, Elkanah," he replied.

Mister Skye approached the cliffside, leading Jawbone with a whang-leather halter. "You're in luck, Elkanah. Jawbone's near hind shoe's loose. I'm thinking to pull it off. Would a horseshoe and eight nails assist your manufactures?"

"That's wealth for us all!" exclaimed Elkanah.

Jawbone eyed them all viciously from yellow eyes. But he let Mister Skye lift the shod rear hoof. The toe of the shoe had worn almost to a razor edge, which delighted Elkanah—an ax! A metal hammer! A striker to make fires! An anvil! The guide wiggled the loose shoe, showing them. All the nails remained clinched down, though.

"I think I can bend those," said Professor Danzig. "Give me a minute to snap off some antler spikes and sandstone them."

"Lots of horn under the shoe," rumbled Mister Skye. "He won't go lame soon."

From the corner of his eye, Elkanah saw Cobb stop and listen to Mister Skye. For some reason the captain seemed interested in all this, even from his distance of several yards and several civilizations.

In a half hour, they'd pried the shoe off without damaging Jawbone's hoof. Instantly, Elkanah and Rudolpho set to work hammering tiny blades of iron with patient taps. It'd take much of the day, he thought. Too much for starving people.

"Rudolpho, let's hammer out only one small knife now, one to cut up some of Mister Skye's leggins. I'm thinking to sew up some moccasins so we can hunt food. We've so much to do. Tonight, around the fire, we'll make things— snares, traps, whatever Mister Skye and his women wish us to make."

"You done with Jawbone?" asked Mister Skye.

They nodded. Elkanah noticed the guide had his ancient belaying pin in hand, a formidable club.

"I'm going after meat," he muttered, clumsily throwing himself over Jawbone's back. He sat barefoot and barelegged.

"When Victoria's back, have her cut some moccasins

with those fancy nails of yours. From my leggins. I'm going meat hunting."

"With a belaying pin?" asked Elkanah.

"I'm hoping to scare up a buffler calf and jump it from Jawbone's back. Club it down."

The thought of juicy calf steaks set juices flowing inside Elkanah.

"Good luck, Mister Skye!" he cried.

Chapter 26

Jawbone topped the west bluff and stepped out upon a flat arid plain of white clay and sparse bunch grass. The wet clay sucked at his hooves. Mister Skye steered him southwest, the direction the Bannocks had gone in the rain two mornings before. He disliked riding bareback. The ugly horse's spinal ridge sliced into his tailbone, and his bare legs and feet dangled uncomfortably without stirrups. The pad saddle Victoria had made him, carefully stuffed with the hair of a buffalo bull, had vanished along with the rest.

He carried his battered belaying pin with him, ancient relic of his days as a seaman, but once he rode out across the Big Horn basin, he realized sheepishly that even if he brained a buffalo calf, he had no means of getting any of it back to camp. He lacked a knife to butcher it and rope to drag it.

He wanted to get away. Back in camp, people would do what they needed to. Elkanah and Professor Danzig would manufacture amazing tools. His wives would gather food. The Morse women would probably gather rushes, weave mats. Percy Connaught, showing some fortitude after all, would amass wood and tend the fire. Cobb . . . he didn't know what Cobb would do. One reason he had ridden out alone was to think about Cobb. He knew what he wanted to do with Cobb: banish him, tell him he would have to make his way alone, tell Cobb that the services, guiding and food, he provided didn't apply to him. And yet . . . he couldn't bring himself to that. He couldn't abandon the man to his wilderness fate.

The tracks of the Bannocks had washed out, and no telltale scrape of travois or hoofprint marred the rain-slicked basin. But he had reasons. Indians discarded what they didn't understand. Their nomadic life kept them from accumulating worthless things. At the times when government annuities were distributed to the far tribes, the Indians dumped the flour—which they didn't understand—and kept the sacks, which seemed valuable to them. He hoped he might find the detritus of their camp if he could fathom which way the Bannocks wandered.

He zigged and zagged generally southwest, hoping to cut a track. Travois poles cut deep into wet gumbo, and he might spot a trail if he persevered. The weak sun rose as high as it would at the start of October, bringing the temperature up into the fifties, he supposed. Maybe warm days ahead. But not today. His bare legs, bereft of the leggins he'd donated for moccasins, felt the chill. He rode worrying—the problems of clothing and food heavy on him. No worry rested heavier than Victoria's near nakedness. She had only Betsy's thin nightdress, having given her own buckskin dress to the white girl. His leggins might make something for her, but they all needed moccasins. That left the cradlebasket outer cover. . . .

In spite of the fire, they were all close to perishing. He'd experienced several starvin' times in the mountains—any fur trapper had—and he recognized the faintness that came over him now and then, knew it for the slow death that crept along on an empty belly. It and cold could addle people, too, turn them mad, trigger senseless fights. Cobb, for instance. Already an outcast; maybe an outlaw when crazed for food and warmth. Once they got moving, what would they do for shelter? How would they make fire again? What would they do for food?

He angled south, the purple hulks of the Owl Creek Mountains looming along the horizon. The Bannocks probably headed that way on a long circling route home, through the lands of their Shoshone relatives. All of it good buffler country. He cut a travois track at last and peered down from Jawbone to examine it. Southwest. He turned again, picking up the faint dimples of horses passing through mud. No debris, no discards. They'd keep all of Elkanah's efficient camp equipment.

A band of antelope watched him progress and trotted off, sliding beyond a low ridge. Food, he thought. And hide. And every one of the prairie goats fleeter of foot by far than Jawbone. That reminded him to look for horses, too. Nothing would solve their problems better than finding their horse herd. With that in mind, he detoured to peer over ridges, detoured to study grassy gullies. Nothing. He sat on Jawbone yearning for horses, aching for horses and mules. With horses he could take them to safety. They might starve and freeze en route, but he'd get them to the Crows or Shoshones, or even to Fort Laramie.

He topped a gentle sage-covered roll of prairie perhaps ten miles from the Big Horn River and spotted the remains of a camp below. Eagerly he trotted down the slippery gumbo slope. Ashes, a pile of unused wood—and the car-

cass of a buffler cow, already stripped to the bone by
wolves and coyotes as well as magpies, crows, eagles, and
all the rest. Flies still swarmed. On the underside of the
skeletal remains, lots of hide remained, nibbled around the
edges, tooth-torn but mostly intact. An eyeless skull gaped
at him, tongueless and hairy. A treasure, he thought.
Rawhide sole leather under there. Bone tools, too. The
remains weren't foul, kept fresh by near-freezing tem-
peratures. He slid off Jawbone, chased away audacious
magpies, and kicked at the rib cage. In a moment he had the
remains turned over, the hide up. Except for a few grubby
things crawling on it, the hide seemed good enough. Eight
or ten square feet of it, he thought. Rawhide soles for nine
mortals in peril. Cut out with Elkanah's tiny nail knives.
He tugged at it, having trouble working it loose. He found
a cannon bone and hammered, finally freeing the soggy
thing. He shook the grubs off it, scraped it swiftly with
pieces of bone, and then collected some useful bone—
ribs for arrowheads and tools, leg bones for war clubs and
hammers. He knocked out some teeth and added them—
maybe Elkanah would turn them into miraculous things.
Satisfied at last, he rolled up his booty and mounted Jawbone again, having a bad time of it, as he always did, without the aid of stirrups. Jawbone peered back at the bundle
nervously, his ears flattened.

"Don't like that, eh?" Mister Skye muttered. "You'd better
like it. Maybe you'll be the only survivor, Jawbone."

Suddenly filled with emotion, he patted the vicious
horse along its black mane, loving the animal that had been
boon companion, brother, and warrior, rescuing Mister
Skye and his nomadic family countless times. His fingers
lingered on the scars. Had ever a horse suffered more
wounds? Arrow and lance and war club, bullet crease, too.

They'd wanted to kill Jawbone for meat and hide. Kill him. And he might have let them. His eyes watered, and he stroked the horse, his brother.

Mister Skye circled the camp again, followed the trail a mile or so west, finding nothing—neither horses nor abandoned loot—and sadly turned back. His stomach howled at him now, and he fantasized buffler rib steaks, tongue, liver, steaming boudins. He worried about Dirk— the adults could understand hunger and cope with it some- how, but how do you explain starvation, poor doings, to an infant? For that matter, how do you explain Cobb? A man who'd rob infants to stay warm would also rob any- one to eat. Mister Skye puzzled Cobb in his mind as he rode, not knowing what to do.

He headed straight back, hoping to make camp by late afternoon, hoping to scare up game—anything. Even snakes, he thought. But the snakes had vanished for the winter. He knew little about snares and deadfalls, but they'd have to try some, bag rabbits, bag anything. He wondered if he could find beaver on the Big Horn, catch them in their stick-and-mud houses. Nothing like good beaver-tail meat . . . Nothing like any meat.

Changing his mind, he steered due east. He'd strike the Big Horn and ride north, and maybe he could brain some game with his belaying pin. River bottoms teemed with animals that might make meat. That and village campsites. A westerly breeze chased him back, sharp and penetrat- ing and chill across his naked legs and feet.

By his reckoning, he struck the Big Horn valley about five miles below his own camp. It coiled green between silvery-white prairie hills, but the green had dappled into yellow with the turning of the leaves. Beyond him angled the Big Horns, blue and snow-tipped from the early storms.

He'd struck the site of a large and recent encampment, a flat beside the great river, gnawed down by horses, muddy and dark. Gently Mister Skye steered Jawbone down grassy slopes and into the camp, his small buried eyes peering sharply for useful things—food, above all food now. He passed rings of stone, black ash shimmering with water, a broken arrow. He slid off Jawbone and picked it up. It had no arrowhead. Its owner had saved that. He rolled the broken arrow into his salvaged hide. Barefoot now, he trudged through the place, desperate for whatever had been missed. He couldn't quite say why, but he felt himself among the Arapaho.

Two worn-out moccasins of wide Arapaho make, holes in their soles. He took them gratefully. A purple rag. He lifted it, tradecloth, once a squaw's long blouse, riddled with holes, torn and nearly useless—except to him. He shook it, sending insects scattering, and wrapped it in his hide roll. An hour of careful searching yielded prizes: several blunt-headed children's arrows, excellent for shooting game birds. Two more moccasins. A hide-scraping tool with a bone blade. A lance point of rusted iron—a great discovery. A shabby chunk of lodgecover, most of a hide, worn and weak. Bits of thong and feather. A long piece of sinew in tiny filaments. A weakened bowstring of twisted sinew, shredded at one end but maybe usable in a very short bow.

But no food. He circled the camp carefully, looking for food, nuts and roots forgotten by squaws, jerky, pemmican, kitchen wastes, fresh bones with marrow . . . nothing. His stomach growled his disappointment back at him. Dizzily—he felt the want of food badly—he gathered his prizes into the roll of wet hide and started north, up the bottoms of the river. Along the way he scared up a giant jackrabbit, threw his belaying pin at it, and missed. Irritably, he clambered off Jawbone to retrieve it. Once, when he was young, he could throw a belaying pin with deadly accuracy. Long ago.

Victoria and Mary found little food. Nine grown men and women, plus a child to feed, and little food. It made Victoria cross and unhappy. Her own hunger ate steadily at her innards, but she ignored it. These whites all seemed to faint and fall into the beyondland the instant they lacked food. Her feet hurt. Even though her soles were much tougher than those of the whites because she had walked barefoot many of the summer moons of her life, they hurt badly now. Dense brush, thickets of sticks lined the Big Horn River, and they'd had to work through the brush barefoot to reach the cattails. Already they'd pulled up all the cattails they could find close to their camp. But they had this last small hard-won pile to take back, rinsed of their grit and the muck on them in the cold murky water.

Victoria felt continually cold, too, in the wool nightdress that was her sole clothing ever since she'd given her buckskin dress to Arabella. Sun wasn't warming her the way he used to. Her old thin body ached, but that didn't matter either. She felt much warmer now than last night just before Elkanah Morse and the little man, Danzig, the one she'd thought was a witch, had made the sparks. She'd felt the heat going away from her, felt the cold coming into her center, and she had prepared to sing her song and go over to the Other Side because the heat had slipped from her. She didn't tell her man about that, how close she'd come. He had enough worries. But she'd brought to her mind the words of her own death song, one she'd thought up when she had been a girl sitting on a grassy hill and think-

ing about serious things the first time, and waited now to
sing soon. She would tell Sun, and the First Maker, to welcome her, and she'd tell them how proudly she had been the
wife of Mister Skye for most of his days. She'd sing to them
of her love for him, and to prepare a place for him, and
Mary, too, in the beyond land where it never felt cold. But
they'd started the fire and she set aside her song for now, for
a little while more. Maybe not long. Oh, she felt hungry!

They'd found few roots, but the ones they found came
easily from the mud, which was good. Their digging sticks
broke at once. No greens at all, for frost had nipped them,
except for a handful of wild onions they'd gathered. Berries had dropped, too, long gone, snatched away by birds
and rodents, bears and women like herself. They'd found
prickly pear, though, and knocked off twenty or thirty of
the thick lobes, stringing them with a cord made from the
whangs of Mary's skirt. And coming back, they'd found a
grove of pines and gathered browning cones that still held
the tiny nuts. Victoria set store by pine nuts, and in her
mind she saw them all going to little Dirk, giving him
strength and life. And at the last they robbed a squirrel,
finding a handful of seeds and nuts cached in a hollowed-
out place in a decaying cottonwood. Not much, she thought.
Not even a whole meal for the nine of them and Dirk.

At least all the whites seemed busy when they got
back. Even the strange white goose-man, Connaught, who'd
patiently gathered an enormous cache of wood, and in between trips had constructed a rock wall, mortared with
mud, along the north side of the overhang to keep the wind
out. The women had collected rushes with Danzig's antler knife, and made thick bedding with them. Betsy had
woven a rush mat and had started a second. Mats wouldn't
help much, Victoria thought crossly. She should be making

baskets to carry food and roots when they began the hard journey ahead.

"Goddamn, make baskets," she said sharply. Betsy stared. They all stared at Victoria and Mary, their gaze glued upon the meager roots and cattails and the prickly pear hanging like giant beads from a thong.

"Cactus?" asked Arabella.

"Hell yes," retorted Victoria. For a reply she tossed several on the small fire, letting them hiss and sizzle. The spines turned black and then flared off the green flesh. Victoria dug one of the lobes out of the fire, let it cool, and then munched on it. The warmed juices and pulp would nourish her. They stared, and then tried it themselves. Cactus! Food everywhere!

"It doesn't satisfy at all," Arabella said, devouring the last of a hot lobe.

"Believe I will," muttered Elkanah, rising from his work. Victoria realized that the things-maker and Danzig had been busy doing something. She peered at their tiny factory, astonished. They had finished two tiny knives, their blades made of horseshoe nails patiently hammered flat and sand-stoned to an edge. These had been driven through handles made of antler that the whitemen had somehow cut off, so that an inch or so of nail projected. She picked up a little knife.

"Son of a bitch!" she muttered.

Beside it lay an awl, made of a nail jabbing out of an antler handle.

"Mister Skye asked that you make moccasins from his leggins with these," Elkanah said as he roasted a cactus lobe. "He's off hunting."

"Goddamn," she muttered. The men still had five

horseshoe nails left, and the shoe itself. She picked up the shoe, ran a finger over the keen edge of its worn toe, and knew how these whitemen had cut off an antler handle for their little knives.

Maybe the things-makers would help after all, she thought. With these things she could make a little bow and some arrows.

Jarvis Cobb appeared, carefully ignoring the others. None of them had any idea how to cope with him, or whether to feed or help him. He simply hovered around. Now, they saw, he'd made some crude weapons. He carried a war club made from a flat river cobble wedged into a split stick, and a lance with a wooden point ground down with sandstone and hardened in fire. He had honed a wooden knife of sorts, too, capable of sawing grasses at least. His gaze focused on the roasting prickly-pear lobes, and some illumination struck him. He struggled off, barefoot, to find his own supply of it.

"We'll have to come to some decisions about him," whispered Elkanah. "I hope Mister Skye returns soon so we can talk it over."

Victoria muttered. She would kill Cobb or drive him out. That's what her people would do to a betrayer, a man without honor. Make Cobb a renegade. But these whites seemed soft and forgiving.

She hunkered beside Mary, who cleaned Dirk and packed moss she'd gathered to absorb Dirk's wastes in the cradle blanket. But the blanket had been fouled, and she thought better of it, and took it off to the river to rinse out. The baby would manage in the leather liner for a while.

They ate and looked as hungry as before. "Well, what's for lunch?" asked Professor Danzig, with a light humor no one felt. The pangs of their bellies told them of looming desperation soon, within hours. They'd had little now for almost two days.

Victoria picked up Mister Skye's leggins. She'd made them for him. She hated to cut them up, but maybe she'd have to. At least she'd wait for him to return. Who knows what he might bring? He had ridden out looking, and nothing could be better than looking. That had always been the way of her people. In trouble, start looking. She huddled closer to the fire because the sun had swung around to the far west, casting their little shelter in deep chill shadow. She peered at her thin white thing disdainfully. How could white women wear something so useless? It held no heat and barely covered her nakedness!

"I think my rock wall is holding the heat in here better, making a deep corner of it," Percy said, hunting acclaim.

"Damn! Good wall!" said Victoria. "Maybe you can take it with us when we go."

The white goose-man looked vaguely crestfallen.

The baby fussed, hungry. Mary pounded nuts and cattails into a nourishing pulp, using her river cobble for a pestle, and then began fingering the stuff to Dirk. He spat it out, but accepted the next finger load.

Victoria heard Mister Skye coming, or rather, heard Jawbone snort and mutter his way through river brush. The guide loomed on the horse and tugged his whang-leather rein in the cold blue shadow of the overhang. They stared at him, seeing something in his lap that wasn't food or meat; he stared at them, his knowing eyes finding heaped wood, a rock wall, rush beds and mats, and an array of tiny tools sitting proudly on the dun rock of their refuge. He smiled one of his rare smiles.

"Got a few things, mates, but not food. Couldn't find buffler, and couldn't get anything else."

But as he unrolled the wet hide, he dropped treasure upon them. Part of a lodgecover! Moccasins! A tool for scraping! Blunt children's arrows. A sinew bowstring, broken at one end. A purple something . . .

Victoria pounced on it, held up a woman's thigh-length blouse, rent with holes and half-unraveled.

"Son of a bitch!" she bawled. "That's for me! And maybe enough of that old lodgecover for a skirt . . . and moccasins." She slid it on and tied it at the waist with whang.

As dusk settled, Mister Skye's women resoled the two pairs of moccasins with rawhide, using awls of nail, courtesy of the things-maker. One pair fit Betsy perfectly; the other larger pair fit Professor Danzig. He slipped them on, tied them over his ankles, and waltzed.

With their little iron knives, they cut rawhide soles from the buffalo cow, not bothering to flesh or hair the rawhide. From the old lodgecover they cut uppers, and all of them worked through the evening punching holes for thong and stringing the uppers to the soles. All of them except Captain Cobb, who stared quietly from the darkness of the corner.

Chapter 27

More than anything else, Captain Jarvis Cobb wanted moccasins. Without them, he would be helpless and probably die. With them, and some hide clothing, he could make it to Fort Laramie. It took a long time to starve to death. Give a soldier shoes and water and warmth, and he could struggle a long way.

In his dark corner, the farthest from the fire, he watched the squaws cut soles from rawhide and uppers from the remains of the lodgecover Skye had found. Betsy and Arabella laced them together, with nail awls and some expert help from Skye's women. No one spoke to him, nor did he feel much like speaking to them. A silly thing threatened his life, and he intended to deal with it summarily. If no one but himself returned to civilization, that would be one way. But he bridled at the thought of something that desperate. Moreover, he'd have to take on Skye. The guide sat with a piece of sandstone honing a rusty, pitted iron lance point he'd found, turning it into a large, effective butchering knife—and a swift, brutal means of self-defense. This point, probably of Santa Fe origin, had a hollow iron socket at one end for the lance shaft, but it had split apart and wouldn't hold much. Even without a handle, it made a useful knife, but Morse patiently whittled a wooden grip for Skye's blade, and they'd probably hammer the metal over it and bind the whole thing with the sinew Skye found.

Cobb felt his hunger and scorned it. Surrendering to hunger seemed infantile, the sort of thing no officer would do. Arabella complained constantly of it, and her whining got on his nerves. He wondered what he had seen in her. Just a wilderness solace, he supposed. He knew how to eat now. Ever since he saw them eat the lobes of prickly pear, he knew. Still, the season had advanced to frosts, and the things he might live on had vanished—grasshoppers, snakes, berries. . . . But he'd roamed the hills of western New York as a boy, trapping and hunting and making deadfalls and snares. He needed thong for snares and intended to get it when the rest slept. He could use some bone or wood for triggers, and certainly needed one of those nail knives to cut it. Grudgingly he admired Danzig and Morse for creating them almost out of nothing.

"Try this, Mister Skye," said Morse, handing him a well-whittled knife handle. It slid perfectly into the socket, and the pair of them tapped the split socket tight, using a heel of the horseshoe as a hammer. A fine knife. Skye handed it to Victoria, who laid it on the rawhide and patiently cut a sheath for it. Soon Mister Skye had the weapon sheathed at his waist.

These people were getting closer and closer to success, Cobb thought. And then he knew what he'd do. Hang around until they had manufactured whatever they needed to journey again—no doubt a bow and arrows, moccasins, clothes, lances, awls, and knives. Then he'd steal everything in the night and be far gone by dawn. And just to fool Skye, who still would have Jawbone and that knife—unless Jawbone could be brained to death—he'd strike for Fort Bridger, southwest, rather than Laramie. Reoutfit there on an army draft. He liked that idea. No murder in it, no violence. They'd perish of natural causes, cold, autumnal snow, lack of clothing—he'd try to get their moccasins if he could—and above all, starvation.

All because of their stupid indignation at him for saving his own life, he thought. He huddled in his corner, scorning cold and hunger, toying with his plans, testing them, applying all he had learned of intelligence to the thing he would do. Much of military intelligence consisted not of facts but of educated guesses, surmises. He had to calculate what he could steal, what he would have to leave to them, what his own resources would be, and just what they—Skye and his squaws, actually—would do when they found him gone. A juicy problem. He enjoyed it. All the

theory he had mastered put to the test. If he won, he'd re-
cover his life and honor. No one would ever know what
happened here, or learn of the unimportant act that threatened his future.

With surprising swiftness they completed moccasins for
all except Cobb. Even Percy Connaught helped, awling
holes in the rawhide soles and clumsily poking thong
through them. Enough rawhide remained to make soles for
one more person.

The question of moccasins for Jarvis Cobb hung in the
air, and he waited, amused. The rest tied theirs on, walked
and exclaimed, their emotions buoyed suddenly by something as important as shoes.

Old Victoria beamed. She'd inherited a pair of the fine
Arapaho moccasins Mister Skye discovered, now tightly
resoled and strong. "Son of a bitch!" she exclaimed. "Now
I got to make a dress." She began to measure out a vest
from the remaining tattered lodgecover. That and the purple blouse and the nightdress poking out below it would
suffice for a while.

But Mister Skye intervened. "Mister Cobb," he said
gently, "come be fitted for moccasins."

They all paused, absorbing that. Jarvis Cobb relaxed. A
major problem had just solved itself. He unfolded himself
from his corner and stepped toward the clammy rawhide
to be measured.

"It's time to get on with living and put the past behind,"
said Mister Skye.

It was a message to all. The guide meant to forget the
incident and draw Cobb back into their small community.

Muttering, Victoria roughly traced Cobb's feet on the
remaining rawhide, using charred sticks from the wicker-
ing flame. Silently, Mary cut the uppers from the precious

soft lodgecover, leaving Victoria less to clothe herself. No one spoke, and yet the atmosphere eased a little. The whites, at least, had been disturbed that they had moccasins and Captain Cobb didn't.

It angered Victoria; Cobb could see that. It amused him. She had it correct, and the civilized whites didn't.

"Mister Cobb," rumbled the guide. "We'll proceed now without thought of the past. We all become desperate. In the mountains, during starvin' time, I'd have likely eaten my partners as not."

It shocked even Cobb, an admission like that.

"Why, yes," said Morse. "Let's be on with it."

Mister Skye continued. "We're all doing what we can, Captain Cobb. Mister Danzig and Mister Morse have made amazing things and rescued us all by finding a way to strike a firc. My women have found food and have made moccasins. Mrs. Morse and Miss Morse have gathered rushes, made beds for tonight, woven mats. Mister Connaught has gathered firewood, built a rock wall for warmth, and made himself useful. There's much more to do, Mister Cobb. You've made some weapons—a lance and clubs. What would you like to do? Hunt?"

Cobb considered. "As a boy I made snares and deadfalls to catch small game. If I may have one of the nail knives and some thong, perhaps I can do that and feed us meat."

"Very well, then," said Mister Skye. "I'll be off hunting in the morning. Before I leave, I'll cut bow wood— chokecherry probably—for Victoria to begin shaping. I know where there's a buffler skull with horns, and I'll cut a horn for a firecarrier."

"A what?" asked Elkanah, excited.

"Moving villages carry a live coal with them, usually in a hollowed buffler horn. Or used to before they got flint and steel, and sulfur matches. I'll need to have you whittle a wooden plug for the top—tight enough to be airtight. They put the live coal in with slightly moist punk and sealed it. Added punk as they traveled, every two, three hours. Regular firecarrier job, with honors, given to someone reliable."

"Consider it done!" cried Elkanah.

Cobb took notice. He'd take the horn and fire, and that'd solve another of his problems.

"I'll help fashion it," he said softly.

Victoria glared at him. Mary awled and laced one moccasin, and Victoria the other, jabbing thong with dark thrusts.

"I don't care about fire; I want food!" cried Arabella.

Betsy Morse laid a gentle hand on her daughter's arm. "Fasting is good for the spirit," she said. "It sharpens the mind and makes us grateful for God's gifts."

"But I'm feeling weak and trembly," Arabella replied. "I didn't want to come on this stupid trip. . . ."

Mister Skye said, "With moccasins we can travel far and wide tomorrow. Miles, in fact. You're all starving now, but tomorrow will be fat times."

"As long as the weather holds," added Elkanah. "We're in trouble if it snows."

Victoria handed a completed left moccasin to Cobb roughly. In spite of her anger, she'd done a careful job, and the upper had been bound tight. It had been cut ankle-high, the customary height of all winter moccasins. Cobb slipped it on, delighted, and laced thong. His numb foot began to warm at once. Mary followed with the right one, and then Cobb had shoes. It seemed late but Victoria began at once to fashion a vest out of the remaining lodgecover, shorter now because of Cobb's moccasins but still hip length. Muttering, the old woman sawed and shaped, using Mister Skye's big knife, and soon created a vestlike garment of the last of the lodgecover.

"Damn!" she muttered, after slipping it on. "I'm gonna feel warm again."

Her joy amused Cobb. He eyed the armless tunic, seeing a useful wind-resistant item that would warm his torso. Something he could well use on his journey, he thought. That and the cradle cover that had gotten him into trouble, which he intended to turn into leggins.

They awoke to a bitter damp day with autumnal slate clouds lowering over them again, blotting out horizons. Worse, they awoke to tormenting hunger and not a scrap of food to be had. Percy Connaught had found he could endure cold, even in his filthy underdrawers and shirt, but hunger made him faint and dizzy. Everything seemed so hard. Even a drink of water could be had only by threading through brush to the river and cupping it up with one's hands. Cleaning himself had become a formidable problem: grass for body wastes and icy water to wash in. The riverbanks here lacked even sand for scrubbing. He completed his morning ablutions grimly, shivering in cold misty air, and hurried back to the fire, grateful to have moccasins.

The lowering clouds with their threat of renewed rain disheartened them all, and he returned to a camp turned sour. Nothing remained of the evening's jubilation at having moccasins. He felt so dizzy from the want of food he thought he might not be able to gather wood much longer. And he needed clothing more than anyone else now that Victoria had fashioned something.

Mister Skye gathered the haggard party together. "Today

we'll start our journey," he said. "We have the moccasins we'll need. Winter's coming fast. Staying here is death."

"But—" cried Elkanah, "we haven't anything to eat. You were going to hunt today. Betsy's so weak she can barely walk. And what will we do for shelter?"

"Food's where you find it, Mister Morse. We've exhausted it here. The cattails and cactus are gone."

"But look at the clouds! We'll be caught in another icy drizzle."

"That's a risk we take to escape the larger risk, Mister Morse."

Rudolpho Danzig said, "How far is it to Fort Laramie, Mister Skye?"

"I imagine three hundred fifty miles."

Elkanah groaned. Arabella began to weep.

"How long will these moccasins last?" asked Cobb.

"Maybe a hundred miles—at the outside."

Dirk began to wail, hungry and fretful again.

"If we make ten or eleven miles a day—all we can expect in our condition, Mister Skye—it'll take a month to walk to Fort Laramie," said Elkanah, sounding more discouraged than Percy had ever heard him. "I don't think we'll make it. Here at least we can shelter ourselves, and make weapons—bow and arrows, and kill game, get hides for coats. . . ."

"Mister Connaught, how far are you going out now to find firewood?" asked the guide.

"Why—I imagine a quarter of a mile now."

"Victoria—how long does it take to tan a hide enough to make a coat—assuming we have the hide?"

"Damn long time."

"And a workable bow and arrows?"

"Damn long time."

"My son is hungry, Mister Morse. Let's be off."

"This doesn't make any sense at all," said Jarvis Cobb. "We'll all stumble and fall before this day's over. Starting now, without proper equipment—it's a foolish thing."

"We don't even have anything made to carry our few things," muttered Betsy.

"Roll them up in the rush mats, mates."

Elkanah stared at the desperate faces around him and apparently came to a decision. "Mister Skye: up to now I've never questioned your judgment. You're the guide, and we've gladly put our lives and safety in your hands. But we aren't equipped to travel. I'm going to have to overrule you. We'll stay until we are properly equipped."

"And die doing it." Mister Skye peered at them from his small buried eyes. "We can't walk to Fort Laramie. It's too far. Most of us would die, between exposure and starvation. But we can walk forty or forty-five miles south along this river to a place that's a kind of crossroads where we'll find help. Down at the south end of this basin is a hot springs—biggest mineral springs I've ever seen. It's a favorite place of Mary's people, the Shoshone. Bands come through all the time, take the waters, build shelters—there'll be brush wickiups, maybe a lodge or two for us—and leave messages. The place is a regular Indian mail place, telling who's been where and who's coming. It's a long journey in our condition, but our only chance for help. And once you're there, you can sit through a blizzard in those hot waters and never know it's snowing."

They stared at the guide, haggard and disbelieving. Connaught heard the sound of false hope in Mister Skye's talk. He himself harbored no illusions. In spite of moccasins and fire, they had come close to the end now, and one good storm would finish them.

Elkanah said, "Do you have any tasks for us before we leave?"

The guide considered soberly. "Yes, Mister Morse. We need some thin poles with loops of hide attached to one end. A lot of animals freeze when we walk by. Rabbits, ducks, prairie hens. With a pole, we can lower that loop over their necks, twist and yank, and we've a meal."

He peered around at hunger-pinched faces. "Mister Cobb, food is your business. If you can make snares to set tonight, do it now. Mister Morse, I'll cut some poles—I have the knife to do it—and you and Mister Danzig can manufacture the loops from our remaining bits of hide. Mrs. Morse, perhaps you and your daughter can turn your rush mats into baskets or carriers somehow, and gather our things together. We'll leave in a few minutes."

"What about breakfast?" cried Arabella. "We've got to find something."

"Nothing left here, miss. Maybe we'll find something as we go. If we snare a bird or rabbit with the poles, we'll stop to eat at once."

"Without fire! And look at those clouds!" snapped Jarvis Cobb.

"We have flint and the horseshoe for a striker. Mister Danzig, perhaps you could gather tinder from our shelter, and whittle tiny bits of dry wood, and find a means to carry it dry."

"Quite an order," said Danzig, grinning.

"We're dying," said Arabella. "Why don't you just say it?"

"I've been in worse trouble, Miss Morse. And here I am."

In an hour they were ready. Connaught stared almost lovingly at the little place that had sheltered them, the wall he'd built, the remaining piles of wood, the fire that would soon die.

"Can't we take some coals?" he cried.

"We don't have a way," said the guide. "But we can strike a fire now, long as it's dry."

They all stared at the life-giving blaze, dreading to leave it.

"I don't have the strength," said Betsy.

Mister Skye turned to her. "I'm going to scout ahead on Jawbone now, for a while. And when I return to the party, I'll put one person at a time on Jawbone. You'll each get a rest while I lead him."

"Things would be so different if we had horses," she said.

The guide, back in his leggins now, and moccasined, climbed up on Jawbone. With the sheathed knife at his side and his battered belaying pin, he looked almost formidable again, a man who could bring home meat in any wilderness. But Connaught knew it wasn't so, that Mister Skye himself had weakened along with the rest of them.

Silently they watched him ride upstream, south, and when he vanished into the river brush, so did their hopes. The dour slate clouds cast a doomspell none of them could shake off. Percy's stomach hurt. What had been a dull ache and sullen need had become urgent need now. He'd eat anything; rob an old carcass.

At camp, Morse and Danzig prepared themselves for the long walk, gathering rush mats, slipping their few tools into pockets, rolling up bits of hide to carry. Then, heavy-hearted, they started south along the bottoms, faint with hunger before they even began.

"Elkanah . . ." Betsy said, and then said nothing. "I'm

dizzy," she muttered. "I don't know how long this torture will last."

Percy settled himself into a weary shuffle, making his feet step ahead. Forty miles would be impossible. Not long now, he thought. Even if they got an occasional duck, or managed to snare a rabbit, it all added up to nothing. He felt a certain sadness return to him. He'd relived a hundred times the moment when the Bannocks made off with his journals, the outpourings of a lifetime. All gone, just as he would soon be gone, a man without family and soon forgotten. He hadn't expected to become a bachelor, but women found him rather undesirable. He learned that early in his life, when his cold intellect and owlish way of observing the world evoked polite refusals. The owl, he'd privately called himself, growing old totally alone, keeping his bookbinding business functioning comfortably, reading, pondering the state of the world, living out his small lonely owlish life.

The loss of his journals had been a kind of death; and soon he would experience the other kind of death, from exposure and starvation. Well, he thought, it hadn't been a good life, and death held no terror to him because he would lose so little. But one thing remained. He hadn't thought about honor until Cobb did the dishonorable to save himself. And then Percy thought a great deal about honor. A man could die honorably—if not for anyone else's sake, then for his own. Or he could save his skin dishonorably, by any means, and without regard of others, as Cobb had attempted to do. The whole business of the cradle cover had set Percy to thinking, and out of it had come a simple resolution: he would die honorably, and perhaps God—if God existed—would smile.

During the whole journey, he'd disdained camp chores.

Those were for menials like Skye and his squaws. His journals, and the careful observations of his good mind, were what counted, not manual labor. But the journals had vanished. Oh, he might recollect some of it, but the truth and immediacy of them could not be recaptured; the detail would blur, the insights would cloud. All gone. And all that remained was a starving man in his underclothing, ill-suited to a frightening wilderness. He could die honorably or not. From the time of Cobb's dishonor, Percy chose honor, gathering camp wood, doing what he could, cheerfully.

From the little blanket bag, Dirk wailed, hungry and sobbing. Percy watched the younger squaw, Mary, stop and slip off her cradlebasket. She pulled out the child to soothe it and clean it with moss. But the little boy choked and sobbed. Frowning, Mary hugged it, giving all she had, which was love.

"I'll go look, Mrs. Skye," said Percy. "I can find cattails as well as anyone. We're close to the river. And with my moccasins, I can manage."

She smiled. "That would be good. We'll be walking ahead."

"I'd hold him for you, but I'm feverish," said Betsy.

Percy gazed at the woman, realizing how bad Betsy looked, hollow-eyed, gaunt, and pale.

"I'm afraid I took a chill the night we had no fire and it was so cold and wet," she added, smiling apologetically. "I'm sorry. I fear I'll be a burden."

"I wish you hadn't come," said Arabella. "Then I wouldn't have had to come."

That seemed unkind. The young woman might have comforted her mother instead, Percy thought. Still, hunger worked on them all now, making minds cruel. He suddenly realized hunger would twist each one of them into some primal character that lay hidden back in civilization. Percy wished he could record all that in his journals. He wondered what he would become when starvation turned him mad—a beast! What would Cobb become in extremity? And cheerful optimistic Elkanah? And Danzig? And indeed, Mister Skye? When hunger madness came, who would become animal, who would become angelic? Who would kill and rob, and who would give his last bit of something to another?

Oh, for a journal to write it, Percy thought.

"I'll be back shortly," he said, plunging into a cold mist that turned his white flesh to ice. He ventured toward the river, feeling his starving muscles rebel and his heart pound unnaturally. He'd have to walk a considerable distance because Mary had already scoured everywhere nearby for roots and cattails. Honking geese burst into air ahead of him, and his mouth watered. He struggled south through dense cottonwood, willow, and alder forest and grassy parks, working to the riverbank every hundred yards or so. But the Big Horn nurtured no cattails there because the banks rose steeply.

For a mile or so he struggled, feeling his weak body protest. He entered a small park of yellowed grasses, gloomy under the slate heavens, passed an upright dead cottonwood trunk, half-rotted and hollow. His eye caught the movement of bees, several of them, almost moribund in the cold. In an oval hollow, a bee's nest. Honey. Food for Dirk. He peered in, noting the lethargic movement of the few surviving bees. He found a stick and jabbed it in, and no guardian swarm rushed to the defense of the hive. Heart pounding, he dared himself to poke a hand in, break off comb. Food for Dirk. He plunged his hand in, felt the mass of waxy honeycomb, broke off a large chunk, and then his hand turned into fire, white pain rocketing up his arm. He pulled out a mass of honeycomb, along with a dozen bees buried in his flesh.

Chapter 28

They found Percy Connaught sitting on a log, babbling, holding a large waxy yellow chunk of honeycomb in a hand swollen grotesquely. Tears streaked his puffy reddened face. A scream had drawn them toward the river from their trail under the brown bluffs.

"This is for Dirk," he mumbled, proffering the honeycomb to Mary.

"For Dirk?"

Connaught smiled crookedly. "He's hungry."

"You took the honey like a grizzly bear?"

"I thought they were dead. They die in the fall."

"You are Grizzly Bear Man," she said. "Here."

She thrust the cradlebasket into his lap. "You feed the boy. Food from Grizzly Bear Man."

He peered up at her, his face streaked purple with pain. "But I never—I've never held a child. I've never fed—"

She knelt beside him and slipped Dirk from his nest. He wailed at the insult of cold air, added to his desperate hunger.

"Madam, I don't know what—"

With his good hand he cradled the infant. Mary broke off a piece of the honeycomb still clutched in his swollen red right hand.

"Put in his mouth, let him suck it," she said.

Percy did, forgetting his pain a moment. The baby gummed the waxy sweet stuff, wailed, and then sucked on it in earnest.

"See, Grizzly Bear Man, he likes your gift."

In minutes, the child had eaten a large amount of it, and drifted off to sleep. Percy Connaught stared at this little creature nestled into his gray-grimed underwear, a kind of wonder upon him. Mary slipped the sleeping child back into his cocoon and hoisted the heavy basket over her shoulders.

"There's enough of the comb for us all to have a piece," said Jarvis Cobb.

"No!" cried Percy. "It's all for the baby."

A flash of hatred crossed Cobb's chapped red face. The others stared at him again.

"I don't know how we'll carry that sticky honeycomb," said Elkanah.

"Gimme the little knife," said Victoria. She headed for a poplar tree, and in minutes skinned off a curl of green bark and rolled the remaining honey in it. "There. You carry it," she said to Arabella. "You ain't carrying anything."

Arabella looked annoyed.

Elkanah wished Betsy could have a little of the honey. He'd been helping her the last mile and feeling her weaken with every step. The hot springs seemed infinitely distant, and slipping farther away with each hour.

"Let's go," said Victoria crossly.

Connaught stood—and toppled over.

"Damn—them bees got him," muttered Victoria. "You wait. I'll go find Mister Skye and Jawbone."

A while later she returned with Mister Skye, and they loaded the semicoherent bookbinder on the horse. He'd grown too weak to cling, so they held him upright as they walked, Mister Skye leading the angry flat-eared horse, and Professor Danzig beside, keeping Connaught from sliding off.

Elkanah virtually carried Betsy, step by slow step.

"I'm sorry," she whispered. "I'm sorry."

Arabella trudged along beside, and then slipped into the red bushes. They waited for her. When she reappeared, Elkanah knew—sensed, rather—that some of the honeycomb had vanished. He wrestled with himself about it. Arabella had eaten. Betsy needed it more. But Percy should have shared. They all might have gotten a boost from the sugary comb. The girl covered herself well, never revealing anything.

"How much did you eat, Arabella?" Elkanah asked.

She glared at him defiantly.

Cobb, tottering nearby, heard him, and mocked.

Beside him, Betsy dragged to a crawl. They scarcely made progress at all. He couldn't support her, either. He felt as famished as the rest, and his strength had slid away, until he tottered under her weight. He didn't know how far they'd come—six or seven miles, he supposed—almost nothing compared to what they had to travel.

"I can't go any more," said Betsy. She sagged into him. He put a hand to her brow and found it feverish. "I'm sorry," she murmured.

He clutched her, keeping her from sliding into the grass.

They rested there where the river ran through a broad silvery valley bordered by barren sage-covered hills. The slate clouds lowered all the more, threatening rain but not issuing it. Except for black brush along the banks, this place lay open and windswept. The minute they halted, Elkanah felt the wind slicing through his few clothes and wondered how Percy in his tattered underwear endured.

Mister Skye and Professor Danzig slid Connaught off Jawbone and onto the grass. Connaught looked worse, almost comatose. The swelling had advanced up his right arm, ballooning it monstrously. The man muttered and babbled incoherently. Bee poison, Elkanah thought. Enough stinging and it could kill a man.

As if thinking the same thing, Professor Danzig peered intently at Connaught's swollen hand and wrist. "I count seventeen or eighteen bites," he said. "It's hard to tell."

Mary gratefully slid the cradlebasket off her back and pulled out the child to clean him with moss. The baby awakened and fussed and sucked at her finger.

"I'll give him more," she said to Arabella.

The girl handed the roll of smooth green bark to Mary defiantly. Mary hefted it, a question in her eyes, and then uncurled the bark. No honeycomb remained. "You have eaten it," she said softly.

"It must have fallen out," Arabella replied haughtily.

Elkanah sighed, heavy of heart. "There's no excuse for lying, Arabella," he said wearily.

"It fell out," she retorted sullenly.

From the nearby grass Percy lifted his head. "If you ate it, then I died for nothing," he muttered, and sank back into a semistupor.

The statement shocked Elkanah twice over. Did Percy think he was dying? Had his own daughter robbed the old scholar of the last shred of meaning in a barren life?

He settled Betsy back in the grasses, noting the goose bumps on her chapped arms, and squatted down beside Percy Connaught, taking his good hand, cold and clammy, into his own. Mister Skye and Rudolpho Danzig hovered close.

"Percy," Elkanah whispered, desperately trying to reach

him, "you did a brave thing. No deed is ever lost. For good or ill we leave our mark on the world. Whatever happens, Percy, you've left a noble mark. We'll remember it and try to live up to it, and tell the world about it."

But Connaught seemed lost in some sort of oblivion, and Elkanah doubted that he heard. His breathing came in snuffles.

Cobb smiled crookedly.

"Best we cover him with a rush mat, mate," Mister Skye rumbled. The guide looked as gray and pinched as the rest, Elkanah thought. They spread two of Betsy's mats over the man and weighted them down with sticks, against the probing wind.

"I'd rig a travois but I've got no harness for it. I need a surcingle or a collar or something like that," the guide muttered. "This is a bad place to stop. Wind," he said.

"Betsy could go no further," Elkanah replied.

The baby whimpered, hungry again. Mary thrust the basket toward Mister Skye and slowly toiled down to the river brush. Victoria followed, muttering.

"Betsy's feverish, Mister Skye," said Elkanah.

"Fine decision you made, Skye. We're a few miles from the old camp and all half-dead," said Cobb. "Where's the food and shelter you promised us along the way?"

Mister Skye didn't answer. Ahead perhaps three hundred yards the silver river swung around a bluff projecting from the west. He tried to climb on Jawbone but lacked the strength. Instead, he left them there on the windswept gray slope and walked ahead, growing smaller and smaller in Elkanah's eye until he vanished from sight around the bluff.

Elkanah felt the presence of death again. The wind cut icily through his shirt and pants, starting him shivering.

The thought that he had organized this journey, brought his wife and daughter to their doom here, desolated him. Connaught lay dying—that seemed plain enough. From bee poison. From despair. From exposure and starvation. And Betsy . . . he lifted her inert icy hand into his, feeling its clammy cold, its weakness. His gaze turned to Arabella, alive and warm and selfish, his own daughter, no better than Cobb, succumbing at first impulse to dishonor.

What gave some men honor, some dishonor? In extremity, why would some people cheat and steal, think only of themselves, while others would sacrifice, love, encourage, buoy the weak along? Had he failed to bring up Arabella correctly? Spoiled her? Lavished too much luxury on her? Let her become thoughtless of others? It had always been a pitfall of the rich, he thought. He'd failed somehow, and now his daughter shamed him. And yet, Cobb had shown the same traits, too, and Cobb lacked the advantages that he'd given to Arabella. Elkanah stared at Cobb, wondering what lay in the captain's mind. The soldier emanated resentments, mockery, and something else, some cunning and calculation that made him rattlesnake deadly. The man would strike at them again. Elkanah felt sure of that. He huddled closer to Betsy, trying to share his remaining warmth with her, protect her from the bitter wind. A few yards away, Danzig had lowered himself windward of Connaught, trying to keep the comatose man warm.

They'd lost, he knew. Good as dead. Idly, he watched Mister Skye toil back, a burly weary figure crossing a vast empty slope. Without the others, he and his squaws would probably survive, Elkanah thought. But the man remained loyal, doing what he could.

Mister Skye stared briefly at Connaught, noting the

bookbinder's inert form, and at the rest. Mary and Victoria toiled up from the river, carrying a few things that looked like roots and cattails. The baby would be fed.

"We've got to get ourselves around the headland there," the guide muttered. "There's shelter in the rock, a good stand of cottonwoods and firewood—and meat, if I can get it. And I think I can."

"Meat? Meat?"

"Lend me a pole with a loop on it. You can get settled out of the wind on the south side of that spur. Victoria will help you get Mr. Connaught up on Jawbone."

Fourteen wild turkeys. They saw him coming and exploded up into the lower limbs of a box elder. They flew easily enough, he thought, but didn't like to fly. If he could slip that loop over the neck of one . . . of all.

Beneath the tree he peered up at the dark birds through yellowing ruined leaves, into a foreboding sky. Some were twenty feet up or so, but a few fools perched low, within reach of his pole. His arms didn't work well now—hunger had robbed him of the adroitness he needed more than anything. But he would climb that tree and wring their necks by hand if necessary.

Mister Skye yearned for a bow. He had the blunt arrows, but lacked even a boy's practice bow. Out of breath, he slid the last distance on moccasined feet until he stood under three of them. They hopped sideways, never letting him come closer than ten feet or so. Meat! He glared at the big nervous birds, mesmerizing them with some violent force of will as he eased the pole toward the nearest. It watched the approaching loop, flapped its wings, but sat. Gently he eased the loop close, and then with a swift lunge he dropped it over the turkey's neck, twisted, and yanked. The big bird fell, flapping and gobbling, to earth. The others leaped to higher branches—except one.

He snapped the caught bird's neck and went for the next one. It seemed warier, dodging the loop. He lunged and missed, but the bird only danced down the limb, clucking at him. He edged the loop close again, hoping the bird wouldn't flap higher and out of reach. He positioned his loop, lunged again, and missed. Angrily, he lanced the thin pole at the turkey, struck it, saw it flap toward the ground, and caught it midair, furiously wrapping his big hams around the flapping feathers. Angrily, trembling, he smashed it dead and walked out of the small forest nested in the ell of the bluff, and dropped the turkeys before them.

Elkanah saw the birds and sobbed. The others gaped and wept, too.

He and Professor Danzig had managed to start a small fire with flint and the horseshoe and tinder, but it'd take a while to become hot enough to cook.

They were too hungry to wait. Victoria and Mary took the turkeys, gutted them with the tiny nail knives, and handed out raw liver and heart and kidney, which were devoured instantly and wildly. Mary saved some liver and gave it steaming and raw to Dirk, who gnawed lustily on it, blood leaking from his small hands.

They would have devoured the rest, tearing off feathers and ripping apart raw meat of breast and thigh and wing, but Mister Skye stopped them.

"There's more birds, mates. You've had a morsel or two. Let's let them cook properly. They'll stay down better. Professor, Mister Morse, Mister Cobb, come along. They're all in a tree and we'll get them all. Bring that lance of yours, Mister Cobb. I hope you can throw it."

They looked unsure, wanting to tear apart more raw

meat, but slowly they gathered the other pole with a loop on it and Cobb's long wooden-tipped lance. More food. Enough for days, and it'd keep well in the cold weather.

The turkeys flapped higher into the tree, and one or two fled to a nearby cottonwood. Small, lithe Professor Danzig found he could climb. Mister Skye was too heavy, and the rest too weakened. The turkeys edged away from him, and several more flapped off to the cottonwood. But he looped one and dropped it, and Cobb clobbered another with his lance as it started to fly off. Cobb threw his lance at one several times, missing, driving the bird higher. Then he spotted one roosting low in a neighboring tree, and knocked it to earth with a lucky throw of the lance. In an hour of trembling labor and endless near misses, they'd knocked down four more birds. By then they'd reached utter exhaustion, and gave up. Six turkeys!

In camp, Mary and Victoria had roughly plucked the birds and had them spitted over the fire, which burnt off the remaining pinheads and feathers, and whirled a wild voluptuous aroma of cooking meat into the eddying cold air.

The exhausted men grabbed a half-cooked bird and ripped half-raw flesh from it, wolfing it down with trembling hands, too tired to care what or how they ate. Only when they'd devoured one of the turkeys did any of them remember the comatose Connaught, who lay inertly near the fire, bee-poisoned and cold.

Guiltily Mister Skye cut some juicy breast meat from the second bird and carried it to Connaught, hunkering over him.

He shook the man, who seemed cold to his touch.

"Mister Connaught," he said. "Meat! Meat!"

But Percy Connaught didn't respond.

Mister Skye shook him. "Grizzly Bear Man. Meat! Meat!"

Only then did he realize that Percy Connaught had died.

He peered up. They'd all drawn around him, frightened. "He's gone," Mister Skye muttered. "The bees and the cold did him. Gave his life for my Dirk."

Mister Skye sat quietly, scarcely aware of the sobbing of the women, peering into the puffed face of a man who no one knew, least of all himself. Percy's opinions, yes. His conceits, yes. But the Percy Connaught who lay behind the life of the mind had been a stranger. A stranger who, in the end, had revealed some strength of character, some courage, some manhood. Whatever his failings, Connaught had been a man.

He stood wearily. "Here was a man," he said softly.

They stood about Connaught, letting the reality of death soak into them. Percy's spirit had fled somewhere, forever gone. Death subdued and chilled them all. Connaught's face had twisted in death into an agony of pain.

"I think he was lonely," Betsy whispered. "He had no one."

Arabella said, "I don't know why you forget so fast. He never did a lick of work or helped out. He complained all the time. I didn't like him."

Uncharitable, Mister Skye thought. That girl would never be charitable. He bit off a withering response, but Elkanah didn't.

"Arabella, Percy Connaught proved to be someone . . . larger than that. Pay your respects!"

They had no way to bury him and could scarcely find enough loose rock to keep the wolves and coyotes off, but they mounded what they could over the puffy body, leaving his filthy underwear but taking his moccasins. They had no strength, and tottered through the job poorly. But in the end, Connaught lay beside the cottonwoods, in a gentle amphitheater opening on the river, protected from the cold wind that had sapped life from him as much as anything else. They labored in eerie silence. Mister Skye knew they were all contrasting Connaught with Cobb, self-ishness with generosity, caring for others in extremity, or caring only for self. Courage to do the dangerous, reach-ing into a hive, all for a hungry infant. In the end, Mister Skye put a finale to it by reciting the Lord's Prayer. He didn't know what Percy believed, if anything, or what any-one else believed. But it seemed fitting.

"I will have a memorial made, and a service back East," said Elkanah.

In the dusk of that gloomy day, they ate another whole turkey, slower this time, gathering life from its sweet dark meat and juices. They made themselves as comfortable as they could in the deep silence, gathering rushes and fire-wood. They built a second fire so that both reflected from the protecting mudstone that became their refuge that night. Filled at last, they would sleep.

Mister Skye looked over his small exhausted band. Betsy—his deepest worry—looked a bit better with food in her, but still hollow-eyed. Sleep might help. Arabella seemed young and vital and too self-engrossed to surrender her courage. Elkanah lay back wearily. He had an innate courage. Professor Danzig seemed indestructible, qui-etly doing what needed doing—he'd gathered the firewood this evening—and making life work somehow. All along the route he'd stripped off buds and seedpods, munching on them, finding bits of nourishment. Now, against the cliff, he emptied his pockets of flint, set the precious horseshoe beside the flint, and arranged his nail knife, antler knife, and awl. Cobb, enigmatic and still vital, made his bed a little off, perhaps still feeling the sting of his shame, Mister Skye thought.

Victoria and Mary had made a place for them near the fire, piling brush on the far side for a windbreak. It would be a good night, even though Percy Connaught's death lay heavily on them and would fill their private thoughts through the long cold dark. He went out as he always did, wrapped his paws about Jawbone, and whispered a few things to the animal who had become a part of himself, and then slipped back to the fire. He set his big rough knife beside him, instantly available, and settled into sleep. He knew they'd all sleep that night, filled to bursting with good turkey meat, with plenty more in the morning.

That was the last he remembered. When he awoke before dawn, with gray light slitting the eastern horizon above the silver river, he knew something had gone wrong. He felt for his knife—missing. He sat up, wary. He counted heads and recounted. Cobb gone. In the gray light he stood up and studied the camp. Cobb gone, and every tool they'd made, every flint, the horseshoe, Connaught's moccasins, and every turkey. They were back to nothing.

He could not bear to tell the others, or even awaken the camp. The news, he thought, would kill them.

Chapter 29

Something sagged inside of Elkanah Morse. Mister Skye watched the man die before his eyes, the gleam of hope and determination fade from Morse's haggard, weathered features.

"All the tools gone," muttered Elkanah. "He took everything—the knives, awls, flint, and horseshoe. He took the spare moccasins and the cradle cover again . . . even the blunt arrows you'd found . . . It's the end, you know. We can't live without tools."

"You're alive, Mister Morse."

"Never should have come. Should have turned back when the season got late. I've killed me, my dear Betsy . . . Arabella . . . Rudolpho. . . ."

"All of you are alive, Mister Morse."

Some terrible pain flashed into his face. He looked awful, a man surrendering to death and guilt; his jaw stubbled with a week's growth of beard, dirty and ragged.

"I have killed us with my foolish quest," he muttered.

"Get wood, Mister Morse. If the fire dies, we'll be in worse trouble than we are."

"What for? Why prolong it?" Elkanah muttered.

Beside him, Betsy sat round-shouldered, gaunt, and dejected. Arabella burned with bitterness, her accusing eyes first on her father, then on Mister Skye. "Well, do something!" she snapped. "I should have guessed about Jarvis. He takes what he wants."

Professor Danzig seemed almost as subdued as the rest, but somehow not broken. "I have a full belly from last night," he said. "I think I'll hunt for cattail bulbs along the river."

"I'll go, too," said Victoria. "Damn, white people give up without trying."

The baby bawled, and Mary dug through turkey bones, finding tiny shreds of meat for the child. Wearily, she trudged into the cottonwoods for some squaw wood as long as none of the whites bothered with the fire. The day had dawned clear and frosty, and without fire they'd perish all the sooner.

"I'll see what I can see," said Mister Skye, hunting down Jawbone. He thought Cobb had probably pitched most of the tools into the river, kept what he needed, and hauled three heavy turkeys with him. Finding moccasin prints would be tough—much harder than tracking horses. All his hunches about Cobb had been true. The man meant to save himself and save his reputation by letting the others die in a wilderness. Mister Skye barely understood a man like that. What would he see in the looking glass when he scraped his brown whiskers off each day?

Mister Skye had mastered the most important lesson of the mountains long ago, and that was to keep on trying. To give up, to sit down and die, would result in exactly that. By tonight they'd be dead unless . . .

He had to make a rein of whangs from his elkskin shirt. He could ride Jawbone with knee pressure alone, but he never felt comfortable with it, and sometimes Jawbone took perverse notions. So he knotted his rein together, and around Jawbone's jaw, and rode off. He spotted nothing on the west bank of the river. He found nothing in a great arc around the camp. So he forded at a likely-looking place with riffles, and the water rose belly-deep but no more. Jawbone shook and sprayed on the other side, almost tossing off Mister Skye. He found no prints there, either. Cobb had made his escape expertly, no doubt with some cunning, the cunning Mister Skye had observed in the man from the first.

Wearily, the guide rode south along the east bank, doubting that Captain Cobb would turn north, even for the sake of cunning. The bottoms lay barren and frost-covered in the dawn light, and virtually devoid of brush or forest. He had only the belaying pin, which Cobb had mockingly tossed a hundred yards off from camp. Cobb would have a knife, the wooden lance, and his stone-and-wood war clubs. Still, Mister Skye had Jawbone. One word to the horse, and Cobb would be flattened.

Laramie or where else? Fort Bridger? Platte River Bridge, off to the south on the Oregon Trail? Mister Skye had been heading toward the Platte River himself, knowing that it would be a great artery, even this late in the year. But Cobb had stayed on the west bank—he felt sure of it. He wouldn't risk a freezing swim across. He'd stay dry, haul himself and his tools and turkeys south or southwest. . . .

Jawbone's ears came up and he froze, a signal as familiar to Mister Skye as shaking hands. It meant horses, and horses usually meant people, friends or enemies. Sometimes Jawbone stayed quiet; sometimes he whinnied or screeched his welcome. This time Jawbone screeched, and Mister Skye didn't mind. Some black heads bobbed up from a grassy crease in the eastern bluffs. He steered directly that way. Four, no five. Odd-looking dark horses, edging away from Mister Skye but not running. No owners in sight. Unusual. Indians rarely lost horses from their herds, and when they did, those animals quickly found new homes in other bands.

The five dark animals turned and stared. They weren't horses; they were big black mules. The guide reined up Jawbone, trembling. Some warriors scorned slow mules. Mules were no warrior's dream of speed and glory, of warhorse or buffalo runner. Some warriors would turn mules loose after a successful raid, or give them to squaws for beasts of burden. But to Mister Skye, those five dark long-eared mules, nervously watching him, meant salvation. He talked at them quietly. They likely knew English, he thought. He talked at them and eased Jawbone forward gently just as the sun cracked over the eastern mountains, sending amber shafts that lit the mules like torches. Each mule had a U.S. brand. Army mules! Captain Cobb had come perhaps one mile and one river away from United States Army mules. But that was a piece of intelligence he'd missed, thought Mister Skye wryly.

They turned out to be docile, humbled by long famil- iarity with profane army muleteers, men who knew how to apply the carrot and the stick, and do it with a briny tongue. He rode among them, talking, cajoling, loving, rejoicing.

"Ah, you bloody buggers. Come to save us, have you? This is how the United States Army operates? Send the bloody mules but spare the men? Captain Cobb should know it. Bloody colonials never did learn how to make an army. All right, you bloody buggers, I'm pressing you into service. You've joined Barnaby's Army!"

He howled. He howled at the sun, at the blue-stained sky, at the frost. He howled at the wolves and coyotes. He terrorized a magpie. He howled at Cobb, wherever he'd gone. He bellowed like a buffler bull and laughed thun- derously across the frosted sagebrush. Jawbone twisted his head back to see this display, and snapped at Mister Skye with vicious yellow teeth.

"Ah, you bloody horse! Think I'm mad, do you? Well, I am, mate. Now, bloody horse, get these four-footed clod- hoppers lined out. Get them moving. The bloody blue army of this here republic has arrived."

With a lunatic hoot, he booted Jawbone. The horse leaped under him, snarled, clacked his teeth, circled mules like some lobo wolf, and set them to trotting, then loping, then galloping and farting and dropping green pies, and shrieking madly, on down to the silvery Big Horn. They never paused, but plunged in, tall fat ears rotated behind them, listening to demons and devils. Jawbone splashed after them, snorting and snarling, screeching to wake up the dead and send Indian spirits into flight. Jawbone bit rumps and shouldered laggards. Mister Skye howled like a hundred wolves, cackled and hooted, roared and bawled.

"Give up, will you, Elkanah Morse. Ye goddamn lily-livered Easterners. Give up, will you? Quit on me, you bloody idjit! Whine and die will you, you miserable excuses for manhood! You damn fools!"

He saw them huddled, dejected, around a thin column of blue smoke. He saw them rise. He saw Victoria and Mary start to dance and hug each other. He saw the others stare, not yet grasping, stare as if the world had sucked them into its belly and no blue sky would they ever see again.

He drove the dripping mules straight into camp. They whirled fearfully, penned by an ell in the bluffs. The Morses stood staring, not really comprehending. Only Professor Danzig really understood.

"I believe the army has come to our rescue, Mister Skye," he said quietly. "They sent these by express, of course."

"Git on board, you idjits!" Mister Skye roared.

"What good will these do?" asked Elkanah quietly. "We have nothing. No tools, Nothing to make meat. Nothing to strike a fire . . ."

"Railroad tickets to Lowell, Mister Morse. What more do you need—? If we push on right now, and if you can stand long riding, we'll get to the hot springs sometime tonight. The springs are on the river, so we can't get lost. You've got full bellies, mates. Ate like hogs last night. If we can't find help at the hot springs, we'll ride down to the Oregon Trail southeast of there. Can you sit an ugly mule for a week? If you can sit a week, you can live to old age."

"I suppose we can try," muttered Elkanah.

Victoria yelled. "Get your goddamn ass on them mules!"

Elkanah looked at her, aghast.

Professor Danzig gaped, and then howled with laughter.

They paused long enough to fashion some reins from Mister Skye's remaining whangs. They weren't adequate but they would do. And then they trotted south, while Mister Skye roared bawdy ditties at the blue sky and Betsy held her fingers to her ears.

From the grassy knoll where they paused, the whole village shimmered before them, silvery and moon-splashed and alive. From scores of lodges amber light radiated translucently, and the soft perfumed smoke of piney lodge-fires drifted lazily east. Beyond lay a massive black hulk of forested mountains, and Betsy caught glimpses of moon-silvered heights far away. The glowing lodges seemed to illumine the grassy alleys between them like porch lights welcoming Christmas carolers, Betsy thought, staring at her salvation. And beyond, shimmering white, rolled silvery water, steaming in the cold night. The hot springs.

She'd passed the endless day in pain and desperation, sawed in two by the bony ridge of the mule beneath her, no supporting stirrups for her aching legs, and constantly chilled by an icy breeze slicing out of the north. That mad guide wouldn't stop, except for a nooning, and spent hours bawling out awful sailors' ditties that numbed her soul. They lacked one mount, so Mary and Victoria rode to-

gether on the largest mule while Mister Skye carried Dirk
in the cradlebasket. They'd nooned beside a whole es-
tuary of cattails, a small swamp of them, and the squaws
had swiftly gathered armloads, peeled off the long blades,
and stored the slim brown and white bulbs in their bloused
clothing.

They'd all munched on the tasteless slimy things, and
no one had gone hungry all day. Still, they'd done over
forty miles this day—a cavalry march, Mister Skye had
pronounced it—across endless sage-covered hills, fording
five or six small creeks, never stopping. She thought her
legs would break off, her spine would snap. She slumped,
clutching black mane, and rode through the chill clear day,
blind to everything except her pain and the numbing cold
within her.

Elkanah rode grimly beside her through the day, absorbed in his own recriminations and doubts, unable to
comfort her as he had always done. She'd never seen her
husband in such a state, his buoyancy gone, natural optimism sucked out of him by crushing fate. Arabella, younger
and defiant about death, sat grimly on her mule, skirts hiked
high, daring her parents to rebuke her. Betsy didn't. Her
own dear daughter had shown the world a streak of selfish-
ness. But what did it matter? Betsy thought she might have
devoured the honeycomb, too, had it been entrusted to her.
How could one blame a desperate girl for that?

Mister Skye had ridden behind them, looking sharply
for Cobb, while Jawbone harried and frenzied the mules
into constant trotting that jarred her body into acute pain.
She'd never known such ache and cold. Her feverishness
had gone with the turkey meat, but this cold brutal day had
been the worst ordeal of her life, and the melancholy of
her family had only deepened it.

Once Mister Skye had pulled alongside Elkanah. "Be hearty, mate. You'll have the best hot soak tonight in your life. And if no village is at the springs, one soon will be. It's the Snake spa. It's where they have fun."

"You're feeding us illusions to keep our morale up, Mister Skye. Without tools and weapons, without shelter and—"

"Things!" roared Mister Skye. "You think only of things! Be thinking of friends! Mary's people! Victoria's people! When you go back to makin' things in Lowell, think about people and friends, family and clan and band. Stop makin' things in your bloody head and start makin' friends!"

"You don't need to shout so," Betsy had said wearily.

"Even friends, and Mary's people, couldn't exist without tools and weapons, Mister Skye," said Elkanah softly.

"Invent a mule, mate. A little bit of jackass, a little bit of horse, and a lot of Elkanah," the guide retorted, and rode off.

Behind her, Betsy had heard something awful, something unthinkable and unforgivable. Professor Danzig had laughed!

Now they sat on the wind-whipped knoll and waited, for whatever mysterious reasons Mister Skye may have had. Jawbone shrieked, and the screech of that awful horse rattled her ears, invaded her head like a violation of her womanhood. She loathed Mister Skye's horse. Ahead, Mary slid off her mule and cried, jabbering wildly, clapping her hands like a small girl, dancing about the frosty sagebrush. From the luminous village, dogs harped the wind now, and dark forms of horsemen trotted toward them.

Then Mary danced and cried in her strange tongue,

and men on horses laughed and talked, their eyes nonetheless observing the rest of the haggard party in the silvery light.

"Her own bloody people," bawled Mister Skye. "Mary's band. Her father and mother, her brothers and her sister. They're all down there. We'll bloody well have a party!"

"I'd never have believed . . ." muttered Elkanah.

Betsy didn't want a party. She didn't want to cope. Her body was a cold-numbed mass of pain. She desperately wanted just a small corner of a warm lodge where she could curl up and feel safe and loved.

Others on horseback rode out, and soon a procession of Snake warriors escorted them into the village, while before them the town crier gleefully announced these unexpected and welcome visitors, and kin. At the edge of the village Mary screamed, slid off the mule, and ran toward a short broad man whose hair had been drawn into a single braid. She hugged him, dancing in his embrace, jabbering in their strange tongue.

"That's her brother, mates. His name is"—he stared nervously at Betsy and Arabella—"name is . . . Strong Stallion. Yes, Strong Horse."

Behind her, Betsy heard Professor Danzig wheezing with laughter again.

They rode the last distance, through the curious, laughing, shouting throng, and stopped at last before a glowing lodge. Betsy clung mutely to the mule, too exhausted to care what happened. Someone lifted her off. She needed to relieve herself, but there seemed no place to go. Someone lifted Arabella off, too, and helped Elkanah and Rudolpho down. Her legs gave under her, but warm hands and arms kept her from collapsing.

"Thank you," she muttered.

A lot of Shoshones did a lot of talking, and all Betsy knew was that their story, their ordeal, was becoming known among the villagers. She sat mutely in a warm lodge, patted and fondled by beaming Shoshone women with seamed brown faces—Mary's mother and other relatives, Betsy gathered. At last, through her weariness, she smiled back at them, and a sense of gratitude at this surprising salvation purled through her spirit like fresh springwater.

Mary seemed to be everywhere, radiant, beaming and laughing, chattering and hugging, smiling. Victoria clucked and muttered, not knowing much of the Snake tongue but welcome here as Mister Skye's elder squaw, welcomed because her man had always been a great ally of these people.

They fed Betsy a bowl of something warm, and it tasted strange.

"Goddamn! Good antelope," said Victoria.

Smiling women plucked at Betsy, beckoned her to go outside. She didn't want to, except to relieve herself. Maybe that was what they had in mind. . . .

"Dammit, git up and go with them women," Victoria muttered. "They gonna give us a hot bath."

"I just want to sleep," Betsy said. "I'm—so tired. . . ."

But the Snake women dragged her almost forcibly into the icy moon-washed night air, dragged her toward a place of white rock stairs that glinted with water. They took her to a shrubbed place first for her needs, and then led her to the springs. The mineral smell drifted to her nose. She didn't want this. She didn't want a chill bath in the middle of a cold night. She didn't want to disrobe before these strangers. But they tugged her onward, laughing, fondling her gently. She wanted Elkanah. She wanted to curl up and sleep for a week.

They paused at last before a large pool that had been dammed at its lower end with rock. She stared into its depths and saw the moon wobbling up at her. The Shoshone women laughed, beckoned.

"Goddamn!" exclaimed Victoria. Betsy scarcely realized Victoria had come. Arabella, too, crossly, some resentment flaming in her.

Victoria didn't wait an instant. She yanked off the leather vest, the riddled purple blouse they'd salvaged, and the grimed nightdress that had once been Betsy's, and slid her slim old body into water.

"Ohhah!" she snorted. "Son of a bitch!"

Betsy peered about. How could she go naked in open air, and a whole Indian village a hundred yards off? But laughing women were peeling off her tattered green dress, until she shivered whitely in moonlight. She put a tentative toe in—hot! She tried a foot and ankle and calf. Delicious! With some gladdening of soul, she slid into the pool, finding a solid smooth rocky bottom, slid deeper into a kind of paradise, feeling hot water, almost as hot as she could stand, flow about her, warming and massaging her aching body, drawing pain out of her like some magic laudanum, lifting her spirits, making things right.

Around her women smiled shyly.

Betsy eyed them dreamily and then she laughed.

Chapter 30

A triumph of intelligence, thought Captain Jarvis Cobb, West Point. He'd made it his business to know everything, and by knowing everything, he'd escape the deadly trap.

He knew about when in the night frost formed, and intended to escape camp before leaving tracks in it. He knew where Danzig emptied his pockets of flints, nail knife, antler knife, and the rest. He knew where Morse would place his knives and the precious horseshoe flint striker and emergency ax. He knew where Skye put his big lance knife. He knew where Skye's squaws would lie, and how to get the knife. He knew how to fool Jawbone. He knew they'd all fall into a deep sleep after that terrifying day.

But that was only a part of good intelligence. He had surmised, from long observation, what Skye would do at dawn, upon discovering that Cobb had left with literally everything. He surmised the weaknesses in his own plan and questioned himself ruthlessly and unsentimentally about what might happen and what he could do about it.

The weakness would be Jawbone. He'd kill that horse if he could; hamstring the animal if possible; poison it, blind it, whatever it took. But in fact, that murderous horse would kill him and instantly arouse the camp. And yet, Jawbone remained the only weakness. It gave Skye mobility, a chance to seek help, hunt down Cobb, ferry them all to some safe place. But Captain Cobb knew his own limits and sensed that the better option would be to elude them all.

He struck out early, after gathering weapons and moccasins and the turkeys with perfect ease. The turkeys—

which would keep for days in the frosty air—he carried on thongs he'd devised. The horseshoe hung from a thong on his belt. He strapped on Skye's big sheathed knife, kept a nail knife, flint and awl, dumped everything else, except Connaught's moccasins, into the Big Horn River. He'd done it all by starlight, too, shadowy and silent. Jawbone scarcely perked up his ears.

He struck due west out of the Big Horn River valley. He knew that you stayed well away from traveled routes when you wished to elude all eyes. A mile west of the river, he turned ninety degrees, and headed south, roughly paralleling the river, and guided by the North Star in the clear night.

In the morning, Mister Skye would mount Jawbone and go search, especially the west bank. Morse would despair. The things-maker, as the Indians called him, wouldn't fathom survival without tools and weapons. Danzig would be stronger. The white women would want to stay in camp. Skye would return after finding nothing, and they'd begin making new tools halfheartedly. Some turkeys would still be roosting in that patch of woods, so they'd make a new pole with a loop, for food. Danzig would hunt flint so they could strike fire from Jawbone's horseshoe again. Some of them would keep their fire going desperately because losing it would be fatal until they got flint. They'd struggle halfheartedly in that protected camp, and then trudge south along the river again after a few days of preparation, but they'd be demoralized and their progress slow. Or maybe they'd roll over and die there, dead of exposure and discouragement. He didn't wish death upon them, but neither did the thought of their death torment him. Life would always be dilemmas, ambiguities, circumstances . . . and the survival of the best.

Captain Cobb paced himself. He'd had a bad day along with the rest, and needed to husband his strength. He wished he could have nabbed Victoria's windproof leather vest. But he couldn't. Even so, he felt content. No plan ever devised had lacked pitfalls. Generals who waited too long usually were crushed by opponents who seized opportunities, stayed mobile, created new chances by flow and advance. Every textbook said it; every lesson they taught at the Point said it. So he paced through the icy night, ignoring the cold, pausing every fifteen or twenty minutes to rest and conserve himself. South to those hot springs for a healing bath and maybe opportunity—his mind danced with the possibility of stealing a horse there from a passing band, and he weighed the ways and means of doing that as he walked, reviewing everything he knew about how Indians guarded their herds. But even if he found no one at the hot springs, he'd follow trails south to the California-Oregon Trail, and go on home, retiring home from the field, as they liked to say in the army, with honor. . . .

At dawn he found a small gully and hunkered down in it, out of the wind. He built a tiny fire with ease, a palm's breadth across, and with it cooked turkey breast he sliced from a bird. Then he settled down for a three- or four-hour rest. He planned to do the same at dusk. And thus dozing as the morning sun probed down into his little gulch, he missed the passage of several horsemen—or mule riders to be more precise—a mile and a half east, over open prairie.

En route again under a pale autumnal sun, he found himself wrestling with his conscience. He regretted leaving Arabella to such a doom. They'd come together only the one time, in the Crow lodge, and once Arabella discovered lust, her appetite grew boundlessly, beyond Cobb's means to satisfy her. Well, he thought, she has had her great moment in life, and will die reasonably fulfilled. Still . . . he wished she might survive. He wished they all might survive. But he could not permit it. They'd die peacefully of illness and exposure and starvation, and no one would know his part in it. All because of a preposterous code that turned a simple act of self-protection against a freezing death into a crime, a blot on his honor. He deserved life! He deserved success! How could such a small stupid thing hang like the sword of Damocles over him?

He sighed. That had been nothing. A desperate small act that came to no bad end. But what he'd done last night was another matter altogether. It could be construed as murder. Angrily, he shook that thought out of his head. Nature would do the killing; he hadn't. He'd be free to pick up his career at West Point, unblemished, but he felt no joy in it. The thing would always stare him in the face. He'd have to be careful. What if he talked in his dreams and Susannah pieced it together? What if, in dying, Skye and the rest managed to leave behind a message, an accusation? The thought curdled him. Well, after all, what would they have? Charcoal, easily washed away by fall rains and winter snows. Tattletale carbon. He wished he'd buried their fire under earth before he slipped away. Too late to worry about that: the odds against messages were astronomical anyway. They'd think only of surviving, making tools, getting food and shelter. Intelligence, the knowledge of how the enemy would act, the educated surmise . . . He felt comforted.

His long walk proceeded like clockwork, and all went as expected except that his moccasins wore out much too fast, and he squeezed into Connaught's pair, worried that he'd be shoeless soon, a long way from the California Trail.

Surely there'd be discards around the Snake encampments at the hot springs. . . . He rested and cooked turkey twice a day, and proceeded by easy stages south, under clear skies, the weather cooperating in his plans and lifting his spirits.

He fought demons the second day and recognized them as phantasms of guilt. As always, he put them front-center in his mind so he could examine them, understand them, banish them. Had he contributed to the death of others? Well then, agree to it. Yes, indeed. But how might he proceed through life staggering under a burden like that? Why, judge them. From a mental throne, he did exactly that, weighing each of them. Skye and the squaws, nothing, barbarians. No loss. Morse, some enterprising genius and inventiveness, but devoid of a soldier's virtue and courage, and in the end a fool to come out here. No great loss. Danzig, a dry-as-dust professor, who had no business out here. Actually, though, the best mind of them. Some loss there, he had to admit it. Betsy, an amiable amateur artist. Harebrained. No loss. Arabella, spoiled by wealth and empty-headed . . . He remembered her passion, and sighed. No loss. No great calamity. Why let it eat at him the way it did? He'd get past it, he knew. As soon as he returned to the Point, all this would vanish. . . .

At dusk of the next day, he topped a rise, saw a flat layer of blue smoke, tiny cones of lodges, and to the south, rising purple mountains. A village! The hot springs! Horses! Swiftly he settled flat in the dry dun grass to observe, to reconnoiter. He needed, simply, one good horse. He had plenty of thong for a rein. One horse.

A time to put intelligence to work! The herd, shifting dark dots, grazed in the Big Horn valley north of the village and rather close to him. Good. He wouldn't even get close to the village. He'd steal a horse and ford the river and strike east and south, and get down to the trail in a few days of hard riding. He closed his eyes, concentrating on what he'd learned of tribal practice. They'd have boys herding by day, warriors of their police society at night. Favorite horses would be tethered or picketed close to lodges in the village. The night guard would look for commotion among the animals, look for horses with ears pricked all in one direction. Usually two guards. He'd either have to elude them or kill them. He chose to elude. He wanted to slip a horse out of the herd undiscovered, perhaps undiscovered for weeks. Not easy. He wouldn't know which horses would be broke . . . unless he hunkered here in the little gulch long enough to see what the youths rode and trained by day. But that would take endless time, cold harsh exposed time. Evening now, and not until the next evening and the following night could he strike. No, he'd strike tonight, select a big docile animal, and hope he had blackness for a blanket. He thought a moment about the moon, observing it. It lay low now and quarter full. Probably set around ten or eleven. He frowned, trying to remember whether it had been rising or setting early evenings. A lapse in intelligence. It irked him, this carelessness.

Still, he'd try. He felt numbly cold here with the wind whipping relentlessly over his back and the ground half-frozen under him. Dark lowered swiftly, and he thought to get his horse at once. Good tactics. They all supposed horse thieves would strike very late, near dawn. He'd fool them. He observed the night riders now—one circling, the other sitting blanketed near a cottonwood, his horse close. Cobb itched for that blanket, but decided not to risk it.

At last he rose, driving numbness from his limbs, and

slid down toward the herd, from the wind side unfortunately. He couldn't get downwind, not with the river to the east and the village to the south. He stole gently into the herd, seeing them shift uneasily from him, like waves from a bow. A horse snorted, and he froze for minutes. Then he eased ahead, and they dodged as he went. One didn't move, though, a big one and fearless, of a color he couldn't determine in the blackness. Familiar with man. Heart stabbing his chest, he slipped closer. This would be it! He unrolled his thong, slid a hand along the big horse's mane and neck, and started to knot the thong around the horse's jawbone. That's when something struck him from behind, and he felt himself falling and then felt nothing.

"This is the one," said Strong Horse. "See, even the horseshoe."

"He's the one," agreed Mister Skye as Mary's brother eased the semiconscious Cobb through the lodgedoor.

Strong Horse laid Cobb flat, while two other warriors entered as well, seating themselves, and waiting for their captive to come to.

"We made it easy for him," said Strong Horse cheerfully. "He saw only Elk Antlers in his blanket under the cottonwood, and Whistling Deer on his pony, riding the herd. He never saw the rest of us, not even when we were very close!" He laughed easily, staring at the foolish white captain slowly coming back into his head. "It was exactly as you said. He came to steal a horse!"

Mister Skye translated all this, with Mary's help, to the Morses and Danzig. Mary's parents, Rutting Elk and Stealing Jay, had turned over their large, luxurious lodge to the Skye party, and had moved in with relatives. Now, in the glow of the tiny lodgefire, they all looked rested after their ordeal, luxuriously dressed in soft skin clothing, quilled and beaded. Professor Danzig looked startlingly Indian in buckskins in spite of his beard, slim and dark and sharp-nosed. Betsy, washed and rested, radiated something vibrant in her doeskin skirt and red tradecloth blouse. His own women, Victoria and Mary, lounged on the thick curly-haired brown buffler robes in happiness and peace.

But now Captain Jarvis Cobb lay before them, intruding upon their idyll. His eyes flicked open and glanced about the lodge, focusing at last on Mister Skye. He groaned, and felt the knot on the back of his head.

Then he shifted his brown eyes away and wouldn't look at them again. Nor did he speak.

"Well, Mister Cobb, it didn't work, did it?" asked Mister Skye.

The man said nothing.

"I'll satisfy your curiosity. The army came to the rescue," the guide rumbled.

Cobb's eyes flicked around, looking for soldiers, wanting soldiers.

"What would you like to do, Cobb? Go back to West Point?"

The man closed his eyes, feeling the antagonism of the Morses on him. He'd left them to die, and they knew it and understood why.

"We should take him back whether he wants to go back or not," snapped Arabella. "And I'm going to tell the world about him."

Mary translated softly for her brother and their guests.

"I haven't made up my mind," Cobb muttered. "This all happened too fast."

"I think we should forgive and forget," said Betsy, always the generous person.

"Never!" cried Arabella. "He takes what he will and he should die!"

The girl's tone was so vehement that the senior Morses stared at her.

Mister Skye had an inkling of meaning in it.

"Mary's people don't mind the horse stealing. That's Indian sport, Mister Cobb. You're not their prisoner, nor ours. Quite free to go if you wish."

"I am?" exclaimed Cobb, astonished.

"Strong Horse, Mary's brother, has even volunteered to give you an old pony."

Cobb considered that. "Will I have my—the . . . weapons?"

"Exactly what you came with," said Mister Skye. "Perhaps the California goldfields, Mister Cobb?"

For a long time Cobb remained silent. "What if I choose to go east?"

"We would escort you to Fort Laramie. These good people have agreed to take us there, even though Laramie is deep in the lands of their enemies, Sioux and Cheyenne, who tried to jump them at the peace conference last year. If you come with us, we'll naturally take your weapons from you. But you'll be free to tell whatever story you wish to the commanding officer there—Captain St. James, I believe he is now."

"Susannah," Cobb muttered, and fell silent.

They waited patiently, comfortable in the warm luxury of the robes, and filled with buffalo tongue and sausages of boudins and two days of feasting.

"I'll head west," Cobb said. "I can't escape the ruin you plan for me with your exaggerated stories. I'll be a deserter technically, but the West is large and empty."

"No one's planning your ruin, Mister Cobb."

"I am!" snapped Arabella. "Ruin for ruin!"

Some sudden awareness blossomed in Betsy's eyes, though Elkanah missed it all.

"All right, then," rumbled Mister Skye. "You'll go west. One thing, though. If you sneak east tonight, these people will kill you. They'll escort you to a trail over the Owl Creek Mountains. Take it and be on your way southwest."

Mary translated, and Strong Horse and the other warriors escorted Captain Cobb into the cold night. He did not look back or say good-bye.

Mister Skye and his people sat thoughtfully in their luxurious robes. Tomorrow they'd begin the trek to Laramie, graciously outfitted and protected by Mary's people. In a week or ten days, the Morses and Danzig would be ensconced in the old fur post the army bought, and would go east with the next army supply unit.

"He might have lived down dishonor easily enough, if he'd wanted to," mused Elkanah. "No one blames a desperate man much for trying to keep himself alive. It might never have come to light anyway. I've never been inclined to tattle about desperate moments and desperate mistakes. I don't suppose the rest of us would have said anything either. The fear was in his head. . . . But the second episode—stealing all we had so we'd die of exposure and starvation and keep his secret by dying—that's something I would talk about, and intend to talk about."

"It can't be ignored," agreed Mister Skye.

"We owe your people much, Mary," said Elkanah.

"My people are always helpful to those in need," Mary replied proudly.

"I want to paint them!" said Betsy. "I'm making images of them in my mind. I think I'll be able to! How could I forget these dear people? I've been remembering each of my paintings and those I painted, and I think I'll be able to do them again, maybe even better. If I have a few things—these beautiful clothes—I'll make them all come to life."

"My mother and my sisters are pleased to give them to you," Mary said. "We are pleased that you'll paint them, and will think of us when you paint them."

"We'll be wintering here, you know," the guide said. "We'll outfit at Laramie—I've a bit in my account with the sutler there, enough for a rifle and a few things—and then we'll ride here. Or walk . . ." he added, remembering he had no ponies other than Jawbone.

Mister Skye worried about that, actually. He'd lost everything, every bit of gear. His account would cover only the barest necessities. But maybe he could trade the army mules . . .

He slid out onto the frosted night, sensing that Cobb had vanished forever from his life, sensing the calculating captain trotting his ancient pony west, escaping from dishonor that had once lain largely in his head rather than in reality.

Barring surprises, they'd make it to Laramie in utter comfort. He peered around this lodge with its warm cowhide skins, parfleches of jerky and pemmican, white backfat—perfect for stews—hanging from lodgepoles, thick robes, medicine pouch hanging in place of honor, and all the rest. It'd be a good winter with Mary's people—a time of hunting for buffler, trapping for skins to trade, eating fat, making love, hugging his women, telling tales, tanning hides and sewing a new lodge, training colts, giving parties, attending ceremonies, all beneath the eastern shoulders of the Wind River Mountains where this band wintered each year, in a paradisiacal valley. Mary's people, like Victoria's, loved him and made him a part of themselves, and he made them all a part of himself, feeling more Shoshone and Crow than he felt whiteman or Briton or Yank. When spring came and the grass freshened, they'd go back to Laramie and do some guiding and trade some furs to the sutler, and wait for the summer trade.

Chapter 31

Captain Walden St. James liked to shout. "What are you talking about!" he sputtered. "Cobb? Head west? Preposterous! He was a year ahead of me at the Point. I know him well enough to know something stinks here! Desert? Head west? I'll hold you all in irons until I get answers!"

The young Fort Laramie commanding officer had whirled like a tornado into the sutler's store where Mister Skye and his party had only moments before arrived in the company of a band of Shoshone warriors.

"I have instructions from the western command—Leavenworth—to send him along as soon as he arrived. Months late now! Cobb and some civilians. What've you done with the man? You're talking about a United States Army officer and West Point instructor and foremost authority on intelligence!"

St. James struck Mister Skye as someone unduly excited, so he said nothing.

"Well, out with it!" he cried, whirling on Elkanah. "Who are you? Where's Cobb?"

"I'm a New England businessman, Morse by name, and these are my daughter Arabella, wife Betsy, and Professor Danzig of Harvard College."

"Well I want the truth about Captain Cobb or I'll detain you until I get it!" bawled the beet-faced captain.

"I don't believe you have authority to detain civilians, sir," said Elkanah. "And in any case, Mister Skye's story is correct. Captain Cobb chose of his own free will to depart and head west, perhaps to the California goldfields."

"I have the authority to do what I damned well please, including detaining who I please. And your story is full of lies. And the squaw man's story is full of lies. Skye is notorious, and a bigamist."

"It's Mister Skye, mate."

"I don't care if it's Honorable Lord Skye. Your story is bull and you'd better give me reasons or I'll have you all for murder and insurrection." He jabbed a finger at Arabella. "You, miss! You tell me what happened to Captain Cobb or I'll put your father in irons."

"Captain Cobb did a dishonorable thing, and chose to escape whatever fate awaited him," said Arabella angrily.

"Dishonorable thing! Cobb hasn't got a dishonorable bone in his body! Finest man to come out of the Point in a decade."

Arabella blazed. "Dishonorable! He took me—took me into his bed. Had his way with me! Ignored his poor wife and children and had his way, and then fled, knowing what would come!"

Elkanah gasped.

"Arabella!" cried Betsy.

"It's true!" she snapped.

St. James sputtered, then turned crafty. "How come this

young lady claims to know things the rest of you don't know? It stinks, all of it."

"I have nothing more to say!" Arabella said, and flounced off.

St. James stared around him. "Get these savages out of here!"

Old Colonel Bullock drew himself up. "I'm sorry, suh, they are my guests and customers, and your writ, suh, doesn't run here."

"Like you to meet my brother-in-law, St. James. This is Strong Horse. Meet Lieutenant St. James."

"It's Captain, squaw man!" snarled the commanding officer.

Mister Skye considered something, and plunged ahead on the proposition that could end up just one way.

"We recovered five army mules some three hundred miles from here in Big Horn basin, Captain. I thought I'd trade them back for a couple of your older mounts for my women."

"Trade them? Trade them, Skye? They're army property. I could have you arrested for horse theft. In fact I will. Guard!"

Elkanah Morse intervened. "If you arrest everyone who returns army property, young man, you'll get no property back. I fear I must say a word in certain places about you. You are a most rash young man, and I fear for your career. . . ."

Elkanah's quiet powerful tone conveyed something to the young commander. St. James glared at them all, grew cautious, and muttered, "I'll get to the bottom of this. Guard, confiscate those mules outside."

He stormed off, and Mister Skye sighed.

"I hadn't expected unpleasantness, mates. I fear your long journey with the quartermaster command won't be very happy."

"We're glad to be alive, Mister Skye. We wouldn't be, but for you and these good tribesmen of yours. I've been thinking. You've been wiped out, lost everything on our account. If Colonel Bullock here could arrange credit, we—Betsy, Arabella, and I—we'd like to buy you horses and make sure you're properly outfitted—and make sure these Shoshone colleagues of yours get their reward. That's the least we can do, Mister Skye. . . ."

"And a way of giving you our love, all of you our love," cried Betsy.

"We've gained everything," continued Elkanah. "I lost a few goods but gained knowledge and—I hope—wisdom. Betsy lost something dear to her, but gained something profound. She just told me that when she does new watercolors, they'll express something—something inside of them—larger than her earlier paintings." He slid an arm about Arabella. "And my daughter's learned, too, bitter lessons, and will return to Lowell a better person."

"I daresay I lost some and gained a lot more," said Professor Danzig. "I have books to write, maps to spin. And memories, my dear friends, memories. I never dreamed that my geology and anthropology would someday save my life!"

"Goddamn!" bawled Victoria, hugging Betsy, then Arabella, and then the rest.

Two hours later, Victoria and Mary had good ponies, clothes, blankets, and kitchenware. Mister Skye had a new Sharps .60-caliber rifle and all the necessaries, along with boots, a fine bowie, flint and steel, and a raft of other things. Their escort of Shoshones found themselves the

...ick new blankets, knives, powder and galena, and red ribbons for their ladies. And buried in Mister Skye's new kit lay a jug of amber stuff to warm him on cold nights.

"What do I owe, Mister Bullock? And will you carry me to the next season?"

Colonel Bullock stared at his old friend. "Mister Skye. Elkanah Morse asked me to tell you the accounts are even."

Mister Skye roared, found Elkanah, and hugged.

"Is this what the mountain men do?" gasped Elkanah, taken aback.

"It's what Mister Skye does, mate."

They made their good-byes with the Morses and Professor Danzig, and the more Mister Skye tried to see them, the more blurred they became.

Yellowstone

For Michael Seidman

Chapter 1

The trouble in Mister Skye's lodge really began with Victoria's medicine. As spring progressed, the old Crow woman turned inward and slipped into a stoic silence. Sometimes she squinted at Mister Skye intensely, as if measuring him for a grave, and then turned angrily to whatever task lay at hand. He didn't press her. When she was ready to tell him, she would. And he would listen. He didn't hold with Indian religion, but he respected it, and sometimes found it uncanny.

His other wife, young amber-fleshed Mary of the Shoshones, was affected by Victoria's gloom too, so Mister Skye's lodge was filled with sighs and sorrow as the bluestem poked through moist clay and leaf buds formed on the cottonwoods along the Platte.

Once he questioned Victoria.

"What is it?" he asked on a blustery March night when gusting winds drove smoke back down into the lodge, making them cough.

"Don't do it," she said. "Bad. We'll all weep."

But that was all she would say, and turned industriously to resoling one of Mister Skye's winter moccasins with buffalo rawhide, fiercely jamming her awl through tough leather.

But he would do it. The draft for five hundred pounds, two thousand five hundred dollars, sealed it. His usual guiding fee was five hundred dollars, but expenses always

ate into that. True, he would spend much of this on harness drays for Frazier's carts, and saddle horses, all gathered from trading posts along the Platte and tribesmen, but
there would be a thousand left over if all went well. Enough
to comfort Mister Skye and Victoria and Mary for years.

In spite of all that wealth, which had been delivered
to his agent, Colonel Bullock, the sutler at Fort Laramie,
Mister Skye thought long and hard about accepting the
offer. When his head quit working he tried to resolve
the matter with a jug of whiskey. But when he emerged
from that winter hegira he had even less notion of whether
to do it than he'd had before he'd soaked his brain in spirits. He'd never guided Britons before, and didn't ever want
to. They stirred memories in him. Even less did he want
to guide this hunting party, formed by Viscount Gordon
Patrick Archibald Frazier, a great landlord near Bury
St. Edmunds, Suffolk. No, he didn't relish it at all, in part
because of a seething rage toward his fellow Britons that
hadn't abated in decades—and in part because in British
possessions he was a wanted man.

"Take it, suh," advised Colonel Bullock, the retired Virginian who was waxing rich selling grog and tobacco to
the small garrison at the new army post, as well as calico,
shoes, fresh oxen, and sundries to the summer hordes en
route to Oregon and California. "There's no danger I can
fathom. Take them to their buffalo and elk. Show them the
geysers, and pocket it."

"There'll be a lot of them. Enough to drag me north
across the line, Colonel. And besides that, every bloody
Briton I meet starts me boiling again. Especially the titled
ones, the ones called Lord and Sir, and Your Excellency
and Mister."

Colonel Bullock looked amused. "They'll have reason

to respect Barnaby Skye," he said. "God knows, they made enough inquiries."

So he would do it. Through the winter he bought horses, and when new leaf lifted the cottonwoods to a mint-colored haze along the Platte, Mister Skye's wives unlaced the small buffalo cowhide lodge, loaded the slender lodgepoles on travois, gathered their few belongings into parfleches and loaded them on Skye's bony black Missouri mules. They struck due north, herding forty-two half-starved and winter-weakened nags, plunging into the land of the Sioux and Cheyenne, deadly enemies of Victoria and Mary's people, and every warrior among them a famous horse thief.

He'd agreed to be at Fort Union, six hundred horseback miles north near the confluence of the Missouri and Yellowstone, on the 15th of June, 1850, along with forty horses, twenty of them broken for harness. Frazier's packet, the *St. Ange*, owned and mastered by Joseph LaBarge, would arrive on the June rise, as the rivermen called the second annual flood of the Missouri. From there, they would start directly up the Yellowstone on the great hunt.

April had always seemed to him the worst month to travel. The grass had barely peeked from the icy earth, and wouldn't support hungry horses. He would need to keep them alive with cottonwood bark. Rivers roared, and innocuous creeks turned into torrents or lakes, forbidding passage. Late blizzards descended, locking the country in a cold blanket. Ponies plodded and slipped and stumbled through gumbo, making heavy work of what would be easy going on drier turf. Game was hard to find, and poor, reduced to bones by winter starvation. Moist cold earth clawed up through buffalo robes. Chill winds chapped flesh and triggered fevers. Haze and icy pellets and sheeting rain worked into his old percussion lock Hawken, dampening the powder so that he sometimes had to claw caked DuPont out of it, pour in fresh, and jam the galena back down the muzzle, riding a patch. Often there was not a dry stick of firewood to be had. But it wouldn't all be bad: the very things that would make his journey an ordeal would keep horse-hungry Sioux and Cheyenne, not to mention Assiniboin, Blackfeet and Gros Ventre, in their lodges a few weeks more. He had forty horses to deliver, and only himself, Victoria, Mary, and Jawbone, to do it.

Jawbone. Mister Skye sat comfortably on the bony, scarred blue roan as they herded the winter-whipped horses out of the Platte Valley and onto endless broken plains, rough and empty and filled with hidden menace. His yellow-eyed evil horse had become a legend among the northern tribes. The terrible stallion bore the scars of arrows and knives, battle axes and clubs. Mister Skye's training, and the beast's own rude intelligence, had given Jawbone an uncanny grasp of danger, making him a splendid sentry. Every warrior of every northern tribe knew the roman-nosed beast was a medicine horse, capable of murder. The thought pleased Mister Skye. They all knew Jawbone as well as they knew him. And when they spotted the medicine horse, or the burly man wearing his battered silk tophat, the unblinking bleached blue eyes, and a nose as thick as a keelboat stem, they thought twice. Or thrice.

For weeks they furrowed the gumbo north, leaving a trail of horses and travois traces behind them like a wake behind the taffrail. Mister Skye studied the bleak brown lands and saw nothing but contentious crows and an occasional hawk nesting in the rigging of the sky. They camped in silent cottonwood bottoms whenever he could find them, and there he slashed bark for his gaunt animals, and studied the country, and sat glare-eyed through long nights beside his picketed ponies, keeping Jawbone loose-saddled and ready.

His weathered sits-beside-him wife watched him, muttered, and then slid into indignant silence. She'd seen visions, he knew. But she'd say nothing about them. He thought Mary might comfort him with her smiles and the trifles of her bold hands, but she rebuffed him too, until they'd become silent strangers on an endless voyage.

They pierced up the sodden grassy ditch of Old Woman Creek, pushed on to the swollen Cheyenne River, cut across angry creeks to the Beaver, skirted the brooding slopes of the Black Hills, sacred ground of the Lakota people and their *Wakan Tanka*; struck the gloomy gorge of the Inyan Kara and then on to the Belle Fourche, past the dark terror of Devil's Tower, which set Victoria to muttering death songs; then on over a pine-crusted divide to the Little Missouri, which took them to the great Yellowstone. They had not seen a mortal the entire distance, even though the mark of their passage rolled behind them as indelibly as sin in the judgment books of God. Mister Skye took it as a great omen, and thought his luck had soared. But Victoria muttered, placed carmine riverbottom pebbles she'd toted a great distance atop Lakota medicine cairns, for reasons Mister Skye couldn't fathom, and refused to sleep in the lodge as long as they traversed this land of the enemies of her Absaroka people.

They struck the roiling Yellowstone in late May, beneath black-bellied thunderheads that soon boomed down the wrath of the One Above upon their passage. Swiftly Mary and Victoria erected their lodge, deep in the cottonwood bottoms back from the river, and waited for the Spirits to descend and drive them back to Fort Laramie. Mister Skye shot a wolf that evening, ending a two-day fast in the very heart of a game-rich land. He gnawed soft gray wolfmeat, while his wives sniffed dourly and starved. Whitemen, he thought, will eat anything. He'd even eat cooties and grubs.

"We're almost at Union," he announced maliciously. "And not a pony lost. Three lame, all gaunt and poor, but not a beast lost. Oh, we're bloody rich, ladies. I ought to shoot one, just so you can say you knew it all along. Haw!"

Victoria glared and muttered. "You'll see," she said. Those were her first words in a week.

They toiled down the Yellowstone, heading northeasterly on a great tribal highway where anyone could encounter anything, usually lethal. But no hunting party or band of horse thieves beset them, and Mister Skye grinned at his silly women, and began bellowing sailor ditties, and bawling at hail, prancing hairy-chested in showers, and blaspheming Victoria's medicine, asking her how eagle claws and moose eyes and red pebbles could affect their passage and Fate.

"You'll see," she said.

They forded the boiling ice-green river badly, taking a cold bath and risking the weary horses. Even Jawbone swam listlessly, letting himself be carried a half mile in the flood. But they lost nothing, and Mister Skye gloated.

"Try frog medicine," he said. "Frogs got better medicine than anything. I always seek my brothers the frogs for counsel."

But Victoria didn't, and didn't smile, either.

They traversed a thin neck of land, hungry again, and raised Fort Union a day later, across the mighty Missouri. It glowed on the north bank, its sixteen-foot palisades golden in the late sun, the heart of empire, the crown jewel of American Fur Company, Barnaby Skye's erstwhile employer. Small figures boiled out of the fort like grapeshot, launched pirogues, and an hour later Mister Skye, Victoria, Mary, Jawbone, and forty-two dripping and shaking horses rested safely in the lee of the great post, an island of comfort in an aching sea of nothingness.

The Viscount Gordon Patrick Archibald Frazier had become a fixture in the pilothouse, but the master, Joe LaBarge, and the pilot, Renfrew, didn't seem to mind. Lord Frazier had discovered that the pilothouse, which perched atop what these Americans called the texas, or officers' quarters, afforded a spectacular view. He also found the packet's bearded master affable but too familiar.

Day after day, the little *St. Ange* had wrestled its way up the boiling Missouri, at first through forested lowlands and then between grassy bluffs in a mile-wide ditch cut through endless steppes. Lord Frazier had devoured every account he could find of the passage up the great Missouri, including those of Audubon and Catlin, and even Prince Maximilian zu Wied-Neuwied and his artist Bodmer in translation. But not even these keen recollections prepared this English lord for what his bright protruding eyes beheld. The distances and magnitudes were beyond his fathoming. His entire Suffolk could lie in some dusty corner of this vast continent, unnoticed.

He was a man of landed estates, a squire lording over a dozen hamlets, but like most Britons his heart lay close to the seas and the vessels that plied them. At first he had eyed the *St. Ange*, which LaBarge had named after Governor St. Ange de Bellerive, as some sort of Yankee nautical claptrap, and had twitted LaBarge about it. The low flat hull that lay on the water like a lilypad and had so little cargo space in its low hold, for instance. Or the great superstructure that lay upon this makeshift raft, making the vessel topheavy and unworthy of Neptune's wiles, and likely to capsize, like a fat man on stilts.

"This is a mad thing you run, LaBarge," he ventured early in their passage. "Are you sure it's quite safe?"

"It's never safe," LaBarge answered suavely, letting that riposte sink into Lord Frazier's skull.

"I should say not!" the lord cried.

"But it suits the river admirably," LaBarge added. "The Missouri knows not where it runs. One day its main channel lies starboard; the next day to port. Underwater demons build sandbars one day and wash them away the next. The river's awash with logs and trees eroded from the banks, which we call sawyers, and they can poke a hole in a hull faster than we can maneuver. Our firebox eats twenty cords of wood a day, and even at that we barely make enough steam to do the rapids, especially when a stiff wind runs against us. We stop for wood each day, sometimes twice a day, and risk our lives fetching it when tribesmen are around."

"I suppose you strike sandbars, then. What do you do once you're grounded?"

"Why, wait for a rise, or grasshopper over them."

"I say. Grasshopper? You'll have to translate, LaBarge. You Yanks contaminate the tongue."

"See those booms and spars, sir? And that capstan on the foredeck? Well, sir, we lower those spars until they rest on the sandbar, and then my men start twisting that capstan until we lift the boat up on those spars, like a grasshopper lifting its carcass, and then the paddles and the angle of the spars propel the boat forward. We repeat that until we're off."

"I think you're joshing me, LaBarge," Lord Frazier muttered, but some time later, in a barren country they called Dakota, he found LaBarge wasn't joshing at all. In fact— though he hated to admit it—he found the vessel admirably suited for its strange locomotion up a river that was about half mud.

He'd spotted the first tribesmen at a place LaBarge called Bellevue, not long after the river had erupted from a dense bankside forest into grasslands with occasional copses of trees along the shores. The half-naked bronzed men watching the passage of the fireboat excited Viscount Frazier.

"What are they, LaBarge?" he cried.

"Omaha, most likely."

"Are they a menace?"

"Usually not. The tribesmen up and down the river rarely trouble us, we are careful. They are subject to excitements now and then, so one never knows. We've had scrapes with the Yankton Sioux recently."

"Trouble?"

"They beg. Want trinkets for the firewood. Shoot their flintlocks as we pass by. Attempt to board. We don't let them, except maybe a headman or two."

"Shoot at us?"

"Oh sure. Most trips. Look," LaBarge said, pointing at perforations in the white enamel. "We dug the lead out."

Lord Frazier felt himself going giddy and tried to hide it.

"I say. Shall I call my men to arms?" He had thirty of them below, and a whole cartload of fine English pieces made by Manton, Dickson and son, James Purdey, Charles Lancaster, and John Rigby over in Dublin. Even his two cooks, wine steward, and taxidermist could fire them after he'd instructed them back in Suffolk.

"Hardly. Lord Frazier, as master of this vessel I'm in command, and that includes its defense. We'll have no trouble unless we make it with rash conduct. Most difficulties can be resolved with small gifts—a twist of tobacco or some vermillion. I'll want you to heed closely, though. The Rees, up in Dakota, can be a trial. They incline to treachery."

"You're addressing a lord of England—" Viscount Frazier cut himself off abruptly, thinking he'd never accustom himself to American democracy and the insolence of servant classes. He smiled, then. "Of course, of course, my good master."

Down on the main deck, Lady Alexandra had spotted them, and had squealed her terror. She had excitable humors, he thought, in spite of flaxen hair and a steady gaze. Too delicate for this, but she'd insisted on coming. He'd rather hoped she'd stay in Bury St. Edmunds, so he could booze with Diana and shoot bison and play tiddlywinks—their private name for carnal delights—in their tent. But Lady Diana simply would not be put off.

"Will we live?" she cried, waving a soft white hand at them far below. "Are we to meet our Maker?"

"Not quite yet," yelled the viscount, uncertainly.

LaBarge laughed, which seemed altogether rude to Viscount Frazier. These Americans, he thought. Not a bit couth.

But the *St. Ange* toiled up the turbid river without troubles, although Lord Frazier discovered astonishments at every bend of the treacherous flood. They rammed into frequent spring showers, which drove Lord Frazier to the men's lounge where he whiled away time with his ladies. These puritanical Americans consigned all female passengers to a separate cabin far aft, and even wives travelling with husbands were compelled to bunk there. But since he'd chartered the ship, except for some American Fur Company cargo, no rules were observed.

They usually anchored nights at islands or sand spits for safety, and Lord Frazier came to admire LaBarge's prudence. Whenever they stopped for wood, the master posted a rifleman atop the texas as a sentry. A shot would hurry wood cutters aboard. But no excitements disturbed their peaceful passage up the muscular river.

One gray day at a place LaBarge called Crow Creek in Dakota, they came upon buffalo, and the viscount and all his men rushed to the rail to study the huge beasts drinking at river's edge.

"You may shoot some," said LaBarge, "and I'll send a yawl. You'll find buffalo hump and boss rib a feast you'll remember."

His lordship wanted the honors, so he had his two Mantons brought to him, and banged away without effect. It puzzled him. The beasts took the balls and scarcely shivered.

"Sir, if I may," yelled the master from above. "Aim back of the shoulders, sir. A ball in a certain area there will drop them."

But the shaggy beasts had taken alarm and lumbered up the grassy coulee, and vanished. Except for one that stood quaking and spraying blood from his nostrils. Lord Frazier took another Manton handed him by his armorer, peered down the barrel again, squeezed, and the beast shuddered and fell. That night, he found LaBarge's estimation of buffalo meat was as good as his word.

They pierced into a land more and more arid, with tufts of silvery grasses that upholstered the yellow clay, and finally LaBarge told him they'd make Fort Union the following day. At once the viscount began to think ahead toward the unloading, and the great hunt. And of course, about Skye.

"Tell me, LaBarge, is this chap Skye to be trusted with our lives?"

LaBarge didn't reply, but stared dreamily up the aquamarine river at white rifts ahead, and paused so long that Frazier thought he didn't hear the question.

"Lord Frazier," said the master softly. "If there's any man on earth who can keep you out of harm's way, who knows the Northwest, who knows the tribesmen, who knows every menace, it's Skye. Skye and his amazing ladies, and that horse of his."

"Horse?"

"Jawbone. An army in himself."

"Are you quite sure?"

"You'll need him," LaBarge said. "Heed his every word, or face doom."

Lord Frazier thought LeBarge's advice perfectly extraordinary, but it pleased him that this barbarian would serve.

Chapter 2

Mister Skye watched for Victoria amid the throngs that erupted from Fort Union to celebrate the arrival of the *St. Ange*. She'd vanished, after a sullen silence all day. He couldn't fathom her dread, but he respected it. Never before had she refused to meet his clients, but now, as the twin-chimneyed riverboat slid past the wooded point below the fort, and the welcoming roar of the six-pounder up in the bastion shivered the air, he knew she couldn't bear to meet these British clients of his. He suddenly shared her dread, and wondered whether he'd gotten himself into something disastrous.

But his jet-haired Mary stood beside him, solemn and determined. She was with child, he knew, and in the winter he'd see the first of his progeny. That would be seven months and a long summer's hunt away. He smiled at her, though she didn't return the smile, wanting only to cling to his arm. Victoria's medicine had afflicted her too, he thought. He pressed her warmly, a burly arm around her, letting his steady strength calm her. She wore her ceremonial clothes for the occasion, white doeskin tanned to the texture of velvet, a bright red-beaded headband, bone necklace, and soft summer moccasins poking from under the fringes of her skirt. It melted him. Her incredible beauty always awakened something in him that he called The Glow.

Around them shouting engagés thronged toward the levee, along with tribesmen of every description, but mostly Assiniboin and Cree, with some Blackfeet and Crow too. Here on the neutral ground surrounding the old fort, ancient enemies jostled but did not war. Mister Skye stood quietly in the hubbub, resisting the flow of humanity racing to river's edge. The white vessel carried the annual resupply for the fur company, and in a few hours robe and peltry trading would begin. But it also carried Mister Skye's destiny in the cabins on its boiler deck.

The *St. Ange* answered the fort's booming welcome with its own whistles, shrilling steam into the dry summer air. The pulse of the great riverboat slowed, while tribesmen gaped at this magical thing, and the splashing wheels at each side quieted as the boat nosed toward the levee.

Mister Skye could see two blue-suited men high in the pilot house, the bearded LaBarge and his pilot. And another. He studied the other one, faintly startled by the man's wine-colored waistcoat and broadbrimmed green hat. Probably Viscount Gordon Patrick Archibald Frazier, he thought. A fine rill of distaste ran through him. Half the lords of England were fops and dandies; the other half arrogant blockheads. Maybe Frazier was both. He suddenly regretted it, regretted ever being tempted by all that money, and wished he could ride quietly home with his dear women and forget all this.

Too late, he thought somberly. He'd do what he'd agreed to do. The gleaming boat slid the last yards to the bank, riding stilled paddles, and rough deckmen tossed hawsers to the fort's engagés on the bank. Skye watched it all with professional interest. The *St. Ange* looked to be loaded to the scuppers, but all riverboats had that appearance. Two women on the boiler deck caught his eye: a slender flaxen-haired one in a nankeen dress and ostrich-feather hat, the other a glossy-haired stocky brunette in a lavender velvet suit and white jabot at the throat. It amazed him to see women dressed like that. It amazed the savage crowd, too.

Mister Skye surmised that his clients were in no hurry to disembark. At least none of them clamored at the rails while the deck hands dropped long planks from the gangway to the levee, enough planks side by side to afford the passage of a wagon. The foredeck was covered with vehicles, two-wheeled carts mostly, which the hands easily maneuvered down the planks. The mob had turned silent at such strange sights. Rarely had they seen a wheeled vehicle of any sort, and here were dozens being dragged off this ship. Frazier's carts, Skye thought. All of them neatly loaded and battened with canvas wagonsheets or wooden covers.

Then they wrestled a cart with iron-barred sides and a roof, full of squirming dogs that were raising an amazing racket. Frazier's dogs! The lord had mentioned he'd bring some, but Skye had scarcely expected a cartload of them. A squat rumpled man in a liverish suit followed this baying cargo to the levee, and Skye perceived something slavic about him, maybe in his Mongol eyes. Assiniboin women stared warily at the dogs, ready to run. The hound-master trudged to the rear of the cart, pulled a pin that anchored two doors, and dogs spilled out, a blur of brown and tan and black. Everywhere around him, engagés and Indians fled as a wave of dogs whirled and eddied and exploded outward like grapeshot, yapping and barking. Bulldogs! Not a hunting hound in the lot, as far as Skye could see.

He heard wild nasal laughing, and discovered Frazier— it had to be Frazier—wheezing up there at the sight of his mutts bowling over Indians and engagés like tenpins. Skye found himself grinning in spite of his better judgment. Maybe Viscount Frazier had a nasty sense of humor, he thought.

The next cart, enameled white with his lordship's crest blazoned with green and gilt on its sides, the deckhands treated as something holy. Eight of them gathered along its shafts to ease it gently down the planks, and Skye wondered about it, while booting at growling bulldogs that threatened to nip Mary's trim ankles. Reverently, as if unloading the Ark of the Covenant, men rolled the cart downward under the watchful eye of what surely was Frazier's own crew, many of them dressed in some sort of simple black livery. Behind this cart wobbled a vast, corpulent man Skye instinctively knew was a Briton, square-faced, ruddy, John Bull-shaped, who watched the progress of this glossy cart distrustfully. Mister Skye sidled over, wanting to peer inside to discover whatever precious cargo it contained, and he was not disappointed. As soon as the crewmen had chocked its fine spoked wheels, the cart's steward unlocked the rear doors with a huge brass key to see if anything was amiss inside. Wine! Whiskey! Scotch! Gin! Barnaby Skye gaped at hogsheads of whiskey, and row upon row of bottles fitted tightly in racks that pinioned them firmly. A faint glow built up in Mister Skye, and visions of rendezvous danced in his head.

"Is that stuff booze, Mister Skye?" asked Mary, faint hope illumining her features.

"The world's best, I'd wager."

"Ah. It will be a good hunt."

Next the hands freed a sturdy blue-enameled cart that had been anchored to the foredeck with cleats and cables. This, too, bore Frazier's coat of arms in green and gilt on its sides, and Skye thought the two-wheeled vehicle seemed unusually heavy as he watched sweating men ease it down the gangway. This too was followed by some sort of specialist in Frazier's employ. Once the wagon rested safely on the levee and out of the way, the man unbolted the rear doors, revealing rack after rack of glowing rifles. And below, kegs of powder, pigs of lead, and other paraphernalia. An armorer, the man was Frazier's armorer, thought Skye. He gaped at the chased and engraved weapons, the glowing stocks, and knew he was seeing a fortune in arms. Tribesmen gawked, thunderstruck, at the weapons, and jabbered among themselves about it. Arms to wage an entire war!

Other carts followed bearing nameless burdens beneath their canvas covers. Kitchens, Mister Skye surmised. Provisions. Mess gear—though he knew Frazier wouldn't call it that. Tents and awnings, quarters for Frazier's large staff. One cart seemed to contain nothing but bagged grain; fodder for horses, Skye supposed. Then at last the weary crew tackled the remaining vehicle, this one no cart at all but a yellow-enameled four-wheel wagon of some sort, with what appeared to be a collapsible duck cloth top. A mobile palace. Surely Frazier's home away from home. For himself, no doubt, and those two ladies, whoever they might be. Frazier had not mentioned women, but the presence of two didn't surprise Mister Skye, who well knew the lords of England. That one would take four big harness horses, he thought, wishing he had some clydesdales or percherons. But he had only the mustang stock of the West, trained to drag carts. Plus some big mules he might break to harness en route. The black mules in his own herd might just do, he thought. But they'd take training.

"Mister Skye, I want to go home," whispered Mary. "I don't like this."

"Don't know that I do, either."

How out of place all these gorgeously enameled wagons looked in this rude place, he thought. Behind them vaulted the silvery cottonwood palisade of Fort Union, and surrounding it were the earthy lodges of countless tribesmen and the gaily bedecked savages. The garish carts didn't belong.

Well, this was Viscount Frazier's lark. At last the great hunter and his party congregated on the main deck, as colorful as peacocks except for one gaunt gentleman in funereal black with a frilled white shirt at his throat. Mister Skye knew they'd spotted him, no doubt because Joe LaBarge had pointed him out, and now they hastened down the gangway to earth, looking as alien in this tawny land as hottentots. And dazzling, too. Cree and Assiniboin gaped at the slender blonde woman with her ostrich plumes and squash-colored nankeen skirts. Never had they beheld such a sight! And at the other woman, built of rectangles, with glossy brown hair and mirthful brown eyes, and wearing a lavender velvet suit that rippled sensuously as she walked, as if this lady lived for one thing that every male could instantly discern.

Barnaby Skye held his ground, finding himself wary and afraid. Not since he'd jumped his majesty's vessel of war long ago had he suffered the company of Englishmen. And never a lord.

Frazier turned out to be a portly man, square-faced, sandy-haired, with those bulging eyes so common among the British nobility and a cool assessing gaze that missed nothing. He carried a handkerchief in hand and dabbed at his bright nose with it, a beak reddened by the expanded capillaries that told Skye of excessive imbibing of spirits.

"Skye, I presume," he said nasally, not offering a hand.

"It's Mister Skye, sir," Barnaby replied, iron in his voice.

"Well, whatever. Have you done your duties?"

"Duties? Ah . . ."

"The drays. The saddle horses. Good stock I trust."

"The ponies, yes. Uh, mustang blood and mules, small but hardy." Mister Skye found himself stammering and defensive before this august lord of England, and hated it. Frazier's very presence here seemed to rob the land of liberty.

"Well, fetch them, fetch them."

"Now? This afternoon?"

"For me to see how you've rooked me."

Barnaby Skye burned, but held his peace. "This is my wife Mary," he said, an edge on his words. "She's a woman of the Shoshones, the Snakes."

"Yes," the lord said, examining Mary cursorily.

Mister Skye waited. Before him stood two ravishing women, dressed for a promenade in Piccadilly, whose names he didn't know. But Lord Frazier did not introduce them, and Mister Skye realized he didn't intend to. The old class divisions he'd hated so much slapped at him here, in the middle of the North American wilds.

Malcolm Clarke, the bourgeois of Fort Union, pushed through the gawking crowds to greet his guests. Lord Frazier eyed him wearily, seeing simply an unkempt long-haired man in a baggy black suit and open shirt.

"Viscount Frazier," Clarke said, proffering a hand. "I'm Malcolm Clarke, in charge of operations here for American Fur. Please accept the hospitality of the company, and make yourself at home. I'm at your service."

"Yes, of course," the viscount said, reluctantly taking Clarke's hand and dropping it instantly. "Very good, Clarke. This is Viscountess Frazier"—he waved at the flaxen-haired woman—"and this is Lady Chatham-Hollingshead."

Both women nodded but did not proffer their hands. Mister Skye waited to be introduced, but knew it wouldn't happen. Nearby, engagés and deck hands were offloading the annual resupply of tradegoods, but for once the tribesmen weren't gawking at bolts of cloth and iron pots. These amazing Britons and their bright wagons riveted them, and they huddled around Viscount Frazier and his party, wide-eyed.

"I must see to the shelving of the trade goods. This is our busiest season, but Mrs. Clarke and I would like you and your ladies to join us for dinner in an hour. Mister Skye and his Mary and Victoria will also join us."

Viscount Frazier's gaze settled on Mister Skye briefly. "Really? How extraordinary. With your kind permission,

I'll alter the list a bit. This man here"—he waved at the saturnine one in black, with evasive brown eyes that studied people when they weren't looking at him—"is my steward, Aristides Baudelaire, who's responsible for everything. And also, the man there, Colonel Boris Galitzin, master of hounds and horses and the hunt." He waved a languorous hand toward the slavic man in brown tweeds. "We'll all pester you with a few questions at table, eh?"

Clarke nodded. "I must tell Kakokima to set two more—"

"No, no, no, Clarke. Set one less. I'm sure Skye and his squaws will excuse us tonight."

"It's Mister Skye, sir."

"Whatever. You, my good man, will report to Monsieur Baudelaire. He's responsible for all matters, my personal aide and secretary. Fetch us the game, and take us up the Yellowstone to the geysers, and that'll be the sum of your duties."

Baudelaire gazed blandly at Skye from moist brown eyes that hinted of raw power and utter ruthlessness.

Malcolm Clarke refused. "I think, Viscount Frazier, that you would be wise to listen to Mister Skye, and place him in overall command. He and his ladies will share our table."

"Ah, yes. American democracy," said Frazier, unhappily.

Mister Skye listened closely. He had always refused to guide any greenhorn party that would not heed his counsel. Their lives and safety and comfort depended on it, as well as the lives of his own family and himself.

"Not democracy, sir. Safety," said Clarke. "You've taken pains to employ the best man available in all the American West. It's a dangerous land, sir. Things happen, things that a seasoned man of the mountains can deal with best."

"Yes, of course, Clarke. I've an army, you know. Thirty stout blokes with the world's best arms to fend off a few savages if need be. We'll be quite all right."

Mister Skye said nothing, but he was swiftly coming to a decision.

"I'll ask my wife to set additional places, then."

"Begging your apologies, Clarke, but we'll decline. I've a splendid field kitchen to put to the test tonight; a trial, you might say, eh? I'm sure all your little tales of savages and furs are quite rich, but we'll hear them some other day, eh?"

The bourgeois of Fort Union was taken aback. "As you wish, Viscount Frazier. If American Fur can be of any service—"

"Why, yes, yes. A buffalo. Have you a fresh carcass hanging? We thought to sample it. My chef, the Abbot Beowolf, there, has some notions about a proper herb for the beasts."

Clarke looked nonplussed, but recovered swiftly. "Our hunters brought in two this morning. Yes, I have one hanging."

"Capital, Clarke! I'll send a man. Now you go put your trinkets on the shelves, eh?"

Clarke stared, locked eyes with Mister Skye, and winked. Then he strode off to the trading room to supervise.

Mister Skye peered around him uneasily, missing Victoria acutely now. A knot of Cree squaws collected around some bulldogs. The women were squealing and exclaiming, clapping hands to mouths, at the sight of dogs with the ugliest snouts they'd ever seen. The bulldogs yapped and snapped, triggering shrieks and nervous giggles. Some roamed the levee, sniffing the carts and lifting legs.

"The horses, Skye. Take me to the horses, and fetch me your bills of sale so I can see the rooking I took." He waved at the master of the hounds. "Galitzin, come look."

"Penned behind the fort," Mister Skye muttered.

"Gordon, dear, I think I'll go in there"—the Viscountess pointed toward the fort—"and sit. My toesies are killing me."

But the other lady, the blocky brunette in lavender velvet, chose to join them and walked with an easy stride as they rounded the east palisade of the fort, deep in shadow, and headed toward some pens at the rear. Just what her relationship was to Frazier, Mister Skye couldn't fathom, but he entertained some educated guesses drawn from a London childhood.

"Twelve-foot palisade, wouldn't you say, Galitzin?"

"More than that, your excellency."

"Keeps the savages at bay, eh, Skye?"

"Trading posts are rarely beseiged, sir. The tribes need the blankets and pots and gunpowder too much to risk it."

"So you say. Galitzin here was a cossack colonel for Czar Nicholas, but I filched him a year ago, eh? He's my man in all matters of combat, and you'll take direction from him on questions of safety, the hunt, and care of the beasts."

"Perhaps you didn't read the terms in my letter, Viscount Frazier," rumbled Mister Skye. "I wrote that I'd insist on overall command because your lives and safety, out among the wild tribes and beasts, depend on my experience."

"Of course, of course. I showed it to Galitzin here, and we thought it a bit cheeky, my good man. We're toothed and fanged and all that, Skye."

"It's Mister Skye, sir."

They reached a pen that had been cobbled together from weathered, silvery cottonwood logs. Within, forty-odd wiry mustangs and mules peered at the visitors, many of them small, misbegotten, and mean. They ranged across the spectrum from coyote duns to blacks. Some were ewe-necked. Most roman-nosed. Their enormous tails swept the manure. The croups of some were lower than their withers. Only a few topped fifteen hands.

Viscount Gordon Patrick Archibald Frazier stared, clucking with his tongue. Galitzin sighed. Lady Chatham-Hollingshead laughed heartily. And that ghost who shadowed Frazier, Aristides Baudelaire, watched blandly, his brain obviously calculating advantage and profit.

"Rooked. I knew it." He pointed at a linebacked dun with a forelock so thick it blinded the animal. "Who's the sire and who's the dam?" he asked, and laughed shortly.

"Mustangs, sir," Skye said. "That's all that's to be had in this land. They endure. They've got hard hoofs that will give you no trouble. They're small but tough. The métis—French and Cree or Assiniboin breeds up in British possessions—use them to draw their Red River carts, which are heavier than yours."

"There goes my dream of racing over the prairie on a noble white steed," said Lady Chatham-Hollingshead.

"Patience, Diana. We'll buy others from that chap who runs the fort, whatever his name. Proper mounts. Rooked. You, Skye, have rooked us. I knew it. The cunning of your class. I saw it at once in you."

"And what would my class be?"

"The sailor class. See it in your gait. You manned a British ship—I can tell from your speech. The rogue and ruffian class."

Relief flooded through Barnaby Skye. "Viscount Frazier, the bills of sale are in my kit, some, anyway. Indians don't write bills. If you want the horses I'll draft you a note for the remaining balance, on account with my agent, Colonel Bullock at Fort Laramie. If not, I'll refund the entire amount. I'm sure you'll find another guide here—just ask Clarke—more to your liking."

"But—" sputtered Frazier. Galitzin hawked up spit. Baudelaire smiled gently. Lady whats-her-name pouted. A black-headed bulldog wet cottonwood posts.

And Mary squeezed his arm and peered up into his eyes, her own aglow.

Chapter 3

Viscount Frazier gaped. "But you can't do that. You're in bond to me, Skye."

"I'm doing it."

"You bound yourself."

"I agreed to guide you if you'd agree to certain terms."

"Terms? Terms? Whatever are you talking about, Skye?"

Barnaby Skye grinned. "You read my letter, mate."

The enormous lout gazed insolently at Frazier. The viscount had scarcely taken the measure of the man, but now that he stared into that alarming, uncouth, scarred face he recoiled. Skye had a nose such as Frazier had never seen, an amazing beak, twisted and bulgy, which rose like a hogback between two obscure blue eyes. The ruffian wore his graying hair shoulder-length, and on his head perched a ludicrous black silk tophat, tilted rakishly. He encased his hairy torso in a fringed buckskin shirt, and square-toed boots poked from under buckskin leggins. The sight was so comic that Lord Frazier cackled.

"I say, Skye. I know your type, and I'm glad to be rid of you. I'll send my man along and you give him your draft. He'll parse your arithmetic and your bills of sale for those jades you call horses, so let's have none of your cunning, man."

"Those ponies are tough, and you'll come to admire them," Skye rumbled. "They're safe enough penned here by day, but you'll want to put a night watch on them when you pasture them yonder. The tribesmen think it's a great honor to snatch a horse."

"I'm sure we'll manage, Skye. Galitzin has managed horses and hounds in places you don't know exist. I've read all about the dubious habits of these natives."

"It's Mister Skye, mate."

"There you go." He chuckled nasally. "Mister Skye. Baron Skye. Lord Almighty Skye, peer of the realm."

Lady Chatham-Hollingshead thought that was hilarious, and laughed gustily, which pleased Frazier.

"I think I'll examine zese beasts," said Galitzin. "Zey interest me."

"Halter's on the rail there," Skye said.

"Yes, Boris. Sort out the rubbish. Keep the rest, if any are worth it. And let me know. I'll have to arrange with that chap—the one that operates this post—for some decent ones."

"Clarke's got none to spare."

The viscount glared. "Stuck with these, am I?"

"Best I could fetch, mate."

"Mind your tongue." He sighed noisily. "Very well then, I'll accept your draft for the balance."

Lord Frazier let the oaf lead them back to the narrow

portal at the front of the fort. Skye had a sailor's rolling gait, no doubt about it. But that squaw of his was comely enough, if one were inclined toward dusky savages. Good riddance. He'd fetch another of these rustics, one with fewer airs and a map of the country etched in his thick skull, and that would suffice nicely. There'd be no quarrels with Galitzin about who would be in charge. And he'd cost less too, no doubt.

They rounded the side of the fort, into tangerine sunlight, and found bedlam everywhere. Rivermen and engagés still toted bundles of trade goods from the bowels of the steamer into the fort, sweating and cursing. Everywhere, half-naked bronzed Indians gaped and pointed at bolts of scarlet trade-cloth, black iron pots, kegs and crates, shining fusils and spools of bright ribbon. Lord Frazier watched his bulldogs whip through the hoi polloi, yapping and growling and scattering squaws and children.

Skye and his squaw threaded through the gawking crowds and into the yard of the compound, while Frazier, Diana Chatham-Hollingshead, and Baudelaire tagged along. Inside, the raucous sound fell away suddenly, and they found themselves encased in a deep quiet. The factor's spacious house looked as if it had been plucked from someplace back East and shipped up the river. All the rest was easy to identify: offices, a fur warehouse redolent with acrid robes, a kitchen wafting scents into the yard, employee barracks, storage rooms, quarters for a few married couples, a mortared stone magazine near the far bastion. Snug, he supposed. No doubt the Hudson's Bay posts were much the same. A fortified village.

Skye led them across the dusty yard toward a small pen that contained the ugliest horse Viscount Frazier had ever set eyes upon. The distrustful blue roan whickered a greeting at Skye, and Frazier knew at once that this demented animal, with evil yellow eyes and scars crosshatching his lumpy body, was Skye's own beast of burden. It fit, he thought. A lout of a nag for a lout of a man. The horse lifted its head, bared yellow teeth and shrieked, a note so shrill it pained Frazier's tender ears.

"I prefer bagpipes," quipped Diana.

"It fits, it fits," Frazier muttered. "His lordship Skye has got himself a blooded mount."

Baudelaire laughed softly. He always laughed softly, Frazier thought.

A small, crabbed squaw sat on a mound of gear next to that demonic horse, glaring at them. Lord Frazier was pinioned by the sheer force of her glare, which lanced from her eyes with some sort of power that made the viscount uneasy. She'd drawn her jet hair back from her seamed face and into two braids that tumbled over a shapeless brown calico blouse.

Skye's other squaw. As rough as the oaf himself. "That's Skye's first wife. He's got two, you know," Frazier said to Diana. "Only decent thing about him."

Lady Diana chortled. "Two's never enough," she said. "Three can be amusing, especially at tiddlywinks." She winked broadly at Frazier.

The viscount found it convenient not to meet the glare of that fierce woman, and watched Skye instead as the guide silently dug into a hide case of some sort—a parfleche, he remembered from his reading—and pulled out a fist full of papers.

The guide squatted down and began totting up figures with a pencil. Obviously he could do figures, which was more than most of his class could manage.

"The horses and mules cost, in dollars, fifteen hundred

and forty-three," he rumbled. "I owe nine hundred fifty seven." He dug a nib pen and an inkpot from the parfleche, along with a blank sheet of foolscap, and drafted a note, poking his nib into the pot frequently. So the guide had written his own letters, Frazier thought. It astonished him. He'd been sure, from the fine copperplate, that someone competent had drafted the letters.

Wordlessly the guide stood and handed the draft to Frazier.

"Read this, Aristides, and check his figures against those bills. No doubt I've been rooked."

"If you can't prove that, don't say it," Skye said. "If you say it again, defend yourself."

"I say—" said Frazier, alarmed. This man might lay hand to him. "You're talking to a peer of England. You're asking for a whipping. Have you no manners? I suppose not."

Skye laughed. "It's Mister Skye, Lord Frazier."

"Oh my yes, I quite forgot!"

Diana chuckled.

Aristides Baudelaire studied the draft casually, and yawned. "I suppose it's quite proper, your lordship. It's for the balance, payable by Bullock, the sutler at Fort Laramie. Insured by bloody nose with fist as collateral. Maybe the bourgeois here will honor it."

"If you're satisfied, then we're done," Skye said, still looming like a volcano beside them.

Why was it, Lord Frazier thought, that the man could seem a blooming menace just standing still?

"Oh, I suppose," he said.

Skye's women beamed suddenly, and the old squaw hugged the rustic fiercely. "Now we go? We can go?" she asked, and Lord Frazier discovered a wetness on the woman's cheeks.

"Touching sight, eh, Diana?"

"Where's the scotch?" she retorted.

The guide never looked back. He tied a rope around the jaw of that appalling horse while it squealed and butted him, and then threw on a primitive pad saddle of some sort, and added other gear. Then he opened the gate and led the monster into the yard.

"Stand back, mate."

"I suppose he kicks, eh, Skye?"

"No, he kills."

With that, Barnaby Skye and his squaws threaded through the crates and barrels in the yard, and through the portal into the vast freedom beyond. The lunatic horse clacked its teeth and laid back its ears. As they plunged through the gates, the yard seemed to shrink and become alien, as if Skye's party had filled it with their very presence. It puzzled the viscount.

"I say, that's something for Alexandra's diaries," Frazier muttered. "Wherever she got to. She gets ethereal this time of day. Odd how that brute came so highly recommended, not once or twice, but by everyone. Even Chouteau himself, down in St. Louis. Everyone. Amazing. He's pulled the wool over a lot of eyes, I'd wager. Imagine Pierre Chouteau touting him. And Robert Campbell down there. And that Senator Benton—who's as wild a beast as this one, I hear. And all the rest. It's perfectly astonishing."

Only golden dust and a faint odor of buckskins lingered behind. Viscount Gordon Patrick Archibald Frazier peered about the shadowed yard, wondering what was missing. Something impalpable had departed, gone from the very air.

"Let's find that chap—the one who runs this place. We'll sup with him and his savage bride after all," Frazier said. "I'll want him to fetch us another bloke who knows this country. Aristides, go tell our chaps to try out the field kitchen, and we'll find whatever his name is, the one in command of this place, and tell him we'll favor him at his board."

Bedlam reigned in the plank-walled trading room. A dozen sweating clerks in shirtsleeves pried open crates and untied bales, shelving a year's trading stock. Over the next months this mound of goods would vanish through the small trading window, an aperture between the inner and outer gates of the fort that permitted only one or two tribesmen at a time to dicker.

The mountain of bright blankets and iron pots didn't astonish the viscount so much as the spectacle of the bourgeois—whatever his name was—in shirtsleeves, engaged in menial labor like his underlings. The chap scarcely understood his own position in life. Even as Frazier and his party gaped, clerks stuffed bold blue and red and green blankets, some of them bearing black stripes, onto plank shelves, while one pale clerk kept inventory and checked goods against cargo manifests. Another clerk lifted shining smoothbore fusils from a crate and stood them on a long rack. Others shelved bright ribbons and poured sacks of glass trade beads the size of peas into bins, and set shining knives, awls, axes, hatchets, lance points, cast-iron kettles, fish hooks, and hawk bells into cases.

He cornered the bourgeois as the man stuffed a bolt of striped cotton ticking onto the shelf.

"I say, my good man, we've changed our mind here. We'll sup with you shortly, eh?"

Clarke stood, winded, absorbing that, his glance taking in the viscount, Diana, and Baudelaire. "Well . . ." he muttered, uncertainly. "Viscount, I've told my lady—" He stopped. "I tell you what. I'll have her entertain you all. I can't attend. The trading season opens tomorrow, and this is the busiest moment of the year—we'll be at this almost to dawn. And then we'll have to roll out and start the ceremonies—a shot or two from the six-pounder, some speeches, some gifts to the chiefs, and all that. I beg your forgiveness, sir. But I'll send word over to Kakokima—my wife—"

"But, but, my good man. We need your counsel, eh? We've discharged that lout Skye and want you to fetch us another. Someone more tractable."

"You what?" Clarke was plainly astounded.

"Discharged him. Pitched him out on his ear. Worst ruffian I've ever seen."

Clarke paused, catching his breath. Around them swirled clerks toting trays of pocket mirrors and other gewgaws.

"There's more to this," Clarke said carefully. "Barnaby Skye doesn't suffer fools gladly."

"What? What? Are you saying I'm a—"

"I'm saying that Skye no doubt turned you down. He never risks his life and those of his wives on—well, certain types."

"Whatever. Find us another guide, eh? Any of your company men, eh? They all know the country. We'll pay his wages for you while he serves us, and you'll be ahead."

The man stood silently so long that Frazier wondered if he'd heard. "I don't have a man I'd spare you, Viscount."

"You've men all over here! If you can't spare an English-speaking one, we'll settle for one of these brute French. We speak the tongue."

"None I'd post to your party, sir. Now if you'll excuse me—"

"See here, now, chap. We need a guide."

"You had the best of all," Clarke said wearily.

"A dishonest scoundrel. Those horses—those ill-made nags—why, we were rooked, sir, rooked."

"Barnaby Skye's as good as his word, always, Viscount. And those horses he bought for you—they're something! They'll keep on kicking through trials that would kill domestic ones."

"Oh, pshaw, I know good horseflesh when I see it. Tell you what, my good man. We'll trade these to the company, and you sell us some real horseflesh, eh? We'll add a few quid to make it come out."

"Don't think you heard me, Viscount. Now if you'll excuse me—I'll send word to Kakokima . . ."

"Never mind, never mind. I can scarcely imagine sitting at table with a red woman of the plains. We'll go try out our kitchen and find a guide to place in our service. La-Barge should know of a dozen."

"By all means ask him," Clarke said, returning to his toil. "See me tomorrow afternoon if the company can help you further."

Viscount Frazier wasn't used to being dismissed, but he took it amiably, and they wandered through the narrow portal. Behind them, some clerk swung the heavy gates shut and bolted them, and the lord found himself locked out of civilization and on a treeless steppe with a thousand or two savages milling around conical buffalohide lodges. It alarmed him faintly until he spied the blessed *St. Ange* docked right there and manned by a doughty band of rough rivermen.

"Hudson's Bay would have treated us differently," sniffed Diana. "Where's the scotch?"

Lord Frazier found his entourage camped under the very palisades of the fort in an area that contained no lodges of the savages. He supposed the company insisted on some well defined distance between the skin teepees of the savages and its walls. Galitzin had organized the camp in his usual competent way, with the bright enameled carts parked to one side and tents erected in orderly rows within, most of them at the foot of the palisade. Several of his men had been detailed to roasting quarters of buffalo over two fires.

"Had a devil of a time finding firewood," Galitzin said. "With all zese savages about, we couldn't manage a stick. I finally bought some from some squaws."

The thought of so many savages camped around them made Lord Frazier uneasy. In the low sun he could see an endless forest of amber cones and black lodgepoles, pulsing with life, a pall of cookfire smoke hanging bluely over a huge village of Crees, Assiniboin, and heaven knew what others. He scarcely knew the tribes, in spite of all the bloody reading.

"Where's my lady, Galitzin?" he asked, not seeing Alexandra about.

"Why, she wandered through, poked around in your parlor-wagon zere, and I haven't seen her since."

No sooner had he asked than he spotted her running wildly toward them, weaving among the lodges west of the fort, clutching her yellow nankeen skirts and screaming. Trouble with the savages, he thought.

She stopped before them, gasping, her cheeks wet and her flaxen hair in wild disarray. "Chesterfield," she gasped, trying to catch her breath. "Where's poor little Chester-field?"

The lady's bulldog. It spent more time in bed with the viscountess than did Lord Frazier, and made twice as much gas.

"In a savage stewpot, I hope," the viscount said.

At which Lady Alexandra sobbed piteously.

"Here now, the pup's about somewhere. Galitzin, where's that pup?"

"Why right zere, gnawing on a buffalo rib, your lordship."

"Chesterfield!" she shrieked, and plunged toward the bewildered bulldog, snatching him from his meat.

Frazier waited patiently. One had always to be patient with Lady Alexandra, especially in her dreamy phases. "Tut tut, Alex. Whatever is troubling you?"

"They eat dogs!" she said, waving a slender arm vaguely. "I saw them. I saw a bulldog's head in a boiling stew, its poor eyes peering out at me. Oh, these bloody beasts!"

"The dogs or the savages, Alex?"

"The savages! Eating our dogs. How could they?"

"Why, it's convenient I suppose. Meat right there on their doorstep."

"Oh, Chester," she cooed. "I won't let them eat you. I'll have them before the magistrates." She carried the wiggling pup to Frazier's parlor-wagon, a bedroom of his own devising that he'd brought clear across the Atlantic, and vanished within.

"Galitzin, we've a little difficulty. That rude fellow who runs this place—can't remember the name—won't trade good horses for that rubbish back of the fort. And he won't spare a man for our service, either. These Americans!"

"I've been looking at the horses, your lordship. Zey seem sound and healthy, and as Skye said, their feet are a marvel. Hard and solid. Zey're small creatures, but I suspect the American mustang is more than it seems. I even see some Arab qualities in them, dished heads, short-coupled bodies. Ze Spaniards brought them here, you know. And you know how Arabs fare even in deserts!"

"You're simply excusing Skye and his vile beasts, Galitzin. But I suppose we're stuck with them."

"I made inquiry about pasture, your lordship, and found zere's none closer than two miles from here, with all the tribesmen and their ponies about. Not unless we cross the river, anyway. So I fed them some oats from our stores, to get them by, and tomorrow we'll be off. I've posted a night guard. They'll be safer here within sight."

"Capital, Boris. Now I've got to track down LaBarge— is he aboard that packet?—and have him post a guide to our service. I imagine any riverman will do who knows the land and where the buffalo are hiding. In fact, the dumber the better. Never say I learned nothing from dealing with Skye, Boris."

But when Frazier pressed Joseph LaBarge to find a suitable guide, the bearded master refused so violently that an ill-concealed tremor ran through him. In fact he seemed astounded that the viscount thought so little of Skye.

"Well, LaBarge, we'll go without one, then. It's simple enough. We'll follow the Yellowstone up to the geysers, and then come down here again. We don't need a guide when we have a river, eh?"

"Viscount Frazier—you need Skye."

"Oh, we know about the savages and all that. I've read the blooming books. I have trinkets to give them and thirty well-armed men. Now one more thing, LaBarge. Would you ferry us across the river tomorrow?"

"You need Skye," said LaBarge. "Yes, I'll ferry you to your doom, if I must."

Chapter 4

In the blue of dawn, Frazier's men wrestled the carts and wagons back aboard the *St. Ange* while LaBarge's crew built up steam. A mob of Cree and Assiniboin in gorgeous festival dress watched silently. Then the deckmen loosed the packet from its moorings and LaBarge's pilot steered it toward the south shore. No sooner had they cleared land than the fort's cannons boomed sharply, a Yankee flag scurried up a pole, and the fort's bourgeois and clerks, in black suits and shining boots, emerged for the ceremonies preceding the new trading season.

"They could scarcely wait for us to be off," Lord Frazier said to Baudelaire as they stood at the foredeck rail.

"The Americans are fond of money," Baudelaire replied.

On the barren south shore of the Missouri, just above its confluence with the Yellowstone, LaBarge's deckmen jury-rigged a gangway to a gentle bank. Frazier's men unloaded the carts and the wagon once again, then drove forty-two mustangs and mules to shore. Baudelaire settled with LaBarge—the price was ten pounds—while the party trooped down to the bank.

Galitzin set to work at once, shrewdly guessing which mustangs were saddle horses and which were trained to harness. The packet's whistle shrilled, and a thunderous vibration and splashing drew the ship out into the main channel. LaBarge waved amiably from the pilot house, and in a few minutes the *St. Ange* had crossed to the north shore.

Not even the hubbub of neighing horses and rattling harness and shouting men allayed the sudden dread that raced through Viscount Frazier as he stood on the hushed and alien shore. Across the wide Missouri lay the only safe harbor in a wild unknown land.

"I say, Aristides, I rather miss that vile place."

"We've brought our amenities with us, my lord. Would you and the esteemed ladies care for something cold and wet?"

"This shore. There's absolutely nothing. Even the Opposition fur post a few miles down is across the river. I have the strangest sensation, Aristides. As if swarthy men will rise out of the sagebrush and send arrows into us."

One by one, Galitzin and his men backed wild-eyed mustangs between the shafts of the carts and hitched them. Other men settled light English saddles over the bony backs of the little horses. One or two of the ugly brutes humped and bucked, but most accepted their burdens calmly.

"You see? Skye sold us better horses than they look, your lordship," said Galitzin. "And more than the forty we required. Two spares, including those mules. I can't fathom what ze mules do, but I fear zey're pack beasts. I've a notion to break them to harness, but I have to see how the teams zere pull your wagon first."

"Quantity for quality," the viscount quipped. "Spares. Have you found a nag suitable for myself? And Lady Diana?"

"Not yet," Galitzin said, returning to his labors.

"This place makes me shiver," Diana said.

"There's nothing amiss," Lord Frazier replied. He peered closely at distant red bluffs magnified by transparent air, at silent steppes lifting upward from the great river, at silvery bunchgrass. A raptor circled far off to the south; eagle or hawk, he thought. "It's because we don't have the fort's protection now," he said.

"I dreamed of riding a charger so fast he'd leave any savages far behind," she said. "But I suppose I'll be riding a mule."

In fact, that's what Lady Diana Chatham-Hollingshead ended up with for a mount. Galitzin discovered the four mules were saddle animals. The lady, wearing bold yellow riding attire with brown velvet trim, bounded up on a long-eared black beast, and howled. "Here we go," she said, steering the wily creature into reluctant figure eights.

Galitzin selected a good fifteen-hand dun for Lord Frazier, and then they were off. The viscount rode out to the right to see his gaudy caravan, bold scarlet and blue and green carts creaking over land where no wheeled vehicle had ever rolled. They made a gorgeous picture, gleaming enameled carts strung in a long line, each with his family coat of arms on the side, a stag's head caboshed on a barry-bendy ground. He watched the yellow parlor-wagon, driven by a coachman with a postilion riding to the left and forward, while his thin blonde viscountess peered from a window. Perfectly gaudy, he thought, against a desert land hued dun and gray and ochre, and a bleached blue heaven. It'd be a splendid hunt.

That afternoon they angled across a humped nose of land just above the confluence of the great rivers, and coiled down a sudden grade to the wooded bottoms along the west bank of the Yellowstone, which flowed due north just there. They found a well-worn trace along the bank and pushed south, up the turbid river, encountering no difficulty of any sort. With each passing mile, Lord Frazier grew more exuberant. For a day or two they'd travel up the river, getting his company accustomed to the daily drill. And after that, he'd hunt. He gazed keenly at the mysterious brown ridges, seeking the black giants of the North American plains, but saw none. He knew he would soon.

Behind him the carts rolled effortlessly, well organized by the valuable Colonel Galitzin. They wouldn't need a guide! They wouldn't stray far from the great river, going out or returning, though he wasn't sure just where the geysers were up near the headwaters. No matter. He'd find some savage to take them. A lot of them spoke a bit of English, he'd read. The lord counted it a blessing to be rid of that bounder the Americans thought so highly of. A blessing not only to his purse, but to his entire company.

Their riverbank passage took them on occasion through gloomy groves of cottonwoods, rising to majestic heights above them, leaving the earth littered with shaggy bark and branches. The stuff burned with a foul odor, he'd noted back at the fort, but seemed plentiful, and would fuel their cookfires all along the way. The shade of the giant trees cooled them, and kept the fierce sun—why did it burn into flesh so intensely at this high altitude?—off their faces and hands. Up on the rocky steppes he spotted yucca and prickly pear cactus, and down along the river grew chokecherry and hackberry, willow and box elder as well as the shimmering cottonwood trees. Along much of the high Missouri they'd spotted white-rumped antelope and mule deer, and an occasional elk as well, and now along the Yellowstone they found the same species in great abundance. Capital, he thought. They'd feast on venison tonight.

He summoned his armorer, Gravesend, and had a

Manton rifle brought him. The next stag, he thought, would turn into a roast. Bucks they called the males here. The next buck. The fine British steel felt sweet in his dry hands. He clasped it, and the burnished maple stock, with sensuous delight. Suddenly his dread lifted, the dark anxiety that had hung over him like the queen's displeasure since the fort had vanished behind them. Fondling a loaded piece fanged a man and drove fear out of his skull. He peered back and found his retainers subdued and fearful, just as he had been, and knew at once the solution.

"Gravesend," he commanded. "Hand out arms to those who want them. We'd best have a few in hand anyway, to deal with the savages."

"Very good, sir. I've those Colt Dragoon revolvers we purchased from the chap in Connecticut. They'll feel good tucked into a man's belt, I imagine."

"Tell the men they'll be docked if they lose them," the viscount cautioned. "You'll be counting them each evening, I trust, Gravesend?"

"Of course, sir."

No sooner were the weapons distributed than the viscount felt a great wave of relief among the men behind him. Their silence melded into hearty conversation and occasional laughter. Who needs a guide, he thought. A little common sense, a little muddling through, a little applied intelligence would see them along. Why hadn't he thought of that earlier? Why hadn't Galitzin?

They would make six or eight miles that day, enough for the first time out. He didn't want to gall those scruffy mustangs or chafe men's feet in new boots. Diana joined him, cussing her black mule, even though she had taken to admiring its huge rotating ears. She had her chased damascus fowling piece sheathed on her saddle.

"Let's fetch us our supper," he said.

"I'm game."

"That you are, and I'll cook you later," he rejoined. "But now we've got to get ahead and drop some stags."

"Bucks."

"Whatever. There you go, sounding like Skye."

He kicked his wiry dun into a bone-jarring canter, but she fell behind at once, cussing her dainty-footed black steed.

"I don't think he likes to run," she said. But she whipped the surly mule into a trot, and in twenty minutes the two were a mile or so ahead of the caravan, walking their mounts silently through a grassy park surrounded by giant trees.

"I've seen the harts all day, scampering one way or another. We'll find some, eh? I don't suppose you plan to shoot one with that piece of yours."

"Gordon, it's your piece that drops things," she said, laughing bawdily.

They were enjoying that, and working themselves toward some tiddlywinks in the grass, when eleven brown savages in breechclouts emerged from river brush, each of them pointing a bow with a nocked arrow at the viscount and his lady.

Old Victoria's spirits lifted when they left Fort Union behind them. All the time they'd lingered there, waiting for the strangers from across the great water, she'd felt a weight on her bony chest heavier than a cast-iron kettle. Her medicine, the magpie helper, had shown her clearly what would happen when those people from Mister Skye's own land employed him. It would be something worse than death for her, Mary, and Jawbone. Much worse. It had made her weep in the night, and resist her man for the first time ever. It had darkened each day and made each rising and setting of the sun a thing that took them closer to the doom that awaited them.

Magpie had come to her in the moon of falling leaves, long ago, strutting boldly about her as she drew water from the Platte River. Magpie had alighted directly on her head, and pecked her once. Then Magpie had flown away, far into a distant tree, and made raucous noises. Victoria had known at once Magpie had a thing to show her, so she had left Mister Skye and climbed a bluff and spent three suns fasting. Her vision had come with a frosty dawn that lay gray and icy over the naked land. They would hold Mister Skye like an eagle with clipped wings, hold him among them and then take him far across the waters to the land where he was born, and keep him there. Keep him in a dark place until he died, longing for his family, for his sits-beside-him wife, his Mary, his medicine horse, Jawbone, and the feel of an open land without fences about him. And that is how life would go on, not only for Mister Skye, far away, but for Victoria, who would never hug her man again, never feel him warm beside her in the buffalo robes, in their own lodge; and the same for Mary of the Snakes, who would never again see Mister Skye. And all the worse for Jawbone, who would pine for Mister Skye, not eat, not drink, not run over the hills, and die.

All these things she saw, and knew they were more terrible than death because they were a living death without end. She could not tell Mister Skye she had seen this; he would scoff, and say it was only a phantasm and not the real world where the sun rose and set. But she knew anyway, knew Magpie had shown her the turning of the circle, and so the old woman had slid into a deep mourning, a widowhood that lacked only death.

But now she witnessed a miracle. Here was her man, Mister Skye, riding Jawbone out of Fort Union, leaving these countrymen of his behind him. He rode through the portal of the fort, and she felt some tension within her ebb away, as if she was leaving a prison behind her. Outside, Mister Skye peered into the lavender twilight of the June night and turned Jawbone east. His women followed. He rode straight past the encampment of the Britons, past those bright wagons and men in identical dark britches and shirts, past the thin blonde woman in the squash-colored cotton dress. The woman waited for him to stop, to say something, to become their guide again, but he didn't. They gawked at him as he rode past, saying nothing, keeping all their dark thoughts to themselves. And Victoria felt joy.

She knew where he was going, and followed behind gladly. He steered the terrible horse gently through the lodges of her people's enemies, the Assiniboin, while the people around them stared at him and Victoria and Mary. They all knew of Mister Skye, and of his medicine horse. Then at last they came to the end of the lodges and he rode eastward across barren clay stripped of every blade of buffalo grass, and finally turned north up a broad coulee with broken sandstone ledges along its periphery. Mister Skye's two black pack mules and Victoria's and Mary's ponies would be there, along with their lodge and possessions, guarded by two Cree boys who were eager to serve the man with the terrible medicine.

Mister Skye found them and the ponies, and paid the boys with a packet of precious gunpowder and six lead balls apiece, a handsome reward. The boys grinned, and danced happily back toward the fort two miles distant.

"Well, ladies, we're far from home and unemployed," he said, a gleam in his obscure blue eyes.

"I am glad!" Victoria cried, speaking up for the first time in many days.

He eyed her affectionately, aware of her feelings. "Is that your medicine barking at me?" he asked amiably.

For an answer she beelined to him as he clambered down from the blue roan, and hugged her man fiercely.

"That's more than medicine," he said, hugging her. "Whatever was troubling you, it's past, old lady."

"I don't like this place," she said, her voice muffled by his pungent elkskin shirt. "It is the place of our enemies. The river Absaroka come here, but not my people, not the Kicked-in-the-Bellies. Let's go to Absaroka, Mister Skye. Let's swim the Big River and go. Right now."

Something of her terror lingered in her and she could think only of flying, of breaking camp and riding down to the great river and making a raft of their lodgepoles and swimming their horses across, away from those people from across the sea.

"Right now!" she cried. "Right now!"

"Belay yourself, Victoria. I've a mind to do something else. We haven't a dime in our accounts with the colonel now. Gave the whole amount back. It's a hard month of travel back to Fort Laramie—bad time with war parties running. And when we get back there, end of July or so, it'll be too late to pick up a client."

She listened quietly, wondering as she always did why Mister Skye needed clients, wondering why he guided whitemen at all, when all he needed was a little powder and ball, which he could buy with robes she and Mary tanned. They could live out their days with her people in the heart of Absaroka, the most beautiful land at the middle of the earth.

"But maybe we can fetch a client over at Fort William," he went on. "Opposition boat isn't in yet. Who knows who'll be looking for a guide when it comes? I'll see what Joe Picotte has to say. We'll camp there a few days anyway, until the boat comes. It's the one chance we've got for a client this season."

The Harvey, Primeau and Company adobe trading post lay down the Missouri a mile or so below the confluence of the rivers. Only a half hour's ride. The companies opposing the giant American fur had come and gone, she knew. The great Rocky Mountain Fur Company had tried it; later, Fox and Livingston. But none had weathered the ruthless competition of Pierre Chouteau's Upper Missouri Outfit.

"Mister Skye," she pleaded. "I still got damn bad feelings. We got to go away from here."

He patted her affectionately. "One quick stop for a talk with Picotte."

She turned silently to her packing, not liking it a bit. That sinister vision still haunted her, piercing every corner of her soul and aching old body, not leaving her as it should now that he'd escaped from the ones with the bright carts.

They left in a blue dusk with a green streak of light still lingering in the northwest: Mister Skye, massive and comforting on Jawbone, his senses reading the twilight; Mary on her light gold pony, young and vibrant; old Victoria, hunched over her rail-thin bay mare; and the two pack mules, each carrying a heavy burden in panniers on pack-saddles.

With each step eastward, Victoria's spirits revived. She wanted distance and more distance between Mister Skye and his childhood people, before they came with snares and brass collars to capture him like a black bear in an iron cage. They rode a short distance along the shore on a well-hammered trace, and soon the adobes of the opposing post loomed up at them. This one had fewer lodges gathered about it, but across the flats were eighty or a hundred, the bands of chiefs who'd been successfully wooed by Picotte or Harvey, usually with extravagant gifts of tobacco and whitemen's suits or blue soldier uniforms, which the chiefs loved as a mark of their warrior status.

The towering plank gates had been shut for the night here too, but Mister Skye's sharp hammering brought young Picotte himself, a lantern in hand.

"Want company, Joe?" Mister Skye asked at the eye peering through the cracked door.

"Barnaby Skye! Sure do, you old coon. I haven't a thing to wet your whistle, but the *Mary Blane*'s overdue. It's above Fort Clark, and that's all I know. They're badly overloaded."

"That's what I heard," said Mister Skye. "I'm looking for a client, if any are wanting a guide."

"Well, come in and we'll palaver," the bourgeois said.

A few minutes later they were ensconced in one of the guest rooms, and the horses and mules were safely corraled in a corner of the yard.

"We're out of coal oil and candles, except what's in that lamp, so I guess we'll just talk in the dark," Picotte said.

Which suited Victoria fine. She loved the soft June night with its restless, eddying air.

"I'm busted," said Mister Skye to his host. "We turned down some porkeaters that would have got us butchered."

"I know about them. Went over myself this afternoon to gawk at those carts and saw how the stick floats. I think maybe you done right, Mister Skye."

"It didn't help my Big Dry any, Joe. Are you sure you don't have—"

"We can't bring the stuff into Indian country, Mister Skye."

Picotte laughed. Mister Skye bellowed. In a moment the pair of them were roaring and bawling like sore-toothed grizzlies, and Victoria glared at the two giants, not understanding whitemen.

Her dark vision refused to leave her mind.

Chapter 5

Savages. Lord Frazier peered wildly about him, and knew he would die. A great sob erupted from him. He, the seventh viscount, a peer of the realm, would feel arrows pierce deep, deep through him, through his vital parts, and that would be the last he'd ever know.

Beside him, Diana burst into tears. He could no longer choke back his own, and that added to his terror and shame. These savages wore paint, greasy black and white chevrons across their wide cheeks, slashes of vermilion on their foreheads. A war party. He knew that much from his readings. And he would die. He flinched, feeling the arrows pierce his tender flesh even before they were loosed.

"I'm going to die," Diana cried. "They'll kill us. Talk to them. I'll do anything, anything—"

Resignation flooded through Lord Frazier, and he felt himself sagging in the saddle, his soul half departed from his doomed body.

One of the savages, a six footer with his jet hair in two braids and a single eagle feather stuck at a rakish angle in his tightly bound hair, walked toward them, the arrow in his drawn bow never wavering from Frazier's chest.

Here it comes, he thought wildly. Not even time to make peace with God. Here it comes!

The savage was a giant, with shoulders as wide as an ox, arms like mizzen-masts, and hands the lord knew could rip him out of his saddle and pulverize his soft flesh in an instant.

The savage spoke in a rumbling voice. Harsh, peremptory words the viscount couldn't fathom. Oh, for a translator, one of these rustics who knew the tongue of this one—whatever tribe he came from. Frazier realized he hadn't the faintest idea which tribe. The savage barked something and the viscount gaped, utterly lost.

Then the savage motioned violently, his arms describing harsh arcs, and this time Frazier understood. He eased out of his saddle, trembling, and slid toward the grass, almost collapsing because his legs refused to prop him. So they'd march him off to a tree and fill him with arrows, he thought.

The savage barked at Diana, some explosion of words, and she crept down, weeping all the while. "They'll have their way with me," she cried.

The leader herded them away from the dun pony and the mule, and then several savages pounced at the animals, grabbing reins, snatching at the sheathed rifle and shotgun, exclaiming at the beauty of the burnished stocks and chased barrels and locks. Swiftly they probed everything else, the scrimshawed powder horns, the pouches of shot and wadding, the mercury fulminate caps, the lord's splendid hunting knives—

The knives. Surely they would scalp him, he thought, his terror ballooning. They'd grab his sandy hair and run a knife brutally across his forehead, and over his ears and around the back of his head, then pull violently; and he'd feel his hair popped from him and his skull naked to air, and a ghastly pain.

And Diana. They'd lift her glowing chestnut locks while she screamed, and they'd run the tip of a knife around her skull, an act so disfiguring she'd go berserk, then leave her heaped on the ground, her remaining flesh bleeding.

The tension gripped him so severely that his body ceased to work; his lungs refused to pump, his heart pulsed faster and faster until its rhythm disappeared and he felt only a hum in his chest and a deepening paralysis. Death, then.

But it didn't come. Not quite yet. The leader, the giant savage, cat-footed to Diana and snatched her hat from her head, exclaiming in his strange tongue at the creamy ostrich plumes curving majestically back from the brown crown. He drew a plume through his fingers, exclaiming, grunting, waving this strange trophy before the others, who flocked around to see this exotic thing.

Just then yet another warrior, this one on a spotted gray pony with chalky handprints pressed into its chest and stifles, rode out of the river brush. He wore only a breech-clout, like the others, and bore the scars of battle on his bronzed body: long puckered scars slashing across his ribs and arms and creasing one calf. This one spoke something sharp, and pointed back on the river trail. Lord Frazier knew at once this one had discovered the caravan, perhaps two miles back, and was telling the others.

The caravan! If only he could survive until it arrived, until his thirty men and his Cossack colonel could drive these beasts away! But he knew it would never happen. A half hour separated him from that plodding column. Still, he had to try something, anything . . .

"Do you chaps speak English?" he asked, his voice squeaky and unnatural. Oh why couldn't he act like a proper Englishman, like a lord, like a peer of the realm?

They stared, saying nothing. If anyone understood, he didn't reveal it. Frazier desperately wished he'd learned the finger language of the plains. He'd read that all these tribes could talk with it, and most of the rough fur trappers and traders knew it too. But he lacked even a rudimentary knowledge. He'd been hasty. Oh, for a guide. For any brute who could placate these savages! Oh, for a company of kilted pipers, screaming out the fierce bloody howl of a hundred bagpipes, a sound that sent shivers through any auditor, civilized or barbaric.

The leader took hold of Viscount Frazier's fine knife, with its Sheffield steel blade glinting in the dappled light, and approached him.

It's coming, my own blade into my bowels, he thought wildly. The savage stopped just before the peer of England, smiling faintly.

"Anything. I'll give you anything!" the viscount croaked.

But the warrior simply motioned. He wanted the viscount to do something, but Frazier couldn't fathom what. Then the savage flicked the knife at a button, terrifying the lord. Others of these brutes swirled around Diana, fingering her velvet riding habit while she whimpered piteously.

"I'll bloody well have you whipped," he cried.

The savage patted the lord's hunting jacket, a plum-colored tweed with leather elbow patches and sleeves, and motioned.

The coat, the coat. The brute wanted his coat. The lord swiftly shed it with trembling arms that wouldn't work right, and handed it to the beast. Lady Diana fared no better. Two of them wrestled her beautiful velvet coat off her while she shrieked and struggled.

"They're attacking me!" she cried.

He couldn't help that. He watched, frightened, as they wrestled her to the grass and pulled her velvet split skirts off, leaving her in white drawers, and danced around with the handsome skirt. Next they tugged at her soft boots, of finest English leather, and popped them off while she groaned, awaiting her fate.

The powerful leader slid Frazier's jacket on, but found it too small, and pulled it off. He pointed at the lord's shiny boots, and Frazier sat in the grass tugging them off. The savage examined them curiously and tossed them aside, and pointed at the lord's britches.

"Not my pants," he cried, but he had no choice. The Sheffield blade waved ominously under his nose.

Moments later he sat naked in the grass, as white as a fish belly, while the savages swiftly gathered everything he had possessed and divided the plunder among themselves. Beside him huddled Diana, equally bereft, but with flesh not so pale.

"They're looking at me," she muttered.

Lord Frazier thought wickedly that on other occasions his lady rakehell would not only have been amused, but probably would have approved and been eager for whatever came next. But now she clutched herself with arms that hid little, and sobbed.

The one on horseback barked a sharp command and the savages fled with their booty, leading away the horse and mule as they vanished silently into brush.

Lord Frazier gaped. Alive. He and Diana lived.

But she had spotted something, and her pointed finger steered him to an awful spectacle. On the sunny bluff above stood a line of horses, more than he could count, scores of them, and on each pony sat a brown warrior, some wearing little more than a breechclout and feather. Several others wore magnificent war bonnets of eagle feathers, with long tails of feathers reaching clear to the ground at the feet of their restless ponies. Frazier shuddered. Never had he witnessed, or imagined, such barbaric splendor. He was too rattled to count, but knew instinctively he saw hundreds, hundreds of savages on ponies, bearing bows and arrows, rifles, lances, and lethal-looking warclubs. Enough well armed warriors to overwhelm his little caravan, toiling along back there somewhere.

He stared, frozen, expecting the crack of rifles and the hoarse cries of battle. Instead, a leader, one of the bonneted ones, lifted an arm, and the whole column of savages wheeled westward, away from the river bottoms and out of sight.

Lord Frazier felt terror drain from him like ale from a keg. Alive. Both of them. Even if the devils had snatched everything they possessed, and he and Diana were as bare as Adam and Eve in this paradise. She grinned at him from a face wet with tears, and he marveled at her pluck.

"Go fetch me some clothes, Gordon, and don't let those bastards see me. I'll have them whipped if they stare."

"But I can't walk up to the carts like this—I can't even walk at all on these sticks!"

"You'll have to, Gordon. You can wear a leaf or two if you wish." She laughed wildly, her guffaws sounding like sobs.

He rose and began his march to the rear, mustering whatever dignity he could manage, knowing he'd bloody well find that Skye and tell him to guide them.

Under a flat gray sky that threatened a drizzle, Mister Skye worked downwind of a small herd of buffalo, about ten miles from Fort William. He and his ladies would make meat while they waited for the *Mary Blane* and whatever it might bring for a client. They'd spotted the herd to the north, black dots grazing a still-green swale in an endless, empty land, and had hastened eastward at once because the beasts were directly downwind.

Victoria rode her bay pony beside Skye, while Mary herded the two packmules which had been brought along to cart much of the meat and the summer hides back to the fort. Victoria's spirit lay as gray as the low clouds. She didn't want to be here in this land of the Lakotah, Cree and Assiniboin, her people's enemies. The blackness that had settled over her with her medicine vision refused to lift, even though the people from Mister Skye's land across the waters had left. She wondered at it, why her spirits remained as dark as before. She squinted angrily at horizons and ridges, seeking out menace along them, but didn't find any. The land slumbered through a chill, sullen afternoon without even a wolf or coyote to disturb it.

She'd resigned herself to his will. She always felt proud to be the sits-beside-him wife of Mister Skye, and wherever he went, there would she go also. But she'd never known a time when her heart lay so heavy within her, and

she glanced at her man often, wondering when he would
be snatched away from her forever.

He circled around the herd and then approached from
the southeast, well out of the wind. They topped a ridge
and spotted the small herd grazing quietly two hundred
yards ahead, and hastened back down the slope, keeping
out of sight. Mister Skye drew his Hawken from its beaded
elkskin sheath, gathered his tied shooting sticks and possibles, and crept back up the slope and over it on hands and
knees while Victoria waited in the humming quiet. A few
moments later the Hawken boomed once, and not again.
Mister Skye rarely wasted a shot, she knew. His head rose
above the ridge and he motioned them forward. She and
Mary topped the shoulder and saw a downed cow, still
spasming, and the remaining buffalo trotting away.

She and Mary set to work at once, cutting out the tongue
and peeling back the hide. She wanted a whole hide this
time, not a split, to repair their lodge, so Mister Skye and
Jawbone helped them roll the big cow over so they could
peel hide from its underside. They cut out the humpmeat
along the boss ribs, and the backfat, and the valuable sinews that ran down the back. Then they sawed tender meat
from the front quarter, until they had all that the two mules
could carry. They'd feast at the fort that night, she knew.
And she'd have a light hide to scrape and tan and sew into
the lodge, and a worn, smoke-cured hide from the lodge
to turn into fine moccasins that would turn water.

But she didn't rejoice at this bounty as she normally did.
She labored silently beside Mary, who had learned not to
try to cheer Victoria while they lingered in this land of
their enemies. She would not be cheered. Done at last, they
abandoned the red carcass to the two coyotes and circling
raptors that had watched and argued, and rode through a

somber afternoon to the fort, Victoria's spirits as gloomy as the low heavens.

She knew, even before they walked their ponies through the massive gates, that Mister Skye was lost. Her medicine told her so; a powerful knowing so intense it racked her small body until she hurt badly. But Mister Skye knew none of it, and steered Jawbone easily into the trading post.

She saw them at once, the two who had come from across the great water, whose names were almost unpronounceable to her: Boris Galitzin and Aristides Beaudelaire, standing beside the factor, Joe Picotte.

"Ah, there you are, Skye," said Galitzin. "We've been looking. Zey told us at the other post you were here."

"It's Mister Skye."

"Yes. I forget. We've urgent business, Mister Skye. We've had a little brush with some savages—not the body of us, actually, but his excellency—in which zey made off with his horse and embarrassed him. He's gone quite daffy about it, though we scarcely see what all the trouble is. At any rate, sir, he sent us back at once with his commission. He wants you and your ladies to guide him at any price, under your terms."

"No."

Victoria heard Mister Skye's resolute reply, and dared to hope a bit. In all her days, she'd never stared at other mortals with such pain and dread.

"Ah, I have a note from his lordship." The colonel dug into the pocket of his new hunting jacket and produced a scrap of foolscap. "It says you are to be in charge."

Mister Skye read it, frowning, while Victoria tried to read his thoughts.

"And this, of course, sir. He's returning your draft on Bullock's account," Galitzin said.

Mister Skye took it. He seemed lost in thought.

"Let us go to Absaroka at once, Mister Skye. My medicine helper speaks."

He turned toward her, his obscure eyes searching her brown ones with an intensity she'd never experienced. "Aye, I've always heeded that, Victoria . . ."

His very gentleness saddened her.

"We're camped a dozen miles away, on the west bank of the Yellowstone," Baudelaire said hastily.

"What happened?"

Baudelaire smiled amiably. "Why, a minor fright. His lordship rode ahead with the lady, and a few savages stopped him and took a few things. He felt the need of someone who could translate."

Mister Skye didn't answer for some while. "What do you wish, sir?" he asked the man in the prim black suit.

"It'd be helpful. Of course it was all exaggerated. His lordship took it too seriously."

Mister Skye turned toward the colonel. "Galitzin. You're a colonel, used to command. How do you feel bearing a note that places me over you?"

"I don't know that it does, Skye. You'll be dealing with the savages is all."

"You've both made light of what happened."

"Why, we both think Lord Frazier's quite unbalanced, and calmer heads ought to prevail. Now if you'd rather not, we'll head back and tell him that you've turned us down, and—"

"I'll talk to him."

Victoria felt herself go faint. She glanced at Mary, who stood tautly, taking in all this too. Already she felt a kind of widowhood settle over her, saw in her head the vision she'd had of Mister Skye being carried off, never to return to her aims. Her man stared at her unblinkingly, and for once she couldn't meet his eye because her own spirit groaned inside of her.

"I'm sure you know the tribe that stole the horse from the viscount, Colonel?"

"We haven't the faintest idea, Skye. His lordship says that the chiefs wore eagle-feather bonnets with long tails of feathers that reached clear to the hooves of their ponies."

Lakotah, thought Victoria at the description of her people's ancient enemy.

"Sioux," said Skye. "I wonder which." He stared at the two men solemnly. "You've not told me everything. You've made light of this, although I imagine the viscount came to the edge of death. Something changed his mind about the value of my services. You've come here on his instruction, but you're doing your duty half-heartedly, eager for me to refuse. You both are disloyal to your employer, then."

"Why—why—you've put a twist on it," said Galitzin. Baudelaire merely smiled and nodded.

"I hear," said Skye.

Victoria loathed them both, but she, knew Mister Skye had discerned their true nature and would not be fooled.

"We'll go talk to Frazier presently," he said. "You go ahead and tell him how it went here. How truly you described his ordeal to me, and how hard you struggled to persuade me."

Baudelaire nodded and smiled.

"—And I'll correct matters when we get there," Skye added.

Baudelaire smiled blandly again, but Galitzin glared.

Victoria knew Mister Skye was politely calling them

liars, and worse, disloyal men. They enraged her. No warrior of the People would betray a sacred trust like these whites.

"Oh, Colonel Galitzin. Your safety doesn't depend on rifles, but on diplomacy. Any of the tribes can gather well-armed warriors by the thousand, and form them into the best light cavalry in the world. Perhaps you were unaware of that. Surely your men are. One reckless shot, and they'll never see England again."

"I'm sure your melodramatics will have their effect on Lord Frazier, Skye, and you'll be our general."

Victoria watched them trot out of the fort, and knew Mister Skye had accepted. He would have to deal with those conniving men all the time he guided them. Dourly, she watched him give some of the meat to Picotte as a gift, and then they took off. They would reach the viscount's camp four hours after Picotte's engagés ferried them across the Missouri. She'd lost, but she knew she would never speak of it again. In the few days remaining of her life with Mister Skye, she would watch over him fiercely, as she always did. But she would not sleep in his lodge. Mister Skye's lodge would be dark.

Chapter 6

When Mister Skye, Mary, and Victoria rode into the camp the Britons had made on a grassy flat along the Yellowstone, Viscount Frazier saw them through different eyes. Barbaric splendor, he thought, discovering safety and comfort in the guides he had supposed he could do without. Mister Skye and his women had not followed the river trace at all, but had emerged as silently as stalking panthers out of a long coulee above the camp.

Galitzin and Baudelaire had returned hours earlier, telling him they'd found Skye and had engaged him. They seemed amused about it, and Lord Frazier scented mockery in Baudelaire's attitude. Both of them had treated the episode as a bloody joke. But it hadn't been funny. He'd limped along toward the caravan, waving a box elder branch before him like a figleaf in the Uffizi Gallery, the rubble along the way biting at his naked feet. He'd worried too about leaving Diana behind, fearing the savages would return and diddle her. Then at last, as the caravan hove into sight, snaking through a grove of looseknit cottonwoods, he'd dodged behind a hackberry bush.

"Galitzin!" he had cried, waving a bare arm and peering around the tree.

Galitzin had reined up, stared, and snickered. "Would your excellency like me to hold up the column while you and the lady, ah—"

"Galitzin, the savages! They stripped us and stole our duds. Go fetch clothing for Lady Diana and me, eh? And stop the men. I'll—I'll have words with you if you let this be known."

It had taken Galitzin an hour to stop the column, fetch clothing, and rescue the viscount and Diana, who'd grown snappish while slapping deer flies behind a chokecherry thicket. The story had raced through the column in spite of Lord Frazier's interdict. Everywhere the louts he'd engaged were smirking. And no one simpered more than Baudelaire, who'd hinted that maybe his lordship's horses had drifted off while his lordship was enjoying the attentions of his lady.

Not even his own Alexandra believed him. "Gordon,

dear, you shouldn't indulge yourself in the middle of the morning," she'd lectured.

But now Skye approached, some palpable barbaric force emanating from his solid body. It was that ineluctable presence again, the thing the viscount had felt at the fort. The man seemed to own this wild land and traveled through it like some lord of the wilderness, that silk top hat jauntily perched over his shoulder-length hair and that black Hawken cradled like a firstborn in his massive arms. Gladly, gladly, would Lord Frazier entrust his life to such a man.

They halted before him, Skye and his women, the old one glaring ominously straight through him, and the two pack mules, one dragging a travois of lodgepoles.

"Will you meet my terms, sir?" Skye asked without so much as a hello.

"Gladly, Mister Skye. I've had a scrape that taught me a bit."

"Did it teach the rest?"

"Lady Chatham-Hollingshead, yes."

"Tell me exactly what happened."

Odd how the man addressed him without a *please* or a *your lordship*. "Ah, later, eh?" he replied, peering about at Alexandra, Diana, Galitzin, and Baudelaire, who smirked beside him near the yellow parlor-wagon. But Skye's stare, striking him like pikes, changed his mind, at least a bit.

"Ah, the lady and I rode ahead a mile or two, intending to shoot a stag—ah, buck—and all of a sudden there they were. Savages! A swarm of them. They snatched everything, ah, quite everything, and rode off. And up on the bluffs were a whole army of them, more than I could count."

"What did they take?"

"Horse. Mule. My Manton. Her Purdey. Ah, the equipage."

Mister Skye said nothing for a moment, apparently pondering it. Then, "Your story seems to amuse people."

"That's right!" snapped Diana. "The beasts made off with every rag we wore. I thought they were going to do me, but they didn't."

"You sound disappointed, Diana," said Alexandra.

Lady Chatham-Hollingshead laughed. "Too many for me, but maybe not for you."

"Mister Baudelaire and Colonel Galitzin appear to take the matter lightly," Skye said.

"Not at all. It's a serious matter," protested the colonel.

Baudelaire smiled blandly.

"I assure you, Skye, it happened, and I never want to see a dozen drawn bows, a dozen arrows pointing at my middle, ever again. Not ever."

Skye nodded. "Painted?"

"Terrible white and black stripes, sir, and red on their foreheads."

"You told Galitzin the chiefs wore bonnets with a long feather tail?"

"Yes."

"Probably Sioux, then. They do that. Maybe Cheyenne who take their ways from the Sioux. They're after the Assiniboin that were trading at the fort. You're lucky."

Galitzin nudged Baudelaire with his elbow, and the viscount caught it. "I'm afraid, Skye, some of my men don't quite believe me—or you."

Mister Skye nodded, and fixed that unblinking stare at the colonel. "You'll learn the hard way, if you live," he said. "All right then, I'll take you. But if you and your men don't heed my counsel, I'll leave you to your fate. That must be understood."

The man sat his battered yellow-eyed stallion, waiting.

The viscount nodded. "Done."

"Colonel?"

"Whatever my private wishes may be, I am in his excellency's service," Galitzin said.

Mister Skye looked faintly amused, and turned his gaze toward Baudelaire, a question in his eyes.

"I am at the service of all masters," the viscount's aide purred. "Set me to a task, Mister Skye, and I will be delighted to do you the favor. Yes?"

Skye grinned suddenly, startling the viscount with the warmth of it. "Well then, we'll be off in the morning. Buffler wherever we find them. Good elk, royal elk, along the river. Pronghorn, mule deer, coyotes—bear. Even an old silvertip grizzly now and then."

But Lord Frazier wasn't really listening. He gaped at the younger squaw, Mary, astounded at her exquisite beauty. Skye's younger woman had flesh the color of honey and peaches, smooth and unblemished. Her face formed a wide oval, with an exotic cast from large, almond eyes set above prominent cheekbones. Her slim figure, barely visible beneath a soft tan doeskin blouse, seemed voluptuous, and the brown calves bared by riding astride her pony were smooth and young and perfectly formed, disappearing beneath her hiked red calico skirts. Why hadn't he noticed her before, he wondered. A peach, a plum, a dusky fruit! A lady made for wooing! A savage damsel—dame, he corrected himself—awaiting his attentions! He had to have her. Surely he could woo her, this exquisite child of the wilds—Snake was she? Yes, Snake. An enchanting Shoshone, snared like some bird of paradise by this brute of a guide who sat his evil beast before him. Woo her, a simple task: he a lord of England, and she a simple child of nature. He'd set Baudelaire to it . . . Ah, Baudelaire. The chap had his uses even if he was French-born.

Skye surveyed the orderly camp that Galitzin had laid out with military insight, seemed satisfied, and turned that blue roan of his into the twilight. He stopped well outside of the camp's perimeter; there Skye and his two squaws slid off their mounts and in the lavender dusk made their own camp, placing some unspoken distance between themselves and these lords and ladies of England.

"Baudelaire," whispered the peer of England. "I want the young one, called Mary."

The frock-coated man smiled, saying nothing.

"You'll give us all cooties," snapped Diana.

"You have such evil habits," said Alexandra.

Lord Frazier laughed softly. "Despicable," he agreed. "Hurry, Aristides. Begin tomorrow. Even tonight. There's a reward in it for you."

"Mister Skye'll kill you," Diana said.

The viscount hadn't thought of that, and it disturbed him. But not for long. What could the brute do, after all? With thirty retainers watching his every move? Nonetheless, he resolved to be cautious. Baudelaire watched him expectantly, nodded, and smiled.

Mysterious Baudelaire, he thought. The man smiled even when being eaten alive by mosquitos. Which in fact were biting the viscount's tender hide. He swatted unhappily at them, wondering if the ferocious things would torment him the whole trip. Some of his retainers had gathered downwind of a campfire, coughing in the smoke they hoped would drive the things off. But his parlor wagon was armed with netting.

"Good night, my little ladies," he said, his voice an invitation.

"I think I want to visit Skye's camp," said Lady Diana.
"He's such a manly animal."

Mary wished she could go out with Victoria each day,
but her task was to herd the mules for Mister Skye and stay
close to the whitemen's carts. Often she rode alone on her
lineback dun pony, driving the mules before her and keeping a sharp eye out for the dangers these blind whitemen
never seemed to see—except Mister Skye. He had Indian
eyes. The big dark mules didn't need much herding. One
drew a travois of lodgepoles, with their small cowhide
lodge anchored to the poles. The other packed the rest of
their things in panniers on a packsaddle her man had made
from canvas duck.

Mister Skye usually rode well ahead on the river trail,
often with the soldier chief called Galitzin and the great
chief, Frazier. His name and title confused her. Sometimes
he was Lord Frazier, sometimes Viscount Frazier, and he
had other names too. But she'd never heard him called Viscount Gordon, or Lord Gordon. So each day she rode
alone, keeping her own counsel, usually just a little ahead
of the carts and the big yellow wagon. That was her duty,
and it didn't occur to her to complain to Mister Skye, her
man, about her tasks. When they camped each evening she
swiftly erected the lodge by herself, intuitively putting it
up in the best place to shed rain water, feed Jawbone, hide
the fire, and minimize surprises from woods and brush
and dangerous coulees. At Mister Skye's insistence, it
was always a little distance from the camp of the ones from
far across the waters.

She didn't really trust them. She'd been influenced by Victoria, who'd turned silent and angry in the presence of these odd white people. Victoria had confided her medicine vision to Mary—the magpie's vision that had foretold what was to come: these people would take Mister Skye away, far away across the waters, and neither she nor Mary would ever see their man again. She believed it, and watched the Englishmen closely, trying to discover the secret things inside their minds that would make them do what Victoria saw in her vision.

That terrified Mary, but still she could see not even a hint of such evil in these strange ones. Instead they treated her politely, though some of the men gazed at her too long, with eyes that told her they wanted her. She ignored that. Among her own Shoshones she'd been celebrated for her beauty. How they all doted on it, exclaiming about it to her mother and father. Many of the young men had courted her, leaving small bone rings where she would find them and playing their love flutes outside her lodge, to steal her heart. But after her eighteenth winter, Mister Skye had visited among them with his sits-beside-him wife, and he had eyes for her. She scarcely dared believe her good fortune: every one of all the Peoples of the plains knew this great white man, his medicine horse and strong wife.

She'd been named Blue Dawn in the tongue of her people, but after Mister Skye had heaped many good things, blankets and rifles and powder and shot and knives and calico and ponies, at the lodgedoor of her rejoicing father, he had taken her to his own lodge and she became Mary in his tongue. He had told her it was a name of great honor among white people. She'd rejoiced in Mister Skye's love. Old Victoria had rejoiced, too, to have another woman to help with the endless toil of making camp, tending ponies, gathering breadroots, wild onions, and camass, brain-tanning robes and hides, and keeping them all in good summer and winter moccasins. She adored the other wife, and rejoiced in old Victoria's company.

Now she wished she could ride with Victoria, far off on the high broken prairie above the river bluffs. Victoria could slide through open country unobserved, like a spirit-fox, seeing but not being seen. And so she always scouted for Mister Skye, off forward and to one side or the other, like cat's whiskers, probing for whatever lay just over a rise or hidden in a swale. Each day at dawn, Victoria sternly tightened the small pad saddle over her bony mare and rode out into the gray sea of land, her disapproval of this hunt and these strange people plain to Mary and Mister Skye, who watched with sadness as Victoria rode away. It was not good, Mary thought, but nothing could be done about it. Victoria and Mister Skye disagreed about these Britons, and this time he was ignoring her medicine.

They'd found no buffalo after three days of travel up the Yellowstone, but Mary knew they would, and then the viscount would shoot some, and they'd all enjoy great red feasts. What strange people they were! The great chief had two men who did nothing but cook. Another who did nothing but walk beside the cart carrying all those spirits, and pour them for the lord and his ladies. And another who was going to tan hides like a woman, and clean and tan the heads of beasts too, and fill a cart with them to take back across the waters. Back there he was going to make bones from wood, and stuff the hides full of his wooden bones and straw and sew them up. And still another man did nothing but look after the lord's guns and walk beside a whole cart full of them.

The one called Baudelaire, who were nothing but black, like a warrior coming back to a village after a great victory, often walked beside her as she rode. He seemed friendly, but she didn't like him much. She didn't dislike him, either. She watched him catch up with her once again, this time riding a pony. He wasn't much of a rider, and bounced painfully as his horse trotted toward her. But soon he caught up and settled his mount into a fast walk beside her, smiling gently but saying nothing. She liked that in him, not talking all the time. Some white people never knew silence and the seeing and hearing of the world.

"Well, our beautiful Mary herds the mules all alone again," hc said perceptively.

"It is my duty."

"But not always so pleasant, I imagine."

"I don't mind. See what a fine day it is. Sunny and not too hot. It could be very hot now."

"You're a fine patient woman to serve Mister Skye so well."

"There is no man that walks upon the breast of the earth mother like Mister Skye. It is only an honor to do his bidding."

"You are not only beautiful but brimming with virtue," he said.

"I do not know the word virtue."

"Goodness."

She smiled, knowing otherwise, and saw him observing her closely.

"His lordship would enjoy the pleasure of your company today, Mary. He mentioned it to me. It is a great honor, being invited to ride with our chief. He stayed with the carts this afternoon, just so he might entertain you."

She knew she must refuse. "This is where I must be, with the mules, ahead of your carts and men."

"Oh, oh. Why, I'll post a man to drive Mister Skye's mules, and you can go back and ride with his lordship and enjoy his favors—and gifts."

"No," she said. "I am here to see the things you don't see."

"See?"

"Yes. White men don't have good eyes. So I am here to give you eyes."

"But—Mister Skye and the colonel ride ahead, watching. And your Victoria rides far to one side, seeking buffalo. And the river protects us on the other side—"

"No, it doesn't, Mister Baudelaire. See there, that wall of brush near the water? It could hide a hundred of the enemy."

Baudelaire peered nervously at the spit of river brush, seeing nothing. She watched him curiously. "Ah," he said at length, "you and Victoria and Mister Skye guard us well, Mary. I must commend you for watching, and for the eyes that see what we don't. Truly, you are a rare and beautiful woman."

She smiled. All her winters she had known of her beauty, and when Mister Skye had given her a looking glass she could hold in her hand, she saw it herself, better than in the mirroring waters of ponds. But she'd always known it, seen it in her firm, smooth, honeyed flesh and the shine of her brown eyes. "It is true," she agreed. "Mister Skye has eyes only for me, and no other. And I am his."

Baudelaire nodded gently. "A beautiful and faithful woman, a crown for Mister Skye," he said. "I'll suggest to his lordship that he come forward and ride with you. He will be honored by your company, even as you will be honored by the attentions of a great chief, a chief above chiefs, of the British."

She nodded. "That is where Mister Skye came from long ago," she said. "But he would never go back."

"No, I'm sure he wouldn't, with a woman like you to keep him here."

"It is more," she said. "He is as big as these prairies and this sky above us. Back there he would not be so big."

"Very well said, Mary. I'll suggest to his lordship that he join you after our nooning."

"That would be fine, as long as he doesn't keep me from looking. I see and hear the things that tell of danger."

"I'm sure there's little danger, Mary. Three days now, and we've not seen any of it. And Mister Skye is just ahead."

She didn't reply. She lacked the words to tell things to someone who would not understand.

"Very well, Mary. You'll be honored by his lordship's company by and by. He rarely favors a woman, so consider it a great honor."

She nodded, wondering.

Chapter 7

Day after day, Victoria rose before the rest of the camp stirred, and rode off to find buffalo. And night after night she slid back about dusk, and reported she had seen none. She ranged far north and west of the Yellowstone, ghosting up coulees to peer over the ridges ahead upon a vast, silent land populated by nothing but an occasional antelope and jesting crows.

Something within her was saying that the sacred buffalo weren't there, north of the river, in the widening triangle of treeless slopes between the Yellowstone and Missouri. Still she tried, ranging farther each day than she would admit to Mister Skye. She needed that distance, and the long lonely hours upon her gaunt bay mare, to prepare herself for what was to come. Soon she'd be alone, an old Crow woman without a man, and the hard solitary hours helped her prepare for the darkness to come. In camp at night. She rarely spoke to her man, and when she was forced to, the answer came in harsh gusts.

"The viscount's growing impatient," he said one night. "He came for buffler and we haven't fetched him any. Says I ought to be out hunting them too, but I told him you have eyes twice as good as mine, and know the way of them far better than I do."

"Not here," she replied dourly. "Not anywhere there." She waved a bony arm in a great northerly arc.

And so they toiled up the river, never sighting the four-foots they had come to hunt. Lord Frazier sometimes made meat because the bottoms teemed with deer, and once he shot a small cow elk. But the land died under the fierce July sun, and gradually even the deer vanished, bedded down somewhere and grazing only in the dark of the night. And the harder it got to feed his large party, the more the viscount complained and accused Skye of failing to do his duty.

They passed the confluence of a braided stream rolling up from the south, the Powder River was what Mister Skye called it, and more and more Victoria knew inside of herself that the sacred buffalo were across the Yellowstone, out there in the lands of the Sioux and Cheyenne. The

peoples of the prairies, like her own Absaroka, didn't
draw sharp property lines the way whites did, but had
homelands nonetheless that they considered their own,
often demarked by an important river. And now she
knew the buffalo languished down there, across the river,
in the heartland of her enemies.

These whitemen and their strange carts mystified her.
They talked as if they were all great chiefs and other peoples of the world were bugs. Never before had she avoided
the people Mister Skye guided, but these were different.
So she roamed far. She really didn't know what happened
among them each day: whether they killed rattlesnakes or
saw an otter or shot a hawk or got sick and died. They had
bad medicine, like the spirits of under-earth creatures.

She had to find the buffalo. She eyed the shimmering
river contemplatively one moonlit eve, and knew she'd
cross it the next morning. It had dropped steadily since the
spring flood; now its green flow coiled around long bars
of sand and gravel, and the waters didn't rage as they had
earlier. And she'd spotted a great buffalo trace into the
water, probably a place where they forded.

She reined her little pony into the cold water before dawn,
and found solid footing and a shallow passage. The water
never reached her mare's belly, though it tugged at her and
threatened to upset her as she splashed slowly across,
wary of a channel and dropoff. But just as the dawn blued
the northeast she led her mare up a shallow bank and let
her shake loose water off. The south bank. She sat in the
gloom, feeling a palpable change. The north bank had
been country almost without owners, hunted by Sioux,
Cheyenne, Piegans, Assiniboin, Cree, Gros Ventre, and her
Absaroka. But now she sensed she was invading, though

all those tribes hunted here as well, and claimed this country too.

This bank too had its river road, but she chose instead to retreat to the hills south and east, staying away from lethal traffic, war or hunting parties who could easily capture on old woman of the Absaroka and enslave or kill her and steal her pony.

The country here was rougher, and off to the south she could see dry prairie ridges, forested with yellow pine, country where the Cheyenne loved to summer because of its abundant wood and shade and sheltered grassy bottoms along ever-flowing cold creeks. To the west lay another great river the whites called the Tongue, that rose far away in the Big Horn Mountains, and some instinct told Victoria she'd find the buffalo there, scattered through the cottonwooded bottoms and parks of the river, escaping the terrible heat.

By mid-afternoon she struck the Tongue a few miles above its confluence with the Yellowstone. From the ridge she peered into a shallow trough, an emerald streak almost a mile wide running between tan bluffs. She paused cautiously in a crevass, studying the empty country and absorbing its menace. Anything could be hidden in the brown shadows of the giant cottonwoods that speckled the bottoms. And indeed something was. The buffalo, shaded up on a fierce day, hiding from merciless sun. More than she could count. Her man always used the word *thousands* but that wasn't enough. She saw thousands of thousands snoozing in the shade, occasionally rising up, rump first, turning around, and settling down again until blessed darkness and its cool would permit them to graze. She'd never seen so many in a wooded place, though out upon naked prairie she'd seen black rivers of them, the sacred provider of meat, tools, lodging, clothing, and so much more for all the peoples. But this herd lay concealed in dappled shade, and she knew the heat had driven the animals to shelter. She felt the heat also from her own terrible thirst, and the whited tongue of her mare, and the sopping wetness of the mare's back under her little pad saddle.

But she did not ride into the shallow trough toward the Tongue and its water. Instead, she turned the reluctant pony toward the Yellowstone, not far away, where she hoped to intercept Mister Skye. This time she would have news. She reached the great river when the sun lay low, yellowing the west sides of ridges and bluing the east, until the land seemed toothed and fanged and ready to strike at her. She chose a broad, gravelly place and forded easily, though the mare dropped briefly into a deep channel and out again so fast Victoria scarcely noticed the wetness of her moccasins. Nothing disturbed her passage, though she set a flock of black and white mockingbirds into a raucous furor, a dangerous thing always because it was a sign.

She studied the trace along the north bank and saw nothing, no linear tracks of cart wheels, or fresh hoofprints in dust, or manure, and knew they had not come this far this day. So she turned downriver and found them after a while, camped early because of the wilting heat that made men sweat and dry at the same time. These people lay about indolently, waving fans of sedge or leaf, gulping spirits from sweaty tin cups. All were dark-tempered because of the oppressive sun that lay over them like fired anvils. How strange that none of them slipped into the cold river to cool down, she thought. Did these whites know nothing about comfort?

And there was Mary, a cup in hand, sipping spirits along with Frazier and the rest and smiling, sitting crosslegged on the grass, her blue calico skirts hiked and her honeyed arms bared. Victoria frowned. She did not see Mister Skye there. She found him at their lodge, lying on a robe within, the lodgecover rolled a way off the ground to permit the breezes to cool him.

"You are not with her," Victoria said.

"If I touch spirits, I'm lost. No one over there with the bloody sense to deal with things. I can't. No buffler. Bad spot here, on a dozen horse-thief trails . . . and me parched worse than ever."

"I found them."

He peered up at her in the buttery light of the lodge, absorbing it, beginning a question.

"Many. Hiding from Sun in the bottoms of the Tongue. More than I've ever seen, I think. What a fine eye I have. I looked a long time at nothing but shadow."

He grinned slowly. "I suppose his lordship will be pleased. We found what he come for. Any sign?"

"No. Maybe people are far away. Not even old tracks."

"Suppose I ought to tell Frazier," Skye said, rising.

"Tell him when the sun comes back," she replied crossly. She had no reason at all, and simply felt like keeping her secret a few hours more.

"They'll want to do some preparing, Victoria—"

"Sonofabitch, you do what you want," she retorted. "You go over there and they'll give you spirits."

He grinned slowly. "Not now. But I got a powerful dry on me, Victoria. Powerful."

She glared at him. "You gonna get plenty dryer when they take you away."

"What are you talking about?"

She glared. "You know damn well."

"I don't, woman. Is this your medicine vision?"

She refused to answer, and turned crossly to the tasks at hand. She wanted food, but Mary hadn't built a fire and she doubted that the party had made meat. She'd make a stew, then. The bottoms were full of breadroots and sego lilies and she still had time to dig some before dark.

"Don't know what you're jabbering about, but it's just hoodoo," he muttered.

Buffalo! The camp was in a perfect frenzy that dawn as word swept through it. The viscount had abandoned his soft berth in his parlor-wagon and now danced about outside, giving nasal commands to everyone within earshot. Diana Chatham-Hollingshead thought his voice had risen at least an octave, and if it kept going up he could join the Vienna boys' choir.

She eyed Alexandra, who lay awake languidly, but probably wouldn't abandon her blankets until mid-morning. That was the way the viscountess lived. Diana knew she was made of other stuff, and plunged through her days like a clipper in full sail. She couldn't stand being left out of anything, especially not the forthcoming hunt. She'd shoot her share of the black beasts and then some. Her head ached a little from the boozing, but some tea would cure that. How amusing that had been, with poor Gordon sniffing around that dusky savage, and Baudelaire smirking about, and Skye's wife sipping scotch and giggling, quite unaware.

She'd frustrated his lordship in the end.

"Mary," Gordon had said huskily, drooling upon himself. "Mary, let's repair to the wagon."

She hadn't understood until he made himself clearer,

and then she had giggled and said, "Ask Mister Skye. If he says I should go to your robes, I will. That is the custom."

Poor Gordon had been nonplussed at that, and muttered something. And Baudelaire had listened intently, smiling.

"I will ask Mister Skye," Baudelaire had said blandly, and Lady Diana knew exactly what was coming. In a day or so Baudelaire would tell Mary that Mister Skye approved. And that's how the evening had ended, with the savage wending her wobbly way back to Skye's lodge. It had amused Diana then, and amused her now to recollect it.

Lady Diana drew up her pink silk drawers and then pulled on her hunting attire, split twill skirts for riding, and a loose silk blouse just right for the hot day ahead. Even as she finished her toilet, she felt the wagon lurch as a team was being hitched, and heard the coachman and postilion going about their work. Lord Frazier wasn't even waiting for breakfast!

She stepped out into a cool, dry morning and discovered that the fat wheezing Abbot Beowolf had at least steeped some tea, something to repair her aching brain, but that would be it. Crossly, she took the cup he handed her and watched Gordon play with rifles like a schoolboy, aiming and dry firing, and wiping every last mote of dust off the stocks.

"You ignored my pleasure last night," she accused.

"Ha! Buffalo! I want a trophy bull."

"Gordon, you should *be* a trophy bull, not shoot one."

"Ha. That's all you think about."

"It's what I do best," she said. "And now I have a headache. I always get a headache when you ignore me."

"They say cow's best to eat. Not so tough. The hump of the cow."

Diana refrained from comment, and found that a groomsman had saddled a pony for her. How she detested these bony, stupid beasts, and longed for a fine thorough-bred with a flowing canter, such as she rode after foxes.

"Buffalo, my lady," he said, helping her up by making a stirrup of his hands.

"Tiddlywinks," she replied crossly. She took the reins and whirled the cold-mouthed little mare toward the front of the column, wanting to see Mister Skye. She detested him, especially since he didn't seem to notice her advances. But at least she could get proper information about the hunt, since Gordon was sputtering gibberish.

She couldn't find him or his dusky tarts. Already the caravan of carts careened up the Yellowstone with the soaring sun white at their backs. She cantered ahead, scarcely remembering the lessons she'd absorbed about leaving the safety of the caravan, and in a while she discovered Mister Skye, Mary, and Victoria, all waiting at a gravelly place beside the wide, glinting river.

"We'll ford here," Mister Skye rumbled, a gnarled hand lifting and resetting his silk tophat at its usual rakish angle. "You'd better wait with us, Lady Diana."

"Where're the buffalo?" she demanded.

"Ahead a few miles. Up the valley of a big stream called the Tongue."

"I want a big bull," she said, glaring at him.

"I imagine you'll see a few."

Then she surprised him. "Where are you from?"

Something changed in his scarred face. "Lots of places, Lady. Fort Laramie in recent years."

"You don't talk like the Yankees. I think you're from Canada, and a subject of the crown."

The older squaw glared at her.

"I've never crossed that line," he said enigmatically.

His small blue eyes seemed to study everything but her, focusing on the far shore, the flight of a magpie, a sudden shiver of cottonwood leaves in a breeze, and even the sullen rock-crusted bluffs that held no secrets at all. His lack of attention annoyed her. She had a gorgeous face and figure; slightly blocky, true, but lushly colored. But he didn't seem to notice, or else he was a lot more clever—or stupid—than she gave him credit for. Stupid, probably. He didn't know a gift when it was laid naked in front of him.

"I think I'll cross," she said, spurring her little mare.

"Best wait," he said.

She ignored him, kicked the horse into the swirling water and felt it step daintily, feeling for a solid bottom with each step.

She heard a splashing behind and an instant later that evil blue roan, Jawbone, plunged beside her with Skye in the saddle, and he grabbed her bridle with one of his ham-handed fists.

"I think we'll wait," he said gently.

She quirted him across the chops, and he jerked back, losing his grip. That weird horse of his shrieked, reared up, and snapped at her, almost biting her thigh. But she spurred her mustang mare forward, not stopping, feeling the restless tug of the river push her pony downstream. In the deepest channel it threatened to topple her pony, suck her hooves out from under her. But a moment later the mare crow-hopped up the far bank and shook icy water in a fine spray that made rainbows.

Nothing happened.

"See?" she yelled, waving triumphantly at the three Skyes from a hundred fifty yards away.

The caravan hove into sight, and she watched the gaudy carts, bright greens and blues and reds, and the yellow parlor wagon, snake down to the river bank and stop. Mister Skye instructed the cartmen about crossings, his voice rumbling clear across the wide flow. Victoria started across the river, her rifle in hand, while the first cartmen whipped their reluctant drays into the boiling river, followed by the next, and then the others, and finally the yellow wagon, drawn by four skittish drays that looked ready to panic. She watched fascinated, wondering if the water at this ford would reach the bottoms of the carts, or invade the yellow wagon. It crept higher on the wheels, pouring between spokes. The sheer force of the river threatened to overturn carts and horses. Creaking hubs vanished in the flow and still the throbbing water climbed up spokes and wet the bellies of the drays, twisting the horses downstream and hammering the topheavy carts. But then the wheels and hubs and forelegs of horses reappeared, spilling water.

Victoria arrived first, glaring at Lady Diana while her bony old bay shook off water, and then the old woman froze, her squint locked on something behind Diana, who turned to look.

Standing quietly in the shade of a giant cottonwood was an Indian youth, eighteen or twenty, Diana thought. A handsome young man, slim and brown, with a diamond face and coal hair carefully braided. He held a bow, and a quiver was slung over his bare back, but he had no arrow nocked and no paint smeared across his face or arms. He observed the fording of the river by the bright carts almost hypnotically, drinking in sights he'd never seen or imagined in his young life.

"Lakotah," hissed Victoria, swinging the muzzle of her battered rifle around a bit, as a sort of warning. The Indian observed her and made no response.

"Dogs!" she whispered. "Enemies of the Absaroka!"

The youth did not abandon the shade of the cottonwoods, and for that reason the cart-men and others wrestling the muscular river didn't notice him. But his face remained expressionless, without the faintest revelation of curiosity, anger, fear, or anything else. At last he slowly made signs, his powerful brown arms and fingers spinning the prairie language.

"Hunkpapa!" Victoria cried, though Lady Diana hadn't the faintest idea what that meant. She eyed the approaching carts yearningly, wanting protection that still lay in the middle of the broad river.

"Big village!" Victoria snapped. "Came yesterday and found buffalo on the Tongue. Camping over there." She pointed up the Yellowstone.

Victoria herself began flashing her ancient arms and fingers, until the youth nodded. "I made the sign of the sky, the heaven," she said. "Now he knows. He sees Mister Skye! And Jawbone!"

Indeed the guide had spotted this, and was splashing his roan through the boiling current. He rode straight toward the youth, letting Jawbone clamber up a steep bank and stand, ears flattened and body dripping, before the young man. Something hardened in the youth's eyes, though Lady Diana couldn't fathom what had changed. The youth stood his ground, even against the menace of Mister Skye above him. Then, in motions so small his fingers scarcely seemed to whisper, the youth conveyed something to Mister Skye.

"He says his name is Sitting Bull. You'd say Sitting Buffalo Bull," Victoria explained to Lady Diana. "He's one of the village wolves—guards. And we must visit the village of these dogs."

Chapter 8

Lady Alexandra discovered that she was not a viscountess but a queen. Of all the wonders that smote the eyes of the Hunkpapa, she plainly excited them the most. Her flaxen hair, pale chiseled features, jade-colored eyes, and tall willowy figure captivated them, so that these Sioux swarmed around her, wanting to touch her silky hair or peer into her gentle dreamy face.

Not even the enameled wagons, gaudily colored and bearing the viscount's crest on their sides, or the nickel-trimmed black harness on the drays caught their eye half so much as her own pale hair and flesh.

After they'd all crossed the Yellowstone, their guide had talked with the young Indian waiting there, sometimes using strange words harsh to her ear, other times swiftly gesturing with fingers and hands that somehow communicated. They had all watched, the cart-men clutching their rifles and revolvers.

"Put up your weapons," Mister Skye had rumbled at last. "We're making a peaceful visit. This young man's not wearing paint, and the Hunkpapa aren't on the warpath. In fact, it's the time of their sun dance—big religious doings this time of year—and some buffler hunting, I suppose."

They had all listened carefully to the guide, grateful for

his expert advice, and then nervously returned rifles to Gravesend, the armorer, though some men were reluctant about it.

"Fetch your gifts, Lord Frazier. Tobacco and a little powder and ball. We'll smoke with the chief and headmen, and they'll welcome us. You'll be safe enough in the village—they treat their guests the same way most folks do. Nothing'll be stolen. Not inside the village, anyway."

The guide's squaw, Victoria, had glared at him and looked like she didn't believe a word of it.

"You'd better not give them spirits, though. Give them spirits and there's no saying what'll happen. Just don't do it and don't let them know you've got a cartload. Some Sioux chiefs won't permit spirits in their village. They've got wiser heads than we do."

Poor silly Gordon had looked upset, but his lordship was hiding it as best he could. Alexandra had gazed at the young Sioux, not finding anything menacing about him, and discovering a grecian beauty in him that attracted her in ways she couldn't put in words.

The Hunkpapa youth had led them upriver toward the village, and before long other warriors appeared out of nowhere—she couldn't imagine how they could rise up out of the earth—and shortly the carts and Englishmen were flanked by a score or so of these Sioux, all of whom wore very little in the fierce heat.

So many! The youth hadn't frightened her, but the others had. She had feared for her life, and so did all the rest, except for Mister Skye, who rode that broken-down horse of his as serenely as if he were going on a picnic. But that old squaw beside him glared fiercely about her, looking murderous herself, and Alexandra remembered that the old woman's Crow tribe and these Sioux—Mister Skye had

variously called them Tetons, Lakotah, and Hunkpapa—
were enemies.

She wore another of her squash-colored nankeen cottons today, this one with split skirts so she could ride. She
didn't enjoy the riding much, but she enjoyed even less the
rocking, jarring wagon, so now she rode toward the village, staying close to her postilion and coachman. She also
wore a wide-brimmed straw hat gauded with feathers, to
protect her vulnerable white skin.

How fierce they looked, she thought. Scores of warriors
formed the escort, with more joining the procession as
they approached the village. Mostly they stared, sometimes riding close to gape at her hair. And then at the
bulldogs, especially at her pugnosed ugly Chesterfield,
who trotted along faithfully ahead of her little pony. Some
of the warriors were at least six feet tall, with angular features, and the scars of battle puckering honey-colored
flesh. Several had peculiar slashes on their chests, and she
wondered about them. The older ones didn't have the
serene handsomeness of that young Adonis called Sitting Bull, and their corded muscles and scars and flat
stares gradually evoked dread in her. They progressed up
the south bank of the Yellowstone, with serrated rocky
hills to her left and thick river verdure on the right. Even
before they rounded a great bend, she spotted a layer of
blue smoke and sensed she was about to see the village.

Ahead lay a broad flat, still green and lush even though
nature's alchemy had turned the surrounding bluffs to
gold. Cottonwoods massed near the river, but on the grassy
meadow yellow cones rose like beehives, each topped by
a small forest of poles. A barrage of gray curs howled
toward them, and she feared for her little Chesterfield,
but the village mutts and the bulldogs simply chased one

another in wide spirals rather than tangling. People boiled toward them too, people in leather skirts and loincloths and fringed leggins. But most of the stocky women wore calicos they'd traded robes and pelts for—bright reds and greens and indigos, sewn into billowing skirts and loose blouses that left arms bare.

Gordon, riding just ahead, looked pale, and she saw sweat rivering down his neck in spite of the dry heat. Even Diana looked subdued, and Baudelaire positively terrified. She found malevolent pleasure in his pale terror. One never saw Baudelaire baring any emotion other than bland amusement. It was like seeing him naked, she thought. Near Skye and his squaws rode Boris Galitzin, ramrod erect in the saddle, trying to look serene in spite of the twitch spasming his lips.

She'd expected an uproar, but except for the whirling dogs, there was none. Instead these Hunkpapas gaped, blotting up sights too astonishing to exclaim about. The procession pierced into the village itself, wending among cowhide lodges, smoke-blackened at their tops, golden below. Many had been rolled up part way to let summer breezes through. Some women had been erecting brush arbors, shady places made by planting four poles in the earth, tying crosspieces to them, and then laying leafy branches across the tops to keep the sun at bay.

There were so many things she didn't understand, such as the tripods before each lodge, each dangling feathers and small animal skulls—and scalps. She recognized the human hair, most of it black, and she shuddered. The lodges had been raised in concentric circles, their oval doors facing eastward, and she supposed there might be some religious aspect to that. But now the crowds pressed so closely about her mare that she could scarcely see the village and all its strange sights. She knew she was a cynosure of a lot of brown and black eyes. Girls gaped and clapped their hands over their mouths. Children peered upward with blank faces.

Her hair. She smiled and undid her wide hat, and pulled a brooch out of her locks, letting them cascade over her shoulders, and knew she'd done something that fascinated the Hunkpapa. She sat her saddle regally. Let them gawk, she thought.

Strange scents thickened the air; woodsmoke, roasting meat, leather and sweat, and less pleasant odors rising from the offal of dogs. And horses! Everywhere she saw restless ponies picketed near lodges, the acrid sun-pummeled scent of them strong in her nostrils, along with the sharp and not unpleasant fragrance of their manure.

Mister Skye halted before a lodge somewhat larger than the others, with feather-bedecked lances struck into the tan clay before it. He peered behind him, studying his clients for signs of folly and finding none. He knew the Britons were much too uncomfortable to do anything rash. Still, the guide's gaze settled steadily on Galitzin, and then the armorer, Gravesend, and others he seemed to have catalogued in his mind as trouble.

Whoever was within that lodge certainly took his time, she thought. Crowds of these Hunkpapa pressed silently around them now, blocking all escape. They pointed at the bulldogs, some giggling or covering their mouths at the sight of creatures so ugly and fierce-looking. One crevassed old man with a buffalo-horn headdress and a dreadful necklace of dried human fingers—she thought he might be one of the medicine men she'd heard of—eyed the ugly dogs with obvious displeasure, as if the creatures had profaned an altar by coming into this village.

Then at last a man emerged from the honeyed darkness of the great lodge, and she watched enthralled. Never had she seen such a beautiful body, tall and perfectly formed, with deeply defined sinews cording through it, and all of his near-naked flesh the sienna color she'd first seen in Italy near Florence. And upon his powerful neck sat a chiseled head with prominent cheekbones, an aquiline nose, and gray eyes with a gaze so observant that she felt chilled as he took her in, and the others, one by one. Nor was that the end of it. He wore an eagle feather bonnet of such wanton savage luxury she could barely fathom it, feathers bound in red tradecloth with ermine pendants dangling from either side, and a feathered tail that extended to his bright quilled moccasins.

Dizzily—for something percolated wildly within her— she met his intense gaze, which lingered on her once again until she was certain of his keen interest in her. She scarcely knew what malady had beset her, and clung to the low pommel of her saddle. But his attention slid swiftly to other things, especially when Mister Skye began making the signs of these lands with his burly arms. This noble chief would fill pages in the journal she was keeping, she knew. Pages!

"*Pte*," the chief replied, nodding, and spoke in a soft tongue Lady Alexandra couldn't fathom.

At last the guide turned to his clients. "We're welcome, and we'll be guests of the village," he said. "We'll have us a smoke now. His name's Bear's Rib, and he's an important chief of these Hunkpapa. Lord Frazier, you'll join us for the smoke. Bring your twists of tobacco and your gewgaws and follow what I do. Colonel Galitzin, you'll join us also. And Lady Alexandra, he asked that you join us too. After the smoke, we'll have a feast, and at dawn tomorrow we'll join the hunt for Pte, the sacred buffler. That's their name for it. They spotted that herd too. They're camped here because it's upwind. And after the hunt they'll have their sun dance, but I think maybe that's something not for your eyes."

Lord Frazier found the chief's lodge more commodious than it appeared from outside. The buxom young squaws— or perhaps daughters—had rolled the hide lodgecover up a foot or so, like most others in the village, turning the lodge into a kind of chimney that drew air upward and out the smoke vent at the top. The chief seated himself at the rear, opposite the door, and motioned to Skye to sit at his right, then the viscount and Galitzin. Two village headmen settled themselves at the chief's left, one of them the fierce chap with the ghastly necklace of fingers. Alexandra was seated separately, near the door and close to a small stack of firewood.

The viscount settled himself on a soft buffalo robe, wishing it might be a chair because he was going to be uncomfortable shortly sitting crosslegged. He had supposed the inside of one of these nomadic tents would be dreary, but instead color rioted at him. Along the sides were bright-dyed parfleches with intricate geometric designs in green and yellow. Above him hung the chief's bow and a quiver festooned with red-dyed quills.

Methodically the chief—Frazier thought him an ugly brute with grossly large cheekbones—pulled his calumet from a soft-tanned bag and tamped tobacco in it. Its bowl was of a rose pipestone, and some sort of burnished hardwood comprised the long stem. Even as he tamped, one of his squaws laid an orange ember wrapped in some large green leaves before him, and the chief nimbly dropped the coal into the bowl and sucked until the tobacco burned, its pungence filling the lodge. Frazier sensed that this would take a while, and that the tribesmen would not be hurried through ceremony.

Bear's Rib lifted the pipe with both hands, saluted the cardinal directions, the sky and earth, and puffed slowly.

"I know a parcel of Sioux, and I'll translate for you," said Skye. "He's saluting the spirits that lie in each direction, *Wakan Tanka* above, and the Earth Mother below. Now I'll do it."

The guide completed the ritual and handed the pipe to Lord Frazier, who took it, wondering if he was going to do something heathenish and sacrilegious. But Skye seemed to read his doubts.

"He's honoring the spirits and expects you to. Best not to violate the medicine of his house, mate."

So the viscount imitated what he'd seen and handed the pipe to Galitzin, who followed. The next, seated separately, would have been Alexandra, but Skye intervened.

"Hand it to the headman," he said.

Galitzin did, and when the pipe had run the circle it was sent around a second time, until the whole charge of tobacco had been burned. The viscount's knees hurt, and he grew impatient.

"Tell him who I am," he whispered to the guide. "The queen's blood runs in my veins."

Mister Skye stared at the viscount as if he were daft.

"Your excellency, I am Lord Gordon Patrick Archibald Frazier, the seventh viscount, Bury St. Edmunds, Suffolk."

Bear's Rib stared blankly.

"Tell it, tell it, Skye."

"It's Mister Skye, mate."

"Whatever, whatever. I won't stand for insolence."

Bear's Rib returned the pipe to its pouch as deliberately as he had pulled it out, and then began some sort of welcoming oration. Mister Skye listened, and occasionally resorted to sign language, so the viscount supposed the lout of a guide lacked a full understanding of this tongue.

"He's welcoming you and urging you to stay in the village and share the big doings. Tomorrow they'll hunt the buffler. They've got some fine buffler runners—fast ponies trained for the hunt—and we're welcome to join them, make meat. I said we'd be pleased to do so, and you have some gifts. Now's the time."

"Ah! Yes!" he said, digging into the commodious pockets of his tweed hunting coat. He handed Bear's Rib two twists of pungent tobacco, some gaudy ribbons in rolls, and the powder and shot, each in a canvas pouch. Then, sighing in the silence, he withdrew another twist and dropped it before the chief. How they all sucked his blood, he thought.

The chief accepted these amiably, and began once again talking to Skye, this time jabbing a finger at Alexandra. Then Skye muttered a while, his burly hands slicing the air when words didn't come.

"He asked about the lady, and I said she's your woman, and that you both are from across the waters. He said he's never seen a woman with hair the color of aspen leaves before they fall, and he wondered whether the color is rare. I told him not at all; lots of people in your land have the color. Then, ah, he said he'd give you ten fat ponies for her—"

"Oh!" exclaimed Alexandra.

"—and I said I'd ask you. That's some price, ten ponies. Does her honor."

"Why, she's my wife, Skye! I can't give her to a savage."

Mister Skye nodded, and said something to the chief, who listened and talked to Skye at length.

"Bear's Rib says he knows that, but he's got two beautiful fat young squaws he'll give you for, ah, Lady Frazier. Plus the ponies. I said it's against your religion, but I'd ask."

"No, no, unthinkable!"

"It's not unthinkable," Alexandra said. "Tell the gentleman we'll take him to England and I'll introduce him to society."

Galitzin was grinning like a well-fed coyote.

The chief tried again, talking animatedly to Skye.

"Bear's Rib says he'd like to borrow her while you're here. Give you a fat pony," said Skye, solemnly.

"Borrow me!" she cried. "The brute! I'm worth two ponies. I'm worth five. I'm worth— Tell him I said yes."

"Why, Alexandra—"

"Try one of his fat squaws," she retorted.

"But, Alexandra—it might lead to— Are you sure he's quite clean?"

"Lakota bathe in a creek most every morning," Skye said, amused. "Is it settled?"

"Settled! See here, Skye, you've gotten us into something—"

"I got us into it," cried Alexandra.

"It'll scandalize the men—"

Alexandra giggled. "Let it," she said. "I'm going to, whether you get a squaw and a fat pony or not."

Skye turned solemn. "He might want to keep you, lady. Chiefs live by whim, same as any bloody king. I'll tell Bear's Rib no—"

"Say yes or I'll discharge you."

Galitzin grinned. "Is this how you got ze ponies for us, Skye?"

The viscount was shocked by the quiet ferocity of Skye's response: "Every pony was bought and paid for with the pounds you sent, Colonel. And no man touches my wives."

"Bear's Rib reminds me of Adonis. I saw the naked Adonis all over Italy," she said dreamily. "He has a beautiful soul."

Lord Frazier sighed. "There's no stopping her when she's being ethereal, Skye."

"Tell him I'll come to him tonight, Mister Skye."

The guide and the chief conferred in that muttering tongue, and then Skye said, "He is pleased, and will bring a fat pony to the chief shortly. As for the lady, he desires she stay and cook him a supper. He's curious about the food a woman with hair the color of the sun cooks. He will lend her a kettle."

"I don't cook! I have servants."

Skye consulted again with Bear's Rib. "He says if you don't cook, you're lazy. But if you are the wife of a chief of the people, he can understand it. He wishes to know what you do."

"I keep a journal. And just what does he do, Mister Skye?"

"He'll tell you he listens to the shamans—the medicine men—and listens to the elders, and then decides things."

But Bear's Rib was clambering to his feet and dismissing them. Lord Frazier followed the others out into a slanting sun and a blast of heat. Outside the lodge, his retainers waited quietly, still surrounded by curious Hunkpapa who were fingering the carts, poking and probing everything except Jawbone. Around that brutal horse lay a wide circle of emptiness. Apparently the beast was known to these people, the viscount thought. Capital. He'd somehow hired a guide and a horse and two squaws who'd smooth everything over.

Skye's squaws, he noticed, stood solemnly near Jawbone, and the old Crow woman glared angrily at the crowd, daring them to come closer to her. Even the evil horse stood with ears laid back and lips distended, baring teeth that could rip flesh apart.

One of the village wolves, or policing society, nodded at them and gestured that they should follow him to a place at the edge of the village, which would become their camping ground. These people didn't seem so bloody frightening now, the viscount thought. Just friendly people like any other.

He was much put out with Alexandra and intended to have a word with her privately, even if she just laughed as she always did. Pleasuring with a savage! Unthinkable! Almost, anyway, he thought, glancing covertly at Skye's young Mary. But of course Skye's woman was half-civilized, and that made the difference.

Well, the buffalo tomorrow. He'd sailed across an ocean for this, and it excited him. These savages seemed to have ponies trained to race among the beasts, but he couldn't imagine why. Surely those lumbering giants couldn't run fast. He intended to have Gravesend drive the cart to the herd, and hand him loaded rifles, one after the next, and bang away. He thought he might shoot a hundred buffalo before growing weary of it.

Chapter 9

Mister Skye awakened to the bustle of men and animals outside of his lodge. He peered upward through the smoke-hole upon an iron sky that told him it was not yet dawn, and very early this July day. His ears registered the hubbub of a rising camp, men coughing, the clank of cookpots, and more: the nasal voice of the viscount like a tolling bell, rousing men to action. The hunt, Mister Skye thought. It'd be only minutes before the eager man came banging on Skye's lodge, sundering the guide's rest.

He peered about in the gloom, sensing the warm presence of Mary in a buffalo robe to his left. But not Victoria. She slept apart most nights, or disappeared long before he went out to greet the sun and make water. His lodge had not been a happy one. He thought to crawl over to Mary's robes and fondle her, but he didn't. She would push him away, just as she pushed him away whenever things weren't good between them. So the two of them lay alone in their robes, as alien and distant as strangers.

He rolled out of his robe, fastened his leggins to his belt, and pulled a patterned red calico shirt over his thick chest. Then he lowered his grizzly bear claw necklace over his head and settled the polished long claws on his shirt. Big medicine. He normally shaved when he could and happened to have a ball of soap, but this morning he didn't bother. He had always scraped away his cheek-bristle for his women, but for days his women had avoided him, so stubble collected on his jaws and forested his face. It was his way of saying his lodge had darkened.

Mary feigned sleep but watched him, he knew. He

yawned, driven by the racket of the viscount's camp outside, and pulled his square-toed boots over his white feet.
He'd never surrendered to moccasins, though he wore them
often enough around camp. He liked boots, and the feel
of half an inch of sole under him like the thick hull of a
man-o'-war.

Then he stood in the sable gloom, completing his toilet
by anchoring his holstered Colt's dragoon to his heavy belt
and screwing his silk tophat over his graying shoulder-
length hair. An odd collection of rags and leather, he supposed, but it suited him. He ducked through the small
lodge door and into a crisp dawn, marked by a yellow
streak fissuring the northwestern sky.

He peered about him at the large village of silent cones
that caught the pale light on their eastern slopes and looked
like fangs against an indigo western sky. Over in the Sioux
lodges no one stirred. No smoke from cookfires rose and
flattened in the air. He turned to Jawbone as he always did
at dawn. The young blue roan nickered. He never had to
picket the animal. After it had grazed its fill, it drifted back
to Skye's lodge and stood sentry through the long night.

Mister Skye scratched Jawbone's ears, and the beast replied by butting him with his massive roman nose. It had
become their morning ritual, an act of love. The stallion
had known no other master, and had met Mister Skye
the first day of its life. Its sire had been a roan mustang,
uniquely large for the feral horses of the American west.
For years Mister Skye had tried to trap and tame the noble
animal, which roamed the high valleys of the Pryor Mountains in the land of Absaroka. He never succeeded. But
he did have a tall roan mare from somewhere back in
the States, a lady of difficult temperament, always half-
rebellious under saddle. So Mister Skye decided that if he

could not capture the stallion, he'd borrow its fire, and arranged the match, picketing and front-leg hobbling his big mare at a place the stallion haunted. He used chain, knowing how hard the stallion would try to steal her. He feared she'd kill herself struggling with her bonds, but she didn't.

Eleven months later Jawbone was born, yellow-eyed and evil, biting the hand that held him. From that day forward Mister Skye shaped his colt into a terror of the plains, a medicine horse so brave in battle and canny as a sentry that he became a legend among all the tribes, something magical, as awesome as Mister Skye himself. Even now Mister Skye's thick fingers probed along the horse's flesh, discovering gouges and pits and puckered flesh where Jawbone had felt the searing pain of lance and arrow and battle axe, and once a ball from a fusil that raked his stifle. The horse squealed and whickered, welcoming Skye even when his wives didn't. Skye curried, inspected hard hooves and hocks and fetlocks, pulled a burr from Jawbone's mane while the stallion nipped and butted and squealed.

"Ah! There you are, Skye," said Frazier. "Let's be off, eh?"

"I think we'd better wait for our hosts."

"Well, let's just shoot a few now."

"The shots might start a stampede that would put the herd twenty miles away. I don't suppose that would please Bear's Rib a bit."

"Well, wake them up. It'll be an inferno soon. I've never felt a heat like this. Over a hundred every afternoon."

Mister Skye had been mulling it since yesterday, when the chief had invited them to join the hunt. The viscount expected to be led up to the herd to shoot them while they grazed or stood, but the village warriors planned to saddle their prized buffalo runners—horses especially trained to race beside a running buffalo so the hunter could loose an arrow or fire his fusil into the heart-lung area just behind its shoulders. The runners were amazing animals, as fast as warhorses because buffalo could gallop at surprising speeds; and fearless, willing to edge close to those wicked horns, dodge them if the great beast hooked toward his tormentors, and go on to the next, guided only by knees because the hunter needed both hands for the killing.

"I'm afraid we'd better wait, sir. It's a courtesy required of a guest here."

"Well, when will they—"

"Later. Mid-day. Who knows? Indians don't live by ship's bells. And they don't get up early, either. That goes double for males, whose entire life is hunting, war, and sport, mostly gambling. The women toil. They cook, sew, dress hides, gather firewood, take care of children, make lodges, cut poles. But not the hunters."

"But it'll be roasting. The sun's barely up and I can feel it burning—"

"They're used to it. When they do get ready, they'll saddle their buffler runners and ride downwind to the herd. The buffler are hunkered in the woods up the Tongue, and the breeze is out of the southwest, so the Hunkpapa'll stay east and north and then start the herd running. Victoria says the buff are pretty much on this side of the Tongue. I thought to take you upstream a way, to an eastern bluff overlooking the valley, and you can shoot from there."

"A bluff? Why can't I be on the level instead of shooting downhill?"

"Safety. Stampeding buffler are frisky."

"I don't like it, Skye."

"It's not our hunt. You don't have a buffler runner. I've never seen them run the buffler out of a woods. It's bad enough out on grass, going a gallop over chuckholes with beasts as heavy as a ton, hundreds, even thousands, boiling by, ready to turn you to pulp if your horse stumbles or you fall. But cottonwood bottoms—I can barely imagine it. Getting brained by every passing limb, running into trunks and thickets."

"Well fetch me a buffalo runner."

Skye shook his head. "On the day of a hunt you couldn't trade for one. And I wouldn't let you ride one through those bottoms without a lot of practice."

Lord Frazier looked annoyed. Lady Diana Chatham-Hollingshead joined them, curious about the day's events.

"Our guide and these bloody savages have conspired to ruin the hunting," the viscount said.

Mister Skye contained the anger lancing through him and explained the whole business once again. He stopped short of saying that if they ruined the Sioux hunt, they'd be in big trouble, worse trouble than Frazier could imagine. That old medicine man—Eagle Beak—had been plenty unhappy about the whitemen arriving just as the hunt was to begin—and then the sun dance.

"Where can I get a buffalo runner?" asked Diana.

"Don't suppose you can today, lady. After the hunt you might try trading."

"I'll run one of these mustangs you got us, then."

"I wish you wouldn't, lady."

She laughed. "That's why I will."

Around noon the village warriors finally collected their ponies and weapons and rode off toward the south. They'd awakened at various hours, made their medicine, usually a morning prayer facing the sun, this time accompanied by a lengthy song about the forthcoming hunt, and finally gathered their weapons and mounts. Each took two ponies, one to carry him to the herd, and the other his prized buffalo runner, kept fresh and unridden for the great race.

"It's afternoon!" cried Lord Frazier. "And so hot I can hardly breathe!"

At Mister Skye's prompting, only the viscount, his armorer Gravesend, and his taxidermist, Will Cutler, came along. Gravesend and Cutler rode the arms cart, while the unhappy lord rode his sweaty pony. Skye took them southeast along a ridge that formed a divide between the Tongue and a creek to the east, and once they topped the grassy ridge they could see the thin green streak of the river bottoms winding through arid prairie. The cottonwoods had thinned here, upstream from the Tongue's confluence with the Yellowstone. Mister Skye led them down a long coulee to a point of land that pierced into the bottoms, and suggested that Lord Frazier shoot from there along with Gravesend, while Cutler waited with their cart out of sight in the draw. And there they waited and sweated, while the ruthless sun and furnace winds sucked the juices out of them all.

Gordon Patrick Archibald Frazier was in a sulk. Had he sailed clear across the Atlantic, suffered the cinders and smoke of barbaric railroads from Boston to the confluence of the Ohio River and the Monongahela, and camped on grimy bed-bug packets from there to Fort Union, months on end, all for this? The heat was suffocating, beyond anything he'd ever experienced in cool England. The sun hammered at him until pain gripped his eyeballs. His shirt dampened until he could no longer tolerate his tweed jacket, and he tore it off in spite of the indecency of shirtsleeves and handed it to Gravesend. That stopped the sweating, at least. But nothing stopped the searing heat that sapped energy from him like a leech dining on his blood.

And that was only part of it. That brute of a guide insisted on joining him on the promontory, and had taken to calling him *mate*, a term common sailors used. That or matelow, British slang for a seaman. Whenever Lord Frazier's noble ears suffered that form of address he winced, but there seemed to be no educating this oaf to the niceties of civilization.

What is more, the guide had lectured him, and couldn't seem to still his tongue.

"Not the best spot, mate, but we're guests. Now I don't expect the buffler to be moving fast. Not in this heat."

"Skye—it's Lord Frazier, Sir, your lordship, or if you must, Viscount Frazier. But never Gordon. No retainer shall address me familiarly."

The big oaf grinned.

"Furthermore, you needn't stay here. My man Gravesend will reload, and that'll be quite sufficient."

"I'll be watching out for Hunkpapa. They'll be coming along with the buffler."

"Gravesend'll watch."

"He'll be loading and you'll be aiming. And I'll be watching. Shoot a Sioux hunter, and maybe your scalp will hang from a lance tonight."

The viscount glared, but said nothing. The barrel of his Purdey scorched his fingers when he touched it.

"Buffler drop fast with a heart-lung shot, spot the size of a hat just behind the shoulders. No sense wasting powder on anything else. Another thing, mate. I'd suggest you lie down, set up some shooting sticks, rest your piece in them. You'll have a better shot than just standing here. Take your time, follow a good 'un—"

"I don't intend to take my time. I intend to shoot as fast as Gravesend can reload. And as long as I'm retaining you, you can reload also."

The guide shook his head. "I'm your eyes, mate," he said.

Lord Frazier stared. Was this man uncivil deliberately? "Skye, you push me to my limits."

The man grinned again, insolently, too.

"Buffler's sacred animals to the Indians," Skye continued. "They're downstream making medicine now, thanking the spirits of the ones they'll take. They make meat and shelter and clothing; make moccasin soles. Tallow makes soup and grease for their clay paints. Bedrobes, tools, and a whole lot more. Hair gets stuffed into saddle pads, children's dolls."

The viscount began to develop a headache, and a terrible thirst in the exhausting heat.

"I say, enough, Skye."

"Trophy buffler, now. You look for a light colored bull. They're mostly lighter in summer. Some even tan and buff. A few famous ones albino—sacred ones to any tribe. A few cinnamons too. Look for the odd color and you'll have a trophy."

"I say, Skye—"

"Mister Skye, mate."

The viscount felt a change come over the land, something not palpable, like thunder too distant to be heard. The earth beneath him seemed less secure, and he gradually perceived a vibration in it, an earthquake under the clay. He peered to the north, staring wordlessly, seeing nothing running the bottoms or dodging the massed cottonwood along the distant river.

"You're right. They're coming now," Skye said.

Then a brown mass, a wall of chocolate, poured into view, and above it a whirling haze of chalky dust that whitened the brass sky.

"Best lie prone, mate. Still have a minute."

"I'll shoot as I will, Skye."

The beasts lumbered closer, not running fast, and he knew he'd drop fifty, a hundred. It enthralled him, this sight of a river of running flesh, flooding around trees, appearing and vanishing as the cottonwoods thinned and thickened.

"Hunkpapa in there, mate."

"I don't see any."

"That's why I'm here."

He aimed into the chest of a distant leader, and fired. The heavy piece jolted into his shoulder, and he handed it to Gravesend, who handed him a John Dickson and Son. This too was so bloody hot he could scarcely touch it, but he swung it toward another leader, two hundred yards to the right, and well below. He aimed the wobbling sight on the beast's chest, and squeezed again. The boom rocked him, set his ears to ringing. He peered into the roiling dust and saw nothing stagger.

"Better to wait for a broadside shot, mate. Shoot midships, not the fo'c'sle."

"You mind your manners!"

Buffalo straggled by, these first lumbering faster than the main body of the herd. The viscount banged at them, feeling the butt of his rifles punch his aching shoulder again and again, and dropping nothing.

"You brought me to a bloody poor place to shoot, Skye!" he cried.

"There's Hunkpapa in there now. Hold up, mate."

"I don't see—" But then he did make out several, racing their dark ponies right through the thundering mass of beasts. Not a one held a rein, yet the ponies seemed to know just where to go. He watched one pony and rider veer tight against a cow, watched the man's corded arms flex, and the cow stumbled at once, tumbling over and over, a thin shaft, feathered and broken, projecting from a place just behind its shoulders.

"More of them, mate. Better hold up."

"I see them, Skye!" he retorted testily.

The hunter who'd dropped the cow never paused, but plucked another arrow from the quiver bouncing on his bare back, and nocked it while his pony closed on yet another cow ahead.

"How can they tell who shot what?"

"Each man's got his own medicine mark on his arrows. And each tribe's got its own way of making and marking the arrows."

Five more warriors swept by, their ponies nimbly cutting and dancing between the buffalo. Briefly he admired them, and grasped the importance of the buffalo runner. Those trained ponies meant food and wealth for any tribe.

"That's the last of the hunters for a bit, mate."

Lord Frazier steadied himself. Odd how his heart banged in his chest, and how his arms trembled under the weight of the rifle. He felt parched, and his dry tongue stuck to the roof of his mouth, as much from thirst as from wild exhilaration.

He swung his wobbling barrel toward a bearded bull that limped slowly by, a trophy beast perhaps, and fired.

His aching shoulder stabbed pain once again, and the beast limped by, unscathed. Surely he'd hit it! He watched, waiting for it to slow, to leak blood, to fall.

And still they came, a river of animals, more four-footed creatures than he'd seen in over forty years of living. He could scarcely imagine a herd this size, or the fodder it required each and every day. He fired a Boss and Company piece at a nearby cow that veered closer and closer, but she never faltered, and he watched enraged as she trotted relentlessly up the river bottoms.

"You've ruined my hunt, Skye. Bringing me here. How can a man shoot running animals?"

"Hold up, mate. More Hunkpapa in there."

He saw them. Eight or ten knotted close, weaving their ponies through the black torrent, effectively dropping cows until the valley before him was littered with kicking carcasses.

He shot anyway, picking a cow that looked wounded and slow. His new piece boomed, spewing blue powder smoke, and he sniffed the acrid odor, mixed with sweat and the stink of manure, buffalo, and alkali dust.

The rifle flew from his grip, some jarring blow wresting it from his trembling hands, and he realized Skye had ripped it from him.

"When I say hold up, you hold up," the guide said in a low voice that somehow pierced through the rumble.

He had never been addressed so rudely by a retainer. A rage burst in him like a lanced carbuncle.

"They're gone. You can shoot now," Skye said, as if nothing had happened.

And Viscount Frazier obliged, again and again until his shoulder could suffer no more. When the last of the great river of buffalo trotted by, the viscount surveyed the carcasses below, and knew every one had an arrow, or arrow wound, in it, and not a one had dropped with one of his lead balls through its lights. He turned a grimy face toward his guide.

"Enough of you. You're discharged, Skye. I came for a hunt, not a stampede."

The insolent guide grinned.

Chapter 10

Alexandra thought she discovered nobility in her chief. They couldn't speak a word to each other, and maybe that was best. He sat in the lodge, eying her, and she found wisdom in his gaze. He seemed to be waiting for something. It thrilled her, seeing these splendid traits in this leader of his people. Everything about him was perfect, even the scars of war, one puckered slash disappearing under his breechclout, another angling across his ribs into his back. She wondered about those peculiar scars on his bronze breast that she'd seen on others of these Hunkpapa. Bear's Rib. A noble name, no doubt, like her own maiden name, Heddonborough, in England. She thought him a royal presence, a majesty, a sceptered and orbed ruler of men.

It thrilled her that he was interested in her, and had invited her to high councils. She'd never had a chief before. That would be like having a king for a lover. He seemed lithe and athletic, unlike Gordon, who was fast deteriorating into soft whiteness. Not an ounce of fat burdened the muscled torso of this barbaric man. She thrilled at the thought of his savagery, and the scalps hanging from the lodgepoles. How she wished she could talk with him, ask him a thousand questions. She knew, though, she'd write epic poems about him—she was a not inconsiderable poet, and had been published several times, once on the same page as Alfred Tennyson. Yes, love sonnets, odes to friendship and savage lovers, something to convey the innocent manliness of this prairie prince.

She'd been so disappointed when he hadn't detained her after the smoke and welcome yesterday. She'd waited, heart pattering, for some indication that she should stay, but he had simply eyed her languidly when Mister Skye, Gordon and the rest, got up and clambered out. She'd followed, her soul wild with need to stay on and feel his cruel touch. But instead she emerged into the coned village and found her way back to the wagon, and spent a miserable night, feeling rejected.

But now she smiled, her eyes feasting on his hard features, the prominent cheekbones, his obsidian eyes that peered sharply outward but let no mortal discern what lay behind his gaze. In his thirties, she supposed. Young. His jet hair, carefully done in two braids, showed no sign of gray. And no beard. She peered again, curious about the smooth cheeks that appeared not to have been scraped at all. Did these people grow no beards? She wished to touch his cheeks, be his woman. She was curious about that, being his woman. The thought sent ripples of excitement through her. Tonight! Maybe now!

She peered about her at the two shy young women who seemed to be waiting for something. Stunning women, now that she looked at them. How she envied them their dusky beauty. She felt weightless and knew she would confide her joy to her journal soon. They sat studying her, especially her flaxen hair, doing nothing. It surprised her.

She had thought Indian women constantly did things; made moccasins, cooked food, skinned hides, sewed calicoes. But these were the chief's wives, and maybe they didn't have to. Lots of servants, like the peerage of England. She had never had to do anything. Always a dozen servants flocked about to dress her, make her bed, help her with her toilet, cook, clean, keep fires burning, run errands, wash, and all the rest.

Plainly these people were superior to anything she'd known in England. What dignity the chief had! With none of the petty little faults that afflicted everyone she knew at home. And how noble the women! Strong and serene and free of all white men's taints and vices. She could see it in their open faces, this vast perfect kindness. She'd never met people without vices before. Her eager gaze traveled from one beauty to the next and to the chief, and she blushed at the thought she had, wondering just how things—happened. It would be beautiful when it came, ecstatic, ethereal, so spiritual rather than animal, because these were people of large soul and exquisite religion and perfect integrity! She closed her eyes tightly, arched her head back, listening to the carillon of the universe, preparing her soft yearning body and soul for all the joys that would transport her onto some true, savage plane her spirit had never penetrated.

She'd been summoned to the great lodge about the time the village emptied itself for the hunt. Bear's Rib's wives couldn't speak words, but made it plain she should come with them, and she had followed at once, walking among young men gathering horses and weapons, past women in begrimed buckskin dresses strapping travois to ponies, past bright children, the little girls in skirts, romping and chattering. She paused once at the sight of Mister Skye and

Gordon and the rest, just beyond the village, heading out toward the buffalo.

To delight her prince she'd worn a suit of jade velveteen that matched her eyes, along with a white silken blouse and a black choker with an ivory cameo, which perfectly framed her oval face with its tumble of blonde hair. It had been a hardship to dress herself this trip, but she'd managed. Back in Bury St. Edmunds there had always been several ladies waiting to perform these things. But she'd managed. One had to sacrifice, keep a stiff upper lip. It had all paid off, though: Bear's Rib's gaze had returned again and again to the velvet dress, and each time he'd smiled gently.

Thus they sat for the longest time through the heat of the day. But the shade of the lodge felt comfortable and breezes eddied in below the raised lodgecover. Then at last some sort of excitement thickened the hot air outside, and she heard women's voices, the sounds of ponies, and cries of joy. She peered under the lodge cover, and discovered blood-smeared women arriving. They were leading ponies that dragged heavy travois, the poles sagging under raw, bleeding meat, huge gory chunks of it alive with green-bellied flies, all of it wrapped in mangy hides. It fascinated her, this savage feeding of the village and the excitement that bubbled up everywhere.

Several squaws with travois stopped at the chief's lodge, exclaiming and jabbering in their strange tongue, and that seemed to be what the chief and his wives had waited for. He muttered something and his ladies rose, beckoning Alexandra to come with them. She followed, curious. The women began unloading the travois, and urged her to help them. But she couldn't! Not in her splendid velvet! They tugged at her, and she felt helpless, unable to tell them the dress was her costliest—at least of the twenty she'd brought—and she wouldn't ruin it. But oh, how she wanted to help. The chief was inviting her to help in this noble enterprise!

She knew what she'd do. She slid back into the lodge and began undoing hooks, her nimble fingers loosening her skirts and blouse as swiftly as if she was mad for a lover, and in moments she stood in her snowy chemise and two flounced petticoats, while the chief gazed amiably. Then she stepped out into the blazing sun and set to work, enchanted by the honor bestowed on her. Something for her journal and poems. The squaws dragged huge bloody quarters of a buffalo off the travois, tugged heavy dark hides with blood on them over to a grassy area near the lodge, and Alexandra joined them, proud to be one of the chief's household. In moments her petticoats were smeared with gore, but it didn't matter. She helped one of the squaws stake down a hide, hair down, and then the woman handed her a chipped stone tool of some sort. A scraper. She would flesh the hide, and it would be a privilege. She watched the other squaw labor, stroking the fleshy gore and refuse away from the skin. It seemed so slow and the hide so large. But Alexandra set to work, scraping diligently, wanting to shine for her chief.

Within minutes her arms ached, but she persevered, enchanted at the thought of noble labor for these noble lords of the American prairies. The chief's other squaw was cutting the buffalo into thin strips and hanging them from a nearby rack to dry. Jerky, she thought. This was how they did it. Tribesmen came and went, and she labored on, oblivious of them, fierce in her zeal to be a worthy Sioux. Day faded, and the redolence of roasting meat filled the village. It'd been a long time since she'd eaten, she thought wearily.

At last the squaws set aside their scrapers and knives and began a meal. Alexandra quit gratefully, her entire body aching beyond endurance. Filth stuck to her, covered her white underthings, gummed her blonde hair. She had no idea what had transpired in her own camp, and she didn't much care. No doubt they were preparing a buffalo roast too. Hump meat would be succulent beyond description, she'd heard, and she intended to find out. From time to time she'd seen the chief peer curiously at her, and she'd redoubled her labors then, wanting to be a perfect savage. Once that creased old medicine man had stared dourly at her and walked off angrily. She feared him vaguely.

The other wives chattered in their tongue, glancing at Alexandra now and then, and she didn't know a word, but she didn't feel lonely. Instead, weary as she was, she felt only loftiness, as if she'd been transported to some finer plane of existence, unspeakably majestic and superior to her conniving, petty, cruel countrymen.

She washed at the tiny creek, yearning for some good English lavender-scented soap. She thought to send for some, but rejected the idea. That sort of luxury seemed sinful to her. She would learn to live just as these magnificent children of wilderness lived, she thought. The chief's wives washed with pulverized yucca root that foamed swiftly when it was immersed, so she borrowed a piece of it and found it made effective suds. She arranged herself as best she could, and by the time the humproast had cooked to perfection she was back in her jade velvet, grinning across firelight to the noble who had smitten her. He returned her gaze enigmatically, nothing visible on his splendid face, which left her anxious and afraid she'd given offense.

They devoured a meal—more meat than she'd ever stuffed herself with—and she learned to let it cool enough so she could eat with her fingers. She felt so drowsy she could barely eat. No one from her own camp showed up to destroy her adventure, and she felt grateful for that.

That night she curled in the dark, curly-haired robe they'd given her, waiting for her savage lover and feeling hard clay beneath her. She knew he'd come sometime. She'd scrubbed in the creek once again after the juicy meal, and then had disrobed silently in the jet darkness of the lodge, her mind transported with visions of ecstasy.

But her savage prince didn't come, and she swiftly fell into troubled sleep.

Mister Skye sat on his impatient blue roan, watching the toil of the squaws in the cottonwood-dotted bottoms below. Actually, he was wondering what to do. The viscount had discharged him—again. It had been the outburst of an empty-handed hunter ashamed of his marksmanship. But it hung there, and Skye was free to leave if he chose. Victoria and Mary would be overjoyed if he did.

He had never guided a party he disliked as much as these. Usually he could negotiate with them face to face, and take the measure of them before committing. But this business had been arranged a year earlier by mail, and he had entered into it blind. It had been disastrous from the beginning, and if Victoria's forebodings were worth anything, likely to get worse. The viscount's station in England had twisted his perception of this wild world where tribesmen roamed free, the writ of courts didn't run, and a lord of England was no more a lord than anyone else. The viscount didn't seem a bad sort, just out of place and expecting a sort of absolute obedience that would endanger them all if Skye ever acquiesced. No doubt the viscount would reconsider back there, among Sioux he couldn't communicate with—not one word—and would send Baudelaire or Galitzin to make amends somehow. But Barnaby Skye wasn't sure he could accept. It was tempting just to let the bloody fool blunder himself, his women, and his retainers into grave trouble, or death. But that very thought largely made up Skye's mind for him.

Below, blood-drenched squaws in old buckskin dresses tugged at dusty hides and sawed at raw meat, loading it onto travois. It was brutal gory work. Already the raptors had collected, whole black flocks of quarreling crows, magpies, red hawks and others he couldn't put a name to. The Sioux hunters had gone back to the village, each leading his prized buffalo runner. Back there they'd celebrate, play the bone game, strut, dance, smoke, brag, and make medicine. The men of every plains tribe Mister Skye had ever seen lived like that, indolently, enjoying gossip and gambling, occasional bouts of hunting, and horse-stealing for the honors that came with counting coup. But the women toiled ceaselessly, cutting and preserving meat, gathering roots and greens, making shelters, tanning hides, sewing clothes and moccasins, cooking, caring for the children, collecting squaw-wood and tending the fires, loading travois, making harness and tack, and most everything else that required grubby toil.

The privileged life of the males had faintly annoyed Mister Skye. It seemed somehow wrong to idle the years away in gambling, gossip, ceremony, and the pursuit of dubious honors, with only an occasional foray required of them. Back in Washington City, dreamers were going to make farmers of them, make them toil like women, but they were only dreamers. These privileged warriors of the plains would either live a subsidized life or die away when the land was settled, refusing to toil like women or white men. Mister Skye hoped it wouldn't happen in his lifetime.

Jawbone grew rank under him, nipping at his boot, so Mister Skye gave him the subtle knee signal that would turn the horse toward the Sioux village. The evil-eyed horse was as ringy and taut-nerved as his wives in this village of their enemies, and showed it in his mincing alert gait. They passed innumerable women driving travois-laden ponies, the poles furrowing the clay under their groaning loads. The village would live fat for a little while, anyway. And the idle warriors would have a wealth of buffalo robes—created through the miserable toil of their women—to trade for powder and ball and knives. It was getting so that a tribesman measured his wealth by the number of wives and daughters he kept busy scraping and tanning robes, he thought. No wonder they all enjoyed capturing enemy women as much as they enjoyed snatching horses.

He reached the busy village knowing what he would do. Unless the viscount were adamant about the discharge, Skye would remain available. He didn't know why he had reached that decision, but supposed it had something to do with old British disciplines long forgotten in this wild land. The viscount would discover himself helpless and in danger without a guide, and Skye hated to abandon former countrymen who were in greater peril than they imagined.

For once the yellow and gray curs didn't greet him noisily. They had all gorged more offal than they could stomach and lay panting in the close heat of the afternoon, unable to stir. The women scarcely noticed his passage among the lodges as they sliced strips of meat for jerking, collected back sinew and backfat, and staked wet hides to the clay for the fleshing. As he rode past Bear's Rib's lodge, his gaze fell upon the astonishing sight of the viscountess in her once-white petticoats, kneeling on a green hide and scraping flesh from it, her blonde hair tumbling over her breast. It amazed him. A noblewoman. A viscountess. Wife of a peer of England, drudging like a charwoman and apparently discovering something romantic about it. She caught him watching and started to say something, but turned her back to him to hide her willowy body and freckled flesh. He grinned, touched Jawbone, and rode to his own camp.

He discovered Mary and Victoria silently building a fire to cook a huge humpmeat roast lying on the grass nearby. They eyed him dourly and busied themselves. Over among the tents of the retainers, the Abbot Beowolf had dropped the tailgate of his kitchen cart and was setting up a spit to cook a vast buffalo roast supper, humming the Agnus Dei cheerfully. The Sioux, unfailingly polite to their village guests, had inundated the viscount's party with the choicest cuts of buffalo, and invited them to the village feasts besides.

His lordship had vanished, no doubt in a sulk, so Skye unsaddled Jawbone and rubbed him, feeling the horse shiver under the massaging it got from Skye's stubby fingers. Then, exactly as expected, he spotted Baudelaire hastening through the heaps of camp equipment like a sallow-faced penguin.

"Ah, Skye. His lordship expressed regret for his tone of voice this afternoon, and wishes you to know that nothing was meant by it."

Victoria stared.

"Mister Skye, mate."

"Yes, yes. Will you accept?"

"Accept what?"

"Continued employment."

"Tone of voice? I heard him discharge me."

"Oh, quite unintended. A moment's disappointment in the hunt."

Victoria set her knife aside and stood, her gaze brittle on Skye.

"Am I to be discharged by the viscount whenever things don't meet his whim?"

"Well, Skye, you understand how disappointed—"

"We are guests here, Mister Baudelaire, and subject to their arrangements. The viscount knew that. He also knows I'll get him to buffler after we get free of the village."

"I'm afraid that's not going to happen soon, Skye. The viscountess is quite determined to stay and enjoy the companionship of chief Bear's Rib."

"They'll want you to leave before the sun dance. That's village religion, not for outsiders. And—Beaudelaire—you won't want to see it."

"Her ladyship is determined—"

"We're leaving at dawn," said Skye.

"But it's impossible. Her ladyship insists."

"My wives and I are leaving at dawn."

"But—we need you. We don't understand a word they speak. Not a word. And not one of us can do the sign language!"

"Then you'll join us when we go. I don't suppose you'll want to be here in a large Hunkpapa village without a guide."

"My dear Skye, you're being quite intractable, and it'll

dismay Lord Frazier. Surely now you'll wish me to convey your delight to him."

A diplomat of sorts, thought Skye. He didn't know what to do. He hated to abandon these greenhorns to their folly. He wanted to leave this semi-hostile village whose warriors he had killed while battling beside his Crow kin. Every man in the village hoped to do something about it, and none more than that young Sitting Bull, whose agate eyes had been full of it. He wanted badly to please Victoria, who even now stared hard-eyed at him, demanding something wordlessly.

Well, these Britons weren't his kind of Britons, but they were his countrymen even so. "One day, Mister Baudclaire. And against my better judgment. You don't understand how things work here, or why I have my reasons. Let the viscountess indulge herself another day, and then we'll leave, and damned fast."

The viscount's secretary smiled blandly, and hastened off like a flapping crow, without a thank you or a nod.

Victoria wept. "You don't hear me," she said. "Magpie told me truly." The wetness streaking her weathered brown face tormented Barnaby Skye, but he'd made up his mind.

Chapter 11

So it would be. Victoria watched the strange man in the black clothing, with a coarse face the color of the belly of a fish, scurry back to Lord Frazier with the news that Skye would stay on. Now she knew what would come. These Britons from across the sea would take her man with them, and she'd never see Mister Skye again. They had some magic hold on him, like witch medicine, so that he wasn't acting like himself.

Twice now Mister Skye had been free to leave, and twice he had chosen to guide these people. He treated them strangely, as if they were chiefs over him, and didn't seem to be his usual self. And they treated him badly, not like a man at all, but a slave, and he permitted it. Oh, he growled a little, but he permitted it, and that seemed strange to her. When Mister Skye felt the presence of danger, he never permitted his clients to dictate to him, but now he was doing it. Truly, Magpie knew.

"Sonofabitch!" she exclaimed to Mary, who looked as troubled as she was. "Soon they will take him away and we'll never see him again."

She could not imagine her life without him. So many winters ago she could barely remember them, when he still trapped beaver for American Fur Company, he had come to her Kicked-in-the-Bellies village and had seen her. She had passed nineteen winters then, and soon he had found ways to spend time with her, often while she gathered firewood. How she'd smiled! What an honor to enjoy the attention of a happy, famous longknife, unimaginably rich, strong, and full of whiteman medicine. He had loved her. She could tell by the light in his small blue eyes, and the way his gaze had possessed her, lingering on her tall slender form as if to wonder what lay beneath her doeskin dress. In time he had laid before her lodgedoor a gift of a fine flintlock Hawken, a pound of DuPont and another of galena, two Hudson's Bay Four-Point blankets, a fine steel-bladed knife, an awl, and twenty metal arrow points. The next dawn her father had gladly taken these things into their lodge, and the compact had been sealed.

So long ago.

"We will not leave this village for many days," said Mary. "I am not happy here."

Victoria thought that was an understatement. They were both miserable in this village of the Lakotah, ancient enemies of the Absaroka and Shoshones. But as usual, Mary avoided harsh words, and that was a sweetness in Mister Skye's younger woman.

Silently they jabbed an iron spit through the hump roast and set it over the tiny fire, neither of them wanting to talk or even share their misery. She loved Mary, but she couldn't really talk with her any more than she could talk to Mister Skye now. The knowledge of her medicine vision burned too heavily inside her breast. But Mary knew. Indians sensed things that these whitemen were blind to.

Victoria had no way of coping with the impending separation except by withdrawing. She'd started that many moons earlier, when the Cold Maker still raged. Once she was certain of the things Magpie had shown her, she had begun to say goodbye to Mister Skye the only way she knew how, which was separation. She couldn't bear to have him torn from her old arms, so she let the distance come early, like cold fog, so the sundering would be completed before it happened. Now the dread was so large inside of her bony chest that she couldn't talk to her man, even when she tried or he wanted her to. So the gulf deepened as Sun made his passages, and she was almost a widow, though each night Mister Skye rolled into his soft robes and waited for her. But she didn't come to him. When the Britons took him away, she would cut off a finger, and half her hair, just as if she were a true widow.

Two days later it happened again. Mister Skye woke early, just as Sun was painting the world with color, and began at once to prepare for a journey. He saddled Jawbone, and wandered out into the well-guarded village herd to bring back the mares and mules. Victoria's heart gladdened at the sight of him bringing his ponies on a picketline. Could it be? Would they leave now? Hastily, her old heart pounding, she began to dismantle the lodge, unlacing the thong that held it together along the seam, while Mary—sudden brightness in her brown eyes—began filling parfleches with their gear and strapping lodgepole travois to the mules.

Oh, the joy of it! Around her the village stirred, or the women did anyway. There would be more buffalo meat turned into jerky or mixed with fat and berries into pemmican this day; more green hides staked and fleshed; more hides rubbed with buffalo brains to begin the tanning. And probably these Lakotah dogs would erect the forked center pole of the sun lodge they would construct from boughs, like an arbor. But maybe Mister Skye would leave! Sonofabitch, it would be good to escape, to breathe air these dogs didn't breathe, wrest away from the dark spirit-persons hovering here, all enemies of the Absaroka!

Several times she had dourly walked through the Hunkpapa village, a small alien woman hearing and seeing the things whitemen didn't see. She knew enough Sioux to make out what the women were saying, and she knew to read the faces of these dogs. Two faces especially. One was that of a seamed old medicine man, whose name, she learned, was Gray Mole. Named after an Under-the-Ground Person! It scandalized her that a medicine man of these people would name himself for the Underworld Persons. Surely he was a witch. The whitemen—not even her Skye— never noticed the way Gray Mole stared at them all with death in his gaze, and barked harsh things to the young warriors crowding about him. But she saw. Sonofabitch, she knew. And the other one, Sitting Buffalo Bull, who peered at Mister Skye with eyes full of something dark. The youth had vowed to undergo the sun torture at the dance, she'd learned, so that Sun and Wakan Tanka would strengthen him for his task—which was to face Mister Skye, killer of Hunkpapa warriors—whenever his medicine told him to. All this she knew, and it had shriveled her spirit and driven her inside of herself until only an ember of life burned deep within her bony breast.

But maybe now they would leave after all! Maybe Mister Skye had come to himself in the night, just as she had begged the true Absaroka spirits. Maybe they would leave this place now, and these countrymen of his too, with their witch-grip on him that troubled her so.

He grinned roguishly at her, cocking his silk hat and then lifting parfleches into panniers that would end up neatly balanced on their packsaddle.

"We can bloody well be away ten miles before the heat's up," he said. "Suppose you'd like that, Crow Woman."

She didn't dare to smile. If she didn't smile they would remain safely far apart, and that was what she could endure. But she met his gaze.

He peered about the silent camp. As usual, the viscount and Diana, along with Galitzin, the Abbot Beowolf, and Baudelaire, had partied well into the night, tapping the spirits wagon. They'd enticed Mary to join them, and she'd stayed late, Victoria knew.

"I told 'em I'd be leaving first thing," he muttered. "I don't see any sign they're coming along. I suppose that pleases you, old lady."

She turned dourly to her tasks, not wanting his cheer to breach the walls. She hadn't slept for days. Not since they'd all left Fort Union. She'd lain awake with her Green River knife sweaty in hand, protecting Mister Skye and Mary. Now tiredness laced her as she hoisted her little pad saddle over the ribby bay mare. She wouldn't let herself hope until they were a day's ride away from these dogs.

A young Hunkpapa warrior in a loincloth stood watching them, and she saw it was Sitting Buffalo Bull. The youth's gaze never seemed to wander far from Mister Skye, and she knew why.

"I'm ready any time you are, mate," Skye said to him in English. "Give yourself a knife or a lance. I'll meet you with my belaying pin."

She wondered if Sitting Bull understood. At least Mister Skye understood. She eyed her man briefly, pleased to see his warrior instincts hadn't diminished. Then she scolded the thought away from her head.

The one called Galitzin erupted from one of the Englishmen's tents, the one always dressed in brown who was chief of all the bulldogs and ponies. He lumbered across the crackling grass, crying out.

"Skye! Hold up!"

Mister Skye paused beside Jawbone, waiting. And so did Victoria pause, already knowing, the thing that had lightened her breath for a few minutes seeping away so that her body felt like the bars of galena the warriors turned into bullets.

"Skye! What are you doing?" Galitzin cried, out of breath.

"I told the viscount we'd be off at dawn, colonel. He's had the extra day he asked for. My terms were that I would be in command, or I would resign from his service."

"But his lordship intends to stay on. Lady Alexandra

insists on it. She can't leave. She's taken to the savage life and plans to write about it." He smiled. "Taken to the chief, anyway."

"Colonel, you don't know what dangers lurk here."

"His lordship insists. He's retained you for a large fee, and expects your loyal, unflagging service, Skye."

"He's discharged me twice, mate. And rehired me twice."

"You'd leave us here, without even the means to understand these savages? You'd do that to your fellow Englishmen, Skye? To a peer and lord of England?"

"I would."

Victoria's heart lifted.

"That's irresponsible, Skye. We can't adjust to your whim every time the breeze turns it. His lordship asks your indulgence for one more day. Surely that's reasonable. Will the sky fall down in one day?"

Mister Skye didn't answer, but gazed out upon the shadow-carved prairie hills, gilded orange by the dawning sun.

"I suppose there's no harm in a day," he said. "Tell the viscount we'll leave tomorrow at dawn."

Woodenly, Victoria began to unpack.

Lord Frazier watched Diana Chatham-Hollingshead lead a little buckskin Indian pony into camp, looking so smug he thought she'd stolen it. She tied it to their parlor wagon and began grooming it, smirking all the while. He couldn't imagine why: the pony stood barely fourteen hands and obviously was mustang stock, with a broomtail and roman nose and narrowset eyes.

"It's a buffalo runner," she said. "I traded for him."

"Buffalo runner?"

"Their prize horses. You saw them run right in beside a buffalo and then duck away before they got hurt."

"Yes, yes of course, but what do you want it for?"

"Hunting buffalo, silly goose."

"You?"

"Of course. Why did I come all this way for? Tiddly-winks?"

"Not a bad reason," he said.

"He cost me my Manton and some powder and balls and caps."

"How'd you manage it? I mean, you don't know a word."

"I watched the horse work during the hunt. And I saw him picketed before a warrior's lodge. So I got my rifle and laid it before the savage and pointed at the horse. He wanted two rifles—two fingers—and I refused. But I got him. I love being a savage."

"So does Alexandra," responded the viscount drily. "But don't call them that around Skye. He'd take offense. Of course the ruffian wouldn't know a savage from an Englishman."

"I'm turning wild," she said.

"Not so I'd notice."

"That's because you can only think of that squaw," she grumbled.

"Ah! It'll happen! Soon! Mary has a weakness for spirits. Maybe tonight!"

"I'm a better savage," Diana muttered.

"We'll see!"

They were all tasting savage living, he thought. The trip was turning out well after all, in spite of that bad fright he'd gotten near Fort Union, and a bad hour shooting at stampeding buffalo. But he could take to this life. Skye'd been a problem from the start, but he'd tamed the oaf at last. His English origins had surfaced after all. A sharp word and a glacial glare, and soon enough a dustman or mechanic like that would doff his cap and remember he stood before a dread lord of England who had abundant measures to deal with insolent conduct. Skye had been no different, even though he'd been out in these wilds for years. That silk hat and the Mister were affectations, his way of playing lord over these savages.

But the problem had ebbed away. Between himself, Galitzin, and the wiles of Baudelaire, the beast was subdued, like a spirited dray, and would now turn his useful cunning toward whatever was needed. Whenever Skye wanted to depart, they just put him off another day. They'd put him off three days now and had him licked. Odd what this wild continent did to the dustmen. Not a bit pleasant to observe. Freedom gave a brute like Skye absurd pretensions.

The Hunkpapa village had ceased to alarm him, and now he wandered through it boldly, watching the savages at their daily life and play. How the women drudged! It amused him. Everywhere vast racks of drying jerky blackened in the sun, while squaws on hands and knees fleshed hides or kneaded slippery gray brains into them for their tanning. The warriors had finally settled down to some interesting work, too. They were building a sun lodge, with a high central pole, roof poles radiating from it, and a covering of boughs. He supposed soon they'd dance and prance and wiggle and wave feathers and pound their drums and gargle out howls, and that would be the sun dance. He intended to watch, even though Skye opposed it and muttered. But Skye no longer mattered.

Some of these savages had been just as curious about the whites, and none more so than the boy Skye called Sitting Bull. He'd come over daily to gawk, peering with unblinking solemnity at everything in the carts. He'd even gotten Gravesend to pull rifles out of the armory cart, and Gravesend had even let the savage heft and dry fire them. The youth made Lord Frazier uneasy, and he thought he'd shoo him off next time.

He made his way through the somnolent village, which had suspended its labors during the worst of the heat, to Bear's Rib's lodge. He'd pester Alexandra a bit. She'd gone tiddly for the savage life—a bit beyond what he'd expected, but she was the ethereal sort, and one never could tell. She'd no doubt have stories to tell back in Bury St. Edmunds, just as he would. In fact he could hardly wait to spin yarns. He approached the larger lodge, brightly stained with umber stick figures he took to be battle scenes, and found Alexandra not where he expected, huddled over some miserable hide, fighting greenbottle flies and scraping stinking yellow flesh from it, but standing quietly in the white sunlight while the chief's squaws took tucks in a fringed white doeskin dress she was wearing.

In fact Alexandra quite took his breath away. A blonde Sioux! The white doeskin, soft as velvet, fitted her willowy form tightly, and was gaily decorated with dyed quillwork over the bodice, red and yellow chevrons, while just above the fringed hem of her high skirt, which bared calf and trim ankle, was another red band of quills. She wore exquisite white moccasins, as fine as slippers for a ball, trimmed with rabbit fur. And over her breast lay a corrugated necklace of ivory-colored bones. A flaxen-haired jade-eyed savage! He gaped, feeling an uproar in his loins.

"Oh, Gordon, we're done with the buffalo. My dear

chief has given me a festival gown for the dances, and my sisters are fitting it."

"You look—ah! Come to the parlor wagon and I'll show you what you do to me, my dear savage."

She gazed at him levelly. "I'm not sure I want to, Gordon. Bear's Rib is such a dear. I think I may stay. He's a perfect prince."

"Really, Alexandra. It's time. Skye says we should—"

"He's a silly man."

"Oh, I quite agree. But he seems to think the sun dance isn't quite what poor innocents like us should be witnessing."

"Do you suppose they do something—" She giggled. "I must see it."

"Where is Bear's Rib?"

"Taking a sweat. They have this marvelous idea that if they sweat, they purge their bodies of evil. So they sweat in a little hutch they make, all bare in there. The squaws bring them hot rocks and water. I wanted a sweat too, but they wouldn't let me. And they're going to make me go away to a separate women's hut soon. Oh well. I'll change all that."

"I'm sure you can change anything, Alex."

He left her there, a blonde Sioux goddess who stirred wild ripples in him. Oh, for a dusky gorgeous savage! His thoughts turned toward Skye's honey-fleshed young squaw, Mary, and he knew he'd force the matter tonight. Oh, he had his ways! A whole trunkload of trinkets, among other things. And an entire cart laden with kegs of bourbon and scotch, hogsheads of ale, red and white wines, ports and sherrys, and a devilish little liqueur called absinthe, distilled from wormwood, angelica root, sweet-flag root, star anise, and dittany, all of which made the heart grow fonder, as the old joke went. Tonight Mary and the emerald green absinthe!

He found his man, Baudelaire, squatting over a privy trench that Colonel Galitzin had ordered dug, army-style. It amused the viscount to catch his man with black britches down and pasty white rear catching the air.

"Baudelaire, here you are. I've been looking. What on earth do you do all day long? See here, Baudelaire. Make sure the squaw comes tonight for a nip, eh? Make sure of it. And tell the steward—I forget how he's called—tell him to bring the absinthe, eh? And tell Lady Diana to be there. Monkey see, monkey do, eh? And have my parlor wagon aired and the bedding too. Sweetened with sagebrush. I'm savage for a savage, eh? This has gone long enough, her coming for a nip and going back to that lout's lodge."

Baudelaire frowned, a sure sign of displeasure. In fact the man's only sign of displeasure, and the viscount took savage delight in catching him at his duties.

"Your lordship, I hear Skye's insisting we be off, for reasons he knows better than we."

"Ah, it's nonsense. Bear's Rib's getting my lady all fetched up in a ceremonial dress for the sun dance. If he didn't want us, he wouldn't be dressing her. She's gone daffy for him, but so what? It's an experience, eh? The Hunkpapa village in North America?"

Baudelaire grunted.

"The squaw, Baudelaire. And think of something to divert Skye while you're about it. Maybe the bloody oaf will drink once you fetch him some whiskey."

Baudelaire smiled up at him. "Count on me, your lordship," he said. "We will all be savage tonight."

Chapter 12

The lodge of Mister Skye had been darkened so long that Mary felt glad to escape each evening. Mister Skye did not come to her in the night, and because of Victoria's vision, neither did she go to him. The old woman had turned silent, and never chattered or cursed or laughed with Mary the way she used to. They had become worse than strangers because they could not reach across to each other. It shocked her that her man didn't heed the medicine of his sits-beside-him wife. Had he no reverence for the ways of the people? This time he had mocked her vision. She'd watched with troubled eyes as he ignored the prophecy of the spirit-helper.

She didn't like being in the village of the Hunkpapa, foes of her Snake people as well as Victoria's. Her spirit ached to be free, free of them all, the Englishmen and the Lakotah, free out on the endless prairies with only themselves and Jawbone, her man's little household. Never was her own spirit far from dread, knowing these treacherous Hunkpapa could turn on them in an instant. Maybe she wasn't even safe as a guest in their village. Maybe they would even violate the sacredness of the welcoming pipe.

Like blind men walking among rattlesnakes, the Englishmen had settled down to enjoy themselves. But at least they remained cheerful and enjoyed their days, unlike those in Mister Skye's lodge. Each evening the one in black, the one who whispered with soft lips while his eyes burned into her, invited her to have medicine-water with them. And she always did, glad to escape the gloom of her lodge. They gave her lots of things, bourbon and a whiskey with a smoky flavor they called scotch, and wines, some thick and red, others amber, some almost white. They made her giddy each night and made the gloom of Mister Skye's lodge go away.

They always invited her to sit with their chiefs and that was an honor too. The others all kept to their own fire and had no spirits to drink, except once in a long while. But among their chiefs the spirit waters flowed generously, and she never had to ask. In fact they enjoyed making her so giddy she could hardly walk back to her own lodge later. They sat in canvas camp chairs, the viscount in one displaying his crest; and Lady Diana, and Colonel Galitzin, and the strange one, Baudelaire, and the Viscountess Alexandra, who stayed with Bear's Rib now. But she preferred to squat in the way of her people.

"And how is our little Mary?" asked the viscount when she joined them. "Capital, I suppose."

She did not respond. Mister Skye wanted to leave in the morning, before they began the sun dance, but had once again been stymied by the viscount. Now it affected her too, and she thought she wouldn't enjoy this evening.

"I don't know this word capital," she said softly. "I want to go away from here. Mister Skye wants to go away and show you more buffalo. It is bad to be here."

"Oh, ho! We're having a fine time, and your man worries too much, little lady."

"That is why you hired him—to worry."

"Oh! You're a clever little wench. No, my dear, we are, ah, chiefs. Heap big chiefs. And your man may advise us, but only that. We decide. In any case, he's gotten quite tractable."

She stared at him, uncertain of the big whiteman words but detecting something condescending in his talk. It angered her. And momentarily she raged at her man, at

Skye, for bowing before these people from his nation, like some slave.

"Oh, see how you pout," he said. "Well, we're going to have something different tonight. Happiness spirits. See the bottle there, green as grass. It makes us jolly, eh?"

"I don't think I will. I don't want spirits this night."

"Oh, now, that's a foolish girl. Here. Aristides, pour her a generous one. Ah, take a little, you lovely wench."

"No, I don't want to. It is the start of the sun dance and we should not be here."

"My, you're being difficult, little savage. Tell her, Diana. Tell her what the green spirits do."

"Oh, my, they make me hot and I giggle and once I took off my clothes and ran," said Diana Chatham-Hollingshead. "But his lordship caught me easily enough."

"I would not do that," said Mary.

They sat quietly while Baudelaire fussed with things at the cart full of spirits. She noticed a strange anticipation among the whitemen tonight, as if something had been planned. Then Baudelaire thrust a glass brimming with the green spirits before her. "Ah, beautiful lady, this will make you happy," he whispered. "So happy."

"I don't think so. I am afraid tonight."

"It's that Skye again," said Colonel Galitzin. "He puts a damper on things. Drink up, my pretty tart. Ze viscount has gifts for you! A Hudson's Bay blanket. A looking glass. Golden ribbons for your hair. He's been waiting to give them."

"Oh, indeed, little vixen. Have a drink now, and when the world seems better we'll laugh and play. I'm a great tickler. I'll tickle you until you shriek."

Baudelaire held the glass before her, its emerald fluid glistening in the firelight; but she shook her head.

"It is a sacred time," she said. "Even these dogs the Hunkpapa know it is a sacred time to honor Sun, who warms us and gives us all."

The viscount looked vexed. "I say, that's just heathen talk, little lady. Surely your man has educated you—"

"You want me to drink it so you can lift my skirts," she said. "You must ask Mister Skye first. That is the custom."

"Usually when they want to lift my skirts, they ask me," said Lady Diana. "I know just how I'll answer."

"My man will tell you."

"Oh! That takes the fun out of it! Have some green spirits and I'll tickle you and you'll giggle and forget all your troubles."

But she shook her head.

"Well, have some whiskey!"

"No, it is time to honor Sun."

"I say, you vixen. I just may cart you off. I just may have the colonel here pick you up like a bag of wool and cart you off."

"You may cart me off," said the Lady Diana. "If you still can. You're running to fat, Gordon."

He glared at the white woman. "You aren't savage enough. I am feeling savage."

"My poor dear savage," she mocked. "How you growl and snap. Next thing you'll insist upon being called Mister."

They laughed, all except Mary.

"Drink up, drink up!" bellowed the viscount, sipping long and deep.

"I will go to my lodge now," said Mary. She rose, but the colonel's hand clamped her wrist, like a manacle of steel.

"No, his excellency will entertain you tonight," he said matter-of-factly.

She tugged hard, but he only clamped harder with a grip like a bear trap.

"Let me go. I will tell my man."

They cackled and sipped the green fluid greedily.

The viscount's lips parted. "I am feeling savage," he cried.

"Come along, you little red slut. The viscount will give you more than you ever dreamed of," whispered Baudelaire. "It's nothing. A moment of joy. An honor. Few women receive the honor of his attentions."

She struggled to free herself, and found she couldn't. Her anger transmuted to dread and hate, even as Galitzin dragged her toward the glinting yellow wagon. She yanked hard, stumbled, heard them laugh.

"Oh, a fiesty wench!" cried Diana, giggling.

"Stop." The voice rumbled at them out of the black shadows, and she cried out to it, her spirit flying to meet it.

Mister Skye stepped into the amber firelight like some Viking giant, hairy and naked save for his breechclout and silk stovepipe hat and ugly square-toed boots. He carried only an old belaying pin of battered hickory. He squinted murderously at one and another of the sports, transfixing them with his glare.

"Let her go."

Galitzin obeyed.

"Pimps."

"I'll have you in irons, Skye. Galitzin. Put him in irons. All he's got is a stick."

"Your lordship. That's a belaying pin, and Skye was a—"

"Arrest the brute, Galitzin."

Mary rubbed her wrist where the man had clamped it, wanting to flee away, away, away from here. But she stayed.

Mister Skye turned to the viscount. "Touch my women and I'll kill you."

Baudelaire said, "My dear Skye, it was all a bit of fun. Oh, a bit risqué, I suppose, but just a little amusement."

"You lie well, Baudelaire."

"See here, Skye. You're threatening a peer of England, and I'll have you in irons, one way or another. Take your red slut, then. I don't want the dirty thing."

Galitzin dug into his brown jacket, and whipped out a small revolver. Skye's belaying pin flicked out, as deadly as a steel blade, and smacked it away, cracking the colonel's fingers.

Galitzin howled and began dancing in pain.

And from the darkness a lithe old woman emerged, pointing an old flintlock straight at Galitzin's heart.

"I say, Skye. You're perfectly insolent," the viscount raged.

A wild shriek, eerie even to Mary who had heard it countless times, pierced the quiet, and Jawbone appeared on dancing hooves, ears back, yellow eyes glowing in the firelight, snorting, teeth clacking murderously.

"I am that," said Skye.

On the first morning of the sun dance, Victoria and Mary silently saddled their ponies and rode out of the village, saying nothing to Mister Skye. He watched them go, understanding their need to escape this camp of their enemies as well as these Englishmen. Victoria's dour stare tore at him. It boiled with rebuke for ignoring her medicine and casting them all into some doom she had foreseen. He loved them both, his old sits-beside-him wife, and lovely Mary, each a gift without price for a roaming man of the mountains, sharing his joys and hardships, feasts and famines. Never before had his lodge been darkened by discord, and it tormented him.

He wanted desperately to go himself, just ride out into the breeze on Jawbone, lean into a shaggy cottonwood in a coulee somewhere, and watch cloud shadows windrow the golden grasses. He needed that. Needed to escape this lord of England and his retinue, all the condescension of his class. The viscount had not reached his position through a natural aristocracy of merit, or genius, or industry, but by hereditary right.

Mister Skye's own origins were far from base. He'd been born into the merchant class, son of an exporter and importer, and had a scholarly career ahead of him before he had been pressed into the royal navy by a roving gang of sailors. At least, he thought, his class progressed to some degree   not all avenues were open to commoners—on merit rather than the breeding of sires and dams. And while a debauched lord could fairly well ruin his estate, a lord of England he remained, while the life of any commoner required more character and courage.

Mister Skye was sick of them all, sick of their lechery, their attempts to seduce his Mary of the Shoshone, their nightly bouts of heavy drinking. Not that Mister Skye didn't drink himself, to excess on occasion. He held it to be a weakness in him. But most of the time he didn't drink spirits at all, and so his world held together—until now.

His heart cried for the liberty of the prairies, but he could not bring himself to leave. He loathed his own weakness. The viscount had some kind of grip on him, awakened something servile in him, rooted in his childhood, in an Englishman's respect for peers of the realm. He hated it. He'd lived in perfect freedom here in the American wilderness until this lord had found some way to reduce him, enticed him to ignore his own judgment. He saw himself becoming a lackey, like Galitzin, and it sickened him.

So he lingered sullenly in the village, making a point of stalking hot-eyed through Lord Frazier's entourage, daring Galitzin and his men to do something. They didn't; the sun dance absorbed them. The first day they stood around the great bough-covered sun lodge, chattering and joking, until Mister Skye told them that what they were witnessing among these Sioux was as sacred to them as Holy Communion was to Christians. That didn't quite stop it, but at least they'd been warned.

Each day fasting warriors chanted prayers, heaped gifts to Sun around the forked central pole that supported the brushy lodge, and recited their exploits in battle, often pantomiming the ways they counted coup.

He had no wish to talk to the viscount, Galitzin, or Baudelaire, but didn't mind explaining things to Lady Alexandra, who watched quietly, full of romantic notions. She fascinated him, this blonde beauty wearing exquisite Sioux ceremonial dress, quilled and beaded so delicately that the work could have won a display in the British Museum.

"It's something you can endure now, Lady, but not on the fourth day. I think you'd better not watch then."

"Oh, it is beautiful. These Hunkpapa souls know only light, unlike ourselves. What are they doing now, Mister Skye?"

"They're giving sacrifices to Sun, to appease Onk-te-gi. That's the spirit in the body of all living creatures. If he's appeased, the tribe prospers."

"Oh, that's beautiful."

"You haven't yet seen one kind of sacrifice, I'm afraid."

The youth, Sitting Buffalo Bull, had vanished, and Mister Skye suspected he was fasting in preparation for the brutal fourth day.

Each evening Skye's women returned out of the prairie, and silently slid into their robes, barely acknowledging him. So his lodge remained gloomy, and he had begun to take his food at the cooking cart of the Britons because no one in his dark lodge bothered to prepare it. As the Hunkpapa sun dance progressed his women seemed more and more distant, and he wondered where out there in the great circle beyond the wide valley they lingered, and what they did during the burning days.

On the fourth day of the sun dance a new mood pervaded the village, as tense and solemn as a crucifixion. And now the villagers stared dourly at their guests, with looks that told Mister Skye, at least, that this part of it was to be private. But the viscount and his minions paid no heed. Skye hadn't spoken to them since the night he'd rescued Mary from rape, but now he decided to say something. That was his job. For this they'd employed him.

"I don't believe we're welcome at today's events, Lord Frazier," he said quietly.

The viscount stared, faint amusement rising in him. "Well, Skye, you've decided to start complaining again. We're doing quite well, thank you. I hear it's quite exciting."

"How do you know that?"

"Why, from my lady. She's learned a bit of the blarney."

"Does she know what will happen?"

"Oh, some sort of bloody pain, I guess. My men are all for seeing it, and so am I, Skye. You fret too much." The lord eyed him. "You're wandering free on my sufferance now, so watch your step, Skye. I'll have you whipped yet."

Mister Skye sighed, as unable to cope with these people as ever, and feeling trapped.

Around noon of a blistering day, Sitting Bull emerged from a special lodge made of brush, looking gaunt and solemn, and Mister Skye knew he'd been fasting. He was the only one to have made the vow. Often several men made the vow. And once in a while a woman would sacrifice for Sun, if she wanted something badly. Sitting Bull had painted himself white and black and red for this occasion, turning himself into a ghastly shining spectre. The youth spotted Mister Skye and paused, staring, meeting Skye's gaze with an unblinking one of his own. Then he smiled slightly and walked on.

A profound silence settled among the spectators as they watched Sitting Bull walk into the sun lodge, accompanied by that craggy-faced medicine man, who was now wearing a buffalo-horn bonnet and carrying medicine pouches in addition to the one he wore around his neck. Two others came also, village elders, each with those peculiar scars across their breasts. The Hunkpapa knew what was to come and waited expectantly, and the Britons, sensing something sacred in this, settled into unaccustomed reverence. Children clutched their mothers solemnly, drinking in this sacred event.

Sitting Bull stretched himself on his back, waiting. The two elder warriors, large powerful men with battle-scars on their flesh and coup feathers in their hair all displaying valor, withdrew glinting knives.

"Oh dear no," muttered Lady Alexandra.

Mister Skye watched dourly. They'd all been warned over and over. Several of his lordship's retainers sweated and twitched. The viscount looked pale, determined to endure whatever sights he must behold.

One warrior jabbed his knife horizontally through the chest muscle until its point emerged inches away. Sitting

Bull groaned in spite of his best efforts not to. Red blood, brilliant red, bright as death, gouted from the wound and sheeted down Sitting Bull's side and belly.

"Oh! Don't do that!" cried Lady Alexandra.

The medicine man glanced angrily at her.

Sweat beaded on Sitting Bull's brow. The warrior slipped a skewer of glossy bone through the wound until both its ends projected from the youth's chest. Then they repeated the whole thing, jabbing the bloody knife through the muscles of the left breast and following it with a skewer. Sitting Bull's body turned red.

Lady Diana moaned, and looked ready to flee. Several of the viscount's men had vanished from the silent crowd, and Skye glimpsed one heading for river brush, holding his stomach.

The warriors tied braided thongs to the ends of each skewer and tugged mercilessly, lifting corded flesh off Sitting Bull's chest until one could see raw red muscle in the leaking wounds. The youth stood up shakily, muttering something that Mister Skye understood, even as the blank gaze of the whole village fell upon him and then the Britons. Mister Skye stood his ground, thankful that Victoria and Mary hadn't heard and the others didn't understand. There were so many young men, in so many villages across the plains, who had made the same vow, often during a sun dance like this. And so far it had come to nothing. But one never knew.

The warriors snaked the two lines up over the fork of the sunlodge pole and tugged higher and higher until they lifted the sinewy muscles from Sitting Bull's chest, forcing him to stand on his bare toes facing the pole. And then they anchored the ropes that way.

"Hiyah!" cried the young man in a voice that carried

eerily out upon the throng and into the prairie. He began his slow, spastic dance, sometimes throwing himself backward until he hung from the bone skewers. Around the pole he went, singing his song, scorning the pain, sheeting blood from wounds that grew with every vicious tug.

"Good God, Skye, when does this end? Will he die?" asked the viscount.

"When he pulls himself free after dancing the rest of the day, mate. The skewers must work through his muscle."

The viscount watched, disturbed. Both Diana and Alexandra fled, the viscountess sobbing as if something inside her had been violated.

"Skye. What did that chap say just before he began that dance, eh?"

"He asked Sun to honor his sacrifice of undergoing torture, and to give him strength to fulfill his vow."

"But what did he vow, Skye?"

Barnaby Skye wondered whether to tell the viscount, and finally decided he would. He lifted his silk hat and settled it again in ritual gesture. "To kill me because I once killed Hunkpapa in a battle. And all white trespassers."

Chapter 13

Sometimes Victoria rode out of the village with Mary, but this day she didn't. She wished to be alone, and learn about aloneness. She could not fathom why Mister Skye still lingered there. His countrymen from across the sea had a witch-grip upon his spirit. She could see that but didn't know what to do. Never before had Mister Skye ignored her medicine. Always he had heeded it, and it had saved their lives several times.

She kicked her slat-ribbed mare over to the Yellowstone—she called it Elk River—and turned the horse upstream, her heart empty but her senses savoring the clean summer air and the freedom of the land. She did not know where she would go. She never did. Her intent was to escape, not go somewhere. Back in the Hunkpapa village, the boy, Sitting Bull, lay in great pain, because the ribbons of muscle on his chest had not parted during the terrible dance until well into the night. Big medicine! That much pain would make him a great medicine leader of the Lakotah nations, and one to be feared.

She rode aimlessly along the river trace, small and weathered, hunched over her little pad saddle, and it was only by accident that she saw the warrior ahead before he saw her. Instinctively she slid her pony into the massed cottonwoods and turned herself into smoke. If he was a good warrior he would spot her anyway, because his pony would tell him where she sat on her mare. She felt no fear. With Mister Skye soon to be taken away, her own suns meant nothing. If this one was an enemy of her people, she would shoot him and then go to the Other Side when the rest caught her.

Painted! This one wore only a breechclout and coup feathers tucked into his braided jet hair. He carried a strung bow and nocked arrow, ready for anything. Great chevrons of black and white paint, made from grease and white clay, or fire ash, slashed his face and arms and announced to any observer that this one was on a mission against the enemies of his people.

She slid off her little pony and clutched the bay's nostrils, intending to clamp them shut at the first sign of whinnying.

She watched the painted warrior from deep in the cottonwoods, seeing and not seeing, following the sunlight and shadow of his quiet alert passage. Her heart lifted into its fear-rhythm, and she slid out her own Kentucky Longrifle, which had a shortened barrel, and poured fresh powder into the pan to prime it. Out toward the riverbank the warrior paused, sensing something from the behavior of his horse. He peered into the shadowed cottonwoods and didn't see her.

At least she thought he didn't. He was a wise one, and knew the birds weren't chirping and everything had become too silent. She waited, ready to cock the old weapon and shoot. The flint would strike the frizzen and make sparks. The powder in the pan would flash through a little hole, igniting the powder in the barrel and driving a ball into the heart of the warrior. White man's magic, and she respected it.

He slid off his pony and pierced into the dense woods straight toward her, his bow at the ready. Maybe she would sing her death song now, she thought. But her medicine vision was not of this. Closer he came, alert and ready, studying all things. She admired his skills. Closer still, and her heart leapt. Absaroka! Everything told her: his moccasins; the color bands on his arrow; the shape of his bow; the way he had painted himself.

A magpie exploded from a branch and he whirled. Odd that a sun-loving magpie would haunt these shadows. But not odd at all if her spirit-helper had come to protect her. The warrior whirled, followed the flitting raucous bird as it hopped toward the river, and at last he made his way back to his pony and headed back up the Yellowstone. She wanted to cry out after him, this one of her people, but she didn't. Instead she turned her pony deeper into the woods until she reached the broken river bluffs, and steered the mare into a tiny coulee leading upward toward the rough plains. Up there, from a position well hidden by the crease in the slope, she might see.

Near the top, she tied her pony in the deep shadow of a three-limbed juniper, and clambered the last bit of slope breathlessly until she could peer out upon the breast of the earth and down into the river valley ahead. They were there, more than she could count. Maybe two hundred Absaroka, painted for war and stalking the Hunkpapa, planning to avenge ancient wrongs. She squinted hard, trying to name names, but they were a little distant for her old eyes. She sensed these were river Absaroka, not her own mountain Kicked-in-the-Bellies. Still, the People of her tongue, within the hoop of her nation. Oh, to go talk with them! To talk in the language of her birth, and see kin! For there would be many she knew and others she'd heard of. And she could tell them much about the village. They were resting their ponies in the midday heat, and soon would ride again, a long bright column of warriors, painted and armed and ready to die.

She crouched uncertainly, a dilemma pinioning her. Her man and Mary and Jawbone were in the Lakotah village. And the first thing the Hunkpapa would do under attack would be to murder them, and the whitemen too. Every one, but especially Mister Skye, who had fought beside the Absaroka against them. It could happen in moments: the village wolves would spot the Absaroka column; Bear's Rib would gather his elders while warriors sprang to their horses and gathered arms; and the wolves, the village police, would turn upon Mister Skye even before her man knew of trouble. The rest she didn't care about. Let the Hunkpapa do what they would to Lord Frazier. But even as she thought it she felt bad inside. Her man had agreed to protect Lord Frazier and his party. So she must, no matter what her feelings.

She slipped back to her gaunt pony and led it away, carefully keeping a high, grassy hump that was famous as a watching place between herself and the war party. After a little while she slid onto her mare and rode across the prairie-tops, well south of the Yellowstone valley. It would be safer than following the river bottoms. She peered back warily, but no one pursued. Sun had already covered most of his day's journey when she dropped down the bluffs, under the watchful eye of the village wolves, and into the Hunkpapa village. She could see it was preparing to move, with the dance over, the entire flat where the Tongue and Yellowstone conjoined stripped of golden grass, and the odors of long habitation dense in the sultry air. It looked peaceful, but in a little while everything would change, and the shriek of the wounded would fill the land.

She had no time. At any moment the police society would spot the Absaroka and the crier would spread the alarm through the whole village. She kneed her sweating mare straight toward her lodge and found her man there, and Mary, neither of them doing anything except waiting for the furnace heat to lift.

She slid down and padded directly to Mister Skye, who peered up at her somberly, a question in his eyes.

"Absaroka! Painted! Many, many!" she hissed.

Mister Skye sprang to his feet even before she'd finished, and Mary started walking swiftly toward the herd to collect their mules and horses.

"How much time?" her man asked.

"No time."

He squinted at the village, knowing exactly what would happen when the alarm sounded. She could see that.

"Leave the stuff," he said.

Her man trotted toward Frazier's camp nearby, while she caught Jawbone and saddled him. The horse watched her with laid-back ears. Then she grabbed halters and raced toward the herd to help Mary, keeping her pace just slow enough not to draw attention.

When she returned, with two mules in tow, she saw her man roaring at Galitzin. Good. The warrior chief, not Lord Frazier. But the warrior chief wasn't listening, and then she saw the viscount emerge from his wagon with no shirt on, and saw them all talking and waving arms. She squinted at the ridges to the west, and saw nothing. No village wolves scrambling down the bluffs or riding the ridge, shooting off their fusils.

As long as they were arguing, she'd save what she could. She threw a packsaddle over a big mule and cinched it, and then stuffed their things, the pemmican and jerky, powder and ball, spare moccasins, Mister Skye's belaying pin, into parfleches and then into panniers. Mary did the same. They would take everything except the lodge. No time for that. And dismantling it would alert the village. At last Mister Skye hastened toward them, and behind him men stirred, heading for the arms cart where Gravesend began handing out weapons.

"What?" she cried.

"Can't get them to leave quick. They want to take the carts. Half hour of harnessing. Frazier says they've got thirty armed men, some with double-barreled scatterguns. I told him they'd be dead in minutes, scatterguns or not. And I'd be dead even faster than that. He called me a coward and other things. I said I'd stay and defend them—if they'd listen. And you'd try to reach your people, let them know. Frazier got excited, said they'd harness up and head for the ridge and watch, like some tournament."

"You'll die. Why do you do this?"

He sighed. "I have to. It's my job. I was paid to do it, even if they ignore my advice. At least Galitzin's been told. He can organize them. If Frazier lets him. His lordship thinks he'll sit on a ridge and watch an Indian war."

Victoria turned away, her old eyes suddenly blurred. She did not want to look at him or let him see her eyes. Moments later she and Mary rode their ponies up the grassy bluffs, leading the packmules, ever farther from her man. And ahead were the warriors of her own people, whose presence might kill Mister Skye. The village wolves eyed their passage, whispered to each other, but did not stop them.

Mister Skye watched his women ride away, growing smaller and smaller until they topped a horizon and vanished. He wondered if he'd ever see them again. They'd attracted the attention of the village wolves, who were collecting up there to talk about it.

The village barely stirred. A crowd of young men played the stick game near the riverbank. Old men gossiped. Only the women stirred, packing their belongings in preparation for the exodus to a new campsite starting in the cool dawn. A few hunters were out in the cottonwood bottoms looking for deer, but not very hard because the village was glutted with buffalo meat. Off in the center of the village Bear's Rib sat before his lodge, listening to medicine men decide where the village should go next. Up on the bluffs the policing society spread out once again, but didn't seem alarmed.

Mister Skye turned toward the activity at hand, and saw at once that it looked too hasty. Retainers were wildly sorting out harness and folding up camp.

"Colonel Galtizin," he said. "Slow down the men. Hide those weapons at once."

Galitzin stared at him, rapping a gold-headed swagger stick against his brown britches.

"Colonel. Your safe passage out of here—if it exists at all—is to leave in a normal way, not a panic."

"Who's in a panic, Skye? His lordship wants us to gather on that western ridge so we can watch ze fight. We must hasten or miss it."

Skye grabbed the man by the brown lapels of his hunting jacket and tugged. Galitzin bounced into him, yanked by a giant hand.

"Unhand me, you oaf!"

Skye didn't. Instead he spat words into the face he had yanked inches from his own. "In that village, Galitzin, are about a hundred and fifty able warriors, capable of becoming an army in about a minute, armed and mounted. Add fifty old men and boys itching to slaughter you. And your ladies. Add a hundred women who can draw a bow as well as their men."

"We'll hold them off. Carts make a defensive ring."

"You'll fail. And you'll never see your horses again."

Something changed in Galitzin's eyes. At least he was listening.

"Stop the panic, Galitzin. It may be too late. It's been noticed. I'm riding to Bear's Rib and tell him we've decided to leave, go buffler hunting again. Maybe—just maybe—I can make this look natural—if you help."

Galitzin didn't reply. Skye let go of the man, and he staggered. A bulldog barked, growled, and bit Skye's boot.

"Your disrespect will be reported to his lordship, Skye," Galitzin said.

Skye ignored the man. He strode away, barely containing rage, and clambered up on Jawbone, who sensed trouble and clacked his teeth, peering about with scurvy eyes. He steered his roan straight through the village toward Bear's Rib's lodge, trying to find a way to make a late-afternoon exodus seem normal. Behind him he heard Galitzin snap orders to hide the weapons, and knew he'd won—for a moment. Still, the feverish activity had alerted the village, and people stared at the whitemen who were frantically gathering their horses and packing up.

He rode past the lodge of Sitting Bull's family and saw the youth lying on a pallet before it, his grossly swollen chest bandaged. It would be a month before the torn flesh would heal. Sitting Bull watched his passage with raptor eyes, mumbling something.

There were no smiling faces in this village now. Sitting Bull's vow had reminded them all that Mister Skye fought beside the Absaroka and made widows in lodges here. His passage past busy women and idling men occasioned stares and muttering, but he ignored them. The lives of all he'd been paid to protect would depend on his skills now. He scanned the bluffs anxiously, hoping not to see a horseman racing along a horizon, firing warning shots or waving a blanket. If only the Crow war party would linger a while more . . .

He dug into his possibles kit and found a pungent twist of tobacco. If he could nerve himself to do it, while his every instinct screamed at him to get out, he'd propose a goodbye smoke with Bear's Rib and his shamans. He didn't know if he had the courage. If the alarm sounded while they were smoking, they'd likely slaughter him on the spot. But only if they identified the enemy as Crows.

He reined Jawbone to a halt a little apart from the circle of village headmen and shamans, and dismounted slowly. He was not a natural horseman, and clambering on or off had never been easy. He took his time unbuckling his holstered Colt revolver, and laid the belt over his pad saddle. It was a sign of peace and trust. He clutched his twist of tobacco, walked to the periphery of the ring, and waited there. These were village leaders, and they were engaged in medicine ceremony, and dressed for the occasion. The selection of a new village site, and even the way to travel there, would be divined by medicine men and war chiefs in congress. The village would need grass, water, trees, and proximity to *pte*, the sacred buffalo.

Time ticked slowly as the headmen continued their divinations, eying Skye occasionally. While he waited, he watched the slumbering hills for signs of the eruption to come, but they lay somnolent in the summer heat, innocent of death. At last Bear's Rib stood and invited him to a place of honor within the circle. Mister Skye settled himself awkwardly—his blocky body never folded easily to the ground—and began at once to say his goodbyes, using what Sioux words he knew, supplemented with his talking fingers.

His party had decided to pull out now, ahead of the village, he said, and head westward on their trip. He brought with him a twist of tobacco for a final smoke, and to honor them for their hospitality.

"Where are the others, the great chief from across the waters, and his headmen, Mister Skye?" asked Bear's Rib. "Have they forgotten us? And why have your women gone away?"

Mister Skye sighed. As usual, nothing of consequence ever escaped a village. By some mysterious telegraphic means, everyone knew everything.

"My women have gone ahead. The ones I guide are busy packing. I will bring them for a smoke soon. But now I have a twist for you, as a gift."

Tobacco was a peace-gift everywhere on the plains, and Mister Skye hoped it might do. He handed it to Bear's Rib, who sniffed its aroma and smiled. He nodded to one of his young women who was hovering near the lodge, and she ducked inside to fetch the pipe.

"It is a strange time to leave, Mister Skye," Bear's Rib observed.

"It will make your passage in the morning easier, Bear's Rib. We will smoke our pipe now instead of in the morning when you will be eager to be off."

Bear's Rib nodded. He accepted the red-quilled pipe pouch, made of the velvety hide from an unborn buffalo calf, and deliberately withdrew the pipe, packing its pink pipestone bowl with the tobacco.

"The woman with hair the color of sun went away after the sun dance," he said as he tamped. "I would trade many ponies for her."

"Ask her man," said Skye. "Perhaps he will trade. He needs good ponies for his carts."

"The carts are strange sights," the chief said, lighting the pipe with an ember passed to him in a green leaf by one of his women. "White men show us astonishing things." He sucked until the tobacco glowed yellow, and then began the ancient ritual, saluting the spirits that dwelled in the cardinal directions, and then *Wakan Tanka*, the One Above, and the Earth Mother below.

Time ground on. Mister Skye studied the ridges. The

pipe made its way around the circle of elders, some of whom watched Skye malevolently, Sitting Bull's vow obviously on their mind. And still time ticked on, as each performed the ritual. Mister Skye's nerves abraded with every salute to the spirits, and he wondered if he could endure to the end of this.

Off at the edge of the village he heard the hawing and bawling of drivers, and the creak of carts, and a moment later the viscount's party wallowed across a soft bottom of the Tongue and began toiling up a western slope. The elders watched curiously, some frowning because of this impolite exodus.

The pipe came to Master Skye, and he ritually saluted the spirits, even while he watched the caterpillar of carts toil up a steep grade toward the western horizon, inching away from the Hunkpapa. Now Skye sat alone in a village of Victoria's ancient enemies, and it made his hair prickle. Slowly the caravan topped the bluff and dwindled into small dots while the elders watched.

Bear's Rib took the pipe and tapped it, dumping the dottle, and turned to Skye. "You did not speak truly, saying you would bring the great chiefs to us, Mister Skye."

His eyes plainly expressed distrust, and something more: the power to do whatever he chose with this famous big-medicine whiteman who sat beside him unarmed.

Just then two Hunkpapa wolf-society warriors, half way up the loaf-shaped signal mound to the southwest, discharged their pieces.

Chapter 14

They topped the bluffs and rode out onto a sun-blasted grassy plateau. It hadn't been a long uphill trek, but enough to wind the drays and horses, so Galitzin ordered a halt to let the beasts blow. Lord Frazier sat his pony, absorbing the empty sweep of land shimmering in a white glare. Just north lay the emerald valley of the Yellowstone, coiling between golden bluffs. Far to the south rose low hills, thickly blackened with pine, toothing the horizon. To the northeast he could make out the green valley where the Tongue joined the Yellowstone. Tiny figures down near the Hunkpapa village were scurrying about, gathering fractious horses. He could no longer make out the lodge of Bear's Rib or see that perfidious guide Skye smoking the pipe with the savages, but it didn't matter.

"I say, colonel, isn't that the war party?" he asked, pointing toward a column of crawling dots in the hazy west. The viscount could see that the fight between the Crow and Sioux would occur right around the confluence, with each side unable to spot the other until the last moment because of the dense cottonwoods.

Galitzin pulled field glasses from his kit and watched. "That's what it is," he said. "A large column."

"I say, Galitzin. Let's watch. Head for that promontory, eh? We'll see a rare thing, oh a proper joust! Have them put up the marquess, eh? The ladies and I'll watch. Set a guard, of course. Some of those blokes might ride up here."

"It might be better to withdraw from sight, your lordship."

"Pshaw! Let's see the fight! The Hunkpapa won't fight

us, and Skye's squaws went off to warn the Crow to leave us alone, eh?"

Galitzin nodded reluctantly, and commanded the column to make for the level bench near the signal hill. A minute later the viscount's retainers trotted out the gaudy marquess tent from a cart and erected it with its open side pointing northeast. The white and green-striped linen chattered in the furnace wind but in short order the noble tent stood, a protection from harsh sun and the hot gale. Swiftly the men arranged camp chairs within, and settled the viscount and his ladies in them.

"Oh, capital, capital, Galitzin! We've a grand view of the whole spectacle."

"I hope the savages aren't cowards," said Lady Diana. "Do you suppose they'd cut and run? I do so want a fight."

"It'd be a pity, my lady," said Galitzin.

"Savages," said Lady Alexandra. "Blood and gore, feathers and paint, medicine and death. Oh, how they send their ghastly vibrations through me! I shall write an ode!"

"You're being ethereal again, my dear."

Baudelaire supplied opera glasses from the viscount's bountiful supplies, one each for the ladies, the viscount and himself, and they settled down to watch while the canvas behind them rumbled and snapped in the gale like God clearing his throat.

"The Crow column's halted," muttered Galitzin, peering through his field glasses. "They're consulting, I think."

"I suppose Skye would tell us they're making medicine," the viscount said.

Galitzin studied them. "Zey're looking this way."

"Colonel, run up the flags, eh? That'll warn them." The viscount didn't relish the attention his candystriped tent was receiving below. "And arm the men, eh? I wouldn't want those naked thieves around our carts."

Galitzin nodded. A sharp command to Gravesend set men running, and in a minute the Union Jack flapped from one pole of the marquess tent, and the viscount's own banner, a green shield on a white ground, flapped from the other pole. The colonel posted an armed guard at either side of the tent as well, just to ward off trouble, and sent the rest of the cartmen and carts back from the promontory, where they would be less visible.

"Ah! That's better, colonel. The savages all know the Union Jack. They've all traded with Hudson's Bay, I imagine."

"What if they come?" asked Diana nervously.

"Why, we'll distribute arms and repel them, my dear. Gravesend's at the ready I'm sure."

"I wish I had my rifle," she said darkly.

"Watch the show, watch the show! Will you ever see the like again?" He turned to his aide. "Say, Baudelaire, let us have some refreshments, eh? Tell the cooks! How can we watch these savages chop heads off without tea and tarts?"

"I want scotch," said Lady Diana.

"I don't believe we have water," said Baudelaire.

"Well fetch some. Send a man."

"Of course." Baudelaire smiled and vanished from the chattering, stuttering tent.

Down in the village warriors were leaping onto bare-backed ponies and urging them toward the river in knots, while others still gathered arms. Most unwarlike, the viscount thought, observing the clots of warriors erupting every few moments from the lodges below. And off to the left, in the Yellowstone valley, the Crow still stalled for some reason, a congregation of them on their ponies collected around one or two with warbonnets. He swept the whole panorama with his opera glass, and discovered two or three savages straight ahead on the lower reaches of the very promontory from which they viewed this grand event. These faced the Hunkpapa, and seemed to be their village police, signaling the whereabouts of the Crow. Ah! What a sight! What a fine yarn to spin back in the clubs!

He wished he had Skye at hand to answer questions. The only thing of any value about that guide was that he knew his savages and what they were doing. But the dustman probably sat back there puffing a pipe in the village.

Off in the heat haze the Crow began to divide into two parties, each under a bonneted chap, he noticed. By George, at least they were organized, unlike the Sioux savages, who all raced hither and yon like headless hens.

"Sketch it, Alex. Have the guard fetch your pad and charcoal, eh?"

"It's too beautiful to sketch. I'd never capture it," she replied.

"Well I'll have them send your things." He clapped his hands sharply. "Guard. You, there. Go fetch the lady's portfolio, eh?"

The Hunkpapa boiled up the Yellowstone bottoms, but were often obscured by the canopy of cottonwoods. Many still straggled out of the village, after snatching ponies from the farflung herd. The Crow, on the other hand, had divided themselves, one wing proceeding down the river straight toward the Hunkpapa, and the other—oh, a surprise!—turning squarely toward the promontory. Why, he thought, the buggers were going to circle around and hit the village from its flank. And they'd pass close enough to give him a dandy look at greased bronze bodies, feathers, painted ponies of every description, the whole bloody thing.

"I think they're attacking us," said Diana nervously.

"Oh, pshaw, they're flanking the Sioux. They'll swoop down on that village from up here. What a sight, eh?"

"Shouldn't we be armed?" she persisted.

Maybe they should. "Galitzin!" he bawled, not seeing the colonel. He unfolded from his camp chair and peered around the edge of the fluttering canvas. There was the colonel, leading a squad of cartmen at a trot, all of them well armed with good British steel, powder and ball.

"Ah, colonel! You're ahead of me. Good thinking, man. Post these blokes round about. If that baggage gets too close, pop a warning shot, eh?"

"Where's the damned wine steward?" asked Lady Diana. "I want spirits. Where'd Baudelaire sneak off to? You can't trust servants to do their duty any more."

"I'm sure he's fetching something, my dear."

"Well, I'm dry as a camel's tit. Tell him to move his arse or I will."

"Where are my puppsies? Where's Chesterfield?" asked Lady Alexandra.

"I think zey took to the shade under the carts, my lady," said Galitzin.

"Have Chesterfield brought! He would enjoy this! He'll snap and growl!"

"I'll send a man, my lady."

"No, you do it. You're master of the hounds."

"As you wish, my lady." Galitzin, sweating in the broiling heat but unwilling to doff his brown tweed jacket, trotted back toward the carts to capture the bulldog.

"Really, Alex. You should be watching this, not worrying about your little puppsie," chided the viscount.

"I want Chesterfield to see it too," she replied coldly. "Oh, the brute strength of those savages!"

They were closing now, around a hundred Crow warriors on thin ponies, each man stripped down to a breechclout, their amber flesh glinting from sweat or grease and slashed everywhere by chevrons of color, vermilion across their brows, white, black, ochre. Some three hundred yards distant they fanned out into a rough line that stretched clear across the western slope of the promontory. At first their piercing cries sounded almost gentle, wafting in against the rumbling breeze. But then the cries grew sharper, like the bark of coyotes under a fat moon, and the thump of distant fusils reached them at about the same time as the ripping sound of balls piercing linen.

He lacked even a moment but he made one. Just as Bear's Rib and the elders sprang to their feet, Jawbone shrieked. Mister Skye threaded through the Hunkpapa, wresting himself away from powerful grips that snared his forearms and ankles. Jawbone knew. The horse bulled in, teeth clacking, front hoofs striking. Mister Skye curled around to the side, quieted the berserk roan with a sharp command, and mounted. His revolver belt had slid to earth; no time to fetch it. He steered around lodges, somehow dodging women, children, old people, and racing warriors, along with curs and loose ponies. Jawbone raced between the cones, tipping kettles, collapsing racks of jerky, scattering embers, pulling picketlines and perforating staked hides.

But Mister Skye wasn't watching where Jawbone took him. His gaze lay on the bluffs and the armed wolves, the police society of the Hunkpapa, who had alerted the village to attack and were even now shouting to each other and urging warriors in the village to ride up the Yellow-stone. And who were pointing at Skye as Jawbone burst around the last lodge at the edge of the village and lunged through the muck of the Tongue. They'd stop him if they could. They'd try to keep him from reaching the Crow and fighting beside those old enemies of the Hunkpapa.

He had only his sheathed Hawken. One shot, if the cap was over the nipple and the powder still dry. He let the weapon rest in its beaded buffalohide nest, and headed straight toward the knot of Hunkpapa. He always did that if he could, and it had become a part of his medicine legend. But it was also the direction in which Victoria and Mary and their packmules had ridden earlier, and the route that Frazier's cart train had taken to the top of the bluffs and out upon a broken land above. He felt Jawbone gather his powerful muscles to bound upward as the bottoms gave way to steep-sided slopes. Ahead, warriors bent short bows and loosed arrows, white blurs that flashed close. Already in range. Jawbone knew. He shrieked demonically, striking terror in enemy hearts, the terror of the yellow-eyed medicine horse bounding in berserk leaps to butcher them with his hoofs and teeth.

One warrior fled, but the other four stood their ground, spitting arrows that hissed past like lightning, one glancing off his boot, another nicking his neck and a third notching Jawbone's left ear. He shrieked, a murderous proclamation of what he intended to do in a moment. Mister Skye glanced behind and discovered half a dozen Hunkpapa mounted and pursuing. They wanted Skye. They might stave off the Crow, but not the Crow plus Mister Skye. And every one of them burned with the medicine power of Sitting Bull's vow, sanctified with pain and blood just days before.

The wolf warriors expected him to race up a coulee with a shallow grade and a worn trail, so they fanned out on either side for the coup. But Skye kneed Jawbone left, toward an impossibly steep bluff, broken by sandstone outcrops. Behind, the village warriors gained ground. Jawbone was far from the fastest horse on the prairies, but Mister Skye treasured him for other things, his staying power and sheer strength. The horse danced, eying the barrier and knowing he would skin his hocks pawing upward over ledges, but he never faltered, and his weird shrieks sounded like a gale in high rigging.

Mister Skye stretched a horned hand with stubby fingers over the animal's sweaty neck and withers, an act of love, and the touch loosed a tremor through the great horse. They picked up cover now from juniper and sandstone outcrops, but still the deadly arrows stabbed in, one through Jawbone's mane, nicking his neck. The horse bawled and leapt, just as another deadly shaft sliced air under his belly. The Hunkpapa pursuing him had edged into range now, and an arrow from the rear glanced off rock as Jawbone boomed by.

"Scared you, Jawbone. Everything scares you and me," Skye said. "All I've ever done is keep you afraid, and steer some." Jawbone's battered ears rotated back, listening to Skye's quiet crooning. The mighty horse reached the first ledge, a five-foot leap coming off a steep incline below. He shuddered, gathered, and sprang, lifting himself and Mister Skye's massive bulk upward, hooves flailing, then spattering chips of yellow stone like grapeshot from a cannon, rear hooves clawing stairs out of rock, and then they were over. Ahead lay two small ridges, easy to leap, and a horizon with anything beyond it.

"Ah, horse, I knew you could. Luff to the crest now, and

we'll raise the stun'sails," he said, sudden joy sweeping through him.

Jawbone limped slightly and Mister Skye knew the horse had skinned a fetlock clawing up the rock facade. He steered the animal toward the rolling shoulder, unsure what lay beyond. Now, he thought. Now pull the old Hawken with its short octagonal barrel, and be ready. Jawbone seemed to gather another wind and pumped furiously upward, sailing over a low shelf of rock, and then out. The whole world grew, horizons suddenly skidding away and away into hazy infinities. He tugged Jawbone down into a walk, squinting behind him to see what came. Nothing. The ledge had foiled pursuit from the rear. Far off on a neck of level land, he spotted the viscount's caravan, and something else—a bright oblong green and white tent with banners flapping hard in the whistling river of air out of the south. A tent? He could scarcely imagine it. He turned Jawbone that way and kneed the winded animal, squinting about for signs of pursuit.

A tent. Men scurrying about among the carts, unhooking the drays. Camping there, apparently. An infinity from water. Puzzled, he rode north across the scooped head of the coulee, and as he turned the horse into that crease of land, he spotted something he wished his eyes could not witness.

There, invisible in that vee to the distant Britons, were a half dozen Hunkpapa wolf society warriors milling about two small figures hunched over their ponies, figures he knew at once. They all spotted him and shouted, and though he could not make out the words, he knew the message. He didn't need words, eddying hard against the gale. His eyes registered the drawn bows, and the nocked arrows pointing at Victoria and Mary, and he knew their lives depended totally on what he did next. He wrestled back his instinct to boot his mad horse into a berserk run, and lift his Hawken and let it spit, for the instant he tried it each of his women would be pierced by three or four arrows, and by the time he got there he'd find them pincushioned with them, minus their scalps, and their breath.

He hunted for a way and found none. The Britons had seen none of it and wouldn't in this sloping trough of land. He would go die with his women, then. And Jawbone, too. Soon, after the battle with the Crows, every Hunkpapa warrior, every woman and child, old man and infant, would count coup on the corpses of them all.

Yet he lived, and they did too. And he'd been in tighter squeaks. He turned the yellow-eyed horse toward the knot of warriors, speaking softly to Jawbone.

"Hold your fire, mate. Hold your fire," he muttered. "They caught my ladies after all."

And no news of Skye had reached the Crow.

He pulled up Jawbone before them, and felt the animal quiver, some wild pent-up thing barely contained within. An elder warrior nodded, triumph radiating from his face. The prize. On all the plains, no prize like this. Especially in war with the Absarokas. This warrior was utterly bald—an odd thing—and murder shone in his eyes. Victoria squinted dourly at Skye, her own features blank. Mister Skye slid his Hawken back into its sheath, but the warrior barked a command, and slowly Skye slid it out again and handed it to the headman, remembering to slide the cap off the nipple as furtively as he could. The headman smiled slightly, and tapped Skye hard with his bow. No coup had ever meant more.

Skye lifted his silk hat, ran a hand through his graying hair, and screwed the hat down again, an ancient signal among them: watch, wait, be ready. Victoria and Mary responded with a faint lift of the jaw. The headman snapped a hard Sioux word, and they filed down the coulee trail toward the village. Mister Skye's back itched with the thought of so many nocked arrows with hoop iron points aimed at it. But he guessed they'd wait. They had a war to fight. And when they drove off the Absaroka, a victory to celebrate. And while they celebrated, the entire village would count coup a dozen times over, each time more painful than the last, until the final cuts and blows would land on corpses tied to poles.

Warriors steered them into an empty hollow-coned village where only a few old people remained, along with some keening women singing their medicine while they made ready for a sudden exodus if things turned against the Hunkpapa. Bear's Rib had gone too, though he was the peace chief. But one remained, still lying on his pallet before his family's lodge, and that is where the headman led Mister Skye, Victoria, and Mary. They stopped before Sitting Bull, who lay gray with pain, with tight-wrapped calico binding his swollen chest. He stared up at them, gathered strength against pain, and lifted himself to his feet, clinging to a lance he kept there for locomotion. The young man's wide-spaced eyes took it all in, and a faint joy flooded through his diamond-shaped face. Sun had been kind. Even before he had been healed of his torture sacrifice, Sun had granted him his vow. He lifted his lance and jabbed it toward Skye. The point pierced through his elkskin shirt and drew blood under a rib. It stung viciously, but Mister Skye showed them nothing in his face. Sitting Bull smiled slowly, and jabbed Mary and Victoria as well. Mary wrestled back tears. He'd hurt her.

And Mister Skye knew that was only a preliminary.

Chapter 15

Viscount Frazier leapt up from his camp chair, aghast. The ball had just missed his head. In the flapping cloth at his side a bright hole stabbed sun-glare at him.

"The savages are shooting at us! It's an outrage!"

The women scrambled up too, alarmed.

"Galitzin! Run out there and point at the flag!"

"He's not here. He's fetching Chesterfield," said Diana.

"Run for the carts," Lord Frazier cried. "We've no protection here."

"Oh, it's so savage!" moaned Lady Alexandra. "Balls and arrows!"

The two ladies lifted their skirts and raced toward the carts.

"Tell them to put the carts in a line!" the viscount cried after them.

Arrayed across the slope, more warriors than he could count raced toward the tent. The cartmen who'd spread themselves around the tent began firing, sharp cracks and blue smoke here and there. One warrior's chest bloomed red and he slid slowly from his pony, which broke free and raced laterally, slowing some of the others. The cries of war sifted to the viscount, sounding like the sharp barks of coyotes.

"Shoot the bloody buggers!" cried Frazier. "I'll go fetch Galitzin. Stand your ground, men!"

The prone cartmen were too busy to notice. Most of them had fired their pieces at once, and were now pouring powder down hot barrels, jamming in balls with ramrods, and slipping caps over nipples. The savages never faltered. Those few with fusils seemed capable of reloading on the run, pouring powder and ball down their barrels and seating the balls by rapping the butt of the weapon on their saddles. Frazier watched, astonished and paralyzed until an arrow sizzled past, and then he broke for the rear. Just as he did, a cartman screamed and tumbled back, an arrow clear through his chest with its point protruding from his back.

"Don't do that! See the flag! The Union Jack!" he cried. Oh, where was Skye. The guide knew the tongue of these savages. He could stop them. Down there smoking with Bear's Rib, that's what. He'd discharge the guide for good this time.

From the carts a barrage boomed and found its mark. Half a dozen ponies stumbled and shrieked, tumbling their warriors. Galitzin's work! Lord Frazier turned and ran, lumbering behind the ladies who screamed their way back toward the loose array of carts. Some of the cartmen who'd been defending the tent ran too, knowing they'd be overwhelmed in seconds.

Heart hammering, his lordship fled along with them. Ahead the cook and the wine steward were prying the carts about, trying to make a barrier of them, while Galitzin and the rest loaded weapons. Frazier's legs began to give out, and he trembled, losing ground. Several fleeing cartmen passed him by.

"Bloody cowards," he bellowed. "Defend me!"

One of them fell just as he passed Frazier, his entire face a mass of red and gray pulp. Horrified, the viscount watched the man flop and flail his way downward, dead before he hit the ground.

"Skye! Where's Skye? Tell them to stop!" he bawled, trembling forward on legs that caved and buckled.

The women reached the carts and tumbled to earth beyond one, sobbing. Behind, the sweeping line of warriors gained ground. Arrows pierced by. One whipped through his left sleeve, scratching his elbow. Other cartmen passed him, bloody cowards.

Behind he felt the tremor of horses, the snorts, the wild cries. They'd have him in seconds. A vicious feather-decked lance whipped by, stabbing clay just to his right.

Ahead fowling pieces boomed, a great belch of them, and he heard screams behind him. The scatterguns! That bloody fool Galitzin was firing scatterguns and barely missing him! He'd have words with that fool colonel!

Wheezing, his chest hurting brutally, he tumbled around a cart just as a second barrage of the fowling pieces caught the attack and decimated it. Horses screeched, warriors fell, and the rest turned and fled out of range. He clung to a cartwheel, feeling its iron tire burn his hand, his wind-pipe afire and his quaking body humming.

An arrow smacked earth beside Diana, who lay huddled there. She jumped. The cart offered little protection. "Turn it over," she cried. "Make a wall!"

Galitzin trotted over. "Get a piece from Gravesend," he said to the viscount. "We've turned them for the moment. The fowling pieces. But zey'll come around."

"Keep a civil tongue, Galitzin," the viscount muttered.

"Hurry! We've two dead and six more wounded."

Diana leapt up and headed for the armorer's cart. Frazier peered out fearfully and saw the warriors sweeping around toward the left, flanking the line of carts. Others gleefully pulled down the marquess tent, which sagged and collapsed like something dying. One ripped the Union Jack from its tent staff and danced with it, finally tucking it around his waist, into his breechclout belt. Another picked up the rifle of the dead cartman there. Others shot arrows into the corpse until it bristled with them. The one who'd gotten the piece whipped out a knife, slashing silvery in the boiling sun, and scalped the man, finally holding up a brown tuft of hair and yelling.

Two cartmen struggled to hold the drays, but a wounded horse galloped into the herd, scattering them like tenpins. The entire herd exploded and bolted off to the east, angling away from the closing Crow warriors.

Several cartmen leapt up and began wrestling the carts around to make an ell, even as the Crows wheeled in from the flank. The cartmen tilted one cart over, and it crashed to its side while everything within clattered and tumbled. A dozen men gathered behind this small barrier, but the Crows kept wheeling and the viscount knew suddenly they'd angle in from the rear.

Wounded cartmen sobbed, some trying to stanch the bright blood gouting from arms and legs. Others just lay on earth, leaking their life into it.

Lady Alexandra peered at them, and turned to the viscount. "Make someone help them," she pleaded. "Do something, Gordon."

"Galitzin! Tend to these men. You've bloody well neglected them!"

The sweating colonel ignored him, and continued dragging a cart around. An occasional rifle blast from the cartmen kept the circling Crows off, but their awful barks and yells caught the breeze and sent chills through the viscount.

A piece. He stumbled to the the arms cart and found Gravesend. The armorer handed him a revolver belt with a Colt's tucked in it, then a good Purdey scatter gun, paper cartridges and caps. The weight of the Colt at his belt and the hot steel in his hand suddenly inflated the viscount.

He stood tall, his heart slowing, and gazed shrewdly about him, taking stock as a commanding lord should.

Gravesend himself had a rifle at the ready, and used it between the moments when he was dispensing his wares. He rested the barrel on his cart, followed a warrior who had edged too close, and squeezed the trigger. The rifle bucked and the pinto pony out there stumbled and fell, its warrior landing on his feet and racing back out of range.

"Very good, Gravesend," the viscount said coolly. "I'll have a feather for your cap when it's done."

A gang of sweating cartmen tilted the taxidermist's cart up until it tottered and crashed onto its side, forming a little protection on the south side. Cutler, the taxidermist, howled at them for wrecking his equippage. Diana, with a small fowling piece in hand, stationed herself behind it. Alexandra peered about, clucked at the wounded, and headed for the gleaming yellow parlor wagon, situated in a jumble of carts that had not been dragged into the defense.

"Do something for those poor fellows, Gordon," she insisted, and stepped inside.

Viscount Frazier hailed the taxidermist. "I say, Cutler. Help those blokes. If you can stuff and sew skins, you can sew up those poor chaps. Give them some water, eh?"

"There's no water, your lordship. We're a mile from either river."

In fact, the viscount felt parched and he peered about looking for water. It should be in the keg on the cook wagon, and he trotted over to it; but a bullet had demolished the keg, splintering a stave.

His dry throat ached. Wine, then. The spirit wagon. He cast about, not finding it, and then spotted it in the north side barrier. Where was that bloody steward with his key?

It had to be locked at all times lest the bloody cartmen steal from it.

"Stauffinger," he roared, not seeing the steward. "Open up. I'm parched!"

Slowly the ruddy wine steward crawled out from under a cart, peered fearfully at the savages who rode back and forth just beyond shotgun range, taunting and working themselves into another assault, and sidled toward the cart.

"Fetch me some port. No, too heavy. Some Rhine. Yes, some light Rhine, eh? And another bottle for the wounded."

"Yes, lordship," he said, his key trembling in the lock.

The viscount peered in and found everything in good shape, although a fearsome arrow point had pierced clear through one wall. The steward snatched two green bottles off racks, uncorked one, let it settle and air a moment, wrapped a white napkin about it and poured a finger of it into a goblet. This he handed to Lord Frazier expectantly. The viscount savored it, decided it was adequate, but just barely. A noxious aftertaste, he thought. "Yes, it'll do. Not very good bouquet, but it'll do." The steward filled the glass and the viscount drank gustily from one. "Now, take this other one around to the suffering blokes," he commanded.

The steward locked up and began his mission, sneaking a long drink himself first while the viscount watched suspiciously.

The wine felt good. The hot British barrels of his double scattergun felt good. The weight of the Yankee Colt's revolver felt good. Galitzin didn't have a perimeter, but they'd managed barriers of some sort. A line of carts on the north; a tipped over cart on the west; the tipped over taxidermist's cart on the south. A jumble of unused carts at the southeast corner. And several enterprising blokes had pulled tents and bedding out of carts and mounded them into two heaps, and lay behind the mounds, at the ready.

The bloody savages hadn't quit, but they'd been scratched by English tooth and claw. They'd lost one warrior at least, and a few others had taken balls. And half a dozen ponies. But it never should have happened. Skye had deserted. The man's squaw was Crow. He could have stopped the whole bloody business with a shout or two, but he didn't. The bloody coward was hiding back there in the Hunkpapa village. Why did all these damned Yanks think so highly of Skye? It didn't make sense. He'd taken the measure of the lout. Maybe he'd shoot Skye for deserting, while his squaws howled. If the deserter showed up, he'd have Galitzin clap him in irons for a whipping. Indignantly, Lord Frazier peered eastward, out toward the Yellowstone valley where that barbarian lingered.

Something caught his eye about a quarter of a mile away, where the grassy plateau ended at the bluffs overlooking the valley of the Hunkpapa. He made out faces just above the grass, tribesmen peering out from below the rim of the bluff. More popped into view, a dozen, twenty, still more. All watching. Crow or Sioux? He didn't know. All savages looked alike to him.

"Galitzin! Over here!" he bellowed, pointing.

The sweat-stained colonel trotted over and stared across the dun flats, muttering. "Who are they?"

"I don't know. If that bloody guide hadn't deserted, he could tell us."

"Where's Skye?"

"In the Sioux village of course. Having a smoke with Bear's Rib."

"I doubt that," Galitzin replied.

"Keep a civil tongue, colonel."

The colonel turned away and summoned some cartmen to barricade the still-open east side, but the faces above the rim of the bluff didn't move.

"Don't shoot. They may be friendly," the colonel cautioned.

Far off to the north, the snap and moan of battle overrode the southwinds to tell them of death and blood and pain. The Crow themselves stayed just out of range, nerving themselves for another assault. They hadn't been seriously mauled. Wounded cartmen groaned in the broiling sun, and no one helped them to shade.

Out of the east a wide line of warriors materialized, trotting over the crest of the bluff. Unlike the Crow, none were painted. Sioux, then, hastily gathered into a defense. They trotted easily, saving their mounts, most of them riding bareback with quivers over their bronzed backs and bows in hand. The Crows spotted them at once, and fierce taunts crisscrossed around the Englishmen. The Hunkpapa stared at the hasty defenses but their real interest lay elsewhere, in the mocking Crow, who outnumbered them twice over. They trotted their ponies northward, away from the Crow, keeping the Englishmen between themselves and their enemies. The Crow raged back and forth, shouting, but unwilling to brave the guns of the whitemen to get at the Hunkpapa.

"Looks like zey're going to flank the other Crows, on the Yellowstone," Galitzin muttered. "Or decoy zese up here somewhere."

Lord Frazier didn't know. Everything had turned oddly quiet. The Crows began wheeling in a wide arc northward, beyond range, to try to pounce upon the Hunkpapa before the Hunkpapa swept down on the rear of the other Crows off to the north.

"I say, Galitzin. It's over for us, eh?"

Galitzin looked disgusted. "We've no water. In this kind of heat, men'll drop from thirst in an hour or so."

"Well, harness up and we'll go to it."

Galitzin sighed, saying nothing.

"Send some blokes out to find the drays, Galitzin."

At last the cartmen tended the groaning wounded, dragging them gently to the only significant shade, beneath the yellow parlor wagon. One chap sobbed and blubbered.

The viscountess watched from her window, annoyed. "Take them somewhere else," she commanded. "It's too savage for me. And fetch me cold water. It's perfectly fierce."

Cartmen stared, and silently dragged their wounded colleagues to the lesser shade of various upright carts.

The silence seemed eerie. The roaring southwind muffled the sounds of struggle off to the north, and Lord Frazier had no notion how it went. He had grown petulant with the discovery he had no horses, no locomotion other than his two feet, and nothing to pull the carts. Bloody damned Skye.

"Galitzin!" he roared.

The weary colonel shuffled up to him. "Sir?"

"Get on with it! They might come back any moment!"

"The cartmen are worn to nothing, sir. They're desperate for water."

"Well, that's regrettable. Have them build a barricade instead of lollygagging about."

"Lord Frazier, I think we'd better retreat to the Tongue. Get to water and safety in the Sioux village."

"Are you daft, colonel? Abandon the carts to those thieving savages? We'd have nothing! Nothing!"

"We may abandon them anyway, sir, without drays."

"Well, fetch the drays. Send a bloke out to find them!"

Galitzin shook his head. "Do you see them? You can look for miles in most directions."

Lord Frazier peered about and fumed. "That Skye got us into this. He should've been here. He knows how to talk to those cutthroats and could have steered them off."

Galitzin sighed unhappily. "We'd better get to the Sioux village while we can, sir. Carry our arms, and whatever we can."

"You're perfectly daft. I forbid it. Send a chap with buckets, then."

"Who'd volunteer, your excellency?"

"Why command it. They're in my service. They owe me total obedience. Tell them duty calls, the duty of any Englishman in service, colonel."

"It's a death trip, sir." He sighed. "I'll go, then."

"Are you quite all right, colonel? You go? I need you. Send some bloke we don't need."

Galitzin stared. Furnace winds eddied across the plateau, whitening nostrils and tongues, parching throats.

"I say, colonel. Have a bit of this Rhine, eh? It'll make you jolly up, take heart. I say, you've no taste for blood, you Russians. Stiffen up, eh?"

He thrust the bottle toward the colonel, who stared at it dubiously, then uncorked it and drank.

"I'll send a bit around to the blokes. Not much. I don't want them tiddly. But it'll wet their whistles."

"It'll make them thirstier, sir."

Lord Frazier peered about him, dreading the sight of a wide line of savages cresting one or another bluff. "I say,

Galitzin, here's what we'll do: Put the men in pairs, and assign each man to a cart shaft, a pair to a cart. We'll drag the carts down to the village. We'll save the carts, and have us a drink, and be perfectly safe from those bloody Crow savages."

It delighted him, his inspiration. He'd save the men and save the carts and save the whole trip. And down there, he'd set the chaps on Skye and have his revenge.

"It's only a half of a mile to the bluff. And after that, it's all downhill, colonel. The blokes can do it."

"I'm sorry, your lordship, but they can't."

The viscount glared at the colonel, enraged at this wanton defiance.

"Even if zey had the strength left to load up the carts, right the ones tipped over, and drag them to the trail down the bluff, sir, zey wouldn't have the strength to hold back the carts on that grade. Half a mile of it to the flats. You can't expect two men to slow a cart with a ton or two on it. The carts would run right over them."

"You Russians are fast to show the white flag, Galitzin. No wonder the Czars lose their bloody wars. Smile a little. See Lady Diana there. She's quite enjoying herself, eh?"

Lady Diana had commandeered a bottle from the wine steward, and was guzzling lustily, growing cheerier by the minute. "Kill the red bastards," she yelled.

The sweating colonel nodded. Men lay exhausted in what little shade they could find, while the dying groaned.

The viscount sighed and straightened himself. His fine British scattergun felt splendid in the crook of his arm, and his deadly black six-shooter weighed menacingly on his hip. "I'll go myself, Galitzin. I wasn't born a peer of England for nothing. Fetch me two pails. I'll bring water for the whole worthless lot, and get some help from my friend Bear's Rib, eh?"

He stood straight, wanting to look like a solid bulldog, the queen's own hussar. But Galitzin wasn't looking. His stare was riveted to the north, where once again knots of savages topped the bluffs and rode out on the plateau. This time they weren't in a line, and they were shooting at each other. The fight had swirled up from the Yellowstone, and was about to engulf them.

Chapter 16

Thick silence pervaded the emptied village, and it slumbered in the sun as if great events were distant rather than close. Mister Skye could hear nothing of battle, no shouts or shots on the breeze, no snort and squeal of horses. He wondered about the fate of the Britons. Perhaps they'd been swiftly overrun and only the quiet of death remained.

He could not know, and might never know because he probably wouldn't leave the Hunkpapa village alive. The police society warriors had returned to the upriver clash, but surrounding Mister Skye, Mary, and Victoria were a score of old men, each with a deadly nocked arrow in his bow. A dozen old squaws added to the force, all of them armed with bows and arrows, or lances. And even a few boys too young to fight managed to aim small bows and short arrows at him. He eyed the boys unhappily, knowing the impulsiveness of children. The older ones would hold him for the coup-counting and torture, but the boys might do anything.

Sitting Bull eased himself back onto his pallet, the pain of his self-torture etched in his face. But also glowing in his eyes was victory. It was the biggest medicine ever made in this Hunkpapa village. His chest muscles were obviously much too torn and painful for him to draw a bow for the coup de grace, nor was it necessary. His medicine had brought Skye here, and the whole village knew it. And the competent old men made sure the legendary whiteman wouldn't move an inch.

Mister Skye eased slowly off of Jawbone, who stood shivering, ears laid back, teeth clicking, his evil eyes measuring foes at every hand. He had no weapon at all save for a belt-knife, but Jawbone could be a formidable one. They knew that; all the tribesmen of the plains knew that, and many of those arrows were pointed at the animal. Their victory over Jawbone would be just as important as their triumph over Skye. But Jawbone belonged to Sitting Bull now, by right of medicine.

Still, thought Mister Skye, one word to Jawbone, and the horse would go berserk. But where would it lead? To a whole flight of arrows buried instantly in himself and his wives.

Mary and Victoria did not dismount. An old headman with notched coup feathers stuck proudly in his white hair watched closely and then gestured at the women, repeating the motion angrily when the women did nothing.

"Should we get down, Mister Skye? I am ready to die," Mary said sadly.

"Yes, Mary. We need time."

She and Victoria slid off angrily, and instantly Sioux boys commandeered their horses and the packmules, taking them some distance away. With them went the women's sheathed flintlocks and the rest of their worldly goods.

"We'll see," muttered Mister Skye.

A sharp gesture from the old headman bid them to sit down, thus reducing the chance of flight. They did so, while Jawbone sidled restlessly, almost berserk. The villagers kept their distance from his murderous hoofs and teeth, knowing the legends about him. It had become viciously hot, and Mister Skye sweated profusely in the glare. They would enjoy that little torture, denying their prisoners shade.

On the lip of the bluffs a herd of crazed horses thundered into the sky, squealing and restless, and then it plunged down the slope to the flats near the village. Familiar horses, Mister Skye thought: the saddle horses, drays and mules he'd bought for the Britons. He wondered if he could make something of that. The herd headed toward its familiar grazing grounds along the Tongue, where the horses had been during the long visit in the village.

Mister Skye watched them intently until they disappeared around a bend in the bluffs, heading for better grass. So the Britons were stuck up there, he thought. Not an animal for those carts and the yellow wagon. Not a pony to ride. It made their prospects much worse.

He wondered if he could slip Victoria out somehow in the night to talk with her Absaroka people who were engaging these Lakotah now. He doubted it. By nightfall, if this village fended off the attack, the three of them would be bound tight to trees, rawhide thongs cutting deep into their ankles and wrists. The whole village would be filing past to count coup, and after that—he didn't want to think about it. He feared pain as much as the next man, and had known his share of it. So had Victoria. But Mary hadn't, and it would go doubly hard for her.

But what about a Crow victory, a Crow rescue? He toyed with hope a bit, and then rejected it. The instant Crow warriors swooped off those bluffs, these old men would bury their arrows in the prisoners. It might save them torture—at the cost of swift death. He lifted his battered stovepipe hat and screwed it down again, his signal to watch and wait. He had no tricks in his kit. So this would be it, he thought. He'd go under now, after a quarter of a century in these wilds. He didn't regret his days here. He didn't lament a minute of the life he'd lived after slipping off of the H. M. S. *Jaguar* one foggy night into the icy water of the Columbia River across from Fort Vancouver.

"He got no medicine," muttered Victoria. "That sonofabitch Sitting Bull got no medicine. It ain't any good."

He gaped at her. She hadn't said much of anything to him for months, darkening his lodge with her silence. A question filled his eyes.

She glared at him. "It don't happen this way. You'll go away from us later and never come back."

He listened carefully. He had scarcely heeded her before because all those English pounds had scattered his brains.

"Tell me your vision," he said.

Something flamed in her old brown eyes, but before she could reply a sharp command from the old headman stayed her. They were not to talk to each other, not to make plans, plot escapes.

She shrugged, smiling faintly. He hadn't seen a smile on her face since last winter, and it affected him crazily, filled him with thoughts like mountain lupines. He began at once looking for ways. He could find none, but talk was always a way. He would make signs, use the little Sioux he knew to talk with Sitting Bull, and see what came of it.

The youth lay on his robe, his eyes joyous even through the veil of pain across his face.

"Tatanka Yotanka," said Skye, "you have made great medicine."

The youth gazed up at him from his bed of robes and nodded. "I made a vow," he replied.

"Soon you will be known everywhere—all the peoples of the plains and mountains—as the one who carries Mister Skye's scalp on your lance."

"Yes. Honor will come, but I will honor Sun for heeding my pain. I have vowed to drive away the enemies of my People, and Sun and Wakan Tanka have heard me. I don't care about honor. It is not for honor I live, but for my People. I live for the People and die for the People. My name will be great, but not because I desired it. Let that be my prophecy."

In a way Mister Skye admired the fanatical Sioux, but set that feeling aside. His life lay in the youth's hands, and he needed to gather what few facts might help him. "You'll count coup on Jawbone, too. Break Jawbone's medicine. You will torture him also."

Sitting Bull gazed softly at the mad blue horse. "No. His medicine is my medicine. After you are dead, he will come with us. He will be free, and no one will touch him. As long as he walks with the Hunkpapa, his medicine is ours, and he will be honored."

The elders listened intently, and some lifted their bows away from Jawbone, turning them toward Mister Skye and his women. To kill Jawbone after Sitting Bull had said the horse would live to honor the People would be to defy medicine.

Mister Skye watched the elders alertly. A sharp command would send Jawbone careening murderously among them, and none of the old men would pierce the great ugly roan with arrows. It was something to consider.

"We are guests in your village, Tatanka Yotanka. We stayed with you in peace."

"You warred against us beside the Absaroka dogs. That woman of yours is one. You killed the father of White Weasel and the brother of Running Moon."

He would not mention the names of the dead, Mister Skye knew, lest their wandering spirits return to plague him. The young warrior looked gray. Even standing for a minute and thrusting the lance at them had been too much for him.

"Jawbone will not let you count coup. He'll kill you if you try. No rope holds him either," Mister Skye said.

Sitting Bull grinned and then turned his face away, signalling the end of the talk. The elders would enforce it, Mister Skye knew. Something accomplished, anyway: Jawbone might live.

Off on the bluffs the sounds of war overrode the hum of the southwind. Mister Skye watched alertly, the muffled booms of barking guns eddying to his ears sometimes when the wind paused. Fowling pieces, he thought. Maybe the Britons lived, or some of them. He couldn't really tell.

Then a wide phalanx of warriors—which side he couldn't tell—rose up from the rim of the bluffs and began a swift descent toward the village, while simultaneously a large party of warriors rode down the Yellowstone toward the village, and Mister Skye could scarcely make out who any of them were.

Jawbone shrieked, turning berserk like boiling water flashing to steam.

But Victoria knew. "Absaroka," she hissed, pointing at the rolling line of warriors pouring down off the bluffs. "Absaroka!"

And probably Hunkpapa coming down the Yellowstone, he thought. The Crows would reach the village after all, but from above. He eyed the elders, who were even then responding to the sudden descent of battle, and Mister Skye wondered how many more seconds he and Victoria and Mary had to live.

Across the plateau, more warriors milled about than Viscount Frazier had ever seen before. Savages everywhere, and he couldn't make out whether they were Sioux or Crow. The bloody buggers all looked alike. Hundreds of them, racing about on their ponies, collecting in knots, the yelps and war-cries subduing the southwind. Rarely did he hear a shot. These blokes used bows and arrows and lances rather than pieces. He watched one devil tumble from his painted horse, which galloped off, and other devils jump off theirs and scalp the downed one.

Amazing!

He peered about. His cartmen had scrambled for protection under the carts, even though Galitzin was yelling at them to complete the barricades. The east side lay wide open, and only a single tipped-over cart guarded the south and west. But the heat lay white upon them, and the weary cartmen had found shade behind the tilted carts.

Frazier leapt to action, running from one cart to another. "Make barricades! Get up now and drag the carts, you chaps."

But no one did. Finally, Galitzin himself, along with Diana and Gravesend, untangled one cart from the others and dragged it off to the east, making some sort of barrier there if war should come that way.

"I say, help them!" cried Lord Frazier angrily, but no one did.

"Them lords and sirs got to wet their whistles," yelled a defiant voice behind him. "We didn't."

Frazier whirled, but couldn't make out the culprit.

Gravesend trotted back to his enameled blue armorer's cart and began filling spare shot pouches and powder flasks. Good man, thought the viscount. Inside that blue cart, which lay in the middle of their hasty perimeter, were twenty or thirty more fine British pieces. That plus two kegs of powder, caps, spare pigs of lead, several casks of fowling shot, and all the rest. Reserves.

He sucked greedily on the bottle of Rhine in his hand, sweating freely in the brute sun.

"Here they come," bellowed Diana. "Blow their balls off."

Odd how bellicose the lady'd become, he thought. That bottle she kept sucking had done it.

"Hold your fire," Galitzin countermanded. "We don't know friend from enemy."

But some cartmen ignored him, and banged away at tiny targets off in the white glare.

Still, a milling clot of savages had gathered to the east, and now rode straight toward their defenses, howling so fiercely Lord Frazier shivered. Frightful! On they came, sundering into two wings and the center, one swirling south, the other north, while the majority plunged straight at them out of the dark east. Cartmen began banging at them, sharp booms and acrid powdersmoke boiling from around the tilted carts.

Arrows stabbed into their refuge, one zipping past the viscount's face. He jumped, and crawled under the nearest cart, one full of Alexandra's evening dresses and a portable chifforobe of linen for her toilet.

Sioux! He recognized two of the buggers as they swept by on their ponies. He knew their bloody savage faces. Village blokes. It enraged him. The warriors circled the barricades, drawing fire from the cartmen, and then it happened: a powerful wedge of the Hunkpapa savages, howling bloody oaths, pierced straight into the fortress, just when cartmen were reloading their pieces. Galitzin banged at them with his revolver, and so did Gravesend, but they swept on, straight toward the blue armorer's cart. Several slid off their ponies, grabbed the tongue and doubletree, and dragged the two-horse cart out of the compound, while knocking Gravesend into the dust.

Nipping the pieces! Viscount Frazier could scarcely believe it. A mob of redmen right there, dragging the cart off! He squirmed around, trying to get his fowling piece free of the spoked wheels to blast the buggers, but by the time he did, they'd fled, leaving Gravesend kicking in the dust. Shots from cartmen followed the buggers, but as far as the viscount could make out, the thieves hadn't lost a man.

Galitzin leapt up and calmly emptied his Colt's at the savages, but no ball took effect. Beyond the compound, savages lashed ropes to the cart and then used their ponies to drag it beyond the range of the British rifles. They leapt off their ponies and swarmed around the rear, distributing the pieces and ammunition, until most of them had a weapon. An eerie howl erupted from them, and they turned their ponies eastward, skirting wide around the Britons, going after the Crows with a firepower they'd never possessed.

Frazier gaped at them, scarcely believing it'd happened. Now his blokes had only the pieces, powder and shot in their hands. He suddenly knew why all the warriors in the village had ambled by the blue cart, stared at it, prevailed on Gravesend to show them the pieces, peered into its dark hold, studying the shining weapons, the kegs of powder and shot, the boxes of caps. Lucky a bullet didn't ignite the powder, he thought. And none had stared longer, or dawdled more, than that young Sitting Bull. Thieves, the whole lot.

"Where's that damned steward. I want some booze," said Diana.

Within moments, every savage in sight had vanished over the northern lip of the plateau. Save for the slap of the southwind, the day had become as quiet as death. The crumpled forms of two scalped cartmen lay off to the north where the marquess tent had been. No sign of the tent or the campchairs remained. Not a dead savage darkened the white spaces. The bloody thieves must have trucked off their dead, he thought. If there was war down on the flat near the village, he could not discern it. The southwind hid it or the bluffs baffled it.

Slowly Gravesend sat up, rubbed a knot on his head where he'd been grazed by a warclub, and wobbled to his feet. "Water," he mumbled, staring unfocused at the rest.

Galitzin approached, looking exhausted. "I'm organizing a detail of twelve men to get water," he said. "We're still armed, and maybe we can make the Yellowstone. It's a mile that way. The fighting's over on the Tongue. That's nearer but full of savages."

"You'd leave me with just a handful to defend my person?"

"Your lordship, the men can't last. The wounded are

dying for want of water. I'm leaving the cooks, the taxi-dermist, the wine steward, and the wounded, with Gravesend in command. He'll be all right, after he recovers from that knock."

"But that's nothing—"

"There's Lady Chatham-Hollingshead and yourself, your excellency. Between you, you're worth a dozen cart-men. You alone could handle ten savages, lordship. There's Baudelaire, too. I don't know where he is, but around somewhere—and three of the wounded can still shoot. Perhaps you've a better idea?"

"Where is that Baudelaire?" the viscount bellowed. "Aristides, come at once!"

The pasty-faced gentleman emerged silkily from the yellow parlor wagon, a baby dragoon Colt's in hand. He smiled blandly. "I was protecting her ladyship," he said. "And just as well, too, because a savage peeked in while she was lying indisposed."

"I see. Summon the wine steward, Baudelaire. We'll have us a dust-cutter, eh?"

Baudelaire nodded blandly. Cartmen stared.

Galitzin snapped orders, and cartmen slowly emerged from their shelters under the carts and unearthed three canvas camp buckets and a wooden one. Lord Frazier didn't oppose. The poor wounded blokes groaned for water. A strong party of cartmen ought to get through and bring enough back.

"I'll take command. Not Gravesend," he announced to the remaining men. "Baudelaire, fetch us some chairs and glasses, and have the awning run off the parlor wagon for shade, eh?"

He watched the water detail stumble north under Galitzin, and then settled into a chair beside the yellow parlor wagon. An unearthly quiet pervaded the place. He peered mournfully at the forlorn carts, sagging on their wheels and shafts, useless without drays. Each of the carts that had been tipped over had been smashed beyond repair. Four carts ruined. Perhaps he should dock the cartmen, he thought. They did it. He gazed furtively at the wounded, lying half in the shade, half out, and wondered what to do with the helpless chaps, especially without a cart to fetch them along. Give them to Skye, he thought. They would be Skye's problem. He didn't have the faintest idea what to do, but he knew where to start. He'd catch that Skye, tie him to a post, and give him forty lashes plus one. The man deserved worse—the entire hunting trip was a botch—but it'd be the place to start. The thought of raising blood on that oaf's back, and hearing his barbarous howls, pleasured him.

Chapter 17

Mister Skye knew he had to control Jawbone. The swirling battle, edging ever-closer, had driven the mad horse to its brink. It didn't know friend from enemy and would shriek into Hunkpapa and Absaroka both. And the instant it did, arrows would bury themselves in Mister Skye, as well as Victoria and Mary. River Crow were pouring down the western bluffs of the Tongue while the village warriors rushed back from up the Yellowstone. He eased to his feet slowly, his body itching with the dread of pain and death, but for the moment the elders' attention had been drawn to the melee.

"Whoa, boy," Mister Skye muttered low. The wild-eyed

horse plotted murder and mayhem, arcing his scimitar nose up and down in terror, utterly unhinged. Mister Skye took one soft step and then another, and still no arrows pierced him, although old men followed with their bows. He caught the single rope that dragged from a crude halter, and soothed the twitching animal.

The horse trembled, and shrieked weirdly, but didn't resist, and something sagged in Skye. Standing up in the face of those drawn bows, walking two steps, and catching Jawbone, had taken all the courage he could muster. He had counted on his medicine reputation—which evoked a fear in the breast of all his captors—and it had held, at least through those seconds, though they watched him closer now.

The fight had become a fluid vortex swirling around the flats near the village, mostly warclub and lance combat at close quarters. Horses shrieked, men screamed, the squaws of the village whined and melted away toward the battle, turning their arrows on the hated Absaroka rather than the Skye family. But the elders held their arrows on Skye. Sitting Bull struggled to his feet and grabbed a lance, sweating with the pain of standing and holding it ready. Crow horsemen raced among lodges, each bent on glory, heading toward Chief Bear's Rib's lodge and the triumph of ripping it down and counting coup.

Jawbone trembled and danced, his feet lifting and falling in wild rhythm, but he did not break Mister Skye's grasp. The old headman guarding the Skyes seemed to approve.

But Sitting Bull, he with the greatest medicine ever seen in the village, thought otherwise. "Let the medicine horse go, Mister Skye," he said in Sioux. "The horse will fight for us. He will kick the dogs to death."

Victoria stared harshly, saying nothing.

"His friends the Absaroka know him," Mister Skye said.

The response enraged Sitting Bull. "He will fight them. My medicine speaks to him. Let him go or he will die."

Once again the elders' iron-tipped arrows turned toward Jawbone's chest.

Mister Skye leaned up to Jawbone's bobbing head and spoke into his ear. "Run," he said. That was not the fight command the horse had heard from its infancy. Mister Skye let go of the rawhide halter rope, wondering if this time the crazed horse would not obey. The battered blue roan quivered, jerked his head crazily, and then trotted off, slowly at first, cutting around lodges, ducking warriors who paused to stare at the medicine horse they all knew and had sung terrible tales about.

The blue horse vanished from Mister Skye's sight, hidden by the concentric rings of lodges stretching toward the perimeter of the village. The lodges hid much of the battle too, except where the land rose toward the southwestern bluffs. He could see no concentration of warriors anywhere. This seemed to be almost entirely a struggle of individual warriors, none cooperating with others, which was the way tribesmen fought. Still he watched, sickened with the thought that his great horse might lie dying, an arrow through its chest.

But then he caught sight of Jawbone again, a blue streak loping easily upslope, far from any warriors, scrambling up the very slope he had tackled before with Mister Skye on his back. With giant leaps, the horse clambered over rocky outcrops, sailing past dark junipers, and with the same mighty leap as before, he clawed up a yellow sandstone cliff and paused, triumphantly above. Then, slowly, he trotted to the crest of the bluff and stood there, his sides panting rhythmically, staring down on the chaos below. And from there, high above the fray, he loosed a scream so crazed and wild, so like the howl of a thousand wolves, that it paralyzed all below. Scarcely a warrior on either side failed to recognize that horse and that berserk howl. The Crow warriors saw an ally—a horse that was a legend among them—and peered about at once, seeking that horse's legendary owner, married into the Absaroka People.

Mister Skye whirled toward Sitting Bull, who watched intently, pain etching his face. "Now you will lose the village, and your life, even if you kill me," Mister Skye said. "He did not give his medicine to you. Your medicine's no good. You're too greedy, Sitting Bull, and now Sun will turn on you."

The Crow warriors, heartened by this great medicine sign above, turned savagely on the Hunkpapa. But the Sioux warriors, terrorized by the sight of this medicine shining in the sunlight on the bluff, fell back. With a fierce howl, Absaroka horsemen swept toward knots of Sioux warriors, driving Hunkpapa before them. In the village squaws wailed, gathered their children, and splashed into the Tongue or fled to the cottonwoods.

Even Mister Skye stood, rapt, watching that horse. What was it about Jawbone? He danced back and forth on that bluff, light shattering off him like some god-horse from Olympus, neck arched, floating above the ground like an apparition, though Mister Skye knew it was only the spring in the beast's legs, muscles spasmed by a strange madness, that created that effect. If Jawbone had sprung wings like Pegasus and flown and swooped over them all, he'd scarcely have been surprised.

He turned, discovering doubt in Sitting Bull's eyes as the youth witnessed the rout of his people.

"I can stop it," Mister Skye offered.

Sitting Bull stared, darkly, pain flaming in his gaze.

"The Absaroka are my brothers. They will listen if I ask them to spare your warriors and headmen, and let your women and children go free."

"I have medicine," Sitting Bull said curtly. "You will see."

They watched quietly, Sitting Bull, the Skyes, the elders gathered around Sitting Bull's lodge, and it grew plain that the village of Bear's Rib might never rise from this onslaught of fierce Crows. Medicine, thought Mister Skye. These peoples of the plains lived by it, heeded it, consulted it always. Let them discover good medicine in the spirit things of the earth, the spirit-helpers, the totems in each warrior's medicine bundle, the signs given by the sacred buffalo, and grizzly bear, and wolf—let them see the good auguries, and they took heart. Let them glimpse the bad, and their courage deserted them like water from a broken pot.

Fierce Crow warriors steered their war ponies through the village now, collapsing lodges with their lances, braining old men, chasing after the squaws and children who would make good slaves. A few Sioux warriors were scaling the bluffs, obviously defying Jawbone's medicine and planning to kill him and turn the tide, but Jawbone didn't wait. He shrieked, that unholy sound shivering flesh and quaking leaves, and leapt clear off the ledge, onto the Sioux party, hoofs flailing, teeth snapping like rifleshots, and those still in one piece fled pell-mell downhill. Gently, Jawbone scaled the bluff again and stood, triumphant, on its crest, his tail arched, backlit by afternoon sun, lord of all he surveyed.

Something bitter ran through Sitting Bull's face. "Do it,"

he said loudly. "I will let you go if you save my people. Some other sun, when my medicine returns, it will be different."

Mister Skye waited quietly for the elders to lower their bows. He was not satisfied with them, and did not trust them. So he stood waiting, even as Crow warriors boiled triumphantly through the whole village, upending racks of jerky, pulverizing good buffalo robes, and collapsing medicine tripods, the final sacrilege. Then at last the one he distrusted most, the glint-eyed old headman, set his bow on the ground, a sign of surrender.

Mister Skye breathed easier. Mary and Victoria relaxed almost imperceptibly. He whistled sharply, not sure the horse would hear in the sobbing of the wind. Jawbone pricked up his ears but did nothing. Mister Skye whistled again, and this time the great horse bowed its neck, stepped tentatively, and began a fluid downhill run, somehow turning the jolting passage into a smooth gallop, his iron shoes spraying sparks.

A moment later the horse appeared at Sitting Bull's lodge, breathing heavily, and Mister Skye quietly mounted. He lacked a weapon other than the greatest of all weapons among these people: medicine. He found the Crow headmen gathering and waiting on sweated ponies, exultant with victory over these Sioux dogs.

"Mister Skye!" cried one. "We did not know."

"We were visiting," Mister Skye said, choosing not to say more. "And they held us when you came."

The headman nodded. "Who are those whitemen above?"

"Ones I am taking across the land to hunt the buffalo."

"Some are dead," the headman said.

Mister Skye nodded, absorbing that. By the hand of the

Crow, probably, he thought. "I promised the Hunkpapa I would ask you something. You have won a great victory, and the Hunkpapa wail now. It is enough. Let the women and children go. Let the wounded live, unscalped."

"You ask too much. It is good to take the hair of the Hunkpapa. The captives will make good slaves."

"I told the young man there, Sitting Bull, I would ask it."

They debated that, not liking it, seeing it as a defeat in the midst of a great triumph. Mister Skye listened patiently, knowing how carefully these things must be deliberated.

"Our warriors will not like it."

"It was Jawbone's medicine that gave them their power," Mister Skye replied.

"That is so," the headman said reluctantly. "But we were winning anyway. We drove them before us down the Elk River."

It took a while more, but within the hour, it was settled. The Crow warriors counted coup on the Hunkpapa wounded, but did not scalp them. And they let the captives go. Young Sitting Bull watched, mortified, his eyes smouldering with a hate that would last a lifetime. Mister Skye, Victoria, and Mary collected their possessions, including his Hawken, loaded their lodge on its travois, recovered the herd of drays and saddlehorses belonging to the Britons, and started up the long trail to the top of the bluff and the plateau beyond, accompanied by a party of Crow headmen, all of them driving the cart horses and mules before them. An unknown number of Hunkpapa warriors still lurked out in the wild, and some would strike boldly, a last desperate act of redemption. But Skye's family and friends scaled the bluff and headed across the plateau toward the Britons unmolested, while the southwind sighed.

* * *

Lord Frazier grew weary of squinting and he ran out of spit to lick his lips, so he repaired to his yellow parlor wagon and found his lady lying abed.

"I say, Alexandra, we've come to a bloody pass. Out here in these wilds, without a dray a pull us. And that bounder Skye, off and gone. A deserter and a coward."

"Oh, the savageness of it! I could hardly bear it, Gordon."

"I thought you liked the savages."

"Oh, I do. They are ever so much finer than Englishmen. I shall write about all that back home. Did you see their nobility? Their bearing? How they stand and walk? Their beauty? I think they're descended from Greeks. Those ancient Greeks were all swarthy, you know."

"I don't think so, Alex. Asian eyes. They're Mongols of some sort."

"They're all gods, except when they do naughty things to themselves. Whatever possessed that boy—Sitting Bull—to hang himself from his chest, Gordon?"

"I haven't the foggiest idea. His headmaster ought to cane him. Such silly business."

"Savage! So perfectly savage," she mumbled. "I will dazzle England with my journals. Alfred Tennyson will be perfectly jealous. Fetch me water, dear."

"Galitzin's getting some. We had a scrape there. But he'll bring some. And then he'll get us horses."

"Have we none?"

"The Crow drove them off."

"Whatever will we do?"

"Buy more, of course. From our friends in the village. They played a little prank on us, taking our rifles. But we'll get them back. Do you suppose they'll take a draft? They could cash it at any Hudson's Bay post."

"Well, I wish the colonel would hurry. I'm quite dry."

"There's wine, Alex."

"Summon him, Gordon. I'm perfectly parched."

"Capital, capital," he said, rousing himself from his chair. He poked his head out just in time to see a terrible spectacle. Off to the east, rising off the crest of the bluffs, came another savage army. A large herd of ponies—what miserable beasts they all were—and some creatures laden with packs and travois, and a knot of warriors, almost naked.

He discovered Diana staring at them. "I wish I could dress like that," she said.

"They look peacable enough, but we'd better prepare. That flighty colonel is off and gone, leaving us exposed." He peered about. "Gravesend—ready your men!"

But the armorer had already deployed what few he had, including the rubicund wine steward, Stauffinger.

About when the savages came into rifle range, a stout bloke on a gray horse pushed forward, and Lord Frazier recognized him at once.

"Why—it's Skye! Hold your fire. It's that deserter, walking right into our hands!"

Oh, the joy of it, the viscount thought. That oaf hadn't run off after all. They'd clamp him in irons for the whipping. Or maybe wait a bit and have Galitzin do it. The savages paused out there, and Skye shouted something, lost in the whine of the southwind.

"We've got your horses," the man shouted.

It was perfectly extraordinary how that bounder's silk topper stuck to his head in the gale.

"Well bring them in," Frazier shouted, testily. "But keep those savages out."

Skye ignored him, and the whole party pushed cautiously into the compound. Horses. Frazier sighed. The bloody guide had done something of value, at last. He couldn't think of anything else the guide had done to earn his piratical fee.

The whole lot trailed in. Skye's squaws, the old one looking sour as usual. Mary smiling. Those mules with their travois. And savages of all sorts, looking peaceable enough.

"Well, Skye, now that the shooting's done, you've crawled out of your hideyhole."

"It's Mister Skye."

"Oh, of course, Lord Admiral Skye."

The guide ignored him. "These are my friends the Absarokas, kin of my wife. We've brought you the stolen rifles and the rest of the truck the Hunkpapa got."

"Well, fine. We were going to fetch it from them in a bit, but you've saved us the effort."

"I don't think so," said Skye, insolently. "The Crows routed the whole village."

"And I suppose you helped them, eh, Skye?"

Mister Skye said nothing, but ran a big blunt hand along the neck of that vile horse. He nodded to these headmen, and they all began handing rifles and shot pouches and powderkegs to Gravesend, who stored them in the retrieved blue cart. The viscount watched narrowly, wondering how many were being held back. These cutthroats would make off with the family silver if you let them.

From under the carts, the wounded watched and groaned. One had slipped into a coma. Mister Skye studied each one. "Have they water?" he asked.

"Galitzin's gone for some. Took a strong party."

"You've lost men."

"Two out there, and these. Your bloody friends there did it."

"We tried to reach them, Lord Frazier."

"You hid in a hideyhole."

The guide didn't respond. He was watching some specks toiling up the grade from the Yellowstone. "Your water party," he said at last, studying the plateau. The savages did too.

"Skye. Take these savages out of here."

The guide turned and fixed him in that stern gaze that Frazier found so hard to meet. "They've come in friendship. They feel bad about their fight with a party guided by Mister Skye. They've tried to make amends by collecting your horses and weapons. They're here to protect us. There's plenty of Hunkpapa warriors out from the village, and every one's got a burning need to count coup, redeem himself, kill if he can. I'd take it kindly if you'd give these Crow friends some good gifts. A few pounds of powder, some shot, some tobacco."

"You're perfectly daft, Skye. They're murderers."

Skye did something astonishing. He dismounted from that blue terror he rode, stalked over to Gravesend's cart, and dug out a pig of lead, a shot pouch, a fine British fowling piece, and then poured a pound or more of powder into a duck bag. All this he handed to the headman, whose eyes glowed with pleasure.

"Why, Skye, you've stolen our things!"

The guide ignored him, and tramped to one of the enameled carts, the one stowing the trade trinkets, and found twists of tobacco there. These he distributed to each of the dozen savages who'd accompanied him. The viscount raged inwardly, but thought it wise to smile, lest the brutes slaughter them all. He'd deal with Skye later. Oh, would he deal with the man!

Skye talked with the warriors in their Crow mumbo-jumbo, and the savages all rode off toward the village they'd conquered. That old squaw of his hugged one, and jabbered with him a few moments, and smiled. The viscount had never seen the old crone smile. But he spotted tears in her eyes as they rode off with the loot.

Galitzin's water party stumbled in a moment later, and the colonel swiftly detailed men to succor the parched wounded. The wine steward brought one bucket to the viscount and his ladies, plus Baudelaire, who had materialized from under something or other, and they all guzzled thirstily.

"It's better than tiddlywinks," said Diana.

Skye interrupted them. "We'll harness and get off this high country fast," he said quietly. "Not a good place to be. We'll head for the Yellowstone bottoms, mate, and hole up a few days in the shade, close to water. Let the wounded heal. And on the way we'll pick up the dead and bury them down there. I trust you'll lead the services. Church of England, I suppose."

The viscount gaped. The coward and deserter stood there resuming command, reminding him of duties, as if nothing had happened.

Chapter 18

The refreshed cartmen gently tended the groaning wounded, packed the spilled goods into the surviving carts, harnessed the drays, and plunged out of that white hell, pausing on the way to collect the rank, flyblown corpses of the ones who'd been killed and scalped near the marquess tent. Then the solemn cortege wended its way back to the Yellowstone river bottoms and their dappled cottonwood shade, pushed a few miles upstream, and halted in a blue glade beside the cold water.

Victoria had watched Mister Skye confront the viscount, and it gave her some small hope that he had found himself again. For some reason she couldn't fathom he'd not been himself among these tribesmen of his, as if they had a right to rule over him and even rule the thoughts in his head. She couldn't imagine it; her man had weakened, and it unnerved her.

They made camp silently in a salmon lastlight, all of them too weary to rejoice at their deliverance. Nothing was settled between Mister Skye and the viscount, but for the moment a truce prevailed. Victoria had no meat. She and Mary would make do with greens and roots gathered from the river bottoms, and a handful of jerky thrown into a stew. She would dig for the roots of the sego lily, arrowhead and tule; the bulbs of the wild onion; and hunt the wild rhubarb, pigweed and pokeweed for greens. This time of year, they would find something.

The wind died with the sun, and smoke from several fires layered lavender over the camp. Galitzin, their war chief, set cartmen to digging graves in the moist soil near the Yellowstone where the spades bit easily into the earth. She eyed the canvas-wrapped bodies, knowing they must be buried at once. Three now, she realized. The cartman who'd taken an arrow through his belly had died, too. At least he had his scalp.

Mister Skye picketed the packmules and mares on bluestem near the lodge, and then roughhoused with Jawbone, their way of loving each other, she knew. The ugly roan had saved them again. Many times had the medicine horse rescued them from death. The Britons didn't know that, and Mister Skye wouldn't tell them. They did not understand about medicine. Their religion seemed strange to her. Whoever heard of such a thing as sin? Not even Mister Skye's patient explaining helped.

Around the yellow wagon the viscount and his women lounged, and Baudelaire too, all of them sipping spirits as if nothing much had ever happened and they didn't owe their lives and freedom and possessions to Mister Skye and Jawbone. She eyed them, wondering if they had the faintest gratitude. She decided they didn't. The wine steward, Stauffinger, hovered over them, and nearby the chief cook, Abbot Beowolf, built fires and began some soup and frycakes from stores because they had no meat either. It was all as if nothing had happened.

Mister Skye caught up with Galitzin, who was supervising the repacking of carts.

"Say, mate. There's a lot of Hunkpapa around, itching to get the horses. You'll want to set a strong guard tonight. Picket the horses close and hobble them. Keep a few right in camp, hobbled and tied, for emergencies."

Galitzin sighed. "I'm sure we'll manage, Skye."

Mister Skye caught him by the arm in a grip of such iron that he winced. "It's Mister Skye, mate. And from now on—for your safety, the viscount's safety, and mine—you'll be heeding me."

Galitzin stared aghast at the lése majestè.

"Set your men to watching those horses, or I will."

"Let go of me. If you were a private, you'd be court-martialed."

"I'm not a private. I'm your guide. And things have changed. I'll never again give you the chance to kill yourselves—or kill my wives and me, mate."

The altercation aroused the viscount, who tumbled out of a campchair. "Unhand him, Skye!" he bawled. Cartmen paused, gaping. The viscount wrestled his revolver from his hip and proceeded toward Skye, bawling at the cartmen. Only Gravesend, bull-sized and hard, abandoned his cleaning of the rifles and sprang toward Skye, fists ready.

Victoria slid into the lodge, along with Mary, reaching for the old longrifles there. Many times they'd rescued Mister Skye with them, because whitemen never paid any attention to squaws. She and Mary walked among them almost invisible to them, she knew.

A swift shove sent Colonel Galitzin sprawling, and a well-aimed prod of Skye's square-toed boot caught Galitzin's hand just as it clamped over the grip of his revolver.

"Skye. Stand quiet or I'll shoot," roared the viscount.

"It's Mister Skye, mate," he said, whirling on Gravesend, who bulled in from his right. Gravesend's massive fists rocked Skye, and a deft thrust of the foot tripped Skye, sending him sprawling.

Jawbone shrieked and began dancing madly, the amber light of fires reflected in his mad eyes. Mary and Victoria slid out from their lodge, each armed with a flintlock, plus their swift silent bows and arrows.

Mister Skye rolled and kept rolling in a parabola that landed him on his feet again. The viscount lifted his pistol toward the darkening heaven and shot, a sharp boom in the quiet.

"Stop at once. Don't move, Skye, or I'll shoot. Galitzin, fetch the irons."

But even as he spoke Skye leapt like a panther, all of his massive frame bulling into the viscount, who staggered back, his finger spasming on the trigger and shooting the stars once again. Skye landed on him and in two swift blows sent the Colt flying and spun the viscount around. The ladies screamed.

Gravesend picked himself up and sprang forward, only to be thrown ten yards by Jawbone, who exploded out of the darkness, his massive shoulder slamming squarely into the armorer, toppling him like a sawlog. Jawbone shrieked, wild and eerie, sending chills even through Victoria, who nestled behind a parfleche, her longrifle aimed at the viscount.

"Arrest him!" squeaked the viscount in a voice that lacked breath.

But Skye lifted the man by the front of his shirt until he dangled upright, inches from Skye's face. Fearfully, cartmen watched but did nothing. Something released in Victoria's chest. Her man was himself again. Even now, he held that chief of England in his clutch, making him squirm. Beside her in the dusk, Mary giggled softly.

"Mister Skye," Mary said. "Your hat is over there."

That was a signal to him, Victoria knew. Between themselves and Jawbone, Mister Skye need not fear any rush from the cartmen, Gravesend, or Galitzin. Or Lady Diana, for that matter, who had slid toward the yellow wagon, unnoticed by all except Victoria.

"You lost men," rumbled Skye, holding the viscount inches from him. "You lost your horses. You lost most of your arms. You and your men almost perished of thirst. You made enemies. You came close to being killed, you and your ladies. You've got the wounded now, the dead on your souls. And all of it because you wouldn't listen to a guide who knows the country and the tribes."

The viscount peered back from embered eyes, palpable rage in them from being manhandled.

"You brought it on yourself," Skye rumbled.

"Are you quite through, Skye?"

"No, mate, I'm not. You've toyed with my wife Mary, forcing your attentions on her. If you touch her, Frazier, I will kill you." The viscount managed a faint smirk, but his eyes still blazed back. "I'll not have you tampering with my wife. Or risking our lives."

"Oh, pshaw, Skye. You make much ado about nothing. We had a bit of a scrape and you make a mountain of it. You're a cheeky bugger, telling us what to do after you hid in the village to save your skin. We'd have fetched our horses from Bear's Rib and our Sioux friends and gotten our borrowed weapons back, and that's all there is to it. Where were you? Cowering somewhere. Not a bone in your spine. Some Englishman, Skye! You haven't earned a farthing of your fee. You're a bloody coward. Now let go of my shirt, you dolt, or I'll have you lashed."

Mister Skye did, so suddenly the viscount staggered.

Cartmen gaped. The Abbot Beowolf let his pots boil. Lady Diana edged from the yellow wagon in the shadows, carrying her small fowling piece. Victoria swung her old flintlock around, ready,

"Frazier," Mister Skye rumbled. "Take your pick. We'll leave now, my wives and I, if you say go. If not, you'll follow my command as long as I'm guiding you in this wild land."

"Oh, pshaw, Skye." The viscount stared about, cunning replacing the rage in his face. "Let's wait until morning, eh?"

Victoria studied the lord in the light of the dying fires, and saw deceit in him. She hoped her man did too.

"Now."

Lady Diana edged out of the blackness toward the light, the fowling piece glinting orange in the crook of her small arm. Victoria watched suspiciously. Jawbone snorted, his ears laid back again. From the ground, Gravesend and Galitzin watched and plotted.

"Why, old chap, we'll agree." The viscount smiled crookedly, filling Victoria with loathing and dread. "You just take us to game and keep the savages under control, eh? Don't run off now. I want you handy."

Something relaxed in Mister Skye. "Everyone here has heard that. And everyone here has heard me. But I'm not sure you heard me, Frazier."

"Keep a civil tongue, Skye. Address me as befits your station."

Lady Diana continued to ease around through deep shadow to give herself a clear shot at Skye alone. Victoria waited, not wanting to do anything if she didn't have to. But then Diana lifted the fowling piece, and Victoria pulled the trigger of her flintlock.

The boom startled Viscount Frazier. Instantly he found himself slamming into Skye, who'd grabbed his shirt again and yanked. The viscount's head bounced off Skye's hard chest, even as the guide's thick arm pinioned him close.

"I say, Skye—"

"Easy, mate."

The viscount managed to extricate himself enough to peer around. He spotted Diana limned by the cookfires, frozen, a fowling piece clutched in her hand. She gaped into the darkness toward Skye's lodge. Over there, in indigo shadow, he made out the old squaw, Victoria, a drawn bow in hand, the arrow pointing directly at Diana. And next to the old squaw, the young one on the ground, her piece aimed at Galitzin and Gravesend. That ghastly horse shrieked and pawed grass. One of the bulldogs yapped and growled.

A swift shove from the guide tottered him backward several feet, and the viscount found himself peering into the terrible black bore of the guide's revolver. The man was about to kill him! He, a peer of England! He gaped at these Skyes, the guide and his squaws, holding engines of death upon him, and felt a terror turn over his stomach and squeeze his guts until they drained. His pulse racketed through his veins like a mad snake in his body, and then he trembled—rattled every fiber of his being—and couldn't stop. His hands refused to quiet down, and the tremors turned his own flesh into an uncontrolled rage.

"Lady," rumbled Skye, "set that piece down slowly."

Diana, rage twisting her face, did so. "You're scum, you Skyes," she snapped. "I'll get even."

The viscount peered around at the whole dark camp. Cartmen stood transfixed. Even the wounded had stopped groaning and stared into the wavering amber light and inky shadows. A vast disgust boiled up in the viscount. This barbarous guide and two savage women and a crazed stallion had overwhelmed Galitzin's entire force. It sickened the viscount, this discovery.

"In all my years of guiding, I've never had clients like you," the guide said in a voice so low the viscount strained to hear it. "I supposed this would happen some day, but I've always been lucky. I chose well. Everyone I've taken into the wilds has sensed its dangers and listened to me. I've prowled these empty lands for a quarter of a century. Most of my friends went under. Maybe nine out of ten went under: mostly caught by the Blackfeet, Gros Ventre, Cree, Assiniboin, Cheyenne, Sioux, Arapaho, Arikara, and the rest. The pox, cholera, ague. Mountain fever. Dysentery. Strokes. Heart seizure dropping a man like he was pole-axed. Blizzards, hailstorms, sun. Lightning and wind. Hydrophobia, heat, thirst. Starvation turning a man's guts inside out. Poisoned on bad berries and roots. Clawed to bits by grizzly bears. Mauled by a moose. Smashed by a rank horse.

"Getting lost and not a familiar landmark anywhere. Wandering mad, full of terrors. Noises out of the night that set a man to sweating. Drowning in the cold sucking rivers. Gyp water, poison springs. Froze solid without a hole in sight. Bit by rattlers. Misunderstandings—man couldn't speak a tongue or talk with his fingers and hands, and died for it. White renegades, living wolves. Breeds, too. Accidents—plugged barrels. Wet powder, bad caps, nothing but fizzle in a barrel. Stomped by horses, broke a leg on ice, died of plain terror. Stupidity, too. Leaving friends to hunt alone and never coming back. A mighty lot of them walked out of camp and were never seen again. Some were fools. Insulting Indian medicine and shamans. Torture—oh, I've seen that, too. Tie you up and peel your flesh. Squaws do it. Cut your fingers, one joint at a time, and the more you howl the slower they go. Stick burning brands into you, right into your privates. Gouge your eyes out. Unman you. Scalp you while you still breathe. Lay with captive women until they die. And some, Frazier, die for no damned reason at all. They just do. Oh, I've seen it all, mate, and I've survived. I learned a few things. Mostly I learned to be afraid. I never stop being afraid, right down in my marrow. A man learns to fear out here, or he dies. I learned all that and now I offer what I know to whoever employs me. And they've all been delivered safe to wherever they were going. I've not failed yet. Not yet, mate. But maybe this time."

The guide stopped, letting all this sink in. He had spoken low but everyone in camp had heard perfectly. Lord Frazier realized the brute had come to the end of his monologue. He meant to put him in his place.

"Keep a civil tongue in your head, Skye. You'll address me as you should," he said, still spasming at the sight of Skye's revolver aimed squarely at his chest.

"You didn't hear a word, but the rest did," Skye muttered. "You're the first one who hasn't listened and hasn't become a friend. Well, if you won't be a friend, at least listen."

"A friend! You're incredible, Skye."

The brute grinned suddenly. "That's what they tell me, mate. Take your pick. Discharge us now, or keep us—my wives and me—and heed what I say." Skye slid his revolver back into its sheath and turned his back on the viscount, as if to tempt him.

Galtizin stood shakily, looking pale even in the wavering amber light. "I think we'd better keep him on, your lordship," he muttered. "I'm perfectly willing to follow his instruction."

"Why—why—Galitzin, are you quite well?"

Baudelaire emerged from somewhere. The man had a genius for wiggling under something when trouble loomed. "Your lordship, to keep Mister Skye present is to enjoy future opportunity," he said softly. "Including, ah, rewards—and punishments."

Lord Frazier, feeling calm settle his trembling flesh at last, smiled.

Something had changed. Well, he thought, let it. If this

rustic wanted to play lord in a lordless land, let him. For the moment, anyway. Oddly, the cartmen looked like they'd enjoyed it. Well he'd have a sharp word for them at the right moment.

He watched Skye assume Galitzin's command, wandering from man to man, quietly learning the cartman's name and issuing instructions. Two cartmen dug up hobbles and hastened toward the picketed horses out in the dark. Two others found halters and lead ropes and began tugging saddle horses into camp, picketing them close to the tents. That annoyed the viscount, who'd commanded that the horses be kept apart because they disturbed his slumber and their manure stank.

The bloody cartmen were responding all too happily, he thought, watching them transform the camp along Skye's design, tugging carts into a perimeter, shafts sideways to make a kind of barrier against riders.

He was famished. No one had yet eaten. It had been a long, exhausting day. And that sluggardly Beowolf hadn't finished a meal, even now in the July dark. Well, he thought, he and the ladies would have a nip and gossip a bit. He wanted to hear what Baudelaire and Galitzin had to say about Skye's histrionics.

"I say, Stauffinger, make yourself available to my ladies," he said amiably. "And fetch me some scotch with a dash of cold river water, eh?"

The rosy wine steward bustled about while Frazier settled his aching bones into a camp chair beside the yellow wagon. If he had to wait for food, he intended to do it comfortably. But no sooner had he settled into his chair, relishing the thought of a jolt of scotch, than the guide loomed up before him.

"We'd best bury the dead, mate. Grave's dug. Vittles are a way off still."

Bury the dead! The viscount had utterly forgotten them. He peered off toward the river bank and the hole clawed out of the moist earth there, and the shrouded forms still lying there like logs. Three now.

"Oh, have the cartmen pop them in, Skye."

"I think they'd like you to offer words, Lord Frazier. It's something you should do for men in your service."

"It's much too dark, Skye."

"You have a coal oil lantern. Several, I believe."

"Command the men if you must, Lord Skye, but not me. It's been a long day."

The guide waited, letting time tick by, a faint scowl across his scarred face. Really, that battered visage was almost too much to peer at. "Give me their names," he said at last.

The viscount didn't know. "I say, Galitzin, who were they, eh?"

The colonel thought a moment. "Milton Ramp, Hardwick Wiggins, and that last one, ah, Abner—no, Adam Quigg."

Mister Skye nodded and walked off, while the viscount eyed him. How he detested that bounder. Stauffinger returned with his scotch, delicious with the cold river water in it, and he sipped, even as cartmen quietly gathered down near the river bank, forming a loose circle around the graves. Mister Skye walked there too, carrying a glowing lamp and a dark book.

The viscount settled back into his camp chair, feeling the honest benefits of the spirits he was imbibing, and watched the Reverend Skye do the funeral.

A cartman held the lantern beside Skye while the guide thumbed through the book—a Church of England prayer book, Frazier realized—and removed his battered silk tophat.

"Oh God, whose nature and property is ever to have mercy and to forgive," Skye read quietly. "Receive our humble petitions for the souls of thy servants Milton Ramp, Hardwick Wiggins, and Adam Quigg, whom thou has bidden to depart out of this world: deliver them not into the hands of the enemy, neither forget them forever; but command thy holy Angels to receive them and bring them into the country of paradise . . ."

The viscount saw tears streaking the faces of the cartmen, and wished he had done his good English duty instead of preferring his comforts.

Chapter 19

Until now, it never had occurred to Victoria that she might be miserable in the heart of her Absaroka homeland. And she'd never imagined that she would ever want to slide past her own Kicked-in-the-Bellies band like a wolf in the night, but that's all she wanted now. This time she didn't want her father and stepmother, brothers and sisters, her relative Chief Many Coups, and all the rest, to know she was anywhere near.

She hunched over her ribby mare at a place she loved, on Elk River just east of the place the white captains Lewis and Clark called Rivers Across, but she was not glad. Ahead the Birdsong mountains rose razor-edged to slice a cloudless sky. The young Absaroka went there often on their vision-quest, to fast four days and supplicate the spirit ones to come. Mister Skye called them the Crazy Mountains, and called Elk River the Yellowstone, and called the cool lush river valley where her people summered the Boulder, but those were not the names painted on her heart.

The whole river valley before her was black with buffalo, but that did not lift her spirits. Usually her heart would soar when she gazed upon so many of the sacred animals. Some lounged under cottonwoods, while others grazed the golden slopes that broke back from the valley. She wondered where her own Absaroka hunters were, and why they were not making feasts and lodgecovers and robes and moccasins of them.

Never had she felt so alone. No one cared if a small burdened woman sat all alone, miles from her man and the ones he was guiding. Magpie's vision lay heavy in her spirit. She might have rejoiced because Mister Skye had taken command at last, and had cast off the weakness that had beset him among those people of his. Always before, the ones Mister Skye had chosen to guide had become her friends along the trail. But not these ones, who scorned her if they bothered to notice her at all. Always before, she had gladly taken the pale ones to her own village, but now she wouldn't. She would not subject her people to the disdain of these strange ones who confused themselves with the One Above.

Mister Skye had finally won his rightful place among them, and things had gone well, except that they'd found no buffalo day after day, traveling up the river. Because he made them, they guarded the horse herd each night and forted behind the carts and kept some riding horses inside for immediate use. The cartmen liked it, but the chiefs pretended not to notice, or grumbled about small things, especially the absence of buffalo and elk and moose and bear, as if they expected to find those four-foots right along the hot river bottoms this moon of the ripening berries.

She did not like these people, and that weighed on her. But she couldn't bear to be around them, so each day she rode ahead at dawn, and didn't slip into Mister Skye's lodge until dusk, and didn't eat with anyone. She made do with roots and berries, and sometimes a bit of meat she brought down with an arrow and roasted on a tiny fire far from the caravan of carts. She knew she brought darkness into Mister Skye's lodge, and her man grieved, but she couldn't help it. Magpie's vision grew heavier and heavier inside of her breast, and the only way she could cope with the idea of eternal separation from Mister Skye was to start it now, riding alone and apart—a woman without home or husband.

Still, she automatically continued her scouting, as she had always done, squinting over the brow of hills for the tiny movement that might mean Siksika dogs, or maybe Lakotah, or—as now—the great buffalo in their shining light summer coats, many shades brighter than their winter blackness. And here were what she had been seeking, many more than she could count.

She faced a decision: to ride back and tell them, or let them come up in a few hours. Something tugged at her, something deep in her spirit. She wanted to stampede the creatures away, yell and shoot and gallop until they all rose up, rear-end first, and began a great gallop that made the earth tremble under their hooves. Send them away, far from the white men. But she didn't. She willed herself to turn back and find Mister Skye so the viscount might have his hunt. Still she wished that these Britons would never see the sacred animal they came to shoot, and that they would swiftly go across the sea again because they found nothing here to kill.

She sat her patient mare, bewildered, tugged by so many things that her head couldn't hold them. What would Mister Skye want her to do? He was her man, and she found her greatest joy in making him happy. At least until the lodge had darkened. The mare switched her tail angrily at big black deer flies that bit deep and tormented creatures whose blood ran hot. How could Victoria sit there in the land of sweet visions, a land of prairie and fragrant sagebrush foothill and rushing icy creeks and thick cottonwood groves, and not be joyous? Not even want to see her own family and clan?

She knew she should ride back and tell her man, but she couldn't. Slowly, she permitted herself to know what she would do. She had never done such a thing, but now she would. She turned her little mare south toward the grassy benches that hemmed the valley, riding into the hot wind. She passed dark clots of buffalo, most of them sprawled on the golden grasses, their weak eyes missing her and their ears deafened by the wind. As long as she stayed downwind, they would barely pay her any attention. She had never done this thing, and she began to chant a strange sad song, begging that the spirits of those that walked the earth might understand.

From a bench south of the river she could see the entire herd, dark masses almost inert in the midday heat. All of them south of the river. She wanted them to cross. A gray wolf skulked behind her, and then another. Every herd had its wolves, preying upon the old and the injured and very young. They eyed her brightly, knowing what she would do, and she looked back and called them brothers.

At the bench she circled westward, quartering into the

southwest wind, and the wolves followed, an arrow-shot to one side. And still the gusty breeze favored her. Soon it would carry the message of her to the sacred beasts, tell them that a horse and a withered Absaroka woman rode up the wind. She paused on a knoll where she could see the entire sweep of the Yellowstone country; the great mountains that roofed the world glistening far to the south and west; the Birdsongs across the river, still creased with white here and there; and broken country lying between and around. Her heart lay heavy. Down near the green sweep of the river, with its silver thread, crows fought over some morsel left by a coyote or wolf, black flocks cleaning up after the fanged ones had finished.

The white people had called her own the Crows, but they had got it wrong. They weren't the Raven People either, but the People of the Great Bird, and this was the heart of their home. Other times she might have been transported into a kind of ecstasy at the panorama before her. It had never failed to suffuse her spirit with things unspeakable, feelings beyond words that flowed out to the tips of her fingers and tingled there. But not now.

She touched her moccasins to the flanks of her pony and steered it westward again, quartering deeper into the wind. Far to her right a sentry cow stirred, turned her massive head and sniffed the eddying air, and lifted her face. The cow circled restlessly, testing the air in other directions, and turned again toward Victoria. The wolves settled on their haunches and watched, panting in the heat.

Victoria rode across the wind again, and saw more sentries rise and sniff the relentless breeze. Others, dozing quietly through a cloudless afternoon, sniffed and humped up upon their feet, scything their heavy heads back and forth. Several calves sprang up and trotted toward the center of the herd. Victoria sang, letting her words ride down the wind.

"This day I am sending you away, sacred ones. Sending you away from these hunters from across the sea. This day I do a thing I will not tell to my man. I will hide from him what I have done. I will save you for the Absaroka, for the Peoples who come to you for meat and robes and the covers for their lodges. Go away, sacred ones, and hide yourself from the ones who come up the river. Hear Many Quill Woman."

More stood and sniffed the wind restlessly, alert but not moving. She turned the pony and kicked into a light, lithe run, jarring down the grassy slopes, into the wide golden bottoms, rolling a black wall of buffalo before her. Her brothers the wolves trotted beside, still a wise arrow-shot away, sending their own scent down the wind. A dozen or so bearded bulls broke into a lumbering trot, and then others, and finally the entire herd bolted toward the shivering river, racing with a muted thunder, narrowing into an arrowhead that pierced through a fringe of bright cottonwood along the bank, and thrashed into cold water until it frothed white with the passage of an army.

"Ayah, sacred ones!" she cried as the great herd twisted into the river, swam, struck bottom on the north bank, and splashed out, snorting and shaking off water but never slowing as it snaked up a distant golden flat along Big Timber Creek and vanished among the cottonwoods. The wolf-brothers patrolled the south bank hungrily but didn't swim, and she knew they'd hunt another supper soon.

The earth ceased its trembling, and a great quiet, save for the moan of the wind, settled upon the sun-drenched valley. She had sent the sacred ones away. And by the time the slow cart caravan arrived, even the sign they left behind would have turned brown in the hot air.

She turned her winded pony, rimed with dry sweat over its withers and hips, back toward the river trail snaking close to the southern benches.

She saw him then, his silk hat cocked against the wind, sitting Jawbone, taking it all in. She had never known his anger, and wondered how it would taste in her mouth and feel in her ears. She turned the little slat-ribbed mare toward him while he watched, and drew up before him, awaiting words that would land like warclubs.

"I love you, old woman," he said, and she wept.

Let's go up yonder," he said gently, and turned Jawbone upslope. She followed, scarcely caring where he took her. He steered up to a bench, and then a second one further back, where golden grasses rippled beneath them, making the land pulse and tremble. On the second bench he slid off Jawbone and gazed silently at the vista, studying it for signs of life and danger but enjoying it too. She could not see through the blur of her brown eyes.

"I imagine your people are up there," he said, pointing toward the Boulder valley and the great blue mountains rising to the south. "They usually are about now. Cool and sweet, plenty of deer and antelope."

She nodded silently.

"I imagine you miss them, this close. All your clan."

She nodded.

"Here now, let's sit down a spell," he said. He slipped his burly arm about her frail shoulders and eased her to the hard clay, facing toward where the Boulder tumbled into the Yellowstone amidst a dense canopy of cotton-woods far below.

He didn't say anything for a while, but let the hot breeze toy with his graying hair and tug at his silk hat. She sat quietly, comforted by the arm about her shoulders and his great paw of a hand encasing her arm.

"The carts are two, three hours back. I left Galitzin in command but told him to heed Mary with any sign of trouble. He's not a bad sort, and he agreed."

She liked his presence, even if she dreaded it. Many moons had passed since he had even touched her because of the darkness in their lodge. She resisted his hand and arm; she should be separating herself, learning to be alone. But she could not take his arm away.

"You never told me your medicine vision, Victoria. The one last winter."

"You never listened."

"I suppose I didn't," he said slowly.

"It is too late now."

"I am listening."

She didn't want to tell him what Magpie had shown her. So she sat still, liking and not liking the closeness of man and woman.

"Sonofabitch!" she muttered.

"Magpie took you up into the hills above Fort Laramie last winter and showed you something. You were gone so long I thought you'd frozen to death."

She did not want to talk about it, so she said nothing, huddling deep into the hollow of his arm and chest.

"I didn't pay it much heed," he said. "You didn't tell me and I was busy with the outfitting. Took some doing to get the ponies and the rest. Next thing I knew, you weren't saying anything and my lodge was dark and sad as death. Even Mary—you must have told her."

"You wouldn't hear," she said. "Just some old savage woman's notions. Goddam."

"I wasn't listening," he agreed. "But I will now."

He wanted to know now. But it was too late. She shook her head.

"You were fixing to ride right past your people. I saw that, Victoria. They're likely half a day away. Usually around here you turn into a girl, beaming at the whole world like sunlight, itching to slip into the lodges of your pa and his new wife, and your brothers and sisters . . . but not this time."

She felt the tears and could not fight them back, so she burrowed her head into his shoulder so he might not see her foolishness.

"You're thinking the viscount and those people aren't fit company for your village."

"Sonofabitch!" she spat. "They treat you bad. They treat me bad. Mary, too. What did they do that they can treat everyone bad?"

"Born to it. Born lords and ladies."

"But what did they do? Were they great war chiefs?"

Mister Skye shrugged. "Their ancestors, maybe. That's the way my country is. Divided up. The lords, the freemen, and lots of peasants who weren't even free until not long ago."

"Goddam, I don't want them in my village. They're damn dogs, like Siksika."

He held her tight, until she could feel the thump of his heart beneath the elkskin shirt she'd made for him. "You go visit your people, Victoria. I'll push along slow, up the Yellowstone, and after a good visit you'll catch us easily enough."

"Sonofabitch," she muttered. "When they hire you they hire me."

He didn't say anything, and they sat quietly, closer than she wanted to be, peering at the restless land, windwhipped and shimmering. Off to the west, an eagle floated lazily in an azure heaven. From where they sat they could see a few buffalo well north of the river, dots upon broken piney hills. They would not be visible to the caravan, toiling along the bottoms.

"My spirit-helper summoned me on a cold day, when the air cut through my bones, even in my robes. I was out gathering sticks. She landed on my shoulder and then hopped to my head and pecked. Who ever heard such a thing? The magpie is a bold bird, but not so bold as that.

"So I went away into the hills with only my robe and fasted. The nights were so cold I didn't think I'd live through them. But Magpie summoned me, and she is my protector and friend, so I knew I would not die."

She didn't want to talk of it, but at last she had Mister Skye's ear, and their lodge was dark.

"Magpie shortened the time because I was cold. She came the third dawn, and I saw—I saw—Goddam."

Far off, the eagle flattened its black and white wings and plummeted downward.

"They will catch you in their talons like that eagle," she said. "I saw lions catch you and take you away across the water, and I could not go along. Not I, not Mary, not Jawbone. They took you away on a fireboat across the water, and I never saw you again. I was worse than widowed. I cut off my hair and a finger and grieved, but soon I died because you never came back. And they kept you there in a cage until you died, even though you wanted to come back to us. Soon they will do this thing."

Mister Skye seemed puzzled. "Why would they do something like that, Victoria?"

"Goddam, I don't know!"

He sat quietly, saying nothing, his mind obviously at work. "Was this a warning? Did your spirit-helper say this might happen? Or did Magpie show you the future itself, something that was bound to happen?"

"I don't know! I saw it when Sun came the third morning."

"You didn't tell me."

"How could I? You were full of pounds and dollars and buying ponies and getting rich. I don't think you hear me now."

He sighed, lifted his stovepipe hat and screwed it down again. "I am listening. I don't know whether Magpie had come to warn you what could be, or show you what will come."

"It's too late! Mister Skye's lodge is dark and soon we will all be torn apart. I don't want to live after that, Mister Skye."

"But there's no reason," he said, puzzled.

She pulled free of him. She didn't mean to let him hold her; that had been too good, and she had to push those things away as sternly as she could. "Your lodge is still dark," she said angrily.

"Victoria—beautiful woman—"

She stood bitterly. She'd told him her vision and he didn't believe. So it would be.

He clambered to his feet slowly, while the southwind toyed with his iron hair and whipped the fringes of his shirt. "I have listened to your medicine, Victoria," he said with a strange quiet dignity. "You are Mrs. Skye and will always be. I am not going back across the sea to England, no matter what. Don't let your good heart carry something so heavy. The viscount may be a lord there, but he has no power here. He can't command the law and the sheriff and the courts here. There are none, and he's powerless. He can't carry me in chains down the Missouri, through St. Louis, up the Ohio, and all the rest, Victoria."

But he didn't comfort her. She watched glinting dots toil toward them far to the east. The caravan, the handiwork of Viscount Gordon Patrick Archibald Frazier and his men. They would reach this place in a while. Not soon, but a while. The sight of them filled her with loathing and dread, and that added to her shame. But now Mister Skye knew, and understood why his lodge was dark.

Chapter 20

Not a buffalo. For days they'd toiled up the broad valley of the Yellowstone without seeing the shaggy beasts. The viscount fumed. He had come clear across the Atlantic to shoot them, and he'd scarcely had a shot. He'd seen more from the river packet than he had in his entire journey with that incompetent guide. Millions of the bison on the North American continent, and Skye couldn't lead him to one. The viscount thought he'd have done better engaging some Hudson's Bay guide in British possessions.

Their food stores had declined alarmingly too. He'd been counting on abundant buffalo to feed those ravenous cartmen and all the rest. Instead, they'd made do with an occasional mule deer and antelope. He could never accustom himself to chewing on those prairie goats, but it was that or starve some nights. It took at least three deer a day to feed this throng, and four were better. Skye and his wives brought in most of the meat, and that annoyed Frazier all the more. He'd come on a hunting trip, and those savages brought in the meat. Once in a while the squaws dug roots and plucked greens, and had instructed Beowolf, so they had occasional stews full of strange tasteless things that needed dosings of salt. But none of it was as satisfying as a boss rib of bison.

Several times he and Diana had saddled up at twilight and chased after the stags that had come down to drink at the river, but the slippery deer had danced off faster than these dismal cobs Skye called horses could follow. So Lord Frazier had skulked back to camp fuming, his hunting trip a ruin.

July slipped into August, and still their menacing guide pushed upriver. They rounded a great bend in the Yellowstone and plunged through a throat of rock, into a vast north-south valley hemmed by spines of indigo.

"Not far to the geysers and hot springs, mate," said Skye one evening as the cartmen made camp.

"Address me civilly, Skye."

The guide grinned insolently. "Sorry, sir," he said, his face belying the apology. "A man should be addressed civilly."

That had been the way with Skye since the beginning. He had no respect. At least the man had run an untroubled camp since that—episode. But at what a cost!

"Skye. I want buffalo. I went to great lengths to employ a guide who'd take me to buffalo, but I saw more of the beasts from the deck of that riverboat than I've seen since you joined us."

Skye peered back at him, his silk hat jaunty on his unkempt skull. "Yellerstone's not the best buffler country, mate. We could swing north to the Judith country—rich with the bluestem they like—and I'd show you buffler by the thousands. Or we can head up the river toward the geysers. There's moose, elk, grizzly up there, and sometimes buffler too."

"You're asking me to choose, are you? That's a novelty, Skye. Letting your client choose."

The guide smiled blandly. "Two, three days more and this valley'll narrow down into rugged country, and we'll start climbing. That's about as far as the carts can go. No roads through that high wilderness, and no ways to drag carts across those mountain streams. The geysers are up there, all sorts of steaming bubbling pots. And big game, mate. Bull moose with racks wider than your outstretched arms. Grizzly ba'r, if you're inclined, but I don't suggest it. Balls take no effect in them."

"You mean we can't take our carts and my wagon up there? Why didn't you tell me?"

Skye didn't reply.

"We'll have to ride in on horses, will we?"

"Three or four days on horseback, sir. You may wish to leave most of your men in camp and bring a small party up on horseback, with the packmules for supplies."

"We'll have to sleep on the ground?"

"Tents, camp foods, sleeping on the ground, mate."

"But what will Alexandra—and Baudelaire. Oh, well. I'll leave them behind. A pity. I think the geysers would excite my lady's sensibilities. She's a poet, you know, Skye."

"If she'll ride, I'll make her comfortable, mate."

"I say, Skye. This mate business grates on me. No, Lady Alexandra doesn't ride much. She usually doesn't adorn herself in split skirts."

"I thought to leave Gravesend in charge of the carts and men at the lower camp, and take those who wish to go, plus three or four cartmen for packers," Skye said.

The viscount had turned testy. Skye did that to him. "Do what you will. But get me to game. I've brought Cutler—my taxidermist—clear from Huddersfield to cure the pelts and save the heads, and he's not had a bit of work—thanks to you. All right then. Take us to moose and elk and grizzly if you must. I suppose a stuffed grizzly in my guildhall will look as fine as a buffalo. And Skye—I'll say it again. Keep a civil tongue and mind your station."

Skye nodded, and rode off on that berserk jade he called a horse.

His lodge remained dark. He'd never known a time when his women had turned silent as death, their faces like obsidian. Mary, too. They rarely even cooked, and stayed away from him as much as possible. In the night she turned from him, and drew her robe tight about her. His young Snake woman seemed as distraught by Victoria's medicine prophecy as old Victoria. Maybe more so, because the child stirred within her. At least he had a reason for all this now.

He took to riding out at dawn each morning, ostensibly hunting but actually just wanting to be alone. He had no home any more. All the Skyes went their separate ways each dawn. Galitzin now ran the caravan competently since Mister Skye had insisted on night defenses, especially a guard for the horses, so the guide felt less and less need to stay close. He'd never guided a party who'd scorned his services, and he felt no compunction about drifting off each day rather than suffer the constant mock of the viscount's cronies.

But mostly he grieved. Victoria slid off into the night, even before dawn, avoiding his company, believing heart and soul in her medicine vision, and preparing herself for some sort of separation Magpie had foretold. It left Mister Skye uneasy about the vision itself and the grip it had on his two wives. They shunned him as if he'd done something wrong, but he couldn't fathom what it might be. Riding out alone was his only solace.

He didn't hold with Indian visions—too many had been nonsense—but he respected medicine, understood the power of its grip upon the people of the plains, and used it ruthlessly to foster a certain perception of himself. He couldn't even talk to his wives in reasonable terms. That evening, after Victoria had finally told him what burdened her, he'd tried to tell them he had no intention of going away. They'd stared at him somberly, and his lodge remained dark.

This dawn he saddled Jawbone before the rest of the camp awakened, as usual, intending to slip away as he had for several days. He had no answers, but lone-riding with his faithful Jawbone offered some small balm, especially in this upper Yellowstone valley he always enjoyed. But before he could flee once again, Lady Diana Chatham-Hollingshead popped out of the yellow wagon, in riding attire, and approached.

"I'm going with you today, Skye," she said. "I'm having my buffalo runner saddled."

It didn't please him. In fact, the arrogance of her class pierced him. She hadn't asked. It had been an announcement. She'd supposed she had a perfect right; supposed he'd be pleased to have the company of a highbred lady. He wasn't pleased. In fact, she awakened an ancient loathing that cut back to his childhood and infected his merchant father as well as himself. It was not enough to be a freeman in England. Not enough even to be rich or to achieve great things, or give splendid gifts to mankind or the Crown or the Church. Never enough!

"Very well," he said, reminding himself she was his client.

A night guard brought Lady Diana's mount to her, and they rode off. From his lodge door, Mary stared.

This day's solitude would be ruined, he knew. And he'd have to remember to address her properly: my lady. He steered Jawbone east of the much-diminished Yellowstone river, across benched flats that shouldered the vaulting mountains. The sun rose behind the giant crags to the east, shining on another world up there while the valley was still bathed in lavender. He'd planned to shoot a good buck or two to feed the camp, and nurse his loneliness while he did it, but now he was stuck.

She kicked her coyote dun forward, until she rode beside Mister Skye. Jawbone didn't like it a bit, and laid his ears back.

"I don't think you like us, Mister Skye," she said.

It struck him that she'd addressed him as he wished. He felt like saying plenty—about lords and ladies, about the viscount, about class and caste, but he bit it off. "Someone has to bring in meat," he said evasively.

She laughed. "There's several good hunters among the cartmen. Gravesend, for instance. No, try again. You detest us, and we detest you."

He glanced at her and found her face lit with amusement. She lacked beauty, having rather blocky features, but she possessed a fine radiant face and a bright mien that gave her a rich handsomeness anyway. "Whatever you say, my lady."

She bellowed at him, a laughter so loud it'd scare off the game he sought. "The thing I like about you, Barnaby Skye, is that you don't m'lady me. Gordon needs sirring and your lordshipping, but I don't."

Mister Skye was determined not to let that pleasure him, and focussed fiercely on the obvious fact that she'd intruded on his morning, and on his peace.

"Won't talk, eh? Gordon says you're an Australian, and no doubt right out of a penal colony."

"Let him think it."

"Where are you from, Mister Skye?"

"If we talk, we'll miss spotting the game. Drive it off, especially this hour when sound carries."

She peered up the valley, still indigo and lavender in its dawn shadow, and misty far upriver. But high above, snow-streaked peaks caught the sun and glowed like embers under a bellows.

"I admire this valley. One of the choice places in the western wilderness," he rumbled.

"Where are you from, Mister Skye?"

He sighed. "London."

"Were you sent to Australia?"

"No."

"Ha! Gordon's wrong. He thought you'd been a common crook, a footpad or a thief sent to the colonies. But he also says you were a seaman and I think he's right."

"I was."

"Gordon says that's a common trade."

"It wasn't what I intended."

"What did you intend, back in London, Mister Skye?"

She annoyed him, probing so much. Yet something responded in him. Her fine clipped English stirred ancient memories: faint visions of narrow streets, half-timbered houses, and always the scent of the not-distant sea sweeping in on breezes.

"I don't seem to be getting anywhere, do I? I've been watching you, Mister Skye. You're a mystery to me. You never touch spirits, do you? You never join us. Mary joined us."

"Was I welcome to join you?"

She laughed. "You have me there, Barnaby."

"It's Mister Skye."

She laughed, a waterfall of music in the cool dawn. He'd forgotten what the music of laughter sounded like.

"I touch spirits."

"But you haven't. The viscount's got a whole cartload still. Scotch, ah, there's a drink to get tiddly with. It improves my shooting too. Give me a good dose and it steadies my hand."

"When I touch spirits, I roar like a grizz, stomp on stars, ride bull moose up the canyons, bugle like a rutting elk—"

"And what else?"

"And make water." He guffawed. "Like the Yellerstone."

"You are a man of many parts."

He hoohawed.

"But you don't touch a drop. It must be our company you don't like."

"I don't touch drops. I touch jugs. Since I don't trust Galitzin to do anything sensical, I don't touch anything. But I'm getting a gawdalmighty dry in me."

"Do you really bugle like a rutting elk?"

"More like a bull moose."

"You'll have to show me," she said lightly.

"I'm dry."

"I'll fix that. I'm a famous boozer and I'll drink you under the table."

She made him uneasy, even though she was good company. He couldn't relax. And mixed into it was the constant sense of her breeding and his lack of it.

They rode quietly a while, topping several grassy benches that seemed to form pedestals for the mountains. She didn't banter, and he felt grateful for that. At the topmost bench he turned Jawbone south and rode up the valley, letting himself absorb its grandeur. Ahead a few miles rose a huge conical peak, still snowstreaked. A splendid hotsprings purled out from its base, cascading into pools, each one cooler than the one above. Victoria's people loved to bathe there. They came summer and winter, but especially winter, enjoying a delicious soak in the steaming water when the land lay burdened with snow. He'd had many a soak himself to drive the cold and numbness from his bones, lolling in the hot water amidst steam so thick he could scarcely see his toes.

But now he studied the valley, his alert eyes focusing slowly on the surrounding country, reading it and the sign it offered him. This had always been a great thoroughfare for wandering tribesmen. For eons they had come this way en route to the obsidian cliffs up a way, a mountain of black glass that flaked into the finest arrowheads in North America. But today he saw nothing. The land lay as somnolent as the horse-latitude sea, sun gilding the western slopes across the valley and driving the blue shadow ever eastward as it climbed above the eastern range.

"What do you see, Mister Skye?" she asked softly.

"The Sargasso sea."

"I've never seen a valley like this. In England things are

small and close. Here, everything is—reckless with size and beauty. A reckless giant made this place."

A glint caught his eye, and he studied the east bank of the Yellowstone far away. "They're starting off," he said, pointing to the shining dots, crawling like beetles along the river.

"How can you stand to be so far away? If it weren't for you, I'd shudder to be here."

"I've lived a quarter of a century in this. It's home— much as anything is home."

"You were a sailor before this?"

He nodded and touched his heels to Jawbone. He didn't really want her probing or even getting too friendly. She wouldn't scruple at much, he knew. Her class rarely did. "Hotsprings a mile or two ahead. Maybe two. You can wiggle your toes in the warm water," he said.

"Hot water!"

"Yas . . ."

"A bath! Oh, how I miss baths."

"Ah—I'll fetch my Mary, to keep an eye—"

"A bath!" she cried, heeling her buffalo runner into a canter.

He cursed himself for mentioning it and followed behind her on Jawbone, sniffing mingled sage and juniper and pine eddying sweetly down from the high country.

She held her pony to a rocking-chair gait until at last they burst into a scoop of land where the waters purled. Usually he surveyed places like this carefully, hidden in shadow, but he'd had no time with this noblewoman racing ahead. He fumed at her recklessness. But this time things seemed to be safe.

"Oh!" she cried, sliding off the dun. She stabbed her finger gingerly in a glimmering little stream, and cried out. "It's warm! Is it hotter higher up?"

He nodded, following helplessly as she dashed ahead, dragging her pony toward a pool partially scooped from the slope and partially dammed by tribesmen some time in the distant past. He peered about nervously, wondering whose eyes surveyed them here. A long shoulder of mountain separated them from the valley now, and its distant caravan.

"I'm going to. Here, Skye, tie my horse." She thrust the reins at him and began at once tugging at her slender riding boots.

"Ah, Lady Diana, I'd better—"

"Oh you ninny. You dither too much!"

"I think—"

"We're going to have fun, Skye. Take your duds off."

She popped her second boot off and wriggled out of her brown riding jacket. Her split skirts came next, and then she undid her silky blouse, until she sat in her chemise and drawers.

"Ah, that's just fine, Lady Diana. Wet your toes—"

"You're a goose, Skye."

"Ah—"

She pulled her chemise off, baring lush brown-tipped breasts and golden flesh, and then dropped her drawers and smiled. "See," she said. "I don't have the best figure, but I still turn a man's head."

Mister Skye gaped at her curvaceous breasts and taut wide belly, and felt a rush of desire he couldn't help. She knew it and posed seductively, her gaze riveting him.

"Take those buckskins off, Barnaby. I don't think you've had a bath in years. You need a bath. You stink. Your hair's greasy. But keep that awful silk tophat on. That'd be the funniest thing I've ever seen. We'll do it in the water with your silk hat on."

"I'll stand guard," he replied primly.

"Stand guard! Against what, Skye? Take your chances. The same as I am."

"I'm married and love my wives, Lady Chatham-Hollingshead."

"Your wives. All two!" She gusted with laughter and slid gracefully into the pool, the shimmering water gliding over her loins and breasts, up to her neck. She rolled and played in it like a dolphin, splashing hot water in sunlit rainbows.

"Oh! Glorious! Paradise!" she exclaimed. She wallowed about in the water, dipping her dark hair into it, sputtering and laughing. "Drop your breechclout, you idiot."

"Sonofabitch!" bellowed Victoria from behind, where she sat her ribby pony.

Chapter 21

Barnaby Skye could delay no longer. He'd gone dry, so dry his juices didn't flow and his soul stiffened like sunblasted rawhide. He'd put it off, fought it off, but now it pounced upon him and he knew what he had to do. In all his days he'd never had such an awful thirst as this.

Without a word he turned Jawbone back to the caravan, leaving the noble lady to her bath and ignoring the hard look in Victoria's eyes. His old Crow woman had come at just the right time. He wouldn't have resisted Lady Diana's voluptuous charms. It had all been too much, with his own lodge darkened, his wives cold as an arctic storm.

And then Victoria had ridden in. His woman hadn't laughed. She should have laughed. She came from the bawdiest tribe on the plains, a tribe whose wild women had made mountain men blush. But Victoria had just hunched on her ribby mare, cursing, reading the faces, and that was all it took. Something collapsed in Barnaby Skye, and he turned Jawbone toward the caravan, leaving the women to their own devices.

He trembled with his need, and Jawbone sensed it. He laid back his ears, hating Mister Skye for it. But Mister Skye had slipped far beyond help. He would take his journey now, and say goodbye to lords and ladies who loathed him and subverted the discipline he established; goodbye to Mary and Victoria and Jawbone, his own family, or what was left of it. He didn't care what happened. The whole hunting trip could fall apart and he wouldn't care. In fact he wished it would.

He rode over the grassy shoulder and spotted the caravan instantly, off in the northwest, toiling up the right bank of the Yellowstone along the first grassy bench above the river. The sight of the enameled carts with their heraldry blazoned on the sides enraged him. They didn't belong here. The viscount didn't belong here, and neither did his ladies, Galitzin, Baudelaire, and all their retainers. Let them take themselves, their oriental carpets, linen tents and all the rest back to England.

He rode dourly down the grass, hoping he'd be discharged and free, hoping for oblivion. Jawbone acted strange under him, snarling and clacking his big molars, sensing what would come. It enraged Skye, this censure from a horse, and he thought to whip the beast or kill it, and then felt shocked at his own wild rage. He spotted Mary ahead of the caravan, riding her dark pony and herding the pack mules and horses that dragged their lodge and lodgepoles on travois. Something steamed within him. He'd throw her out. He'd get rid of Victoria too. He'd toss their worldly goods out of his lodge, every last thing they owned, throw them out, cast them loose, divorce them Indian-fashion, cut free of his damned women and all their damned superstitions and hoodoo. It was over. He'd gather up his packmules and git, out to the high lonely, away from his dark lodge and these asinine lords and ladies and their whole retinue! But not until he pillaged a certain wagon. The thought of it turned his tongue dry and parched his throat.

"Take them to the hotsprings," he snapped at Mary as he passed her. They could all go there, these lords and ladies, and prance around naked in the hot water. She stared at him, recoiling from the harshness in his voice. "Victoria's there. So's the fancy lady."

She nodded gravely and turned her pony to the east, tugging on a picket line to swing her packhorses off the river trace.

"Follow the squaw," he snarled at Galitzin as he passed the colonel. He wouldn't call Mary wife any more. He rode down the caravan, passing drays and carts, scattering bulldogs. Jawbone minced along with laid-back ears, menacing everything around him, but Mister Skye paid no heed. His thoughts focused on a single gorgeous cart near the rear, and the fleshy man walking beside it. He passed the yellow wagon, drawn by four mustangs, and saw no sign of Lady Alexandra. But the viscount sat beside the coachman, eyeing the banks of the river with a small field glass.

"No game, Skye. My hunt's a ruin, thanks to you."

The guide ignored the man. The viscount no longer mattered. "We're heading for a hotsprings, Frazier. Your bawd's already there."

"I say, Skye—"

"Discharge me, Frazier," Skye snapped.

Lord Frazier winced, and then withered under Skye's glare. "I think I might. I've endured enough of your insolence."

"Say it, Frazier."

The viscount looked pained. "You tempt me. But I'll wait a few days. Take us to the geysers. Get me to the moose and bear and elk you promised, and after that we'll find our way back down the Yellowstone without your, ah, assistance. And after this, if you've anything to say to me, tell it to Colonel Galitzin. I won't suffer your rudeness any more, Skye."

"It's Mister Skye, matey. When you start calling me Mister, I'll start calling you Sir." He hoped that would get him fired. "Meanwhile, you're whatever I feel like calling you." Angrily, he heeled Jawbone off, leaving his lordship to his glassing of the riverbanks for deer. Things had come to a fine pass. His lordship didn't want Skye's words reaching his tender noble ears.

Near the back of the procession he spotted what he'd come for, creaking along like a mirage, an oasis splashed across a desert sky, with gaudy palmtrees and shimmering brown waters. Grimly he steered Jawbone toward the apparition, knowing he'd take by force whatever he needed.

"Mister Stauffinger," he said with controlled politeness. "I have come for refreshments."

The rosy-fleshed steward looked dubious at first. "I'd better ask his lordship," he said.

"Open," roared Skye in a voice that brooked no disobedience.

"We'll have to stop and I'll get too far behind," the man complained.

"Keep going. Hand me the key."

"Oh, his lordship would—"

Skye glared at the man until the steward wilted under his stare. Stauffinger swung to the rear and unlocked the double doors of the creaking cart, nervously eyeing both Skye and Jawbone.

Skye steered Jawbone behind, and peered into the darkness. "What's in there?"

"Wines, two barrels of scotch, a hogshead of American corn spirits for the cartmen, and—"

"Any empty jugs?"

"Why yes—"

"Fill two with corn whiskey."

"But his lordship hasn't—"

"I'll do it then," said Skye, heeling Jawbone closer.

But Stauffinger scurried into the creaking cart and began drawing the whiskey from the bung in the hogshead, filling one jug and then the other while Skye studied it.

"Hand them to me," Skye roared.

"I—I'm afraid of your horse."

Wordlessly, Skye slid off Jawbone and grabbed the jugs, feeling the cool heavy porcelain in his big hands, and enjoying an ecstasy that stole into him even before he uncorked one.

"I'll be back," he roared, as the steward clambered out of the squeaking cart and locked the doors. Behind, other cartmen and the horse herders gaped.

Ahead, the caravan veered to the left, abandoning the

river trace to climb a grassy slope leading toward the conical peak. He watched, knowing the squaw was taking them to the hotsprings. The two gray jugs felt good in his palms. He clamped them to his belly with both hands, full of juicy joy. He kneed Jawbone away from the caravan, and the evil horse responded sullenly, lashing his tail and sulking with every step. It didn't matter. He'd lodgepole Jawbone too. He'd had all he could take. Off to the south, puffballs hung on peaks, and by late afternoon they'd turn into mountain showers. But here in the golden valley of the icy Yellowstone, the benign sun coddled him and warmed the jugs in his horny hands.

He veered away from the gaudy carts, feeling cleansed by every yard of distance he put between himself and the loathsome caterpillar wending up a shallow coulee toward the springs. He stuck to the shoulder of the nameless mountain, wanting high ground. He would find a place high above, a place with a few pines to sough in the breeze and a warm boulder to lean against, a vast view of the upper Yellowstone valley before him, and maybe the hotsprings off to his right. That's where he'd slide off Jawbone and go away into his own world for a while.

He rode ever higher, sometimes in sight of the caravan snaking toward the springs below. Once he rode across a dish of land where he could see the hotsprings. A tiny white figure still lolled in the waters, but Victoria had vanished. Not far, he knew. She wouldn't leave the noblewoman alone in that wilderness. But it didn't matter. Nothing down there mattered.

He found a drinking place beside a tiny alpine lake and sighed happily. Tension leaked away from him as he slid off the horse, clutching the jugs, and turned Jawbone loose to graze. He could wait no more. A great boulder rose like a breadloaf before him, and he sank gratefully to earth before it, and settled into it. He eyed the jugs, wondering which; finally uncorked the left, and lifted it to his lips. The stuff gurgled into his parched mouth burning like fire, and he gasped, choked, and laughed. His lordship had bought raw whiskey for his cartmen. He swallowed again, gasping, feeling fire burn out his insides. And then, slowly, the thing he'd needed began to creep through his tormented body and soul.

"I quit," he bellowed, lifting his jug toward the sky.

The competent Colonel Galitzin had known exactly what to do, much to Lord Frazier's relief. It wouldn't do for the cartmen and retainers to be about while a peer of England and his ladies were disporting themselves at the hotsprings. So the colonel had established two camps, the one for Lord Frazier at the springs, and the other for the cartmen, half a mile down and slightly around a bend. The runnel ran tepid down there, but what did it matter? The cartmen could dam it into a little pool, and make do. The important thing was to keep their mean eyes and thoughts away from the ladies and himself.

There'd be some slight inconvenience because the Abbot Beowolf would have to cook at some distance, and the wine steward, Stauffinger, would have to bring his wares. But that was proper and necessary. Lady Alexandra had demanded that canvas walls be erected about the pool, but Lady Diana, lolling perfectly bare in the pond when they'd arrived, had scoffed at that. Lord Frazier suspected she rather enjoyed making a spectacle of herself, even in front of the mechanics. Baudelaire and Galitzin, of course, would camp at the springs. They were the souls of discretion, and if they saw the ladies cavorting, not the slightest hint of it would ever pass their lips.

The hotspring purled out of a meadow near the foot of a vast pineclad slope that vaulted upward to cloud-shrouded high country. It lay in a natural vee that opened to the north, protected by a root of the conical mountain, perfectly private, except, of course, to his dear Alexandra, who couldn't imagine disrobing out of doors. And indeed, there remained one little problem. Those savage squaws of Skye's had erected their cowhide lodge right there at his lordship's camp. It was a perfect breach of manners, insolent in its very nature. They didn't belong here, but seemed to think they did.

"I say, Galitzin," he yelled. "Tell them to be off."

The colonel sighed. "I'll try. They do what they choose."

"It's unthinkable. I haven't seen that lout of a guide all day, but he has no business here. Tell them to mind their manners, eh?"

Lord Frazier refused to speak to any of the Skyes. They'd become so insufferable to him that he left communication to the colonel. The light had turned dusky, and he looked forward to a plunge before full dark, but he'd be damned if he'd bare his flesh before those squaws. The water felt delicious to his immersed hand, and he could barely wait to plunge into it. He watched the colonel approach the savage women, talk and point down the slope, and finally turn away.

"They say no, they're here to protect you," the colonel said.

"We can take care of ourselves! We don't need the bloody common squaws!"

"That's what I told them. They said no; with the cartmen so far away, we needed them all the more, and they are staying."

"Blast!"

"I can remove them by force, your lordship."

"Then that lout of a guide will make a fuss. Oh, well, Galitzin, the evening's ruined. Lady Alexandra won't unhook a shoe with a commoner around. I suppose we'll just suffer their disrespect."

"After it's dark, sir, she might—"

"No, never. Not with that pig of a guide watching. By the way, have you seen him?"

"Gone all day, Lord Frazier."

"Deserted us. It tallies."

"The cartmen say he compelled Stauffinger to give him some spirits."

"Ah! Theft. I knew his boozy nature would show itself. He's London dregs, penal colony stuff. I'll cane him personally if we can catch him."

"Ah, your lordship, what are we to do about food?"

"Have Beowolf bring it. Have him stop a hundred yards from us first, eh?"

"We're down to nothing. Skye didn't bring in any meat."

"Deserted us, Galitzin. Stole spirits and abandoned us! Tell Gravesend to start hunting at once. But not around here. If he peers over that ridge, he'll be flogged. Send me spirits, Galitzin. I'm famished. Have Stauffinger leave some with us and then retire to the lower camp."

It was tempting to have that monk of a cook and the wine steward stay and wait on them, but that would be unthinkable. They'd see and hear things not meant for common eyes and ears.

Lord Frazier had worked himself into a temper because

nothing was going well. Still, a lavender dusk had lowered upon the hotspring, and soon enough he and his ladies could have their delicious sport.

Far above him, on the grassy shoulder of mountain that hid the camp from the Yellowstone valley, something bawled like an old buffalo bull. He'd heard the very sound from the deck of the river packet. Buffalo! Up there in the settling dark! Meat! That grating noise had scarcely subsided when wild bawling laughter erupted—the laughter of a man or a spirit, he scarcely knew which. But sure enough, the bellowing seemed human, Skye's squaws stared upward, a frown etched deep in the old one's brow. Skye? Was it Skye, drunk as a lor—ah, oaf? A horse screeched. He knew the horse. Only one horse in creation screeched like that, the bag of bones called Jawbone. Its shriek shivered through him, and no doubt woke the dead for miles around.

Lady Chatham-Hollingshead giggled. The viscount stared at her, still lolling in the pool. Why didn't she fetch a robe instead of displaying herself shamelessly to commoners?

"It's Skye," said Baudelaire.

"Warn him off! Tell him to head for the cartmen's camp, eh?"

Far up a grassy shoulder, a horse and rider appeared in the dusk, the rider bawling and bellowing and weaving about on the angry animal.

"It's Skye all right, flying his true colors," Alexandra said shortly. "Make him go away. I want a bath."

But the insufferable bellowing and bawling continued as the horse picked its way down into the narrow flats.

"Sonofabitch!" muttered the old squaw.

Jawbone sugarfooted forward, with that hog on his back

weaving to one side and then the other, righting himself at the last moment before tumbling in a heap.

"Frazier!" bawled the guide. "You and me's going to have us a toddy!"

The very thought of it drained the viscount's energies from him. He peered about for Galitzin, and remembered he'd sent the colonel to the lower camp. He'd have to deal with this brute himself. He and Baudelaire, who was worse than useless in moments like this. He spotted his aide peering from the wagon window.

"Frazier, you old coon, fetch a cup," Skye bawled, the rasp of his voice shivering the air. "Tell the ladies to join us. We'll have a little spirits, and then have a splash."

The viscount gaped.

"Shed your skins, Barnaby," yelled Diana from the hot pool. "The water's divine. Hurry up before my flesh puckers."

The viscount was aghast. Skye's squaws stared angrily.

"Everything but my hat."

Mister Skye sagged over the near side of Jawbone, righted himself, teetered toward the off side, shrugged too late, and tumbled in a heap while Jawbone snarled and shrieked.

"Goddam," said Victoria.

Ponderously, Mister Skye hoisted himself from the grass, rear end first, and peered at him. In one massive hand, he clutched a gray jug. He wobbled uncertainly, while Jawbone skittered sideways angrily, snorting and clacking his teeth.

"Go eat," said Mister Skye. He lifted his battered silk tophat and screwed it down again, and turned to the viscount. "Have a slug," he said, proffering the jug.

Lord Frazier recoiled.

"Won't booze with a commoner, eh?"

The viscount refused to speak. Let Galitzin convey messages if there must be any.

"Ah, paradise," Skye said, uncorking the jug again and quaffing juices that gurgled out of his mouth and dripped on his elkskin shirt and over his grizzly bear claw necklace. "Ah!" He belched like a dyspeptic Turk.

Tenderly he fondled the jug, lurched down, daintily placed it upright, and teetered back to his feet again. Then he veered toward the pool, while the viscount followed, speechless. At the rippling pond, with lavender lights lifting from it in the dusk, he peered about serenely, set his silk hat on the ground, fumbled with the laces of his crude square-toed boots until he could wrestle them off, releasing a vast noisome odor, fought his elkskin shirt off, baring a massive chest with hair going gray, unbuckled his heavy belt, which supported his leggins and breechclout, along with his revolver and knife scabbards, and let it all fall.

"Ah!" he said, retrieving his silk hat and screwing it down over greasy gray-shot hair. He maintained a perfect dignity, even wearing nothing over his hairy flesh except a black silk tophat.

"I knew you would," said Diana.

"I think I'll retire to the wagon," said Lady Alexandra, but she didn't move, and watched Skye, her gaze riveted on his massive frame. Something excited her. "Oh!" she exclaimed.

Lady Diana whooped and splashed water at Skye.

Mary giggled. Just like a squaw, thought the viscount. Then Victoria giggled too, the pair of them grinning like strumpets. Had those savages no decency?

"Come on in, yer lordship," bellowed Skye. He turned

slowly, tread his lordly way to the pool, and toppled in like a felled oak, landing in the pond with a crash that sounded like a plugged cannon exploding, and shot tidal waves of hot water roiling over the banks. The tophat bobbed. Mister Skye surfaced and gently settled it down upon his dripping hair.

"Diana, come out of there!" the viscount demanded.

"Tiddlywinks," she retorted.

It enraged him. "You—you—in there with a common criminal?"

Lady Alexandra started dithering and muttering.

"A common sailor, you mean. Royal Navy," bellowed Skye.

"I thought so—I thought so!"

Mister Skye splashed mightily, spraying showers of hot water into the dusk. Lady Diana whooped and splashed too, soaking the viscount's pants. He danced back from the bank.

Mister Skye belched joyously and bugled like a bull elk. Then he roared, shivering the dark slopes. "Pressed in on the banks of the Thames; jumped ship at Fort Vancouver."

The news froze Viscount Frazier. "What did you say, Skye? You deserted the queen's navy?"

Skye bawled at the distant ridges. "Overboard with a belaying pin, foggy night, second watch."

"You deserted her royal majesty!"

"Naw, she deserted me. Press gang snatched me at age fifteen, just as I was about to start at Cambridge. Made me a bloody slave, a powder monkey. Your bloody queen and her bloody lords don't care anything about that."

"A common deserter. A thug and a lowlife!"

"A freeman, yer holiness."

"Oh, tiddlywinks, Gordon." Diana wallowed over to the

deserter who stood in the pool, ludicrous in his silk tophat, steaming water lapping his waist. "Let's all have a splash."

"I think I will," whispered Lady Alexandra in a strange squeaky voice.

"Goddam," muttered Victoria. The squaws trotted toward the inviting dark water.

Lady Alexandra Frazier and the two squaws began pulling and tugging and unhooking and squirming.

But Viscount Gordon Patrick Archibald Frazier, peer of England and seventh of his line, refused to budge. He had the man now—deserter, traitor to the queen. But it would take some planning.

Chapter 22

Victoria endured. She would not sleep. She'd never quite grown used to sitting awake all night, but whenever Mister Skye crossed over to the Other Side, she watched over him ceaselessly. For as long as she'd known him he had taken these occasional journeys, and been helpless as a newborn. She couldn't fathom why he drank the spirits. Mary drank too, sometimes. And that left only her, Victoria, Many Quill Woman, to guard over the lodge of Mister Skye.

She sat crosslegged outside of the lodge, a thin two-point blanket drawn close about her to ward off the sharp chill of a mountain night. Her man snored peacefully, a white mountain under the buffalo robe she'd roughly thrown over him, afraid someone would see tenderness in it. Earlier, he'd wallowed to the bank of the hot pool, let more of the spirits gurgle down his throat, and then had fallen asleep in the water, bobbing on it like a great otter. She and Mary had pulled him out and covered him, setting his silk hat at his side. And she'd settled into her own blanket to watch through the night, as she had countless times before.

She would not weep. Neither would she sort through the confusion that snared her. It had been a dark evening, sinister with portents that she felt in her flesh and soul. She didn't want to watch over Mister Skye, but ancient habit made her do it. Soon he would be taken away, and nothing would remain of Mister Skye's lodge. She had felt something new this night, some fierce power radiating from the viscount, who'd prowled around the lip of the hot pool like a panther looking for a way to pounce.

No sooner had Mister Skye fallen asleep in the water than the ladies abandoned the pool and hurried off through the dusk to their yellow wagon, mincing barefoot through grass and clutching their skirts and linens. A swift silence settled around the hotsprings. Even Galitzin and Baudelaire had vanished to the cartmen's camp far away, leaving only the lord and ladies, and that little bulldog, Chesterfield, who trotted along with Lady Alexandra everywhere. The ugly mutt lay in moonshadow under the yellow wagon.

She sat with her old muzzle-loader across her lap and Mister Skye's heavy dragoon revolver close by. She and Jawbone. The horse cropped meadow grass angrily, his temper even more vicious than usual because Mister Skye had gone to the Other Side. The horse was staring now, his ears pricked forward, but in the light of the small moon she couldn't see anything upslope. If it was thieves from other tribes, he'd bugle and begin that unearthly howling. Many a night his bloodcurdling shriek had awakened them in time to avert theft or murder. But he wasn't shrieking, and whatever was up the slope did not have a human spirit. She watched anyway, waiting to see the creature that engaged Jawbone's attention. Usually she loved this place, a favorite resort of her Kicked-in-the-Bellies, but this night she dreaded it. Evil lurked and danced, and she knew it was the spirts of the dead that had gone to the Beyond Land without the scalps and ponies and weapons and eyes and limbs they needed over there. She watched sharply, half-afraid of the spirit people.

So far she'd had health. She was actually a year younger than her man, but her flesh had withered sooner and she'd grown small and light, while he stayed the same. But maybe this evil night the spirits would cast a spell upon her body and make her sick. Maybe that was good, to die before Mister Skye was taken away from her.

Something lurked out upon the slope. She couldn't see it, but she sensed it. She squinted into the slit-mooned murk, seeing not even a hint of motion. Nothing stirred. A few embers still glowed in the remains of a tiny fire Mary had used to make a broth of jerky, and she wondered whether to build them into a flame again. She thought she would. The thing out there wasn't human, but a creature. She creaked to her feet intending to find squaw wood. Little of it remained here where whole villages camped. But Mary had left some she'd gathered earlier, so Victoria fed sticks into the coals and blew gently until a cold flame awakened out of its womb of ash and cast a somber glow into the night.

Goddam! she thought. This was a night when the dead danced. Nearby, Mister Skye snored suddenly and rolled, a shuddering mountain under the curly black robe. A beefy white calf flopped out upon grass. And just beyond Mister Skye sat a small wolf on his haunches, its eyes dancing a phosphorescent orange in the wavering light.

Startled, she slid back to her blanket and her battered rifle there, keeping an eye on the bold animal, which stared brightly back at her, its muzzle oddly turned and jaw hanging. A wolf. Not a large one. Solid gray, except for a black diamond rising over its brow and into the ruff of hair back of its ears. A strange mark, she thought, suddenly afraid. She'd never seen a wolf like that. It panted, its tongue slavering even in the chill of the night. One of its yellow eyes seemed larger than the other, or radiated more light from the guttering fire. It sent fear piercing through her, though she couldn't say why. She'd never known a wolf to venture so close. The creature watched her while she studied it, slowly easing her rifle around, and then deciding Mister Skye's Dragoon Colt would be better for close work.

Chesterfield came alive over at the glinting yellow wagon and growled. The little bulldog stood up, bulbous-eyed, and muttered like distant thunder. Then the dog yapped and barreled toward the wolf, which leapt lithely toward the smaller bulldog and bit it, breaking its neck with one crunch of its heavy jaw. Chesterfield's yowling died along with the writhing dog. The wolf sat back on its haunches again, panting.

"Chesterfield," said a woman's voice from within the wagon. "Do stop annoying us, dear."

The wolf turned, listening to the sound emerging from the yellow wagon, and walked lazily toward Victoria and Mister Skye, slobbering strangely, grinning at her madly. And then she knew. Madness! Hydrophobia, Mister Skye called it, though her people called it spirit-madness. Hydrophobia! She had heard the whispered stories in the light of a hundred campfires. The fearlessness. The slobbering. The bite that always killed. The wolf grinned at her, reading her mind, laughing at her because a bad spirit possessed it, peering out from its mad eyes.

Kill it! She clawed for Mister Skye's holster and found it, and lugged the cold steel from its sheath on his belt, but the wolf was trotting toward Mister Skye's bare white calf. Too late, too late. She whipped her weapon around, cocking the heavy hammer, just as the wolf snarled savagely and sank its fangs into Mister Skye's flesh. She shot, the explosion blinding in the night. Mister Skye roared, flailing legs, erupting from his robe.

She searched for the wolf but it had vanished into the gloom, its evil spirit hiding in the darkness. She heard talk in the yellow wagon and saw it creak on its leafsprings. But even as she watched, a terrible realization sliced through her: Mister Skye had been bitten, and he would die.

Mister Skye clambered to his hands and knees, fighting off his own fogginess, rumbling and muttering. Victoria gaped, seeing death upon him, seeing the slow, mad, crazed dying that would possess him in about two moons, maybe less, until he slavered his life away, foaming at the mouth, unable to drink, spasming and convulsing, berserk and tied down to keep from harming himself and everyone else.

"Sonofabitch," she wailed.

Skye stared at her, alert now, no longer over on the Other Side.

He stared at the four fang holes piercing his calf. "Hydrophobic?" he asked quietly.

She nodded, tears welling up.

Swiftly he yanked his Green River knife from its sheath, paused, and then slashed across a fang mark until blood welled up freely. He groaned, but didn't hesitate. The knife ripped into his own flesh across the other small wounds until all four bled copiously, the red blood gouting to the earth. He sobbed, anguish shaking him.

"Heat the knife and the iron spit, Victoria. We've only got seconds."

She was never sure what he meant by seconds. A white man's concept. But it meant little time. Wordlessly she plunged the knife in the coals along with the iron cooking spit, grateful she'd built up the fire. She heated the metal, barely aware that the viscount had crawled out of his wagon.

"Get back in, mate," Skye commanded. "Hydrophobic wolf."

Viscount Frazier gaped.

Her man found a stick of squaw wood and clamped his teeth over it. He gripped two more pieces in his massive hands and lay back. "Don't spare me, woman," he demanded, an urgency in his voice she'd never heard before.

She didn't. She jammed the smoking blade down into the first fang wound to cauterize muscle, recoiling as his flesh fried and the stench of charred meat assaulted her nostrils. Mister Skye's body jolted, he screamed, and his spasming legs rocked her away and catapulted the knife from her grasp.

"Goddam," she muttered, crying, unable to find the blade in the dark.

Far away, in the direction of the cartmen's camp, she heard shots thumping through the night.

Skye groaned and then sobbed. She saw tears glinting on his face. She found the knife and stabbed it into fire again, her heart hammering, and pulled out the smoking iron rod. Somehow, Mary appeared beside her, still wearing nothing, and stared, horrified, her eyes welling tears of her own.

"Hurry," muttered Skye. "If it gets into the blood, I've gone under."

About the time that the viscount finished lacing up his boots, Colonel Galitzin loomed out of the night.

"Your lordship, there's trouble," he said.

Testily the viscount pulled aside the canvas flap of the parlor wagon, leaving his ladies staring at him in the darkness, and stepped down to earth. Galitzin seemed to be half-dressed, in boots, a nightshirt, and brown tweed jacket.

"I say, colonel, you're a sight." The viscount chortled at the spectacle.

"We've had a wolf. Hydrophobic, we think, your lordship. He bit Cutler about ze face."

"Bit Cutler?"

"On the neck. Sank its fangs into his cheek. We tried to shoot it, but it vanished in the dark."

"Cutler? The taxidermist?"

"Yes, I fear he faces a horrible death. There's none worse, or drawn out so terribly."

"I see. Anyone else?"

"No, Lord Frazier."

The viscount eyed Skye, who lay groaning and sobbing beside the small fire before the lodge a few yards away. That mad nag, Jawbone, stood beside the guide, screeching and carrying on.

"Did you take any measures?"

"There are no measures. Poor Cutler—he's doomed. It'll take a while, and the last will be frightful."

The viscount sighed. "Skye was bit. First thing I knew he was stabbing himself, and then his squaws were heating a knife and cauterizing the holes. Savage nonsense, I think. I don't suppose it'll save him."

"I can't imagine it."

"Now I'll have no one to preserve my trophies, Galitzin. What a piece of bad luck, eh? Losing my taxidermist. I suppose we'll have to put up with his howling, too. Keep him at the end of the caravan, as far from my wagon as possible. I don't want to listen to all that howling."

"I think he'd welcome a visit from you, sir. He knows his fate."

"That's your business, Galitzin. You're in charge of the blokes. And say, Galitzin—when Skye begins to rave, snatch him from his squaws and throw him back with Cutler. And then drive the squaws away."

"Why not just send them packing, your lordship?"

The viscount peered through the darkness toward the two Indian women, hovering over their groaning man. "I say, Galitzin, I found out something this evening that changes everything. The drunken fool's a deserter. He was in the Royal Navy and jumped ship at Fort Vancouver. I've got him now, oh, I've got him! I knew it; I knew him for a scoundrel. I want him with us just in case he lives, just in case all that cutting and burning works. In truth, Galitzin, I'm a bit disappointed he got bitten. I had better plans for him."

"They might just leave us, sir, and go off somewhere to let him die."

"Don't permit it! Keep an eye on them, Galitzin. I'm charging you with it."

"Very good, Lord Frazier."

"We'll know if the hydrophobia takes soon enough. And even if it doesn't, I've made new plans."

Lady Alexandra poked her head out of the wagon. "Chesterfield, sweetie, Chesterfield. . . . Where are you, my little poopsie."

The bulldog didn't come.

"Chesterfield!" she cried nervously. "Find him, Gordon. Find my little poopsie."

Galitzin pointed. Off a few yards, barely lit by the flickering fire, lay a mound of hair. They trotted over and found the bulldog dead, its neck snapped and its throat ripped open, its bulging eyes turned milky.

"Gone!" exclaimed the viscount, poking the soft little body with the toe of his boot. "Killed by the wolf. While protecting his mistress." A sob rose in him. "Was there ever such a noble pup, colonel? It touches my very soul, the courage of this loyal little bloke. I wish men were half as loyal." He sighed heavily, absorbing the terrible reality of death. "Tell the lady, Galitzin. And then fetch men with a spade and we'll bury the little chap with honors, eh?"

Grief pierced him as he stood in the eddying night-breeze, watching Galitzin walk over to the bed wagon and say something to Alexandra. Her shriek shattered the night, and the sobs that followed racked his soul.

"Oh my little poopsie!" she cried, sobbing and gulping. "Oh my baby, my baby."

The lady shuddered and wept, and finally withdrew from the door of the carriage and tumbled back into their bed, her sobs rising muffled from within. The viscount felt her pain deeply, and resolved to bury the manly little bulldog with all the honors due him. He was a true English bulldog, fierce and loyal and noble, the best that England could make.

"Galitzin," he said softly. "We'll wait for dawn. We're going to have a proper burial for that noble creature. We'll lay him to earth with a prayer and raise the Union Jack and fire a salute. And I'll say some words, eh? And, blast it, colonel, you could have broken the news to her more gently. Have you no sensibility?"

The colonel didn't respond, but stood in the wavering firelight looking sheepish. He annoyed the viscount. Was there no competent help anywhere on earth? Why did retainers all turn out to be boneheaded and coarse, if not crooked? He had no answer to it, but knew it had to do with breeding. The world's ruffians, like that groaning Skye over there, were simply brutes.

"Galitzin. Take Chesterfield with you. Sew him into wagonsheeting for the burial. I don't want him lying there when dawn comes up. The sight would grieve my ladies. Do it up proper, Galitzin, or it'll be a mark against you."

"Very good, sir."

"Post a guard, Galitzin. Why wasn't a guard posted? The pup might be alive if there'd been a guard."

"You sent us all to the other camp, sir—"

"No excuses, Galitzin. Negligence. I detest negligence."

"You had the Skyes guarding, sir."

"You should have been. Nothing but an old squaw watching for trouble."

From beyond the fire, the old woman stared at him, along with the young one, who sat shamelessly unclad beside that cowardly oaf who groaned and wept and kept running those big paws of his along his bloody left calf. Well, he was done for, and a pity. He deserved a worse fate.

Galitzin picked up the dead bulldog awkwardly and made off into the night with it, while the Skyes all watched. It grew quiet, save for the constant sobbing and grunting of that lout. The viscount walked over there, as far as he dared with that vicious yellow-eyed horse snarling at him.

"I say, Skye. If you're going to groan and weep all night after butchering your own leg, take your lodge away, eh? It'll ruin our sleep. But not far, mind you. We're still retaining you, Skye, and I won't have you sneak off."

The guide peered up at the viscount, from a face raked with pain and weariness. "If there's any chance at all with hydrophobia," he said hoarsely, "it's by bleeding the wounds and frying the flesh around them. Saw it work once. Saw it fail many times, back in the trapping days."

"Whatever," the viscount said. "Now be a man for once, Skye, and stop the blubbering."

Skye didn't respond. The calf looked ugly, with black holes of charred, fried flesh pocking it, while blood and gore caked the whole swelling limb. The guide turned silent, his mouth clamped shut even though his eyes still leaked.

Jawbone snarled and clacked his teeth. The viscount thought to shoot the animal as soon as Skye died. If Skye died. If by any chance that drastic treatment kept him alive—well, all the better.

The viscount wished it would happen that way. Skye living. That would change the whole trip. Instead of heading up to the headwaters of the Yellowstone to hunt and see the geysers, they were going to head north. He would insist on it. Somewhere, perhaps two hundred miles north, lay the boundary, and beyond it, the Queen's possessions. And beyond that, the Hudson's Bay Company's Rocky Mountain House in Saskatchewan. Once they hustled Skye across that line, the viscount's word would be law, and when they reached the Hudson's Bay post, he'd give the command that had tickled his fancy all evening. He'd clap irons on Skye and haul him back to England as a deserter from the Royal Navy, and see to it that the scoundrel rotted away the rest of his days in a dungeon.

If Skye lived. The viscount earnestly hoped he would.

Chapter 23

Victoria wept. Loss engulfed her. Mister Skye would die. Shame pierced her too, because she had failed to drive the wolf away, even though she'd been guarding her man. It'd happened so fast she scarcely had time to act. But mostly she wept because her man would die, and she would be alone and a widow, and the lodge of Mister Skye would be cast to the winds.

Dawn came slowly in the blue valley where the hotsprings purled. She sat in the dark lodge beside her man, who lay half-covered by a buffalo robe, groaning occasionally. His swollen calf projected from the robe, because the slightest weight on it was more than he could bear. After things quieted outside, he'd crawled in beside her and Mary, silent and somber. His trip to the Other Side hadn't lasted long this time, but it was too long—much much too long.

The knowledge that he would soon die crushed her so much her lungs didn't pump right. Her man, gone! Not because of arrows or gunshot or knife or a stumbling horse, but because of the bite of a mad wolf. She had darkened his lodge these past moons, darkened his life, darkened Mary's because she couldn't bear to become a widow. She'd fled to the hills each day, not talking to him, not doing her work, not hugging him. And now her selfish deeds were upon her head. She had made him unhappy; she had driven him away to others; she had not helped him deal with these strange people; she had thought only of herself and her own future.

She slumped in the gloom, not wanting sleep but weary,

feeling tears streak down the seams of her weathered cheeks, registering the unsteady breathing of her man and his occasional groans. She felt his heat and knew he'd become feverish from the brutal knife-work and cauterization. He had settled himself on his robes and said only one thing: "I'm going under."

He might last one moon; two moons; three moons. That was the way of hydrophobia. His fate would hang over their lodge like a thick snow waiting to avalanche, filling the next moons with dread and finally terror as the disease pounced on Mister Skye. She knew what she had to do. Even as gray dawn began to filter through the umber cone of cowhide, she knew she would darken his lodge no more, and make his last days as happy as she could. They would be unbearable, those last days. But she would do what she could; she owed it not only to Mister Skye, but to Mary too. She reached out in the murk and found his sweated palm, and held it tightly. He moaned. But it was a beginning, and he would know his lodge was darkened no more. She sobbed, knowing how good it was to hold her man's hand.

Mary saw, and smiled somberly. They had both heeded Victoria's medicine vision, the gift of Magpie, and now all that seemed an aching mystery. Had Magpie's guidance been wrong, or was it yet buried behind mysterious veils that would be drawn apart, one by one? How could the Englishmen take Mister Skye away to a place across the sea if he no longer lived? She could not fathom all this, and set it aside as something beyond her frail knowing. She knew only that she'd failed her man and that she would pour out her love upon him during his last days, so he might go to the Spirit Land comforted.

"I think we should leave these people now," said Mary softly from across the lodge.

Mister Skye's voice startled them. "I've been thinking on it. We're close to Victoria's people and I'd like to go under there. With old Many Coups telling jokes."

"Ah!" exclaimed Victoria. "You are here."

"Need a day or so. My leg hurts so much from that carving I can't ride. Puffed up now. I'll tell the viscount we're quitting—I'll write him a draft for the balance—and we'll cut free of them. They'll find their way up the Yellerstone, I imagine."

Victoria's tears welled up again at the sound of his somber voice. Impulsively she squeezed his clammy hand and held it fiercely. "I've darkened your lodge. I won't darken it any more," she cried.

She waited for him to say something. He caught her small hand in his and held it tightly. "I'm glad of that, Victoria. Makes it easier to go."

She wept bitterly, remembering every day of every moon she'd darkened his lodge.

Mary crawled over to them from her robe and held his other hand tightly, and in that sweet dawn quiet they banished darkness from Mister Skye's lodge forever.

"You are hot," said Mary softly.

"I'm some fevered. But that'll pass unless my leg takes to mortifying."

"Oh, why did it happen?" Mary cried.

"My weakness," Skye said somberly. "My weakness for spirits, that did it. I knew it would do for me some day. For twenty-five years I've lived careful as a doe, except for the times when I take spirits. I always slept light as a cat, ready to leap. Recent years, Jawbone helped, like a sentinel in the night—if I wasn't too far gone with the spirits . . ."

"No, not you. I was watching. I always watch when you are gone to the Other Side." She fought back tears again.

He clutched her hand tightly. "I know, Victoria. Saved my life more'n I can remember. Watching over me. Don't you blame yourself any."

He was reaching to her, she knew, and it warmed her a little.

"I don't want to go under. I want to see my child. I've fought off wolves and bears, snow, freezing, starving times, thirst, ambushes and thieves—all of it. I didn't expect to have a hydrophobic wolf cash me in. I can hardly make it real—that I'm going under."

The dawn light intensified outside of the lodge, and she could see him now, see the vicious wounds, scarlet and charred black, each the size of a brass trade dollar, pitting his purplish calf.

Daylight triumphed but they didn't stir. The disaster had drawn them together again, for a last forlorn time before they scattered to the winds.

"Worried about Jawbone. Don't know what'll become of him," he muttered. "He'll turn outlaw around anyone else. Victoria, maybe you could take him out to a band of wild ones up in the Pryors, let him run free after I go under. I'd like that."

"Don't talk of that," she replied crossly. A helpless anger welled through her. She had no medicine for this, and no shaman of her people did either. The tears rose again, unbidden. Mister Skye gone. Jawbone gone. Mary gone.

Colonel Galitzin's voice eddied in from outside, and they heard men busy themselves with morning tasks. Apparently the whole caravan had been pulled up to the hotsprings, and morning chores were underway. But it didn't matter. Within their little world inside the cone of skin they did nothing, wanting only to share a reconciliation that was precious to them all, even if laced with sorrow.

Sun struck the lodge, turning its eastern flank into a wall of amber light that radiated on those within.

"Are we ready, colonel?" asked the viscount, outside.

"Bring Lady Alexandra, your lordship," Galitzin replied.

Victoria slid her hand out of Mister Skye's, tugged a soft doeskin dress over her small frame, and tied her moccasins. Then she stepped through the lodge flap into a glaring sun, and blinked. Off a little way, beyond the rippling pool in the meadow, the cartmen had gathered around a small grave chopped out of the turf, along with the lord and ladies and all the rest, it seemed. Lady Alexandra wore a black dress with a veil over her face. And Lady Diana as well, looking solemn.

Had the cartman died so fast? Puzzled, she walked toward the gathering, her gaze settling at last upon a small canvas sack resting on the yellow meadow grasses. She found a place at the rear edge of this solemn assemblage and waited.

"We will begin with a prayer," said the viscount earnestly, opening his black book. He cleared his throat portentiously and read, and she wondered at the smallness of the man they were burying. Then he closed his book and handed it to the lady, whose eyes brimmed with tears. Victoria had never seen Lady Alexandra cry. But now she grieved, along with the lord and the other lady.

The viscount paused, pregnantly, waiting for a hush in the assemblage that would amplify his words.

"We have come to bury a great Englishman," he began sternly. "Never was there a nobler breed, a more perfect expression of the courage and daring of our island race, a finer example of the faithful steward, the loyal soldier, the sentry who never abandoned post or duty—than the one we lay to rest here today.

"Chesterfield was no ordinary dog. He was a noble dog, of a noble English breed bred on our own little island for its loyalty, courage, daring, and honor. Let us think about Chesterfield now, and how he dashed, full of fury, into the jaws of his giant adversary, the mad wolf, to protect his mistress Viscountess Frazier, and gave up his little life doing it for her . . ."

Victoria listened, astonished, as the eulogy droned on and Lady Alexandra wept softly, a steady flow of tears sliding down the alabaster face under her veil.

"We will have an oil rendered, and it will occupy the place of honor in my guildhall," the viscount went on. He wiped a tear from his eye. "We will have a great medal struck, both silver and gold. We will petition the Queen, God save her soul, for a decoration for this noble breed, our own Chesterfield . . ."

At last the viscount wound down, and with a curt nod to Galitzin he stepped aside so the cartmen could lower the little gray sack and shovel sod over the little grave. This they did while the lord and ladies watched, and added a cap of rock clawed out of the bluffs above to mark the place. Then the viscount led a final lengthy prayer, commending Chesterfield to earth and his dog-spirit to God. And at the last, ten cartmen lifted their fine rifles and fired three volleys that echoed slowly and somberly across the valley, into the rising mountain beyond.

"Sonofabitch!" she muttered, and slid back to Mister Skye's lodge.

"What was all that about? Cartman die?" Mister Skye asked, from his robes.

"No, Mister Skye. They buried Chesterfield."

The viscount commandeered Colonel Galitzin's black and gold kangaroo leather-wrapped swagger stick because it suited him. With every passing moment he felt his military soul burgeon in his breast. It lay buried in him, that hawkish blood of his warrior ancestors. The Lords Frazier had been generals and chieftains, marshals and admirals, coming alive to the howl of bagpipes, lancers, archers, and cavalry.

The hunt was a ruin, but it didn't matter. He had a nobler mission now, to bring a foul deserter to England to taste the queen's justice—if that drastic surgery saved him from the hydrophobia. It'd be a lesson to every skulking limey in her majesty's vessels of war. Not even the distant wastes of North America could hide a traitor to the Crown. He'd come to these wastes on a lark, but high duty called now, and fired his blood with visions of liege-duty to his queen and his country.

He rapped sharply on the guide's silent lodge, feeling cowhide give under his baton. "I say, Skye, let me in."

The flap parted and the older squaw squinted out. The viscount didn't wait, but pushed in, finding the lodge filled with a soft brown light from the translucent cowhide skins. The ruffian lay at the back in his buffalo robe, except for the swollen left leg, which bore evidence of ghastly self-mutilation, its burnt-black wounds suppurating yellow fluids. The scoundrel peered up at him sharply.

"I say, Skye. We've a change of plans. Instead of going further up the Yellowstone to hunt, we're going to start north to British possessions—to Rocky Mountain House, the Hudson's Bay post on the Saskatchewan River."

Mister Skye absorbed that, keeping silent.

"Have you nothing to say, Skye?"

"It's a long way—longer than you imagine," the guide said at last. He looked feverish, now that the viscount could see him in the dim light. "Up past Bug's Boys, all three tribes of them . . . Piegan, Blood, and Northern Blackfoot."

"They trade with Hudson's Bay, don't they?"

The ruffian ignored the question. "Why?" he asked. "Why go there?"

"Because I wish to," Frazier replied coolly.

"Long way home. You can't take your carts from there back East. It's packtrain, canoe and portage."

"I'll deal with that when I get there. I'll have an HBC escort, no doubt."

"You didn't answer my question, Frazier."

"Keep a civil tongue, Skye. I don't choose to answer it."

Skye sighed softly. "I won't make it. Going under, one month, two, three. Go ahead, Frazier, but don't count on me. We're resigning. I'll give you a draft on my accounts carried by the sutler at Fort Laramie. I'm going to choose the place where I go under."

"I won't permit it."

"We're doing it."

"I need you for a guide."

"I'm going under. And any Blackfoot can take you there. They'd kill me anyway."

The revelation delighted the viscount. So Skye had his enemies up there!

"As you wish, Skye," the viscount said, carefully. "We're leaving in an hour. Perhaps you'll come with us as far as the great bend of the Yellowstone and help us ford."

"Galitzin can lead you now. I can scarcely get out of my robes."

The viscount nodded, his mind made up. He peered about the lodge. Skye lay naked under the robe. The squaws had set their weapons near the lodge door, along with his Hawken. That's all he needed to know. The old woman stared at him, as if transfixed, as if reading his mind, and the younger one peered at him also, rank hostility in her savage face.

"Very well," Frazier said, backing out into bright sunlight.

It had to be done at once.

He found Galitzin organizing the departure from the hot springs, and rapped sharply on the colonel's shoulder with the swagger stick.

"I'm taking Skye prisoner, colonel. The bird was about to fly the coop. Go away to die, he said."

"Prisoner, your lordship?"

"Of course! Deserter! We're going to Rocky Mountain House on the Saskatchewan. HBC post."

Galitzin gaped, absorbing that. "Without a guide, sir?"

"Skye, if he lives. If not, any Blackfoot. They've been allies of England all along. We'll have a royal reception from the northern savages."

"Have you a right, sir? To take Skye, I mean. Zese aren't British possessions."

Frazier glared, and smacked his swagger stick in his palm with a resounding crack. "The eye and arm of the queen reach anywhere on earth, colonel! Go find Gravesend and the best ten cartmen you've got, and issue them arms. And then do your duty."

The colonel nodded, and trotted off to collect the men while the viscount stood watching, snapping the swagger stick sharply against his britches. He fancied that the cracks, which sounded like rifle shots, stirred the fiery blood he'd inherited from the first Lords Frazier.

Minutes later cartmen filtered around Skye's silent lodge, armed and ready. The viscount watched, approving, feeling the power of steel. A stiff morning breeze hid their movement. Not even that vicious blue roan horse paid any attention.

"All right then," he whispered to the colonel. "Skye's naked in his robes. Their weapons are heaped just inside the lodge flap, to the right. But his belt with the dirk and revolver's a bit closer to hand. Skye's at the rear. Don't announce. Just send Gravesend and some others in."

The colonel nodded, saluted smartly, and deployed his men quietly, with whispers and gestures. The three who were to plunge in formed a wedge and drew their revolvers. Others surrounded the lodge, rifles at the ready.

"They'll rush at the crack of your stick, your lordship," the colonel whispered.

The viscount felt a strange joy well up in him. All about the camp men paused to watch, and a deep silence stained the bright morning, except for the groaning of poor Cutler, lying bitten and no doubt dying in a cart off a way.

He peered about and then cracked his swagger stick sharply in the palm of his hand. It sounded like a cannonshot. Gravesend leapt, piercing into the Skye lodge, followed by the two others.

He heard a muffled roar, and the cursing of the savage old woman, and a few thumps, and soon enough the lodgedoor belched out a squaw, the old one, who sailed through and tumbled into the grass. The younger one followed, on her feet, her arm pinioned by a burly cartman. And finally, Gravesend pulled Skye out, naked and white and so weak he could barely stand. The deserter stood in the sunlight, blinking, absorbing the armed men, the pieces aimed at him, the captivity of his wives. In the light his calf looked ghastly, swollen into a tree trunk, scarlet and black.

Gravesend motioned, and a cartman ducked into the lodge, pulling out Skye's Hawken, the squaws' flintlocks, Skye's belt with its sheathed revolver and knife, and finally Skye's robe.

"I suppose you want an explanation, Skye."

But the guide said nothing, staring at them all from small blue eyes burdened with pain.

"You're a deserter! And I'm taking you to the queen's justice! If you die of hydrophobia, justice will be done at last. If not, you'll taste the justice of a good English court and an English dungeon."

"Sonofabitch! Magpie said it true," muttered the old squaw.

The statement puzzled him, but it didn't matter. "Keep a civil tongue, old woman. Next time you profane the air, you'll be whipped."

She stared at him, almost shrinking before his eyes.

He nodded, and the cartmen dragged Skye off. The fevered guide didn't resist, but mustered what strength he could while Gravesend and another cartman marched him toward the distant cart where Cutler lay, a tumbril now devoted to carrying the two hydrophobic men to their doom.

"Fetch his robe but keep him naked," the viscount commanded. "He won't go anywhere naked."

Skye paused before the viscount. "Hope you'll let my wives pack up the lodge, mate. They can guide you, even if I can't. Make sign talk with the Blackfeet."

The viscount had been wondering about the squaws, whether to confiscate in the name of the crown their shabby lodge and ponies and drive them off or not, but now he realized they'd be useful. He nodded curtly, and the cartmen released the women.

"One thing, Galitzin. Take Skye's clothing. Don't let them pack that."

The colonel nodded and began supervising the squaws. He found Skye's silk tophat and grinned, setting it on his head rakishly.

The cartmen helped Skye into the tumbril and threw the robe over him. Skye stared sharply at Cutler who lay beside him, his face and neck a gashed ruin from the rabid wolf, and sighed, knowing. Cutler stared back, his gray eyes wet.

And the viscount watched, exultantly.

Chapter 24

Barnaby Skye lay in the bouncing cart, his mind upon medicine rather than the violent jolting that rocked and bucked his bruised body. At least the cart had bows and a ragged canvas wagonsheet over it to keep sun and chapping wind and rain off him, as well as the icy night air of September.

The caravan had retreated down the Yellowstone to the great bend, and had forded just below there at a place Victoria knew of, and now pushed north up the Shields River valley, an ancient Indian route that would take them ultimately to the lands of the Blackfeet, up near Canada, on the eastern flank of the Rockies.

In the week of travel his fever had died and the swelling of his leg had diminished, and he had recovered strength, at least temporarily—until whenever the hydrophobia pounced on him. He could walk now, and even resume his guiding, but he decided against it. If they knew he was strong enough to escape, they might well clamp him in the manacles Colonel Galitzin had with him for disciplinary purposes.

He wanted only to die free, in a place of his choosing, with Victoria's people. It seemed to him he had a good chance at that, if he and Victoria and Mary could slip away in the night. He'd do it naked if he must. Victoria's people would take them in.

The first two days, while he still lay fevered, Victoria slid over to him at dawn or dusk and they talked in Crow to keep Cutler or anyone else from understanding. But the viscount had heard about it and forbidden Skye's women to go anywhere near him. Still, they knew how to signal to him and he knew how to answer, and they might yet arrange the escape, a last melancholy trek so he could die in peace.

He feared for his women. Once this party reached Blackfoot country, anything could happen. The viscount might well turn them over to his Piegan hosts and his wives would either be tortured to death, as enemies of the People and especially as Skye's wives, or else made slaves and treated almost as badly. Somehow they had to escape. He ached to tell Victoria to flee while they could, but he had no way to talk with her now. And she and Mary were resolutely sticking with their man, rather than considering their own fate.

Jawbone had followed along puzzled and unhappy, sometimes edging close to Skye's cart. But he'd learned to accept the people in any Skye party, and still accepted these Britons, not grasping that friend was no longer friend.

Mister Skye feared for his horse; feared what might happen if Jawbone took a notion that all wasn't well; feared that the viscount might simply have the horse shot. The thought was so unbearable to him that he resolved to do something at all cost, even if he were murdered in the process. He would tell Jawbone to go! And hope the horse would obey this last heart-rending command.

Beside him in the jolting cart, Cutler sat up and peered out the rear.

"It's coming," he said. "I can feel it."

"Hope it's not, mate." Skye studied the taxidermist, noting the fang wounds in the man's neck and the furrows gouged across his cheek and brow and ear by the mad wolf's crazed biting. He didn't know much about hydrophobia, but he knew a victim took the disease faster from a facial wound than one lower down, like his. A man bitten around the face might die in two weeks. The disease seemed to attack a man's throat, torturing it until he would no longer drink, even if he lay famished for want of water.

"It was rabid," Cutler said. "I'll never see England again. If I go mad, Skye, kill me. Don't let me suffer."

Cutler had struck a nerve. If the taxidermist did go mad at the end, he would quite likely bite Mister Skye, dooming him to an earlier death. Mister Skye stared bleakly at the man. "I won't let you suffer the last," he said slowly.

"It's revenge. The animal kingdom revenged itself on me," Cutler said. "I preserved their hides and stuffed them with straw, and now they're having their revenge."

"I don't follow the reasoning."

"How'd you liked to be pickled and stuffed, Skye?"

The faintest amusement crept into Skye's thoughts, but he pushed it aside. "You didn't kill them. Hunters killed them and brought them to you."

"It's revenge," Cutler insisted. "The mad wolf wanted me pickled and stuffed and mounted." He sobbed, and Mister Skye could think of little that would comfort the doomed man.

"Maybe the wolf wasn't rabid," he muttered, which evoked only a scornful snort from the taxidermist.

Mister Skye lay back in the cart, pondering once again the nature of Fate. His imminent death lay like a stone upon his soul, infusing his every thought with desolation. He'd weathered it all for twenty-five years in these wilds, surviving with caution and cunning, only to die from—this. He desperately wanted to live. He peered out upon the azure sky and loved it madly, its transparent blue. He gazed at the vaulting mountains hemming in the Shields River, the soaring Crazies to the east and the rising hills of the Rockies to the west—and ached within, for they were his wild home. He smelled the sage, pummeled by the mid-day sun, and it was incense in his lungs.

It was all more than he could bear, but not the least of his sorrows. For soon he'd never see his dear Victoria again, she of infinite resources, who always gave—and still gave—the whole of herself to him, for his pleasure and comfort and safety. And his dear young Mary, of the golden flesh, laughing and lusty and eager to give her love to him—a hallowed gift—and receive his. Gone. Soon a swift dark wall would arise between them all, terrifying and impenetrable, and they would be drawn farther and farther into a blackness, taken away forever. He sighed, loving life more than he'd ever loved it before.

They nooned on an oxbow of the lazy little river, in a place where the breezes made the yellow grasses shimmer, and the blue peaks of the mountains danced under a golden sun. There'd be no food, he knew. Now that the Skyes were no longer hunting, there'd been precious little of it—not enough to feed a large caravan. Gravesend and the other hunters, including the viscount and Lady Diana, had proved inept, and the caravan had slowly begun to starve on half rations the last few days.

He heard voices outside of the canvas walls of his prison, and then Frazier and Galitzin appeared at the back of the cart.

"Skye, step out," Frazier commanded.

"Weak," Skye responded.

"Step out or we'll drag you. I suppose you're not too weak for a few lashes."

Galitzin dropped the tailgate. Mister Skye reluctantly pulled himself to the rear, not wanting them to see the healing. He slid to the grasses, clutching his robe about him. Galitzin yanked it off.

"There!" said the viscount, pointing his swagger stick at Skye's calf. "Healing over. Swelling's down. No flush in his skin any more. Take him to do his duties, and put the manacle on. I won't have this fish jump back into the water."

"You might attend to Cutler," Skye said softly. "He's feeling thirsty and feverish."

"Yes, yes. And from now on, Skye, don't speak unless spoken to. If you speak, we'll devise appropriate punishments. Don't talk to your squaws, the cartmen, or Cutler either."

Fury welled up in Skye, and he could barely contain it. He could strangle the viscount before they could claw him off and shoot him. But if he did, they'd brain Victoria and Mary next. He walked barefoot toward the riverbrush, wary of rattlers, ignoring the stares of cartmen watching his naked progress. Galitzin followed behind, revolver drawn. The viscount stood at the cart, snapping his swagger stick against his britches. Far off, he spotted Mary and Victoria observing solemnly. Victoria lifted a hand and ran it through her ebony hair, an ancient signal among them: watch and wait.

Jawbone whickered and approached, and he felt a sudden terror.

"Away!" Skye cried at the eager horse. It paused, unhappy, ears flattened back, and reluctantly turned to graze.

"That's one lash for talking, Skye," the viscount announced. "Galitzin—when you're done, shoot that horse."

Something terrible flooded through Skye. Had it all come to this?

"Away!" he yelled at Jawbone. "Away!" He roared it hoarsely, his voice choked in his throat. Jawbone stopped grazing, peered at his master, and whickered. The sound was love, Mister Skye knew. Love that Mister Skye returned with his eyes and outstretched hands.

"Ten more lashes, Skye."

"Go!" cried Skye. "Go!"

Victoria rode toward them, an old squaw no one paid the slightest attention to, until her little dark pony stood a few yards from Jawbone. "Come," she said softly, and the ugly blue roan followed, slowly at first, and then ever faster as the old woman heeled the ribby mare into a gentle trot.

Mister Skye watched, the faintest hope rising in him. Sometimes Jawbone obeyed her. But not usually. In the distance, Victoria drew up beside Jawbone, took his ear in her hands, and said something. The horse trotted, and then loped, and then stopped about a thousand yards distant.

Galitzin laughed. "Your ugly brute didn't go. Too bad

for him. And there went your escape plans, Skye. We'll have some rifle practice when I'm done with you."

Barnaby Skye watched the small form of Jawbone standing on a distant mound, and hot tears welled up from his eyes.

A few minutes later, after he'd done his duties in the river brush, Galitzin escorted him back to the wagon and clamped heavy hobbles around his ankles and locked them. The rusty steel bit at his tender legs, and the chain links rattled with his every movement. But Galitzin wasn't done.

"Hold out your wrists," he commanded.

Skye thought to bash the man, but thought better of it. He slid his thick arms forward, and Galitzin clamped lightweight brass cuffs over his wrists, and pocketed the key.

"That should stop any thought of running off," he said. "If you resist, I'll chain you to the cart, too. Now stand quiet while I get the whip."

Nothing in Victoria's life had prepared her for the next moments. The crack of Colonel Galitzin's lash across the back of her man pierced across the campground, each terrible blow vibrating in her own small body. It pushed her to madness. She could kill Galitzin. In a pocket of her high moccasin, beneath her voluminous skirts, nestled a Green River knife they hadn't found. She could do it—whitemen rarely noticed the movement of old Indian women—but she would die for it. They'd club her with the butts of their rifles, cave in her skull, and toss her unburied into the brush for coyote food. So she stood and trembled, berserk within but rigid as stone to any observer, across the camp where they'd pushed her, with only the ripping sound of the whip across Mister Skye's naked back in her soul.

He didn't cry, at least as far as she could hear at her distance, but absorbed the blows silently. They waited for him to resist, so they could kill him. The viscount himself stood near Galitzin, revolver in hand, waiting for their erstwhile guide to roar and fight. She feared only that he would, in despair, since he would soon die anyway. At last they finished and threw her man back into the cart. His crime had been talking, begging his horse to save itself.

"Savages!" she spat.

From out on the bench where Jawbone stood she heard a whicker, and a whinny, the love-noises of Mister Skye's faithful horse, reaching toward his master. The noise paralyzed her. Soon he'd trot back to camp, and his doom. Even now, Galitzin was commanding his cartmen, forming a squad of them to shoot their fine British pieces at Jawbone. She watched, paralyzed, as they formed smartly into a line, lifted their rifles, aimed at the distant roan, and waited for the command to fire.

The viscount laughed. This would be sport, and would destroy Skye's outlaw horse as well as one more avenue of escape. "Aim high, lads. He's far up that slope. We'll have dogfood, anyway."

Jawbone stood, facing them, whickering, uncertain, pleading, loving, wanting to come to Mister Skye's lodge. He lifted his head and shrieked into the noon sun, and then trotted down the slope toward them.

The viscount laughed again. "Hold your fire, lads. He's making it easy!"

But a cartman shot, and they all did, a ragged volley that battered Victoria's ears and left blue powdersmoke drifting off in the zephyrs. Something hit Jawbone. He screeched and began bucking, berserk, confused. He knew the sound of rifles and knew pain, but this volley had erupted from his own camp, his master's camp. She saw blood then, even at that vast distance, rivering over a shoulder.

"Goddam!" she cried, her eyes welling up tears.

"Damn you!" cried the viscount. "I didn't give the order. Now you've driven the outlaw off!"

The cartmen hastily reloaded while the viscount raged. But Jawbone didn't flee. Confused, he milled about, out there on the sunny slope, bleeding scarlet, whickering for Mister Skye, unable to come to grips with murder.

She couldn't stand it. Beside her Mary slumped to the ground, sobbing. Cartmen grinned. Victoria whirled toward her lodge, trotting toward her ribby old mare. Too late, too late. She'd die now, time to die, time to sing her deathsong and go to the Beyond Land. She clambered painfully up on the mare, bareback because she had no time, using the halter rope for a rein, and kicked her mare with her moccasins.

Nearby, the cartmen were finishing their reloading, and Galitzin was rebuking them for driving Jawbone off. She trotted past them, an old, small squaw, hunched over the withers of her mare, rode straight past them, trotting toward Jawbone.

"Stop her!" Viscount Frazier roared.

A few ran after her, but she lifted her mare into a lazy lope, leaving them behind. She heard the harsh bark of rifles. The snap of bullets. A good time to die. Only let her lead Jawbone away first. Tears blinded her. She deliberately rode toward the flank, drawing fire from Jawbone, then jagged back the other way.

"Stop that squaw!" Frazier roared. "Can't any of you aim?"

In truth, she'd progressed three hundred yards on her loping mare, becoming smaller and smaller to them. But then her pony shuddered and stumbled, and sagged slowly into the grass. She wept, feeling life falter in her faithful old mare that had carried her for so many winters. The mare caved to earth, landing with a lurch that threw Victoria sideways, slamming her into clay. She gasped, winded, too stunned to move.

Jawbone raced toward her, coming back into the range of the terrible rifles. She sobbed.

"Go!" she cried. "Go, Spirit Horse!"

But Jawbone screamed, some wild bleat erupting from its throat, and bulled toward her, even as ragged shooting lifted puffs of dirt around him. Behind, men came running now.

She'd lost her wind, and her limbs felt like bars of lead, but she willed herself up and stumbled toward the great horse, the medicine horse, the storied horse of all the plains and mountains. "Go!" she screamed, sobbing, her eyes so wet she could not see.

He whickered and dashed toward her. Now she could see the wound, a vicious crease just below the withers that leaked a sheet of bright blood. She wept. A day to die. A bullet caught her blouse, ripping fabric, the force so terrible it spun her. She sprawled, leapt, and ran again, small and hunched. Behind, they came closer, and she heard the roaring of the viscount, like a rabid bear, shattering the air.

A ball parted Jawbone's forelock, grazing his skull between his ears, and he shrieked, bewildered, bucking and snorting.

"Go!" she cried, panting, her breath cauterizing her lungs and throat.

But he didn't. Berserk, teeth clattering and snapping,

yellow-eyed and evil, leaking blood and foaming at his mouth, he limped toward her, a demon beast, a monster from the Under-Earth spirits, limping and blowing until he pulled up beside her, trembling, and shrieked, deafening her with his trumpeting.

"Go!" she panted. But he stood, trembling. She peered behind, terrified, as men lifted rifles. She grabbed his mane and clambered on. He shivered as her old legs slid across his cut flesh, and then they exploded away, even as murderous bullets pecked and probed the space they'd vacated. She steered him by leaning, just as Mister Skye did, this way and that, zigzagging, becoming ever smaller to the cartmen behind, until at last she slowed him down on a knoll. His sides heaved and he trembled, bobbing his massive roman nose up and down, wild-eyed, brimming evil and love.

She let him catch his wind. She hunched lightly on his bony back, feeling him tremble under her. If she could hold him still a while, the blood oozing from the wound would coagulate. She reached her small strong arm forward and ran her palm tenderly under the mane, along his sweated neck, calming him.

"They are no friends now," she said to Jawbone. She talked to him, trying to convey meaning to him, knowing that Mister Skye talked to him constantly, with English words, because the terrible horse seemed to fathom something of it. "He is alive," she said. "But maybe not for long now. The mad-spirit is in him, waiting to burst out and kill him. We can't go back. They'll kill you and bash my head in and throw me away."

She hunched in the zephyrs, unaware of the caressing breeze, weeping. "I wished to die with him, so we might go to the Beyond Land together," she said, feeling tears river down her seamed cheeks. "But now we must go away from them, Jawbone. He asked me to do something, and now I must do it."

She watched the tiny distant figures trudge back toward the noon camp. They congregated around the black heap of what had been her mare, and shot their revolvers into it. Victoria bled inside. But she was safe, and so was Jawbone. Mary wasn't, and neither was her man. She wiped her eyes, trying to think what might happen, but she couldn't think. Perhaps they would murder Mister Skye for this. Perhaps not.

Beneath her, Jawbone calmed, and stopped shivering, except when buzzing flies landed in the long bloody crease. Mister Skye wanted her to take Jawbone high into the Pryors, there in the heart of Absaroka, and release him among the wild ones, where he'd be a great stallion-chief among them and make his blood to flow in many colts. She could do that. She could slip away now, before they tried again. Only one horse in camp could keep up with Jawbone, even wounded, and that was the buffalo runner Lady Diana had purchased from the Sioux. Maybe Lady Diana would come with a gun and shoot her and Jawbone. But she didn't think so. Victoria didn't dislike the lady who hunted and rode and wouldn't bend to Lord Frazier's will.

Not yet. Not until after her man died from the mad-spirit fever. Then she'd take Jawbone on the long sad journey to his home. But now she would shadow the caravan, out of sight mostly, stalk it like a cat, watching and waiting for the time she could help her man, help Mary, help them escape. It'd be hard. She had only a knife for getting food.

She spat. "Sonofabitch," she exclaimed to the zephyrs and the warm sun. "I can outsmart them all."

Chapter 25

Mary found herself alone, with all the burden of holding Mister Skye's lodge together. Never in her young, happy life had she experienced such desolation as she felt now, her man doomed by the madness-fever and a prisoner in chains, lying naked in a jolting cart. And old, wise Victoria gone too, in a sudden, desperate flight to save the medicine horse.

At least Victoria and Jawbone lived. They roamed ahead a few miles, invisible to these blind whitemen, but visible to her. Victoria had deliberately walked Jawbone along soft river sands and moist earth, leaving Jawbone's tracks and sometimes her own Crow moccasin prints for Mary to see. And Victoria had left the mark of her digging stick in the earth, as she gathered cattail roots and arrowhead and sego lily along the bottoms of the Smith River, which they followed north into a jumbled, wild land broken by sinister yellow coulees and tattooed by long black arms of jackpine reaching toward the canyon.

Mary discerned a limp in Jawbone from the way his prints marked the soft earth, but at least the horse lived. It brought a bit of gladness to her, even though everything else lay dark upon her bright spirit. She ached to tell Mister Skye, who lay in torment back in the rear cart beside the one who was dying of the fever. But they watched him day and night and kept him chained like a beast, and prodded her away whenever she tried to slip close. Raw open wounds festered on his back where the whip had lacerated his skin. They'd seen each other from time to time, but he'd said nothing, staring at her silently, unable even to lift his hand to greet her. But at least he knew she was present, and knew Victoria was not.

She kept the lodge and lodgepoles on the travois now, not erecting it at each night's camp the way she and Victoria usually did. These people had ceased to feed her, and had taken away her hunting weapons, her bow and quiver, and her flintlock. A little jerky remained in a parfleche, but she refused to touch it, knowing it might save their lives if they could escape. Instead, she did what Victoria did, gathering buffalo berries and bitter chokecherries and digging up edible roots, surviving somehow.

The foreigners themselves weren't any better off. They all proved to be inept hunters, driving away game with their noise, not understanding the spirits of the creatures they stalked. They were poor marksmen even when they did occasionally spot a distant deer or antelope. And so they starved, grew cross and mean, and blamed the Skyes all the more for their dilemma. She sensed they'd stopped feeding Mister Skye at all, letting him starve and grow weak, hogging what little meat they shot for themselves and the remaining bulldogs. How foolish they were, even when they shot meat. Didn't they know of the succulent marrow in the bones, or the goodness of a tongue? Or the broths one might make of the things of the belly that they threw to the dogs? How strange whitemen were. In spite of all their medicine, guns, and metal, they didn't know the earth and its creatures. They looked straight at muledeer without seeing them, ignored the four-footed creatures at every hand, the ones they called skunks and raccoons and badgers, scorned coyotes and wolves as food as if they were unclean, and scarcely bothered to gather purslane, milkweed, cattail, wild onions, wild grape, pokeweed, rhubarb, or anything else that lay thick across the land these last days of summer. Neither did they fish for trout. They could not even fashion traps and deadfalls to snare rabbits.

She listened to the cartmen complain about half-rations and then quarter-rations, and the weakness that smited them, and she knew it wouldn't be long. She slid out each dawn, a wraith invisible to Colonel Galitzin's guards, and gathered her berries and roots and greens in the Smith River bottoms, devouring as many as she could in the pale gray light, and then filling a small duck pouch of Mister Skye's with them. She had to try to reach him in the night; nourish him.

With each passing day the luck of the hunters turned even worse; the country seemed utterly devoid of game, even though they worked through a rich jumbled foothill land with all sorts of forage for the four-footed things of the earth. Once they passed a grassy valley where buffalo had grazed and wallowed and rubbed against the bark of cottonwoods not long before, but the white hunters didn't even know it. Mary knew it, and knew why the buffalo had gone away. Victoria, ahead, drove them away, as well as every other four-foot her sharp old eyes spotted. She was fighting her own war her own way against these inept whitemen, making their hunters return each day with nothing but shame upon them. Secretly Mary exulted, but it was a bitter pleasure, knowing her man lay in chains, doomed either to death or a dungeon.

One chill evening the viscount approached her. She watched his measured tread with hatred and terror, wanting to flee from him like a wild thing flees from evil.

"I say, woman, we're having a bit of bad luck hunting. You'd think a wild place like this would be full of game. Not even a buffalo. The men have had all they can bear of it."

Mary said nothing, meeting his arrogant stare with the steady gaze of her own bright brown eyes.

"I'm giving you your flintlock and a bit of powder and two or three balls. The savage has his skills, I suppose. Beginning at dawn, you'll ride out for meat. Each evening you'll return the piece to Colonel Galitzin."

"No," she said softly.

"What? What?"

"You heard me."

"I'll make you. I'll whip you until you do."

"No," she said.

"You're a prisoner, you know. An accomplice of the deserter. We can turn you over to your enemies the Blackfeet if we wish."

"No."

"You must be hungry. Or maybe not. I'll have my men search your parfleches. If you've got jerky in there, we'll confiscate it. You've been getting by on something, that's plain. If you want to keep your dried meat, you'll hunt."

"Perhaps I will waste the powder and shoot at the sun, Frazier," she said, curtly.

"Keep a civil tongue. You're a savage and don't know who it is you're talking to, but that's no longer an excuse."

She thought a moment. "If I hunt, will you feed my man and take the chains off?"

From the kindling realization in his face, she knew at once she'd made a grave mistake.

"No, I won't. But you will hunt each day, and each day you fail to bring in meat, he'll be whipped. Five lashes a day ought to move even the savage paramour to hunt."

"Give me the rifle, then," she retorted slowly. "And powder and three balls. I will make meat. With the first ball I will shoot you. I think you will taste bad. With the second, I will shoot Galitzin. And with the third, I will shoot Gravesend. After that the cartmen can kill me."

"By God, you little savage. I think you would."

She smiled scornfully at him, and he whirled away.

A little later she heard a shot from the direction of the horse herd, and walked that way swiftly, wanting to know what it was. She found a dark corpse of a mule humped obscenely in the grass, leaking blood on the clay and twitching its last. A Skye mule. One she used to carry the parfleches on a pack saddle. Even before the mule breathed its last, cartmen began slicing down its belly, desperate for the mule steak they'd devour that evening.

She turned away, feeling the hopelessness of her fate. Not that it mattered now, with Mister Skye dying. But she hoped to escape, hoped to give birth to Mister Skye's child which lay inside her belly, and tell the child some day about the great one who had sired it. Let them shoot the mules, then. She could slip away on foot any time unless they chained her too. But as long as Mister Skye lived, she would accept her fate among these ruthless men.

They celebrated that night with an impromptu party. The hardy, stringy mule meat didn't last long among so many starving men, but it filled them; and Lord Frazier, his ladies, and Galitzin and Baudelaire, drank themselves into a silly glee beside the yellow wagon, while the cartmen ate, snoozed, and neglected their duties. She watched them closely, biding her time as the night thickened. The crickets chirped their last hymns of summer, and one by one the men dozed off and neglected their three campfires until only embers remained.

She dared not wait too long. She slipped through the

nippy moonless dark to the rear, where the cart rested on its tongue and cumbersome wheels, its slant making life miserable for the two within.

"Mister Skye," she whispered.

"Mary!"

"Eat this first."

She handed him the duck bag full of berries, and listened to the soft clink of his chains as he devoured handfuls of them.

"Needed that. Perishing of thirst. They forget to take me to water."

"Do you hurt?"

He sighed softly. "Can't sleep on my back. Can't sleep anyway with these irons, and the slant of the cart."

"Victoria and Jawbone are safe, ahead. They hurt him and he limps. She's driving away game."

"Do they know it?"

"No. They are blind and deaf."

"They shot our mule. They're down to that now."

"Are you—sick yet, Mister Skye?"

"Sored up some from the lashing. But my legs are healing. I'm strong as I ever was, but . . ."

She waited, afraid.

"Cutler's took the fever. Throat's swollen up, and he's going fast. That wolf was hydrophobic, Mary, and it'll be my turn soon. I'm going under. I'm done. Don't wait around to fetch me away. You and Victoria slip off while you can, because any time now we'll meet up with some Piegans, and then you can't. Forget me, Mary. Go, now. Save your lives! Don't let the Blackfeet get Jawbone! I'm glad you and Victoria and Jawbone . . ."—his voice broke in the dark—"you three'll get loose. Just remember me, Mary. I loved you all."

"I am staying close to you," she replied stubbornly, not letting him sense the tears welling into her eyes.

The taxidermist, Albert Cutler, died on a cold morning, but the cartmen didn't discover it until evening. Mister Skye felt pity and relief. The man had thrashed and foamed and spasmed, his throat virtually swollen shut, in such obvious torment that the sight terrorized Skye and made him dread what was to come. At the last, Skye had wrapped himself in the buffalo robe, skin out, as a sort of armor against the man's slobbering. He feared being bitten, which would only shorten his own life. But Cutler slipped into a coma, lying inert and hot until fever took him off.

Barnaby Skye watched and wondered how he might kill himself before that final torture. He'd try to escape, he thought. They'd shoot him down, and bullets would be better than the sort of misery Cutler had been forced through. The taxidermist had been a decent man, lamenting that he could not return to England and be buried close to his parents there. Toward the end he'd choked out his goodbyes to Skye from a throat that barely worked, and then sobbed through convulsions that spasmed and twisted his helpless body. It would have been a mercy to shoot him then, he thought.

They'd had a bad time of it that day, working through rough country never before traversed by wheeled vehicles. Often they were forced away from the bottoms of the Smith River to crawl over a headland or escape a gorge. The two-wheeled carts did well enough but the heavy yellow parlor carriage didn't belong in this sort of country. It careened half-uncontrolled down slopes, and had to be dragged up other slopes by double-teaming.

Mister Skye lay beside the dead man, feeling the cart

tilt downslope one moment, and uphill the next, rolling with every jolt of the wheels, sometimes feeling his irons bite his flesh. He felt, actually, healthy enough with his blistered and gouged calf healing and the hydrophobia not yet showing itself. But the days had become increasingly miserable, and sheer starvation kept his stomach rumbling and slowly weakened him. Some days he scarcely even got water. The late September nights bit at him under the loose buffalo robe. His nakedness magnified every eddying breeze that pierced the robe to torment his flesh. Skim ice had shown in buckets at dawn, and winter would pounce on them any time—sooner than they realized, he knew. He'd seen many a blizzard in this country, this time of year.

He felt, at bottom, a terrible helplessness. Being naked, unarmed, chained like a beast was only part of it. He couldn't even speak without risking more lashes across his aching back. Not even Mary and Victoria paid the slightest attention to his will. He'd commanded them to escape while they could, but Mary stubbornly stayed close, risking herself and the little one that would be the only thing Skye would pass on to the world. His mind turned endlessly to that tiny bit of life growing in her belly, the bit of life that he would never see, but which would be something of himself for the future. He had no other future but that, and as long as Mary insisted on staying close, she jeopardized herself and that small miracle within her.

He could not be angry with her. Everything she did now was pure love. She'd managed to feed him berries and roots each night at terrible risk, and whisper a few things to him before slipping off into the blackness. But the moon was pregnant again, swelling each night, and in a few days sentries could spot her in the silvery light. He welcomed her nocturnal visits more than anything else, even as he worried about her fate.

By noon it had clouded over, high streamers out of the northwest first and then a heavy overcast with a whiff of snow in the wind, and he knew he was in for it. There'd be the usual equinox storm common to these parts, snow at the higher elevations, icy rain below. Snow here. The thought of his own lodge with a hot fire at its center and his wives close by ravished him. Robe or not, he'd come close to freezing tonight in the drafty exposed cart. He toyed with the idea of hobbling, chained, to Mary's lodge tonight after they'd all settled down. Surely tonight she'd erect it, lifting the heavy rawhide-bound tripod of lodgepoles first and then adding the rest, nine others, and then wrestling the cumbersome, leaden lodgecover over the poles, prying it higher, lacing its seam, inserting the windflap poles and adjusting the flaps, finding rocks and setting them in a ring around the lodge to anchor the cover to earth so wind didn't slide in—either that or staking the cover down if they hadn't taken away her hatchet; hauling robes and parfleches from the pack animals, gathering wood for her fire . . . together Mary and Victoria managed it with difficulty; alone, Mary would stagger under the burden of it.

If she couldn't do it, he prayed she'd bring him a blanket to slip around himself under the robe, and then pluck it off again just before dawn. A lot to ask of her.

Mid-afternoon he heard shouting, and then the caravan halted on a steep slope, the cart beneath him pitched forward so steeply that he could barely keep from sliding into its front planks. Cutler's inert form, cooling beside him, did flop forward and roll until the cart-wall stopped it. In irons or not, he couldn't stay in this position long with blood bursting his head. He hauled himself to the rear, dragging the robe with him, and eased himself clumsily over the tailgate, tumbling into sandstone detritus on the steep slope. His cartman had vanished. He settled himself on the earth with the robe about him, knowing he risked another whipping. How easy it'd be to crawl off, he thought. The quarantined prison cart always trailed the rest by a hundred yards or so. The herders followed, driving loose stock, but not always. Sometimes they trailed the loose horses far to the side, or even pulled ahead. He could drop off some morning and his absence wouldn't be noted for hours. Not that it would do him much good, bound hand and foot in irons.

Down below, in the bottoms of a giant coulee that dumped toward the distant Smith River, the yellow parlor wagon lay on its side, its undercarriage shattered and its off-side wheels a ruin. No one seemed to be injured; at least both the ladies stood nearby, gawking at it. Cartmen struggled with the tangled four-horse team. Two drays were on their sides, pawing the ground, thrown down by the tongue and harness. A ruin, Skye thought. They'd failed to lock the wheels properly going down that slope. Or maybe they'd locked the wheels but failed to add a drag, a log on a chain behind for a spare brake.

He pulled the robe tight about him, aware of the cruelty of the ruthless wind, and grateful that no one saw him out of his prison up on the slope. No one but Mary, who glanced upward with troubled eyes. Below, both the viscount and Galitzin shouted orders while cartmen eviscerated the shattered parlor wagon, toting wardrobes, bedding, chamberpots, field desks, lanterns and wigs toward carts emptied of foodstuffs earlier. The lord and ladies would either move into a cart, or camp out. By the time they'd finished, the castiron skies had darkened noticably, and he could see Galitzin motion toward a small flat in the coulee bottoms, apparently a place where they would spend the night. Cartmen spread out toward their vehicles, including the one who teamstered Skye's prison-cart. Skye, still unobserved, hobbled to the rear and clumsily threw himself as high as he could over the tailgate, feeling the wood bite into his belly, and tumbled back into the cart, bruising his shoulder.

The cart jolted down a grade so steep he slid helplessly into the front wall, pinioned next to Albert Cutler's stiff blue body. The cartman was having a time of it in spite of locking the creaking wheels. The cart skidded on its iron tires, hurrying the dray that pulled it, alarming Skye with its uncontrolled lurches. But at last the cart pulled out onto a small flat hemmed by towering ridges, a flat lying squarely in the coulee bottoms. Mister Skye didn't like it a bit, especially with a fall storm brewing and himself in chains and unable to swim, or even walk at any speed other than a painful hobble.

The viscount's dour visage appeared at the rear. Frazier noted the body sprawled grotesquely at the front of the cartbed, and sniffed.

"I say, Skye, you could have told us."

Mister Skye said nothing.

"Speak when you're spoken to, or you'll taste the whip again."

"He died this morning," Skye said.

"This morning, your lordship," the viscount corrected.

Mister Skye nodded. "May I address you about a matter of some importance for your safety—your lordship?"

"No. I'll fetch Galitzin. We'll have to bury this fellow, and far from camp. Terrible pity, and all that. The sooner the better. Your turn next, eh, Skye?"

The guide nodded.

The viscount turned to leave, and then remembered something. "Say, Skye. I'm confiscating your lodge. We had a bit of a mishap here, and my ladies and I need it. I'll give the savages credit—they invented a snug tent that could handle a fire, eh? We'll be cozy."

"I believe my wife needs it, sir."

"Oh, pshaw, Skye. Those savages can manage in any weather. In any case, it's yours and I've taken it for the Crown. She can bed under a cart."

"I have a suggestion concerning your safety, sir."

The viscount stared, his face pained. "I've already told you no. Galitzin is perfectly competent. And one more impudent word from you and I'll fetch Gravesend and the whip."

Chapter 26

Victoria sat Jawbone atop a vast shoulder of land, near the edge of a ponderosa forest that blackened its upper reaches. The long-needled pines cut the sharp wind but offered no other comfort. She had only the thin summer clothes she was wearing when she fled with Jawbone.

The object of her attention, far below, was the Englishmen's camp on a golden flat in the bottom of the coulee. The castiron clouds and late hour made the light tricky, so she wasn't certain what she was witnessing, but she sensed things as well as saw them, and trusted in that as much as in her eyes.

Beneath her, Jawbone twisted restlessly, itching to gallop down there to his master. He'd become so fractious she'd been forced to cut a thin coil of doeskin from her skirt with her Green River knife to fashion a loop rein, tied over his ugly nose. Even as she sat lithely on him, near the edge of the forest where she could observe without being noticed, she felt the evil horse's muscles ripple, and knew he was thinking black rebellious thoughts about her slender control over him. But she had to keep him here; death awaited him below, so she cursed him soundly, that being the only language an evil medicine horse could comprehend, yelling whitemen's blasphemies first in one ear and then the other, while the horse pawed pine needles and snorted.

The damp wind cut into her in spite of the trees, and she knew the storm would pounce soon. She had no shelter at all. This time of year, this kind of storm spat either snow or icy rain, and murdered the unwary. She might make a crude shelter of boughs or find some cranny in a bluff. But she scorned that now. She would endure until the last heat left her.

That day she had ridden far ahead, down the giant ridges toward the valley of the Big River, the Missouri, and peered into the distant haze, seeing the long tendrils of the storm sweeping across an endless sky. She knew trouble would come soon. But on the last ridge she discovered a more profound menace. In a sheltered hollow on the Smith River, not far from its confluence with the Missouri, lay a giant village. Siksika! The word filled her mouth like spit. She didn't know which ones, Piegan, Blood, or northern Blackfeet, but she knew instinctively it was one or another.

She'd peered around warily, hunting the Mad Dog Society warriors, the village police who'd be patrolling even this far away, along with its hunters. She saw nothing, but sensed she hadn't been seen there in the shadow of the pines. The Englishmen would encounter the village the next day or so, and that'd be the end of Mary and Mister Skye. Those Siksika dogs would discover Mister Skye in chains, his medicine shattered, and demand to have him, count coup—the whole village—and then torture him to death. They'd take him from the viscount, no matter what the viscount said or did. And Mary'd fare no better. Neither would she or Jawbone, if she were caught.

She'd run out of time. Not a trace of blue smoke marked the village. Instead, the sharp wind blew it off and made the village wobble and dance in her eyes, and brought it closer because the air was so clear. The Siksika village writhed in the distance, like a snake ready to strike, and she knew she'd have to act that very night because there'd be no tomorrow. She'd eyed the advancing palisade of clouds anxiously, and trotted back up the Smith River canyon toward the caravan.

What she saw in the Englishmen's camp alarmed her just as much as the village of the Siksika dogs. They'd picked a site that would flood if it rained hard. A wall of icy water could roar down the cavernous coulee. The cart that held Mister Skye—how well she knew its sagging sheet and its green bones of wood—had been unhitched squarely in the dry watercourse, where it tilted crazily on its tongue and two wheels. Nearby, the wrecked yellow parlor wagon lay on its side like a smashed grasshopper, its wheels spinning in the wind. And just behind that her lodge was being erected, but not by Mary. Cartmen wrestled the poles up and laced the heavy cover over it, while the lord and his ladies watched, their backs to the icy wind. They had taken it from Mary. She peered about for Mary, not seeing her in the slate light, as anxious about her as she was about Skye. The lord and ladies would be snug tonight with a fire to warm them—unless the coulee ran, and then they'd learn another lesson, and fast.

That disappointed her. She wanted the lodge. Mary had ceased erecting it these past days, and that suited Victoria perfectly. She would have to carry Mister Skye on a travois because his legs and hands were chained together and he couldn't ride Jawbone. But the Skyes' two travois had always been made from the lodgepoles, and these had been commandeered by the viscount.

She would have to make a travois before dark with only her Green River knife. And out of crooked, twisted jackpine instead of the slender lodgepole pine. She peered about, knowing at once the task lay beyond her. And yet she had to have some way to carry her man away in the night. He could lie over Jawbone's back, like a dead body, for only minutes.

She heard a shot clatter up to her on the cutting wind, and saw another mule slump. For several days now they'd eaten mule—the Skyes' horses and mules. That was the bitter price she'd paid for driving off game. But she could steal animals tonight from the stupid guards, especially after the storm hit. They'd crawl into their tents and tell themselves no savages would prowl in such a storm. She felt a gust of bitter air cut through her blouse, and shivered. The storm might be a blessing—if she lived through it. It'd cover her tracks.

Below camp, men scratched at the bottoms with spades, and she realized the cartmen were digging a shallow grave. Was it Skye's? The very thought clutched at her. She watched tensely, wondering, seeing the evidence of death. Two men shoveled, and two more broke the breast of Earth with pickaxes, and others gathered loose sandstone for a cover. Probably it was for the other, the one who stuffed animal skins with straw. They would not be so kind to Mister Skye, but leave him for the coyotes. She waited, transfixed by the spectacle. At last, in a thickening gloom, four of them approached the cart that held Mister Skye, and pulled a body from it, one man grasping each limb. Not Skye. Even from her vantagepoint high above, she could discern that. They toted the flopping body to the shallow hole and dropped it there and began piling the yellow clay back in with no ceremony at all. It shocked her. Did no one down there care about the brother they buried or wish to say words or weep?

In the last of the murky light they finished with the grave and carried the pickaxes and shovels back to the tool cart, resting them on its dropped tailgate. She watched, a desperate idea forming. On the grassy flat several campfires blossomed orange, guttering wildly even behind rock barricades cartmen built to hold off the wind. They'd eat their butchered mule half raw tonight, she thought. Or entirely raw if the rains deluged them. Except for the lord and ladies, of course, who had discovered the comforts of her lodge.

She did not see Mary. And the figures below had become black blurs, indistinguishable from one another. It troubled her. She had to know where Mary would be. She needed to know where the Skye parfleches lay. She wanted to know which cart Mary would crawl under after losing her snug home.

She cursed and spat, wondering what it all was for, this desperate plan of hers. Mister Skye would die soon anyway. She could leave this instant, turn Jawbone south and reach her own Absaroka people, if she could find them, and if she could endure the icy cold. But she wouldn't. She had only one goal, and that was to take her man away from here, with Mary and Jawbone, and flee to a safe place so her man could die of the mad-fever among friends.

She'd risk her life for that; readily die for that small thing. Her medicine seemed an aching mystery now, this vision sent by Magpie of Mister Skye being carried off across the waters, never to return. He lay dying instead, his lodge lying apart because of mad-fever. Sonofabitch, she couldn't understand these things.

A gust of cold air sliced right through her blouse, so that its tendrils froze her ribs and robbed her breasts of warmth and nipped her calves. Jawbone turned crazy under her, sawing air with his head, and she realized he was about to whicker his piercing greetings to the herd down there. She yanked a rein to turn him, and slid off, pinching his moist nostrils just as they erupted. He bobbed his massive head, fighting her hand, yellow eyes looking murderous, but she held on.

"They kill us!" she snapped at him. He seemed to calm down, and she released his nostrils. Then he shrieked.

"Sonofabitch!" she yelled at him, kicking him fiercely with her moccasin. He backed off.

Below, an animal neighed. Frightened, she peered into the deepening gloom, wondering if they'd noticed. Everything had melted into blackness now, except for what she could see from the glancing amber of the fires. She waited angrily, ready to kick the evil horse again, but nothing much happened. She felt numb and walked to the lee of the horse, pressing into his high warm withers to warm herself. He let her.

That's when the sleet hit. One moment there'd been damp cold wind; the next, a wave of stinging pellets that soaked her miserable calico blouse in moments and sucked life from her with each passing second. Below, men abandoned the cooking and hastened into their dark tents. Even from where she stood, she could hear Galitzin's larger tent chattering and rumbling in the gale. In moments the sleet had murdered the fires, except for the one that glowed in Skye's lodge, where the lord and ladies lay comfortably in the bright cone, no doubt enjoying a mule supper.

It wasn't late but blackness engulfed the camp. She couldn't wait. She needed just a bit of light to find her way around. So much to do there. And the storm would kill her in minutes. Kill Mary if she lay outside. Kill Mister Skye under the bowed canvas with both ends open to weather. She clambered up on Jawbone's slippery back, feeling the ice soak through to her loins, and steered him urgently down the slope, with only the translucent glow of the lodge, in the blurry distance, to guide her.

Stringy mule loin didn't appeal to Lady Diana. As she gnawed at the miserable meat her formidable temper boiled higher and wider. Gordon had turned perfectly daft, heading for Canada, abandoning the hunt, alienating the Skyes, who had been the steady provisioners for the entire party, all because that splendid man Barnaby Skye had once jumped one of the Royal warships. She liked Skye, totally male beast that he was. And at the moment she was ready to strangle the viscount, who sat across from her in the warm lodge, looking smug as he gnawed a revolting gray haunch.

Beside him sat Lady Alexandra, who'd abandoned her meat after a few bites and stared unhappily at the fierce little blaze in the center of the lodge. She'd turned as dour

recently as Diana, talking of home and snapping at
Gordon Patrick Archibald Frazier, who had been growing odder by the day.

Outside, volleys of sleet rattled the lodge, and gusty
winds thundered around the ears that drew the smoke off,
shivering them like angry sails. Diana found herself fairly
comfortable, except for an occasional billow of smoke that
didn't escape into the blizzard. The viscount had dug
the inner lining out of the Skyes' belongings and had
commanded that the cartmen tie it up to the lodgepoles
and anchor it to earth with stakes. She was, she knew, far
more comfortable than she would have been in the un-
heated wagon.

"Well, aren't we snug. These savages don't live half
badly," the viscount said jovially between bites.

"This meat's disgusting. It's getting cold. We should be
halfway down the Yellowstone by now," Diana muttered.

The viscount turned grave. "We have higher purposes
inspiring us now."

"I would think that decent meat for ourselves and the
men is a high enough purpose. I haven't had a decent meal
since—since you put irons on Skye. Really, Gordon, you're
perfectly daft, and I'm perfectly tired of it."

"That mule is disgusting," Alexandra said. "Why don't
you do something? Why doesn't Beowolf cook something?
Why doesn't Stauffinger bring wines any more? Why don't
we have greens? I need greens but no one brings them to
me. Really, Gordon, this is quite enough, and I shan't put
up with it. Take us home at once."

The outburst surprised Diana. Lady Alexandra had
never displayed temperament before.

"The men are complaining, too. They're all half-starved
and angry. Maybe they'll run off," Alexandra added.

"I hope they do! That'll put some sense in you, Gordon," Diana snapped.

Slowly the viscount set his Wedgwood plate aside and dabbed at his greasy lips with a linen napkin. He looked pained, and Diana feared he would begin one of his lectures, which he'd delivered to them frequently these last weeks. He sat crosslegged on a feather mattress salvaged from the yellow wagon, looking ruddy from the summer's outing, his eyes piercing and bright.

"I'm going to bear this criticism with some nobility," he said, his face infused with suffering. "And I don't suppose you ladies understand the half of it."

"Oh, hell, Gordon, stop it. Stop it!"

He turned to her, his eyes ablaze. "I'm doing it for England. Have you no loyalty? No thought of England? No love of the Crown?"

"We're starving. The men are miserable. Just because Barnaby Skye chucked the Royal Navy long ago you've wrecked our summer. He was pressed in. Doesn't that mean anything to you? Stop being a silly goose and let's go home. He's half-dead anyway."

"Never," said the viscount sternly. "They all say they were pressed in, and even if they were, that's what brutes like him deserve. It's no excuse for deserting. I say, we'll proceed. I'll take him to Canada and justice, and even if he dies, his last thought will be of an English dungeon and my resolute purposes."

"I'm quitting. I'm going to find that poor squaw we stole this lodge from and have her take me to Fort Union."

He stared at her, aghast. "You can't do that. I forbid it."

"I'll do what I choose."

"I'll prevent it. And don't pity that squaw. Savages can

survive in any weather. And she willingly allied herself with that deserter."

"I do pity her. Here we are in her warm lodge. And the men are freezing in tents or under wagons. I pity them all."

"The low classes endure well. Don't waste your frivolous sentiments on them."

She knew what she'd do the moment the storm abated. She'd find the squaw, pay her well, saddle up the buffalo runner, gather her own weapons from Gravesend, and ride for Fort Union. To hell with this mad lord.

A gust of icy air billowed down the smoke hole, bringing sleet and woodsmoke with it. The viscount coughed.

"Blast!" he exclaimed. "Wind's shifting." He stood up and walked to the doorflap, and pulled it aside, letting in a gust of air. "I say—Galitzin. Galitzin," he yelled. "I say, adjust the flaps, eh?"

No one answered him. The viscount bellowed into the night but his voice drowned in the wind.

"Worthless help. Why is it help has gone bad these times? I've never seen retainers so insolent. We'll do something about it when we get back. This American wilderness subverts their good conduct."

Angrily he donned his tweed coat, a hat, and gloves, and crawled into the night. She watched the smokeflaps move in the dim light high above, and then they stopped chattering and driving smoke back down. The viscount crawled in, coated with white, and huddled over the tiny fire.

"These savage lodges are clever, but they take doing," he muttered. "It's a bit nippy out. I'll have words with Galitzin tomorrow. It's a stain on his record, this indolence."

"I want some booze and some tiddlywinks. If I can't eat

because you're being such an ass, I'll booze. And then we'll have fun. I'll play squaw, long as I'm decorating a teepee. Where's Stauffinger? Your hunting trip's turned into a crashing bore."

"Oh, tiddlywinks," Alex said. She smiled for the first time in hours.

"I'm going to get so crocked it'll be noon before I remember I'm here," Diana announced. "I suppose he's in one of the tents. I'll get him to unlock—"

"Don't you do it. Call Baudelaire. He's our domestic man."

She ignored him and clambered past the doorflap. A stinging barrage of icy pellets sliced into her as she peered into a whirling white murk. She could barely see the tent shared by Galitzin and Baudelaire, much less the little hovels beyond.

Angrily she yelled at the shivering tent. "Baudelaire. I want scotch," she bawled. "And now."

A dark head emerged from the tent flap, stared, and then retreated. "And hurry!" she snapped. She'd have her booze. Nothing else would do. As long as that ass she'd come with had wrecked the hunt, she'd have her booze.

Back inside the Skye lodge, she tossed sticks on the fire and tried to drive the numbness out of her limbs. If those servants didn't bring the scotch, she'd wring their necks tomorrow. She thought to roll herself in blankets on one of the feather mattresses and guzzle until she passed out.

But Lord Frazier had risen, and stood near the center of the lodge, smoke coiling around him as if he were emitting it, and snapped that swagger stick he'd plucked from Galitzin smartly across his palms, cracking it almost in rhythm with the volleys of sleet outside.

"You need moral instruction, Diana. There'll be no, ah, frivolities tonight. No scotch. No, ah, tiddlywinks. From now on, we shall contemplate higher matters."

Scarcely hearing, she stared at the stranger he'd become.

Wordlessly he thumbed through a morocco-bound book, one of several salvaged from the wagon. "Ah, here!" he exclaimed. "Now listen and let it be a lesson. This is from King Richard the Second: 'This other Eden, demi-paradise, This fortress built by Nature for herself against infection and the hand of war, this happy breed of men, this little world, this precious stone set in the silver sea, which serves it in the office of a wall or a moat defensive to a house, against the envy of less happier lands, this blessed plot, this earth, this realm, this England.' "

He peered at her, eyes burning, his countenance triumphant. "You see? For this we live. For this we suffer. For this we'll devour mule meat and starve, endure rain and sleet and a harsh continental winter. For this we'll show our steel, our backbone, our fierce execution of duties. For this we'll take Skye in chains back to our sceptre'd isle and show him, and all the brutes of the world, what it means to be one of us, an Englishman."

"Gordon, you're such a goose," said Alexandra.

Chapter 27

Mary did not exclude murder from her thoughts. She huddled against the northwind, hoping they would leave her good four-point blanket capote alone as they pillaged. They scarcely noticed her as they led the last

Skye mule away to be shot and began erecting the lodge themselves. Lord Frazier intended to occupy it—he and his ladies—now that they had no wagon.

She made her spirit lie very still within her, though every fiber protested. She wished to shout at them that they were desecrating Mister Skye's home, that they took what was not theirs. But instead she huddled against the blast of arctic air and watched, knowing they didn't have eyes for squaws except when they lusted. Mister Skye's big medicine lay scattered upon the trembling grasses, just like his possessions. Galitzin found their small hoard of pemmican and jerky in a parfleche and exclaimed. But the viscount commandeered it.

They'd already pillaged the parfleche that contained Mister Skye's clothing, and had long since distributed it to ragged cartmen. Skye's moccasins, especially, had been snapped up by cartmen with tattered boots. And Mister Skye's grizzly bear claw necklace, filled with the shining gray talons of the king of the mountains, hung from the viscount's leathery neck, a perfect symbol of medicine shattered and medicine won.

"I say, what's this?" asked the viscount as he withdrew Mister Skye's battered belaying pin. "A belaying pin. Hickory, I imagine. Royal Navy. The scoundrel stole it. There's a bit of evidence I'll just cart along." He set it in the grass.

She heard a shot and saw the mule sag and then collapse heavily. Even before life fled, cartmen began eviscerating it. The last mule, she thought. But she had her mare, and Victoria had Jawbone somewhere. The Britons had eaten the rest, grumbling all the while. The light had gone gray, draining life from the world. No four-foot remained to drag the travois. But it didn't matter to the viscount. He'd throw the lodgecover and poles into a cart after this.

She eyed the battered belaying pin, remembering how Mister Skye used it as a weapon in the days of his medicine. She thought she might use it too, once, before they swarmed over her. Once to crush the skull of Viscount Frazier.

"The squaws' stuff," Colonel Galitzin said as they emptied a parfleche. Mary's own doeskin skirts and calico blouses tumbled to earth, along with her double winter moccasins, the outer ones with soles of rawhide cut from a bull. "Capote there—nice little trinket for the ladies. Something to parade in around London, I suppose."

Her winter capote. She could no longer repress the turmoil within her. Mister Skye had bought her the blanket at Fort Union, thick wool with four bars in the corner, creamy wool with green stripes at either end. She'd carefully cut and sewn until she had a fine capote with a hood, against the times when Winter Man came from the north to torment her.

"It is mine," she said.

They peered over to her amazed, unaware that this squaw of Skye's had been watching.

She walked resolutely toward these men, aware that her medicine had gone bad, and theirs was good. She would take it from them. She would need it.

"There now, little lady. We have it. You're Skye's wife and the man's a criminal."

"They are mine. All these. And those are Victoria's. I will take them." She reached for her winter moccasins, but the viscount yanked her away, his cold hand powerful on her arm.

"Your medicine is bad," she said softly.

"The savage mind at work. Here now, you're looking for a bit of warmth to crawl into tonight. Take a robe. I'm going to trade the rest at Rocky Mountain House. But you can have that one."

She followed his pointed finger to one that had been Victoria's. "I will take my capote, too," she said, but the viscount dragged her away again. "And my moccasins."

"We're taking them. They'll be a great curiosity in London. All this truck. Beads and feathers and dresses of hide. That elktooth blouse you have here, that's a sensation. Maybe I'll donate it to the British Museum. You've got moccasins, little lady; you don't need any more."

She clutched her robe angrily, watching them pillage the kitchen things; the copper kettle, spider, the iron spit they used to hang kettles. The whiteman's bowls and plates.

"Maybe your medicine is bad sometime soon," she said.

The viscount responded thoughtfully. "Keep an eye on her, Galitzin. Who knows what evil lies in the savage breast?" He turned to her. "Why aren't you fetching us greens? Helping the men? In fact, why don't you just go back to wherever you came from? We don't need you now."

"I will stay."

"Then you'll work, little lady. And you'll walk. Tomorrow we'll have that worthless mare for breakfast."

She stood her ground as the light thickened, and watched them pillage all that had once belonged to the lodge of Mister Skye. She didn't know what the British Museum was, but with each discovery of things she and Victoria had quilled or beaded, or woven feathers into, or tanned, the viscount babbled about what a sensation they'd make in London, and what a contribution they'd be to the museum's collections.

She watched the cartmen stake down her lodgecover, collect firewood, hang the liner, tote in the viscount's featherbeds and blankets; watched the viscount's shivering ladies duck inside. Tonight would be miserable, but at least she had the robe. A thought came to her. Maybe two robes.

She wrapped the robe about her, skin-side out, and walked swiftly down the coulee to the Smith River bottoms a long way distant, and there found a stick. She had to feed Mister Skye something, anything, because they gave him so little now. And feed herself. She felt faint with a hunger that wouldn't let go of her. But it was too late. The cruel dark snuffed her vision, and she could see nothing—no roots or berries. She wanted cattails at least, and found none here where the river cut through rock and hammered an opposing bluff.

She ached to find Victoria too, but the older Absaroka woman wasn't here. It had turned too dark to see hoofprints or messages that Victoria often left in plain sight for Mary. She remembered the old woman wore nothing but summer things, a hip-length blouse belted at the waist, a doeskin skirt, and low summer moccasins with no warmth in them.

Sleet and blackness hit her simultaneously, a stinging blast of it, followed by gusts that laced her face. She had to get back before she was lost! No food at all this time. Wearily she toiled back to the camp, steering by instinct, climbing steep slippery meadow, somehow hewing to the watercourse up the coulee that might run later. Ahead, finally, she discerned the vague, bobbing light of the lodge, the only light because the wet sheets of sleet had doused the campfires. In just moments she'd felt her body go numb with the cold, and knew she in her robe was better off than Victoria, who rode almost naked to the ice.

Not a cartman remained out in the weather. She glided swiftly through camp, the gale whipping through her robe and piercing to her thighs and belly. She sensed the horses nearby, their rumps into the storm, tugging at their pickets. Galitzin had learned: he always kept two or three hobbled and in camp now, to chase after the others. She noticed one tethered to Galitzin's own tent, looking miserable as sleet whitened its body and lodged in its dark mane.

No one. It pleased her. She stumbled through the bitter air, feeling the sleet lace her neck and collect in her hair until she came to the cart set apart, a little lower than the others, a black forlorn thing whose sheet chattered in the gale. Its front end opened north, letting wind and sleet whistle through. She found the tongue and slowly twisted the cart sideways, its creaking wheels yielding bit by bit until she had one side athwart the wind. Then she felt her way to the rear.

"Mister Skye," she breathed.

"Mary!"

"They are not watching tonight." She crawled over the tailgate and slid beside him in the icy dark.

"Don't get close or you'll take the hydrophobia."

She ignored him, found his heavy form on the slanting bed of the cart, and pulled herself to him. His hand found her icy one.

"Want to hug you but I can't," he said.

She knew. She felt the icy brass between her breast and his. But at least she could make them warm. She pulled her own robe over his, the skin sides to the weather and the warm curly fur tight against their flesh. She tucked both robes carefully around their feet, and drew them over their heads to make a small cocoon that might hold a little heat.

"You are so cold," she said softly, just barely clinging to calm.

"I am that. I'm feeling well enough, but this cold might have put me under. Not much I could do. You saved me, Mary."

Tears came, and she hugged him, giving him what little heat she possessed. Slowly the double robes warmed them while the thundering wagonsheet above held off the sleet and most of the northwind.

"Mister Skye, they've taken everything. The lodge now. The viscount's in our lodge. I don't even have winter clothes."

"Not much time left," he said slowly. "You'd better get out while you can."

"They're eating our horses. Only my marc is left. Tomorrow I walk or ride a cart."

"Mary—you hitch up with Victoria and get out."

"I didn't find roots. I'm so hungry. You're hungry."

He remained silent and she knew how starved he felt.

"Need to hug you goodbye," he said. He made a loop of his arms, stretching the chain that pinned his wrists. She felt what he was about and slid into the circle, and felt his massive strength surround her, along with his broken medicine.

The footing became treacherous as the sleet turned the gumbo slope into a greased chute. Jawbone skidded and floundered, his hoofs flailing, but he pressed on eagerly because Victoria steered him toward his master. Only a faint amber glow from the lodge gave her direction. Closer in she discovered a second glow, often shrouded by the whirling white flakes that began to replace the sleet. A coal oil lantern in Galitzin's large wall tent, she surmised. Probably for warmth. He and the privileged Baudelaire weren't suffering.

She'd never been so cold. Sleet and snow whipped out of the blackness, plastering her entire body, hair and face, thin calico blouse, hands, skirt, legs. It had soaked through her meager clothing instantly, turning it into a sodden clinging sheet that magnified the cold and sluiced heat from her. Her feet turned numb and then she ceased to feel anything except a strange white pain there. Her bony hands fared little better, though she buried one, then the other, in her armpits. Her fingers ached and then died, sensation abandoning them so she could not know whether she held her makeshift rein or not. And at last, near the camp, spasms convulsed her, a violent shaking she could not control.

I will do it, she thought. I will not let Cold-Maker win. She steered Jawbone past the cart where Mister Skye lay. He resisted, turning his head and threatening to screech, but she guided him resolutely toward the cartyard, keeping a sharp eye on the huddle of dark tents where cartmen lay awake in blankets and shivered through the miserable night. She needed to find the tool wagon. If it had been left just as she saw it from above, they would have a chance; if not, all would be lost.

So opaque was the blackness that she could not tell one cart from another. They lacked color and form and looked utterly unfamiliar, alien beasts faintly limned in the lodge-light. She hunted desperately among them, ignoring the shaking that racked her, wanting the one with the tail-gate down. At last, despairing, she slid off Jawbone, landing in a heap in icy grass because her feet never felt the earth. Then, leading Jawbone, she worked cautiously among the carts, stumbling once over a tongue or a shaft. She located one of the food carts and found it empty. She stumbled into the cart that held the spirits and found it locked tight.

Her strength ebbed even as the convulsions of her slim body defied her will. Soon she would no longer be able to walk. Her cheeks still stung, but she was losing feeling in her arms. Then she lurched into a sharp projection that bit her hip, and found herself at a cart with an opened tailgate. She crabbed her hand around until it caught on something she couldn't feel.

"Sonofabitch!" she exclaimed into the wind. Her arms refused to lift the heavy thing. Panting, she began running in place, making her heart pump hot blood into limbs that no longer worked, and slowly she felt life, a thousand painful prickles, course down her arms. Her hand clasped a wet pickax. And then the spade.

She carried them over her shoulder, not able to hold them in her hands, and slid through the camp watching sharply. At Galitzin's tent stood a picketed horse, which lifted its head sharply and whickered. Jawbone whickered back, and Victoria froze. Nothing happened. She studied the colonel's glowing tent in the shrouded dark, and still nothing happened. Maybe these whitemen heard only the bitter wind, or maybe they were just too lazy to check during a storm.

She hastened toward Mister Skye's cart, plunging back into utter blackness on the edge of the camp. Jawbone followed, shaking his head and bobbing it in some eerie horse mood she couldn't fathom. She tripped over the tongue and fell, the spade and pickax clanging as they flew from her grasp.

"Sonofabitch!" she bellowed.

"Victoria!" The muffled voice of Mary lifted from within, and that instantly solved a major problem. Victoria had had no idea where Mary lay, and hoped Mister Skye would know.

Warm hands pulled her over the front of the cart and drew her down under two robes. She lay shivering while Mister Skye and Mary pressed her tight. From outside, Jawbone whickered, and Mister Skye barked a sharp command at the animal. They couldn't see him, but sensed his ugly head close by, perhaps poking into the cart.

For a long time she lay between them, feeling her tremors slow, even if her body still felt like ice and her arms and fingers refused to work. But time flew.

"Goddam it's cold," she muttered. "I tell my arms and fingers and feet to go and they don't go. They got a mind of their own, worse than Jawbone."

"He's all right?"

"Got a crease across a shoulder. He's coming fine. Limped a few days."

"Victoria—take him to your people. Set him free high in the Pryors. Let him breed the mares. That's all I want. All I've got left."

She listened to her man, dreading to refuse him. "This morning I found a big Siksika village ahead. They find this camp soon, maybe tomorrow. We got to go tonight—use the storm."

She waited for his objections but didn't hear any. Her man seemed to be in an odd mood. Maybe he'd given up too soon, waiting for the madness-fever to eat him.

"Good enough way to die," he muttered at last. She lay so close she felt his warm breath as he muttered. "I'm not much for walking barefoot in chains. You got a pony and travois?"

"It's too cold," Mary said. "You've got nothing to wear. Mister Skye's naked. They took everything in our parfleches. We have nothing. Not a blanket. Not a moccasin. Not even pemmican."

"Goddam, we got to go—now!" she whispered fiercely. "I got ways."

"Two buffler robes and one horse," Mister Skye said. "You git to your people with Jawbone and leave me. It doesn't matter if I die now or in a month."

"Mister Skye," she whispered fiercely—but outside the darkness danced and bobbed. She pulled free of the two robes and peered out, seeing a coal oil lantern swinging on its bail. Someone was coming.

"Coming!" she hissed. "They check. Hide Jawbone!"

Lithely Mary slipped out the shadowed rear of the cart while Victoria slid deeper under the robes. Mister Skye swiftly wrapped the robes tight about her, concealing her under the dark curly hair.

The light bobbed, making shadows dance, and even under the robe Victoria could see its steady approach. Then, she knew, the whole interior of the cart blazed white above her.

"Gravesend," muttered Mister Skye.

"Just checking. Show me your hands."

Mister Skye reluctantly drew his arms out of the robe and let the light fall on his chains.

"Show me your ankles, Skye."

Victoria worried that her own moccasins would be exposed, but her man worked slowly, tugging the robe back until his ankles lay bare in the wavering light, and the chains around them shone.

"That do it?"

Gravesend laughed. "You ought to pitch the robe out and just freeze up, Skye. That'd beat dying of hydrophoby, or rotting away in a British gaol. Not that you're going to live. We buried Cutler, and that's how it'll be, Skye."

Gravesend lifted the lantern and vanished into the

swirling white. Victoria peeked out and saw downy flakes boiling down, making walls in every direction. The sleet had turned to snow, and the wind had ebbed.

Moments later Mary clambered over the tailgate and crawled, shivering, into the robes again.

"Jawbone's safe?"

"Yes. Right here. The snow hides him good. The man could not see more than a little way."

"They'll be back," he muttered.

"We go now!" she hissed.

He sighed but did nothing.

"Outside I got a spade and pickax."

She felt him listen in the dark. But he said nothing. She'd never known him like this, giving up, not trying. It was the madness-sickness coming to him.

"We take the pickax and land it on a chain. Make the point go through a link. Pop the link. Then you can walk. You ride Jawbone away."

"Barefoot and naked."

"No! I fix that too!" She slid a hand down to her Green River knife in its moccasin sheath. "Here! Feel this!"

His hand closed over hers, and the knife. But he said nothing.

"The wagonsheet. I'll cut it off. And keep the cord too. I'll make three ponchos, slice a neck hole. There's lots more canvas than we need. We'll take it too. For a tent. For leggins. For—after we get away, I'll make what we need—moccasins, leggins."

"Horses?" said Skye, a change in his voice.

"Jawbone. And I'll steal Galitzin's. It's picketed at his tent with a saddle on it. We put the saddle on Jawbone for your feet."

"Bare feet in a blizzard. You figure I'd make it in just a canvas poncho? I'm bare-ass naked."

"Goddam! You want to die your way or their way? The Siksika, they see your medicine's all goddam busted up, and they take their time torturing you."

He was weighing it, she knew. "You'd have a robe too. Me and Mary, we got the other one and ponchos."

"You'd both ride Galitzin's horse?"

"Yes. We're light. We bust your chain, make ponchos, take the rest of the wagonsheet, take the two robes, steal the pony, take the pickax and spade. We go maybe half a night. Then maybe dig us a dugout. And now it's snowing to cover the tracks. In a few suns we're with my people."

"We're half-starved, Victoria, and weak as pups."

He seemed to be objecting, but she heard something else in his whisper.

"You want that goddam viscount to throw you in a shallow hole like they did the other one? Cutler? You want that? While he gloats and laughs and they all have a drink?"

"You warmed up?" he asked.

"Yes!"

"Well, don't figure on staying that way," he said, tossing aside the robes. "Where's the pickax?"

Chapter 28

Mister Skye poked his head out of the wagon, feeling snow slice across his cheeks and seeing nothing. At last he made out a dim blur, so veiled and subtle through whirling snow that he wasn't even sure whether it was light from his lodge or from Galitzin's lantern within his tent. He could not see his own hands or the ground beneath the cart, even though white snow accumulated on the grass. He knew, with a sudden black epiphany, that the thing Victoria proposed was impossible. They needed light.

He pulled back in and drew the robes about him. "I need light to drive that pickax into the chain. Got to sit in the snow, legs apart, drive that point into a link. I could spend all night pounding at it, like some bloody fool. Victoria, you'll need light to cut that wagonsheet into ponchos."

"I can cut the wagonsheet from the cart in the dark," Victoria muttered. "It's tied down with puckerstrings."

"Maybe we can harness the cart and drive off," Mary said. "They always leave the harness next to the carts."

"You think you can fetch two drays from the picket line and harness in this kind of dark? You'd get lost out there. I can't help in these chains."

She said nothing and Mister Skye sensed her discouragement.

"Sonofabitch!" Victoria exclaimed. He felt her crawling about on the tilting bed of the cart, and then a sudden gust ripped in from the north, and canvas flapped like a shivering trysail. He felt the cart creak again, and suddenly the canvas sagged, free of its anchors, riding over the bows. A blast of arctic wind instantly destroyed their snug world.

"Now we're in trouble," he muttered. "Can't put this back together in this blackness and cold."

"Damn right," the old woman snarled. He heard her clamber out, cursing and muttering, felt the wagonsheet drop from the cart, and then heard the clink of metal.

"All right, get out," she snapped. "Bring the robes."

He sighed. Something desolate had crept back into him,

paralyzing his will. All right then. Death by freezing would be better than death from hydrophobia. But he wasn't quite ready for death.

"Hurry up—you freeze your ass."

He grabbed a robe and sensed that Mary had grabbed the other. He heard the tailgate drop, and knew the old woman had made it easy for him. But the chains impeded all movement, and his linked wrists kept him from pulling the robe close. His feet landed in snow that bit at them swiftly. Then he felt her small hand.

"Come," she said.

She dragged him forward while he hobbled, his steps reduced to mincing because of the ankle irons that scraped and chafed him. Then he stepped onto the wagonsheet.

"Sit on that, and hold them tools," she whispered at him. "Mary, help me pull."

He felt himself sliding over snow and grass and rock on the wagonsheet, straight toward that single dim source of light that lay veiled by swirling snow. The sheer audacity of it amazed him. He worried then that any of the cartmen would step out to make water and spot them; that Galitzin or Gravesend would hear and rush out; that his women would suffer endless pain for their efforts to free him. And still the women tugged relentlessly, dragging him straight toward the lodge and the light, which slowly enlarged so that he could see the forms of his women, and even see his leg chain.

They circled wide around Galitzin's glowing tent and the saddled horse outside. He wondered where Jawbone was, and spotted him ghosting along, and worried that the horses might greet each other. But it didn't happen. His women dragged him well around behind the lodge, opposite the doorflap, and then stopped. Snow eddied down, and he felt a deepening numbness even though his robe hung over his shoulders.

"You got eyes. Do it now," she whispered. They had halted scarcely twenty yards from the lodge. He could see his chain, but couldn't make out one link from another except for a wet glint.

"Mary," Victoria whispered urgently. "You go get that horse and put the saddle on Jawbone. Then you look around the camp and find what you can find. Horsemeat, maybe."

Mary nodded and glided into the snow, swiftly walled from their sight.

Mister Skye crabbed forward until his bare ankles and feet rested in the snowy grass. Then he grasped the wet pickax, feeling his numb fingers clamp the slippery wood. One end tapered to a point; the other tapered to a chisel two inches wide or so.

"Hurry!" she snapped at him, anger suffusing her voice.

He lifted the pick and arced it down sharply. The act caused his knees to lift and his legs to buck, and the pick buried itself in the unfrozen clay.

"I hold your legs," she whispered. "Be careful."

She crawled clear over his lap, pinning down his legs. He was conscious of warmth.

He arced the pick down again and missed. He pulled the point out of the earth savagely, and arced it again. It struck metal and clanked. He waited, expecting the lodge and tents to disgorge men. Nothing happened. Snow whirled, numbing his face. His ears hurt. His feet had turned prickly.

Viciously he struck at the links again and again, missing, clanking, pinging, but not sundering a link. He lost his breath, sobbed, and struck again, feeling the clay trap the point and not let go. His hands had quit hurting, and he could no longer feel the pick in them, but he kept on, naked in the snow, seeking the eye of the needle and never threading it.

He rested, wheezing, his heart racing. They were in for it now. They couldn't go back to the cart. The best he could imagine was to have Jawbone drag the canvas with him on it far enough away so that maybe they could bust the chain in the morning. The snow might cover their exodus. But he knew they'd not make half a mile that way, and would be found swiftly at dawn.

Smoke from the lodge whirled back down on him, searing his lungs. Within, someone stirred, the shadow lapping the cone's translucent side. Putting wood on the fire. Then a figure loomed outside, vaguely male. Frazier. About to make water.

"Goddam," Victoria muttered, swiftly lifting the white wagonsheet up around them both, making them virtually invisible through the veil of snow. They watched closely, waiting for whatever came. Mister Skye worried about Mary. Frazier walked toward Galitzin's tent.

"I say, Galitzin, we need more wood. Fetch some sticks, eh?"

They saw the colonel emerge and stand, a blurred figure beside the viscount. He talked but Mister Skye couldn't hear what they were saying.

"Well, fetch it then. And tomorrow load a cart with wood. I won't have this sort of neglect," the viscount snapped.

Galitzin ducked back into his tent, and emerged carrying his coal oil lantern on its bail. He walked through the snow toward the carts and disappeared back there, hidden by snow and the various conveyances. Frazier dashed back into the lodge, and Skye watched his shadow bob across the cowhide.

Galitzin appeared a while later, carrying two lanterns, both lit. At the lodge he summoned Frazier. Skye couldn't see what transpired because he was on the rear side, but in a moment he watched lights dance within. Galitzin had given the lord and his ladies both lanterns and had returned to his darkened—and colder—tent.

A quietness settled over the snowy camp. If anything it seemed darker without the faint glow from Galitzin's tent adding to that of the lodge.

"That lord sure don't leave nothing for his brothers," Victoria whispered. "They'll be warm enough with two lanterns."

Barnaby Skye thought about warmth. His ankles and calves had gone numb again and he'd lost track of his bare feet. He turned the pick around idly, until its chisel edge faced the ground. He arced it down angrily, and felt its edge strike metal with a thud. Suddenly excited, he reached forward, found the chain with his hands, but his fingers had lost their touch. Then he sensed Victoria's hands probing along the chain, and she muttered something.

"Ah! You cut a link but it ain't open yet. One side cut."

"Victoria! Help me. I'm going to drive the chisel edge into the ground until the point sticks up. Then I'm going to lie on my back with my legs up in the air. Fit the weak link over the point and I'm going to jerk my legs down."

He didn't wait for an answer. He drove the pick down, burying the chisel point. He felt her lift his legs and guide the chain until the weakened link lay over the point. He jerked his legs downward—and nothing happened.

"Yank down, Victoria!"

He felt her try, felt her fail, heard her curse. He sobbed.

He felt her tremble, knew the cold stole her strength from her, just as it robbed him. She yanked. They yanked together. The link didn't yield. He fell back exhausted, feeling snow collect on his goosebumped flesh wherever the robe failed him. Felt his butt freeze on the wet duck canvas.

Defeated. He'd take a few more whacks at the link with the chisel point, and that would be the last of it. Freeze up and die, then. Tonight. He lay panting, nothing left in his cold, starved body to give to this desperate enterprise.

"You sure that link's cut on one side?"

She snarled at him in Absaroka.

"Drag me," he said. "Get Mary and Jawbone."

She nodded. But even as the old woman began to unfold, they spotted a form gliding toward them in the snow. They froze until they knew it was Mary. She was carrying things.

She looked like a ghost with furry snow clinging to her robe and hair. Gently she set some things down on the wagonsheet, and Mister Skye strained to make them out in the murky amber. A horse collar. A cylindrical thing— his old belaying pin, the hickory covered with snow. An excitement built in him.

"Goddam!" the old woman cried. She hefted it, pleased. "Maybe you fix us, Mary."

Mary looked mystified.

Swiftly they positioned themselves again. Mister Skye settled on his back, legs up, while Victoria settled the weakened link over the point of the pick. Then she whacked the chain. He felt cold iron jerk his leg. She tried the other side, her hammering making sharp cracks in the night. He peered fearfully toward the lodge.

She paused, feeling the pick point and the weakened link with her fingers. "It's coming," she announced. She hammered again, each blow cracking woodenly into the night. "Mary— Don't just stand there. Get that horse."

Mary started—and froze. Ahead, Galitzin poked his head outside, curious about the sharp noises. He had only the glow of the lodge for vision now, and Mary edged softly away from his view. Snow whirled, but the wind no longer whipped and roared, drowning noise. The colonel clambered entirely outside, and peered about.

"Gravesend," he roared.

From obscure darkness a man loomed, and the two conversed in low tones Skye couldn't make out. More men appeared, some relieving themselves and others collecting around Galitzin's tent in light so obscure Skye couldn't even count them. Beside him, Victoria eased the white wagonsheet upward to conceal them. In the whirling snow they'd be invisible even from a few feet, with the sort of light they had.

Someone, Galitzin probably, approached the lodge. "Your lordship?" It was the colonel's voice.

Skye saw shadows flitting across amber cowhide, then heard muffled talk around the other side of the lodge. He heard fragments of talk, and the words alarmed him: lantern, pounding sounds, patrol, check the squaw, Skye . . .

They were going to patrol. They'd find Mary up and around; read her moccasin prints. Discover the cart with no sheet, and Skye missing. He knew they'd run out of time. He saw the lantern now, illumining Gravesend's burly features. The armorer formed a party of six cartmen and plunged into the snowy night toward the horse herd, probably intending to check that first. Galitzin crawled back into his blackened tent.

Only a minute or two, then. Victoria threw back the wagon sheet, found the weak link and once again settled it over the point of the pick and cracked the belaying pin over it sharply, the sound like a rifleshot. He sensed her hands feeling the link and exclaiming, and then some gentle tugs, and his legs fell free, chain dangling from each ankle.

"Ah!" she cried, too loud. She sprang up. He did too, onto feet that had ceased feeling. He walked stiffly, joyous, hearing the chain-ends clink softly. But she was already smoothing out the wagon sheet to make ponchos.

"Hold the damn thing," she growled. "This here is hard work." She began sawing savagely at the sheet, muttering and cursing, finding that her small knife didn't easily sever the tough duck canvas. He peered about as she sawed, seeing nothing but whirling white, worrying about Mary, worrying about getting the horse they needed desperately. It occurred to him he was half-starved, mad with hunger. He stood, dancing, making his dead feet hop and whirl, jumping crazily on free feet, wanting his hands freed to. But that must wait.

"Haw!" he roared, and then chastised himself. Much too noisy.

He saw shadows bobbing about within the lodge. And then, near Galitzin's tent, the vague figure of a woman leading a horse. Mary!

Victoria sawed away fiercely, muttering, and then she lifted up a large rectangle of canvas with a slit in its center. "Try this," she whispered.

But he couldn't, not with his wrists still chained. Clucking, she lifted it up and pulled it over him, jamming his head through the slit, tucking the front side between his chained arms. It didn't warm him at all. In fact, the wet snow on it stung his flesh and chilled him anew. But still it was clothing of a sort. She found the cordage she'd salvaged and tied it around his waist, pinning the poncho to him.

Mary drew up with the bay horse and swiftly undid the cinch, intending to transfer the saddle to Jawbone. Skye knew the saddle, a good English make with tie-down rings fore and aft, and light, slender stirrups. He was glad of the stirrups, knowing they'd help support his iron-weighted legs.

Shouting. They'd been found out. Skye squinted into the blur, discerning the bobbing lantern ghostly in the distance, near his prison cart. Men running. Men boiling out of small tents that shed snow in heaps when they were jarred. Galitzin bolting out of his larger tent.

"Sonofabitch," Victoria muttered. Swiftly she jammed her Green River knife back into its bullhide sheath on her ankle, and snatched up the wagonsheet. "Let's get."

Mary threw the saddle onto Jawbone, who screeched when she did it. The other horse sidled backward, tugging at its reins and then pulling free of Mary's one-handed grasp.

Mister Skye dove for the reins, but the horse sidestepped back, closing toward the lodge.

Mary returned to her saddling. Victoria clawed at Skye. "Don't. Let me. Them chains spook him."

Skye stopped at once. If anyone could catch the spooked horse, which sidled closer and closer toward the lodge and light, toward the viscount, who carried a fowling piece that glowed amber, it would be Victoria.

"Stop!" bawled Galitzin, but he was facing and yelling the wrong direction, tricked by eddying snow.

"Mister Skye—come. I'll help," whispered Mary.

She drew him to Jawbone. He needed help. He couldn't feel the stirrup. His legs trembled and wouldn't lift. She guided a cold bare foot into the near stirrup. Jawbone felt the chain smack him, and squealed. Then she lifted, and he, found himself sprawling atop Jawbone, trying to stay on his slippery back, finding the cold wet saddle, and dropping onto it. She ran around to the off side, found his bare foot and jammed it into a stirrup. He felt nothing except an anchoring of his numb legs.

"Stop!" cried the viscount, and this time they were shouting in the right direction. Just beyond, men tumbled out of the flurries, one carrying a dancing lantern. Off behind the lodge, Victoria caught the horse and threw herself up onto it, teetering over its wet back for a long instant. And then she righted herself and steered it back from the light, the dark horse much more of a target than Skye's blue roan.

The viscount lifted his fowling piece toward them and fired, a shocking report in the night. Shot seared past. Now men boiled toward them and Skye saw sidearms on several, including the colonel.

"They're out there. Stop them, blokes."

Shots.

Mary, tugged desperately at the pick, but the clay of Earth Mother wouldn't surrender its prize. Viciously she yanked, and this time the pick popped up, spinning her backward. She thrust it toward Skye, and then the wagon sheet. He grasped everything in his chained hands.

Men twenty yards off. More shots, white flashes in snow. Mary running toward Victoria's horse. Mary pausing to catch the remaining buffalo robe lying in a heap. Mary picking up the belaying pin. Men closing on Mary, bulling in. Mary clawing at Victoria. Victoria clamping Mary's arm, dragging her up. Horse sidling away from running men. Shots, white flashes. Jawbone sliding into deeper gloom. Jawbone shrieking. Shots whipping close.

The dark horse plunged past him, Victoria and Mary riding double. He followed, plunging into absolute inkiness without knowing where they were going except that it was uphill and the northerly winds quartered at him from the rear.

Behind, volleys of shots, white flashes, shooting blind. The shouts grew faint.

"Talk to me. I can't see you."

"We will talk," said Victoria, just ahead. "You talk too."

They set the horses into a quiet walk. The horses minced, unable to see, groping into a murk.

"Free, I guess," he said. "They can't follow. And we don't know where we're going. Victoria, can you cut more ponchos by feel? We might as well, before we freeze solid."

They stopped only a short distance from the camp, but it could have been a hundred miles in a night like that. Mister Skye sat Jawbone and held the rein of the bay horse while Victoria and Mary worked in the blank dark, muttering and mumbling. He heard the faint sound of a knife sawing at canvas. He clamped the pickax in his numb hands, knowing it'd free his wrists in the morning. He loved the pickax like a brother.

He felt someone wrap his feet in canvas and tie the bandage. He felt someone lift his poncho off of him and then slide a buffalo robe over him. The robe had fresh slits in it for his head to go through. He felt warm fur slide over his shoulders and then his chest and back like an angel's caress. Then he felt hands pull the poncho over and tuck it between his chained wrists. Then he felt the loving hands of his good dear women tie his makeshift clothing tight about him. He could make it to the Kicked-in-the-bellies now.

"We'll go now. Keep the wind at our back so we go

south. You talk, Mister Skye, yes? We'll talk. We got to talk for a long time now."

"I'll talk, mates," he said. "I could eat a grizzly ba'r right now."

They laughed, or was it crying?

Chapter 29

Escaped! Lord Frazier gaped at the wall of snow that hid that deserter and his squaws from good British justice. He could scarcely believe it. How had it been done? He glared at those around him, wondering who had betrayed him. Galitzin, maybe. The colonel had the keys to the irons

"After them!" he cried. "I want them stopped. For God, for England, for the Queen!"

Cartmen gaped at him.

"Really, now, Gordon, don't be silly," said Lady Diana. He whirled to find her standing there in dishabille, a blanket wrapped around her.

"You've taken his side," he accused.

"It's snowing. It's black as ink. The man was pressed into the navy, made a slave. And it happened a quarter of a century ago. Really Gordon, you're so silly."

She enraged him. "Into the lodge. I'll speak to you later. Not in front of these retainers. He deserted. If we let him perform these criminal things, then every other dustman and lowlife in England will too."

She laughed, and it infuriated him. Around him cartmen smiled, their grins hideous to him in the swirling snow and yellow lantern-light.

"Your lordship, the man's as good as dead from hydrophobia," Galitzin said.

"That's not it, not it!" the viscount cried. "He's dying the way he wants, escaped and free. He must die in irons. And speaking of that, Galitzin—how did he get your key?"

"He didn't." Galitzin pulled the keys that locked several of the carts—the armorer's cart, the spirits cart, the carts carrying silver and china for the lord and ladies—as well as the simple skeleton key that unlocked his irons. He jangled them before the viscount's nose, most rudely, the viscount thought.

"Someone has betrayed me, and the crown," he announced darkly, while surveying the villainous faces about him. "Well, get on with it. We will bring them back. If they resist, they'll die. I don't suppose they have weapons."

"Your lordship, it isn't practical in this—"

"Practical, practical. Here is a lantern. Out there are tracks in the snow. Take spare oil for the lantern. Saddle up. Take a squad, Galitzin. You shall lead it. I shall come along. I want every man saddled in five minutes. I want Gravesend to issue sidearms and rifles and rounds."

"With one lantern, sir, the men could hardly find mounts, or saddle—"

"Do it!"

Lady Diana laughed. "Gordon, dear, come play tiddly-winks. You'll get over it."

He paused before her, noting her amused smile, her insolence. "You are perfectly worthless. Trash. Go join Skye. If you return to England, it shall be in shame."

The amusement vanished from her face, and she stared at him contemplatively. "You've changed, Gordon. For the worse."

"Your lordship, what are we to do for rations?" Galitzin asked. "The men are starving and weak. A horse a day is vile fare."

The staring cartmen suddenly turned solemn, and the viscount noted it. "Bring Skye back dead or alive; then I'll stop the caravan for a few days and we'll hunt. Every last one of us. But only if you bring him back, and his squaws for good measure. They're all horse thieves. Stole Galitzin's mount."

Diana started laughing again. "And just what were we, eating Mister Skye's horses and mules day by day? Be consistent, Gordon."

"Out of my sight, you—"

She chuckled, obviously enjoying it. "Oh, pooh," she said. "I'm glad Mister Skye's free."

He could barely stand it. Had she not been nobly bred he would have ordered ten lashes. But he didn't wish to give the cartmen ideas. Instead he pulled his revolver from its sheath. "Go saddle," he said coldly.

Reluctantly, cartmen dispersed to their small tents to pull on clothing.

"And saddle a mount for me," he roared.

It took an hour. Lord Frazier stalked around his lodge, raging, fuming, checking his revolver and his rifle; glaring at Lady Alexandra, who cowered in her blankets, and ignoring Lady Diana, who dressed in her hunting attire as if she intended to go along.

Then, at last, he heard that bloody fool Galitzin outside the lodge. "We are ready, your lordship," the man proclaimed.

"It took you long enough," Frazier muttered. "I hope the tracks haven't snowed over. I don't suppose you thought of that—or did you?"

Lord Frazier peered about him. Ten cartmen wrapped in blankets sat their mounts. Galitzin sat on a gray, holding the lantern by its bail. Diana sat on her buffalo runner, looking ready for a hunt, snow collecting on her split skirts.

"You're not going."

"I wouldn't miss the fun for anything, Gordon."

"Dismount."

"Make me, dear."

He thought he might. But it was unthinkable to tell a cartman to manhandle a noblewoman.

"Have you spare oil for the lamp, colonel?"

"A tin."

"Very well then. We will all do our duty."

Galitzin touched heels to his mount and the viscount fell in beside him, the two of them studying the ground for the snowed-over dimples that remarked the passage of Skye and his squaws. The cartmen strung out behind.

He and Galitzin picked up the trail easily enough, the dimples left by the passage of two horses. And no blood. He'd been hoping for blood in the snow.

"I am a man of iron, eh, Galitzin?"

"A determined leader, sir."

"Where do you suppose the scoundrel's going?"

"South of course, sir. As long as zey have a little northwind on their back zey'll manage it—unless the wind shifts. I think it's out of the northwest, myself."

"Very good, Galitzin. Even if we lose the tracks, we'll head south. By the way, did you leave anyone in command at the camp?"

"I'm sure Mister Baudelaire—"

The viscount snorted. "A pimp in command."

The strangeness of everything subdued them. They

drove through a low tunnel of whirling white, scarcely knowing whether they were climbing or descending, walking the edge of a cliff, or circumventing a forest. There was only the fast-filling string of dimples in the lantern-yellow snow, sucking them through nothingness.

"Faster," he said at last. "The trail's dim."

Galitzin set them into a trot, and behind he heard horses wheezing, gear clattering, weapons rattling in their sheaths, and the jingle of bridles. The sound satisfied him. Good British steel.

They clambered up a vast slope and then the trail vanished where wind had scoured the snow. It alarmed him.

"We'll go until we strike snow again," Galitzin said. "Then I'll halt the column while I work to either side. I'll pick it up."

"Excellent, Galitzin."

They crossed the barren ridge into snow, and in a few minutes Galitzin spotted the trail.

"We might lose them, your lordship."

"Pshaw. They're going to go south to the band of that older squaw—what's her name. We'll just press ahead and intercept. They'll cross the Yellowstone about where the Shields joins it. They must be weak as pups, and the oaf is probably half-dead by now. Canvas wagonsheet won't warm him, eh? How do you suppose they took it? Did you miss a knife?"

"I've learned not to underestimate the savages, your lordship."

"Very good, Galitzin. But that old squaw must have hidden a dirk."

Diana drew up beside them and it annoyed him, but he said nothing.

"We're catching up, aren't we. We have the lantern, but they have to feel their way along," she said.

"We'll have them soon," Galitzin replied.

She sighed unhappily, and the very sigh curdled the viscount's thoughts. An insufferable woman.

They rode relentlessly, while snow caked on their clothing and cold bit their toes. The temperature had barely dropped to freezing, the viscount knew, but the fall storm came fanged with wetness and bitter air. The ride had become eerie, a steady plodding across a white island in a black sea, without the faintest guidepost.

The light wavered, and Galitzin stared at it. "We'll stop and fill the reservoir," he said. He tugged his horse to a halt just as the light blued and vanished. Instantly the blackness closed in around them, clamping them in a stygian vise.

"I say, Galitzin, you brought some matches—"

He heard Galitzin rummaging in a leather pouch slung over his shoulders, and then white light blossomed in his hand. "I've plenty. Bring me the tin, Wiggins."

It took them a few minutes, while the viscount chafed. Once Galitzin lit a match so the cartman could see where to pour the coal oil. He spilled some, and the viscount caught a whiff of it in the air. But at last the colonel struck a sulphur match again, cupped the bright flare, and the lamp sprang to life. Galitzin carefully replaced the glass chimney, and they started off again.

But while the colonel refueled the lamp in the dark, the viscount thought he spotted something. He peered into the night, straining his eyes to catch it again. And yes, there it was. Off behind them and to the right, he saw two or three stars just off the horizon. He realized even then that the snow had diminished, and so had the wind. There'd be little more snow or wind to obscure Skye's tracks, and just enough on the ground to leave an indelible trail. He exulted. The Divine hand, reaching out on behalf of mighty England and the Queen once again, as always.

"Look over there, Galitzin. Stars. It'll clear off in a few hours. And the snow's stopped. Now we have them."

The snow died and the wind died. Victoria knew the snow had stopped because it no longer stung her hands or dampened her cheeks. With the death of wind came the death of direction. She had no idea whether they progressed southward or meandered. She could not see the trail behind for reference. The horse would follow the path of least resistance.

"Talk to me, Mister Skye," she said. They'd neglected the contact

"I'm here," he said, behind her. "Jawbone knows to keep up."

"I don't know where I'm going."

"We might head downhill. Any coulee should take us to the river. I'm used up. Hope we'll find some shelter down in the bottoms."

The thought gladdened her. She was used up too. She had Mary's warmth pressing her back, but the horse's hard backbone sawed her in two, and her legs ached.

"Are you cold?"

"Feet ache. My legs feel the way they did when I was making beaver. I'd climb out of those icy creeks and they'd hurt for a day."

He never talked about the aches in his bones from all the years he'd trapped beaver. He'd kept his hurts to himself, but she knew every scar in his battered body tortured him through the winters.

The earth tilted to her left, and she felt the horse's gait change, jolt more, on a downslope. She felt the darkness thicken even more, if that were possible, and felt the presence of forest, though she couldn't see a tree. Then a branch brushed her, and she felt its shower of snow. She turned the horse into the downgrade, and felt it skid slightly.

"I am going down, Mister Skye."

He didn't answer.

"I'm going down," she said louder.

"Feeling bad," he muttered, and the words relieved her as much as alarmed her. "Like to stop. Can't stand my hands chained up any more. Can't stand my feet hurting."

"Soon!" she cried. "Not now."

The medicine vision had returned to her, Magpie's prophecy scorching her mind even as she peered blindly into nothing.

"We're safe," said Mary. "I need to stop too."

"No! sonofabitch!"

"Magpie talkin'?"

"Yes!" In truth, her mind crawled with the vision, almost as if Magpie were there in the dark, on her shoulder, showing her Fate.

"Funny thing," Mister Skye muttered behind her. "That medicine vision was plumb right. The viscount fixing to haul me off. But how come I'm free? How come I'm dying of hydrophobia instead of being carted off to England?"

"Are you dying?" she cried.

He didn't answer for a while. "Don't want to go under. I want to see the baby." He paused again. "Die free. Die without these chains on. Die with you—" His voice broke hoarsely, and she heard him sniffing and muttering back there. She ached to hug him, dismount, help him off, bury themselves in the robes and hug. But it could not be. Something crabbed at her.

Victoria felt Mary's hands tighten around her waist. The horse skidded down a sharp defile, careened into a trunk, and righted itself. She felt the lash of needles.

They pierced into deeper forest. The horse picked its way along, stumbling frequently, its hoofs barking logs and rocks, skidding on wet unfrozen ground covered with needles. She peered upward through the canopy and saw stars off to one side, and sensed the night blooming open. A while later the heavens were clear. Cold deepened, hurting her. She could make out the snow on the ground, dim in starlight. Not much. The September sun would demolish it in a few hours.

They bottomed out onto a flat, emerging from the pine forest at the same time. They sensed looming shoulders of the earth catapulting upward, lifting horizons. Probably the Smith River, coiling in oxbows toward the Missouri.

"Northstar back off to our left. Dipper," muttered Mister Skye. "We're going southeast."

These whiteman's directions meant little to her. She took her directions from places. Now they were going to a place she loved.

"See!" cried Mary.

Victoria peered about, seeing nothing at first. And then, far away, atop the black ridge, just where it touched the open heavens, she saw a tiny bobbing light. They stared as the little light slid off the horizon and down into the blackness of the slope.

"Magpie's right, Victoria," Mister Skye said quietly. "They've got a fresh trail in snow to follow. But we've got a light to watch for. Armed to the gunnels, I imagine."

"That viscount—he's got one thing in his head."

"You have any notions, ladies?"

She peered sharply at him. He sat Jawbone, a ghostly figure in the dark, but visible now. She had never known him to surrender himself like this. The onslaught of death had robbed her man of will.

"You got that pickax?"

"Not much of a weapon, Victoria."

"Get down," she yelled at him. "I got to do something."

He obeyed, sliding clumsily off Jawbone and falling, unable to right himself with chained hands and legs that had ceased to function. She helped him up.

"Come here," she said. She lifted the pickax from the snow and steered him toward a downed tree. "Now get down. Put your hands out. Make that chain tight across the log."

"In the dark? You'll hit my—"

"Goddam, just do it. That chain, it locks your spirit worse than it locks your hands."

"But it's too dark—"

Mary said, "Do it, Mister Skye."

He stared from one woman to the other. Then he settled himself over the log, his arms out, the chain taut over the bark.

She lifted the pickax, turning it to make use of the chisel edge. A faintness undermined her, and she remembered how long it had been since any of them had eaten. She aimed carefully, and drove the heavy tool down. The chisel buried itself in wood. She yanked it loose, muttering to herself.

"Careful, Victoria," Skye muttered.

She drove the pick down again, and felt it drive into the link, burying chain in the rotting log. She tugged the pick out, and pulled the chain up. It fell apart, the links of drawn wire easier to cut than the forged links of the leg irons.

Mister Skye stared, seeing liberty in the starlight, and slowly drew his arms apart, chain-ends dangling from each wrist. He did not speak. Slowly he stood up, lifted his gaze to the infinities above him, lit now by a rising quarter moon, and stretched his freed arms upward, wanting to touch the stars, reaching, arching his back, straining his arms, his reaching fingers lifted to touch the music of creation. Then at last he lowered his thick arms and turned to her.

"Victoria. Mary," he whispered, and the two words made love.

She hugged him. They both hugged him. Then they turned toward the bobbing lantern, now visible, now obscured, as the viscount's men worked down the trail toward the bottoms.

"The river," said Mister Skye. "We'll head north, downstream in water. They'll look to the south."

Swiftly they mounted, gathering their few things: the pickax, spare canvas, and belaying pin. Liberty infused Mister Skye with an energy she hadn't seen in him. She grunted, satisfied, knowing she'd acted wisely.

He took the lead, steering Jawbone into brushy bottoms, and she and Mary followed on the dark horse, pushing now through whipping branches. Then, ahead, Jawbone stopped abruptly. She could hear water.

"Damned cutbank here. Ten-foot drop, looks like. Maybe more, hard to tell. Go back. We got to cut south a bit—make them think we're heading south."

They pivoted and worked their way back from the bank, pushing through clawed brush. When they broke out on meadow at last they whirled south, alarmed by the bobbing light, now three-quarters down the black slope and only minutes away.

They trotted furiously along the bottoms. Then Mister Skye pushed Jawbone back into the brush, cutting for the river again. On the trail above, a horse heard them and whinnied. Victoria's horse squealed back. Discovered, then. This time they struck the riverbank at a place where the water undulated three or four feet below the cutbank, wobbling the stars that rode its surface. They stared, not knowing how deep the river lay. It could be a pool, and they could drop into a spot that would drench and kill them. The water boiled evilly by, oily in the night.

Behind, they heard distant shouts and the motion of horses as the viscount's men reached the open bottoms. No choice. The cartmen didn't need their lantern any more, and were closing fast.

"All right, you bloody horse," Skye said, kneeing Jawbone. The great beast poised on the lip of the cut-bank, shuddered, and then let himself slide in, his fore-hoofs plowing down clay, slowing the descent in some small way.

Jawbone struck water, staggered under Skye's weight, and righted himself. The river scarcely reached his pasterns. Only inches deep.

Mister Skye laughed softly. "Come along, ladies," he whispered.

Victoria and Mary had a bad time with the dark horse. They kicked and cursed, while just beyond the brush the noise of horsemen pierced to them.

"I will make him," said Mary. She turned, the belaying pin in hand, and cracked it over the horse's rump. The animal careened forward, dove off the cutbank and landed with a splash. It staggered, almost dumping its bareback riders, and then stood in starlit water that didn't reach its hocks.

"I hear you, Skye!" the viscount called. "Surrender now, or we will shoot to kill. All of you."

Chapter 30

Mister Skye sat quietly on Jawbone, listening. Beside him, Victoria and Mary sat waiting on their dark horse. Beyond, walled by a thick band of dense brush, his pursuers collected on a meadow. He heard the mutter of horses and talk, and then the movement of horses. Up and down the stream, he surmised. They were fanning out.

The Smith River ran in great oxbows here, walled by brush and contained by steep cutbanks in spots. Across the slender river a six- or eight-foot cutbank loomed, trapping them in the water. If they could scale that, they could vanish in the brush on the far side easily enough. The cartmen had light enough from stars, a slim moon, and a few inches of snow, but it was tricky light, and all three Skyes wore white ponchos cut from the wagonsheet. He doubted that all the cartmen would shoot to kill, but he couldn't count on that. He felt like a fox beset by hounds, with only his guile to protect him.

Jawbone stood quietly, ears laid back, ready to shriek. Skye, enjoying the lush pleasure of freed hands, ran one up his neck, under the mane, quieting the horse. Downstream lay a high cutbank with dense brush on top. And across the oily river there, a low bank, maybe three feet. Something they could negotiate if they had to. He signaled to the women and gently turned Jawbone in the water, letting the animal pick his way along, step by slow step, toward the moonshadowed pool of blackness below the bluff. Victoria's horse, less disciplined, splashed, and he heard her cursing softly.

"Mister Skye." The voice was a woman's and rose from some distance, beyond the brush. "Will you marry me?"

He paused, astonished.

"I'd love to be your third wife—even for the—the little while left."

He turned. Victoria and Mary sat grinning at him.

The viscount yelled at her. "Have you no decency?"

"Mister Skye—" Diana called again. "I don't know if you're there or hearing me. They've divided into two parties. Galitzin went down—"

"Stop that," roared the viscount. "You're betraying the crown. I'll see you brought to justice!"

"—and Gravesend went upstream with the rest."

He heard a sharp crack, like a slap or the blow of a swagger stick across her face, and a small scream, followed by groaning and weeping. He used the noise to dash swiftly through the water. As they slipped into the shadow below the cutbank the river deepened suddenly, and Jawbone plowed water rising to his knees and hocks. Skye peered around swiftly. Safe enough for the moment, with an escape into brush across the river, and up the steep fissures of land beyond. From both sides now he heard crashing in the brush as cartmen spurred horses into the red willow and chokecherry and hackberry that massed along the creek.

"Skye," yelled the viscount. "We have you. Surrender or die. We'll have mercy on your squaws if you do. Otherwise—death to all of you. Prepare your villainous heart to meet God!"

Mister Skye said nothing.

"You're not armed, Skye. You haven't the faintest chance."

Mister Skye thought he might be armed at that, but the thought lay bitter in his soul. He knew then what he'd do, if he had strength enough after being starved for weeks and now chilled to numbness. His women wouldn't like it.

He nodded to them and began pulling his poncho over his head, luxuriating in the liberty of his arms. Then he pulled the buffalo robe off too, wrestling with its heavy weight. He rolled the robe into a compact cylinder, and tied it behind the low cantle of the British cavalry saddle he rode, and slid the poncho over him again. He wanted freedom.

"Goddam," muttered Victoria. "I tell you about medicine and you don't care." She sounded angry.

Mister Skye held out a hand toward Mary. Wordlessly she reached over and handed him his belaying pin. Then he quietly slid off Jawbone into the river. He ran a loving hand down Jawbone's neck, steadying the great horse. Icewater blasted his feet and calves and knees, but he was used to that. For years he'd braved the bitter waters of the north setting his beaver traps, seeing how the sticks floated day after winter day. The old pain flared at once but he ignored it. New pain from wounds barely healed bit at him too. It didn't matter.

He stood listening. Horses and men beat the brush above and below. A pancake cloud, silverlined by the moon, skidded across the sky and would darken the land in a moment. Good. He began a slow, quiet plowing against the current, feeling his way along the slippery bottom until he found a spot where roots gave him toeholds up the cutbank. In a moment he crouched numbly in brush, feeling his near nakedness in the bitter night.

He enjoyed what he was going to do. If he died doing it, that would spare him a worse death shortly. Audacity had saved his life several times, and ultimately had become part of the legend of Barnaby Skye told in the council fires of the western tribes. He'd grown aware of the legend and used it, called it medicine, and turned his medicine legend into a powerful weapon. Even now, he knew, his own women hunkered in the moonshadowed lee of the cutbank, wondering if he had gotten back his medicine.

"Very well then, Skye. You've signed your warrant."

Good of the viscount to announce where he stood, Skye thought. He slipped gingerly forward, knowing how to stalk, how to test the ground ahead for sticks that might snap, branches that might whip. He focused on one thing, the viscount, and scarcely registered the cold on his flesh. Off to either side he heard the thrashing of horses and the voices of men. He might die at that. Most of the cartmen were near.

He slipped into a dense grove of young cottonwoods, their naked branches praying to the moon, and steered through them warily, afraid of snapping a stick. But his medicine held. He pushed gently through brush he knew would look red by daylight, and then found himself peering out upon the rough flats—and the lord and lady, both sitting their horses. He had drawn his revolver and pointed it at her.

"Go ahead and shoot, Gordon," she said mockingly. "Mister Skye! Take me to your bed." She laughed. "I'm mad for you, Skye. I'll be the third wife, Skye!"

She obviously enjoyed taunting the viscount. And she

was obviously missing the sudden murderous calm that settled across the lordship's face, something Skye sensed even in the dim light.

A volley of shots split the night, shots from downstream, where his women hid. Shouts drifted to him, and more shots, and violent crashing in brush. Alarmed, he squinted into the murk, seeing nothing, worried about Victoria and Mary. Had the cartmen shot his women in cold blood?

The viscount and Lady Diana stared northward, wondering. Whatever the viscount had intended had been arrested by the commotion. Skye considered slipping back through the brush to his women, then decided to wait. Off in the north he saw Galitzin's lantern bobbing, and the blurred forms of men and horses. Some rode; some led their horses. Skye could scarcely make them out. But then his gaze settled on something that roiled his stomach and caught his breath in his throat. Over one led horse lay a body. A gray thing bobbed and dangled and leaked blackness. Mary! Victoria! Oh . . .

They came swiftly now, cartmen trotting, until they reached the viscount.

"Get back out there, I say," yelled Galitzin.

"No, we'll eat!" cried a cartman.

"Do your duty first. The lord insists."

A cartman paused defiantly. "The bloody hell with that. We'll eat and be damned."

Men slid a slain doe off the nervous dancing horse. Skye gaped, a sudden tremor rattling through him.

From the south, upstream, men trotted back, drawn by the commotion.

Galitzin waved his lantern. "I command you to do your duty. You can eat later," he said. "There'll be severe discipline—"

"Shut your scurvy mouth. We didn't eat today. We've downed stringy horseflesh for a week. We'll—"

The viscount's revolver blasted. The jostling cartmen froze in place. "Two things," said Lord Frazier. "I'll shoot the first bloke who touches that doe. And second, I'll shoot any man who doesn't go back out immediately and hunt down Skye. Get Skye. Then eat. If he escapes, you won't eat. I'll confiscate the carcass."

Men gaped. Any one of them could have lifted his rifle and shot the viscount, but they didn't.

Diana laughed. "You're such a goose, Gordon. These chaps don't want to hurt our Mister Skye. They like him. He and his ladies brought in meat. They kept us all safe and got us out of some bad scrapes. There's not a one who'd shoot at Skye."

"I beg to remind you that a lord of England has measures," the viscount replied coolly. "Colonel Galitzin, make note. This one here, that one there, the ringleaders. We will deal with insurrection as it must be dealt with, with the lash and the noose."

From the edge of the brush Mister Skye watched the cartmen acquiesce. He was so relieved that the body was that of a doe that he trembled. He'd watched that body in the stealthy dark, watched and felt his soul die. Now he crouched transfixed, seeing the surly cartmen yield their wills to the one they'd always called lord.

The soft voice just behind Skye galvanized him. "Up with those big paws, ye bloody oaf."

He whirled, too late. Just behind him in the brush stood the armorer, Gravesend, with a cocked double-barreled fowling piece pointed squarely at him.

Gravesend grinned from behind the weapon. "And drop the hickory stick, sailorboy. Now, or—never, eh?"

Slowly Mister Skye let the belaying pin tumble to earth, and stood.

"Cassocked like a bishop and ready to pray," Gravesend said. "All right, matey. For'ard march."

Mister Skye turned and walked, emerging from the brush and exciting the mob a few yards away.

A sudden hush fell over the cartmen. Lady Diana Chatham-Hollingshead watched bleakly as Gravesend prodded the erstwhile guide into the circle of lanternlight. Somehow, though she couldn't fathom why, the act seemed shameful. Something loathsome was happening. Like the assassination of a king or the murder of Thomas a Becket. The cartmen sensed it, and looked solemn.

Gravesend halted Mister Skye before the viscount. "Here's the bishop, your lordship," he said cheerily.

The viscount nodded benignly.

Skye stood pale in his poncho, naked otherwise except for the tied-down canvas that shrouded his feet and calves. She'd seen him in similar condition many times these past weeks, ever since he'd been captured and his clothes taken from him. By good English models Mister Skye didn't look like much. His torso formed a great barrel, and it rested on massive haunches, tilted slightly forward. He wore his graying hair shoulder-length and loose, like any mountain ruffian. The great body under the poncho was blocky, like her own, and perhaps that is what always started something pattering inside of her when she glimpsed it. She'd long since recognized that sensation as lust, but now, as he stood helpless before his tormentor, she felt no such passions, but only a sadness, and that stain of shame she'd noted.

"Well, Skye," said the viscount blandly, some deep

pleasure in his eyes. "You departed without a stitch and now return in a burial shroud." He smiled.

The guide did a strange thing. He didn't speak, but he rumbled in a most peculiar way, almost as if in some sort of pain. Maybe he was, she thought. His flesh must suffer in the icy air.

"Galitzin, go find the squaws and shoot them. And that bloody horse once and for all. We can't be fending off rescues and plots and all that."

"As you wish, lordship. Come along, come along."

But no one followed. She saw at once the cartmen had no intention of shooting squaws, and half of them looked to be on the brink of rebellion.

"Go along," said Lord Frazier sharply. "I will suffer no insolence." He snapped his swagger stick against his britches smartly.

It occurred to Diana that she held fate in her hands. Or would, as soon as she eased her fowling piece from its sheath hanging on her saddle. She managed it without difficulty, because Skye remained the cynosure of all eyes, and she sat her buffalo pony well back in the darkness.

But Skye saw, and his sharp quick gaze surprised her. For an instant their eyes locked, and he nodded slightly. Then he made that strange noise again, roaring like a grizzly bear, and she saw spittle collect at the corner of his mouth. Sick! Hydrophobia! The sight desolated her. Others saw it too, and muttered.

"Your lordship, you've caught me. I'll shake your hand, then, and we'll be off," Skye said amiably. He stretched his right arm forward. The locked manacle and severed chain shone amber in the lantern light.

The viscount sniffed, stepped back, and glared. "Shake

hands with a lord, would you? And you, the scurviest scum alive?"

Skye grinned, and lowered his arm slowly.

"How'd you sever the link, Skye? We'll make sure it doesn't happen again."

"Take a look yourself, matey," Skye said. He held his hands forward, letting the links dangle.

The guide was certainly acting strange, she thought. Pity seeped through her. She'd come to see this man in a new light during their long passage through a dangerous wild. She'd discovered education in him, and courtesy, and a commanding way of dealing with crises along the trail. She'd thought him a barbarian at first, and found him an eminent citizen of a wild kingdom. By degrees, she had learned to admire him, and particularly his grace under pressure, the thing she called courage.

The lamp shattered. One second it stood on the snowy ground shedding gold; the next, it flew apart, glass splintering, and the whole scene blanked black. Her light-blinded eyes could see nothing.

Men exclaimed.

"Goddam," muttered someone, and it sounded like Skye's older woman. Diana scarcely understood the whirl of motion about her.

"I say! Take your bloody paws off me!" the viscount roared.

She heard scuffling in the dark.

"All right, mate," roared Skye. "Tell them."

The viscount whined.

"Tell them or I'll bite you."

"Bite me?"

"Right at the base of the neck. Here. Right here." Skye's voice. Somehow close to the viscount.

"Bite me? Bite me?"

"Like the wolf." Lady Diana heard an awful gnashing of teeth. From somewhere out in the darkness, close by, that awful horse screeched.

"Bite you," said Skye. "Sink my teeth right in. Chew your flesh and spit it out."

The viscount made some sort of noise that sounded like a gargle. Then, "Don't kill me, Skye. Don't bite me. Galitzin. Gravesend, don't try anything. Not a thing. He'll give me hydrophobia."

Skye roared, and the sound shivered Lady Diana. The man had turned into a hydrophobic lunatic.

Jawbone shrieked.

She could see a little now that the lantern-blindness was fading. Skye stood behind the viscount, pinning him within his massive arms. His face was poised just over the viscount's right shoulder.

"For God's sake!" cried Lord Frazier. "You're oozing hydrophobia."

Skye laughed wildly, and the sound echoed up the coulees.

Diana watched a dark form edge around behind Skye. Galitzin, intending to brain the guide. She lifted her fowling piece, and then knew it wouldn't work. She needed a revolver or a carbine.

"Colonel, one more step and I sink my teeth into this meat."

"For pity sake!" cried Lord Frazier.

"Gravesend, you might hit me—or the viscount—but before I die, I'll sink my teeth into his lordship."

Diana watched Gravesend, over on her right, falter. Then something hit him. He fell, poleaxed, tumbling in the snow. Diana had the distinct impression she'd heard the sound of hardwood striking the skull. And at last she made out the wizened figure of Skye's woman, holding something like a club in her hand.

Skye laughed, his bellow eerie in the night. "I suppose most of you cartmen would be pleased if I bit," he said amiably. "Set down your pieces, and we'll palaver a bit."

They hastened to do so.

"Lady Chatham-Hollingshead, please keep your scattergun on them."

"Don't bite," cried the viscount. "I'll do anything."

"Of course you will, mate. To save your hide. All right, Gordy, or is it Pat or Archie? Here's what you'll do. You'll say 'Damn the bloody Queen,' eh?"

Diana waited, some wild amusement welling up in her.

"Say it, matey, or I'll bite. I'll count to three and bite, your holiness. One, Two—"

"Damn the bloody Queen," croaked the viscount.

"Why, matey, you're a deserter!"

Cartmen laughed. Diana chortled.

"Sir, you are an abomination," said Colonel Galitzin.

Skye addressed him benignly. "First brave thing you've said or done, colonel. And I respect it. You've been a toady from the beginning, bowing and scraping. No wonder the Czar's hussars promoted you, and no wonder your army's full of lickspittle officers. Where'd you learn English, Galitzin? Cambridge?"

The colonel muttered something.

"Here's what you do, Galitzin. You're taking charge. Somewhere inside of you is a competent officer. You'll march your caravan up to Fort Benton on the Missouri— the Blackfeet'll steer you—and my friend Alec Culbertson will see you all down the river. Tell him I said hello—and goodbye."

"Very good, your excellence."

Barnaby Skye roared. Jawbone shrieked.

"Don't bite!" cried the viscount.

"My lady," said Skye, and Diana realized suddenly he was addressing her. "The viscount was about to do you harm a few minutes ago. You are welcome to come with my wives and me. Not, as you may suppose, to become my third one, but because we offer you safety and friendship. I am going to Victoria's people to die. They will see you safely to Fort Laramie."

She didn't hesitate an instant. "Bye, Gordy," she said.

Skye continued: "I'm going to borrow a few things, Lord Frazier. That tweed jacket for one, and those lace-up boots. My feet have forgotten what warmth feels like. And a few arms, of course. We'll have to disarm you. And a good horse. We'll take a haunch of that doe, and leave the rest for your men. Unless you'd prefer I bite you. And then you can trot off to Alexandra's featherbed and Baudelaire's comforts."

"Anything, anything. Don't bite!"

Chapter 31

The waiting seemed worse than the dying. That fall had been glorious, with mild days and frosty nights and azure skies. It grieved Mister Skye to know that he was enjoying these things for the last time. As the cottonwoods and aspens turned golden and lost their leaves, he saw his own doom in the naked limbs that pressed against an enameled sky, and it lay in him, haunting and dark. He felt well through the Moon of Falling Leaves, but that meant nothing. Hydrophobia lurked and waited and in-spired false hope and wild relief—until it sprang.

They had found Victoria's Kicked-in-the-Bellies band on the Stillwater, and had been warmly welcomed by Chief Many Coups and all the people, who counted Mister Skye as one of their own and who honored his feats of battle beside his Absaroka brothers. They listened raptly to their story of the viscount, which Mister Skye told in halting Crow, while Victoria embellished easily in her own tongue. But when he'd told them of his wolf-bite, the death of Cutler, and his own certain fate, they saddened and began their mourning.

That afternoon, the great medicine man Red Turkey Wattle had examined Mister Skye's calf. Wordlessly he felt the puckered scars and pink flesh where the swift knife had bled each fang puncture and Victoria had fried the sur-rounding flesh, leaving a wrinkled red pocket and unend-ing ache in the calf. The skeletal shaman peered up from rheumy eyes and said only that he would fast and seek a vision in his lodge for four days. Mister Skye thanked him, but did not delude himself into believing it would alter his fate.

The whole band vied to reprovision the Skyes. Young women hiked high into the mountains to the south, to a grove where young lodgepole pines grew dense and slen-der after a fire, and cut new lodgepoles. Older women tanned cowhides from the fall hunt, then laced them to-gether into a shining lodge. Others made luxurious winter moccasins for all the Skyes and Lady Diana too, with thick bullneck soles sewn to softer uppers. Victoria's step-mother fashioned a splendid elkskin shirt for Mister Skye, with dyed quillwork across the chest and long fringes under the arms. Young men brought them meat, choice buffalo hump and boudins, haunches of elk, and soft rabbit pelts for moccasin lining and warmth. Older men, proud of their bow and arrow-making, honed seasoned chokecherry into fine bows for Victoria and Mary and supplied them with carefully wrought arrows with hoop-iron points. And so the Skyes were made new with an outpouring of gifts from the Absarokas.

Mister Skye felt well. In fact, he had never felt better, apart from the ache in his calf. But that new ache mingled with ancient ones that cried at him in the onslaught of each winter, aches from the days he waded hip-deep in icy streams, setting beaver traps, pulling wet, drowned beaver from their watery tombs. The Kicked-in-the-Bellies had chosen a dazzling place to while away the fall. Their vast pony herd fattened on rank golden grasses that grew along the river flats. If they chose to winter near here, hoary cottonwoods would offer fodder for the ponies. Beyond the flats, tumbled foothills dotted with juniper and jackpine vaulted toward the purple mountains to the south, already snow-tipped and beyond mortal reach. Often, Mister Skye took all this in, staring at the tawny collection of lodges, the drying racks of meat, the transparent sky, and the noble mountains, and wept.

But he did not let any one see his tears. Not even Victoria and Mary. All three of them huddled close in their new lodge each night—and waited. As long as he felt well, he tried to be of some use. He made a point of taking Lady Diana around the village and introducing her, and she responded with childlike joy. He wanted to be alone with his women during his last days, so he introduced Diana to Pine Leaf, the legendary old warrior woman of the band, graying now but greatly honored, and powerful in the councils of the whole Absaroka nation. Pine Leaf had never married, but for years she had been the lover of that scamp Jim Beckwourth, and knew English perfectly.

"My lady," she said graciously, "I'd be delighted if you would stay with me. We'll hunt. You love the hunt and have a fine buffalo pony. So do I. We'll see who hunts best!"

"Pine Leaf, I'd be delighted!" Diana had said, and Mister Skye was pleased. Almost every day from then on the pair rode away at dawn, and returned in a crisp fall evening with spare ponies loaded with elk and deer and quarters of buffalo, outstripping all the young men of the band in their successes.

Mister Skye watched approvingly as the young noble-woman transformed herself into an Absaroka huntress, swiftly mastering the Crow tongue, dressing herself richly in Crow attire, and letting Red Turkey Wattle give her a Crow name, which was Grizzly Sow Woman.

"Am I a grizzly sow?" she asked Mister Skye.

"You're more fetching," he replied.

"I'd like some cubs."

He laughed.

"I don't want to go to England."

"Then don't. But I'd better warn you, the winters are often starvin' times."

"Many Coups has asked me to be his fourth wife. It must be my blue blood. Do you think I should?"

"You'll make up your own mind, Lady Diana."

"I'm Grizzly Sow Woman." She laughed, and then turned somber. "I'd hoped it might be you, Mister Skye. I've never known a man like you. You're so full of— innocence! Innocence."

"I jumped ship."

"Oh, Barnaby. They pressed you in. You were going to go to Cambridge, like your father."

It startled him. "How'd you know that?"

"When you drink, you babble on and on."

"Do me a kindness, Grizzly Sow Woman. Keep that to yourself."

The trees lay naked, and ice formed along the edges of the Stillwater, and Mary's child grew in her belly, making her large, and still the hydrophobia did not pounce. He dared to hope a little, but found hope worse than the surety of doom. With hope came an ache for living that he'd ruthlessly driven from his soul. But he could no longer contain his hope. Each day he examined himself anxiously, and each day his body replied with bright strength and ease. His women had stopped weeping at night, clutching him, and saying goodbye; now they peered at him shyly, contemplatively, sharing his hope but not daring to express it.

His lodge was no longer dark, at least in the sense of divided souls and hearts, but death lurked at its doorflap and Mister Skye's great medicine lay in balance. He felt an unfamiliar helplessness. It chafed him that he could do nothing. But at least he could die well. He lavished love on each of his wives, making them smile, letting them bask in his caring. And he roamed the village each day, bringing a kind word to old men and encouragement to young hunters and warriors, and a gentle flirtation to women young and old. Yes, he thought, he could die well. That alone was left to him, dying well.

One cold day a French trapper named Jean Gallant rode into the village on a shaggy winter-haired pony, and presented himself to Many Coups first, then Mister Skye. He'd come, he said, at the request of Alec Culbertson, bourgeois at Fort Lewis—soon to be renamed Fort Benton. The British, he said, had arrived half-starved and petulant at the

American Fur Company post, along with a Blackfeet escort, and had negotiated for two mackinaws to float them to Fort Union. There they would embark on a waiting Chouteau keelboat that would float them down to St. Louis.

"Monsieur Culbertson, he ask me to find out if you live, and I will say zat you do. And he ask me to give this—" he reached into a sack he was toting—"to your good widows." He pulled out a battered silk tophat. "Zee colonel, Galitzin, give it to the bourgeois."

Mister Skye roared. "My medicine hat! I've got my medicine again. Good as new! Burnt and bled the hydrophobia out. Haw!"

Victoria plucked up the battered hat and set it rakishly on his head, grinning.

"Sonofabitch, you got your medicine," she bellowed.

Author's Note

This story, like each of my Skye novels, is pure fiction. But it follows history loosely. This story was inspired by the exploits of Sir St. George Gore, eighth baronet of Gore Manor in Ireland.

In 1854, after outfitting at Fort Leavenworth, he set out on a three-year hunt across the American West that became a legend in its time. His caravan was composed of four six-mule wagons, two ox-wagons, and twenty-one Red River carts. One wagon was filled entirely with the best arms England could manufacture, made by Purdey, Manton, and Richards, and numbering seventy-five rifles and a dozen shotguns. Another contained nothing but fishing tackle. He had greyhounds and staghounds with him, as well as one hundred twelve horses, eighteen oxen, some milk cows and various mules. One of his horses was a Kentucky thoroughbred called Steel Trap, which got to live indoors during the winter encampments, enjoying corn meal fodder.

He had a personal wagon with a collapsible roof (which inspired the parlor wagon in my story), a fancy green-and-white striped tent, a luxurious rug, washstand, brass bed, and other accoutrements of civilization. He even brought a telescope with a six-inch lens for star-gazing. And of course he had a large retinue, about forty men plus several guides, including Jim Bridger for a while. These included cooks, secretaries, dog-tenders and even a professional fly-dresser.

Unlike my fictional viscount, Gore knew how to hunt, and he slaughtered game in prodigious quantities. By his own estimate, he killed two thousand buffalo, sixteen hundred elk and deer, and a hundred bear. Most of this meat was left to rot on the prairies. His chosen method was to shoot standing up, his weapon resting on a forked stick, while his gun-bearer stood beside him with a re-loaded rifle. Even in those days when game seemed inexhaustible, his slaughter aroused indignation among the western tribes as well as back East in Washington, where officials pondered ways to curb his hunting and stop his illegal trading with tribesmen.

Like my fictional viscount, Sir St. George Gore eventually prevailed on Major Culbertson, of American Fur, to help him head back to St. Louis on mackinaw boats. Culbertson, glad to get rid of Gore because his profligacy had enraged the tribes, swiftly built the mackinaws, and sent him on his way after several contretemps.

I am indebted to John I. Merritt, whose *Baronets and Buffalo*, Mountain Press Publishing Company, contains a brief, excellent account of the Gore hunt. It became the germ of my novel. As is commonly the case with Old West material, the historical reality is wilder by far than anything rising from a novelist's imagination.

Turn the page for a preview of

Anything
Goes

Richard S. Wheeler

*Available from Tom Doherty Associates
in December 2015*

A FORGE BOOK

Chapter One

The silence was deadly. The show might as well be playing to an audience of cigar store Indians. Half the seats were empty. August Beausoleil hoped that Helena would be one of those cities where people habitually arrived late. But he wasn't seeing any new arrivals pushing their way along the rows. The opera house seemed a giant cavern. Opera houses were like that. They seemed largest when they were empty, more intimate when they were jammed.

From his perch at the edge of the proscenium arch, he studied the vast gloom beyond the hissing footlights. Ming's Opera House, in Helena, in the young state of Montana, was a noble theater just up the flank of Last Chance Gulch, where millions in gold had been washed out of the earth just a few feverish years earlier.

And now, opening night, those who had braved the chill mountain winds were sitting on their hands. Who were they, out there? Did they understand English? Were they born without a funny bone? Why had a sour silence descended? A miasma of boredom or ill humor, or maybe disdain, had settled like fog over the crowd, what there was of it.

The show had opened with the Wildroot Sisters, Cookie, Marge, and LaVerne, strutting their stuff, singing ensemble; Sousa marches melded into a big hello, we're starting the show. And all it got was frostbit fingers tapping on calloused hands. Beausoleil could almost feel the dyspepsia leaking across the arch onto the wide stage.

The show was his. Or most of it. Charles Pomerantz, the advance man, owned the rest of it. He had done his usual good job, plastering Lewis and Clark County with gaudy red playbills and posters touting the event, booking hotels, hiring locals, stirring up the press, handing out free passes to crooked politicians, soothing the anxieties of clergymen with bobbing Adam's apples, and planting a few claques in the audience. Who weren't doing much claquing at the moment.

Beausoleil doubled as master of ceremonies, and that gave him a chance to stir the pot a bit, sometimes with a little jab, or a quip, or even a hearty appreciation of wherever they were.

He grabbed his cane and silk top hat and strutted into the limelight, Big City man in gray tuxedo, in the middle of arctic tundra.

"Ladies and gents," he said. "That was the Wildroot Sisters, the Sweethearts of Hoboken, New Jersey. Let's give them a big hand."

No one did.

"LaVerne, Cookie, and Marge," he said. "Singing just for you."

Dyspepsia was in the air. Time for some quick humor.

"Citizens of this fair city—where am I? Keokuk? Grand Rapids? Ah, Helena, the most beautiful and famous metropolis in North America—yes, there you are, welcoming the Beausoleil Brothers Follies."

Well, anyway, waiting for whatever came next. No one laughed.

"We've got a great show for you. Seven big acts. Please

welcome the one, the only Harry the Juggler, who will do things never before seen by the human eye."

Harry trotted out, bowed, and was soon tossing six cups and saucers, breaking none. And when it was time to shut down, he pulled one after another out of the air and set the crockery down, unharmed. He bowed again, but the audience barely applauded.

"And now, the famed Marbury Trio, Delilah, Sam, and Bingo, from Memphis, in the great state of Tennessee, doing a rare and exotic dance, a lost art, for your edification."

It was, actually, a tap dance, and they did it brightly, the dolled-up threesome syncopating feet and legs and canes into rhythmic clatter that usually set a crowd to nodding and smiling. But the applause was scattered, at best. This crowd didn't know a snare drum from a bass drum.

"Next on our bill is the monologuist and sage, the one, the celebrated, the famous Wayne Windsor. Welcome Mr. Windsor as you would a long-lost brother fresh out of the state pen."

They didn't.

Wayne Windsor trotted out in a soft tweed coat, a string cravat, and a bowler, which he lifted and settled on his balding head. He would do his act in front of the silvery olio drop downstage.

Another bomb, Beausoleil thought, retreating into side-stage shadows. Windsor was also known as The Profile, because he thought he had a handsome visage from either side, with a good jut jaw and noble brow and long sculpted nose. He had contrived to take advantage of this asset, speaking first to the left side of the audience, giving those on the right a good look, and then when that portion of the audience had absorbed his famed profile, he shifted to the other side, treating the viewers on the left to his noble nose and jaw.

The act was a good one. The Great Monologuist always began with an invitation.

"Now tonight," he said, "I'm going to talk about robber barons, and I want anyone who is a genuine, accredited robber baron, or any other barons, please step forward so we can have some fun at your expense."

That was good. Robber barons were in the news. Helena had a few. The Profile had a knack. Beausoleil thought it might crack the ice this sorry evening, but it didn't even dent the silence. The Profile fired off a few cracks about politicians, added a sentiment or two, and finally settled into one of his accounts of bad service on a Pullman coach, while the Helena audience sat in stony silence. It was getting unnerving.

Was something wrong? A mine disaster? An election loss? A bribery indictment? Nothing of the sort had shown up in the two-cent press before the show. The trouble was, the week hung in balance. A bad review, three bad reviews in the three daily rags, and the Beausoleil Brothers Follies would be in trouble. A touring show bled cash.

He eyed the shadowy audience sourly, and came to a decision. He talked quietly to two stagehands, who told him there were few tomatoes this time of year in Helena, but plenty of rotten apples, which would do almost as well.

"Do it," he said.

They vanished, and would soon be sitting out there in the arctic dark, surrounded by surly spectators and bystanders little comprehending the subversives in their midst.

"I knew it," said Mrs. McGivers. "I saw it coming. You should pay me extra. It grieves my soul."

"I didn't know you had one," he said.

Mrs. McGivers and her Monkey Band would follow, after The Profile had ceased to bore his customers. Like most vaudeville shows, this one had an animal act, and the Monkey Band was it. Mrs. McGivers, a stout contralto, would soon take the stage with her two obnoxious capuchin monkeys, Cain and Abel, in red-and-gold uniforms, and an accordionist named Joseph. Cain would pick up the miniature cymbals, one for each paw, while Abel would command two drumsticks and perch with a little drum in front of him, looking all too eager.

And then the music would begin, with Cain clanging and Abel banging, and Joseph and Mrs. McGivers setting the pace and melody, more or less. It was usually good for some laughs. And sometimes the beasts would add a flourish, as if they were caffeinated, which maybe they were. The result was anarchy.

August Beausoleil loathed the monkeys, who usually spent their spare time up in the flies, careening about and alarming the performers. The Profile had complained mightily when something had splatted on his pompadoured hair. Beausoleil sometimes ached to fire the act, but good animal acts were tough to find and hard to travel with, and Mrs. McGivers usually gave better than she got. It was better than any dog or pony act he'd seen.

But he had one surefire way to turn a show around, and this was it. When at last The Profile had ceased to bore and offend, the master of ceremonies announced the one, the only, the sensational Mrs. McGivers and her Monkey Band. Quick enough the olio drop sailed into the flies, revealing Mrs. McGivers, the monkeys seated beside her, one with cymbals, the other with drumsticks. And Joseph, the accordionist, at one side. The audience stared, lost in silence. Would nothing crack this dreary opening night?

Mrs. McGivers had come from the tropics somewhere, and the rumor was that she had killed a couple of husbands, but no one could prove it. She used a jungle theme for the act, and usually appeared with a red bandanna capturing her brown hair and a scooped white blouse encasing her massive chest, below which was a voluminous skirt of shimmery blue fabric that glittered in the limelight. She looked somewhat native, but wasn't. She wore sandals, which permitted her smelly feet to exude odors that offended performers and audience alike.

Her repertoire ran to calypso from Trinidad and Tobago, mostly stuff never heard by northern ears, which usually annoyed the audience, which would have preferred Bible songs and spirituals as a way of countering the dangerous idea that man had descended from apes. There, indeed, were two small primates, wiry little rascals dressed in red-and-gold uniforms, making dangerous movements with drumsticks and cymbals in hand.

She turned to Beausoleil.

"You're a rat," she said.

Joseph, the accordionist, took that as his cue, and soon the instrument was croaking out an odd, rhythmic tune, and she began to warble in a nasal, sandpapery whine stuff about banana boats and things that no one had ever heard of.

Mrs. McGivers crooned, repeating chords, giving them spice as she and her monkeys whaled away. The capuchins gradually awakened to their task, led by the accordion, and soon Cain was whanging the cymbals and Abel was thundering the bass drum, with little attention to rhythm, which was actually intricate in Trinidadian music. The whole performance veered toward anarchy, which is what Mrs. McGivers intended, her goal being to send the audience into paroxysms of delight.

Only not this evening in Helena, in the midst of stern mountains and bitter winters.

Were these ladies and gentlemen born without humor?

Abel rose up on his stool and began a virtuoso performance on the bass drum, both arms flailing away, a thunderous eruption from the stage. And still those politicos out there stared across the footlights in silence.

Very well then. Beausoleil quietly waved a hand from the edge of the arch, a hand unseen by the armored audience.

"Boo!" yelled a certain stagehand, now sitting front-left.

"Go away," yelled another stalwart of the show, this gent sitting front-right, four rows back.

The capuchins clanged and banged. Mrs. McGivers warbled. Joseph wheezed life out of the old accordion.

The two reporters, front on the aisle, took no notes.

"Boo," yelled a spectator. "Refund my money."

The gent, well known to Beausoleil, had a bag in hand, and now he plunged a paw into it and extracted a browning, mushy apple, and heaved this missile at Mrs. McGivers. It splatted nearby, which was all Cain needed. He abandoned his cymbals, leapt for the mushy apple, and fired it back, any target would do. It splatted upon the bosom of a politician's alleged wife.

This was followed by a fusillade of rotten items, mostly tomatoes, but also ancient apples and peaches and moldering potatoes, drawn miraculously from sacks out in the theater, and these barrages were returned by Cain and Abel, who were born pitchers with arms that would be the envy of any local baseball team.

Mrs. McGivers was miraculously unscathed, the war having been waged by her two capuchins. Joseph, too, was unscathed, and continued to render calypso music, even imitating a steel guitar with his miraculous wheezebox.

It was a fine uproar. Suddenly, this dour audience was no longer sitting on its cold hands, but was clapping and howling and squealing. Especially when Abel fired a soggy missile that splatted upon the noble forehead of the attorney general. The Helena regulars enjoyed that far more than they should.

After a little more whooping, Beausoleil, in bib and tux, strode purposefully out onto the boards, dodged some foul fruit, and held up a hand.

"Helena has spoken, Mrs. McGivers," he said. He jerked a thumb in the direction of the wings.

She rose from her stool, awarded him with an uncomplimentary gesture barely seen on the other side of the footlights, and stalked off, followed by the capuchins, and Joseph, and finally some hands who removed the stools and instruments.

"Monkey business! Give them a round of applause," Beausoleil said, and immediately the audience broke into thunderous appreciation.

The two bored reporters were suddenly taking notes.

All was well.

The rest of opening night was well nigh perfect. Indeed, Mary Mabel Markey, the Queen of Contraltos, got a standing ovation and repeated demands for an encore, which she supplied so abundantly that Beausoleil almost got out the hook to drag her offstage. Mary Mabel was getting along, was fleshy, and used too much powder to hide her corrugated forehead. She was sinking fast, and Beausoleil had hired her mostly out of pity, since she could no longer find work in the great opera houses of the East and Midwest. But she was also becoming impossible.

There were more acts after the intermission and, finally, the patriotic closing in which all the acts combined with a great huzzah for the waving flag.

The rotten vegetables had rescued the show, once again. It annoyed August Beausoleil. It meant his acts weren't working. It meant financial peril. It hurt the reputation of the Beausoleil Brothers Follies. There were neither brothers nor follies in it, but that was show business. The audience had gone home happy.